The king — Falkieri An... ...
Duke Phelan of Tsaia an... ...
before the fire, brooding, hi... ...ogether before
his face. "I have heirs enoug... ...ow; my lands are safe. It is
time to undo the damage my folk did long years since.
Time to redress old grievances, time to bring ancient
enemies together in peace."

"Are you sure this is your task?" The woman stood by the
fireplace, leaning one arm on the mantel; it shadowed her
face, but the firelight brought out the gleam of silver in her
belt, in the hilt of a dagger at her hip, and glinted from the
crescent symbol of Gird that hung from a thong around
her neck. And in shadow or sun or firelight, nothing
dimmed the silver circle on her brow. Paksenarrion,
paladin of Gird, the king's friend and former soldier.

"I'm sure. My grandmother, that Lady you met, said the
present ruin was in part my fault — I cannot argue...." He
stared at the fire. "If it were possible to find some buried
talisman, some ancient relic...."

"Is a sword worth more than a swordsman?" Paksenarrion rested in her chair as if weightless; no hawk ever had
more vigilant eyes.

"No, but I'm not likely to find a convenient army of
Aareans ensorceled for an age, ready to my command — "
He stopped abruptly; she had held up her hand. Her face
seemed closed a moment, then she grinned as happily as
the young girl he remembered.

"Are you not? Can you doubt the gods' influence, sir
king, in asking *me here?*"

"I would never doubt the gods where you're
concerned...."

THIS IS WHAT IT COST HIM . . . .

Baen Books By Elizabeth Moon

The Deed of Paksenarrion:
Sheepfarmer's Daughter
Divided Allegiance
Oath of Gold
(*also available in one volume as a trade paperback*)

Surrender None: The Legacy of Gird
Liar's Oath

Lunar Activity
Sassinak (*with Anne McCaffrey*)
Generation Warriors (*with Anne McCaffrey*)

LIAR'S OATH

AUTHOR OF *THE DEED OF PAKSENARRION*
CO-AUTHOR OF
SASSINAK AND *GENERATION WARRIORS*

ELIZABETH MOON

BAEN
FANTASY

Copyright © 1992, by Elizabeth Moon

A Baen Books Original

Baen Publishing Enterprises
P.O. Box 1403
Riverdale, NY 10471

ISBN: 0-671-72117-8

Cover art by Gary Ruddell

First Printing, May 1992

Printed in the United States of America

Distributed by Simon & Schuster
1230 Avenue of the Americas
New York, NY 10020

● Prologue

The king — Falkieri Amrothlin Artfielan Phelani, once Duke Phelan of Tsaia and now ruler of Lyonya — sat before the fire, brooding, his fingers tented together before his face. "I have heirs enough now; my lands are safe. It is time to redress old grievances, time to bring ancient enemies together in peace."

"Are you sure this is your task?" The woman stood by the fireplace, leaning one arm on the mantel; it shadowed her face, but the firelight brought out the gleam of silver in her belt, in the hilt of a dagger at her hip, and glinted from the crescent symbol of Gird that hung from a thong around her neck. And in shadow or sun or firelight, nothing dimmed the silver circle on her brow. Paksenarrion, paladin of Gird, the king's friend and former soldier.

"I'm sure. My grandmother, that Lady you met, said the present ruin was in part my fault — I cannot argue. And the original problem, too, comes from my ancestors." He gestured to the table behind him, with its litter of scrolls and books. "The Pargunese, in their rough way, have the right of it: they were free Seafolk, whom my ancestors sought to enslave —"

"As they had enslaved the Dzordanyans?"

"Perhaps. I don't know that, but I do know — I am sure — that the Old Aareans routed the Seafolk from their homes. They came here, to the Honnorgat valley, and settled the north shore of the river as far up as they could sail or row — and then found themselves faced with the Aareans again, moving north from Aarenis."

"A long time ago," said Paksenarrion, frowning.

"Very long, for humans." The king smiled briefly. He himself looked no older than she, though in truth he could have been her father; he had not seemed to age for a score of years. He would live as long again, or more: his elven mother's inheritance. "But when I asked my lady grandmother, she confirmed the Pargunese account. They sailed upriver; the Tsaians and human

1

Lyonyans came over the mountains. And a few have memories of complaints made then, and wars begun then. The Pargunese and Kostandanyans have quarrelled with Tsaians and Lyonyans as long as any human remembers. And now with Sofi Ganarrion's heirs loose in Aarenis, with Fallo and Andressat at odds—"

"Not all that is your fault," Paksenarrion said. She moved to the chair across the firelight from him and sat down. "Surely you know that."

"As I know what *is* my fault," he said. "A king must never excuse himself. Gird would say that."

"Gird did," she said wryly, with a grin. "But how will you proceed?"

He stared at the fire, as if it had answers to give. "I must find some way to convince the southerners that I do represent Old Aare as well as the north. You remember Andressat: those old lords believe no northern title. If it were possible to find some buried talisman, some ancient relic . . ."

"Is a sword worth more than a swordsman?" Paksenarrion rested in her chair as if weightless; no hawk ever had more vigilant eyes.

"No, but I'm not likely to find a convenient army of Aareans ensorceled for an age, ready to my command—" He stopped abruptly; she had held up her hand. Her face seemed closed a moment, then she grinned as happily as the young girl he remembered.

"Are you not? Can you doubt the gods' influence, sir king, in asking *me* here?"

"I would never doubt the gods where you're concerned, but what—?"

"Kolobia," she said. Kolobia. His breath caught in his throat. Where she had been captured by iynisin, the elves' cruel cousins who hated all living things, who corrupted the very stone by dwelling in it. Where she had lost what made her what she was, a paladin of Gird . . . he thought of what she had gone through to regain it and winced away from the memory. She shook her head, impatient with his sentiment. "Kolobia," she said again, joyfully. "Luap's Stronghold—the sleeping knights there—"

"But you told me they waited some god's call to wake—"

"So Amberion said, when we found them. But as you know the Marshal-Generals have sent scholars there to read through their archives; they have not shared all they learned abroad. Those were not Gird's closest followers, as we first thought, but mageborn, descendents of those lords against which Gird fought. And in their own time, they believed themselves descended from the lords of Old Aare."

"Were they?" he asked.

She shrugged. "How can we know? We know what they said of themselves in their records, but not if they spoke truth — or even knew it."

"And you think I should try to wake them?"

"I think you should ask the gods, and possibly your elven relatives. The scholars found as many mysteries as answers; they are not sure why the stronghold was founded, or why an end came — even what the end was. The records end abruptly, as if it came suddenly, or as if the writers expected no one to read their words again."

The king stood and paced the length of the room without speaking. Then he came back to the table, and leaned on it, as if reading the maps and books thereon. She watched him, silent.

"I know the way," he said finally. "I know, and cannot tell you, how to wake the sleepers . . . but without knowing why they sleep, and if some great power intended another awakening for them, dare I intrude?"

"The gods will tell you, if you listen," she said. He grunted; she always said that, and for her it was true: she listened, and the gods guided her. That was the essence of a paladin. For himself, it was more of a struggle. A king could not merely follow; a king had to understand. She had said more than once that paladins were not meant to govern.

"And what of the iynisin in Kolobia?" he asked. "If I waken the sleepers, what about them?"

A shadow crossed her face, as well it might. "Sir king, if you could persuade your elven relatives to explain more of the iynisin presence there it would help us all. In all the records from Luap's time, there is no mention of iynisin, and only one or two comments of some mysterious danger. The neighboring kingdom was said to believe that demons of some kind lived in the canyons before Luap came. Perhaps they thought iynisin were demons, but that doesn't explain why Luap and his folk never saw them."

"It would help," the king said, "if we knew more about Luap himself: who he was, and why he journeyed there, and what he thought he was doing."

● Chapter One

Fin Panir in summer could be as hot as it was cold in winter; every window and door in the old palace complex stood wide open. Luap had started work early, before the heat slicked his hands with sweat to stain the parchment. Now, in midmorning, the heat carried ripe city smells through his broad office window. He paused to stretch and ease his cramped shoulders. For once Gird had not interrupted him a dozen times; he had finished a fair copy of the entire *Ten Fingers of the Code*. He reached for the jug of water and poured himself a mug, carefully away from his work. Could he write another page without smudges, or should he quit until evening's cool? He wondered, idly, why he had heard nothing from Gird that morning, and then remembered that a Marshal from a distant grange had come to visit. Doubtless they were still telling stories of the war.

He stretched again, smiling. It was nothing like the life he had imagined for himself when he was a boy, or a young farmer, but somewhat better than either of those vanished possibilities. As Gird's assistant and scribe, he had status he'd never had before; he was living in the very palace to which his father had never taken him. And he knew that without him, Gird could not have created, and revised, the legal code that offered some hope of lasting peace. His skill in writing, in keeping accounts, in drawing maps, had helped Gird win the war; his skill in writing and keeping records might help Gird win the peace.

"Luap . . . " One of the younger scribes, a serious-faced girl whose unconscious movements stirred him brought her work to his desk. "I finished that copy, but there's a blot — here — "

"They can still read it," he said, smiling at her. "That's the most important thing." She smiled back, shyly, took the scroll and went back downstairs. He wished he could find one woman who would chance a liaison with him. Peasant women, in the current climate, would not have him, as some had made painfully clear. They had suffered too much to take any man

ith known mageborn blood as lover. The few mageborn
omen who sought him for his father's name he could not
ust to bear no children; he suspected they wanted a king's
randson, and in his reaction to their pressure he could
nderstand the peasant women's refusal. As for those women
ho sold their bodies freely, he could not see them without
inking of his daughter's terrible death. He needed to feel
at a woman wanted him, the comfort of his body, before he
uld take comfort in hers.

But he knew that would not happen, any more than wishing
ould bring back Gird's wife or children, or restore any of the
sses of war. All the Marshals had lost family; everyone around
im had scars of body and mind both. His were no worse, he
minded himself, and decided to work on another page. Work
sed his mind, and kept it from idle wishes — or so the peasants
ways said, in the endless tags and ends of folktales that now
lored every conversation. He was lucky to have his work
doors, in this heat, or in winter's cold. He was lucky to have
ird's understanding, if he could not have his indulgence.

He had just pulled another clean sheet toward him when he
eard the old lady's voice all the way up the staircase. He
vered his inkwell; perhaps he would be needed. With that
cent, she had to be mageborn, and with the quaver in it, she
ad to be old. The young guards, he suspected, would have no
xperience with her sort.

"I don't care what you say, young man." A pause, during
hich some male voice rumbled below his hearing. "I must
e your Marshal-General, and I must see him now."

Luap rolled his eyes up and wondered how far the respect
r age would get her. Her voice came nearer, punctuated by
uffs and wheezes as she came up the stairs.

"Yes, it *is* important. It is always important to do things
ght. If your Marshal-General had had the advantages of
ood education, he would know that already, but since he has
ot — " A shocked interruption, from what Luap judged to be
very young yeoman, whose words fell all over each other in
isarray. He grinned, anticipating the old lady's response. She
id not disappoint him. "You see, young man, what I'm talk-
g about. You're very earnest, I'm sure, and very dedicated to
ur Marshal-General, but you cannot express yourself in
ain language with any grace. . . ."

Just as he realized that she would inevitably end up in his office, the yeoman's apologetic cough at the door brought his eyes to the spectacle. She was, undoubtedly, mageborn: a determinedly upright lady with snowy hair and slightly faded blue eyes, who dressed as if the former king were still ruling. A pouf of lace at the throat, a snug bodice with flaring skirt and puffed sleeves, all in brilliant reds and blues and greens: he had not seen such clothes since childhood. Luap wondered how that gorgeous robe had survived the looting. Then, with the appearance at her back of a stout, redfaced servant in blue and brown, he realized she must have impressed her staff with more than her money. The younger woman gave him look for look, challenging and defensive both.

"This is the Marshal-General's luap," the yeoman said. He was sweating, his eyes wide. "He'll be able to help you."

"I want the Marshal-General," the old lady said. Then, as Luap rose and came toward her, she raked him with a measuring glare, and her voice changed. "Ohh . . . *you'll* understand. Perhaps you can help me." Whatever she had seen convinced her he was one of *her* kind. Behind her, the peasant woman smirked, and Luap felt his ears redden. Of course everyone knew about him — at least that he had mageborn blood on his father's side, which was not that uncommon. But the way this woman said it, she might have known who his father was.

The old lady favored him with a surprisingly sweet smile and laid a longfingered hand on her chest. "Could I perhaps sit down?"

Luap found himself bowing. "Of course . . . here . . . " His own chair, onto which he threw a pillow. She rested on it with the weightless grace of dandelion fluff, her rich brocaded robe falling into elegant folds. The peasant woman handed her a tapestry bag, then settled herself against the wall. The old lady rummaged in the bag, her lips pursed, and finally drew out a strip of blue gorgeously embroidered in gold and silver; it glittered even in the dim indoor light.

"You will understand," she began, peering up at Luap with a smile she might have bestowed on a favorite nephew. "They all tell me that the Marshal-General doesn't like fancy things, that he was a mere peasant, but of course that's nonsense." Luap opened his mouth, then shut it slowly at the expression on the peasant woman's face. Best hear the old woman out. "Being a peasant

6

doesn't mean having no taste," she went on, looking up to be sure he agreed. "Peasants like fancy things as much as anyone else, and some of them do very good work. Out in the villages, you know." She seemed to expect some response; Luap nodded. "Men don't always notice such things, but I learned as a young wife — when my husband was alive, we used to spend summers at different vills on his estates — that every peasant vill had its own patterns. Weaving, embroidery, even pottery. And the women, once they found I was interested, would teach me, or at least let me watch." Another shrewd glance. Luap nodded again, then looked at the peasant woman leaning against the wall. Servant? Keeper? The woman's expression said *protector*, but it had to be an unusual situation. Few of the city servants had stayed with their mageborn masters when Fin Panir fell.

"So I know," the old woman went on, "that Gird will like this, if he only understands how important it is." She unfolded the cloth carefully, almost reverently, and Luap saw the stylized face of the Sunlord, Esea, a mass of whorls and spirals, centering a blue cloth bordered with broad band of silver interlacement. "For the altar in the Hall, of course, now that it has been properly cleansed." She gave Luap a long disapproving stare, and said "I always told the king, may he rest at ease, that he was making a terrible, terrible mistake by listening to that *person* from over the mountains, but he had had his sorrows, you understand." When he said nothing, finding nothing to say, she cocked her head and said "You *do* understand?"

"Not . . . completely." He folded his arms, and at her faint frown unfolded them. "This cloth is for the Hall, you say? For the High Lord's altar?"

She drew herself even more erect and almost sniffed. "Whatever you call it — we always called Esea the Sunlord, though I understand there has been some argument that the High Lord and the Sunlord are one and the same."

"Yes, lady." He wondered what Arranha would say about this. For a priest of the Sunlord he was amazingly tolerant of other peoples' beliefs, but he still held to his own.

"I could do nothing while the Hall was defiled. And of course the cloths used then could not be used again; I understood that. But now that the Hall is clean, these things must be done, and done properly. Few are left who understand that. You must not think it was easy."

"No, lady," Luap said automatically, his mind far astray. How was he going to explain her to Gird? How would Gird react?

"First," she said, as if he'd asked, as if he would be interested, "the wool must be shorn with silver shears, from a firstborn lamb having no spot of black or brown, neither lamb nor ewe. Washed in running water *only*, mind. And the shearer must wear white, as well. Then carded with a new pair of brushes, which must afterwards be burned on a fire of dry wood. Cedar is best. Then spun between dawn and dusk of one day, and woven between dawn and dusk of another, within one household. In my grandmother's day, she told me, the same hands must do both, and it was best done on the autumn Evener. But the priests said it was lawful for one to spin and another to weave, only it must be done in one household."

She gave Luap a sharp look, and he nodded to show he'd been paying attention. He wasn't sure he had fooled her, but she didn't challenge him. "It must be woven on a loom used for nothing else, the width exactly suited to the altar, for no cutting or folding of excess can be permitted. No woman in her time may come into the room while it is being woven, nor may touch it after; if she touches the loom while bleeding, the loom must be burned. Then while it is being embroidered, which must be the work of one only, it must be kept in a casing of purest white wool, and housed in cedarwood."

Luap nodded, tried to think of something to say, and asked about the one thing she hadn't mentioned. "And the color, lady? How must it be dyed?"

"Dyed!" She fairly bristled at him, and thrust the cloth toward his face, yanking it back when he reached out a hand. "It is not dyed, young man; that is fine stitchery." Now he could see that the blue background was not cloth, but embroidery. He had never seen anything like it.

"I'm sorry," he said, since she clearly expected an apology. "I don't think I've ever seen work that fine."

"Probably not." Then, after a final sniff, she gave him a melting smile. "Young man, you will not guess how long I've been working on this."

He had no idea of course, but a guess was clearly required. "A year? Two?"

She dimpled. How a woman her age had kept dimples he

also had no idea, but they were surprisingly effective. "*Ten* years. You can't work on this all day, you know. No one could. I began when the king made that terrible mistake; I knew what would come of it. I tried to warn him, but . . . " She leaned forward, conspiratorial. "Would you believe, the king thought I was just a silly old woman! You may have been my mother's best friend, he said, but she only liked you because you were too stupid to play politics. Safely stupid, he said. You needn't think I'll listen to you, he said, you and your oldfashioned superstitions. *Well!*" Old anger flushed her cheeks, then faded as she pursed her lips and shook that silver hair. "When I got home, I told Eris here — " She waved a hand at the peasant woman. "I told her then, I said, 'You mark my words, dear, that hot-blooded fool is leading us straight into trouble.' Though of course it didn't start *then*, but a long time before; these things always do. Young people are so rash."

A movement in the passage outside caught Luap's eye — Gird, headed downstairs on some errand, had paused to see what was going on. For someone his size, he could be remarkably quiet when he wished. From his expression, the old woman's rich clothing and aristocratic accent were having a predictable effect on his temper. *Go away*, Luap thought earnestly at Gird, knowing that was useless. Then *Be quiet* to the old lady — equally useless.

She went on. "And that very day, I began the work. My grandmother had always said, you never know when you'll need the gods' cloth, so it's wise to prepare beforehand. This wool had been sheared two years before that, carded and spun and woven just as the rituals say: not by my hands, for there are better spinners and weavers in my household, and I'm not so proud I'll let the god wear roughspun just to have my name on it. Ten years, young man, I've put in stitch by stitch, and stopped for nothing. The king even wondered why I came no more to court, sent ladies to see, and they found me embroidering harmlessly — or so the king took it." She fixed Luap with another of those startling stares. "I am not a fool, young man, whatever the king thought. But it does no good to meddle where no one listens, and my grandmother had told me once my wits were in my fingers, not my tongue."

Gird moved into the room, and the old lady turned to him, regal and impervious to his dangerous bulk. He wore the same blue shirt and rough gray trousers he always wore, with old boots worn thin at the soles and sides. He stood a little stooped, looking exactly like the aging farmer he was.

"Yes?" she said, as if to an intrusive servant. Luap felt an instant's icy fear, but as usual Gird surprised him.

"Lady," he said, far more gently than her tone deserved from him. "You wanted to see the Marshal-General?"

"Yes, but this young man is helping me now." Almost dismissive, then she really focussed on him. "Oh — *you* are the Marshal-General?"

Gird's eyes twinkled. "Yes, lady."

"I saw you, riding into the city that day." She beamed on him, to Luap's surprise. "I said to Eris then, that's no brigand chief, no matter what they say, even if he does sit that horse like a sack of meal." Gird looked at the peasant woman, who gave him the same look she'd given Luap. Gird nodded, and turned back to the lady. "Not that you could be expected to ride better," she went on, oblivious to the possibility that a man who had led a successful revolution might resent criticism of his horsemanship. "I daresay you had no opportunity to learn in childhood—"

"No, lady, I didn't." Gird's formidable rumble was tamed to a soft growl. "But you wished something of me?"

"This." She indicated the cloth on her lap. "Now that you've cleansed the Hall, the altar must be properly dressed. I've just this past day finished it. Your doorward would not allow me to dress the altar, and said it was your command — "

"So you came to me." Gird smiled at her; to Luap's surprise the old lady did not seem to mind his interruptions. Perhaps she was used to being interrupted, at least by men in command. "But we have a priest of Esea, lady, who said nothing to me about the need for such — " He gestured at the cloth.

"Who?" She seemed indignant at this, more than at Gird. "What priest would fail in the proper courtesies?"

"Arranha," said Gird, obviously curious; surely she could not know the names of every priest in the old kingdom.

"*Arranha* . . . is *he* still alive?" A red patch came out on either cheek. "I thought he had been exiled or executed or some such years ago."

"Ah . . . no." Gird rubbed his nose; Luap realized his own mouth had fallen open, and shut it. "You said you were in the city when it fell — when we arrived. Surely you came to the cleansing of the Hall?"

"No." Now she looked decidedly grumpy. "No, I did not. At my age, and in my — well — with all due respect, Marshal-General, for those few days the city was crowded with — with noise, and pushing and shoving, and the kinds of people, Marshal-General, that I never — well, I mean — "

"It was no place for a lady of your age and condition," Gird offered, twinkling again, after a quick glance at Eris, the peasant woman. "You're right, of course. Noisy, rough, even dangerous. I would hope your people had the sense to keep you well away from windows and doors, most of that time."

"In t'cellar, at the worst," said Eris, unexpectedly. "But the worst was over, time you come in, sir. Worst was the other lords' servants smashin' and lootin' even as the lords fled. Runnin' round sayin' such things as milady here shouldn't have to hear. Though it was crowded and noisy enough for a few hands of days. And when th' yeoman marshals sorted through, takin' count o' folks and things. But they didn't seek bribes, I'll say that much for 'em."

"They'd better not," said Gird, suddenly all Marshal-General. Even the old lady gaped; Luap, who had seen it often enough not to be surprised, enjoyed the reactions of others. He had never figured out what Gird did to change from farmer to ruler so swiftly, but no one ever mistook the change. "So," he went on, this time with everyone's attention, "you did not come to the Hall that day, and had not known Arranha was with us? You should know that I've known him for some years — he'll tell you in what tangle we met, if you wish. I knew he'd been exiled, and nearly killed, but for all that he's a priest of Esea, one of the few left alive these days."

"He's a fool," said the old lady, having recovered her composure. "He always was, with his questions into this and that and everything. Couldn't let a body alone, not any more than a bee will give a flower a moment's peace to enjoy the sun. Always 'But don't you think this' and 'Well then, don't you see that' until everyone was ready to throw up their hands and run off."

Gird grinned. "He did that to me, too. You know he took me to the gnomes?"

She sniffed. "That's exactly the sort of thing I'd expect. Gnomes! Trust Arranha to complicate matters: mix a peasant revolt with gnomes and both with religion." The flick of her hand down her lap dismissed Arranha's notions.

"Well, it worked. Although there were times, that winter, when I could happily have strangled your Arranha."

"He's not *ours*," the old lady said. "A law to himself, he is, and always has been. Although you — " She gave Gird a look up and down. "I expect you give him a few sleepless nights, and all the better."

"But my point," Gird said, now very gently, "is that Arranha is the only priest of Esea now in Fin Panir, serving his god within the High Lord's Hall, and he has not said anything about needing such cloths . . . although your years of labor should not be in vain, you must know that we are not such worshippers of Esea as your folk were."

"Even he — even he should realize — " Abruptly — Luap wondered if it were all genuine feeling, or a habit known to be effective with men in power — the old lady's eyes filled with tears that spilled down her cheeks. "Oh, sir — and I don't mind calling a peasant *sir* in such a case — I don't care what you call the god: Sunlord, High Lord, Maker of Worlds, it doesn't matter. But he must be respected, whatever you call him, and I've made these . . . " A tear fell, almost on the cloth; when she saw it, her face paled, and she turned aside. "I must not — cry — on the cloth — "

Eris came forward, and offered her apron, on which the lady wiped her damp face. "She really believes, sir, that if the altar's not cared for, it'll come bad luck to everyone. It's no trick, sir, if that's what you're thinking."

The old lady's hands, dry now, fumbled at the cloth, to fold it away safely. She didn't look up; her shoulders trembled. Luap felt a pang of emotion he could not identify: pity? sorrow? mean amusement? Gird sighed, gustily, like his horse. Luap knew what he wanted to say; he had said it before. *You should have worshipped better gods* he had told more than one mageborn survivor who wanted enforced tithes to rebuild the Sunlord's lesser temples. Only Arranha's arguments had kept him from forbidding Esea's worship altogether, although Luap couldn't see how the god could be responsible for his worshippers' mistakes. What he could see were any number of ways to placate the old lady without causing trouble among Gird's followers. Give the cloths to Arranha, and let him use them once or twice . . . the old lady would not make the journey from her house too often, he was sure. Agree to use them, then not — only she would care, and she would not know.

But he knew as well that Gird would not take any of these easy ways out. He would refuse her utterly, or agree, and use the damn cloths, and leave Luap to explain it all. Or Luap and Arranha together, an even less likely combination. Luap squeezed his eyes shut, wishing he could think of a deity who might be interested in this minor problem, and untangle it with no effort on his part.

"Luap," said Gird. Here it came, some impossible task. He opened his eyes, to find Gird's expression as uncompromising as ever in a crisis. One of those, then. "You will take this lady — may I have your name?"

"Dorhaniya, bi Kirlis-Sevith," said the old lady.

Eris spoke up again. "Lady Dorhaniya, as a widow, was entitled to revert to her mother's patronymic and her father's matronymic, sir. . . . ." As if Gird really cared, but he smiled and went on.

"Luap will escort you, Lady Dorhaniya, to confer with Arranha. I presume there is some ritual . . . you do not merely lay the cloths on the altar yourself, at least not the first time."

"N-no." Her voice was shaky. "N-no. Properly — " Now it firmed; clearly the very thought of propriety and ritual gave her confidence. "Properly new cloths are dedicated by the priest . . . it's not . . . it's not a *long* ceremony," she said, as if fearing that might make a difference.

"I understand. Then you will need to speak to Arranha, tell him what you've done, and have him arrange it."

"Then you will — you give your permission?" She looked up, flushed, starry-eyed as any young girl at her first courting. Gird nodded, and her smile widened, almost childishly, the dimples showing again. "Oh, *thank* you, Marshal-General. Esea's light — no — " and the smile vanished. "If you don't honor Esea — "

"Lady," said Gird, as to a frightened child, as gently as Luap had ever heard him. "Lady, I honor all the gods but those who delight in cruelty; in your eyes, Esea's light is kindly. May Esea be what you see; you need give me no thanks, but your blessing I will take, and gladly."

She had not followed all that, by the bewildered expression, but she put out her hand, and Gird gave her his. She stood, then, and said "Then Esea's light be with you, Marshal-General, and — and — then I can rest, when I see the altar dressed again as it should be."

• Chapter Two

Arranha had a favorite walled court, on the west side of the palace complex, edged with stone benches and centered with a little bed of fragrant herbs. Against one wall a peach tree had been trained flat: something Luap remembered from the lord's house in which he had grown up. Most mornings, Arranha read there, or posed questions for a circle of students. Luap led Lady Dorhaniya by the shorter, inside, way, ignoring her running commentary about who had lived in which room, and what they had done and said. When he reached Arranha, the priest responded with his usual cheerfulness to the meeting.

"Lady Dorhaniya! Yes . . . weren't you — ?"

She had flushed again, whether with anger or pleasure Luap was not sure. "Duke Dehlagrathin's daughter, and Ruhael's wife, yes. And you — but I'm sorry, sir, to so forget myself with a priest of Esea."

"Nonsense." Arranha smiled at Luap. "This lady knew me in my wild youth, Luap, and like her friends gave me good warnings I was too foolish to hear."

She softened a trifle. "I blame my sister as much as anyone, she and your father both. If he had not tried to force a match, or she had accepted it — "

"I would be a very dead magelord, having fallen honorably on the turf at Greenfields with my king," said Arranha. "If, that is, your sister had not knifed me long before, for driving her frenzied with my questions. She threatened it often enough, even in courtship."

"Well . . . that's over." With a visible effort, the old lady dragged herself from memory to the present. "And my business with you, Arranha, is about the Sunlord, not about the past."

At once, he put on dignity. "Yes, lady?"

She sat on the stone ledge beside him, and recited the whole

14

tale again. Arranha, Luap noted, actually seemed to listen with attention to each detail — but of course it was his god whose rituals mattered here. But when she started to pull the cloth from her bag and unfold it, Arranha put out his hand.

"Not here, lady."

"But I wanted to show you — "

"Lady, I trust your piety and your grandmother's instruction, but you have now told me — Esea's priest — about them. From here, the ritual is his, not yours or mine. Give me the bag."

She handed it over, eyes wide, and Arranha held it on outstretched hands. A pale glow, hardly visible in the sunlight, began to gather around it. Luap realized that the sun seemed brighter, the shadows of vineleaves on the wall darker . . . stiller. No air moved. The glow around the bag intensified, became too bright for eyes to watch. Luap felt a weight pressing down on him, yet it was no weight he knew, nothing like a stone. Light. But very heavy light.

Abruptly it was gone, not faded but simply gone; he blinked at the confusing afterimages of light and shadow. A cool breeze whirled in and out of the courtyard. And the bag on Arranha's outstretched hands lay white as fresh-washed wool, only less white than the light itself. The old lady sat silent, mouth open, eyes wide; her companion's face had paled, and even Arranha had a sheen of sweat on his forehead.

"Lady, your gifts are acceptable, and we can now, with your help, restore Esea's altar to its proper array."

"What *was* that?" Luap asked. Arranha merely smiled at him and shook his head; a fair answer. He offered his arm to the old lady, who roused suddenly from her daze and stood, more steadily than Luap would have expected.

"You should come too," Arranha said, as he guided the women toward the High Lord's Hall. Luap knew better than to ask why; he suspected the answer had to do with his ancestry, and only hoped Arranha wouldn't think it necessary to tell the old lady about *that*. He tried to think of a duty he must perform, right now, somewhere else, and couldn't — and in Arranha's presence, he could not make one up.

Fortunately for his composure, the walk through the maze of passages and little walled yards that had grown around the old king's palace kept the old lady breathless enough that she had no questions to ask. When they finally came to the great court before the High Lord's Hall, Arranha led the way straight across it to the main entrance. Whatever the door-wards may have thought, they offered no challenge to Arranha and Luap.

Inside, the coolness of stone and tile and shadowed air. Most of the windows shattered when the city fell had been boarded up. Luap supposed that someday artists would design new windows to fill the interior with manycolored light, but for now Gird had no intention of spending the land's wealth on such things. The great round hole in the end wall, above the altar, had been left open, for light, and through it the sun's white glare fell full on the pale stone of the floor, a bright oval, glittering from minute specks in the slabs of rock. Luap noticed how it was all the brighter for the shadows around it, focussing the eye on what lay within the light.

Arranha walked up the Hall, followed by the other three, their footsteps sounding hollowly in that high place. They walked through the sun, and back into shadow, halting when Arranha did, then moving at his gesture to stand at either side, where they could see. At the altar, he bowed before laying the bag atop it. His prayer seemed, to Luap, unreasonably elaborate for something so simple as the consecration of a handwoven cloth for its covering, but he omitted none of the details the old lady had mentioned, from the selection of the animal, to the washing and spinning and weaving. From time to time, he asked the old lady for the name of the person who had performed each rite. At last, he came to some sort of conclusion. By then Luap was bored, noticing idly how the sun's oval slipped up the floor, handspan by handspan, as the morning wore on. Arranha's shadow appeared, a dark motionless form; when he looked, the sun blazed from Arranha's robe. It shifted minutely to catch the edge of the altar, which would be in full sun any moment.

Abruptly, in silence, Arranha came alight. As if he had turned in that instant to the translucent stone of a lamp, his body glowed: Luap could see the very veins in his arms, the shadows of his bones. Once more he prayed, this time in a resonant chant. Without haste, yet swiftly as the sun moved, he opened the bag and drew out the cloths, unfolding them with cadenced gestures. In the full light of the sun, that rich embroidery glittered, shimmered, gold and silver on blue. Arranha's hands spread, and passed above the cloth. Its folds flattened as if he'd soothed a living thing. Blue as smooth and deep as the sky . . . light rose from the altar, as light fell from the empty window, to meet in a dance of ecstasy.

Luap did not know if Arranha kept on chanting, or if he fell silent. Until the sun moved from the altar, as it passed midday, he stood rapt in some mystery beyond any magicks he'd thought of. Then the spell passed, and he looked across to find the old lady's face streaked with tears; she trembled as she leaned on Eris's arm. Arranha folded the cloths, just as ceremoniously, and returned them to the snowy bag for storage. Then, stepping away from the altar, he turned to her.

"Lady, Esea accepts your service, and I, his priest, thank you for your years of diligence."

She ducked her head. "It is my honor." From the way she said it, Luap wondered if she had anything else in her life to look forward to. He smiled at her when she looked up, but none of them said anything as they left the Hall. Back outside, she seemed to have recovered her composure, and turned to Luap with a sweet smile.

"You will thank the Marshal-General for me? I will come again, but now — I am a little fatigued. Eris will see me home; please don't trouble yourselves."

"Of course, lady," he said. He might have offered to escort her anyway, but she'd already turned away, and something in Arranha's expression suggested that Arranha wanted to talk to him out of the old lady's hearing. For a few moments, Arranha was silent, then he shook his head abruptly and smiled at Luap, a smile twin to the old lady's, before leading the way back to his own chosen courtyard. There he waved Luap to a seat on the stone bench and sat beside him, hot as it was now in midday. Luap was about to suggest that they find a cool inside room in the palace when Arranha shook his head slowly. "I had forgotten her, you know. Until you brought her, I had not thought of Dorhaniya for years."

"You knew her," Luap said. "A . . . duke's daughter?"

Arranha sighed, and nodded. "Yes — longer ago than I care to think." He gave Luap a searching look, then went on. "You need to know some of this, and you probably don't remember it."

Luap felt himself tense, and tried to relax; he was sure

17

Arranha saw through that, as he did through most pretense. "Don't remember what?"

Arranha peeled a late peach with care, and then handed it to him before starting to peel another for himself. Luap bit the peach fiercely, as if it were an enemy, and Arranha talked as he peeled.

"You need to know that we both saw you, as a child. Dorhaniya and I."

"What!" It came out an explosive grunt, as if he'd been punched in the gut, which is what it felt like.

Arranha gave him an apologetic look. "I didn't remember, until I saw her, and she started talking. Then, thinking of places we'd met before, I remembered. She will remember, too, once she thinks of it. She's the kind of old woman who thinks mostly of people, and where she's seen them. She will tease at her memories, Luap, until your boy's face comes clear, and then she will come to ask you. Be gentle, if you can; that's what I'm asking." He started eating.

Luap could not answer. He had locked all that away, that privileged childhood, a private hoard to gloat over when alone. Now he realized that no one had ever claimed to know both of his pasts . . . the nobility had left him strictly alone, a pain he had thought he could not bear, and the peasantry, where he'd been sent, had not known him before. He did not even know, with any certainty, just where his childhood had been spent. It had never occurred to him, during the war, that he might come face to face with anyone but his father who had known him . . . that the other adults of his childhood might still exist, and recognize him.

He felt that a locked door had been breached, that he had been invaded by some vast danger he could hardly imagine. His vision blurred. In his mind, he was himself again a child, to whom the whole adult world seemed alternately huge and hostile, or bright and indulgent. He could remember the very clothes, the narrow strip of lace along his cuff, the stamped pattern on the leather of his shoes. And someone else had seen that — someone who knew him now — someone who could estimate the distance between that boy and this man, could judge if the boy had grown as he should, even if the boy had potentials he had never met.

"I — didn't know —" It came out harsh, almost gasping. He

could not look at Arranha, who would be disapproving, he was sure.

"I'm sorry." Arranha's voice soothed him, sweet as the peach he'd eaten and which now lay uneasily in his belly. "I was afraid she would tell you and cause you this grief in a worse place . . . here, you are safe, you know."

He would never be safe again . . . all the old fears rolled over him. He had been safe, secure, in that childhood, and then it was gone, torn away. The farmer to whom he'd been sent had not dared cruelty, but the life itself was cruelty, to one indulged in a king's hall, a child used to soft clothes and tidbits from a royal kitchen. All around, the walls closed in, prisoning rather than protecting. He could hardly breathe, and then he was crying, shaking with the effort not to cry, and failing, and hating himself. Arranha's arm came around him, warmer and stronger than he expected. He gave up, then, and let the sobs come out. When he was done, and felt as always ridiculous and grumpy, Arranha left him on the bench and came back in a few minutes with a pitcher of water and a round of bread.

"I daresay you feel cheated," Arranha said, breaking the bread and handing Luap a chunk. "Those were your memories, to color as you chose, and here I've pointed out that others live in them."

Luap said nothing. He did feel cheated, but it was worse than Arranha said. Someone had invaded his private memories, his personal space, and torn down his defenses. The only thing that had been his, since he had had neither family nor heritance.

"I don't remember much," Arranha said, musing. "You were a child; I was a priest, busy with other duties. Not often there, in fact."

Luap noticed he said *there* instead of *here*, which must have meant he had not been brought up in Fin Panir — at least, not in the palace complex. That made sense; he remembered a forecourt opening on fields, not streets. He got a swallow of water past the lump in his throat, and took a bite of bread. If Arranha kept talking, he could regain control, re-wall his privacy.

"Someone pointed you out. I was in one of my rebellious stages, so I remember thinking what a shame it was —"

"What?" That came out calmly enough; Luap swallowed

more water, and nearly choked.

Arranha chuckled. "Well — she's right, Dorhaniya, that I was troublesome. I questioned — as I do to this day — whatever came into my head to question. Her sister threatened more than once to cut the tongue from my head — and might have done it, too, that one. Anyway, I not only thought the lords' use of peasant women was wrong, I thought it was stupid — and said so. You were an example: a handsome lad, bright enough, eager as a puppy, and by no fault of your own the hinge of great decisions. All the talk was of your potential for magery: not your wit or your courage, not your character or your strength. I thought you had the magery, but that fool of a steward had frightened it out of you; others were hoping you had none."

"Why? Didn't the king have legitimate heirs?" He would be reasonable; he forced himself to ask reasonable questions.

"You didn't know — ? No, of course, how could you? Luap, the king's wife lost four children, either in pregnancy or birthing, and died with her last attempt, who was born alive but died within the year. By then he had taken the fever that left him no hope of children, even if he married again. He did, in fact, but to no purpose. He had sired you just before his wife's death; his older bastards had shown no sign of power, and most — for three were the children of a favorite mistress — died in the same fever that left him sterile."

Luap had never thought of his father as a king with problems. Whatever the king's problems, they could not have been as great as those he gave Luap. It gave him a strange feeling to hear him spoken of, as an archivist might write of a figure of history. In his mind he could see the very phrases that might be used of such a king.

"And his brother and brothers-in-law, and his cousins — all would have been glad to have him die without an heir. As in fact he did, before you were grown."

"But — but then the king Gird killed was not my father?"

"Oh no. Although when Gird told me you were the king's bastard, that's who I thought of, naturally. It was the simple answer, and like so many simple answers, it was wrong." Arranha shook his head, presumably at his own foolishness. "Seeing Dorhaniya again brought it back to me, and then I realized the child's face would grow into one very like yours. The king Gird killed was . . . let me think. First there was his brother, but he died in a hunting accident. So-called. Then his eldest sister's husband, who caught a convenient flux. The king Gird killed was the fourth, or fifth, since your father, a cousin."

"But she said she knew him — when she was talking about mistakes — "

"Well, she knew all of them. So did I. Her father was a duke, her husband one of the cousins — not one who became king; they killed him, I've forgotten how. She did know your father — "

"Does Gird know?"

"Know what?"

"That the king he killed at Greenfields — the king who defiled the Hall — was not my father?"

"I . . . I would have thought so, but . . . perhaps not." *Does it matter?* was clear on his face, then his expression changed. "I see. Of course he must be told, in case he doesn't know. You are not *that* man's son; you would have been the heir, but of a different man. A better man than that, though not much wiser. I'm sorry, Luap, but your father was, for all his troubles, a blind fool. I said it then, and spent a year in exile for it, and I'll say it now, to his son."

"He . . . didn't hate me?" It took all his courage to ask that; it was the deepest fear in his heart, that he had somehow earned his father's hate. Against it he had mounted a fierce defense — it wasn't his fault, it wasn't fair.

"Esea's light! No, he didn't hate you. He put all his hopes on you, but understood only one thing to hope for, and pushed too hard. He was desperate, by then, but that doesn't excuse him."

"No." Luap stared at the pavement under his feet. He had held that grudge too long; he was not ready for a father who had had problems of his own, who had been desperate, who had placed a kingdom's weight on the hope that his latest bastard would grow to have the tools of magery. He was not ready to consider how a king might be trapped by something more honorable than his own pleasure. "My . . . mother?" For the instant it took Arranha to answer, he held the hope that she had been mageborn too.

Arranha gave a minute shrug and spread his hands. "I'm truly sorry; I know nothing about her. When I saw you, she was nowhere in evidence. A tutor had you in hand, and bragged to the king of your wit."

"I don't remember her." He said that to his locked hands, staring at his thumbs as if they were the answer to something important. "I never knew — except that I couldn't ask. It made them angry."

"I daresay it frightened them as much as anything. You know the peasant customs: the mother's family determines lineage. We overrode that, whenever our law intruded into the vills, but quite often the peasants evaded our law one way and another. If you had found your mother, if she had claimed you, her people might have helped her get you away and hide you."

"But she didn't." Luap strained for any memory of his mother, forcing himself to imagine himself an infant, a child just able to stand. Surely he would remember who had suckled him, that first deep relationship; surely he could raise it from the deep wells of memory. A face hovered before him, dim and wavering like the reflection of his own in a bucket of water.

Arranha shrugged again. "It's likely she couldn't. She may have been sent far away; she may have died. That I don't know. Your problems were not her fault, Luap, any more than they were yours."

Too much too soon. His mind ached, overstretched with new and uncomfortable revelations. He had had it all organized, he thought, his past tidied into a coherent tale of childhood wrongs and struggles flowing logically into the conflicts of his adult life. He had constructed it of his own pain, his own understanding, and he had become comfortable with it. Now he must revise it, and found he was unwilling to do so. Tentatively, somewhere in his head, a new version began to take shape, safely remote from the other . . . something he could revise, to bring it into conformance. A tragic king, struggling against destiny — an equally tragic peasant victim, a child doomed from the start to be less than anyone's hopes, including his own.

He spent the rest of that day pretending to write, hoping no one would ask what he was doing. He wanted no supper, but knew that if he did not eat with the others, someone would ask questions. So he forced the food down, complained with the others of the heat, and spent a restless night by his window, staring at a sky whose stars held no messages for him.

The old lady returned days later, as Arranha had predicted. In those two days, Luap had struggled to regain the balance she had disrupted. Arranha had told Gird which king had really fathered him; Gird had grunted, scowling, and then given Luap one of his looks.

"What difference d'you think it makes?" Gird had asked. Luap felt abraded by the look and the question, as if the mere fact of stating his real parentage had been an evasion, or a request for something Gird could not approve. He realized he'd hoped for understanding, for Gird to move toward a more fatherly or brotherly relationship, but now he saw that could not happen. Anything that reminded Gird of his father's blood and rank — even this, which should have made it better — aroused the old antagonism.

This day she came early, before the late-morning heat. He heard, again, her voice below, and went down to meet her. *Be gentle*, Arranha had said; he wasn't sure he could be gentle, but he could be courteous. She wore a dress equally costly, but different, from the day before, more blue and less green in its pattern. Lady Dorhaniya's servant gave him another warning look, as he led them toward an inner room on the ground floor. He had no idea what it had been, but recently it had housed scribes copying the Code from his originals. These, at his nod, left their work gladly enough. The room had a high ceiling and tall narrow windows opening on a court shaded by trees and edged with narrow beds of pink flowers; it held night's coolness and the scent of the flowers as well as the tang of ink and parchment.

"No need to climb the stairs," Luap murmured, offering her a chair. Lady Dorhaniya smiled, but tremulously. Clearly she had something on her mind.

"Thank you, young man. Now let me just catch my breath—"

"A drink of water?" The scribes kept a jug in their room; he poured her a mug. She took it as if it were finest glass, and sipped.

"You should sit down, young man. What I have to say is . . . is very important to you."

Luap tried to look surprised. "I thought perhaps you'd come about something in the Lord's Hall."

"No. It wasn't that." She peered at him, then sat back, nodding. "I wasn't wrong, either. I may not be as young as I was, but I've not lost my memory for faces. Tell me, these men call you Luap, but do you know your real name?"

"I've always been told it was Selamis," Luap said.

"Ah. You have reason to wonder?"

He shrugged. "Lady, by what I was told, my mageborn father chose my daily name, and gave me no other — common enough with such children."

"You know that much," she said, her eyes bright. "Do you know which lord fathered you?"

"I've been told it was the king," Luap said with more difficulty than he'd expected. "But many bastards dream of high birth."

She bent her head to him, in so graceful a movement that he did not at first recognize it as a bow. "Then I will confirm what you were told: you were the king's son — not this recent king, but Garamis. I saw you many times as a small boy, and you have the same look about the eyes you had then. Your mother was, it's true, a peasant lass — a maidservant in the summer palace — but some said she had mageborn blood a generation or so back."

Even knowing it was coming didn't help. He felt the same helpless rage and fear that had overwhelmed him while listening to Arranha. This old lady, so secure and decent, had *seen* him, remembered him. She had seen his mother, no doubt; she had known his father. He shivered, and looked up to find them both staring at him. The old lady's servant — Eris, he remembered — had a look he could interpret as contempt.

"Does it bother you?" Lady Dorhaniya asked. Her eyes were altogether too shrewd. "You were a charming boy, very well-mannered, and you've grown to a charming man. . . . " It was almost worse, though he could not explain it. If he'd been a bad child, cruel or wicked or dull, that could justify what had happened to him. If his father had been the last, most wicked king, that could justify what had happened to him. But he could see, against the inside of his eyelids, the child he had been, the child she was now describing so carefully . . . the child who wanted so much to please, the child alert to the wishes of those who cared for him. " — you brought me a little nosegay," she said. "So thoughtful, for such a young boy. . . . " He had learned that from a mageborn youth, a few years

24

older, and found it impressed ladies visiting; he had made nosegays for all of them. " — and recitations. Your father had you stand up one night before dinner, and speak the entire text of *Torre's Ride*. You must have been nine or so, then — "

That he remembered; it had been just before he was sent away, and at first he'd thought it was because he'd made an error. His tutor had scolded him for it. He had known, then, that the king commanded that performance, but not that the king was his father. And then the steward had come, with a false smile on his face, to take him to an outlying vill and deliver him to the senior cottager.

" — Just before your dear father died," Lady Dorhaniya said. "I don't expect you remember it. They closed the summer palace, and I suppose you went somewhere else."

She could not know where 'somewhere else' had been — to someone like her, the closing of one palace meant the opening of another. His mind, running ahead on its own track, tripped on the memory of " — your dear father died," and came back to the present. "He died after that — not long after that?"

"Yes, that's what I was saying. Before Sunturning, it was, and then Lorthin took the throne, and sent my dear husband into exile for a time. So of course I wouldn't have been to the summer palace even had it been open."

"What — " His mouth had dried; he swallowed and tried again. "Did you know my mother — I mean, her name?"

"You don't remember — ? Oh — yes; they sent her away when you were just walking. Her name . . . no, I don't . . . but she was a comely lass, never fear. Darker haired than your father, but with red in it; that's where you got the red highlights in your hair, and your eyes are more like hers. Your face is his, brow, cheek and chin."

That didn't help; she seemed to realize it, for she made one of the meaningless comforting sounds old ladies make, and reached to pat his knee. "There, young man — young prince, I should say, for you alone survive of the royal blood, though it won't do you much good. You've nothing to fear in my memories of you. . . ."

But I do, he thought, feeling himself squeezed between intolerable and conflicting realities. Already I have much to fear from you, and I can't even tell what it is . . . but I feel it. "I . . . don't remember much," he said with difficulty. Even as he said it, details he had forgotten for years poured into his mind as pebbles from a sack, each distinct. Yet it was not a lie, for he could not remember what he most wanted to at the moment, what this old woman had looked like, which of the many noblewomen she had been. He could not remember what she remembered; he had nothing to share, no memories that would make sense to her.

"I expect you remember more than you want, sometimes," she said, surprising him again. He had scant experience of old women, and none of his own background; when he met her eyes, they seemed filled with secret laughter, not unkind. "Most men remember the bad things; my husband, to the day he died, remembered being thrashed for riding his father's horse through a wheatfield near harvest. Yet in his family he had the reputation of being a rollicking lad no punishment could touch. You look now as you did then — sensitive enough to feel a word as much as a blow. That's why I thought, perhaps, my memories could help you. Show you the way you seemed to others — "

"No!" It got past his guard, in a choked whisper; then he clamped his lips tight. Tears stung his eyes. He swallowed, unlocked his jaw, and managed to speak in a voice nearly his own. "I'm sorry, Lady Dorhaniya, but — that's over. It's gone. I don't — I don't think about it — "

She sat upright, her lips pursed, her expression unreadable. Then, as if making a decision, she nodded gravely and went on. "Prince, you cannot put it aside that way. It's true, the world has changed; you have no throne, and no royal family to sponsor you. But you must know your past, and make it your own, or you cannot become whatever Esea means for you."

The god's name startled him; he started to say that he was no worshipper of the Sunlord, but stopped himself. Instead, he said, "I swore that I would give up all thought of kingship."

She nodded briskly. "Quite right, too. Pursuing such a claim could only bring trouble to the land and people. And you have had no training for kingship. But this does not mean that Esea has no path lighted for you."

Luap shrugged, easing tight shoulders. "As Gird's chronicler, scribe, assistant . . . it seems clear to me that this is my task." Listening to himself, even he could hear the lack of completion; he was not surprised when she shook her head.

"For now, prince. For now, that is your task, and see that you do it in the Sun's light! But you have more to do — and don't laugh at an old woman, thinking me silly with age." For an instant, she looked almost fierce, white hair and all, though he had not laughed, even inside. "You have a position no one else can share: you are the royal heir, though you have no throne. But you — and only you — can lead your own people —"

"Which of my people?" Luap asked irritably. She was beginning to sound like the Autumn Rose, and he had a sudden vision of that dire lady in old age, still pursuing his irresolution with her own certainty.

That got him a long straight stare; he could feel his face reddening. "That," she said severely, "was unworthy of you. You know quite well I meant your father's folk, the mageborn. I would have thought Arranha would have spoken to you. . . ."

"He has," said Luap, suddenly as disgusted with himself as she seemed to be. "He and the Autumn Rose both. I am supposed to do *something* — but no one can tell me what, or how, or even more how to do it without breaking my oath to Gird —" *And the gods.* Sweat came out on him. What kind of leadership could he give, without using magery he had sworn not to use? What kind of leadership without usurping Gird's authority?

"Of course no one can tell you," Lady Dorhaniya said tartly. "You are the *prince*; you inherited the royal magery — oh yes, I have heard that, too. As the prince, the Sunlord's light is yours, do you choose to ask such guidance. Have you?"

To such a question only a direct answer was possible. "No, lady," said Luap, sweating. He had had a child's knowledge of the gods when he was sent away; after that, among peasants, he could not have worshipped the Sunlord even if he'd wanted to. He had not wanted to; he had been abandoned by his father and his father's god, and he would not pay homage to either of them.

"Well, you should. Esea knows you had a poor enough childhood, with that prune-stuffed steward and whatever happened after your father died, but the fact remains that you are what you are, and unless you learn to *be* that, you're as dangerous as a warsteed in the kitchen." She looked around for her servant, and then hitched herself forward. Luap rose and offered his arm. "Yes — I must be going. I've said too much too

27

soon, it may be. But your father, prince, had more sense than his brothers; somewhere in your head you have it. I suggest you ask the Sunlord's aid, and soon." Then she stopped again. "And who is this Autumn Rose you mentioned?"

That he could answer. "A mageborn lady, a warrior from Tsaia, who joined Gird's army after —"

"Oh, *her*. The king-killer. Some nonsense about her having been involved with the king before his marriage." Lady Dorhaniya sniffed. "She was a wild girl, willful, always storming off about this and that. It's one thing to learn weaponlore, if you've the strength and stomach for it, and another to be starting quarrels just to have the chance of settling them. Not that the prince — later the king — wasn't as bad, for he loved to watch her flare out at things. So she's calling herself Autumn Rose, is she?" From her tone, that was just more foolishness.

"Do you know her name from before?"

The old lady's eyes twinkled in mischief. "Of course I do, but if she hasn't told even Gird, why should I tell you? I doubt she has much family left to be embarrassed, but it's her business, silly as she is." Luap could not imagine anyone thinking Autumn Rose silly. Dangerous and difficult, but not silly. "You might just tell her it sounds more like a title than a name."

Luap grinned. It had not occurred to him that the old lady would have known the Autumn Rose, or, knowing her, might disapprove. She sounded as she might about an errant granddaughter. "I think of her as Rosemage," he said. "Some call her that."

Another sniff. "It would not hurt either of you to ask Esea's guidance," she said. "You've no time for foolishness, either of you, at your ages." Then, with a last nod, she left, leaning only slightly on Eris's arm. Luap followed silently to the outer door, then climbed the stairs to his office. He felt even more unsettled than usual. Everyone wanted something from him, but none of them agreed on what it was. All the decisions he'd made so firmly, in good faith, seemed to be coming apart, unravelling in his hands like rotting rope.

• Chapter Three

Through the hottest days of summer, Luap kept to his work. Gird wanted copies of the newest version of the Code spread widely by late harvest; he asked no more about Luap's real father, only about how the copying proceeded. Aside from the heat, the work suited Luap well. He could concentrate his mind on accuracy, on the precise flavor of a phrase, on Gird's intention and its best expression. He had little time for memory, though he found forgotten courtesies creeping into his speech. "It's that old lady, eh?" asked Gird. Luap agreed it probably was, or perhaps Arranha. He tried not to think about it, and claimed his work prevented visiting Dorhaniya until he'd finished the Code. It was safer not to think of it, to submerge himself in Gird's plans, to become, if he could, the eldest son or younger brother that Gird so desperately needed.

But at last the copying had been done, and in the cooler fall weather, he had more than an excuse to leave Fin Panir — he could best be spared to carry the copies to the larger granges, where more copies could be made to send elsewhere. So it was that on a dank autumn day he found himself peering along the bank of a stream for the overhanging rock and dark entrance to a certain cave.

He did not let himself wonder why he chose not to stay overnight at Soldin, knowing he could not reach Graymere by sundown. When the chill autumn drizzle thickened to gusts of rain, he made for the cave directly. It was the only thing to do. It was logical, reasonable, and he did not have to manufacture an excuse.

It bothered him slightly that he could think of making an excuse. He had legitimate business, Gird's business, in Soldin and Graymere both. No one would have questioned his spending a night in the cave, even if anyone had seen him. The yeoman-marshal in Soldin had suggested that he stay the night there, but obviously saw nothing amiss in Gird's luap choosing to press on, even in bad weather. Young and earnest, he expected such dedication in Gird's personal staff.

Luap had wondered if other travelers used the cave . . . surely they did. But on this dank, dripping evening no smoke oozed from the entrance, and no tethered mounts or draft teams snorted or stamped as he legged his own mount along the creek bank. A pile of blackened rocks marked a firepit, obviously in recent use — but not today. He would have it to himself, unless someone showed up later. He hoped no one would, but he was grateful to the previous users, who had stacked dry wood inside the entrance, out of the rain.

He got his fire going, and went out to gather more wood to dry beside it. Someone had improved the path down to the creek, cutting steps and anchoring them with stone; the single plum he vaguely remembered had suckered into a thicket, now dropping their narrow leaves to the sodden ground. By the time he had found wood to replace what he expected to use, it was nearly dark.

His wet cloak steamed as he set his traveling kettle to boil. So did his horse's coat, and the smell of horse expanded, he thought, to fill the cave as well as his head. Wet wool, wet horse . . . almost as bad as the stench of their army, the last time. And then someone else had done the cooking. His head felt heavy, stuffed with thick smells and memories . . . including that final memory, of Gird's fist against his skull. He ran his hands over his wet hair as if feeling for that old lump. There — it had been there, and another bruise on the other side, where he'd fallen against stone.

He had eaten his soaked wheat and beans, and a lump of soggy bread that wrapping had not kept dry, had gone out into the fine rain to use the jacks he'd dug, and was back in the cave's relative warmth and dryness, when he admitted to himself just why he had chosen that trail, that day, in that weather. Of course he didn't expect anything to happen. He had had his revelation, first from the gods, and then from Gird: you are a king's son, and (or but) you can't be a king. One revelation to a lifetime, Gird had said after Greenfields, and would explain no more than that.

But for Luap it had happened here, and he still did not understand it. As with the rest of his life, he had been shown something, a small glimpse of some mystery, and then it vanished. He had learned to hoard such glimpses, to keep them hidden deep in his mind, until he found another — and another — and could try to make them fit some pattern. He had learned, he realized, in all the ways Gird despised . . . that he himself despised, when he thought how he admired Gird . . . but ways he could not change. Not now. Gird had all the pieces of his pattern — had always had them. He had always known who he was, and what his place was, growing out of his own ground like a young tree. Luap had had sidelong looks, sly taunts, occasional brief phrases, whispers, suggestions, riddles. "Don't you know, boy?" he remembered an older youth had asked once. "Only bastards don't know who their fathers are." The boy had been yanked away by someone in guards' uniform, and disappeared; Luap never saw him again.

He sat staring at the flames, ignoring the dancing shadows on the walls that shifted, bowed, straightened in answer to the flames' movement. He had come back because . . . because he was going back in there, to the place where he got one straight answer, for once in his life, and might — no matter what Gird said — get another.

But that means, one of his inner voices said, *that you are not content to be Gird's luap.* Was that true? Alone in the cave, in the orange firelight, he let himself think about that. *Feel* about that. He did not resent Gird. Gird had won his heart, that first night, when he had had to confess his duplicity, when Gird had let him sob out the agony of loss. Gird had defended him against the other peasant leaders. And even the blow that felled him had been, he realized, justified. In the years since, he had come to believe that Gird, with all his peasant coarseness, all his human failings, had the intrinsic greatness of an ancient tree, or a mountain.

Yet he did not want to be *only* a luap forever. He let himself remember, cautiously, his life before the war. His wife and children were long dead, their suffering ended. He would regret his treatment of them for the rest of his life . . . but that was in the past. Tonight . . . tonight, he would like to have had a woman beside him. A child leaning against his knee. A place where he, not Gird, was paramount. A kingdom, however small, in which to be king.

Here, inside a whole mountain, on a black night of dripping rain, no one would see him use his power; no one could see his light. It could not be betrayal if no one knew. He felt his way to it cautiously, even here — a little light, just enough to see by — and his hands enclosed it, glowing. He felt the hairs rise on his arms. He could still do it; it had not vanished. Despite Arranha's assurance that it would not, he had doubted. Around him, in the throat of the cave, the walls showed their stripes of gray and pink and brown. There was the ledge over which Gird had stumbled . . . there, the opening beyond.

Gingerly, he edged toward it. The little chamber opened, then enclosed him, as if he completed it. Its walls held the same graved patterns he remembered, that Gird had traced with his thumb, that Luap had devoured with his eyes, trying to remember them. Spiral on spiral, coil in coil, lacing and interlacing. He turned, slowly, following the pattern . . . it felt *strong*, and meaningful, but he could not read it. A bad taste came into his mouth: another failure.

On the chamber's floor, curiously clean of dust, multicolored tesselations glowed in his light, inviting. A different pattern, in which color as well as line interacted, in which his eye was teased, frustrated, satisfied, and finally released with a *snap* that echoed in his head. He looked up.

And up.

He stood, not in the small bell-shaped chamber of the cave, but in a lofty hall, larger than the Lord's Hall in Fin Panir, lit by unshadowed silvery light. He could see no windows, no source for the light. He stood on a pattern like that on which he began, but set on a raised dais large enough for a score to stand uncrowded. All his hair rose; cold chills shook him; his own pulse thundered in his ears.

At last he could hear and see clearly again, only to find great silence and unmoving space about him. He did not want to speak, and risk waking whatever power held sway here, but courtesy demanded some greeting. In his mind, he recited the opening phrases to the first ritual he remembered, something out of his childhood, the morning greeting to the Sunlord. Around him, unbroken silence changed its flavor from austerity to welcome. Was he imagining it? He took a slow, shuffling step forward, away from the pattern. Nothing. He was not sure what he half-expected, but he felt like a child exploring forbidden adult territory. For an instant, such a moment flashed before his eyes, a tower bedroom crowded with furniture, rich hangings, a bed piled with pillows, and the furious eyes, four of them, that glared at him before an angry voice rose and whirled him away on its own power.

No. He was grown, and whoever that had been must have died in the war, if not before. He fought down the fear that trembled in his knees and walked forward, off the dais, across a pattern of black and white stones, to the high double arch that closed the end of the hall. Not truly closed, for he could see less brightly lit space beyond, but he didn't want to walk under those arches. At the top of one, a harp and tree intertwined; on the other, a hammer and anvil. He shivered: he could not imagine a place where elves and dwarves would both choose to carve their holy symbols. He turned back.

The dais, at that distance, seemed apt for a throne; he closed his eyes, and let himself imagine seeing one there, and himself —no, not on the throne, but walking up the hall toward it. His imagination peopled the hall with vivid colors, the richly dressed lords and ladies of his childhood. Music would fill the hall, harp and drum and pipe, and from that celebration no one would be sent away, solitary, to cry in the dark. His power prodded him from within, responding to some influence he could not directly sense.

He opened his eyes. He could still see what it would be like, but — he shook his head to force the vision away — that was daydream, and this was — if not reality — at least something less tuned to his wish. It lay empty, gracefully proportioned, but blank stone, not filled with the friends he had never had.

Soon he realized that it must be all under stone somewhere, for in his cautious exploration he found no window, no door, no hint of outside weather or time. Fresh air, in currents so gentle he could not detect a source, lighted corridors and chambers, all carved of seamless red stone, all empty, all silent but for his footfalls echoing from the walls. No sign of living things, not the Elder Races he assumed had built it, or the animals that should be inhabiting any such underground warren. He dared not explore too far; he went cold again at the thought of being trapped here forever, in some vast nameless tomb, if he lost his way back to the main hall.

Then it struck him that he might be trapped anyway. Would

the pattern work again, and if it did would it bring him back to the cave he knew? Trembling, he placed himself on the dais, on the pattern, as precisely as he could. With a last look around, he concentrated on the pattern, and his own power. A cold shiver, as if touched by ice, and he was back in a bell-shaped chamber. The same such chamber? He intensified his own light, and went back toward the cave mouth . . . to find there the embers of his fire, his blanket, his damp socks now dry on the hot stones. He felt almost faint with relief.

All that night he sat crosslegged with his back against the rock, hardly aware of the rain outside or the smell of horse. In his head, the puzzle pieces would not merge, made no sense. What kind of place was this? What kind of place was *that*? Twice he found himself on his feet, headed back to the chamber to see if it would work again, and twice he forced himself back to the fire. He shouldn't try it again until he'd thought it out, and thinking *at* it wasn't the same as thinking it out.

Should he tell Arranha? He could imagine the priest's eager questions, his childlike curiosity. Arranha would tell everyone else, hoping to stumble on someone with more lore, if it were but fireside tales. He didn't want others to know yet, not until he knew more himself. The Rosemage would want to come try it for herself; she might keep it a secret from everyone but Gird, but she would not let the knowledge rest idle — she would insist that he *do* something with it. And telling either of them meant that Gird would find out, and Gird would not overlook the use of magery if he found out through someone else. So — should he tell Gird first? That would mean admitting the use of magery, unless he could claim that the pattern acted without his power — and lying to Gird was always, no matter how good the reason, tricky. At best. At worst, Gird would hit him again (he rubbed his scalp, remembering.)

The next day, in the rain-wet woods between Soldin and Graymere, he argued with himself and his internal images of Gird, Arranha, the Autumn Rose. Surely the gods would not have given him the power, shown him the inner cave, if they had not meant him to use them. In his head, Arranha agreed, pointing out that using magery where no one could see it, where it could affect no one but himself, was very like using no magery at all. It had not been oathbreaking, because he had not sought power, or influenced anyone, or taken command unbidden. The Autumn Rose also approved; he imagined her striding along that vast hall as if she owned it: she fit that sort of space. She would want to know where it was; she would want to know who had been there before, who built it, who used it now. He had a moment's vision of her confronting a troop of very surprised dwarves somewhere in those warrens, and almost laughed.

Gird, though. Gird stood in his head foursquare and awkward. *You used magery*, that image said, scowling. Only a little, and it didn't hurt anyone, he answered. And look what I found. *Excuses*, said Gird's image in his mind. *Truth's truth, lad: you swore to give up the mage powers, and you used them.* Even in his own mind, Gird had the stubbornness of a great boulder in a field, or a massive oak; he felt that his own arguments scratched around and around, going nowhere and moving that obstruction not even the width of a fingernail.

By Graymere, he'd convinced himself to tell the Autumn Rose and no one else until she'd had a chance to try the pattern herself. She might agree to keep it secret from Gird until she had used it, or tried to; perhaps Gird would accept that if Luap explained he had wanted confirmation from someone else before "bothering" Gird. Between Graymere and Anvil, by way of Whitberry, he changed his mind, and planned to tell only Arranha. Arranha, for all his skewed approach to things, would be more likely to know what those symbols carved in the arches meant, if there had been a time when elves and dwarves worked stone together. Approached carefully, he might be willing to keep this secret, at least for awhile. But on the long, muddy track back to Fin Panir from Anvil, he realized that he would have to tell Gird, and risk the consequences. If Gird found later that others had known, he would not forgive — he would not even listen. His one chance was to tell Gird first, and hope that curiosity had not completely abandoned the Marshal-General.

He wanted to keep it secret. He wanted one place, one small corner of his life, in which Gird had no standing. He rode hunched against the wind, eyes slitted, remembering that vast silence, that sense of absolute privacy. He did not have to decide *now* — for certainly he was the only one to have this knowledge. As long as he did not choose to share it, he could have his secret kingdom. His mind flinched from the words— he was not to seek a kingdom. It was more like the memories he had once held privately: a secret, but nothing so dangerous as a kingdom.

But he would have to tell Gird, he argued to himself. It would not be honest to do otherwise. Although it *would* be important to pick exactly the right time to tell Gird — when the Marshal-General was in the right mood, when he had no pressing worries, when they had ample time to discuss it. From experience, he knew the first few days back in Fin Panir would be a chaotic jumble of work. It might easily be a hand of days, or two, before he could find time to tell Gird about something which, after all, was of no practical importance to the Fellowship.

"Luap . . . sir?" Luap glanced up to see a strange yeoman in the doorway, twisting his conical straw hat in his hand. "It's about Gird. . . . "

Luap realized he had not heard anything from the other end of the corridor for a long time. He had been working steadily through the mass of accounts and correspondence that had, as he expected, kept him at his desk every day since his return. Gird had been out much of the time, busy with court work. Now his heart faltered — had Gird died? But the man was already speaking, concern overcoming nervousness.

"He come in for a meal like he does so often," the man said. "And then he sees this old friend from back at Burry or some-such place. And they gets to talking and taking a bit of ale, you know. . . . " His voice trailed away. He didn't want to say it. Luap sighed.

"You'd like someone to help him home?" he asked.

The man nodded. "This friend, see, he's eggin' him on, like, and Gird won't listen to the innkeeper or even the cook. . . . "

Luap realized that he'd seen the man before after all. He worked in the stables at the largest inn down by the lower market. He groaned inwardly. It was going to be a hard job getting Gird back up the hill. "Do you have a spare room, perhaps?" he asked.

"Well . . . I suppose maybe, but after what he called the innkeeper . . . "

"I'll come now," said Luap, standing. Whom could he call?

He'd need more arms than two, if Gird had drunk his fill. He flung his blue cloak around him, and took the stout stick that had become a Marshal's insignia, though all knew he was no Marshal. A glance out the window of the room across the corridor located Marshal Sterin, and a yell brought him in, sweaty and cross from drilling novices.

"Gird?" he said. "What's the Marshal-General want now?"

"A friend's help to come home," said Luap. "He's down at the Rock and Spring."

"Ahh . . ." Sterin cut off whatever he'd almost said, with a glance at the man from the inn. "Met an old friend, did he?"

"From Burry, this man thinks. Got to talking about the war—"

"I see. We'll need another, and it can't be a novice. Too bad Cob's not here. Tamis Redbeard?"

"Good," said Luap. Tamis Redbeard stood a hand taller than he did, and could probably lift Gird in one hand. If he wasn't fighting back.

They could hear Gird and someone else before they came in sight of the inn. Singing, none too melodiously, one of the songs written after Greenfields. A small crowd loitered outside the inn, a few lucky ones close enough to peer in the windows. It parted like butter before a hot knife, then flowed back as seamlessly, as Luap led the others through the door.

"There was a man rode out one day
Upon a horse, a horse of gray
And all along the people saaaay
He must be such a king, oh . . ."

The man from Burry, or wherever, had one arm around a post, and one around Gird's shoulders. He had reached the green stage; Luap thought he would vomit in a moment or two. Gird had still the flush of early drunkenness, a red rim to each eye and a glitter in them.

"Marshal-General, we've need of you up the hill," Luap began. It wouldn't work, but he could start with respect and good sense.

"No court today," said Gird, head thrust forward. He belched, grinned at his companion. "So we're just taking a bit of ale, like, and singing the old songs. No harm in that. Everybody's got to have some time—"

"No, it's not court," Luap said. "It's something else."

37

"I know," said the other man, slurring the words. "You think we're drunk and ye've come to nursemaid th' old man." Luap glared at him; that would end any chance of Gird cooperating. Gird glowered, first at his companion and then at Luap.

"Is that what it is, you think I need a keeper?"

"No, sir. We've need of you, that's what I said."

"And you need me so much you brought two Marshals along? Can't you ever tell the truth, Luap? Did you think I wouldn't know Sterin and Tamis, big as they are, with their staves?"

Luap gritted his teeth. It was not *fair*, in front of all these people, and in such a cause. Confront drunks directly and start a brawl — even Gird said that, when he was sober. It wasn't as if he himself hadn't used subterfuge on other drunks, from time to time. Rage scoured his mind, eroding the controls he placed so carefully. He opened his mouth, but Sterin was before him.

"Aye, Father Gird, if you'll have the truth of it, we was told you'd drunk more'n was good for you, and would be the better of friends to bring you home. Yer friend there's had more'n his fill; he's green as springtime berries, and the both of ye smell like ye've emptied a barrel —"

"Lemme alone," began the other man, when Sterin reached to unhook his arm from Gird's shoulder. Then he turned even greener around the mouth, his eyes widened, and he spewed across the floor, then fell headlong in the mess. Sterin had stepped back, not quite in time, and now gave Luap a disgusted glance. He shrugged.

"I'll get this mess clean," he said, meaning man and floor both. "You and Tam get the Marshal-General back before he doubles it." Luap fought down another surge of anger. Sterin was in his rights, as the senior Marshal present, but did he have to make it so obvious that Luap had no right of command?

"Yes, Marshal Sterin," he heard himself saying, the effort at courtesy clearly audible and destroying the effect he had meant to produce. He and Tam moved around the man from Burry, now struggling to sit up, and moved into position beside Gird. He put his arm under Gird's elbow, ready to lift or push or whatever would be necessary.

"Let's go now," he suggested, in the calm quiet tone that

worked best with most drunks. Gird glanced from one to the other.

"I am not drunk." As always in this state, his words came slow, the peasant accent distinct. "My father wouldn't put up with it."

"Your father's dead these many years." Luap heaved, as effectively as he might have heaved at a live, deep-rooted oak. "Come on, now, man . . . you've got to get back home."

"No home." His forehead knotted. "Gone. Went away."

The other drunk, still pale from throwing up the first wash, tittered weakly. "I'm not that drunk," he lied. "*My* home didn't go away."

"Shut *up*," Luap muttered at the man from Burry. "Sterin — get him away." He had seen the expression on Gird's face before, the swift change from hilarity to grim sadness. It had something to do with whatever happened the morning of Greenfields, which Gird would not speak of — but he was more dangerous in this mood than any other. The man from Burry vanished, and in a few moments Sterin reappeared. Luap could feel the tension in Gird's shoulders, some mingling of rage and sorrow.

"No home," Gird said again. "Never . . . it will never be. . . ." All around the eyes stared, the ears listened; Luap could almost see the legend growing. In a moment someone would decide it was prophecy, that Gird had the foreseeing gift beside all his others. He caught Tamis's eye, and Sterin's, and gave a minute nod. "It is not finished!" Gird's voice sharpened, and Sterin, who had reached for his other arm, stopped to give Luap a worried glance. Somewhere outside, Luap could just hear pattering hooves of sheep or goats, and a voice calling to them. Everyone in sight was silent, motionless, waiting Gird's next word. And this, too, he would have to explain, somehow, when Gird sobered up the next day, for all that some thought the gods spoke truly to men drowned in wine.

"It is not finished!" Gird said again, louder. "Not until mageborn and nonmage live in peace, not until the same law rules farmer and brewer, crafter and crofter, townsman and countryman. Not until they agree — " He paused, breathing hard, as if from battle, then he shook his head. "And they won't," he said quietly, sadly. For all Luap's recent annoyance, he found himself moved, almost to tears, by that tone. "They want what cannot be — " He turned to face Luap. "You do,

39

whether you know it or not — and they — and maybe I myself wish for what cannot be." He spoke still quietly, but with such intensity that everyone around stood breathless, straining to hear. "It should not be so hard, by the gods! To agree to live in peace: what's so hard about that? Or is it because I didn't die at Greenfields?"

Luap stared at him, feeling the hairs rise on his scalp and along his arms. Die at Greenfields? What did he mean? He peered around Gird to meet on Tamis's face the expression of what he felt: fear and confusion.

"They told me," Gird said, now almost conversationally, "that I would not live to see the peace. I came down from the hill to die — and then lived. Is it that?"

"Thank Alyanya's grace you *did* live, sir," said Tamis quickly, and Sterin murmured something similar. Luap couldn't say anything; his mouth was dry, his tongue stuck to the roof of it. He had never believed in the drunkard's truth, but this was truth if ever he heard it.

But Gird was shaking his head. "My head hurts," he said. "It's hot. I think — I think I'll go back — if you'll settle with the innkeeper, Luap?"

He walked off, not quite steadily, Tamis and Sterin at either elbow, leaving Luap to pay and — since Sterin had gone — to help the innkeeper in mopping the stinking floor. *That's what I'm good for,* Luap thought. *Pay the bills, keep the accounts straight, clean up after him.* That wasn't a fair assessment, and he knew it, but he indulged himself a little anyway. It wasn't fair that Gird had called him a liar in public, when he was only trying to be tactful.

When he had finished mopping, much of the crowd had melted away, as crowds do. Not as interesting to watch a sober man mop a floor as watch a drunk foul it . . . and Gird hoped to make a strong and peaceful society out of these sheep? The innkeeper accepted his coins with a sour look, although he'd added a sweetener to the total. "Great men!" the innkeeper said, leaving no doubt that he was still angry. "I'm not saying a thing against what he did, y'understand, but that doesn't give him th' right to call honest men thieves or cowards."

Luap couldn't decide if an apology would do any good, and his momentary silence seemed to irritate the innkeeper even more.

"I know what you're like," the man went on, feeling each coin ostentatiously before putting it in his belt-pouch. "You won't tell me what you think, but anything I say goes straight to *him*."

"He's not like that," Luap said.

"Huh. He's not, or you don't tell him everything?" Shrewd hazel eyes peered at him. Luap shrugged.

"Tomorrow he'll be sorry he insulted you; surely you know that. Bring it up at the next market court, and he'll fine himself and apologize before as large a crowd as heard the insult."

"Oh, aye. Apologies don't mend broken pottery or put wool back on a shorn sheep. My da said them's don't make mistakes don't have to waste time on apologies." Luap wondered where the innkeeper had been during the war. The innkeeper answered that, too, in his final sally. "We've had royalty in here, you know, before the rabble — before the revolution. Dukes, even a prince of the blood. Knew how to hold their wine, they did, and it wasn't any of this cheap ale, neither."

Luap's temper flared. "Well, you've had another prince of the blood, for what that's worth."

The innkeeper's eyebrows went up. "Who, then?"

"Me," said Luap, turning to go, sure of the last word. But the innkeeper cheated him of that, as well.

"But raised with peasants, weren't you then? Makes a difference, don't it? It's not like you're a real prince, just some summer folly, eh?"

And if that's not enough to sour a day, thought Luap as he climbed back to the upper city, there's maudlin Gird, who will no doubt spout more difficult prophecy I'll have to explain.

Down below conscious thought, he was not aware of the relief he felt: another day in which he had a good reason not to tell Gird about the cave.

41

● Chapter Four

Raheli leaned against the barton wall, arms folded, watching the dancers through the open grange door. Out of courtesy for her, to spare her the long walk to the traditional sheepfold, they had brought the musicians here . . . they were dancing *here* . . . and she could do nothing but watch. She knew the music, the same as she'd heard all her life, and every step the dancers danced. She could remember, as if it had been yesterday, the night when Parin's hand on her arm changed her from girl to woman. When the dance had changed from entertainment to courtship, and they had begun the dance of life that ended with his death.

She tried not to think of it; she had pushed it aside, so many times, from the moment the mageborn lords had broken his head. She would not let herself brood on it; it did no good. But the old songs ran into her heart like knives; for an instant she almost thought she felt the flutter of that life she had never actually borne. Her child, and his. The face that had come to her in dreams, as her mother had said her children's faces had come. She could smell the very scent of him, feel the warm skin of his chest against her cheek.

The dancers shouted, ending one dance, and a short silence fell. In the torchlight, the dancers' faces wavered, bright light and black shadow, as strange for a moment as ghosts. Raheli had the feeling for a moment that Parin and the child both were in there, somewhere, waiting for her. She had pushed herself off the wall before she realized what she was thinking. Her movement had caught someone's eye; before she could return to her place, she saw people watching her. She would have to go in, and greet them. She tried to smile, and walked forward.

"Rahi! The Marshal's back!" yelled some of the younger yeomen. A way opened for her. They had been dancing a long time; the grange smelled of sweat and onions and the torches and candles, more like a cottage during a feast than a grange. "Now we can dance the Ring Rising."

They meant it as an honor. They could not know she had danced the Ring Rising with Parin, that first time. Rahi blinked away scalding tears, put off her old grief, and accepted the role they demanded of her. The musicians finished their mugs of ale, and picked up the instruments again.

Ring Rising had been, Gird told her once, older than any other dance. Something about it had to do with the old Stone Circle brotherhood, that Gird had turned into the Fellowship, in his own way. But long before, so the oldest tales went, the dance had raised stones, rings of stones, on hill after hill, until the mageborn came and struck them down with their new magic.

Hand in hand with her senior yeoman-marshal, Belthis, Rahi began the dance to the beat of the finger-drums. Couple after couple fell in behind them. It felt strange to dance this indoors; the walls seemed to lean inward, pressing on them. What if it did move stones? Rahi concentrated on the intricate steps, feeling her way back into the rhythms. Heel, toe, side, back, skip forward, stamp. A step, a double-stamp. Now a double-line of couples, two concentric rings, then a swirl that twisted them to interlocking rings, dancing in and out of each other's patterns. Soon all there had joined in, children and elderly as well as the young adults. Rahi found herself moving through four interlocked rings, touching hands with one partner after another for a quarter-turn, then swinging to find another.

It was in the midst of the dance, with the grange full to bursting of music and dancers, that she came face to face with her dream, the child she would have borne. Dark hair, dark eyes, Parin's smile, soft fingers, light-footed and blythe. Her breath caught in her throat, but they had danced the pattern and separated again before she could get a word out. Tears burned in her eyes; she felt them on her cheeks, on the scar . . . and someone she could not see for tears put an arm around her shoulders, making sure she did not falter in the dance, until her breath came easily again.

It was not fair. It had never been fair. She rejected bitterness as instantly as she would have fear. Fairness had nothing to do with it, and everything, and was all Gird had wanted, and more than she would ever have. From bootheel to the top of her head, she felt the beat of that ancient dance, and from hand to hand the warmth and love of her people, and in the middle where the cadence and warmth met, she could feel her heart beating, expanding and contracting, as if it had grown larger than her chest.

Around her the faces glowed, all the children her children, all the men and women her brothers and sisters, her aunts and uncles, fathers and mothers. Her own scars bound her to them, to all those maimed or sickened by life's disasters. *Her* people, with their ancient link to land and deeper magic than the mageborn would ever know . . . and it had not been fair, but she would make it fair. Light and dark, true and false, as simple as the realities they had all endured: hungry and not hungry, cold and not cold, pregnant and not pregnant. She felt herself rising above them, lifted on their affection and trust like a leaf on a summer wind, like the stones of the great rings in which peace and plenty dwelt. Here was the child she had lost, and the love she had lost, and here she would serve.

When the music stopped, she did not know it; she came to herself slowly, realizing silence and space around her. The torches had burned low, but gave a light unusually steady. Then, as she drew a long breath, the murmurs began. The senior yeoman-marshal of the grange bowed to her. "Marshal — it was our honor."

"My pleasure," she replied, hardly thinking. She felt different, but could not yet define the difference; she would have to think about it later. She glanced around. They were all watching her, most smiling, as if she were the favorite grandchild at a family gathering. *Once, I was*, she thought, and felt the scar on her face stretching to her grin. Now they moved closer, touching her arm, her shoulder; her heart lifted, suddenly exultant. She could have hugged them all, but had no need — she could tell by their expressions that they felt what she meant, just as she felt what they meant. Once, and again, she had a place, the place she had thought lost forever.

The next morning, she set out for Littlemarsh barton with a lighter heart than she'd had for years. She felt in place, comfortable; she thought of Gird suddenly with a warmth that surprised her. Could he have felt estranged, in these past years? She thought of him once more as a father, as the father he had been to her. Not perfect, not with his temper and his occasional bouts of drunken depression, but a man who loved his children even more than his beloved cows. For the first time in years, she let herself think of her mother: her face came to memory only dimly, but her words, her movements, the very smell of the bread she made and feel of her strong arms were as clear as if she'd died the day before. That was what she'd hoped to be — another woman like her mother — but time and chance had stolen that from her, as the lords' cruelty had stolen her mother's life, robbing her of peaceful old age.

Yet this morning, bitterness could not swamp the better memories. Mali had laughed a lot; even her scoldings had held warmth and good humor in their core. They had been, within the limitations of hunger and cold and fear, a family drenched in love. From that love, Gird had found the strength to hold and lead an army; from that love she herself had found the strength to come back from an easy death, lead others in battle, and care for them after. For all that had gone wrong, all the wickedness loosed on innocents that she had seen, love and caring had not abandoned the world — or her.

"Alyanya's blessing," she murmured, feeling the tears run over her face, knowing they were healing something. She was not cut off, alone, alienated from her people, a useless barren woman who could only hope for death. She had a family: all of them. She had given her blood, though not in childbirth, and this day she knew that gift had been accepted, by the gods and by her people.

I will go to Gird, she thought, half in prayer and half in promise. *I will tell him he has a daughter again, and not just another Marshal.* In her mind's eye, she saw him grin at her; she saw his arms open; she felt the welcoming hug she had told herself she would never seek again.

Raheli dismounted stiffly. After six days in the saddle, she felt every one of her old wounds, and twice her age. She led her brown gelding into the stable, shaking her head at the junior yeoman who would have helped her. Taking care of her own mount came naturally to a farm girl. She stripped off the saddle and rubbed the sweat marks with a twist of straw. The junior yeoman had brought a bucket of water and scoop of grain; when her horse was dry, she put feed and water in the stall and heaved the saddle to her hip, closing the stall door behind her. Gird's gray horse, in the next stall, put its head out and looked at her.

"You," she said, with emphasis. The gray flipped its head up and down. Cart horse, she thought. Da should know better than that. She would never forget how it had shone silver-white in the sun at Greenfields. Here, in the dim stable, it looked gray enough, but she knew its coat would shine in the sun. It took her sleeve in its lips, carefully, its eyes almost luminous. She rubbed its forehead, scratched behind its ears, and it opened its mouth in a foolish yawn. "You don't fool me," she told it, and it shook its head. "Right." Gird had loved cows, from her earliest memory, as much or more than people; she wondered that the gods had sent him a horse and not a magical cow. A snort from the gray horse. "I know — I'm not supposed to know the gods sent you." She herself had discovered an affinity with horses, and the gray had responded much as others did, with its differences in addition.

Out of the stable, across the inner courtyard. In her Marshal's blue, with the saddlebags that proclaimed her a visitor from some outlying grange, she found a way opened for her in the crowds (they seemed like crowds) that thronged the court and the passages of the old palace. The two guards at the outer door had nodded to her, not questioning her right to enter. Up the stairs, along the corridor, to the office where Luap — she had come to calling him that after Gird did — kept accounts and made the master copies of Gird's legal decrees. She looked in — empty, but for the sick lad she'd heard about, asleep again. Gird's office, near the end of the corridor, was empty too. She frowned. Usually this time of day one or both of them were at work here. She left her saddlebags on his desk, and went down to the kitchen.

"Rahi!" One of the cooks on duty recognized her at once. "When did you get in? How long can you stay?"

"Just now," she said, pouring herself a mug of water. "I'm not sure how long I'll be here yet — where's Gird?"

A sudden silence; eyes shifted away from her. She felt her heart quicken even before the first woman said anything. "Oh — he's not feeling too well today. Nothing serious — "

He'd gotten drunk again. She was sure of it. She had come here to make peace with him, to restore their family, and he had gone off and gotten drunk. Rage blurred her vision, and

46

she fought it down. She would not ask these people; it would embarrass them. She made herself smile. "Well — if he's not up to work, perhaps I could find something to eat?"

"Of course." In moments, a bowl of soup and a loaf were before her. "I don't know if you remember me . . . ?" The woman looked to be her own age, or a little older, not so tall and plumper. Rahi tried to think, but nothing came back to her. "Arya, in the third cohort of Sim's . . . " the woman prompted.

Yes. Arya had been thinner — they all had — but strong and eager, one who never argued about camp chores, either. "I do now," Rahi said, pulling off a hunk of the warm bread. "You taught us all a song about the frog in the spring, I remember." She hummed a line, and Arya grinned.

"You look like your da when you smile," she said. "But dark hair . . . "

"My mother," said Rahi, around the bread, relaxing. Arya had come from a vill much like her own; the talk about which parent a child resembled was as comforting as old tools. Next the talk would turn to their mothers' parrions.

"Since you're here . . . " Arya said, then paused, floury hands planted firmly on the table. Rahi swallowed the bread in her mouth and waited. Arya looked away, but didn't move, and finally came out with it. "There's some of the Marshals saying that now the war's over, there's no need for women to be taken into the bartons. There's some of them saying the Code's too partial to wives. Have you heard of that?"

Rahi nodded. "Mostly in the bigger towns, is where I've heard it. Mostly from men who weren't in the fighting at all, crafters and traders and such."

Arya sat down across from her. "It's the same here, but some of the Marshals — I'd have thought they'd have more sense — some of the Marshals have taken it up. Taken it to Gird, even. I heard it myself, one evening: pecking at him like crows at a sack of grain, all about how there's no need for it now, and the women won't make good wives or mothers if they're always drilling in the bartons. That in the old days our women had parrions of cooking or healing or clothmaking, not parrions of weaponwork."

"He won't listen," said Rahi. "He lost that argument a long time ago." She didn't realize she was grinning until she felt her scar stretch; she was seeing in her mind's eye the blank astonishment on Gird's face that day in the forest camp.

"For you, maybe," Arya persisted. "He would never try to stop you — but what about the rest of us?"

"But you're a veteran," Rahi said. "No one could put you out of the barton now — "

"Not exactly. Not yet." Arya spread her hands. "I shouldn't be bothering you, maybe, but you were the first — and we all look to you. Some of us don't intend to be wives, or go back to farms; we like what we're doing now. And if anyone can keep Gird from taking it away — "

"Don't give it up." She knew now what was coming, and hoped to head it off with a short answer.

"That's what I say," said the other woman, coming now to sit beside Arya. She was younger, darker, with the intensity of youth. Rahi wondered if she had ever been really tired. "It's not up to Gird; our lives aren't something for him to give or take. Arya's a veteran, same as anyone else who fought; why shouldn't she live however she wants? It's not like she was a mageborn lady who needed watching."

"But you know yourself, Lia, it's not that easy — "

"Gird always said nothing's easy that's any good — isn't that right?" The other woman faced Rahi with a challenging stare.

"But are you really afraid he'll change the Code?" asked Rahi. "I'm not the only woman who's a Marshal, you know." But some gave it up, she reminded herself. Some went home, back to a family if they had one, or to start a second family if they'd lost husband and children. When she ran through the list in her mind, perhaps half the women who had won Marshal's rank still held it. In her own grange, fewer women came to the drills as the memory of war faded, as fear of invasion lessened. She had not pushed them, she suddenly realized, as she pushed the men — she had accepted all the usual reasons: pregnancy, a new baby, a sick child, an ailing husband or parent.

"It's not just the training," the other woman — Lia — went on. "Who wants to fight in a war, after all? I was too young for fighting then; I train now because Arya tells me I should. Without her, I'd wait until trouble came before I picked up a sword. But the rest — you know how it was. Under the lords' rule, women could hold no land, even as tenants; in the city, women couldn't rent buildings or speak before a court for themselves. *Father's daughter; husband's wife; son's mother* — that's how it was for all but the mageborn ladies. My mother was a widow; she had no son. She had to ask her brother for houseroom for us, and I had to take him for my da. If the war hadn't come, he'd have married me to the tanner's son, and taken his share of the bride-price. The mageborn didn't have that problem — that woman everyone calls the Autumn Rose, or the Rosemage — "

Rahi snorted; she couldn't help herself. Arya grinned. "I remember what you called her, Rahi."

"Don't say it!" Rahi held up a hand, chuckling. "I've been told often enough how rude I was. Am. And if my mother were alive, she'd say throwing a name at someone is like throwing mud at the sky. It always comes back on you."

"But what I meant was it was different for them," said the younger woman, earnestly. "Their ladies had the right to choose; they had the right to learn weaponscraft — "

"Easy, Lia," said Arya. "Rahi knows all that, none better." She took the younger woman's hand in hers, squeezed it. "Rahi's not going to let her da, even the Marshal-General that he is, change the laws back and put free women under men's thumbs again." The look she gave Rahi said *Are you?* as clearly as words.

Rahi shook her head, and bit into the bread as if she hadn't eaten in days. It made her uncomfortable, the way so many women acted around her, as if she were a sort of Marshal-General for women, and Gird was the one for men. Whenever she traveled, women would come to her with their problems, things their own marshals should have handled, things she had no idea how to handle. She supposed she deserved it: she had been the first, and the arguments she'd used on Gird still seemed reasonable. But when she heard them coming back at her from someone else's mouth — and when some women went far beyond anything she'd ever meant — she never knew what to say.

They didn't want to hear what she really thought. If she had had a family to go back to . . . if she had been able to bear children . . . she would not be a Marshal. She would have been happy to center a family as her mother had; she would have enjoyed (as, in her short time as a young wife she had enjoyed) the close friendship of other women in a farming village; she would have liked growing into the authority the old grannies had, when younger women came to her for help, one of the endless dance of women who passed on the knowledge and power that came with the gift of life. The peasant folk had always had a place for those who loved for pleasure, not bearing, but most of those married for children, and loved where they would. She had no way to understand those who were content outside the family structure, women who not only loved women but wanted no home as she knew it, wanted no children.

And even with those whose needs she understood, she felt she was the wrong person to help. She wasn't the right age, the right status. To be one of the old grannies, you had to be a wife and mother first; you had to give the blood of birthing, the milk of suckling, proving your power to give share life to the family, before you could share it abroad. She was no granny; she was barren, a widow, a scarred freak who would not fit in. The comfort she had felt at the dance vanished, and she blinked back the tears that stung her eyes, hoping the others did not notice, and finished her meal. Her past was gone, no use crying over it. That cottage would not rise from the rubble; those poisoned fields would not bear grain in her lifetime, and Parin would not rise from the dead to hold her in his arms, however she dreamed of it. And hers was not the only such loss; the only thing to do was go on. She struggled to regain the vision that had brought her to Fin Panir. She had said she would do what her people needed; if these women needed her, she must be what they asked.

"I don't think Gird would change the Code that way," she said slowly. "Not just for me, but because he really does believe in a fair rule for everyone. But I'll keep my eye on it, how about that?"

"And on that luap of his," said Arya, scowling. Rahi looked up, startled. He had seemed loyal to Gird, these last years — was he changing?

"What about him?"

Lia sniffed, and Arya's scowl deepened. "He's too thick wi' that Autumn Rose, is what. And that old woman that brought fancy cloths for the altar in the Hall, she's been telling him he's a prince — "

50

Rahi shrugged. "Gird knew that, and told others. So?"

"But she *treats* him as one. What if he starts thinking he'd rather rule than be Gird's luap? What if he has another child? What if the other mageborn are turning to him . . . eh?"

Rahi considered this. She had never liked Luap as well as some, or disliked him as much as others; in later years she'd come to think of him as important, even necessary, to the success of Gird's purposes. A bit too confident in situations where an honest man wouldn't be confident, but as Gird had said, if the gods could make a commander in war from a plain farmer, anyone could change. Yet — she doubted the gods had anything to do with Luap's change, if it was a change. "I don't know," she said. "You know I don't like the Rosemage, but Luap — he's not the same as he was when I first saw him, and he's not to blame for his father's acts."

"If you say so." Both women had a sullen look Rahi could not interpret; she wondered what Luap had done or said.

"Rahi!" A man's voice, from door to the courtyard. Marshal Sterin, she remembered after a moment. "When did you reach the city?"

She looked at the angle of sun through the tree in the courtyard. "Perhaps a hand ago." Then it occurred to her that he had phrased his question curiously. Why? Why "reach the city" instead of "arrive?"

"Th' old man's had a bad morning," Sterin said, coming in. The two women got up, silently, and went back to their work. Sterin sat where they had been. "He'd gone down to the lower market, on some errand, and met an old veteran from Burry."

She had figured it out for herself; she didn't want to hear it from Sterin. "He went drinking with him, did he?"

"Yes. We got him home all right, but — " Sterin leaned closer; Rahi noticed that he looked worried. "Did he ever talk to you about Greenfields? About *before* Greenfields?"

"No." She had not seen him before Greenfields, except that one glance across the field; she had heard from others that he came down from the hill just before the battle started, and looked, they said, "strange." By the time she saw him again, they had other things to talk of than the morning — and by the time she thought to ask, a season later, he would not speak of it. Everyone knew he would not speak of it.

"He said something," Sterin said now. "He was drunk, yes,

but his voice changed, and he said things. . . . I wonder if the gods gave him the words."

Rahi doubted that. She waited; Sterin was silent a moment then told her the rest.

"He said he should have died, at Greenfields, and that all the troubles we have now come because he didn't."

"What!"

"Aye, that's what he said. Plain as if he was in court, giving judgment. 'I should have died,' he said, 'and that's what's wrong.' The gods gave him a vision that day, he said, of a land at peace with him dead, and shattered with war if he wasn't willing. Well, we were there, you and me, Rahi — we know how he fought. He didn't save his skin by shirking danger; he and that horse were right in the middle of the battle. When he charged the magelords' cavalry, I thought sure he'd be spitted."

"Yes," said Rahi, trying to remember anything but a confusion of noise and fear and stench. She could remember faces in her cohort, the thrust of pike and spear, the moment she slipped and fell, and someone yanked her up, but she could not remember anything of the shape of the battle. She had heard about Gird's charge at the cavalry, but hadn't seen it. All she knew was that it ended, at last, with the old king dead and victory for the peasants.

"So if the prophecy was that he'd have to be willing, I'd say he was — he proved that. Yet does that mean the prophecy was wrong, or he's remembered it wrong, or is this something new?"

"I don't know." Rahi shook her head fiercely when Sterin kept looking at her. "I don't, I tell you. He gets drunk sometimes, you know that, and drunken men spout nonsense. Why believe it's prophecy? He may not remember anything of that morning but the end of it."

"You could ask him," Sterin suggested. "Maybe he's willing to talk about it now, the morning after . . . maybe to you, especially. You are his daughter — "

She started to blurt "Not anymore!" as she had so often, insisting on her separation from all that *daughter* meant, insisting on her status as a yeoman and then a Marshal. But after all she had come here to regain that family name, and angry as she was at him for being drunk at such a time, she could not now deny that he was her father. "I'm a Marshal," she said, after too long a pause. "Just like you: a Marshal."

"If something's gone wrong, something more, we need to know it," Sterin said. "People heard, Rahi: people heard him say that, in the inn and on the street. They will talk; they will make stories about it. Luap is worried, too," he finished, as if that would change her mind.

Rahi snorted. "Luap worries: that's his duty. He thinks he'll have to change the records, that's what it is." But Sterin still looked worried, his blunt honest face creased with it. "All right, I will ask. When he wakes, when I can see him." Another task set her because she was Gird's daughter, another burden she'd never asked for and did not want. The entire time she'd been insisting she was only a yeoman like any other, a Marshal like any other, people had expected her to have Gird's ear: find out this, please make sure he does that, don't let him do this other. Make him change the Code, don't let him change the Code, tell him the Code will never work, explain that granges need more grange-set and that the farmer shouldn't have to pay grange-set in a bad year. She wondered if anyone bothered Luap asking for Gird's favor—it was his job, after all, to deal with such things.

Sterin left the kitchen, clearly relieved to have handed her the difficulty. The two cooks did not come back to chat, for which Rahi was glad. She wanted a few minutes of peace to think about all this, and decide which end of the tangled knot to grasp. Perhaps she should start with Luap, assuming he hadn't been drunk, too. She wished she could stay in the kitchen, with its good smells of baking bread and stew and bean soup. She wished she could discuss it, parrion to parrion, with Arya, going back to the comfortable time when the way to chop onions, or season a soup, or preserve fruit, had been the most important topic of the day. She had not cooked, really cooked, for years; she eyed the great lump of dough Arya pummelled and wished she could sink her own hands into it.

But she would have to talk to Luap and Gird, bearing the grievances of some women and the fears of some men, worrying about prophecies and law instead of bread and meat. She sighed, finally, and pushed herself away from the table. Her bowl went into the washpot; she doused it and rinsed it and set it aside before Lia could intervene, and grinned at the surprised younger woman.

"My parrion was cooking and herblore," she said. "In the old days." Arya looked up at that.

"D'you still?"

"No — not much. I've five bartons and the grange to oversee, and the market courts as well."

"Someday we won't have parrions," Lia said. "Someday we'll be able to choose what we like."

Rahi just managed not to stare rudely at her. "Parrions *are* what you like; I had my mother's gift for it, and nothing made me happier than using it."

"Not me," Lia said. "I'd have learned leatherwork, if I could, but my uncle said girls must choose needlework, weaving, or cooking. And at that, he wouldn't let me choose, but left it to my aunt."

It must be the city way, Rahi thought. "A parrion is a talent," she said firmly, "talent and learning both. If you're not happy as a cook, why not learn leatherwork now?"

"It's too late, and none of the leatherworkers would have me as prentice," Lia said. She seemed to grow angrier as she talked about it, as if Rahi's interest were fat dripping on hot embers.

"There's a woman in my grange does that work," Rahi said slowly. "She's got a girl prentice." She was realizing that even now she understood very little of the structure of city crafts; had city women been restricted in their parrions? Had the village girls? None of them, after all, were ever swineherd or tanner or — except in emergencies — drove the plough-teams. She had assumed those differences resulted from the magelords' rules, but they didn't really know all that much about their own ancestors. How much of what she saw now, in the villages and towns, was new, a still fragile structure?

Lia shrugged, the shrug of someone more ready to complain than change, if change requires effort. "It's all right; I'm here and doing useful work. And with Arya."

Another tangle. She wondered who would know how the crafts had been organized, which were traditionally men's and which women's. And how Gird could possibly come up with a law that would satisfy those who remembered the past and those who wanted a wholly new future.

● Chapter Five

Patiently, Luap trimmed another goosequill for the boy who might, if he lived long enough, make a scribe. The broken quill had not been the boy's fault; he could not control the spasms of coughing when they came. Garin was asleep now, and when he woke would find a new quill ready-trimmed. Luap wished he had better skills, some magic to heal whatever raged in the boy's lungs. So few had his gift of language, almost elven in its grace. He concentrated on that task, to avoid thinking about Gird's "prophecy," and the rumors already coming back to him in colorful variety.

"You spoil them," came a voice from the doorway. Luap set his lips in a smile and turned. Not the woman he'd wanted to see, this gray morning, but Gird's unmanageable daughter, back from the eastern wars to quarrel with her father . . . or so he saw it. In all fairness, Raheli often had the right on her side, but she had even less tact than Gird, if that were possible. And with Gird sleeping off a drunken binge, her tongue would be all edges; he wondered when she'd arrived, and if anyone had told her yet. In answer to her complaint, he tried a shrug with one shoulder. She scowled.

"The boy's sick," he said. "It's not his fault. I don't trim quills for all of them."

"I should hope not. D'you have the latest version of the Code?" Just the slightest emphasis on "latest"; whatever she thought of Gird's incessant revisions, she would not criticize her father to him. In the same way, copying her father's courtesy, she had continued to call him Selamis long after everyone else used Luap. Now she and Gird both used his nickname more often than not, but he remembered their care to preserve his own identity.

"Three copies." He stood, foraged in the pigeonholes above the work table, and handed her one, hoping that hint would keep her from taking it.

"Good," she said cheerfully; he anticipated what she would say and managed not to wince visibly. "Then I can have this, and you'll still have some . . . I'll have copies made for the eastern granges. You won't need to worry about it."

The end of his tongue would never heal, he was sure, from biting it. Rahi's eyes challenged him, daring him to argue. Tall as Gird, not quite as broad, though the padded tunic she wore gave her more heft than she owned, she stood foursquare in his doorway and dared him. Despised him. *Lord of justice*, he let himself pray, and then dropped it. She was Gird's daughter; he was Gird's luap; he had no right to do whatever he thought of.

Not that she'd ever know what he thought of. *That* he hid far inside, from both Rahi and Gird . . . that Rahi reminded him of his dead wife, that he had waked from dreams of stroking her scarred face back into beauty with his magery, erasing the ruin of war, pretending (how long would such pretense last? he had demanded of himself) that she was Erris come back . . . and making her love him, as Erris had.

Which would never happen, no matter what magery he used; he could not do it.

"It would be a help," he said mildly, handing over the thick roll, enjoying her surprise at his cooperation. She even relaxed, a rare sight, and came forward to take it, bending then to look at the sleeping boy.

"One of yours?" The implication was clear: one of *his* meant one of the mageborn. Luap shrugged again.

"I don't know, to be honest. No parents he can remember . . . he came out of the taverns here in Finyatha. Voice like crystal, and had taught himself to read. He has a talent for words, that one, and takes in knowledge as damp clay takes footprints. The singer's gift is no commoner in my father's people than in my mother's — " At that not-subtle reminder of his dual heritage, he saw the long scar on her face darken. He went on smoothly. " — so he could belong to either, or both."

"That priest says the mageborn need no training to wake their powers." *That priest* was Arranha, but Raheli would not say his name. She liked nothing mageborn, and Arranha's mildness irked her, giving no excuse for her dislike.

"Not to wake, but to use . . . or at least, to control." Luap wondered what she was getting at now.

"So how can Gird say the children are safe?" She sounded puzzled more than angry, but underneath that puzzlement Luap sensed a decision already reached. She did not understand her father's reasoning, and would go her own way.

"I'm not sure—"

Her hand flashed outward, demanding silence; Luap bit off the rest of his words and waited. "I'm trying, you see, to follow him. I know it is not the child's fault, to be mageborn, to have the magicks inborn, any more than it is a strong child's fault to have strength. But the magicks are weapons; it's like handing a strong child a sword or a pike — pots will break, if not heads. If the powers can wake without training, and it takes training to control them — but we cannot let them be trained, lest they turn against us—"

"Why would they?"

Her eyes were dark, her mother's eyes Gird had often said, but they seemed full of light as a hawk's eyes, staring through him to distant lands he could not see. "Why would they not, knowing we killed their parents . . . or most of them? Knowing their magicks gave them power of vengeance, power of rule . . . why would they not turn against us?"

"You don't trust fairness? Gird does."

She did not quite snort at that, but she glared, this time directly at him. "Fairness! Gods know we need fairness, and demand it, but for all the fairness lodged in human hearts you might whistle down a hedgerow forever, hoping to call out a skreekie with a bag of gold. I've seen little enough fairness, nor you either. Fairness would have had you on a throne—"

"Fairness forbade me," said Luap. "Your father — Gird — trusts fairness. In the end, he says—"

"In the end, when all men are wise and honest . . . and do you, too, believe that will happen?"

He had changed this much: he could not lie to her, even though he wanted Gird to be right, and her to be wrong, as much as he'd ever wanted anything. "No," he said. "I don't. But I think it's worth working toward."

"Men and women aren't gnomes," said Raheli, as if he'd argued that point.

"No," he said. "They aren't." He wished she would go. He wished she would go now, quickly, before the Autumn Rose arrived . . . or he wished the Rosemage had his sensitivity and

57

would delay her arrival until Rahi left. But she would not deviate a hairsbreadth from her way, that one, and if her way now aimed at more than her own pride's joy, it was still a straight uncompromising trail. *Go away*, he thought at Rahi, knowing it would do no good. Even if she could feel a pressure from him, she would resist it.

"Will you marry again?" she asked, in a tone consciously idle. He knew it was not. Several of the men had offered for her, before she made it clear to everyone that she would not remarry. She probably thought women had offered for him.

"I doubt it," said Luap. "You know my story . . . and besides, a man marries to have children. What could I offer mine, but suspicion? You — everyone — would think it meant I was still thinking of the throne."

"I thought you might marry . . . her." Only one *her* lay between them. Luap said nothing, but Rahi persisted. "You know. Calls herself a rose . . . I say thorny. . . . "

Luap closed his eyes against the explosion: the Autumn Rose was in hearing distance, only a pace or so away. Silence. He opened his eyes, to find Rahi lodged in his doorway like a stone in a pipe, and the Rosemage's light streaming around her like water.

"You don't have to like me," the Rosemage said. "You don't have to understand one tenth of what I have done — "

"I understand quite well." Rahi's accent thickened; her back held the very shape of scorn.

"You do *not*." The Rosemage angry regained her youth; color flushed her cheeks and her light blurred lines of age and weather. Luap's mouth dried. He was bred to find her beautiful; her voice and the magic she embodied sang along his veins. Despite himself, he could not believe that the peasants knew what real love was. They could not feel this wholeness, this blend of body, mind, spirit, magery. "You hate me for things I never did; you despise me for not doing what in fact I accomplished."

"You never bore a child." Rahi, like her father, seemed to condense in anger: immovable, implacable.

"That's not *fair*!" That shaft had gone home; the Rosemage's light flickered, and true anguish edged her voice. "You know it's not — it's — "

"It's women's warring," Rahi said, her own voice calm now

that she felt her victory. "And for all that, lady, neither have I. You could have thrown that back at me." She glanced over her shoulder at Luap. "Don't marry this one, or they'll never believe you a luap." Before either of them could answer, she'd shouldered past the Rosemage and disappeared down the corridor.

"That miserable . . . "

"Peasant she-wolf is the term you're looking for," Luap said softly, nodding to the still-sleeping boy. "Prickly, a trait you both share. Is it, in fact, an effect of barrenness?" He hated himself for that, but he dared not show his very real sympathy, not now. Her face whitened, as her light died, and then her intellect took over.

"I don't know. Possibly. Her people, with their emphasis on giving as the sign of power, would obviously value childbearing . . . but all peoples must, or they die away. So she and I, childless, though each with good reason, know we cannot meet our own standards. I never thought of it that way, but it could be." She sounded interested now, not angry. She hitched a hip onto his work table, and swung the free foot idly. Even relaxed like that, she had more grace than Rahi.

"I try to think what the difference is, between her and Gird," Luap said. "Surely it's not that women bear grudges more — at least, Gird says his wife never did. But Rahi is not going to trust us, not ever."

"Not me, not ever." The Rosemage's hands clenched, then relaxed. "I suppose you've heard the full name she gave me?"

Luap had, but he was not about to admit it. She waited a moment, then went on. "I suppose it doesn't matter. I might even think it funny, if crude, if she'd pinned it on someone else. Thorny bottom . . . and she's as thorny as I am. . . . "

"True enough." Luap let himself smile in a way that had, in his youth, worked its way among girls. "And here I am, poor lone widower, caught between you two briars, like a shorn wether in a thicket."

She laughed. "You? Don't try that with me, king's son; you are no gelding. Far from it."

"By choice. . . . "

"By choice and good sense, you've chosen to father no more children. You know what would come of it; you would not risk the land or the child. But you need not forswear the love of women, especially women who can't bear children. And the two of us — you may feel caught between us, but not in impotence."

"I do wish," Luap said, turning away as he felt his face grow hot, "that you were not my elder in years and experience. It's difficult." He hoped she had not caught his surprise: he had not thought that he might lie safely with barren women. Already his mind ran through the possibilities.

"So it is. So I might intend it to be. D'you think I like having that name tacked to me? Do you not realize that she has seen to it that no man will even ask?"

"Are you suggesting — ?"

"Maybe." She eyed him; he wasn't sure she understood what he'd meant. When the boy stirred, choked, and began coughing, he was glad.

"Easy, lad." Luap lifted the boy's shoulders, offered a spoonful of honeyed fruit juice. He felt a constant tremor, as the boy tried not to cough.

"And how are you today, Garin?" the Rosemage asked.

"Better, lady." The boy's lips twitched, attempting a smile, then another cough took him. He curled into Luap's arm; Luap stroked his hair. This boy would say "better" on his deathbed, which, if he didn't really improve, this would soon be.

"You *could* heal that," came the Rosemage's murmur, just within hearing. Luap could feel his teeth grating; he could *not* heal it, not without claiming the king's magic as his own, using it . . . and he had sworn he would not. Sworn to himself as well as to Gird, to the gods he believed in a little more each year. His father had used magery for darker aims, yet Luap believed he had intended better . . . surely as a boy he had not been wholly cruel. He had never asked any who might know, including the Rosemage.

"You know better," he said to her, wishing he dared a slap of power at her and knowing she would laugh at him even if it worked.

"Even the peasants know we had healing powers once," she said conversationally. Garin's coughs slowed; he gasped, his heart racing beneath Luap's hand.

"Little enough lately," Luap said. "Gird says he heard rumors, tales from old granddads, nothing recent. You say *you* lack them."

"Mmm." She didn't pursue it, for which he was less grateful than he felt he should be. By her tone she would pursue it later. Garin lay back, spent and silent, barely able to sip a few spoonsful of broth. He was going to die, and not sing those songs, and although there was no way Luap could blame Gird, he did anyway. Gird cared for this boy no less than any other, but no more. It had seemed to Luap that if he could interest Gird, if he could only get Gird to understand *why* the boy was important, he would then do something and the boy would live. What that something might be, he could not of course define. But Gird's response had been, as always, impersonally compassionate. He hated seeing anyone suffer; he had sat beside the boy while Luap slept, on the worst nights, comforting him as tenderly as a mother; but he had shaken his head at Luap's vehemence, insisting that this boy's death was no more tragic than another's.

Was it because so many of his own children had died or disappeared? Because Raheli would bear him no grandchildren? Or was it the gnomish influence?

"I can't believe Gird would really mind that," the Rosemage said softly. Luap started, and glanced at the boy, who lay dozing now, unaware. "Healing, I mean."

"I can't do it." His hands had fisted; he flattened them with an effort. "Arranha says I'd have to claim all the magery — that it would be like trying to use only green, or only red, to use only the healing. And he's not even sure I've got it. Besides, as you very well know, I promised Gird and the gods that I would not become a magelord. No more magicks: that's what I said, and what he holds me to."

"You've asked him about this?"

"Not specifically, no. He knows, though. He knows what it would take, and my oath binds me." Never mind he had broken it more than once, by intention and later by accident. Never mind that time in the cave; no one would know that until — unless — he told. Where he could, he was loyal to it.

"You should ask him. He's a farmer; they care about living things. For healing, he might let you try — "

"No." His power bled into that; the word ached with power. She looked at him, opened her mouth, and shut it again. He wondered if she knew he was lying. He wondered so many things she might know, and he dared not ask — better that she

61

think he knew already, or didn't care to know, than that he hungered for that knowledge he lacked.

"I hope he's better soon," the Rosemage said, putting out a hand to Garin's hair. Then she left, without saying more, and Luap sat struggling with his unruly desires.

Soon enough he heard, from down the corridor, Rahi's voice raised to Gird, and Gird's gusty bellow in reply. He did not want to know what she said, or what Gird said to her; he could imagine it well enough. Gird's taste for ale had been nearly disasterous once in the war; he'd conquered it then. Now, in peace, why shouldn't an old man have some pleasure? But Rahi would have none of that; he had overheard much the same quarrel before. She would drag up times past, from her childhood; Gird would glower for days.

The silence, abrupt and startling, drew him from his musings. Had the woman murdered him? Had he clouted her? He heard what might have been sobs. Should he investigate, or leave them to settle things?

"You blundering old fool!" Rahi said. She had waited in the corridor, trying not to hear Luap and the Autumn Rose, trying to calm herself, but when she looked in Gird's door, her anger flared again. Gird slouched against his work table, eyes red-rimmed and bleary. He and his clothes were clean enough, but the room still smelled like a hangover. "I come all the way to Fin Panir to — to tell you something important, and you've gone off drinking with some lout who probably wasn't even a veteran —"

"He was!" His voice rasped, as if he had a cold as well as a hangover. "He was from Burry, and I remembered him —"

"Better than you remembered your vow not to drink so much." She bit back the other words she wanted to say; disappointment soured her rage. She had hoped for so much from this meeting. She needed so much from it.

"We're not at war!" Whatever energy he'd summoned to achieve that bellow brought life to his eyes. "It's not the same thing!"

"It's still wrong." Rahi realized she was going to cry an instant before the tears came, but too late to turn away and hide them. Sobs choked her as she fought them down; she could say nothing. Gird's face changed, concern replacing anger.

"Rahi! What is it, lass?" He was still bigger than she, more massive; the hug she had imagined enclosed her before she knew it. He pulled her head to his shoulder and stroked her hair, murmuring soothingly. She gave in to it, and let her tears fall. When they ceased, she felt odd, empty. Gird released her before she actually moved, and waited silently for what she might say. She wished that blowing her nose could take longer; she wasn't sure what that would be.

"I . . . wanted to change my mind," she said at last.

"About marrying again?" he asked. His voice held a note of hope. He had insisted all along that she could remarry, even if she could not bear children. With all the orphans war had made, he'd said, she could have a dozen children.

"No." She took a long breath, swiped at her face with her sleeve, and looked him in the face. "I said once that I was your daughter no longer, only your soldier. But you're right, the war's over."

"Lass — " A tentative smile, that widened when she managed to smile back. He reached out again, and she moved into another embrace. "Rahi, lass, you don't know how I've needed that. . . . " She felt him sigh. "And there I was drunk, as you said. You're right, it was stupid."

"It's all right," said Rahi softly, "but not if you keep doing it." She felt his chest shake with an almost-silent chuckle.

"Eh, that's the daughter I remember. Tell me now, what changed your mind?"

Rahi told him about the dance in her grange, and the way she had felt restored to family connections. "And so I thought you might be feeling the same — not fitted in, with no vill or family — "

"I have, sometimes. I've tried to tell myself they're all my kin, but I know they're not. After Pidi disappeared that winter — " Gird shook his head. Raheli remembered her younger brother, her only surviving sib, riding off into the snow and never arriving at the next grange. She had not known until spring that he had disappeared; she would never know what had happened. That was the spring she had almost hated the grain that sprang green in the furrows.

"Da," she said, feeling that old comfortable word in her mouth again. "Da, I still can't marry — I still can't have children — "

63

"I know. It's all right, Raheli Mali's child, it's all right." His eyes squeezed shut a moment; she saw the shine of tears when he opened them.

It was not all right, but it would be later. She still felt angry that he had been on another drunken binge; she could see by the color of his face and the change in the texture of his skin that he was not well. But her impulse had been right, to restore the family link she herself had broken — not broken, she told herself now, but set aside.

They sat awhile in silence, one on either side of the work table, then Rahi remembered the other good reasons she had found for coming the long way to Fin Panir. He had set her saddlebags on the floor; she retrieved them, and spread out her grange records and the comments from the past year's courts.

"The soil's different, where I am now, from home — where we lived before. The Code allows for easing the grange-set in a dry year, but where I am the farmers lose grain more often to mold in a wet year. If you allow the local Marshals to adjust the grange-set based on the yield of sound grain — that wouldn't take a complete revision of the Code — "

"Ummph. You're right. It already says at the Marshal's discretion, so if we struck out 'because of drought' that would do. What else?"

"We had an odd case last spring come into the grange-court: a man, not mageborn, claimed to do magicks a new way."

"A new way?"

"As scribes study writing, he said, so he studied magicks and performed them — for a fee. The judicar brought him to me because some of the people wanted him killed as a mageborn using forbidden power, or as a demon. When I investigated, it seemed to me that he performed what he agreed to, although I found the fee unduly high. And he had none of the appearance of a mageborn, and explained his magicks sufficiently that I feel sure he was not."

"So what did you do?" asked Gird.

"Treated it as a matter of commerce. As someone in an unknown profession, of no registered guild, he had to demonstrate that he was honest and gave good weight, so to speak. The Code allows Marshals to impose a good-faith tax on newcomers who have no guild to speak for them, until their honesty is proven. He had not earned that much with his little shows of colored fire and magic crystals. I told him plainly that too many people disliked all magic for me to keep him safe, and if someone broke his head for him, he'd have only himself to blame. He got out of town safely enough, for I told the judicar and those listening that I would not take lightly an injury done him when he had done none yet himself. Since then I've heard nothing; he never came to the next grange west."

"A new kind of magic . . ." said Gird. "I wonder what it could be."

"He thought of it as a craft, not some inborn talent, and I believe he was honest in that, at least." Rahi frowned. "But without a guild, without knowledge of what his work is worth — assuming it's honestly done — we have no way of knowing if his price is fair."

Gird leaned back and tucked his fingers in his belt. "I suspect we can't protect the sort of fool who will pay a man to work magicks. You were right, Rahi, to treat it as commerce, as a matter of contracts. Make sure he fulfills what he said; the buyer must decide if the price is fair." He shook his head. "Though where we can fit *that* into the Code, I don't know. I'll talk to other Marshals about it."

"I . . . quarreled with Luap, on the way here," Rahi said. "It's not his fault; I was angry about you." She felt a childish pleasure in confessing that; he had always been more understanding with the child who confessed wrongdoing.

"He's easy to quarrel with, this harvest time," Gird said. "I don't know what's bothering him, unless it's the old lady with her notions about royalty."

"Someone mentioned an old lady. . . . " Rahi said. He looked as if he wanted to tell the tale; she wanted, at this moment, to listen to him talk.

"A good woman," Gird said, lips pursed. "Her servant Eris says so, and so does Arranha. Widowed years ago. Very pious: but for worshipping the Sunlord, she's much like old Tam's mother, back home. She came in asking permission to put altarcloths she'd embroidered in the great Hall; it was clear she meant no mischief, so I said she might talk to Arranha about it."

"But she's mageborn? She knows Luap's the king's son?"

"Aye. She knows more than that — seems he's not the last king's son, but one before that. Garamis, his name was. She saw

Luap himself as a child, when he lived in some lord's house. It's that, Arranha says, which upset him, though I can't see why it would. Until we're the oldest, if we live that long, there's always someone who knew us as children. What harm in that?"

Rahi thought about it. It had been years since she had seen anyone from her vill. Would she feel anything strange if she met someone on the street who remembered her as a child? No — she had enjoyed being that child, that young woman. She would like to meet someone who remembered that. Had Luap not enjoyed being that boy? Surely it must have been easier than growing up a peasant child.

"It's the change, I expect," Gird went on. "Having to leave the lord's house for a farmer's cottage; he's said before that was hard. He's tried to forget that first bit, in recent years. And now she brings it back. One of the yeomen even told me she calls him 'prince.'"

"But she shouldn't!" Rahi was more shocked than she'd expected. Gird shook his head.

"She's an old lady, lass. As stubborn as any village granny, for all she wears a fine dress and wears jewels. You know yourself that arguing with old ladies is like plowing water. If she wants to call Luap prince, she will; all I can do is hope it won't go to his head." He tried to stretch again and grimaced. "As yesterday's ale has gone to mine. I'm too old for that, you're right."

Rahi grinned at him. "Remember the time that old dun cow got after me, for trying to ride her calf?" Gird's slow smile widened, and he began to chuckle. "You told me that fools earned their lumps."

"So I did. But that's enough of that, lass, or I'll decide you're only my Marshal again. Marshals don't lecture me —"

"I would," said Rahi boldly. Gird groaned.

"You would, and your mother would have made a fine Marshal. Will you give over, now?"

"Aye. Shall I make up with Luap?"

"You might soothe his prickles a bit, and you might keep the edge of your tongue off the Autumn Rose, too. Don't think I missed that bit of the quarrel."

He had surprised her again. He could always do that, manage to know what no one suspected he knew, manage to do what no one suspected he could. Yet once he had done it, it always seemed right, inevitable.

"She irritates me," Rahi said, "like a bed of nettles."

"And why did we gather nettles?" He did not wait for her answer. "Because the plant is not evil, but harsh, and needs the right cook. Nourishing inside; irritating outside. There's virtue in the Autumn Rose you've never found, lass: take it inside next time."

Rebuke for rebuke, and although it stung, she could feel that he was right. She had never looked for anything in the Autumn Rose but what she knew she disliked. Finding that, she had been satisfied to despise her. She tried a last defense. "I have heard gossip that they might marry, Luap and the Rosemage."

"Neither of them are such fools," Gird said. "Nor are you, to believe it."

"Well, if that's your wish, I will study to adopt her as a sister," Rahi said, half-joking. "No more quarrels, by my will."

"You could have a worse sister," Gird said. "She is as true as Luap once was false. Strange to us, but true." He sounded very tired, now, and Rahi realized that it was nearly noon.

"I could make you a brew," she said, half-shyly. "If Arya will let me use her hearth — "

His eyes brightened a moment. "That black stuff? No one else can do it right, lass, and if you'd fix that I'd be grateful."

"Take your rest, then, and I'll be up with it when it's done." This felt right, felt normal, even if it was the result of a drinking bout. She had Mali's parrion, and her own skill; she knew she could mix healing brews better than most. She settled Gird with a cloth over his eyes and his feet propped up, then went back to the kitchen to ask permission to use the hearth.

She found Luap there, with a cook she had not met; Arya and Lia, the woman explained, had finished their day's work. "Bakes the best bread, Arya," the woman said. "But she trusts me to finish it now. I'm Meshi."

Rahi explained what she needed, eyeing Luap, who looked completely comfortable as if he had been there awhile.

"Of course. No need to ask. The herbery's through there — I expect you know — and I'll just fetch the pot — " Meshi was a bustler, whose brisk busy movements around the room could make it seem crowded with only a few people in it. Rahi went out to the herbery, wondering why Luap seemed so relaxed with someone like that, and so tense with people she found more soothing. She found the herbs she needed, hardy aromatics that could be picked green until the first hard freeze. The rest of the ingredients were in the pantry, in neatly labelled pots and sacks: the same roots and barks used in cookery, most of them.

She set to work acutely aware of Luap watching her. Had he ever seen her at her own parrion? She couldn't remember. She chopped, grated, and squeezed, as each ingredient demanded, then put all to simmer on the hearth. Meshi bustled past her one way and then the other, chopping vegetables into bowls, stirring them into a huge kettle of stew, taking Arya's last batch of bread from the oven and putting the loaves on racks to cool, washing up behind herself as if she had an extra pair of hands. Rahi did not miss the looks Meshi gave Luap, or the occasional sharp glance she herself received. When she had the pot simmering to her satisfaction, Rahi offered to help with whatever Meshi had planned.

"Oh, dear, no — no need." Meshi hardly paused in her path between pantry and kitchen. "I'm not rushed. Just you sit there and keep an eye on your own pot, so I won't worry about it." She came back from the pantry with an apronful of apples, and sat down to peel them. Rahi, rebuffed, ventured a smile at Luap. He nodded and gave her a smile that seemed more forced than natural . . . although after their earlier encounter she had to admit that only a forced smile would be natural.

"Meshi likes to feed people almost as much as I like to eat," he said, with a nod to the cook. She smiled warmly at him, a curl of apple peel dangling from the knife.

"I like to feed those as know good cooking from bad," she said. "Luap's one to know if I change a single spice in my preserves."

"My parrion was cooking and herblore," Rahi said, feeling unaccountably shy.

"Was it now?" Meshi looked up, interested. "I thought you looked more deft than most who cook for need and not love. And you gave that up to be a Marshal, eh?" Rahi wondered where Meshi had been during the war. She looked to be Luap's age, and perhaps, like many city people, she had simply stayed home and hoped the war would not disrupt her life.

"I had no choice," Rahi said, feeling her face flush. She had assumed that everyone knew her story. "And now — "

"Raheli has no village to return to," Luap said smoothly. "Surely you knew, Meshi. . . ."

"Oh." Now it was Meshi's turn to flush. "I'm sorry. I should have known . . . it's just these dratted apples . . . all full of core and I wasn't thinking — " Her hands twitched among the peels.

"It's all right," Rahi said. "I must get used to those who don't know the whole story."

Meshi turned to her. "As you had a parrion for it, would you want to help with these apples?"

"Of course." Rahi moved to the table, and picked up an apple. "Sliced or just cored?"

"Sliced, not too thin." Meshi put an earthenware bowl between them. "If old Gird's feeling better by suppertime, he'll have some of it."

They worked companionably until all the apples were sliced. Rahi got up to sniff her brew, and Meshi continued with her apple dish. Luap had snatched a slice on his way out, and Meshi laughed at him. "That man! There's not another in this place like him. Those two, Arya and Lia, they don't like him for being half mageborn, say he puts on airs, but I don't see that. He likes to eat, but what man doesn't?"

"He's been with my — with Gird a long time," Rahi said, stirring the brew. It smelled about right; she found a cloth to wrap the hot pan, and a mug for Gird to drink from.

Meshi stopped short and looked at her. "It's hard for me to believe, Gird being your father. Him so fair and balding, and you so dark — "

"My mother," Rahi said. "She was dark."

"Ah. And a parrion of cooking, like you? Surely it came from her family, for old Gird, bless him, can hardly boil water."

Rahi laughed, surprising both of them. "I know. When my mother died, he had to cook — and I learned very quickly."

"It's none o' my affair," said Meshi in the tone always used by those who say it anyway, "but your Da needs a family. Why not come here to live? You'd be happier in your parrion than off somewhere being a Marshal."

Rahi smiled at her, but shook her head. "I have to be a Marshal," she said. "I don't quite know why, but I know it's right." Then she took the brew upstairs, and woke Gird from a restless doze. When he asked her the same question, she was ready with the same answer . . . and he smiled at her and agreed.

● Chapter Six

"I want to see the Marshal-General," Aris said. Seri pressed close behind him.

"Run off, lad, and tell your Marshal your troubles," said the big guard. The skinny one said nothing, but his eyes laughed. Aris felt his anger glowing, and fought it back. He knew what the Marshal-General thought of boys who lost their tempers. They had not come this far to make fools of themselves.

"The Marshal-General," he said again. "It's t-too imp-portant for just our Marshal."

Brows went up on both guards. "Oh?" said the skinny one. "Would your Marshal agree?"

Aris just stared at them, one after the other. Finally the skinny one flushed, shrugged, and said, "Gran'ther Gird won't mind young'uns. He never does." The big guard glowered, but finally shrugged as well.

"All right, but you stop first at Luap's and ask if the Marshal-General's got other business right now. Upstairs, second door on the right." He stepped aside, waving a vast meaty hand. Aris and Seri scampered past. The guard yelled after them, "No running! This isn't some alley, brats!" Seri giggled. Aris was at the landing before he figured it out: alley brats, just what everyone called them, but the guard hadn't meant it that way. Exactly.

"We made it," she whispered. "I didn't think—"

Aris shushed her. Another flight to a passage . . . panelled walls, a floor of patterned wood, dark and yellow. Once it would have been polished; now it was clean, but scuffed. The first door on the right was closed. The next, open, gave on a sun-barred room lined with shelves. A tall man in Girdish blue sat at a table, facing away from them, looking at someone on a low pallet under the windows. Aris peeked around the door . . . the youth on the bed lay pale as milk, bones tight under the skin of his face, eyes deep-shadowed. Seri, bolder now that they were upstairs, rapped on the doorpost. The tall man swung around, finger to lips, then stared at them, clearly surprised. With a glance at the sleeping youth, he rose and came to the door.

Aris had heard the tales. Gird's luap, the Marshal-General's scribe and friend, was supposed to be mageborn on his father's side. *Royal*, whispered some. King's bastard. Uncanny, born with great powers but promised not to use them. Can't trust that kind, most muttered, making one or another warding sign. Their Marshal said the same, glowering when another leaf of Gird's Code came down, scribed in the luap's elegant hand. To Aris, he looked like just another tall, dark-haired adult. An uncle or father, not a grandfather, and no more magical than a post. Seri pinched him. His mouth came unglued, and he said, quietly enough, "Sir, they said downstairs to tell you we've come to see the Marshal-General."

The tall man had graceful brows, but they still rose. "Children, now, they're letting in to pester the Marshal-General? Or do you bear a message from your Marshal or some judicar who could not come himself?"

"It's *our* message, sir!" Seri pushed past Aris; she knew his temper and its limits. Her single braid hung crooked over her shoulder, already fuzzy with escaping hairs, for all that she had rebraided it neatly just before they came into the Upper City. "The Code says, sir, that all come equal before the Code —"

His wide mouth quirked. "True, young judicar, but it also sets up the courts in which to try cases; not all come before the Marshal-General."

"This does." Seri gave him a flat stare for his amusement, and his face sobered. "It is a matter the Marshal-General must decide, and we must see him. If he cannot see us now —"

"If you'll allow, I'll let him know you're here; so far as I know he has no one with him." The man slid past them, and strode down the hall. Aris looked at Seri, not knowing whether to follow or not. She leaned against the doorpost, peeking in.

"I wonder if he's dying."

Aris looked too. Unbidden, his magery stirred; he squashed it down. "I think he must be," he said.

"You should," Seri said, flicking him a glance. "Even if we haven't seen the Marshal-General yet."

"It's against the Code; it's not right."

71

"You should." He wondered if the Marshal-General himself were that certain; Seri had the rooted integrity of a tree, that cannot be but what it is. Were all the old peasant breed like that, so sure of themselves, so all-of-a-piece? What would it feel like? He himself, his magery flickering inside him, often felt he was made of shadows and flame, shapeless except in opposition to each other. He could just remember, in his early childhood, someone explaining that light existed by itself, but shadows only when something stood before the light. Now Seri nudged him into the room. "Go on, Aris. I'll tell the Marshal-General —"

The boy — man? — on the bed was older than either of them; Aris could tell that, but not how old he was. He would be tall, if he stood, and would grow taller yet, if he lived. *Can I?* he asked himself. He had never actually healed someone so close to death, not a human person, not someone so large. Did that make a difference? He wasn't sure. Seri nudged him again. She would not give up, but she had no parrion of healing, the way her people thought of it. *Our* people, he reminded himself. He and Seri were one people, whatever anyone else said. She had stood by him in the grange, and he would stand by her . . . meanwhile, he felt his mage powers lean toward the sick youth, as if they could reach out of himself.

He came closer. From the shallow, uneven movement of the chest, he deduced lung trouble: he knew that much from animals. Was the thinness from that, or from not being able to eat for coughing, for lack of breath? With a sudden lift, he felt the power take him over, an exhilaration like none other unless birds of the air felt this way, swooping and gliding. He let himself flow with it, barely aware that he murmured words he'd overheard in childhood. His hands glowed; he laid them carefully on either side of the youth's sleeping head, ran them down to his shoulders, then over his chest. Something prickled in his palms, harsh as nettles or dry burs. He wanted to pull back, but knew he must not. Behind him, he heard Seri's indrawn breath, but he paid no attention to it. She had seen him do this before; she always gasped, but he had learned it meant nothing. She would watch and wait, and be there when he had done.

Darkness retreated slowly, grudgingly, from his light; he could feel, in his hands, the slow withdrawal of something dire from the youth's body. He had no name for it, and it didn't matter. The light either worked, or it didn't; when it worked, it healed old wounds as well as new ones, fevers as well as wounds. If he could hold his focus until all the damage had been repaired, the youth would wake whole and free from pain, healthy as if he had never been sick.

But that was the limit: his own strength, his own concentration. He could feel the sweat trickling down his face; he knew his sight narrowed to a single core of light, and he dared no attention to interpret what his eyes could see. Only with the vision of power, which perceived each strand of disease or injury, which knew when the light had worn or driven it away, dared he perceive. Hearing had gone, and most of eyes' sight, and even the sense of where he was, when the last dark shadow fled. At once, his power snapped back into him, and with it, all his strength. He fell, knowing he was falling, trusting Seri to be there, to catch him, as she had been from the first time he'd used this power.

Hearing returned while he was still crumpled untidily on the floor. Seri's voice, sharp, and a deeper rumble somewhere overhead.

" — because *I* told him to, sir! He would not break your law, but — "

"Will you just stand back, child, and let me see the lad. I'm not going to hurt him. He's fallen."

"He always does," said Seri, somewhat more calmly.

Another voice — the man they had first met. "You mean he's done this *before*? Healing?"

"Yes, of course. He's always done it, until the new Code came out, and the Marshal said he couldn't. That's why we came."

Aris managed to open his eyes. His vision had not cleared: would not, for some little time. But he could see Seri, standing stiffly, ready to fight if she had to, and the man whose office this was, and a great lump of a man who must be the Marshal-General. Aris swallowed, with difficulty, and smiled. "Please don't worry," he said to the Marshal-General. "I'm all right."

The man grunted, and came nearer; Seri moved out of his way, scowling. "You're the color of cheese-whey, lad, and your eyes no more focus on me than a newborn's. If this is 'all right,' I would hate to see you sick or wounded."

"Is *he* all right?" Aris asked. The Marshal-General, so close,

73

looked even bigger, heavier, almost as if a great oak had chosen to move and lean over him. He glanced down, half-expecting roots instead of worn boots.

The other man answered, in a lighter, clipped voice that carried some emotion Aris could not read. "He's got the color you had before; he's sleeping peacefully and breathing normally, and I could swear he's gained a half-stone.... I suppose we'll know when he wakes."

The Marshal-General's hand, hard and warm, cupped Aris's chin. He felt no fear; here was nothing uncanny, but strength and gentleness allied. Less frightening than his father's steward had been, less frightening than his father, for that matter.

"Lad — from what your friend says, you knew you broke the Code, to use such magic."

"Yes, sir." He didn't try to explain.

"Your friend says you did it because she told you to — was it then her fault you broke the Code?"

He could feel himself turning red, hot to the ears. "No, sir, of course not!" He quoted carefully: "'Let each yeoman take heed for his own deed, for if one counsels wrongly, yet the ears which listen and the hands which act belong to the doer.'"

"Mmm. You have learned to recite, but yet you do not obey. What then should the judicar say, in such a case?"

Behind the Marshal-General, Seri opened her mouth; Aris shook his head at her. "It is my deed, and my fault, sir. I know that. But . . . but the boy was so sick, and if I waited he might not live. That's why we came, to ask you to amend the Code to allow healing. The judicar should say I was wrong, and punish me — but you, sir, can amend the Code."

"To save you punishment?" The Marshal-General's face gave nothing away to his still blurred vision. Aris shook his head. "No, sir. Even if you amend the Code, I broke your rule before you changed it. But others who heal won't have to be punished later."

"Alyanya's flowers!" Strong arms gathered him into a rough embrace. "D'you really think I'd punish a boy who healed another, who gave his power until he looked near death? If you need punishment, the way your power wounds you is punishment enough. I had thought the healing magery all destroyed, and all rumors of it lies, with the sick charmed perhaps into thinking themselves well. But I saw this myself, saw you heal — "

"It's not really me, sir; it's the power," said Aris. He was too old to let himself be comforted like this, but he wished he weren't. He had never had that much of it. "It's the light — "

"I don't doubt it's some god's power," said the Marshal-General. "But you're the one they gave it to, and you're the one must decide how to use it. Now: the two of you will come with me, and have more to eat than you've had lately, by the look of you."

Aris found himself standing, but with the Marshal-General's arm half-supporting him. His vision reddened, then cleared; he looked at the youth on the bed, who had slept through all this undisturbed. *He's tired*, Aris thought. Seri gave him one of her looks; he was not sure what it meant, but he would find out. She always told him. The other man, the Marshal-General's luap, had another look, or series of them, that flickered across his face like cloudshadow over a meadow. In the aftermath of using his power, when he felt unusually sensitive, he felt the man's own magery as something cold and hard, and wondered that he could have missed it before.

"Food," said the Marshal-General, and urged him forward. Then, to his luap, "I'll take care of these two for now, but find them a place to sleep. Wherever they've come from, they aren't going back today."

Out in the passage, with its scuffed patterned wood, and along it to the right. The Marshal-General said, as they passed a door, "That's my room, if you need me later, but I think you should eat and rest now. The kitchen's down this stair." Aris stumbled in the change from lighter passage to darker stair, and the Marshal-General's arm steadied him. Seri padded behind, silent for once.

The kitchen, warm, smelling of rising bread dough, some kind of stew, lit by both fire and windows open to an enclosed courtyard, promised safety and comfort. Aris sank down on a bench beneath a window and let himself relax. Seri sat beside him; the Marshal-General murmured to someone working at a long table, and fetched a cut loaf of bread. The other person vanished into a dark door, then reappeared with a jug and brought over jug and several mugs. A tall woman, that was, wearing an apron over trousers and tunic.

75

"Milk," said the Marshal-General, pouring it into the mugs. He handed one to each of them, and then lifted his own. Aris sipped, cautiously. Sometimes his belly objected to milk or meat after a healing; this time it lay quiescent. The milk slid down, cool and sweet. The Marshal-General sliced the loaf, and offered it. Seri fished a dirty lump of salt from her pocket and offered that on an open palm. The Marshal-General pinched off a bit without speaking, sprinkled it on the bread, and waited until she took a slice to bite into his own. Aris swallowed the last of his milk, and filled his mouth with bread and salt.

They had eaten bread and stew, and drunk more milk than Aris had had in several years, before Gird let them talk more about it. Aris felt sleepy with all the food; Seri looked ready to leap at some task, her braid already more than half loosened, the tendrils curling around her face, her eyes sparkling. In the kitchenyard, in the shade of an old apple tree, the Marshal-General looked like an old farmer, not a judicar — and certainly not like what he was. But food had not dulled his wits, Aris found.

" — and your father was a mageborn noble?" he asked. "Did he have the power of healing?"

"No, sir." Aris numbered his father's magery, what he knew of it, on his fingers: light, fire, sending arrows where he would. "He died when I was very young — " In the Marshal-General's war against the magelords, though it would be rude to say so. " — but no one ever said he could heal. Nor my mother either." Seri made a small noise; Aris hoped that would be enough for her. She had never liked his mother.

"And both are dead now?"

"No, sir." He said no more, even when Gird's eyebrows rose in a clear demand for more information. Seri took over.

"She went off with another 'un, sir, after the old lord was killed. He didn't want Aris, her new man didn't."

Gird looked at Aris; Aris said nothing. Whatever Seri thought, his mother was his mother, and he would not speak ill of her. Gird turned to Seri. "So, then — how long ago was this, and how long have you known him?"

Seri grinned, glad to take over. "I've known him always; we grew up in the household together. Aris was youngest, and they were always busy — "

"And I was small for my age," Aris added. "Easy to misplace in a crowd."

"*And* you had none of your father's magery," said Seri. "He didn't know what you did have." She turned back to Gird. "My mother's sister was Aris's nurse; 'twas not her fault he grew no larger. But she was blamed for it, and then his mother wouldn't have him by because he fretted so about sickness. They thought he was afraid of it."

"I am," Aris said. "I didn't know what to do, then."

"And now you do?" asked Gird.

"Not . . . completely. There's too much — Seri's people have ways of healing with herbs I don't know, and she's told me of hearth-witches who can draw pain and lay it on stone or iron. But I know some of what I can do with magery." He yawned, fighting the sleep that tried to overwhelm him. He felt he'd been running for hours, or heaving stones. Why was healing, that required only concentration, such hard work?

"He needs to sleep," he heard Seri say. A chuckle shook the shoulder he leaned against.

"I can see that for myself, child. Let the lad rest, then, and you tell me your tale. You're not mageborn-bred, are you?"

A snort from Seri. "No, sir. Not a drop of magic in me, just peasant common sense." *You have magery, Seri, but it's not my kind*, Aris thought, then drifted into sleep.

He woke on a pallet on the floor, a clean soft pallet. The room was almost dark; the window above him glowed deep blue: late evening. He heard no one near, and stretched at leisure, his spine crackling. He loved to think of the little spine-bones clicking against each other in some language he didn't know. Cats stretched, but he never heard their spines crack. He blinked at the window; one star had pricked dusk's curtain. As he watched, another, and two more. He felt safe, and happy, and thought of going back to sleep. He would wake early, if he did, but no matter. Then he heard voices in the distance, coming nearer. Seri and the Marshal-General, still talking. He grinned in the dark. Seri could talk all night and half the day; now that she'd decided she liked the Marshal-General, he'd have a time getting rid of her. She had missed her grandfather after he died.

"He should be awake," Seri was saying. "And if he goes back to sleep now, he'll wake with a headache before dawn. He always does."

The Marshal-General's voice carried a hint of humor. "So what should we do, lass, to keep the lad healthy?"

"Feed him. He won't think he's hungry, but he needs it."

The light they carried warmed the passage outside, began to gleam on the edges of the furniture. Aris grabbed his wandering mind by its scruff. This was not the time to fall into a trance and let the light play in his mind. So far the Marshal-General had been understanding, but he mustn't push his luck too far. He sat up, rubbing his eyes, as they came in. With the candlelight, the window looked darker, more true night.

"Aris — " An edge to Seri's voice, a warning. Did she think he'd let himself be caught by light-trance in front of the Marshal-General?

"I'm awake," he said, yawning hugely. "Just woke." He looked for the Marshal-General; in candlelight, his broad lined face looked entirely different. "I'm sorry, sir, I fell asleep and keep yawning."

"Seri explained." A long pause during which Aris wondered if Seri had explained too much, then, "Come, lad — there's soup and bread left for you."

He stood without assistance, and didn't argue about the meal; Seri was right, as usual. By the time he'd eaten two bowls of soup, and three slices of bread, he felt solid to himself, firm on his feet. The Marshal-General, he saw, recognized the difference.

"So, lad — are you able to tell me your side of it, or would a night's rest improve your tale?"

"I'm fine now, sir." He felt Seri stir, beside him, but she said nothing.

"Good. You'll need the jacks, I expect, and then come up to my office; Seri can guide you." The Marshal-General pushed himself up and left the kitchen. Seri gathered the bowls and the end of bread.

"I'll help," said Aris, but she shook her head.

"You go clear your mind, Ari. The jacks are across the court, through the gate: there's torches. And the washstand's by the well. I'll do this." When he came back in, all traces of his late supper had vanished; the kitchen looked vast and bare in the candlelight, warmth radiating from the banked fire on the hearth. The cooks had put beans to soak; the faint earthy smell made him think of cellars and small-gardens. Seri took his

78

hand, one quick clasp, then led him back upstairs. He thought he could find Gird's office on his own, but he was glad of her company.

She left him in the passage outside the lighted room, with a single hug. Inside the room, the Marshal-General sat with another man, the luap, and when Aris tapped at the doorpost, they both looked up to stare at him. "Come on in, lad," said the Marshal-General. "Come and tell me your story, and Luap here will write it down."

Aris felt a mild reluctance to talk in front of the luap — Luap, he must be called — but with the Marshal-General's eye on him, he could not argue. He took the stool the Marshal-General pointed out, and wondered where to start. What had Seri already said? He didn't want to bore them. Luap, he noticed, had what looked like an old, rewritten scroll on the board in his lap. Luap smiled at him.

"Start by telling me your name, if you will, and what you know of your history."

Perhaps Luap had not taken down what Seri said. Aris began with his name, his father's name, the place of his birth. That was enough of family, he thought, and said, "When I found I could heal — "

"Wait." Luap held up his hand. "Were you the only child?"

"No, sir. But the youngest, by several years; my next older brother had already begun arms training when I was born. That's why I was so often alone with Seri and her family and the other servants; my parents were away at court, or visiting other domains, or — by the times I remember at all — at the war."

"Do you read, then?"

Aris nodded. "Until near the war's end, I had a tutor my father provided. He taught me to read and write and keep accounts, and I taught Seri — "

"A servant's child?" Disbelief edged the Marshal-General's voice at that.

"She's my friend," Aris said. "It was more fun, to have someone to read with, to write to, and as for accounts, she is faster than I. It was a game to us."

"So," Luap said, with a glance at the Marshal-General, "Seri was your companion in childhood, and much of that was during the war. Did your tutor instruct you in magery?"

"No, sir. He had none himself; he said my father would have me taught later, if I showed any ability. But then my father was killed, and my mother — " He stopped, feeling the heat on his face. His mother could not have known what he overheard; surely no child was supposed to hear things like that. He had tried to forget them.

"Seri said your mother married another lord after your father died in battle," the Marshal-General said. "Seri said the other lord didn't want to bother with you. Is that what you think?"

The last time his father had been home, his mother had said those things he wished he'd never heard. *I didn't want the last brat,* she'd screamed. *It's not my fault he's too young to help.* There was more, that he carefully did not remember. Then his father had come for that last moment, scooping him into a tight hug, telling him to remember. Not what he'd just heard, he was sure: his father could not have known, any more than his mother, that he'd been awake with a headache. *If only you had the magery,* his father had whispered. *But it's too late, now.* He had been frightened; he had started to cry, partly with pain of his headache and partly with fear, and his father had put him down gently and gone out the door.

Aris realized too much time had passed, and his hands had knotted in his lap as they did when he thought about his mother. "She — she grieved at my father's death," he said finally, in a low voice. "The lord Katlinha swore to protect her."

His throat closed on another memory he had not quite buried. The lord Katlinha's long black moustaches, which had fascinated him with their stiff curl. The lord's hand stroking Seri's cheek and neck, and the drawling voice in which he'd said, "Of course you can bring your sweetling, lad, though you're really too young to appreciate her. . . . " Something wrong: he had realized suddenly that Seri was frightened, Seri who was never frightened — her eyes dilated, her breathing shallow. "But you'll both have to mind me," the lord had said, laughing at something Aris couldn't understand, because Seri afraid was nothing to laugh about.

Then his favorite pup, the lame one, had chosen that moment to nip the lord's other hand, and the lord's hard bootheel had stamped. The pup squealed, Seri jerked free, Aris had flung himself at the injured pup, ignoring the lord's command to let the beast die. In the end the lord had shrugged. "I'll have you, lady, if

80

it's your will, but I won't bother with that worthless scrap. There's no mageblood in him; you said you weren't willing, and no doubt you withheld yourself."

They had gone, and left him. He and Seri had run off to join the blueshirts, with the surviving servants, and spent the last of the war fetching water and digging trenches for the peasant army. That he could say; he could not say the other.

"The lord didn't want another son," he said, half-gasping with the pain of remembering it.

"And your mother?" The Marshal-General's voice held no anger, but also no space for refusal.

"Didn't . . . didn't want me," said Aris, eyes down. It was his greatest shame, that he had been the kind of boy a mother would not want.

"Did she know you had magery?" asked Luap.

"No, sir. She was sure I had none; my brothers, she said, had shown it younger than I did."

A silence followed. Aris looked up to see that the Marshal-General's face had contracted in a black scowl. Luap stared at nothing, across the room. Finally the Marshal-General shook out his shoulders and looked at Aris. "Well — she was wrong, quite clearly. When did you find out what powers you had?"

"It was the puppy." He hadn't told them about the puppy; he tried to make it brief, and avoid that difficult moment with Seri. A favored pet, accidentally injured, and the pressure of his grief. "The cowman had already told me I was good with animals," he said. "I liked the stables and byres; the beasts were quiet with me, and the men showed me how to work with them. But all I'd done was what they told me, until the puppy." The huntsman had said it was hopeless; the cowman had said the same. Broken spine, soon death, and the sooner the better; the huntsman wanted to put the pup out of its misery. He had burst into tears again, and again an adult had been disgusted with him, though this time not cruel. *Yer not cryin' 'bout the pup,* the huntsman had said. *Yer cryin' 'bout yer ma and da and that sun-lost count, may he die in the dark.*

He had held the whimpering, shivering pup, that had made such a mess in his arms, and felt Seri behind him, also shivering. Then the familiar prickle he had felt so often before without doing anything — without guessing what it was. His hands itched, stung, moved almost without his knowing. He ran a finger down the pup's back to the soft pulpiness where the count's bootheel landed. He tried to imagine what should be there, what it should feel like. The pup rolled in his hands suddenly, squirming, and slapped his face with its wet pink tongue ... and he'd fallen asleep where he sat, with Seri holding his head.

By the time he'd wakened, the pup had run off somewhere; Seri, the cautious, had said it was best. Before he could argue with her, the remaining servants had rushed in with word of an advancing peasant army. He never saw the pup again, to be sure he'd healed it. But in the next few seasons and years, he had plenty of opportunities to try out his powers. Seri argued for caution, for secrecy, but later helped him use — and hide — what he could do.

"I thought at first it was for animals only," he explained, now once more calm, with the story far enough from his mother. "After what the cowman said — well — I asked to work with the beasts, wherever I was, and found I could help them. Seri said to start with little things, so if I couldn't do it, it wouldn't matter so much. Scratch on a cow's udder, a sore teat, lameness from stepping on something sharp, that kind of thing. I couldn't always heal it, but I could usually make it better. Then one place at lambing time, the shepherd wanted my help because my hands were so small — "

And lamb after lamb he delivered, in the cold rain of that week, had lived ... they had all lived. The shepherd, who had taught him the old hard truth that sheep are born looking for a place to die, had taken his hands and spread them, looking for the gods' mark, he'd said. He'd found nothing, but Aris had slept for a week when the lambing was over, so deep asleep that Seri had had to clean him where he lay, like a baby. It was natural, then, when the shepherd's wife's next baby came out blue and still, for the shepherd to thrust the limp bundle into his hands and growl, "It's a lamb, lad — save it!"

"The baby lived?" asked the Marshal-General.

"Oh, yes. She's a healthy child; it was just something about the birthing." He paused, trying to think what to tell next. Not how frightened he had been; Gird wouldn't want to hear that. The shepherd had assumed his talent came from Alyanya; he himself wasn't sure. The only magery he'd seen was a dance of light by his father and brothers when he was very small, one Midwinter Feast. He'd been told Esea gave them magery, and that made sense, for the light dance. But healing? No one had even mentioned the possibility. In that remote village, once the war passed, all anyone cared about was sowing and tending and harvest, the daily routine, into which he fit happily. No one really cared how he healed, or where the power came from, so long as it worked.

"But you had no family — who'd you live with?" asked Luap, leaning forward. Aris grinned and spread his hands.

"After the war, sir, there's many not in the right place . . . we worked in well enough, here and there, until things settled a bit. Then that shepherd, he took us into his family."

"It must have been — " Luap coughed, spat, and went on. "It must have been very different from what you knew before." Aris did not miss the keen glance the Marshal-General shot at his luap.

"It was, sir, but — but for missing the people I knew, it was better."

"Better!" That from both of them, clearly surprise and disbelief.

Aris felt his face reddening. "Before, sir . . . my tutor and some others, they didn't think I should spend so much time with Seri, or in the stables with the animals. We've been lucky; I know that. Except for that one bad winter, we've always had enough, and we've always been together. Once I found out what I could do, what the feeling was for, I felt happier than I'd ever been."

"Hmmph." That was the Marshal-General, giving his luap another look Aris couldn't read. "Well, then: if things have gone so well, why come to me?"

This part he could tell without a hitch. From the shepherd's child, to another in the vill born apparently dead, from those to a child with fever, a man injured by falling rock, a woman poisoned by bad grain . . . he had begun testing his powers on people as well as livestock. When the village saw how each attempt at healing wore on him, they were careful in their requests, and Seri protected him as best she could. Then came the first request from a neighboring vill in the same hearthing, a child kicked by a plowhorse. Another, from another vill, then another and another. He had come to be known all through that hearthing, the boy who could heal what herblore could not. Most of the time, he worked with animals, learning all he could of each kind, but when the calls came, he would go and heal the sick and injured. Seri stood between him and the world, the warm hand at his back, the one who remembered that he needed food after, the one who would sometimes scold those who hadn't tried herblore first.

"Then the Code came," Aris said, meeting the Marshal-General's gaze directly. "Of course we'd all heard of you, sir, and I'd seen a Marshal in the market towns. Our vill has a yeoman-marshal; Seri and I drilled with the other younglings as we grew tall enough. No one thought anything wrong about my healing and being in the barton as a junior. I don't know how many knew I was mageborn, but no one questioned me. Until last harvest-time.

Last harvest-time, the new Marshal of Whitehill grange had come to inspect each barton on his rolls, and with him, he'd brought the new version of Gird's Code. All the village stood in the barton to hear him read it, nodding their heads at familiar phrases — it wasn't that different — until the clause about magery.

Aris felt the now-familiar tremor in his hands, and locked them together. "It said, sir, that no form of magery could be tolerated, that what seemed good was really evil in intent and act, and forbade the mageborn to use, or anyone to profit by, magery. Of course everyone looked at me, and the Marshal stopped reading. 'Do you have a mageborn survivor in this vill?' he asked. Some nodded, and some didn't — I think they wanted to hide me, protect me. I raised my hand, and he called me forth. 'Do you practice evil magicks, boy?' he asked. Sir, I could hardly answer. I had healed, yes: that hand of days, I'd healed a serpent bite. But evil? I said so, that I had healed, and he drew back as if I'd thrown fire at him. Our yeoman-marshal stood up for me, then, and said I'd caused no trouble, nor had a bad heart, but the Marshal was firm that my magery was evil. If I had no bad heart, he said, I'd be willing to forswear it, never use it again. The people sighed at that, but he overrode them. I could not be in the barton, he said, if I used magery, nor could they harbor me. It was in the Code, he said."

"What did you do?"

"I said I was sorry, and would do so no more, though I couldn't see how healing was evil. He bade the yeoman-marshal watch me closely, and warned me that he would tolerate no magery in his grange." Aris looked at the Marshal-General again. "He said you knew best, sir, and if you said it was evil, then it was. I did my best, after that. The village folk were troubled in their minds; a few said I must have charmed them, to make my power seem good, but most wished naught had happened. They still came to me, many of them, when someone was sick, or a beast hurt. The yeoman-marshal tried to make them quit, but he couldn't. He asked couldn't I do something, short of using magery, but I don't have what Seri's folk call a parrion of herblore: I don't know any way but the power. And it came to hurt, sir . . . it rises up in me like water in a spring, when I see someone in need . . . I fell sick myself, late in winter, and Seri said that caused it. She said we had to come to you, because the Code is yours, and perhaps you didn't know that magery could be healing power."

"I had heard it could be; I never knew it so." The Marshal-General leaned forward; Aris could see doubt in his expression. "You say you had seen little use of magicks by your own folk before — did you never see someone charmed?"

Aris shook his head. "Not that I know of. Others have told me . . . it makes them think they want to do something, or like someone."

"And people do like you." The Marshal-General said that flatly. "Seri says everyone in your household liked you."

"You think I *charmed* them?"

"Perhaps you didn't mean to; a child may not know what it does. But I worry about it, lad. From what Seri says, even my own reaction to you. . . ."

Aris could not think of anything to say. He had been ready for anger, even punishment . . . but he had not expected this. The Marshal-General, looking steadily at him, apparently saw an expression that meant something, and relaxed, sighing.

"No, I don't think you are using magicks, not even without your knowledge. You're too relaxed; you weren't like that while healing. I've seen Luap here make light; he gets a faraway look. But I'm still worried. You seem a nice enough lad, no harm to you; Seri's talked my ears half off explaining about you and your family. Yet . . . there was a reason for the Code to forbid all magicks."

Aris let out the breath he had held. Gird waited, as if for Aris to say something, then went on.

"The magelords misused it, misused it so badly that what

85

everyone remembers is the misuse, not the right use." He said "right use" as if it hurt his mouth. "None of us know what the right use would be like, not having seen it, so judging the difference — knowing when the use is right and when it's wrong — would be difficult, if any of us could do it at all. Tell me, lad, have you ever misused your healing magick?"

Aris had followed the argument Gird was making; it made more sense than what his own Marshal had said, that magery was inherently evil. He spoke his thoughts aloud. "I had thought, Marshal-General, that healing was good in itself — and because it was good, then that use of magery was good. I never used it for anything but healing, but . . . " He stopped, trying to remember all the details of each healing; even in that abstraction he noticed that Gird's luap watched him closely. "I suppose, sir . . . if the gods meant someone to die, for some reason, then healing that person would be bad, and not good. Or not being able to heal completely . . . " He remembered the child kicked in the head by a horse, whose life he had saved, but the child remained mute and subject to fits, dying a few years later of a fever . . . the parents had not sought his help then. He told Gird about it. "Perhaps that was a misuse of magery, although at the time, I thought only of the child's life."

Gird nodded. "It may have been, though I agree you did not mean harm. But I've seen a man who meant no harm bury the tip of his scythe in a child's belly during harvest: the harm is done, with or without malice. I am glad to see that you recognize that, that you are willing to consider what harm you may have done." He glanced at his luap before going on. "Have you ever used your healing magicks to gain something unfairly? To force others to do what you wished? To cause a pain that you might gain approval for relieving it?"

"No!" Aris heard his voice rise, childishly, and took a long breath before continuing. "Sir, I would not know how to cause a pain; the pains people come with hurt enough. I have — I have told people what they must do to help me, sometimes, as in pulling a broken limb straight, or cleaning a wound. As for gain — some have given me food, afterwards, and if that is wrong, then I have been wrong, but I never asked, sir. Seri will tell you."

"Seri," Gird said gruffly, "is a young lass growing into a woman, and you are a young lad; in Seri's eyes you are a hero who will never do wrong."

Aris felt his face burning; it took all his will to meet Gird's eyes. "Seri doesn't lie, sir," he said through locked teeth. "She wouldn't, even if she were —"

"A lass in love?" finished Gird when he hesitated. "You may be right — but even if you are, I had to hear it from you. You are about to cause me a lot of trouble, lad, and I want to be sure it's worth it."

"Cause you trouble?" The last thing he wanted to do was cause trouble, and he could not imagine what trouble he would cause.

Gird's deep laugh surprised him. "Yes — how do you think your Marshal will like it when I change the Code to allow healing? Or the others who think as he does that all magicks are evil, that there are no good uses of a bad tool? And Luap here will have a lot of work to do, writing out new versions of the Code to be sent all over. I will have arguments from the Marshals and others who are afraid of any magicks; I will have complaints about changes — you don't think that's trouble?"

He could hardly believe what he was hearing. "Then —"

"Aris, I believe your healing is good, and your intentions good. I will insist on some restrictions, both for your own good and to calm peoples' fears: you are still young, you would have guidance if you were a farm lad learning to scythe, let alone someone who can save lives. But of course you must heal, and more than that I give you leave to train other mageborn in the use of that gift, if you can. If anything will reconcile our peoples, it will be the right use of magicks, using them to help and not harm."

87

• Chapter Seven

Gird's ideas of proper guidance surprised Aris and Seri both. For a hand of days, they lived in the old palace, free to run about and meet the others who lived there. The lad Aris had healed woke to comfort and health; he was shy at first, but soon treated Aris like a favorite brother. Gird's luap tested their knowledge of reading, writing, and accounting, and argued that they should be kept among the clerks where those skills would be most useful. Aris decided he liked the man, though he didn't want to spend all his time hunched over a desk. He found Luap's mixture of grave courtesy and sadness fascinating, and hoped that he would be able to learn the healing magery. Seri, for once, did not agree with him; she didn't exactly dislike Luap, but she could not, she said, see any reason for Aris's fascination.

On the fifth day, Aris widened his explorations to the stables and cowbyres, where he met Gird's old gray horse.

"You're — you're not old at all," Aris said, staring wide-eyed at the gray. It looked nothing like a carthorse now, in the sunlight that speared through the doorway. Hammered silver, an arched neck, great dark eyes that looked Aris full in the face. Then it turned to Seri, whose breath caught in her throat.

"It's not just a *horse*," she said softly. The horse fluttered its nostrils and made a sound like a growl. Aris, entranced, put out his hand. Warm breath flowed over it.

"I don't think anyone's supposed to know," he said. The horse bumped his hand with its muzzle. He wanted to touch it, stroke that head and that glossy mane. With a twitch of its ear, it gave permission. His hands moved without his thought, gentling and caressing, as he would have touched any horse. He always liked handling animals; he felt better when he touched them. This was more; he felt strong, safe, and alert. "Does Gird know?" he asked softly, into an iron-gray ear. The horse drew back its head and favored him with a look combining mischief and warning.

"No," said Seri, coming up beside him to fondle the horse's other ear. "Father Gird doesn't know, and he — " she meant the horse, " — thinks it's funny. And in the legends, no one quite believes it. They don't want to think about it. But how can anyone think you're an old broken-down carthorse?"

In the way of horses, each of them received the full power of one dark eye, then the horse seemed to collapse in on itself. Suddenly it was thicker, stubbier, paler — no longer hammered silver, but the dirty gray of white cloth left out to mildew and weather. The hollow in its back deepened; it stood hipshot, head sagging over the stall door. It yawned, disclosing long yellow teeth; its lids sagged shut over those remarkable eyes.

"But why did you show *us*?" Aris asked. He was sure it had, that the horse had its own reasons for revealing to them what it concealed from others. Without a change in shape or color, this time, the eyes opened, and the horse looked deliberately from one to the other. Aris felt the hair rise all over his body, as if he'd been dipped in cold water. He felt even more alert, as if some great danger had passed near. Every sense came to him sharply. He could hear a horse five stalls down licking the last oats from its manger, and another slurping water. The voices of men in the yard outside, bantering about their work, were almost painfully loud. He could smell everything, from the pungency of the horses to the smoke to the last apples frost-pierced on the trees in the meadow. He could feel the clothes on his body, the slick hair of the horse's neck, the pressure of the air in his nose that promised an autumn storm.

He glanced at Seri. She looked as if she felt the same. Her hair stood out from her braid as it did on cold clear winter days, more alive than some people's faces. Now she looked the old horse full in the face. "We're supposed to do something? *We* are? But we're newcomers; we don't know anyone. What — "

As if a large, warm hand had touched his shoulder, Aris felt calm rest on him. Not his calm: the horse's. The horse shook its head sharply. "Not yours, then," he said. "A god?" No answer, but it must be. A god wanted something from them, which meant they must give it, whatever it was. And they were to be ready — that much was clear — but whatever it was would come later, not now.

The gray horse yawned again, and when it was through stood looking even more aged and decrepit, if possible. "So," said Gird from behind them. "You've found my old horse." Aris managed not to look from the horse to Gird and back again. "He's a good campaigner," Gird said, rubbing the horse's poll, "but getting long in the tooth." The eye nearest Aris opened an instant; he felt the horse's secret laughter. "You said you liked cows, boy," Gird went on. "Come see ours. We've got two of the dun milkers and four of the spotted ones." Aris glanced back as they left the horse stables and saw the gray horse watching them.

Gird lavished the attention on the cows that Aris and Seri had given the old horse. He and the cowman discussed them in detail, from their broad black nostrils to their carefully curried tails. Gird ran his hands over them, looking inside their ears, stroking their broad sides and velvety flanks, feeling the udders for any inflammation. Aris liked the smell of cows, and their complacent belief that grass counted for more than anything else, but he could see that Gird's affection went beyond that. Finally Gird was done, and led them out into the meadow west of the palace complex. A few fruit trees, the remnants of a larger orchard, clung to their last leaves and some wizened apples.

"If you could live as you liked," Gird said, "what would you do between healings?"

Aris thought. "Well — I could work in the stables — or I suppose with your — with Luap in the copying rooms."

Gird looked at Seri. "I'd like to work with the horses," she said. "If Aris is, that is."

Gird nodded, as if that confirmed something he'd been thinking about. "That's about it. You two have lived and worked together for years, but — but if one of you died, what would the other do? You, Aris, are willing to do whatever's needful; you have the mageborn courtesy; you won't say what you want most, and I'm not sure you know. Seri knows, and will say it, but then thinks she must stay with you. I would not split brother from sister or friend from friend, but the two of you need to learn that you can live out of each other's pockets."

Aris felt cold. Would Gird send Seri *away*?

"I've been talking to Luap and the Marshals," Gird went on. "I don't like to see younglings cramped inside with scribe's work. Unless that's what you wanted most, I wouldn't have it so. You both need grange discipline, and you both need a chance to find your own balance. So here's my thought." He looked from one to the other, as if to be sure they were paying attention. Aris could hardly hear over the blood pounding in his ears.

"You, Aris, need to know herblore as well as your own magicks, and you need to be around others who heal in different ways. There's a grange in the lower city that has three women with parrions of herblore in it; they have agreed to teach you what they know, and the Marshal can supervise your use of your own healing. You will be a junior yeoman, as you were in your own barton; you will spend your days in grange work and healing and study. And you, Seri, seem like to grow into a Marshal someday. For you I've found a grange with a healthy group of junior yeomen; if you have the abilities I suspect, you will be a yeoman-marshal soon enough. And yes, before you ask, these are separate granges. But both are in Fin Panir, and you will live here, near me, for the first year. You will still be together part of every day; but you will learn to trust others, and work with others, not just yourselves."

This was so much better than what Aris had feared that he felt himself flushing with relief. "Thank you, sir," he said. Gird smiled at him, obviously well-pleased.

"All right, then," he said, "let's go down to the city, and I'll introduce you."

Marshal Kevis of Northgate Grange welcomed Aris as warmly as any mageborn could expect. "A healer, the Marshal-General tells me. Gods, lad, if we'd known about you during the war! But you would have been too young, then, I suppose?"

"I didn't know what I could do until later — at least, I thought it was only animals."

"Gird said that, yes. Well. Suriya is our oldest herblore-healer; she wants to meet you at drill tonight. Her daughter Pir and her niece Arianya are the others. We have the same drill-nights as the other granges here, and I'll expect you to attend unless you're sick — or do you get sick?"

"Yes, Marshal," Aris said. "I don't think I can heal myself — if I could, I wouldn't have gotten sick in the first place."

"That's sense. Well, then, be at drill, study healing with Suriya, and when someone needs your skill, come and tell me. If Suriya has nothing for you to do, there's always work at the grange. Gird says you'll be staying up the hill, with them — even so, you're to come to me before you go healing someone."

Aris nodded. He felt half-dressed, with Seri off somewhere

else, but he understood what Gird was trying to do. Not split them apart, but teach them to grow on their own. When he asked, the Marshal had several chores he could do that day, until time for drill. The yeoman-marshal, a young man a few years older than Aris, put him to work chopping wood and carrying water.

Suriya was a gray-haired woman who looked old enough to be his grandmother. She laid a gnarled hand on either side of his head, and hummed, then nodded sharply and spoke to the Marshal. "He'll do. The Marshal-General was right, Alyanya bless him! Here, lad, see what you think of this — " She handed him a small cloth bag of aromatic herbs. Aris sniffed.

"I don't know much, but it smells like what my folk called allheal and itchleaf."

"So it is, lad, with a pinch of dryhand, for them as gets the sweats without need. Scribes use that sometimes, that shouldn't, for a natural sweat keeps the body pure, but they don't like smudges on their scrolls." She waved at two other women, who came nearer. "This is my daughter, Pir, and my niece who's just come into her full parrion. You'll learn from her first, if it doesn't bother you to learn women's things."

Aris shook his head. "No, why should it? The law's the same for all, and the gods gift whom they will."

The women looked at each other, the family resemblance clear in the angle of eye, the set of the mouth. "Well, then," said Suriya briskly, "we'll get along. Aris, your name is, so I've heard — has that a meaning, in mageborn speech?"

"I don't know," Aris said. "I think it may have been a child's name, and I never learned the other."

"Ah. Well. It's the wrong time of year to gather most herbs, but we've still some collecting to do: barks, roots, that sort of thing. We'll meet you here at sunrising tomorrow, shall we?"

Aris ran back up to the palace, excited and worried both. He found Seri in the same mood, but in her it came out in chatter. "I like our Marshal," she said. "I only wish you could be there — but I know what Father Gird means, and he's right. He's made me his yeoman-marshal's helper, already, and I had no idea how much work there is in a city grange. I missed you, but I like it."

That set the pattern for the next two seasons. Before dawn, both were off to their granges, to learn from the best their Marshals could find. They drilled with the junior yeomen, and both assisted the yeoman-marshals and Marshals in any grange work to be done. Aris spent hours with Suriya and Pir, sorting herbs into packets and sacks, learning to identify by smell dozens of different dried leaves, roots, barks. They taught him to brew some into thick dark teas to drink, and mash others to a paste with lard, to be spread on the skin. He went with Suriya to the people who asked her help. Many times his own gift did not wake; he simply watched as she applied her herbs, and saw how her very presence soothed the worried families. At night, back in the old palace with Seri, they compared notes. Her days, spent almost entirely in grange work, were very different from his. Beyond the usual drill, her Marshal had begun giving her extra classes in weapon skills. The first time she was allowed to use a sword, she came back almost glowing with glee.

"But Seri — " Aris didn't know how to disagree with her; in all their life he never had. But swords were for hurting people; he knew she could not really want that. Not Seri, whose warmth was almost a healing magic in itself. Besides, swordfighters — soldiers — died younger than most.

"I am not becoming a bloodthirsty warrior," she said, almost angrily. "You're as bad as my Marshal. Stopped in midswing, he did, to ask what I was grinning about and scold me for it."

"I know you're not bloodthirsty," Aris said, rubbing her shoulder where a knot of pain resisted his fingers. "That's why I worry. If you wear a sword, someday you'll have to use it, and you'll feel bad about it."

"I'll feel worse if I don't know how, and get killed. Or if others get killed because I didn't learn enough. The Marshal-General didn't like killing people, but he did it. He did it as quick and clean as he could." Seri, unlike Aris, had actually watched some of the final battles, despite being warned off more than once by the rear ranks. She had come back white-faced and shaky, but ready to help tend the wounded. Aris had stayed near the fires, tending the wounded as they came from the field as best he then knew, unaware that the pounding headache and itching of his palms came from something more than tending smoky fires and boiling whatever herbs someone gave him.

"I don't want you to die," Aris said softly.

"I won't," she said. "I will work hard, and be *very* good." It should have sounded arrogant, but it didn't.

By the time Suriya was ready to send Aris and Pir out to collect the early summer herbs in the fields far from the city, Gird had decided that the two should live away from the palace, in or near their granges. Aris moved his small pack down to Suriya's house, and slept on a pallet in the kitchen. He had been called out at least once every hand of days for a healing; it would be simpler to live here. But he knew he would miss Seri. The first time he had healed in Suriya's presence, she had gasped and turned pale. Now she knew what to do, what he needed of rest, quiet and food afterwards. But her hands, warm and strong as they were, were not Seri's hands; he never felt the same afterwards until, in his rare free time, he could get up to the grange where she lived and worked, and tell her what had happened. She seemed cheerful enough, but her face always lighted up when he came, as if she, too, needed the familiar audience for her own tales.

The young man strode into the courtyard like someone who had never been thwarted. *Marrakai.* Luap struggled against a lance of envy that pierced him. He had known, as a boy, what the Marrakai were; he had been taught, in those early years, the high nobility of both realms. He fought the envy down, refused that easy resentment. Marrakai, according to Gird, had lost their magery early, and adapted. Gird no doubt thought he had much to learn from the Marrakai. Perhaps he did, though he was sure that learning to live with the loss of a talent was not the same as learning not to use one.

The young man went to one knee before Gird, surprising everyone, including Gird; Luap saw the flush of red that darkened his neck.

"Get up, young Marrakai: we don't do that."

"You have my respect, Marshal-General." He stood straight now, almost quivering in eagerness for something . . . Luap could not imagine what. What could a man like that need from Gird?

"Aye, well . . . " Gird rubbed the back of his neck with one broad hand. "You have mine as well, and your father. How is he?"

The young man grinned. "He's still in some trouble with the king, Marshal-General. For all the king needs his support, he wishes it need not be so."

"That bad, eh?" Gird waved the others aside, called Luap with a look, and sat heavily on the bench beneath the plane tree. "Here — sit and talk." He reached beneath the bench and pulled out a water jug. "Thirsty?"

"No, sir — Marshal-General." The young man leaned back, and stripped off his dusty gloves. "My father thinks the king will settle. He's not like the old one; he's got sense and no wish to evil. But he finds it hard to forgive my father's support of the peasants."

"I thought your father was going to stay at home and pull his woods up around his ears."

The young man shook his head. "That was not his nature, Marshal-General, as I think you know. He could no more ignore a war than a fine horse can ignore a race . . . it began with sanctuary given to fugitives from other domains."

Luap watched the Kirgan closely. The boy had Gird's confidence and no wonder: he hung on Gird's every word, eyes wide with admiration. Luap eyed the thick, lustrous cloth of his tunic, the oiled leather, finely tooled, of his belt, the carved bone hilt of the dagger in his obviously new boot. He remembered cloth like that, boots like that; the boy was rich, and had enjoyed a lifetime of such riches . . . which was fine; Luap could understand that. What he could not understand, or accept, was the way Gird accepted this youth, and his equally rich and powerful father, as friends.

I have served you honestly, he said silently toward the back of Gird's head, and pushing aside the memory of that time when he hadn't. *And I would have been this boy's master . . . but you never trust me this way.*

"But in spite of that your father is satisfied?" Gird asked. Luap had already told him that, as had the first messengers back from troubled Tsaia. "He is sure the new king has no such powers?"

"He swears it," the Kirgan said. "He considers the Mahierian branch the best choice, for all it angers the Verrakaien." Luap wished he knew more about the Verrakaien, who seemed, by the rumors, to be as powerful as the Marrakai but utterly inimical to them. Rumor also gave them the largest remaining store of magery, along with whispered tales of its source. He watched the young man's face, wondering how Gird was so sure the Marrakaien were telling the truth.

"And he has not taken the field at all?"

"No, although some of the local bartons sent volunteers. You did know that father allowed the bartons to organize openly?"

"Oh, yes." Gird's deep voice broke into a chuckle. "That news reached us quickly, I suspect." It was not quite the reaction the Kirgan had expected; Luap recognized the flicker of eyelid, the tension of shoulder quickly controlled. "Luap — "

Luap recalled himself and said, "Yes, Gird?"

"The Kirgan Marrakai confirms our reports that Tsaia's new king has no powers of magery, and that the merchants and craft guilds support his rule, while our supporters have mostly returned to their homes. I see no purpose in pursuing the war, with the most dangerous magelords dead — "

"Except the Duke Verrakai, Marshal-General," murmured the Kirgan.

Gird's shoulders lifted. "Far to your eastern border, Kirgan, and well beyond my reach. Those of you who know him best must do as you think wise, but you are not asking my aid, are you?"

"Well — no." He had the look of one who would have taken help if it had been offered, and had been hoping for that offer.

"Then I see no cause for quarrel between your land and this. Is that not what your father meant by sending you?"

"Well . . . yes. To ask, rather, if it satisfied you."

Gird heaved the kind of sigh that Luap had learned was intentionally dramatic. "Lad, I would be happiest if all the kingdoms lived in peace and plenty, but that's not like to come in *my* lifetime. Men delight in quarrels, as cows in summer grass. But your father's gold bought our freedom, in those steel points we used to let the mageborn blood run out — " Luap could not see the slightest flush, any sign that the youth considered mageborn blood his kin. Gird had told him the Marrakaien magery had been lost long before. How long? Long enough to consider themselves peasants? Not likely, with that air of mastery, that rich embroidery on sleeve and hem, those supple boots, that elaborately tooled belt. Was their friendship then pretense? What other motive could the Kirgan Marrakai have, coming to Gird, than that which he spoke openly?

He felt uneasy, all along his side, as he walked the Kirgan to the common dining hall. Gird had said, with a look that might have been meaningful (but which meaning?) to take care of him.

"He's not changed." The Kirgan sounded happy about that. Luap eyed him.

"Did you expect him to?"

"No. I suppose not. But my father told me that men in power often do." A pause, in which they entered the dining hall, and Luap's look quelled those who would have challenged the Kirgan. He showed the young man where to wash, and led him to the serving table. Would he expect fancier food? No — he dipped into the mutton stew as if he liked it, tore off a hunk of bread just as Luap did, and sat on the bench as if his rump were used to no better. "I saw that myself, in the new king we have."

"Ah." The new Tsaian king, which Duke Marrakai had backed against other contenders. "You are at court much?"

"Only to carry my father's messages. He says court life is not healthy for young men — or for him, at present." The Kirgan chuckled as he said that, and Luap smiled responsively. He could not decide if the young man's frankness were what it seemed or not. He wished the Rosemage were there; she had known Duke Marrakai when he was young, though she would not talk much about him.

"So — how has your new king changed?"

The Kirgan looked thoughtful and clasped his fingers as if that would help him decide what to say. "He was . . . they had always made fun of him. I heard that in the years I was in Valchai's household. The king — the old one, I mean — had the mage powers our family had long lost, and some said that his cousin's lack proved his bastard blood."

A white rage shook Luap as a dog shakes a rag, then dropped him, leaving him hot and cold at once. He could feel his power struggling to escape, prove itself, but held it in check. He would not let this — this *boy* push him into anything rash. "Are the gifts then proof of pure blood?" he asked, as calmly as if discussing the color of a new calf.

"No. At least my father says not. Once perhaps they were, but when our folk came into the north, they began to fail, unaccountably and unpredictably. Some families accepted this as the gods' price for the gift of a great new land, and others fought it . . . but that you know."

"Yes." It was all he could say, through clenched teeth; luckily, the Kirgan seemed not to notice.

"At any rate, the new king had been considered of no moment so many years that some thought he would be unable to rule. He was known to spend his days in the stables, training his own horses and even grooming them."

"And what's wrong with that?" Gird asked, setting his own bowl down on the table and grunting as he swung his leg over the bench. Luap bit his lip. Even now, he'd find Gird down in the cowbyres of a morning, humming over some cow as he brushed her. For himself, if he never saw a cow except on the table, ready to eat, it would be well enough. The Kirgan flushed, and Gird relented. "I know: your great lords aren't supposed to do their own work. But if the man likes horses, how can he keep away? Still, he'll be busy enough now to have no time for that, as I have no time for farming. . . . "

"Would you go back to it?" No one else had asked, that Luap knew; trust a rash youth to open his mouth and say it.

Gird sighed. "Now? I — I like to think I would, if the chance came. I miss it, the smell of the grass and the cows, the feel of a scythe handle as the blade bites into the stems. But my farm's gone, my family's gone — and that's all part of it, you see. Not just any field, but the field I knew from boyhood, and the same cottage, and my family around the table. Friends beside me in the field, all that. If I went back to farming, took a vacant place, I'd have to do it all alone. That I don't want: their faces would hover over the table, and I — I'd be alone."

For a moment, Luap saw Gird in some cottage, surrounded by children and grandchildren — but it would not happen, and they all knew it. He suspected that Gird would make a less than perfect grandfather anyway.

The Kirgan said, "I have thought long on what you told me before, sir. I have been learning the skills of farming myself." He opened his hand to show Gird the calluses on his palm as if they were battle scars. Perhaps they were, Luap thought. Gird clearly approved, and his nod seemed to mean as much to the boy as any praise. What kind of duke would he make, with the attitudes he learned from Gird? As difficult as the blend of mageborn and peasant in Fintha, Luap could not imagine how it would work in Tsaia, with the mageborn retaining their right to rule. His envy ebbed, thinking on the difficult task the Kirgan would face as time went on.

* * *

When Arranha invited him to one of the courtyard discussions, Luap went hoping to hear something which would help him deal with his own confusion. Instead, Arranha spent the whole afternoon propounding the idea that common daylight and inspiration were analogous: that the gods gave light to see with eye and mind both, that the mere exposure of evil by such light somehow ensured its defeat, that all good men would naturally choose to be flooded with that light, so that any errors could be seen and corrected.

Luap could not explain what bothered him about that doctrine. Gird, somewhat impatient after a day spent settling quarrels between granges, had no sympathy with his imprecision.

"He's a priest, and a Sunlord priest at that. Why should you understand what he says?"

"He thinks we all should." Luap rolled the quill in his hand. "He thinks we should all understand the gods . . . that the Sunlord's light enlightens everyone. . . . "

Gird snorted. "There's some as stumble into holes in broad daylight. Granted, we all stumble more in the dark, but — "

"That's what I mean. If . . . if you're thinking about something *else*, if you're not using the light, you can run square into something . . . and if you're trying to see, you can see better in dim light sometimes than midday glare. I think the mind's light is the same, but Arranha doesn't."

"Mind's light, or god's light?"

"They're the same, aren't they?" At Gird's expression, Luap tried again. "I mean, once inside your head — how can you tell? Light is light."

Gird's expression might have been pity, or contempt, or some combination. "I think if you ever have a god in your head, Luap, you will discover the difference. Now — about those grange rolls — " And he refused, with a glower and another question about the grange records, to enter into that discussion again.

Luap puzzled over it himself, day after day. Somewhere in that concept of Arranha's something didn't fit his own experience, his own knowledge of himself. Was refusing knowledge the same thing as choosing evil? Was his desire for the privacy of his childhood memories, his instinctive distaste for Dorhaniya's reminiscences, the same as turning away from the light? He could not tell, and he could not tell if that failure meant something.

Chapter Eight

Luap did not, after all, have to decide when and how to tell Gird about that distant land. Gird himself suggested they travel together, when it became obvious that the Marshal-General's presence would settle some festering disputes in outlying granges. The cave lay on the obvious shortcut from one problem to another, and Luap took that as a favorable omen.

"I don't know that I like this any better than I did the first time." Gird's voice rang off the stone walls.

"You don't have a cold." Luap grinned over his shoulder. Gird had one hand on the wall, feeling his way. He wouldn't fall over the ledge this time.

"And you don't have that tone of voice you had." Gird's look was friendly enough, but unsmiling.

"Yes." Luap remembered the previous occasion entirely too well; he had been almost hysterical with fear and elation. Now his mouth went dry. He had sworn and been forsworn, all in less time than heating a kettle of water. This place was the very focus of Gird's distrust of him, however he'd proven himself since. How could he expect Gird to believe him now?

"Yes," he said again, flattening his tone to avoid the least taint of charm. "But I will tell you what I can. You remember that you, too, felt an influence here?"

"I felt the god's presence, not an *influence* like your magery." Gird had decided to be difficult; Luap smothered a sigh. Gird's expression, in the gloom, looked one with the rock walls. Luap felt as bruised by that as by his memories.

"I felt both." Luap paused, and thanked the gods' mercy that Gird did not comment. He drew another long breath and plunged on. "That inner chamber, floored and ringed with strange designs . . . ?"

"Umph." More grunt than word, it meant *Go on, I'm listening.*

"It can take you to a place."

100

That should have been clear enough, but Gird stared, eyes suddenly brighter in dimness. "Take you? How?"

"I don't know how. And — " forestalling another question, "I don't know where the place is, or why, or anything else. I don't know if it will take you, or only me. But I thought you should know."

Gird had that crafty look Luap most disliked. He would complain. He did. "Gods' teeth, lad, you keep thinking I should know things that don't help at all."

Damned mulish peasant, thought Luap, an indulgence he allowed himself only in the dark. Gird read his face too well.

"You told me to assess all magical dangers. This may be one. If I can go somewhere and return, so may others."

"*Your* kind."

"Or others. I think the Elder Races have used this."

"Gnomes?" Gird sounded almost cheerful about that; unlike Luap, he still got on well with his former advisors.

"I don't know. You might know the symbols I found in that other place."

"So — have you asked them?"

"Not without talking to you. I wondered if you'd try it with me."

"Try — you mean go *somewhere*?"

Luap nodded. Gird heaved one of those sighs Luap had learned were as dramatic as necessary. "Has the place gone to your head, then, as it did last time? Will you try another of your tricks?"

"No." Surely he knew that already.

"Well, then. Yes. I will. But — " a blunt finger hard against Luap's chest. "— But I still own a hard fist and strength to use it."

"I know." He let his own light come, in this hidden place, until it shone as bright as needful, looking away from Gird's face in conscious courtesy. . . . Gird still hated to see magelight, even Arranha's. Then he led the way to the chamber for which he had no proper name, the bell-shaped space with its carved decorations, its inlaid design on the floor. "We'll stand here," he said, stepping boldly out onto it.

"You're sure?" Gird edged his boot forward as if he thought the smooth stone might be glass, and break. In here his voice echoed, waking a resonance more metallic than stony. He spoke more softly then. "I don't like this — the gods — "

"Will sense no impiety." Luap waited until Gird moved

close to him, the broad shoulders slightly hunched, apprehensive. He stretched his own chest, wondering, in the last possible moment, if this was wise. But he had to try; the need for that squeezed his mind painfully. He felt inside for the power he had inherited, that the Rosemage was so determined he would learn to use. As if his feet were moving in a dance, he could feel the interlacing patterns below him in the stone, and his mind sang a response. . . .

And they stood in the great hall with its arches at the far end. He felt Gird's sudden shift of weight, heard the indrawn ragged breath, that came back out as a shaky whisper.

"*Somewhere* . . . you said . . ."

"This is . . . it. Wherever it is. Whatever it is." However it works and we got here, he went on silently, hoping Gird wouldn't ask about that. At least not yet. "We can walk around," he went on, taking a step off the pattern's center. He could damp his own magelight; the place lay under the cool silvery glow of deeper magic. Would Gird notice the difference? Gird did.

"More magicks than yours," he said. "And how big is this place?"

"I'm not entirely sure. I didn't go far." He watched Gird move around, and finally leave the pattern that here centered a raised area of the floor. The man could still surprise him . . . an old man, a peasant born, distrustful of any magicks . . . and here after being snatched from a cave to a hall, he was looking around with alert interest and no apparent fear. He could still taste the fear that had choked his own throat the first time he'd come — but of course he'd had no warning. No . . . Gird was simply the braver man. He followed him down the hall, noticing without analyzing the odd ring of their boots on the stone floor, the way the walls threw the sound back less harshly than he'd expected.

"Harp and tree . . ." Gird muttered, looking up at the carving. "The treelords, the oldsingers, that would be. I wonder if the blackhearts ever had a place here."

"Blackhearts?"

"I may not have told you." A long pause, in which Luap tried to remember if he'd ever heard of blackhearts. "And I'm not sure this is the place for it. There's a feel . . . a good feeling here." Gird looked around. "Anvil and hammer . . . Sertig's folk, then."

102

"Gnomes?"

"Nay. Dwarven; the gnomes follow the High Lord as judge. But I heard the lore of Sertig there, and from the first smith I knew, back in the woods. 'Tis said all smiths learned metalcraft of dwarves, and the dwarves say Sertig hammered out the world on his anvil. Gnomes themselves think the High Lord ordered chaos as we might sort seed or stones for building — at least I think that's what they meant."

"And elvenkind?"

Gird's face wrinkled. He had never said much about the elves, receiving the first elven ambassador with evident embarrassment and awe. "Think that their god made the world like a harper makes a song, if I understood what I was told — and I doubt I do. A song's not a thing, like a stone you can count, or a lump of iron you can shape . . . it's . . . it's just a thought in the mind, until someone sings it again. It's not really there, between singings. So how can the world be a song?"

"Maybe it's not finished." But even as he said it, Luap felt a shiver go down his spine . . . the world *was*, as Gird said: you could touch it, smell it, taste it. He could not imagine it as something becoming, not in its essence. Humans might move across the world, even change it, as the Aarean lords had laid waste some tracts of forest, but its basic reality didn't change. He hoped.

Gird had grunted; now he prowled near the arches. "Dwarfkind, elvenkind, and this . . . I suppose . . . is for the gnomes?"

"What — lords of light and shadow!" That was a magelord's oath, and earned him a sharp glance from Gird, but he could not help it. Luap swallowed an angular lump of confusion, and wondered if he should tell Gird that the arch he stood under had not been there before. Not there the previous trips, and not there a few — minutes? — ago when they'd first arrived.

"I don't remember seeing this at first," Gird said. His voice was husky; was he finally afraid of something? Luap swallowed again and forced the truth past his teeth, which wanted to grip it.

"It wasn't here." Gird gave him a long level stare. "I swear, Marshal-General — " in this context the title came easily, more easily than his name. "It was not here when I came before, and it was not here when we arrived."

Over his head the arch bore the single unflawed circle of the

High Lord, glowing with its own light, as the harp and tree, and the anvil and hammer. Up either column ran the same intricate interlacing patterns as on all other columns in that place, patterns he had seen in weaving or pottery all his life, now graved deep in polished stone. Gird's hand reached out, drew back, went out again, thumb first, to follow one of the lines a short way.

"It must . . . must mean something. . . ." All the resonance had left his voice; his brow wrinkled. Of course it meant something; what else? But Gird stared up, mouth gaping as he leaned back. Luap wanted to say something, do something, but couldn't think of anything effective. He wanted to think Gird was disrespectful, but couldn't manage that, either. Gird reserved disrespect for humans. Now he gave Luap another one of his looks. "Did you go through, before?"

"Through one of these?" At Gird's nod, he shook his head. "I would not chance it, marked as they were. And it felt wrong."

"Humph." Gird shook his head, to what question Luap could not guess, and turned away from the middle arch to Luap's great relief. Back up the long, silent, echoing, empty hall, around the dais. "Back there?" Gird's broad thumb indicated the openings hewn in the wall. Luap felt himself flushing, though why he couldn't imagine.

"Yes . . . I did. Not far; I wasn't sure of the light, of the directions—"

"Show me." That was plain enough; Luap shrugged and led the way through the left-hand door. Heartwise, the peasant lore had it. Sunwise, to Arranha and the magelords. The passage ran as he remembered, with no surprising additions, level and dry, wide enough for three men to walk comfortably together. Gird crowded him, nonetheless. "Find any stairs to the outside?"

"No." That had worried him; he knew there must be ways out, for the air to be so fresh. But in his limited explorations, all he'd found were empty chambers and these passages. Around a corner, then another. Ahead the passage forked. "I stopped here, and went back."

"Wise, I would think." Gird licked his finger and held it up. "Ah . . . we'll try the left again."

"Doesn't it bother you?"

"What?" Then he grinned, mischievous; Luap could have

smacked him. "You mean being understone like this? That's right — you came later. You knew I was with the gnomes, but not how long. All the winter that was, and never a day's clean light, or living air. An hour or so of this won't bother me."

He wanted to believe that negated the courage, but he knew better. Gird had earned the right to be casual here, in those months with the gnomes. He followed Gird left away from the junction of passages, hoping his trailsense would hold here. Empty corridor followed empty corridor. Rooms opened here and there, blank and empty, floors gritty under his boots. Gird seemed to know where he was going, and Luap followed, stubborning forcing his fear under control. Finally Gird stopped, and leaned on the wall.

"I'm tired. This could go on forever."

"Mmm." Luap leaned on the opposite wall, and looked down at his scuffed boots. He felt as if the stone were leaning back against him.

"We'll go back." Gird sighed. "I'd like to know where this is — which mountains. Dwarves would know."

"Would they?" asked Luap. "If it doesn't come out somewhere, maybe they never saw the outside. . . . "

Gird snorted. "They had to, to take out the stone they cut. And I've heard they know stone by its smell and taste . . . that a dwarf will know a rock brought from leagues away. The gnomes could do that, and they said dwarves could too." He pushed himself off the wall. "Well. Back we go." He led the way again, and Luap came behind, trying not to look back over his shoulder at what might follow the clangor of their voices. "You found a good surprise, Luap, I'll give you that. Not like before, indeed." He led on at a good pace, and soon they came back to the great hall; they could hear their footsteps ring in it before they arrived, as if it were a bell.

Luap let out breath he had not realized he held. "How did you know your way?" He could ask, now that they were safe.

Gird's brows rose. "You didn't? You count the turns, the doorways you pass, keep track of lefts and rights — "

And this was the man who formed half his signs wrong in writing, whose brow furrowed over a page of clear script, who could not reckon except by placing objects in a row and counting them. Luap managed not to shudder or glance back through the doorway. "And now?"

"Mmmm." Gird looked around, up, around again. "I would still like to see the *outside* of this rock."

And I, thought Luap fervently. He opened his mouth to say "Then we'll go back," and shut it, for Gird was strolling with perfect assurance — or what looked like it — down the hall toward the arches. He had never heard Gird pray, and he did not hear him pray now — but he was sure that pause before Gird walked under the arch with the High Lord's sigil had in some manner been a request for permission. He himself did not run to follow, because (he told himself) it was disrespectful — he walked, quickly and quietly, and was in time to see Gird standing straddle-legged at the foot of a narrow curving stair that rose into the first darkness he had seen in this place. Gird turned and gestured.

"Come *on*, Luap; if it didn't scorch me, it's not going to hurt you." Luap would have liked to be sure of that, but stepped gingerly through the arch, his heart pounding. It had *not* been there before, and now he had walked through it, and — he glanced back, to find the hall just as visible, just as empty, just as silent as before. From this side, too, the arches stood clear, each with its holy symbol.

Gird had already started up the staircase, grunting a little. Luap sighed and followed. He might as well. If something happened to Gird, he could not go back without him. The stair rose in a spiral around a central well; Luap tried to keep a hand on the wall, but felt that the stairs tipped slightly inward. The staircase had no railing; his stomach swooped within him like a flight of small birds. His legs began to ache. From silver light, they passed to dusk, and then to dark. Gird stopped abruptly, and Luap almost ran into him.

"Why is there no light here?" His voice sounded flat, almost as if they were in a tiny closet, then it rang back from far below.

"I don't know." Luap felt grumpy, and his voice sounded it.

So did Gird; he heard a grumbling mutter, then: "Well, *make* some, then." That was a concession. Luap called his light, dim enough after the gloriously clear light below, and close above Gird's head the stone sprang into vision, arced into a shallow dome, scribed with patterns as intricate as any below. Within Gird's reach was a doubled spiral; Gird reached a cautious hand toward it.

"You know that?" asked Luap.

"Gnomes used it." Gird's broad peasant thumb traced the spiral in, then out, missing none of the grooves. He looked up, and said, "At your will." Not to Luap; Luap's hair rose. Suddenly a gust of cold air swirled in, and he felt the sweat on his neck freezing. Above the red stone vanished, and out of a dark gray sky snowflakes danced down upon them. "Blessing," said Gird, and climbed on. Luap followed, pushing against the gusting wind and shivering in the cold.

He came out over the lip of the opening onto a flat windswept table of red stone. Gird crouched an armslength away, back to the wind, eyes squinted, hair already spangled with snow. Luap looked around. He had never seen anything like their surroundings. They seemed to be on the flat top of some mass of stone, like a vast building. To one side — in that storm he could not guess the direction — rock rose again, a sheer wall as if hewn by a great axe. On the other sides, their table ended as abruptly. Snow streaked the rock, packed into every crevice, but swept clean of exposed surfaces. Its irregular curtains cloaked more distant views, but gave tantalizing hints of other vast rock masses.

"Not a place I'd expect to find elves," said Gird. "Not a tree in sight. Gnomes and dwarves, though . . . I'm surprised we haven't seen them."

Luap shivered. "If we stay here, they'll find us frozen as hard as these rocks."

"Not yet. I've never seen any place like this — or heard of it, even in songs."

Luap sighed, and climbed the rest of the way out, shivering, to crouch beside Gird. "Probably no one ever saw it before." At Gird's look, he said, "Human, I mean. Gnomes, dwarves, elves, yes." He squinted, blinked, and realized that the snow came down less thickly . . . he could see downwind, now, to the dropoff and beyond. . . . "Gods above," he murmured. A wet snowflake found the back of his neck and he shivered again.

"Uncanny," said Gird. It was the same voice with which he'd come down from the hill before Greenfields, quiet and a little remote. As last of the snow flurry wisped past, scoured off the stone by the incessant wind, Gird stood and looked at the wilderness around them.

It seemed larger every moment as the veils of falling snow withdrew, and a little more light came through the clouds.

Vast vertical walls of red stone, cleft into narrow passages . . .
Luap realized that Gird was moving toward the edge of their
platform, and followed quickly.

"Don't get too near —"

" — the edge. I'm not a child, Luap." A gust of wind made
them both stagger and clutch each other. Gird pulled back and
glanced upward. "Nor a god, to stand in place against such
wind. I will be careful." He looked back and up. "There are
trees — up on that next level — " Luap squinted against the
wind and saw an irregular blur of dark and white, that might
have been snow- covered trees. He looked into the wind, and
saw the edge of cloud, with light sky beyond it, moving toward
them, visibly moving even as he watched. He nudged Gird,
who turned and stared, mouth open, before turning his back
to the wind again. "A very strange place indeed, you found.
Not in the world we know, I daresay."

As the cloud's edge came nearer, the wind sharpened, probing daggerlike beneath Luap's clothes. He found it hard to
catch his breath, but he no longer wanted to retreat to the
safety of the magical place . . . he was too interested in the
widening view. Light rolled over them from behind, as the
cloud fled away southward and let sunlight glare on the snowy
expanse. Luap squinted harder, suddenly blinded. Then, as
his eyes adjusted, he stared until his body shuddered, reminding him of the cold.

Wall beyond wall, cleft beyond cleft, stacked together so
tightly he knew he could not tell, from here, where those clefts
led. Stone in colors he had not imagined, vivid reds and oran-
ges, and far away a wall of stone as white as the snow — unless
it was a snowfield on some higher mountain. And a distant
plain, apparently almost level, glaring in the sunlight until his
eyes watered.

"Not good farmland," said Gird. Now even he shivered; he
swung his arms and added, before Luap could replay, "Now
let's get back in; I'm famished with cold."

They struggled back against the wind, eyes slitted, and
found the entrance by almost falling in. Luap led, this time,
and nearly fell into the stair's central well when his boots
slipped on inblown snow. He did not care. He felt that something had opened, inside his head, a vast room he had not
known he owned, furnished with shapes he had not known he

108

wanted to see until he saw them. *Beauty*, he thought, setting one foot carefully after another. *It's beautiful*.

Behind him, he heard Gird's comments about the impossibility of farming in land like that with inward amusement. He had nothing against farmland; he liked to eat as well as anyone. But these red rocks, streaked with snow were not meant for farmland. Trumpets rang in his head. Banners waved. *Castles*, he thought. And then again: *Beauty*. And then, slowly, inexorably, *Mine. My own land. My . . . kingdom*. As in a vision, he saw the arrival of his people, the mageborn, saw them come out into the sun atop that great slab of stone, saw the awe in their faces. He went down slowly, step after careful step, listening to Gird behind him. He did not notice how far they had gone before the cold wind no longer whistled down the central well; he simply assumed, he realized later, that the entrance would close itself.

He waited for Gird to reach the bottom of the stairs, and let Gird lead the way back into the hall. "I wonder if it's the same every time you go up," Gird said, in the tone of one who would find it reasonable if either way. Luap almost turned and went back to find out, but restrained himself. He could come again, alone: he could find out by himself if his land (he thought of it already as his, without noticing) was there. He didn't notice that he had not responded until he realized that Gird had stopped and was peering at him. At once he felt the heat in his face, as if he had been caught out in an obvious lie. But Gird said nothing about that.

"You must have been cold," he commented. "And now your blood's coming back: your face is as red as raw meat. Mine feels like it too." And indeed he was flushed, almost a feverish red. Luap felt an unexpected pang of guilt.

"I'm sorry —" he began, but Gird cut him off.

"Not your fault. I'm the one insisted we stay out up there so long. Brrr. It may be spring in Fintha, but it's winter here — let's go back, unless you have a magical feast hidden here somewhere."

"Alas, no," said Luap. He led Gird back to the center of the pattern on the dais, and reached for his power, this time with confidence. It seemed but a moment, a flicker of the eyelid, and they were once more in the cave's inner chamber. Gird coughed, and the cough echoed harshly, jangling almost. Luap led him out, with a concern more than half real, to their campsite just inside the cave's entrance. Their horses, cropping spring grass outside, paused to look, and Gird's old white horse whuffled at him.

Outside, the day had waned to a moist, cool evening. Luap built up the fire quickly, noticing that Gird still shivered from time to time.

"Are you all right?"

"Just cold." He sounded tired as well as cold. Luap wondered if that way of travel, which he found exhilarating, felt different for the one who was taken, like a sack of meal in a wagon. "I don't *like* caves," Gird said, peevishly. "They all have *something* . . . this one that chamber, the gnomehalls their secret passages and centers, and gods only know what in that place you found, whatever it is." He hitched himself around on the rock, and spread his hands to the fire Luap had built. "And I'm still not sure why you showed me that. Do you know yourself?"

"Not really." Luap put the kettle on its hook, and added more wood to the fire. He should have brought a keg of ale. That would have kept Gird from asking awkward questions . . . but Gird being Gird might have thought that a suspicious thing to do. "I thought you should know about it; I thought it should not be a secret."

"Umph. It was meant to be a secret, I'd wager. Meant to be, and kept a secret, all those years, until you stumbled into it. And that's something I've always wondered about — " He coughed, a long racking cough, and Luap offered him water. Gird gulped a mouthful, and coughed again. "Blast it! You'd think I was an old man, hacking and spitting by the fire." Luap said nothing, in the face of Gird's shrewd gaze. "So . . . is that what you think?" Luap managed a shrug he hoped looked casual.

"You're older than I am, but Arranha is older. To us you're just Gird." Not quite true; others had commented, this past winter, on that same enduring cough.

"That horse has slowed down," Gird said, jerking a thumb at the white blur standing hipshot just outside the cave. "He hardly moves out of an amble, these days." Luap looked at the horse, and met dark eyes that looked no more aged than a colt's. Gird never admitted anything unusual in his horse, but everyone else realized that it had never been a stray carthorse. Where it had come from, no one knew, but Luap had heard more than one refer to it as "Torre's mount's foal."

110

"Horses age faster than men," Luap said, ignoring the snort from the cave entrance. "And you were willing to sit out in that snowstorm longer than I was."

"That's true." Gird prodded the fire with a stick; sparks shot up, and shadows danced on the cave walls. He looked around. "It was homelier with an army in it."

Noisier and smellier, Luap thought, remembering quarrels and hunger. Now they had plenty of food, warm dry clothes without holes, warm blankets to sleep in. "Sib's ready," he said, lifting the lid on that aromatic brew. "We'll be back to a town tomorrow." If he was lucky, Gird would not get back to his previous topic. He dipped a mugful for Gird, another for himself, and set the loaf by the fire to warm. They had an end of ham, the mushrooms they'd gathered on the way, a handful of berries, a few spring ramps. Gird drank his sib in three gulps, then held his mug for more. Luap served him, silent and hoping to remain so. He offered a slice of warm bread, with a slab of cold ham. Gird took it as silently, and bit off a chunk.

Silence lasted the meal, then Gird belched and sighed. "Strange place. A long way from here or anyplace I ever saw. They don't look like the mountains near the gnome princedom. Elves . . . dwarves . . . they will not thank you for sharing their secret, when they find out."

"I thought perhaps they'd lost it." That sounded strange, even as he said it. "Forgotten it," Luap amended. "There's no sign anyone's used it."

Gird blinked. "But you haven't been watching. How would you know?"

"I — don't." He had been sure, from the utter blankness of the chamber in this cave, the empty hall *there*. No smells of occupation, no stir of air, no sounds. He was sure the place had been waiting for him, would be empty any time he returned to it, until he took others there. *If* he took others there. His heart quickened, and he took a long breath. He would not think about that now.

"How much sign did we leave?" Gird went on. "In a day or so, whatever snow we tracked in will have dried. That's large country, out there. You could take an army through this cave, a tensquad a time, and send them out into that, and a day later no one could tell."

Luap hoped his face showed nothing; he felt the sweat

spring out under his arms and on the back of his neck. He cleared his throat and forced a shrug. "But until we know where *there* is, what good is that?"

Gird nodded. "That's sense. We're not wandering folk, any more; we have no need of more lands. There's plenty amiss here to clean up. You're right, lad; my mind just wandered a bit. And I should thank you for showing me, not keeping it to yourself. You're right; someone else should know it exists, someone human, I mean. But it's lucky we didn't know during the fighting. Some would've wanted to hide from trouble that way."

He almost told Gird then. His mouth opened; he said the first words that came into his head . . . and they were not those words. "It would have complicated things," he said, and ducked his head and pretended to yawn. Towers, walls, *castles* slid through his mind, peopled with mageborn men and women and children, living together in peace, far from the quarrels Gird never wanted to hear about, where he could learn the ways of his powers, and use them to prove they were not dangerous.

"Tires you, does it? Traveling that way?" Gird prodded the fire; Luap managed another yawn as the flames danced high for a moment, and nodded. He was tired but not from that. From being caught in the old trap of Gird's mistrust, from being penned in too small a pen.

• Chapter Nine

Gird came from court as grumpy as Luap had seen him. "Your folk I expected to be difficult; mine I thought had more sense."

"What now?"

"A petition from over northeast somewhere, to have all the mageborn children tested for magical powers and then destroy them. The magery, not the children. I think. I don't know how many times I have to *tell* them — !" He broke off, scrubbing his forehead with a fist as if to wipe out the memory. "It will work in the end; it has to work."

"Maybe it won't," said the Rosemage quietly. "What then?"

"Not another war," said Gird. "We've had enough of that." That *no war* didn't mean *no killing* they all recognized. "Look at Aris and Seri: they're fast friends. They get along with both peoples." The Rosemage opened her mouth, but closed it again. Gird knew, as well as she and Luap, that few mageborn had Aris's talents, and few peasant-born had Seri's experience of friendship. You can't, Luap thought, make an alliance work because two children get along. More likely, Aris would trust too much in his own goodwill, and some superstitious peasant with no goodwill at all would bash his head in for him. That Seri would then gleefully avenge him wouldn't help at all. He wondered what Gird would do if someone killed Aris as a mageborn — would that finally convince him that the two peoples would never mix? Or would he ignore that as stubbornly as he'd ignored all the other evidence.

"We could leave," Luap said, as if continuing the conversation interrupted long before. No need to say how or where: Gird had not forgotten that.

"All of you?" Not quite disbelief, but a tone that made clear Gird's opinion. Root and branch, child and lady and old and young?

"All of us." Luap shut his eyes a moment, *seeing* them all in

113

the echoing arches of that great hall, hearing in his mind's ear the voices racketing off stone. How could he feed them? "We could farm that other valley," he said. "Small-gardens . . ."

"Most of us aren't farmers," said the Rosemage. Damn the woman — she should realize it was their best hope. "Small-gardens don't yield grain. . . ."

"There's a plain beyond," he said. "Maybe that would produce grain. Or something Arranha said, about the terraces used in Old Aare; we could build terraces. And if we aren't farmers now, more of us are than were. We can learn. Better that, than — "

"You want to run away!" Gird's anger blazed from his eyes. "You won't give it a chance!"

"I've given it a chance!" The moment he said it, he knew he'd lost; if only he had said *we* instead of *I*. He got his voice under control and tried to mend the unmendable. "Gird — sir — however much *you* want the mageborn to blend in, most of the others don't. They've told you themselves. Even some of the Marshals; you know why you didn't send Aris to Donag's grange. And Kanis, in the meeting two days ago — "

"Kanis is a fool," Gird said through clenched teeth. "And you're another. You ought to see it, you of all of us, if blood-right stands for anything. Does your mother's pain mean nothing to you? You are *ours* as much as theirs — " He flicked a glance at the Rosemage, not hostile, but acknowledging, and went on. "You could be the bridge between us, Luap, if you'd work at it, instead of haring off after some scheme to make yourself a comfortable niche with your father's folk. You don't have the right to say: the peoples must say. The mageborn, if they want to leave *on their own*, can go without you. They don't need you, except to cause them trouble: you've sworn to take no crown, and what can you be, without one, but temptation?"

"That's not fair!" He wanted to say more, but he had ruined his chance, and knew it. Gird would not budge now, not for a season or so. Yet he could not keep quiet. "You know I have traveled the land, more than you yourself, carrying copies of your Code, and trying to show your — the people — how harmless, how loyal, a king's son can be. And they don't trust me yet. What more can I do?"

"Quit saying 'my people' and 'your people,' for one thing. Quit thinking it, for another. The distance between a

114

merchant trading across the mountains and a shepherd lass who's never been away from home is no less than the distance between the mageborn and the . . . " Even Gird wanted a name for the others, and though he refused to say "my people" the words hung between them in the impervious flame of reality. He cleared his throat, avoiding the term, and kept going. "If I can expect the merchant and the shepherd, the cheesemaker and the goldsmith, to live under one law, what is so hard about the other?"

The Rosemage warned him with her eyes, but he could not desist. Gird must someday see the truth, he was convinced, and if he kept at it, perhaps it would be sooner. He did take time to choose his words carefully. "Gird, you set no limits on craftsmen or merchants or farmfolk, so long as they stay within the law, but what would happen if you told farmers they could not farm, or a weavers they could not weave?"

"Why would I do that?" Gird asked. "And what has that to do with — "

"The mageborn powers, Gird. You want them given up, as if they were wicked in themselves, rather than talents like a dyer's eye for color or a horse-trainer's skill with horses."

Gird cocked his head. "Talents like other talents? I think not, lad, and if you believe that you're fooling yourself."

"You let Aris heal: that's a mageborn talent." He hoped his envy did not bleed into his voice. Every time he saw Aris, his own talent ached within him . . . perhaps he too could heal, if only Gird would let him try.

"Healing is a gift of the gods. Yes, I know, it was said to be a mageborn talent, but what mageborn in my lifetime had it? We saw no healing; we saw wounding and killing. I let Aris heal, yes, because some god's light shines through that boy like a flame through glass, but you notice I haven't let him do it without supervision. The gods I trust; his mageborn talent I trust no more than this — " He flicked his fingernails in derision. "Healing is a service; it's not a way of getting power over others. Will you — you of all people — tell me the mageborn don't use their talents to get power?"

"That's not *fair*!" It was already too late; Luap felt the last strand of control fraying. "You trust that Marrakai whelp — born and reared in the privilege you claim to despise. You trust a stripling boy of whom you know nothing but another child's report — and I've worked with you for years, gone everywhere at your command, and you don't trust *me* — "

"And why should I?" Luap had not seen Gird that angry at him for years. "You tell me that — and remember what you did, Selamis-turned-luap. The first time I saw Aris use magery, it was to heal, and he gave his own strength to it. The first time I saw *you* use magery, you tried to kill me, to force me to accept your rule. Right after swearing you sought no crown, you tried that — should I then trust you?"

"Then why did you make me your luap? Why expect me, whom you don't trust, to join our peoples? Why not pick someone you do trust — that Marrakai Kirgan, or Aris?"

"To give you the chance to change, rare as it is." Now Gird looked more tired than angry. "D'you think I don't know men can change? The High Lord knows I have, from the boy I was, from the farmer I became, from my first year as a rebel. Some say no one changes, that cows can't turn horses, or wolves into sheep — but I know change is possible. That's what I hoped for you, that you'd grow out of envy and lying, and into some understanding of responsibility. You've worked hard — yes, and I've praised you for it — but you've never given up wanting what you think you should have had."

"I . . . tried." His throat closed on the rest. He had given Gird everything he could, every talent he knew he owned, except the one Gird would not accept, the magery. And what he had really wanted, Gird had never given him — not easy praise, but the trust he saw given to others for nothing.

"I know you did. In your own way. But — how many more like you, who still want power, would reach for it if I let active magery return? Yes, it's hard on the mageborn to lift mud with a shovel when magic might do it, or rely on candles when they could have magelight — but it was hard on everyone else, when the mageborn chose to use their magicks as they did. We can't have that again; we can't have you, *trying* to control your wishes, and not doing it."

If he had not felt Gird's fist before, he would have thought the words hurt as much. Remorse lay a bitter blade at the heart of his pride; he wanted to throw himself down and plead; he wanted time to unroll its scroll and let him unsay what he had said. But it would take more than a change in the day's writing; he had years of error to undo, and time flowed like the

116

great river, always one way, always down to death. He swallowed the knotted anguish, in all its confusion of meanings and feelings, as he had swallowed so much, and felt an insidious relaxation. He had tried; he had failed; he should have expected that. It wasn't his fault; he had done his best.

He wanted to shrug, but he knew that would anger Gird even more. Instead, he sat very still, avoiding everyone's eyes. From the corner of his own, he could see the Rosemage's expression, composure over disappointment over frustration. She had as many layers as he did, was as different from Gird's singleness of heart as he was, yet Gird, though he did not fully trust her, never subjected her to the criticism he aimed at Luap. He glanced at Gird, ready to be dismissed again, only to meet a steady look of regret that almost broke his determination.

As if no one else were in the room, Gird spoke. "You know, Selamis, you reminded me of my brother from the day I first saw you. My favorite brother; he died in a wolf-hunt, years before the war started, but I never forgot him. I thought 'Here's Aris back again, and this time I'll protect him as he protected me.' There were some who didn't like your ways from the first; I argued that they were unfair. When you told me you had lied, and what had been done to you, I wept — do you remember that?" Luap nodded; he could not speak. "I knew that any man could be driven to lie by enough pain; I never blamed you for it. But you lied afterward."

I told the truth afterward too, Luap thought. *More often than I lied. You might give me credit for that.* Aloud, he said, "I'm sorry. I am not the man you would have me be. But since I am not, give your task to someone more fit to handle it, and let me go."

"I wish I could." Gird looked at him. "But you know why I cannot, if you will only face it. You are who you are, your father's son — and you came to me. That old woman knows, and Arranha: I know they've told you."

"And they've told *me* that my magery is part of it. That I must tap that power to do what you ask — yet you ask me to do it without. How? I have tried, and failed." For the time, his bitterness had vanished, leaving him at peace, a still pool in the calm before a winter dawn. "Since it is my lies that made you distrust my people — " There. He had said *my people* blatantly, just as he saw it in Gird's expression. " — rid yourself of me and you and the others may be able to trust them."

"I don't want to trust them, you purblind fool! I want to trust *you*. I want you to deserve my trust." He had never heard such anguish in Gird's voice; it shook his certainty. "I want you to be the Selamis we all see you could be."

"And not the luap you all see?" The moment it was out of his mouth, he could have bitten his tongue in two. It was like slapping the old man's face; nothing would heal now. But Gird looked more sad than angry.

"No, not the luap. If you could think past your balls, Selamis, and past your own losses, you could see that not all fatherhood involves a woman, and not all kingship requires battle."

"I'm sorry." It seemed he was always saying that; it tasted of long chewing, its meaning leached away, its savor lost. Yet he meant it; he would say it until he died, if he must. He shivered, and made a warding sign; he hoped he would not need to be sorry so long.

"Well." Gird shook his head, refusing further debate on that subject. "You're not going; I need you. And your people are not going out to your mysterious land, wherever it is. We will work through this; if I can lead peasants to war, surely I can lead them into peace. Although I remember Arranha saying that would be harder."

Luap found the look on Arranha's face worse than anything he might have said. He wanted to scream back at it, he wanted to run from it, he wanted to be what all these people wanted him to be . . . that they expected him to be without explaining beforehand. He was supposed to guess, to figure it out from the hints that were enough for others but had never been enough for him. He could always see more than one direction behind each hint, always see more and more complicated patterns radiating from a simple one. Arranha would say more light would help, but more light simply revealed more complexity, more ways to go wrong.

"What is the one thing you truly want?" Arranha asked, after a silence that seemed very long to Luap.

Cascades of images flowed through his mind, each begetting a dozen more. Each made of dark and light, color and its absence, lines and spaces, textures. . . . "To be whole," Luap whispered, into the hollow space of his dream, the secret chamber of his mind, to which no god's voice had come. To have this space filled, this chamber habited, the voiceless voiced, the blind — but he was not blind; he had all Esea's light he could tolerate, and what it revealed was emptiness. "To be whole," he said a little louder, putting voice to something without a voice.

"To *be* something," Arranha said. Nothing colored his voice, neither approval nor disapproval. "Or to *do* something? Or to *have* something?"

Luap sat silent, trying to keep his hands still. Arranha's questions always had traps in them; that parallel series must mean more than it seemed, must be more than the reflection of his own words from Arranha's mind. He had been, he thought, plain enough. He wanted to be whole, more than anything. But to *be*? Not do? What did he want to be whole for? Had he a purpose? Had he some other desire which this phrasing veiled?

He wanted . . . he wanted to hear that voice, the one he had not found in the chamber that lay in no visible mountain, the one no one could find but himself. He wanted to hear that voice say . . . but that was nonsense. Children hoped to hear adults praise them; children hoped for approval. He was grown, a man old enough to have his first grandchildren on his knee, if his children had lived. It came to him in a sudden storm that his son had been killed, not as a whim of the soldiers sent to command his mission to Gird, but because he was a son — a potential heir in time of rebellion. Why had he not seen this before? Because his grief for the boy had eased before the much harder grief of knowing how his wife and daughter suffered when he did not betray Gird?

In the memory of his children, his longing for something only children wanted ebbed, leaving him aware of nothing but exhaustion and the hollow he so desperately wanted filled. "To be whole," he said finally to Arranha. In his own ears, his voice held conviction. "That's all. And — and I don't know what that would be. With magery, without . . . just whole."

Arranha's expression softened. "I wonder sometimes if any of us have understood what your boyhood was like. Did you have any feeling of being in a family?"

"No." Luap swallowed. "Or I supposed I may have, very young, but not later. I never knew where I fit; I never knew exactly what they wanted, except that I wasn't right." He did not try to express the memories that flooded him now: other children had brothers and sisters, parents, a pattern into which they fit. All those patterns excluded him; he had been defined, he realized, by negatives. *You're not my brother*, one boy had said, shoving him away when he would have made friends. He had learned not to ask the adult men if they were his father; he had learned not to ask women if they were his mother. When he had asked those questions, in his innocence, he had been thrust away: you are not my son, you are not my child. He had learned not to ask the most important questions that crowded his head, for that would risk the little he did have, the little he did know. And in the unknown spaces, he could make up his own answers, safe as long as he did not ask, did not seek the truth, which always told him what he was not. His dreams were not lies if he did not ask.

Arranha stared at his own hands as if they were new to him. "I have been an outcast most of my life — causing trouble, as Dorhaniya told you, even as a young man — but at least I always knew what I was an outcast *from*. I knew my father's face, my mother's hands; I scuffled with my brothers, teased my sister . . . and I cannot imagine what it would have been like without them. Would I have gone my own way, if I had not been sure what that was? What I was? Have I taken pride in being true to my own vision without realizing how lucky I was in having such a vision?"

"For some," Luap said, looking down, "the truth is a blessing. For others, the truth can only be pain."

"Surely not!" Arranha's voice shook. "Even if it seems painful, the truth is better than lies; light is better than darkness."

Luap did not argue. He had lost that argument a long time ago, as a small child. Safer to guard his dreams, his private corners of the mind, his small comforts: what truth could improve them? In his mind, Gird could be the loving father he had never had; in truth Gird loved him no more than anyone else, perhaps less. How could the truth be better? What could anyone build from truths that only took away, that never gave?

But he felt Arranha's gaze on him as he would have felt the sun's heat. For all his apparent gentleness, for all his mild good humor, the old man had his passions, truth and light among them. "You cannot be whole without truth," Arranha was saying. "You cannot be whole without the light."

But he was wrong. What would make me whole, Luap thought, is something to fill the dark places, the inside places that have never seen light.

For some days, he and Gird trod gingerly around each other, much like lovers who have quarrelled and want to make up. Luap said little, but remembered to say that little pleasantly, allowing no hint of his misery to color his voice. He drove himself in his work, beginning at the first hint of daylight, writing until his hand cramped and his arm ached, until he could scarcely stand. Gird gave his orders quietly, commended Luap on the neatness of the finished scrolls, asked necessary questions about accounts. And as time passed, Luap felt they were easier with each other. Gird would accept the help of a flawed luap as he would have used a flawed tool if a good one were not available. He himself basked in a gentle melancholy — resigned to his failure, to a future in which he satisfied no one, achieved nothing he wanted, never found trust or acceptance. He could at least be better than Gird's fears, if not as good as his hopes.

In this mood, he found strange pleasure in visiting Dorhaniya and enduring her mild scoldings, in seeing the Rosemage's doubts flickering in her eyes, in noticing how Arranha worried. He might not be what they wanted, but he had their attention. Perhaps it was not possible to be what they wanted — those several contradictory things they wanted. Perhaps the best he could hope for was their continuing interest and attention. It wasn't the trust he craved, but it was better than being ignored.

He had fallen into a reverie one day, staring blindly out his window as he stretched his fingers to ease a cramp, when he felt someone watching him. He turned. Aris stood beside the door, one foot hooked on the other ankle.

"You seem tired, sir," the boy said. He had grown at least a head in the past year, and was as skinny as ever.

"A cramp in my hand," Luap said, smiling. "A problem all scribes share."

"Would you like me to heal it?"

Luap stared. Would he expend his power on so small a thing? "No, Aris," he said. "It doesn't matter; it's just a nuisance."

121

"Father Gird asked me to see if I thought you had the healing magery," Aris said. "I told him I thought you would know best yourself, but he said he had forbidden you to try."

"Yes," Luap said with difficulty. "He did." Something about Aris's posture communicated unease, though he seemed relaxed. "And what do you think?"

"I . . . don't know, sir. Do you want that magery?"

I want all magery, Luap thought, and hoped it did not show in his face. "Yes," he said. "I would like to heal the sick and injured, as you do — it would be a great good. But I know so little of my powers I cannot say if this is one of them."

"Do you want me to attempt to find out?" The obvious answer was *Yes, of course*, but for some reason the obvious answer did not come. Why had Aris asked, instead of simply obeying Gird's request? Was he trying to convey another message?

"Can you?" Luap asked. "What would it take?"

Aris untangled his ankles and came into the office. "I'm not sure, sir. Perhaps if I held your hands — but I don't know if that would work. I've never done this before."

Reassuring. Luap wondered if he'd told Gird that, and how Gird expected to get useful information from so young and inexperienced an examiner. The proof that one could heal was a healing: what did it matter what a boy thought of the possibility? But it did matter; he could feel his heart pounding in his chest at the very thought of it. If Aris, whom Gird trusted, said he had the healing magery, surely Gird would let him learn to use it. He held out his hands for Aris to touch. The boy took them, his own hands warm and dry, their bony length promising size and strength later.

"Did you ever feel your hands itch when you were near someone hurt?" he asked. Luap shook his head. Aris peered at his palms. "You have scars here — what happened?"

"Burns," said Luap. He felt sweat start in his hair, under his arms. He did not want to remember that, not now. "When I first came to Gird's army," he said quickly, as if speed would protect him from the memory, "I had burned hands. They — the men who came to my farm — they burned them." He blinked away the tears and looked up to find Aris's bright eyes watching him steadily.

"I'm sorry," Aris said, almost whispering. "I can't do anything now. But perhaps that's why you don't feel it."

Luap sat back, shaken. What did the boy mean? That he had the healing magery, but didn't feel it because of the burns? That he had once had it, but the burns had destroyed it? Aris still held his hands, and now Luap felt a slow, langorous warmth moving through his own fingers and wrists, up his arms to relieve tension in the elbows he had not even known he felt. Then it receded, and he felt a coolness replacing the warmth. His own magery rumbled inside him like a simmering pot just coming to boil, and he shunted it aside. His head throbbed a moment, then eased.

"It hurts you not to use it," Aris said. "Does Gird know?"

"Do I have the healing magery?" Luap countered. Gird was this boy's hero; he would not complain of Gird.

"I don't know," Aris said, releasing Luap's hands. Luap flexed his fingers: no cramp now, nor any residue of tension. "I feel great power, but it's not like mine. That doesn't mean it's not the healing magery," he said quickly. "I can't tell."

And since he could not tell, Gird would not release him from his oath, and the power would continue to fret in its cage. Luap hoped the boy would not feel his frustration. He did not want to come between Gird and Aris, though he would have liked to convince Gird that his own magery had some good purpose.

Aris left, to report to Gird, and Luap stared blindly out the window. So long as Gird refused to see how many of his people — our people, Luap reminded himself — did not want his vision of peace, he could do nothing. He had to abide by his oath, even when Gird thought him foresworn, and hope that things would change. Either the peasants cease hating the mageborn — which he felt would never happen — or Gird recognize the problem and let him take the mageborn to safety somewhere else. Not *somewhere*, but there — to his own land that he had found.

In the meantime — he picked up his pen and went back to work — in the meantime he must be Gird's most loyal assistant and scribe. The work would ease his mind; it always did. And if nothing changed, if he spent his life this way, it could have been worse spent. He knew that; he accepted it, struggling to crush the doubts and desires that rose from his magery.

• Chapter Ten

Luap and the Rosemage met on the road below Fin Panir; he had been to a barton with a message from Gird to its yeoman-marshal, and saw her coming along the road. He drew rein and waited for her. She looked best, he always thought, on horse-back, her slenderness all grace, her innate arrogance appropriate to the task of mastering her mount. She wore her old armor; she often did, riding out, though it made her more conspicuous than he would have thought comfortable. Perhaps she did not think of it. But on this day, hot and sticky, he wondered how she bore the heat. As she came nearer, he saw the flush of sunburn on her cheek, on her nose.

Before he could say anything, she said, "I was a fool to wear armor on such a day, with no reason." Her gloves were dark with sweat. "Although I suppose I could consider it proper training. That's what I was taught: you don't know the day you will need to fight, so you must be trained for cold and heat both."

Luap smiled. "I must say I'm glad I'm not wearing that."

"So you should be." She reined up beside him. "Gird's right: all these pretensions of our ancestors were more trouble than they were worth. There you are, in soft pants and shirt, with a hat that shades your head instead of cooking it — and I wanted to feel grand, so I'm basted in my own juice."

"Well, you'll be back in the city soon, and into a cool bath—"

"No such luck. I've agreed to teach a class in longsword — that's why I'm back so early — and while I can get out of this cooking kettle, I'll be in a hot banda soon enough."

They rode on to the city gate, and almost at once heard the unmistakeable grumble of an unhappy crowd. Luap might have turned up an alley to avoid it, but the Rosemage pressed ahead, straight toward the noise. Luap shrugged and legged his horse up beside hers. Traffic thickened around them, slowed, became the back of a crowd. Luap stood in his

124

stirrups, peering over the nearest to see the usual small opening in the middle. A man had hold of a boy; and several people were yelling. He could not make out the faces at that distance. Just another brawl, he thought, and would have backed his horse away. He looked at the Rosemage; she turned to him and nodded.

"We need to do something about this."

"Us? Why not a Marshal?"

"Didn't you recognize that boy? He's one of ours." She urged her horse on; around it, people backed away, scowling and muttering. Luap followed, getting the same scowls and mutters, and handsigns that he knew all too well. These were the peasants who never forgot or forgave anything the mageborn had done; his skin prickled all over. Slowly, pace by pace, the horses forced their way into the crowd. One man, enormous of girth and shoulder, refused to give way.

"We don't want *you* here," the big man said. Luap thought he remembered the man as a troublemaker in the last assembly. At least he had the same build and resolute scowl as the one who had stood up in the back and told Gird he was an old fool to trust the surviving mageborn.

"Perhaps not, but I am here, and I'm staying. What is this?"

"None o' yer business, magelover! Think we don't know how ye put it in Gird's ear, and you with that fancy magelady at yer side?" That was someone much shorter, who ducked quickly into the crowd; even from horseback, Luap could not see the man's face.

"That's right, Luap," the big man said. "You always claimed to be no threat, a true luap, even a steer, but day after day we see you with that sorceress and that old mageborn priest. Think we don't know you lust for magery like a boar for a sow? Think we don't know you hoard every scrap of power Gird gives you, may his eyes clear? Seems every time he sits in a court, he's come more to favor *your* people: we know who to blame for that. And every year he ages; he's not half the man he was the day of Greenfields, but you haven't a handful of gray hairs yet. What're ye doin, stealing his life from him bit by bit?"

An ugly sound, not quite a roar, from the crowd, showed their agreement. Luap's horse flattened its ears and tail, and shifted nervously under him. He could not have spoken, for the rage and contempt that filled him — these *dolts*, these *fools*,

125

to think this of him, to blame Gird for partiality to the mageborn, when anyone with sense could see that Gird trod a knife-edge between the resentments of his people.

Anger roared through him, a cleansing wind that swept away the memory of his own half-loyalties, his own errors.

"I would give him my years, if it would help," he said, in such a tone that the crowd stilled. He meant it at that moment. "I am but a child, and he my wise elder. What is this, that you will not let Gird's luap know?"

"A mageborn brat causing trouble, then," said the man, in the tone of one who means *And what will you do about it?*

The crowd opened just a little, showing a scrawny lad, much-bruised, in the grip of a husky man with his other fist cocked. Parik, that was, a member of one of the three granges in the lower city. His scribe's mind read the details off the last grange report: Marshal Donag, veteran of the war in its last year, and known for his dislike of the mageborn. Gird had commented on that when choosing another grange for Aris's training; Donag had later complained that he spoiled the boy. Parik he did not know, though he remembered the man's name on the grange rolls; he could not remember his craft or trade. He could not recognize the boy with all those bruises.

"Let him go." The Rosemage, in her gleaming armor, shone in the sun almost as if she had called her light. The crowd shifted slightly away from her, enlarging the central space. Even the man barring her way moved aside. "Is it Gird's way to batter children?"

"He's no child. He's a mageborn demon; he put fire on me." The man shook the boy, who wobbled and nearly fell.

"Let him go," Luap said, this time releasing enough of his own magery so that the man obeyed, as if his hands were not his own. The boy staggered across the open space to the Rosemage, bleeding from a broken nose and split lip, one eye rapidly swelling shut. She steadied him; Luap could feel her anger's warmth, like a banked fire, and hoped the boy would realize she was not angry at him. He was wondering how to get the boy to safety, how to send word to Gird, when he saw a disturbance in the crowd across the way. He saw sidelong glances, heard the murmurs that ran faster than an old man could walk. *Gird.* He hoped fervently that it was.

The crowd parted for him, reluctantly it seemed, and Luap

watched that heavy-shouldered figure stalk into the sunlit opening. He could think of nothing to say; he watched Gird eyeing Parik and his bruised knuckles, the Rosemage and the bruised boy. It had gone far beyond I-told-you-so, and Luap felt no satisfaction in that. Gird's glance had lost none of its edge; he raked the crowd, and Luap saw many of them flinch from it.

"Well?" His voice cracked; Luap suddenly felt his own throat close in pity. Gird had not been well — really well — since Midwinter Feast, when he'd insisted on showing everyone how to do the Weaving dance in the snow, in and out of all the doors of the palace. It was monstrous that they would not let him rest and heal, that they kept pecking at him with one little problem after another.

Parik, insolent to the bone, tried to pass it off as the boy's fault, a misuse of magery, and then insulted Gird into the bargain, mocking the old man's sayings. Luap saw Gird turn pale, and hoped it was anger — it would have been anger, in the old days, but now it might be illness. Gird's next words did not reassure him; Gird's voice shook. The crowd stiffened; they did not quite growl. Parik pushed his luck, as such men always did, Luap thought, with a viciousness intended to break Gird's authority completely. He felt so angry he could hardly keep from attacking Parik — but Gird would not want that. He must fulfill Gird's trust, at least until Gird died. He was promising himself that he would kill Parik without pity the moment Gird died when Gird surprised him again.

Across that space, in the face of those who despised both of them, Gird met his eyes, nodded, and said, as casually as if they were relaxing after dinner, "You were right, and I was wrong. Are you still of the same mind?"

It could only be the plan he had forbidden so angrily. Luap felt the heat mount to his face; he stammered his answer. Of course he was of the same mind — but to say it *now* —!

"They are not all Parik." Luap winced; Gird, of all men, should not have to plead that way to him. He nodded. He saw that Gird understood that, trusted him now as he had never trusted him before. What Gird might have said next, he never found out, for Parik interrupted, furious that Gird would dare speak to a mageborn. Rude, loud, insolent — and this at last roused the old Gird, the Gird who had settled more than one dispute with his fist. He rounded on Parik with the same intensity, the same deep roar, stalked up to him as if he would as soon clout the lout on the ear as take another breath. Parik backed away, as so many bullies had backed away, making excuses. . . . Luap smiled inwardly. That would do him no good with Gird; excuses never did. Gird went on, inexorably as always, digging at the root of the matter: what really happened? Who did what first?

Luap had not noticed the girl before she spoke; he doubted anyone had. But the boy the Rosemage held shivered as she came forward. *He* knew her. The girl's evidence made it clear that Parik's sons had started the trouble, and then their father had intervened, to help his sons beat the boy bloody, for no more reason than being mageborn and deft-handed. Parik claimed the boy had "put fire" on him then; the girl claimed that if he did, it was to save his life.

Again an interruption, this time Marshal Donag, who tried blustering and sarcasm. To hear him talk, Luap thought, you'd think he'd fought the whole war at Gird's side — or by himself, with Gird coming in at the end. He didn't really hear what they said, concentrating instead on being ready for the trouble he knew was coming. This crowd was as ripe for riot as the summer air for a thunderstorm. Thus it was only the Rosemage's gasp of surprise that brought his attention back to the actual words, and he was as astonished as any in the crowd when Gird suggested exiling the mageborn. " . . . Send them all away," he heard. "Will that satisfy you? Let the boy go, and any like him."

His own plans in Gird's voice; his own dream exposed, taken over.

But the crowd wanted none of it. Like the brooding menace of a dark cloud on a sultry day, the crowd's mood darkened, threatened; he could almost see the murderous anger. Luap struggled to meet it with calmness, to convey that he was not part of this — that he would not meet that anger with his own, that he would honor the oath he had sworn. As if he could reach Gird's mind with his own, he held his thought before him in clarity: *We will not fight. We will not break your peace.* He was sure they would die here, he and the Rosemage and the boy, and probably Gird as well, when the crowd finally stirred, but at least he would have kept his oath.

The change in Gird's expression, the shift from grief through resignation to wild astonishment, brought him back to full attention. All those who could see Gird were locked in the same pose: rigid, staring. All at once, the old man seemed to come alight, not the magelight he knew, but something else, something that made magelight look homely and comfortable.

Then Gird spoke. The words . . . the words had meaning, but no form; sound but no meaning. He could not follow them; he could not do anything else. They battered at him, shattering walls of reticence, caution, prudence, opening up spaces in his heart which he had hardly known existed. As a house unroofed by storm seems suddenly small and full of light, its furnishings dim and shabby in the open air, his mind looked strange to him. Yet as Gird continued to speak those words he could not quite hear, he felt cleansed. He had not wanted to furnish his mind's walls with such shoddy ideas, or its rooms with such ill-made decisions. He could let go, now, of his fears, his spite, his wish that things might have been different . . . he could trust others, as Gird was trusting him. He was scarcely aware of the tears that streaked his face, and only slightly more aware of the Rosemage's voice, murmuring a counterpoint to Gird's.

But this would kill him. Surely this would kill him. Luap blinked away his tears; it was not fair that Gird, who had earned a peaceful old age, should be the one to die of this. He wanted to help, wanted to do something to save Gird, but he could not speak. A voice spoke; he knew what it was, as Gird had always suggested he would if it happened. He had his command. This was not his task. Something else was.

Gird fell silent. Luap could tell that others had been affected as he was; faces had softened from angry hostility to the surprised bewilderment of children who do not understand. He looked up, and saw what might be the cloud such summer days breed, but one that boiled with malice . . . he knew what it was, the dark malice of them all, in a form visible to some . . . and now cleansed, but for how long?

Gird's face changed again, this time through disbelief to calm acceptance. The cloud contracted, condensing around Gird to a black fog that seemed to weigh on him, pressing in on him until he collapsed slowly. Even as he watched, even as he stood paralyzed by awe that such a thing could happen, Luap was aware of part of his mind trying to fit what he saw into words. He would have to write it; he knew that as surely as he knew this would kill Gird. He would have to write it, and how could he possibly convey, in mortal language, what he was seeing? No one could possibly believe it. The cloud thickened as it grew smaller, as Gird struggled to stay upright, and sank to one knee, then to both, then fell on his face. The cloud vanished, and Gird lay motionless. Luap knew he was dead, even as he found he could move again, and came to Gird's side to touch him.

In his own mind, in the faces of others, Luap saw changes he could not yet analyze. Fears vanished; all the nagging barbs of envy and irritation ceased . . . sorrow pierced him, but he knew, even then, that sorrow would heal.

Free, a corner of his mind whispered to him. *You're free, now.* But in the silent space where he knelt, holding Gird's cooling hand in his, he felt not free but rebound to Gird's service. All the rancor, the quarrels of the past days . . . none of that mattered. He had never realized how he loved Gird, how he respected him; he had fooled himself with his ambitions. *I'm sorry*, he said silently. *I will do better.*

In that peace of mind which perfect sorrow brings, he and the others carried Gird's body back up the hill, to lie in the High Lord's Hall a brief space before burial. Silence followed them, spread through the streets, and despite crowds packed breathless-close, no noise intruded. In one brief, almost cordial meeting, the Marshals then in residence in Fin Panir, Arranha, and Luap agreed that Gird should be buried in what had been the palace meadows, and his name carved in a stone of the Hall's nave. No argument, not even a hint of discord, marred that meeting, or the solemn ceremonies that followed. Messengers rode out at once to distant granges; Luap felt only sorrow that Raheli, at the eastern border of the land, could not possibly arrive in time for the funeral.

Despite the crowds that poured into Fin Panir from every town and vill and farmstead within two days' travel, the crowded streets never erupted into argument or brawl. People hugged each other, crying, then walked arm in arm, smiling through their tears. Peasant-born greeted mageborn, and mageborn greeted peasant-born, all at peace and willing to meet as equals. With hardly any formal organization — for the peasant folk had no tradition of elaborate funerals, and no one consulted the remaining mageborn — the city orchestrated a spontaneous ceremony unlike anything its citizens had ever seen. "It seems right," someone would say, and others would agree, as if they had had the same idea but had been slower to speak. They would have a procession from the city wall to the High Hall, and then follow as Gird's body was taken out to the meadow for burial. The family-centered verses of a village funeral would be spoken by volunteers, who had come forward to tell Luap "I want to say the younger sister's part" or "We want to sing the brothers' song."

Two elves brought a length of white cloth bordered in intricate blue embroidery, finer than any Luap had seen, to wind the body in, and herbs to preserve it until the burial. The Gnarrinfulk gnomes sent a squad of gnomish pikes to stand guard over the body. A squat, red-haired, bandy-legged horse nomad appeared the second day with a sack of horsehair he claimed was the forelock and tail of his clan's lead mare and stallion. The horse hair was to be plaited, it seemed, into rings for Gird's great toes and thumbs, the remainder to stuff a pillow for his head. When the nomad found no one skilled at such work, he muttered but sat down in the main court to do it himself. Then, before the funeral, he rode away. Luap hoped he was satisfied; the horsefolk made difficult enemies, and might easily consider that Gird's death dissolved any agreements with his successors.

The funeral procession began at the city gates, by the river. Veterans of the war marched, all in blue shirts or with blue rags around their arms; Marshals and yeoman-marshals marched with their staves; craftsmen and merchants and farmers walked in more ragged, but no less fervent, processions. Some groups sang, others marched in silence. Luap, along with the more senior Marshals, carried the poles on which the body rested. Out the palace gates to the west, into the meadows where someone (Luap had forgotten to think of it) had scythed the long grass and the city's gravediggers had dug the grave. Now the little group came forward, and said the ancient words familiar in every peasant village: the father's lament for a son, the mother's lament for her child, the older and younger brother and sister. No one had spoken for the role of wife, and since Raheli lived, no one could take her place as a child, but the crowd together sang the short farewell.

When Gird's body sank into the grave, and the first clods fell, the crowd wept as one, but they rose from that weeping refreshed again, sad but not despairing. Luap, standing by the heap of dirt, felt someone's arm around his shoulders, and looked up to see Cob at his side.

"I'd hoped not to see it," Cob said, shaking his head. "But then, when it came, I was glad — and that makes no sense at all. They say you were there?"

Luap's scattered wits came back to him. Cob, he realized, must have ridden fast to make it here; he'd been at his grange, a hand of days' normal travel from Fin Panir. "I was there," he said. He felt tears rolling down his face again, as if a wound had opened.

"I was at the market," Cob said, as if Luap had asked. "There was some dispute the judicar couldn't settle, and they'd called me in. One of those days when you think everyone wants to quarrel and is looking for an excuse. I was ready to break a few heads myself, just to let some sense in, although I told myself it was the weather. Then like a weather change it came over us — I could see it in the faces of the others, as well as feel it. I even looked to see if the wind had lifted the pennants, or a storm had neared, for the change was that sudden, and that strong. One moment scowls and whines and angry voices; the next moment smiles and apologies and . . . I've never known anything like it. The two men who'd started the fuss turned to each other and shrugged, and the quarrel unknotted like greased string. I felt suddenly stronger and young again, convinced that Gird's latest revision wasn't silly after all, but would work."

Luap had not had leisure to wonder what had happened beyond the immediate environs of the city; he was both fascinated and surprised. Had no one else seen the dark cloud, or recognized it? "How did you find out what really — ?"

"Gnomes," said Cob. "Don't ask me how they knew, because I couldn't tell you. The rest of that day went by with everyone in a holiday mood, and no reason for it. I would have worried, but couldn't. Then that night, someone knocked on the grange door, and when I went to see, there was a gnome. 'Your Marshal-General is dead,' he said. 'He has taken away the darkness from your human sight; he has freed your hearts from unreasoning fears and anger.' I'd only met gnomes once before, at that Blackbone Hill mess you were lucky enough to miss; *they* didn't talk like that. Afore I could ask any questions, he was

132

gone, and I heard the beat of their boots, running all in step in the darkness." Cob paused for breath, and cleared his throat. " 'Course, the darkness wouldn't bother them, living understone as they do. But then I roused my yeoman-marshal, and called out the grange, and before dawn I was on my way. Rode day and night, I did, as if I'd lost thirty years, changing horses wherever I could. Met your messengers at Hareth—"

"Come on back," said Luap. "There's plenty of beds here—"

"He threw me, you know," Cob said. "I was with him from the first, from the forest camp Ivis had, back in the Stone Circle days. I remember him coming in with his lad and his nephew, all hollow with hunger, and Ivis bade me wrestle 'im, and he threw me. Flat on my back, I was, before I knew what happened." He shook his head. "Not many of us left, that started with him there, and I don't suppose anyone from his vill at all, barring Raheli."

"I wish she had been able to get here in time," said Luap, meaning it.

Cob shrugged. "You sent word; that's all you could do. Rahi's got sense; she'll understand."

"And now what?" Cob scratched thinning hair. Every Marshal in Fin Panir and all those visiting had gathered in the old palace. "Th' old man's dead, gods grace his rest, and we've to decide what to do. Did he ever say, Luap, aught about what came next?"

"No . . . not really." Luap looked around the table. "He wouldn't be king, remember — I know he didn't want to see a return of kingship. He wanted just what he always said: one fair law for everyone, and peace among all peoples."

"So we've got a Code he revised every half-year, meaning he wasn't convinced it was one fair law yet, and quarrels enough to break his heart—" That was a Marshal from the east, someone Luap barely remembered from the war.

"Not now," Cob said. "No one's quarreling now — it's as if Gird himself cast a charm at us." Even that word, so potent for strife, brought no frown to any face. "It's in my heart that's about what he did, him and the High Lord. Gave us some peace to sort ourselves out and have no more stupid quarrels, no more need to knock heads. But we'd best decide how to do that before everyone wakes up."

"We could have a council of Marshals," said Sekkin.

"We *are* a council of Marshals." Cob scratched his head again. "Thing is, will that be enough? Gird himself knew we couldn't go back to steading and hearthing organization, and the bartons aren't large enough either, no more the granges. We've got to have summat up top, if not a king someone who'll do what Gird did, at least in a way. . . . " His voice trailed off. No one could do what Gird did, and they all knew it. Even Gird, for all his talk of every yeoman's abilities, had known it.

Eyes came back to Luap. Now, if ever, he could take what Gird had never offered, become Gird's successor. He knew the Code better than any of them, having written more copies than he cared to remember of each revision, and he had traveled more than most of them, carrying Gird's letters to each corner of the land. It would be logical — would have been logical, if he had been other than he was. Might still be logical, except that he had promised Gird, albeit in silence, in that last moment.

"I think," he said slowly, picking his way through possibilities as if along a steep mountain path, "I think Gird thought of Marshals selecting another Marshal-General. Perhaps a council of Marshals, perhaps all of them — I don't know exactly what he thought. Whoever was chosen ought to have been a Marshal, I would think . . . "

"In other words, you don't want the job." Cob had Gird's directness, if not all his other qualities. Luap spread his hands.

"I was never a Marshal. As well, you know my heritage, and my vow to seek no command."

"Aye, but you're the one man might stand to both folk as the right person to lead now. It's not like you're taking anything from Gird; he's dead." Others nodded, around the long table. "You know the Code and the land; you were his choice for many things. And it's not like you'd be a king — you'd have plenty of Marshals making sure you didn't revert to that nonsense."

It made sense, but he felt repelled. What he once might have thought his due, for all the work he'd done, what he had wanted when he thought no one would give it to him, he now did not want. The thought of having to perform Gird's daily duties shepherded by Marshals who would no doubt look for any deviation from Gird's custom made his skin itch. If he took command — any sort of command — it must be *command*. And besides, he'd promised Gird he wouldn't.

"It would break my vow," he said. Cob nodded.

"All right. Whatever anyone's said, you've always been true to Gird; I've seen that. It's not your fault who your father was, nor any of the rest of it. But that leaves us still with no decision."

He might have changed his mind if they'd pressured him more, but he felt that even with Cob the offer had been as much courtesy as anything else.

"I do think," Cob said, "that we ought to start calling you Marshal — you may not have sought command, but you've been doing Gird's work all this time. If you're not to be Marshal-General, you'll still be needed in any councils, as you were with Gird."

The word popped into his mind from some forgotten conversation. "Why not Archivist?" he asked. "Someone who keeps the records — that's what I really am. You all earned the title of Marshal, leading yeomen — I haven't done that."

"Makes sense," said Donag, down the table. "Like a scribe, only more so, eh? Judicar and scribe together, maybe. You'll write Gird's life, won't you?"

He had not actually thought of that, in spite of having written accounts of the war, battle by battle. He had been hampered by Gird's insistence that he include only the barest facts; the time he'd tried to explore the meaning of a battle to the morale of both sides, following a model in the old royal archives, Gird had insisted he rewrite it. "You don't know what they thought, or even what most of our people thought: you only know who was there, and who won." But it came to him in a rush how much good he could do, writing about Gird, making Gird come alive for later generations, so that those who had never met him would understand how great a man Gird had been.

"Yes," he said to Donag, to all of them, to his own memory of Gird. "Yes. I will write Gird's life."

Aris, dressing carefully to take his part in Gird's funeral procession, felt guilty that he felt no more pain than he did. He had loved the old man as the grandfather he had never known; he had admired him as the hero who had singlehandedly routed the wicked king. How could he be taking this so calmly? Only last Midwinter Feast, when his healer's eye had recognized

135

that Gird's health was failing, he had spent several miserable days trying to hide his grief until Seri talked it out of him. He was not ready to lose Gird's wisdom, he told himself. He was not ready to lose that straight look, the one that made him feel as if Gird were seeing into his head, finding all the messier corners of his mind. Yet — he had cried only briefly. His appetite was good. He had carried out his duties as yeoman-marshal of his grange, to his Marshal's evident surprise and possible distrust. Could he really have loved and respected Gird, if he was acting so normally? Even Seri, usually level-headed and calm, had flung herself on Aris, sobbing wildly, in the first hours after.

You know better, said an almost familiar voice in his head. Better than what? he wondered, and answered himself: better than to think tears define sorrow. Of course he'd loved Gird, and Gird had loved him. But now they had to honor Gird's memory, and go on with the work.

He rubbed at a possible smudge on his belt-buckle and went out to face his Marshal's inspection. He had advanced from junior yeoman to senior yeoman with the others his age, as had Seri. To his surprise, he had been offered a trial period as yeoman-marshal in this, his second grange assignment. His first Marshal, Kevis, had recommended that he change granges for the next stage of training, and Gird had concurred. Seri's promotion had surprised no one, except perhaps the pompous Marshal she had once played tricks on. And now he would walk at Marshal Geddrin's side, at the head of the third grange formed in Fin Panir.

Geddrin, a massive man whose freckled face usually looked surprised, was frowning at his own image in a polished shield. By its shape, it had been captured from a magelord in the war. "Cut myself," he said out of the side of his mouth. Shaving was a new fashion in the past few years, taken from the merchants and much commoner in cities than in rural granges.

Aris wondered whether to offer to heal it. Geddrin had accepted Gird's word that Aris must be allowed to heal, but it clearly made him nervous to watch. And he might take the offer as an accusation of softness. He moved closer until he could see the cut, then whistled softly. "It'll drip, Marshal, sure's you start singing, where it is. Let me close it for you, and it won't stain the cloak. . . ."

"*Heal* it, you mean," said Geddrin, but without heat. "Say

what you mean, Aris. But yes, go on — Gird's seen my blood before; I've no need to look like I was showing off for him."

"Yes, Marshal," said Aris. So small a wound, clean and new, took only his touch and enough breath to make his knees sag. It vanished, leaving Geddrin's face just as rough-scraped and freckled as before.

"If all the mageborn were like you . . . " Geddrin said, wiping the blade with which he'd shaved on a cloth, and slipping it into its sheath. He didn't finish that, though Aris knew the thought in his mind. If all the mageborn were like him, there would have been no war.

One step to Geddrin's rear, Aris led the grange's cohort of yeomen around to the city gates where the parade would start. There the most senior Marshals decided the order of march. Aris listened to the mix of accents, the muttered comments on various Marshals, the rumors already abroad over who would be the next Marshal-General.

" — An' I said to him, your Marshal may be a veteran but he's all hard stone from his eyebrows back. Old Father Gird was tough, but he wasn't stupid."

"What I always say is, the ones you've got to watch is them quiet ones. The nicer they are, the more they're looking for a way into your beltpouch, eh? Isn't that so?"

" — So there we was, Geris and me, not an arm's-length away from old Gird on that horse. An' he was bashing heads, lads, like you wouldn't believe, till one o' them poles got him under the armpit and I was sure he was killed — "

"*And* you and Geris got him back up on his horse. Alyanya's tits, Peli, we've heard that story every drill night since the war. . . . "

"I dunno why they don't get his horse, the way we always heard in the songs. . . . "

"*I* heard nobody's seen that horse these two days."

"Eh? T' old man's horse?"

A silence spread; Aris could pick out the speaker now. A tall, stout woman with graying hair, whose old blue shirt hardly stretched across her front. She nodded, decisively. "I heard it from my daughter, who heard it from a lad who cleans the stables. That very evening, he said, going to tell the old horse, he found the stall empty. And the latch fastened, he said, and that's what she told me."

An excited murmur ran through the crowd, though no one

broke ranks; Aris shivered as if a cold wind had touched his neck. He had not had leave, in the days since Gird's death, to go up to the high city; he had assumed the old gray horse still dreamed in its stall. He looked beyond the dust-clouds rising from the crowd assembled to march, as if he half-expected to see a gray horse in a nearby field. But he saw no animals at all, and in a moment Marshal Geddrin called the grange to order.

Through the old massive gateway they marched, one grange after another, singing the old songs from the war, that Aris had learned as a child. Far ahead, the first marchers were soon out of time with those behind, but no one noticed or cared; those who had come to watch shouldered their way in among the marchers, so the entire route soon resembled a vast segmented monster in tortuous motion upward.

Aris gave himself up to the movement and emotion of the crowd, willing himself to melt into it, be part of it. Not until the silence around the grave did he think to look and see if Gird's gray horse was visible anywhere. He saw no horse in the crowd, or near the grave, or — when he narrowed his eyes to see beyond, to the far edge of the meadows — anywhere on the grassy expanse. Then a flick of cold air, sharp as a tail's lash across his cheek, drew his eyes upward. A fair wind, fresh and fragrant, blew tumbled clouds across the sky, and by some trick of eye and mind, one of them seemed to run, its mottled gray suddenly gleaming white in a streak of sunlight. Then he could not find it among the others, and when he dropped his eyes they were full of tears.

Geddrin's arm came around his shoulders. "S'all right, lad," he said. "It takes some longer to find their tears, that's all. I knew you cared — go on now, give him that gift." The tears ran down his face, and he felt the knot of grief inside loosen enough to let more fall. What he really wanted was time alone with Seri, time for both of them to cry together, and comfort each other. But Geddrin, unlike Kevis, did not know him well enough to know why he needed that. When he followed his Marshal and grange back through the city, he felt bruised and lonely.

138

● Chapter Eleven

Even in the changing climate that followed Gird's death, Luap could not forget the cave and that strange place to which it had taken him. It had not been his imagination, a sort of dream or enchantment: it had taken Gird, too, the last man who could be fooled into believing what wasn't there. And Gird had seemed to say, in that crowded few minutes before his death, that Luap was right . . . that he should take his mageborn relatives and go.

Had that been a gift of knowledge from the gods, a private message to Luap before the general message he had given them all? Or had it been Gird's despair, the last of his human — and thus fallible — utterances? Should he act on it? Was the place even there, now?

As the new council of Marshals dithered about appointing a successor, Luap's mind wandered often, always in the same direction. As it was now, the mageborn didn't have to leave. Things were better, not worse. Gird's dream of compromise and cooperation might well come to pass. But did that mean that none of them could leave, or should leave? The Marshals were, if not as hostile, still clearly frightened by the idea of the mageborn using their powers. Using the powers safely required training . . . and that distant, empty land would be a safe place to acquire that training. No one there to be frightened by a sudden light, a clap of thunder, a gust of wind. No one there to argue that a child who could lift buckets of water from well to water trough could also lift coins from one purse to another. And if the mageborn learned to use their powers safely, with guidance in the ethics involved, then perhaps they could demonstrate to the others how such powers should be used, and that would erase the old fears, and even improve on Gird's vision.

"Luap!" Sterin touched his shoulder. They were all staring at him.

"Sorry," he said, feeling his ears redden. "I was trying to remember something and just . . . "

"It's all right," said Cob, "but even if we bore you, you shouldn't go to sleep: you've got to keep the notes." He was grinning to take away the sting, but Luap felt it anyway.

"I wasn't bored." Of course he was bored; they'd been hashing over the same argument for a hand of days, with the same three or four people saying the same things, only louder. He was hot, his back in the sun from the windows in the council's meeting room, and he could smell the stables all too clearly. "There's something in the gnome laws Gird told me about one time, that I thought might help, but I just can't remember." Apparently that convinced them, or most of them; everyone shrugged and went back to the same things they'd said before. Luap took careful notes, even though he already knew what Foss and Sirk would say.

His own arguments continued in the same trails as well, but more smoothly, more logically, as time passed. It did make sense. The mageborn needed to learn to use their powers safely and properly; the safe and proper use of their powers would reassure those without them, as people recognized the safe use of any tool. They could not learn to use their powers here without frightening people, and threatening the fragile peace that Gird had bought so dearly. Therefore, they needed to find a place — far enough away that accidents or mistakes, common in learning, could hurt no one — to get that practice. Then the community Gird envisioned could be made of mageborn and former peasants, all using all their talents to the fullest, for the benefit of all. As for a place . . . well . . . it was logical to use a place which no one without the mage powers could stumble on by accident, and get hurt. The only such place he could think of was wherever the cave took him. Only a mageborn, he was sure, could do whatever he had done to make the pattern work.

It all made sense; it all fitted like the interlocking gears of a mill. If you start here, and the parts all fit, you come out over here, inexorably. Arranha had said that about logic: arguments are not made, he said, but found, by following all the rules of logic from any starting place. If the rules are not broken, the conclusion cannot be wrong, and has existed from the beginning of the world. He had not made it true that the only way to get to Gird's dream from present reality was by taking the mageborn to the distant land of red stone towers, but he had found out, by logic, that this was true.

Of course he still might be wrong, and he would have to test it. Arranha taught that all human vision lacked completeness. Conclusions must be tested. At the least, he would have to return to the cave and see if he still arrived at the great hall, and if the stair still came to the same outside. He would have to take someone else, as witness and test both.

He found it easy to arrange some days away, on a pretext of gathering material for his *Life of Gird*. Not entirely pretext, for he intended to do just that; he foresaw that his work would be the foundation text, the way that Gird would be remembered generations after those who knew him had died. He intended to make Gird's greatness come alive, breathe from the scroll, and to do that he wanted as much detail as possible. Still, he intended to visit the cave, and he was not going to tell the others about it until he knew if it still worked.

He arrived, on a mild sunny afternoon, in a very different mood than before. Sunlight glittered on tiny crystals in the gray rock; lush green grass and scarred bark showed where years of travelers had tethered their mounts. The creek purled over its stony bed, hardly disturbing the summer growth of mint and frogweed. Luap dipped a pot of water, and sniffed the mint's crisp aroma. He was aware that weather influenced his moods, but this was more than sun-induced relaxation; it was also the inner calm that had followed Gird's death. He was not afraid, this time, of consequences; he was not stirred by useless ambitions or wracked by guilty memories. Signs of recent campfires in the cave did not disturb him; he knew that others sometimes used it for shelter while traveling.

When he had watered and fed his horse, he sat in the sun outside the cave, thinking about the stories of Gird he had heard so far, and how best to arrange them. In the old archives, the stories of great kings and mages began with a childhood full of portents. He wondered if all those tales were true. One young prince had been born, so the tale went, with heatless flames around him; another had brought frost-killed flowers to life in a snowstorm.

Gird's life, as others remembered it, was depressingly free of portents. He had found no one from Gird's original village, for one thing. Perhaps, he thought, squinting into the late slanting light, Raheli would know some childhood stories about her father. The few things Gird had told Luap weren't much use. He'd been chosen for the count's guard because of his size, and left it because of some misunderstanding. He'd never actually said what it was, but Luap assumed it was because he'd gotten drunk. That wouldn't be impressive in a legendary figure. A mother dead of fever; a brother killed by a wolf. Half a life spent farming, apparently with enjoyment — he certainly retained a fondness for cows and even scythed the meadows a few times at haying time.

Luap shifted on the rock he'd chosen as a seat. None of that made a good story. Who, in a hundred years or so, would believe that a simple peasant lad with no more training than that could lead an army to victory? It had happened, yes: It was true, yes: But it was not *reasonable*. He had to make it believable to people who had never seen Gird, who had no idea what force of character lay in that lumpish peasant head. At least, he thought, the man was bigger than average, stronger than most. That would help. He might have been handsome when he was younger; that would help, too.

As the sun sank, he rose and stretched, watered his horse again, and made his own tidy campsite well inside the cave. He needed no fire, but he needed an explanation for the tethered horse outside, so he rolled his blanket and set his pack at one end before calling his own light and going back to the inner chamber.

On this, his fourth visit, the bell-shaped chamber with its walls covered in intricate patterned relief seemed almost homey. He did not hesitate to step out onto the central design of the floor; he felt no real apprehension before calling on his power. As smoothly as ever, as swiftly and silently, he was elsewhere, in the grand high hall he remembered. It, too, looked familiar, and the third arch, which had appeared when Gird visited, still opened off the far end. He thought about going out, up the stairs, to the outer world, but decided against it. This much worked as it had; surely the same world would be outside. And now he wanted a witness to share the wonder. He returned as quickly as he had come.

The next morning, he went on as he'd planned. He interviewed a veteran farming newly cleared land, who remembered Gird telling about the first winter in the forest, and two more in the next vill, who wanted to complain about the current edition of the Code rather than talk about Gird himself. Most of them had only secondhand knowledge; he had known Gird as long as they had, but he wanted to be thorough. The details that would make Gird's life come alive later might come from anyone. By the time he returned to Fin Panir, he had two scrolls full of such tales. He had also decided that he must tell Arranha and the Rosemage, even though he foresaw awkward questions. With that decision made, he wasted no time, and the next day sent word to both asking them to meet him in his office.

The Rosemage, who had been teaching the more advanced yeoman to use a longsword, arrived with a bandage around her left hand. "Clumsiness," she said, before anyone could ask. "Mine, as well as the yeoman's. And no, it's not dangerous, and yes, I would let Aris heal it if necessary."

Arranha, Luap noticed, gave her the same smile he gave Luap. "Lady, no one doubts your ability."

She chuckled, pulling one of Luap's chairs to her, and sat down. "The class I was teaching no longer thinks I'm beyond injury, using magery to protect myself while thumping them. I think the fellow actually expected that his blade would turn aside rather than hit me. Luckily, he's still using wood. Unluckily for me, it still hurts." She had placed herself so that the injured hand could rest on a table, Luap noticed. He wondered if she were certain no bones had broken.

"We need to train more healers," Arranha said. "Surely there are others among us who have, or can learn, that magery. Luap, would the Council of Marshals approve the use of healing magery in someone other than Aris?"

"I'm not sure," said Luap, well-pleased that Arranha had given him an opening without needing any hints. "Aris had trained himself, in a time before the uses of magery were against the Code; whatever mistakes he made then, when he appeared here he functioned as a successful healer. That certainly influenced Gird's decision, and the reaction of the other Marshals. The Marshals know, in their minds, that a child with Aris's talent must learn to use it, just as a child must learn any adult skill, with many mistakes in the process — but in practice, they so distrust all magery that, without Gird, I suspect they would forbid it."

143

"Mmm. So the child would have to be trained to be approved, and would have to be approved to be allowed to train — is that what you're saying?"

"Yes. I may be wrong, but this is the impression I get." Then, before the others could speak, Luap went on. "In fact, I asked to see you because of just this problem and a possible solution."

The Rosemage looked up sharply. "A solution!"

"Yes. You weren't with us when I first discovered that I had some magery; Arranha may remember the incident — "

The old priest hid his expression behind folded hands, peering at Luap with bright eyes over his fingertips. "Are you certain you want me to tell all that tale?"

Luap smiled. "Enough know it already, or think they do. But I'll be brief: we were camped in a cave, lady, and deep within I found a small chamber and had a . . . what I suppose you could call a revelation. A voice spoke, naming the king my father. And my magery woke, so that I had light in my hands. Unfortunately, the shock of that so unhinged my wits that I tried to argue Gird into a command — and sought to use my magery on him to convince him. You tried that yourself; you know its effect."

"Gird knocked him flat," Arranha said when Luap paused for breath. "Told everyone — perhaps especially me — that he'd kill him the next time he used his magery. Luckily, by the time you forced that, lady, Gird had changed his mind."

"Not my most impressive moment," said Luap wryly. "But some years later, after the war, and after Dorhaniya told me my real parentage, I went back there. I was hoping for another revelation, something to settle my mind."

"The study of logic . . ." muttered Arranha. Luap shook his head.

"Such studies settle *your* mind, Arranha, but don't help me. At any rate, I returned, while on a journey for Gird, and found something quite different. I found a place — a far place — to which magery can travel."

"A place." It was almost the same tone as Gird had used. "What sort of place? Where?"

The same questions, and he had hardly more answers. "It's a great hall and many chambers, all carved from living rock, and outside is a strange land of red stone, great towers and

144

mountains and narrow steep valleys. Where it is from *here* I cannot say, but it's apparently in a colder land than this."

"And you can get there by magery . . ." Arranha mused. "So —"

"I took Gird once," Luap said. "That is the place I meant, the time we quarreled so about moving the mageborn. As far as we could tell, it was a great land empty of all people; I thought it would suit us well. He said no — but you remember the day of his death —"

"And you think that's what he meant, when he said you had been right, and he had been wrong? You think that was permission to take the mageborn there?" The Rosemage sounded doubtful, and in her voice he could doubt Gird's meaning himself.

"I think you should come see it. No one knew, but Gird and I; he's dead, and someone else should know. What I'm thinking now is that it's a place no one without magery could stumble upon, a place where the mageborn could learn to use their powers safely, without risking harm to others, and without a chance to use them wrongly: there are no peasants to rule. With such training and discipline, our people might be more acceptable to those without magery — at least, there would be no beginners' errors to be explained away."

"Ah, that makes sense." Arranha nodded, his eyes bright. "As weapons-practice is done in the bartons and granges, not in the marketplace or inside a home — this is a place for our young ones to learn properly." Luap kept quiet, waiting for the Rosemage's response.

"I'm surprised you didn't tell us before this," she said. Luap shrugged.

"Gird preferred that no one else know," he said. "He thought it was a secret best kept close, lest disaffected mageborn try to use the cave. Now, I think you two should know, but no one else, until you've seen the place and considered how it might be used."

"Tell us about it," said Arranha. "What sort of great hall? How large? How many could stay there at once?"

"I'd rather you saw it for yourself," said Luap. He could not possibly describe it all, and besides that, he wanted their reaction; he wanted to see someone like himself arriving.

"How far from here is the cave?" asked the Rosemage.

"A few days' travel by horse; it's between Soldin and Graymere. At this season, the ford at Gravelly should be passable, which cuts a day off."

"It will do my hand no harm to rest from teaching swordwork," the Rosemage said. "Why not leave tomorrow?"

Luap opened his mouth to protest, and then shrugged. If they were that eager, why not? He had planned to suggest a more elaborate, less obvious journey, with each arriving separately, by a different route, to meet by "coincidence" if anyone found out. "Very well," he said. "I'll tell Marshal Sterin or Cob that I won't be at the Council."

Traveling with Arranha and the Rosemage was nothing like traveling alone. Arranha wondered, aloud, about half the things he saw: what was that rock, and why did it break into squarish lumps when another rock the same color didn't? Why would any bird build a nest that hung swinging from a limb? If the weaving patterns of peasant women had the names of plants and animals, why didn't they look like that plant or animal? He noticed everything that Luap normally rode by without seeing it: tiny wildflowers, the speckles on river frogs, the relative numbers of red and spotted cattle in fields they passed. He greeted everyone they met on the road, and if Luap had not reminded him that they had a goal, would have stopped to talk of anything that caught his mind.

He's like a bur, Luap thought. Everything clings to him; he could stop and be stuck anyplace until some stronger attraction yanked him free. By the end of the first day, Luap was exhausted by the relentless intelligence with which Arranha attended to his surroundings.

The Rosemage, on the other hand, seemed to view the country as a military map: this position defensible, that one not. She said little, in contrast to Arranha, but the little she did say had to do with the possibility of brigands up a narrow valley, or the way someone with any knowledge at all could control the trade roads. Luap had not, since the war's end, felt nervous about trouble on the road, but he found himself eyeing places where travelers were vulnerable. Then Arranha would exclaim over some novelty, and he had to make some comment in response.

The cave, when they reached it on the fourth day, felt

146

welcoming. Luap thought longingly of the silence in that distant hall, and was tempted to vanish there, leaving his companions behind. Instead, he took the horses to the creek, while Arranha and the Rosemage set up their camp inside. It was hot, even standing above cool water; he felt itchy and obscurely distressed. Here, with the water chuckling softly around the horses' fetlocks, with their gentle sucking, he began to relax. No one pointed out the swirl in midstream where something had come to the surface from below — he noticed it, which he would not have four days before, but in silence.

Arranha's horse lifted its head, water dripping from its muzzle, and yawned. It shivered its withers, and Luap saw its knees begin to buckle.

"No, you don't," he said firmly; the other two lifted their heads to watch as he yanked Arranha's horse back to dry land. It blew, spraying him in the face. Muttering, he got them all back from the bank and safely into the trees. The Rosemage was coming from the cave when he came in sight of it. She waved and came down to help feed them.

"I've never seen a cave like this," she said, almost eagerly. Sunburn had given her a rich color. "Where I was in Tsaia, the caves were dank little holes under graystone bluffs — big enough for one shepherd and a few sheep in a blizzard, no more. This thing's big enough for an army."

"That's what we had," said Luap.

" — And that chamber," she went on. "Arranha says those designs aren't anything from Old Aare. If Gird didn't recognize them as his peoples', what could they be?"

"You've been in the *chamber*?" Anger raged through him; he had expected them to *wait*. It was his secret, after all.

"We didn't try to use it," the Rosemage said. Luap managed not to say anything sarcastic, and she went on. "Although it's thick with magery in there — I suspect anyone sensitive at all could trigger it." She put two handfuls of grain in the nosebag of her bay horse and tied it over the halter. "How long do you think we'll stay?"

"Not above a glass or so, I think. Time enough to see what Gird saw." Luap finished with the other two horses and led the way back to the cave. Deep inside, where dimness should have faded to blackness, a faint glow showed that Arranha had no qualms about using his magery here. Luap called his own light — if the old priest could be that bold, he wasn't going to chance falling over any stones.

As he came past the ledge where Gird had stumbled, Arranha said, "It's very interesting, this pattern."

"It's more than *interesting*," Luap said.

"Oh yes — I know — but my point is, I doubt if it's a pattern wrought by humans. It's not Old Aarean, nor any pattern of the northern branches, and you say Gird did not recognize it . . ."

"By the gods?" Luap felt a cold chill down his back and arms.

"Perhaps. But the Elder Races, particularly the sinyi, use patterns of power. Have you asked any elves about this, Luap?"

"No. Remember, Gird wanted it kept secret."

"Hmmm." Arranha's bright eyes glittered before he blinked and turned away. "Strange — he had scant love for secrets, in most things. 'Bury a truth, and it rots,' he told me more than once."

"Well — I never asked him if I could ask the elves; it never occurred to me. His reasons concerning the mageborn seemed so strong, to him — "

Arranha said, "I daresay it doesn't matter. You've used this pattern three times now; if it were a matter for elves, you would surely have heard from them."

Another shiver, as if icy water had funneled beneath his shirt; Luap twitched, but said, "Then let us go, and you judge what you see."

This time his mind clung to the pattern and the remembered place; almost before he could think, they had arrived. He did not know which face to watch. The Rosemage, to his quick glance, seemed almost turned to stone. Her face paled, then flushed; her eyes widened. Arranha, too, seemed stunned to silence.

Luap repeated the same prayer he had uttered the first time he came, and heard Arranha and then the Rosemage repeat it. Then he led the way off the dais.

"We can talk now," he said quietly, looking back. They had said nothing but the prayer. They were looking up, around, faces as full of awe as Luap had wished. The Rosemage brought her gaze back to him.

"It's — impossible," she said, shaking her head.

"That's what I thought the first time. That I had dreamed it, perhaps. But Gird saw it too."

"If the gods did not make this, they blessed it," said Arranha softly. "I have never felt such presence, not even in the Hall in Fin Panir when Esea blessed Lady Dorhaniya's belief."

Is that what happened? thought Luap. He felt uncomfortable thinking of Dorhaniya in this place.

Arranha had moved down the hall, slowly; now he approached the arches at the far end. The Rosemage stayed near the dais. "Do you know what this is?" called Arranha, his voice louder than any Luap had heard in this place. He was pointing at the arch with the harp and tree entwined.

"Gird said it might be an elven symbol," Luap said.

"As you should well know," Arranha replied. "And the other — that is surely dwarfish. And you did not think to ask them?"

Luap felt his face burning. For a moment he was not sure what to say, but the great place eased him, as it had before. "Gird saw what I saw; it was his decision. Perhaps he was upset enough with me that I had used magery to bring him."

Arranha did not reply, but walked, as Gird had, through the arch with the High Lord's circle above it. Luap followed, and behind him he could hear the Rosemage coming.

"Up those stairs," Luap said, "is a land unlike any I've seen. Bare red stone, deep canyons with trees and rivers — " He had not actually seen the rivers, but where there were trees, rivers must be also. "Not good land for farming, Gird said, but I think it would support a small number."

"Mmm." Arranha looked at the stairs. "Shall we go up, then?"

"Certainly." Luap led the way, wondering again why the light that filled the hall and passages below did not extend to this. Because it was an entrance? As before, the sound of their boots on the steps echoed off the floor below, and as before they came to a darkness close above their heads. But this time Luap called his light before it was too dim to see, and pointed out to Arranha the whorls and interlacements Gird had noted. He himself, this time, put his thumb in the groove and traced the interlocked spirals in and out, and Arranha prayed.

When the ceiling close above them vanished, Luap half-expected the snowy blast of his first visit. But even here — wherever here was — spring had come, and warm sunlight spilled down the stair. Only a light breeze stirred his hair as he climbed the last few steps and came out to the view he remembered so clearly.

It was still there. He had been afraid, in some corner of his mind, that it was less majestic than he remembered, but in the clear cool sunlight that land lost none of its grandeur. The vast blocks of red stone, the endless vista of stone and sky. He could see farther than before, but still had no idea where the place lay, or how deep the canyons were.

Arranha and the Rosemage reacted as he had hoped. "It's . . . like nothing I've seen anywhere," Arranha said. "Certainly it's not anywhere near Fintha, nor down the Honnorgat valley as far as I've traveled, nor like anything I heard of Aarenis or Old Aare."

"It's so — big," the Rosemage said. Luap glanced at her. Few things ever seemed to daunt her, but this did. "Even the sky seems bigger. And how do you get down from this, or up into those trees?"

Where Gird and Luap, in the cold and snow, had seen what might be the bristling thatch of a forest above another level of stone, now the forest showed clearly. It seemed to stand on the topmost level of the stone, far above their heads or across great crevices on other blocks, as if Luap's imagined city of castles were roofed with trees and not slate.

"We didn't stay long enough to find out," Luap told the Rosemage. "It was snowing when we got into the open, and though the snow ceased, it had been blown away by a bitter wind. We were glad to get out of it."

"And you never came again, to explore?" Arranha asked. He had put back the hood of his cloak, and turned his face up to the brilliant sunlight. With his eyes closed, and his arms held out, he looked to Luap a little like a bird drying itself after rain.

"I had no time," Luap said, "and no reason. I suggested to Gird that he allow me to bring the mageborn here, when all that trouble started. But you know what he thought of that."

"Mmm. Yes." Arranha opened his eyes, as bright and penetrating as hawks' eyes. They seemed to have absorbed the brilliant light and now it poured from them. Luap blinked. It must be something to do with being the Sunlord's priest. Arranha stared in all directions, as if looking for something in particular. "I don't feel anything dire," he said finally. "I see no sign that anyone inhabits this land. Do you?"

Luap shook his head. "It felt empty to me from the first.

That's why I thought it would bother no one if we came here."

"Lady?" asked Arranha of the Rosemage. "What can you sense about this land?"

"Its size," she said, her voice still muted by the land's effect on her. "It is so large, so empty . . . it does not care about us at all, did you realize? Everywhere in Fintha or Tsaia, there's a sense — I think the elves call it taig — that the land is almost aware, that it cares what we do. I've heard the farmers say a field is generous, faithful, or that another field is bitter and hard-hearted. When I had sheep, I felt that way myself at times, held in the land's palm. Nothing so grand as Alyanya's notice, but perhaps some of her power running over into the land itself. But here — " she shook her head. "If this is even in Alyanya's realm, it would be hard to think so. This land has no interest in us, in our welfare; it is neither generous nor mean. It has its own affairs, and what they are I cannot imagine."

"Does it frighten you?" asked Luap.

"No. Not as a threat would. But that indifference feels strange; I did not know how I had depended on our land's sensitivity until I felt nothing like it here."

"I felt it as cleanliness," Arranha said. "As if this were new-made land, its stone washed clean by light and water on the first day, untouched by history. And yet it feels old, at the same time. I wonder if it is just untouched by *our* history — we have no little stories about this rock or that, about who chased a stray cow into which canyon — and so we feel it has no history. Surely it must." His face sobered. "And surely we should know that history, however strange it is, before we lay our own upon it. As there are metals that must not touch, for they cause corrosion in each other, so there may be histories that must not be laid one upon another." He looked from one to the other; Luap wanted to argue that expression, but could not. Then Arranha sighed and shook his head. "No — I feel no menace here; the Rosemage is right. But it is in the nature of Esea's priests to seek knowledge and more knowledge, the god's light upon ignorance. We expect trouble to come from ignorance more than malice — our weakness, as Gird showed, but nonetheless trouble can come from ignorance. Here is a land — a great land, as the Rosemage has said — about which we know nothing, not even how to find our way to water. So I have qualms, which will probably be foolish in the end."

"I hope so," said Luap soberly. "I feel nothing but promise here, a promise of peace and — with enough hard work — security. If you have definite warnings —"

"No," said Arranha. "Nothing definite, and not really a warning. Just the awareness that what you don't know can kill you."

"We'll learn," said Luap, feeling confidence rebound in him. "And the first thing, I suppose, is to map the inside of this place, and find another outlet. Surely there is one." He gestured. "Shall we go back inside?"

Down the stair, under the arch, into the great hall. With their footsteps behind him, he could feel it a procession, almost a homecoming. He led them past the dais, into the corridors behind. To his surprise, he remembered clearly which turnings he had made, both on his own and with Gird. Both Arranha and the Rosemage were more uneasy than he felt; his courage rose as he perceived himself the boldest of the party. He chose a downward-trending ramp at one turning, and found himself in an unfamiliar passage.

"Listen!" The Rosemage held up one hand. They all held their breath. A distinct musical plink repeated at irregular intervals. "Water," she said finally. They followed the sound along the passage to an opening in one wall; it gaped a few handspans wide and high, dark within, unlike the regular doorways they had seen so far. Luap put his hand through, made his magelight, then looked. A chamber as large as the common dining hall in Fin Panir held clear water . . . he could not tell how deep, but he could see the stone below it clearly. Its surface lay within reach of his hand. Above, the chamber rose higher than the passage ceiling, marked here and there with the dark stain of dripping water. From a line around the chamber, Luap saw that the water rarely if ever rose as high as the opening in the wall. He stretched his hand down and touched the surface: ice-cold. He sniffed it: pure, with no hint of salt or sulphur.

"We need not fear thirst," Luap said. He stepped back; Arranha and the Rosemage both leaned in to look, kindling their own light. "Now if we can find a lower entrance —" He was sure a lower entrance existed. It must be there. Farther down, they found a great room that could only be a kitchen, with hearths and ovens cut into the stone. Here was a draft of cool air, sweet and fresh, from the chimney shaft. Another passage, that seemed darker, less full of that sourceless light. Luap headed for it. The spiralling stair had been darker . . . did all the outside ways begin where the light failed?

The passage ended in a blank wall; Luap was not surprised. Nor was he surprised when his own light revealed the same incised patterns on the passage wall to one side. He traced them carefully as before, and as before the wall melted away, letting in a fresh breeze, pine-smelling. The opening let in abundant light; Luap thought two horsemen could ride through it abreast. They looked out onto a narrow terrace supporting great pine trees, and heard the cheerful gurgling of water among rocks below. One tree, larger in girth than Luap could span, stood square athwart the opening . . . clearly it had grown there since someone last used the passage. Luap edged past it, and came out into the sunlight. Some small animal let out a squeak and fled upslope, a flurry of gray fur, hardly seen. High above a hawk squealed; Luap could not see through the pines where it flew.

"With running water so near, why store water inside?" asked the Rosemage, coming out into the sun. "There's enough in there for three rivulets this size." She had moved to the lip of the terrace, and was looking down into the minute creek, which made far more noise than its size suggested. Then, before Luap could answer, she had moved lightly downslope and skipped across, a matter of hopping on two rocks and grabbing the drooping branch of a bush on the far side. She climbed out of Luap's sight; he followed her, out from under the pines, and then realized how narrow the place was. The Rosemage stood atop a cottage-size boulder at the foot of a rock wall that matched the one they'd come out of. He looked up . . . and up. Those soaring red walls, so near and high that he could not see the flat shoulder of the mountain, or its higher forested crown, delighted him even from below. Nothing had ever looked so impregnable, so defensible. Once inside, no imaginable army could possibly harm him or his people.

● Chapter Twelve

Once they came out of the passage, Luap began to wonder if he would ever get his companions back inside. Arranha clambered up and down the narrow cleft in which they had come out, observing the angle of the sun and attempting (as near as Luap could understand it) to determine from that where they were. The Rosemage followed the water up to its source, a crack beneath a wall of stone, and then down to its joining with the larger stream Luap had been able to see from above, a stream that ran almost sunrising and sunsetting. She came panting back with her hands full of red berries, having seen, she said, two deer, fish in the stream, frogs and strange shapes of rock she wanted Luap to look at.

Luap followed her down the streambed. It felt like returning to childhood, when one could explore a new corner of the garden, or a stretch of meadow or woods. Surely he should be more careful, he thought, nearly turning his ankle on a loose stone, but he could not imagine how, in this unknown land, he should know what hazards to watch for. The walls on either side ended as suddenly as the walls of a building; he found himself looking across a wider space, with a noisy stream racing down to his right, to the facing wall. Low bushes, some laden with berries, tufts of a coarse tall grass, and — on this side of the narrow valley — no trees. The trees — more pines and others he did not know — filled the space between the stream and the foot of the opposite cliff.

The Rosemage touched his shoulder. "The deer . . . there." He followed her pointing finger and saw four of them, tails twitching nervously, ears wide. Then three of them returned to browsing. They seemed larger and grayer than the deer of Fintha, but he was not sure . . . everything seemed larger here. He gazed down the valley. On either side, high walls of red rock shut out any distant view. The valley seemed to widen somewhat at its lower end. He saw more trees there, many that

154

were not pines. Up the valley, it narrowed, the walls closing in; it seemed to be cut off by another wall of rock. He tried to remember what he could see from above, but he could not make sense of it.

What he did understand was the sheer size of it. From above, the larger valley had seemed a narrow slot, hardly wide enough to walk in, but he thought an archer would just be able to shoot across it. Hard to tell, with the steep slopes of broken rock below the cliffs, but if it were level . . . it would be large enough to farm. He tried to convert its irregular slope and shape to something approximating the teams and selions by which traditional fields were measured. At least they would have plenty of stone for building, if the day came they wanted to live outside the — he wondered what to call it, that vast hall understone. Castle? No . . . more a fortress, a stronghold. Stronghold: he liked that.

He imagined stone-walled cottages nestled against the walls, fields terraced and leveled, green with young grain, fruit trees trained against the foot of the cliffs. In his mind, laughing children played in the noisy stream, scampered along the narrow paths between plots of grain and garden vegetables, climbed the great rocks. He saw the harvest festival, with everyone gathered in the great hall, and a feast prepared in that huge kitchen; he could smell the food even now. He imagined caravans coming and going from Fin Panir, bringing news of the Girdish lands, bringing those who wanted to study Gird's life, taking back the freshly copied scrolls, the memory of great beauty.

"Luap!" That was Arranha, who had now made his own way down into the larger valley. "I think I know something of where we are."

"Oh?" At the moment Luap didn't care.

"But we'll have to go back, and then come back here, and do it again at night. On a clear night in both places."

"What?" The Rosemage looked as confused as Luap felt.

"I think we may be very far west of Fin Panir," Arranha said. He looked about, then headed for a sandy area near the stream. "Come here; I'll show you." Luap followed him; Arranha squatted and began drawing in the sand with a stick. "Here — this is the world." It looked like a circle to Luap, but he knew better than to argue. "If the sun rises

155

here — sunrising — in Prealith on the eastern coast, it's overhead there before it's overhead *here*, in Fin Panir." He pointed to a spot near the center of the circle. "Now — if it's overhead in Fin Panir, where is it on the sunsetting edge of the world — here?" He pointed to the circle's rim.

Luap said, "Well . . . if it comes first to Prealith, and then to Fin Panir, then the other side of the circle will be . . . later. But are you sure about that?"

Arranha nodded. "You can see the sun move across the sky. It must be going from one place to another. Just as you walking past the High Lord's Hall, let's say, are first opposite one corner and then the next. Morning must be earlier as you travel sunrising, and later as you travel sunsetting. That's clear, isn't it?"

It wasn't clear at all to Luap. "And you got this from what you were doing up there?" He jerked his chin at the narrow cleft from which they'd come. Arranha nodded again.

"I was noticing how quickly the sun moved across that narrow space. When we came out, the sunlight came in the opening and lay full on the rocks above. Even as you and the Rosemage were coming down here, it moved far enough to put that in shadow. It occurred to me that if you had both large and small sandglasses, you could measure how long it took for the sun to cross that space, and thus how fast it moved . . . and from that discover how far apart any two places were. Far apart in the sunwise direction, that is." From his expression, he expected that to make sense to Luap. Luap glanced at the Rosemage; she was scowling in an effort to understand. Arranha sighed and tried again. "If you are walking, you know how far apart places are by how long it takes you to get there, isn't that right?"

"Yes, but — " But some roads were harder than others. Uphill took longer, hilly roads took longer. " — does the sun move more slowly in the morning?"

"No." Arranha frowned. "At least — I don't think so. I don't know if anyone's ever measured it with a sandglass. Perhaps the sun, as Esea's sigil, moves uphill as fast as down. That would be something to do, measure its progress before and after noon. I was assuming its speed stayed the same. If it does stay the same, then it travels across a certain space of the earth in each measure of time."

Clearly Arranha was going to keep explaining until Luap said he understood. He saw no chance of understanding, but he could, perhaps, save himself further confusion. "I see," he said.

Arranha smiled at him. "I knew you could follow that." The Rosemage stirred, as if she had a question, and Arranha turned to her. Luap shot her a glance over Arranha's head, and she made some quiet comment about the tameness of the wildlife.

"I think," Luap said, "that they see few people, if any." He was thinking to himself that there must, however, be something which fed upon the deer. Wolves? Bears? Would these attack humans in daylight, or should they return to the stronghold? He wanted to explore, but not foolishly.

"I'm going across," the Rosemage said. "I've never seen trees like those." Luap started to tell her to be careful, but didn't. She was older than he; she didn't need a keeper. She went slightly upstream, to a narrow place where she could jump from boulder to boulder and make her way across the stream and up a bluff of earth to the trees. Definitely pines, Luap thought, but so much larger than any pines in Fintha . . . and yet they looked small against the cliffs.

"I've seen similar trees in the Westmounts," Arranha said. "But there they grew in solid forests along the mountain slopes." As they watched, a bright blue bird flew from one of the trees, screeching, and into another. A smaller bright red and yellow bird flitted from bush to bush on the near side of the stream. A loud thud caught Luap's attention; he looked and saw that one of the browsing deer was stamping a forehoof. On the third stamp, the group bounded away upstream, leaping over the rocks as if they were floating. He looked around for the source of the danger, and saw nothing — but the Rosemage, working her way upstream through the trees. Arranha said, "There's plenty of wood in those trees . . . enough for fuel and building both, if we're careful. Some of them would have to come down anyway, to make fields. And that one in the entrance . . ."

"And there's more forest on top, if we can find a way to that upper level." He had no idea if the internal passages went that far. "We should be careful; these trees may take a long time to grow. But perhaps some are nut trees or have wild fruit, as these bushes do." He had lost sight of the Rosemage, and felt an urge to follow her upstream on his own side of the stream.

"I'll stay here," Arranha said, still peering at his designs in the sand. "I would like to find this out for myself."

Luap moved along the near bank of the creek, noticing how clear the water ran. He dipped his hand in. Cold, too, and sweet to the taste. The red rocks of the creekbed seemed to sparkle; when he looked closely he saw tiny flecks of gold. His heart pounded. It couldn't be *real* gold . . . but perhaps it was an omen. Certainly that might explain the almost magical shimmer of the cliffs in the sunlight, those myriad flecks of glittering gold. A frog popped up from the water to perch on a rock . . . the frog's skin, too, seemed dusted with gold. And the fish, hardly a hand long, that held its place in the current with its tail just waving, had speckles on its side of rose and gold.

It had not seemed hot, when they first came into this valley, but now Luap could feel the sun's heat reflecting from the cliff to his left. He noticed when it eased, and looked left to see another narrow cleft leading away in the direction of the one outside the stronghold. Should he explore it? No — it would take too long. He kept on his way, watching from time to time to see if he could see the Rosemage among the trees. He caught one glimpse of her, but she was still ahead of him, upstream. The sun baked him; he thought he knew now why the trees stayed on the other side. He was glad when the stream twisted, and he moved into the shade of its opposite bank for a few minutes. Here he found delicate flowering plants hanging half in the water, their starry blossoms stirred by the current. Ferns, too, clung here, and a low herb holding juicy berries just above the earth. A great rock hung out over the water on the other side, with a pine angling up from it.

"There's a very big fish in that pool," the Rosemage said. Luap looked up, and saw her lying stomach-down on the rock, peering at the water. "It's deeper than it looks." Luap squinted and found an angle where the reflections didn't obscure his gaze. What had seemed a pool perhaps knee-deep showed itself much deeper.

"How big a fish?" he asked, thinking of dinner. She held her hands apart to show him. Big enough for all of them, if he could catch it.

But he could not stop for that, and they could not stay past sunset — that much he was sure of. He scrambled past a fall of rocks and found that he was now on the same level as the Rosemage, some distance away. He could just see Arranha's white hair glowing in the sunlight downstream. The sun had moved too fast, he thought; he dared not go much farther. Echoing his thought came the Rosemage's call. "We should go back. . . ." From the tone she was no more eager than he. With a last look around, he spotted yet another cleft leading to the north, winterwards. From above, he remembered, he had seen narrow ridges of rock standing on end, finlike. Did each have its cleft, and could each cleft conceal another stronghold, or part of the same one? He tried to estimate how thick the fins were . . . thicker than the city walls of Fin Panir, thicker than half the city, he suspected. His skin prickled, imagining those walls hollowed out for dwellings, imagining the rock full of his people, his mageborn survivors, all secure in their stone castles. But the sun's angle warned him. He jumped down from that boulder and made his way as quickly as he could back down the stream.

Even so the sun had disappeared behind the cliffs sunsetting when he reached Arranha. The sky, still bright, gave light enough in the larger valley, but up in the small one, under the great pines, it seemed already dusk. Far overhead, he could just see the top of sunlit cliffs, still blazing red, but he stumbled over rocks in the gloom. At first, he could not remember exactly where the entrance lay; the tree in front of it obscured it more than he had expected. But they found it at last, and after a last drink from the rivulet outside, came in to the silence and shadeless light of the stronghold.

None of them said anything on the way back to the great hall. Luap, counting turns and hoping that he remembered them all, had neither breath nor attention to spare for his companions. He had not realized how far down the sloping passages had taken them; going back uphill he could feel the pull on his legs. At last they came to the level ways he remembered clearly, and then to the hall itself. There they paused.

Arranha sank down on the dais, breathless.

"Are you all right?" the Rosemage asked. Luap felt guilty; he had not remembered that the old man might have even more trouble with the climb than he had.

Arranha nodded, but waited a moment to speak. "I'm . . . fine. Just tired. I haven't climbed so much in years. . . . "

159

"I'm sorry," Luap said. "I was trying to remember the turns—"

Arranha chuckled. "And I'd rather you remembered the turns, lad, than worried about me and forgot them. But we must mark the route, next time, eh?" In a few minutes he was able to stand. "I would like to see more — I would like to explore every passage and room — but I think we should return to your cave, Luap. My bones crave a night's sleep, with a blanket around me."

"We could come back and bring food," the Rosemage said. "And blankets. Spend a day or two here—"

"We can't leave the horses there, untended," Luap said. Then he and the Rosemage looked at each other, bright-eyed. "Bring them!" they both said. Luap went on. "We could explore more easily — see more — perhaps reach both ends of the valley in one day." He wondered if a horse would fit into that inner chamber. Its head, yes, but all of it? What would happen if all the horse didn't stand on the pattern? Surely it would all come, or all fail to come . . . not sever the beast. He shuddered. "Arranha's right," he said. "For now, we go back and have a night's rest."

Although he had not thought it took so long to go from the lower entrance to the great hall, when they emerged from the cave in Fintha, the last glow of sunlight was just fading from the sky. "I thought so," said Arranha, with some satisfaction. Luap presumed that meant his idea about distance and time, whatever it was, made sense to him.

"I'll feed the horses," he said, forestalling further explanation. Once more he led the tethered horses to drink, then fed them. Even after sunset, it was much hotter and stickier here than there; he missed the clean bite of that distant air. When he climbed back to the cave entrance, the Rosemage had a fire going, and had started cooking. He gathered more fallen branches for fuel, broke a few switches of flybane and stripped the leaves from them, and went back to rub the horses with the sticky sap. Arranha peeled redroots and sliced them for the pot, quietly for once. He offered no theories about the origins of redroots, the different ways they might be peeled or sliced. . . . Luap decided the old man was really tired.

He himself was tired, he realized, after sitting to eat the stew the Rosemage had prepared. He was stiff from the climbing, and mentally tired from the excitement. He wanted to talk about everything he'd seen, check his memories against theirs, and at the same time he wanted to fall asleep right where he sat. He took the pot to the river to clean it, and came back to find Arranha already asleep and the Rosemage yawning as she piled turf on the fire. So he lay down and dreamed all night of the red castles of his future home.

The next day dawned fair and hot. Luap woke early, and went down to water the horses. He wanted to escape to that cool, crisp air of the stronghold. He imagined what dawn might look like, rising above sheer red rock walls, the first sunlight spilling over the cliffs like golden wine. Here, the air lay heavy, a moist blanket on his shoulders; he was sweating already.

"It'll storm by nightfall," the Rosemage said. Her shirt clung to her, already sweat-darkened. She dipped a bucket in the river upstream of the drinking horses, and put her hand in. "It's hardly cool at all. Your country must be fierce in winter, but it's certainly cooler in summer."

"I know. I was wishing we could go back there today." He backed Arranha's mount out of the water, and fetched hers. "But we're short of fodder for the horses; we need to move on to the meadows and let them graze."

"They could graze there if we could get them there," she said. "If they'd fit into that chamber . . . but then they'd come out in the great hall. That's no place for horses." By the wrinkle of her nose, he knew she was thinking of the mess they could make, the damage they could do. True — that hall was no stable, and they would not have the means to clean it. And if a shod hoof damaged the pattern on the dais, could they get back? Best not to risk it. But he wanted to go back, wanted to taste that cold water again, breathe that air.

Arranha woke as they came back up. He, too, commented on the moist heat of the morning, and the difference from the crisp air in "Luap's country" as he called it. But he did not want to go back — not then. "At dawn, precisely, or sunset — yes. With a sandglass to measure the time."

So after a cold breakfast, they saddled the horses and rode back toward Fin Panir. Just after midday, when they were too far from a village to find shelter, a violent summer storm broke over them, drenching them with rain so they rode the rest of the day with the odor of wet wool. Luap tried to fill his mind with the scent of those pines.

Raheli ran her hand along the shaft of the pike the yeoman had brought to replace one he'd broken in drill. Good seasoned wood, shaped well and rubbed smooth. She nodded her approval, and he grinned at her. He had the agility and grace of an ox, she thought, but made up for it with strength and goodwill. Now may I do as well, she thought, to amend my own faults. She had had so short a time with Gird to renew their family relationship, to feel how she might be truly an elder even without bearing . . . she still found herself mired in bitterness some days. She and Gird had not been meant to do new things, but to do old things well, she was sure. They had done new things because they must, not like those for whom this was their parrion.

Yet she did new things constantly. She had been listening to the women, since her visit to Gird, and even more since his death, noticing much she'd ignored before. She had, after all, lived in the one vill all her life until the day she still thought of as the day the war started. She had never been as far as a big market town, let alone a city; she had known nothing of how city folk lived, or peasant folk across the Honnorgat. Or even peasant folk before the magelords came. She listened to old grannies tell of their grannies' times; she listened to women who had the life she had lost, and women who wanted the life she had as a Marshal. Even mageborn women . . . they had not all been wealthy, arrogant mageladies who delighted in beating peasants. In fact, most of them were more human than she had imagined from meeting the Autumn Rose. She had met Dorhaniya now, and listened to stories that sounded much like those she'd grown up hearing at her own hearth.

So the burden that women wanted to place on her — the way they wanted to see her as the women's Marshal-General — bothered her less and less. She would not be *the* Marshal-General, but she could make sure that the code that bore his name remained fair to women. And that, she was convinced, began with women drilling in the bartons alongside men. Even to Gird, that had been what mattered: if the women risked the same in war, then they deserved the same from the law. Men could not argue against that, as they could if women did not willingly risk the same in times of danger. That women — as she knew from her own past — were always at risk did not help; being a victim won no respect.

Convincing the women of all that, in peacetime, was another matter. Once she thought of it, she quit accepting so easily the excuses that came to her, and applied the hard logic of the war she'd survived. If there were war, she said firmly to the woman (or more often man) who came to explain why Maia or Pir or Mali wasn't coming, she would learn to fight, or be killed. Have you all forgotten? Do you want to see the slaughter of untrained peasants again?

Gradually, she had increased the number of women in her own grange and bartons who actually appeared reasonably often of drill-nights. Ailing fathers and tired husbands found they could survive a cold supper; when they complained to Raheli, she suggested tartly that they come to drill with their wives and daughters. Some couples began to do so, and that heartened others. The young girls she caught early, insisting to their mothers that such drill would not make them unfit to bear. "I am barren because my husband and I did not know how to fight," she had said more than once. "Not because I fought in the war."

But it wasn't the reluctant ones who bothered her most. She had been reluctant herself; she knew what was in their hearts. And while she didn't share the feeling, she could understand those like Seri, who enjoyed drill for its own sake, and dreamed of using their weapons to protect others. No, the ones who bothered her were the few — usually town girls, she liked to think — who were eager to learn the drill, eager to learn weaponlore, and even more than that eager to shed someone else's blood. Those made her shiver. How could a girl, whose life should be risked in giving life, be eager to end it? She did her best to make explanations. This one had a brutal father; that one had been estranged from her natural family from birth.

If she had thought about it beforehand — and she hadn't — she might have thought that girls who had no interest in boys would be like that, but the difference between those who loved women and those who loved men ran across the difference between those who liked to hurt and those who did not. She herself had been angry, after Parin's death, after the loss of her child; she had been so angry she dreamed night after night of striking at others the blows that had struck her. She had expected to exult in mageborn blood, when her chance came . . . but in fact the first time she had hit an enemy she had almost

163

dropped her weapon and apologized. The memory of that first battle in the forest, the feel of striking another human being, still came back to her on bad nights. She did not tell the young ones that — she had, after all, become good at soldiering, or she would not have survived — but she did not understand those who wanted to hurt others.

"Marshal?" A girl's voice brought her out of her musing. Raheli looked at her, noticing how the face had lengthened in the past year, how she had grown so much taller. This was not one of her problems, but a delight: a girl she would have been glad to have as a little sister.

"Yes, Piri?"

"The lads say you'll be looking among the junior yeoman for a yeoman-marshal —"

"Yes, from the eldest group. Whoever it is will be sent to another grange to work with that Marshal for a few years. Why?"

"Sent away — ?"

"Yes. It would be hard on a lad to have his friends beneath him, wouldn't it?"

"Yes, Marshal." Piri had the dark hair and gray eyes common to this cluster of villages; now she flushed and looked down. "I just wondered, Marshal, if you ever thought of a girl."

"A girl? You?" Raheli was startled. Piri came to drill faithfully, but seemed perfectly suited to follow her two sisters into marriage. Had she quarreled with the boy she seemed most likely to marry?

"No — but there's Erial." As if anticipating her Marshal's reaction, Piri rushed on. "She's better at drill than most of the boys, she never gets tired, and she doesn't flirt."

"With boys," said Raheli drily. "She flirted with you last year, until you made it clear you preferred young Sim."

"Well . . . yes . . . but that won't cause any trouble because most junior yeomen are boys."

"And she asked you to ask me?" Raheli said.

"No . . . she didn't. I just thought . . . " Piri looked down. Raheli sighed. The two had been best friends as small children, then that simple relationship had been complicated for them by whatever god governed the loves of adults. Piri had a soft heart; she would not want to hurt her friend, but she felt uncomfortable with her.

"Piri, you're right that Erial is good in drill; she might make a good yeoman-marshal. But one thing any yeoman-marshal needs is a desire to take on that job. Yes, it would be easier on you if she moved away, or was busy with something like this . . . but none of us can live Erial's life for her. She understands that you love Sim; you must understand that she may not want to go away."

"If she asked would you consider her?"

"Piri, is she bothering you?"

"Not really — I mean she's not *doing* anything, but I know what she's thinking about."

Raheli snorted. "I doubt it, child. Most of us think we can read thoughts like scrolls, and yet we have no idea what's behind someone's eyes." She looked at Piri's red face thoughtfully. "Is it Sim? Is he upset about Erial?"

Piri turned even redder. "He did say — that when I wasn't looking he saw her watching me."

"Watching you. And Sim thinks no one has a right to look at you but him, is that it? Boys! At that age, Piri, they're like young bulls, jealous of everything. If he knew a sheep looked at you he'd probably drive it away. No, lass: from what I've seen, Erial understands very well that you prefer Sim; she may not like it, but she's no worse than you are and unless you have something more than 'Sim says she looks at me' you have no real complaint. What did your mother say?"

"That Sim's a young cockerel crowing over his first pullet." Raheli grinned; Piri's mother had come closer than she had. Sim was much more gamecock than bull. "She said Erial'd been my friend all my life and it was silly to fuss now. But I thought maybe — "

"You thought maybe there was an easy way out that would please Erial and Sim both, didn't you?" Piri nodded. "Piri, the easy ways we see out of things are usually full of traps: think how we tempt an animal into a pen. We make the gate look like the easy way out of trouble. Learn to look on both sides of the gate before you walk through it. Now. About Erial. If *she* wants to be a yeoman-marshal, and she asks me, I'll consider it. Not for you, but for her and the yeomen she will serve later. But she has to ask, and I don't want you hinting to her in the meantime. Does Sim know you came about this?"

"No, Marshal. It was my idea."

"Good. Then you don't tell Sim, because the way he is, he would go straight to Erial and tell her."

Piri nodded, somewhat shamefaced, and turned to leave. Raheli called her back.

"It wasn't a bad idea, lass, and I'm not angry. You're one that doesn't like angry words or bickering: that's good. But sometimes there are things worth angry words; you must have the courage to endure the anger when it's needed. I know you have that courage, but you may not have recognized it yet."

Raheli was not surprised when Erial showed up later that day. Piri and Erial had been friends too long for communication to fail, no matter that certain words could not be said. Erial's approach, like Piri's, began obliquely.

"Marshal, do you think married women can become Marshals?"

"Become, or stay? A few wives commanded cohorts in the war, but those whose families lived preferred to return to them afterwards. I think it would be hard to do a Marshal's work and a wife's work as well. Even more, a mother's work. It would be like trying to be the wife of two families. Marshals are, in a way, the grange's wife and mother."

Erial grinned at her. "*You* are, Marshal, the way you visit everyone and help those in trouble."

"Good commanders were the same way: a cohort's not that different from a family. It needs food, healing, comforting, and someone to resolve disputes." Raheli wondered why Erial had started from that direction, but never missed a chance to teach. "Why did you ask — are you planning to combine the two?"

"No. You know better." Erial scowled and looked away.

"Some like you do, to have children. Half the time I see you, you've got all your cousins trailing behind; for all I knew you wanted some of your own."

"It's because my aunt's been sick; you know that. And they like to play marching games, but none of them remember the commands." Nonetheless, Erial had a sheepish look; Raheli suspected she enjoyed watching her cousins more than she would admit. She had lived with her aunt since her own mother died. "No — " Erial went on, sobering, " — it's about a friend, that I think would make a good Marshal, only she'd have to be a yeoman-marshal first, and she thinks she can't do that and be married."

"Piri," Raheli said, seeing no purpose in dragging this out.

"Yes, Pir. She used to talk about it a lot, learning to do what you do, protecting the vill — all until she got silly over Sim."

Raheli had no trouble with this one. "She's not 'silly over Sim' — she wants to marry him, and he wants to marry her. And I can't agree with you: Piri would not make a good Marshal except in wartime, if then — she had a youngster's taste for adventure, that's all, and now she's grown out of it." Erial opened her mouth, shut it, and scowled fiercely as a young wildcat.

"But I know someone else who would make a fine Marshal," Raheli went on. She hadn't meant to, but in thinking over the prospects earlier she'd realized just how outstanding Erial was. "If someone else wanted it, that is. Even though it would mean moving to another grange for part of her training, and who-knows-where after that." Erial turned red, then pale, and her eyes shone.

"Me?" she squeaked. It was a safe guess; there were only seven girls in the older group of junior yeomen, and Erial had to know she and Piri were by far the best.

"You." Raheli ticked off the reasons on her fingers. "You know the drill; you learn fast; you can teach — your cousins prove that. You have no betrothed to go into a decline when you leave. You don't stir up trouble with lads or lasses —"

"Sim's mad at me," Erial muttered.

"Sim's a young lad crazy about Piri, and jealous as . . . as a cockerel. That's not your fault. I'm not blind and deaf; I know how you've acted, and you haven't put pressure on Piri. Sim has. And you're the one who had that notion of being Marshal in the first place; Piri was following you, the way she always did until she veered off to follow Sim."

"You're saying I haven't grown out of it?" Erial asked in a shaky voice.

Raheli chuckled. "*And* you've got the resilience, the toughness, to survive some hard years with another Marshal, among strangers. And even more important to me, while you like the work and the weaponlore, you don't like to hurt people. Alyanya forbid, but if you ever had to fight in battle, you might like it more than I did — but you wouldn't turn cruel. I can trust you for that. So — do you want to be a yeoman-marshal?"

"Yes!" Erial said. Then her face fell. "No . . . no, I can't. There's my cousins; if my aunt dies —"

"We'll let Piri lead your cousins around for awhile: you'd trust her, wouldn't you? And if your aunt dies, the grange will help; you know you can trust me. Take your chance, Erial, when it comes. Unless you don't want it."

"I do." She glowed with delight; Raheli grinned at her.

"Now mind, you'll have some problems with the lads when they hear about it, and I don't want any nonsense. You're not a yeoman-marshal yet; I'll send you to — " And who would she send Erial to, who could be trusted? " — someone I trust," she said finally. She would have to look up the rolls; they really needed a better way of training youngsters who might become Marshals. Cob would be best, but did he have an opening? "Go on," she said. "I'll be along after awhile to talk to your aunt and uncle about you."

She sat at her desk, for once well content with her role as Marshal and a woman other women could come to. It wouldn't always work out so neatly, any more than every loaf came from the oven with a perfect crust and crumb, but when it happened she could take pleasure in it. The next time she went to Fin Panir, she thought, she would bring up this matter of Marshals' training with the Council.

168

● Chapter Thirteen

Luap and the others had been back in Fin Panir only a few days when Raheli arrived. She wanted, she said, to see what progress Luap was making on the *Life of Gird*. He showed her the racked scrolls of notes, explained about the interviews.

"Did you get the ones I sent?" she asked.

"Oh, yes. You are the only source I have for his early life, you know. Can you tell me anything more about his childhood? Anything that would fit well?"

"Fit well?"

"You know — something that would show the reader that he was going to be what he became. That story about his brother dying of an attack by wolves — where was Gird then? What did he do?"

Rahi stared at him. "Arin went out with the hunters; he was the elder. Gird stayed — you know my grandparents were still alive then, don't you?"

"I'm not sure." Luap pulled out the scroll she had sent and looked. "No — all you said here was that Arin died, and Gird succeeded to the tenancy."

Rahi frowned. "It's more complicated than that. It was before I was born; Arin and his wife Issa and their children, and Gird and my mother Mali, lived with their parents. Gird's and Arin's. The eldest son in each cottage could be called out for a hunt; I don't know if Arin had to go, or if he chose to, but he went with other men out to a distant sheepfold. When wolves came, he ran out after them; they tore him but were beaten off by others. Gird said when they brought him home, the steward came, and granted a sheep's carcass to the family. Even remitted the death-duty. But within a year, his father died, and the cottage and all the family came to him. Issa and her children, his mother, his own children — for I was born later that year."

"But Gird didn't go out to hunt the wolf that killed his brother?"

169

"No — the other men had killed most of them. And he had to do the work Arin had done, as well as his own."

"It would have made a better story," Luap said. Rahi gave him a strange look.

"It's not a singer's tale," she said. "It's what really happened."

"Another thing I don't understand," Luap said, avoiding that implied criticism, "is when he actually began working against the magelords. From what you've written, and from what I heard others say, his own liege was harsher than most, deliberately cruel."

"Indeed he was!" Rahi's face stiffened; her scar stood out white as bone.

"Then Gird must have resented it all along; he was no man to put up with cruelty lightly. Why didn't he join the Stone Circle earlier?"

"Do you think he never asked himself that?" She sounded angry; Luap could not understand why. "Do you think no one else ever asked? Why did he have to wait until the count's meanness killed his mother and his wife, until starvation and disease picked off children and friends, until his best friend died beneath the very hooves of the lords' guard, until I — " She drew a long, shuddering breath, and flushed and paled again. "Until they killed my husband and nearly killed me, and I lost his first grandchild. Why did he wait and wait? I don't know." She shook her head slowly; her accent thickened. "I would not call it cowardice, nor stupidity. He knew it was wrong; he knew it was worse; he thought — as much as I can know what he thought — that the Stone Circle way would be no better. It was throwing lives away, not saving them. He did give grain, and pull his own belt tighter, that I know, once his friend was killed. But he had sworn to follow Alyanya's peace, and seek no mastery of steel."

"But *why*?" asked Luap. He had never heard Rahi speak even this much of her father; he was fascinated.

She sat for some time in silence, her face grave. She, like Gird, had gained weight with peace and prosperity; she had grown almost massive, like a matron with many children. "You know he was once in the count's guard," she said finally.

"I had heard that, back during the war; someone said it was where he learned the craft of war. But others said he had been a farmer all his life. Which was it?"

"I don't know this of myself," Rahi said. "I don't know if I should tell you; he never told me about it and I heard it only in bits and pieces, from my mother and the village women her age."

"If it made him the leader he was, it should go in his life," Luap said.

She nodded, slowly. "Very well — but understand that this is a tangled story, and I was a child when I heard it." He waved a hand to urge her on; she continued. "Gird was big and strong, even as a boy; the count's steward saw that and suggested he join the local guard. He trained part time, and his father had payment for his service. When he came to manhood, and would have been made a guard, the count chose to torture a boy who had stolen fruit, and Gird ran away. Arin — the same Arin the wolf killed — brought him back, and the count did not kill him, but the fine and the count's enmity destroyed my grandther's standing in the vill. So Gird gave up all thought of soldiering, and became a farmer in his father's cottage; he had learned, the women said, what came of following foreign gods of war."

"But he had been in long enough to have knowledge — " Luap prompted.

"No — it's before you joined, but remember that he spent that winter understone, with the gnomes. He said himself that what he learned from his old sergeant in the guards was to real soldiering as his own breadmaking was to my mother's. He knew a few things, more than the men who had just run away to live like animals in the woods — but he could not have led an army in war without the gnomish training." She stretched, then pushed herself out of the chair to prowl around his office and peer out the windows. "I think myself, Luap, that his very slowness, his very reluctance, to oppose the magelords openly is what made it work. He had no hothead enthusiasm, no boyish illusions, such as I see in the lads and lasses in my grange, who dream of glory. He had a grown man's thought, slow but sure, and when he finally moved it was like a mountain shifting its place."

She looked back over her shoulder at him. "Of course, it would be nice to think he had been working against them secretly his whole life. If he had organized the Stone Circle, if he had planned it all. But if he had, that would mean he had planned to let his mother and mine die of fever, rather than risk the count's ban against harvesting herbs in the wood. It would mean he had planned to use the anger generated by one outrage after another to rouse the peasants . . . that his own anger was false, assumed for one occasion and put off for another. And a false man, Luap, could not have done what he did."

Luap felt hot. She had made no direct accusation, but he felt as he had often felt when Gird insisted on strict, literal truth where a little pruning of a tale would make it more effective. He had been thinking that she would like his story of Gird's life, the way he had emphasized what was really important, and treated the more noisome moments lightly, as necessary contrasts to the main theme. Now he felt uneasy about that.

"Now it's your turn," she said, smiling. "You have said you have part of it written, the part you know from your own experience. Read it to me."

He spread his hands. "Rahi, you've just told me things I didn't know, that will make some changes necessary. Not changes in what happened, but in what the events mean. I'm not writing for the people alive now, who knew him personally, but for those in the future to whom all our time will be as dim as eight generations back is to us. So I must make it clear not only what happened, but why — not only what Gird said, but what he thought."

She frowned at him. "I don't see why that would change anything from the war years."

"It would," Luap said firmly, now determined not to let her see the *Life* until he had added and adjusted and rearranged the new material. "Consider his interaction with the first Stone Circle group he met, for example. Cob has told me that they all thought he had been a soldier, not just a boy in training. It would have been different if he had been — "

"But the facts don't change," Rahi said. "What happened is what happened. At least for what you yourself witnessed, you should have no changes to make."

"I can't agree." He laid his hand flat on the work table. "When I have had time to consider what's already written, in light of what you've told me today, *then* I will show you — but not now."

She looked more puzzled than angry, though he had expected anger at any confrontation. "I don't understand,

Luap. You wrote to tell me your *Life* was coming along well; you wanted me to see it; you clearly expected me to approve — and now you look like a man who knows someone else's gold has found its way into his pack."

"It's not that!" he said, feeling his ears redden.

"I didn't say it was — but I don't understand why you've changed your mind. Da said you had notions sometimes —"

Notions. Gird had said that about old women who accused each other of being witches. He had also said it about Luap, in one of their arguments. Luap struggled to find his dignity. "I do not have *notions*," he said. "I am doing my best to make Gird's life memorable and accessible to people who never knew him. I want to do a good job. What you've told me today makes me realize that I haven't done as well so far as I thought. And I'd rather show it to you when I'm more satisfied with it myself."

"As you will." Rahi shrugged, as if to show she didn't care, but the tightness of her expression said otherwise. She was probably thinking *notions* even if she didn't say it again.

For the rest of that visit, she remained more pleasant than he expected, if somewhat cool. She did not quarrel with the Rosemage — in fact, Luap realized, she had not quarrelled with the Rosemage in a long time. She did not upset anyone at the Council meetings, except in quietly insisting that Marshals should accept and promote girls as well as boys in barton training.

"It's not necessary any more," Marshal Sidis said. "You know yourself Gird only allowed it because you started it, and you were his daughter. There's no reason for women to waste their time in training to use weapons, when there's no war."

"That's not so," Rahi said firmly. "You weren't there, but Cob can tell you — he was. Gird came to believe it was both necessary and right — the only fair way. Some say there's no reason for anyone to train, when there's no war — but without training, we'd have the same mess Gird started with. If we're to be safe from another invasion, we must know how to fight — and for the same reasons as last time, women need to know as much as men." She surprised herself by having little anger to control. Sidis, from the northwest, had hardly made it to the war before it was over; he had the title Marshal only because he had led his small contingent and Gird confirmed most such leaders as Marshals if they fought at all.

"The horsefolk women learn weaponskills," she added, "and they were never conquered by the magelords."

Sidis snorted. "No one can conquer them — they simply ride away."

The Rosemage shook her head. "The mageborn tried, Marshal Sidis, in the early years; they wanted to settle the rich pasturelands along the upper Honneluur but the horsefolk drove them back. And it's in our archives that the horsefolk women fought as fiercely as the men, making our defeat sure."

"That may be," said Sidis, "but if every glory-struck girl spends her days in the barton, who'll be weaving and baking, eh?"

"Do the glory-struck boys spend all their days in the barton, in your grange?" Rahi wasn't sure if it was his tone, or the dismissive gesture in which he had indicated that the girls were not serious, but now her anger stirred.

"Well, no, but — "

"And do you find they cannot learn to scythe a field or dig a ditch, because they swing a hauk at drill?"

"That's not what I meant, Marshal Raheli!" His use of her long name was the final flick of the lash.

"Wasn't it?" She had both hands flat on the table, the broad hands she had inherited from Gird; her mother's had been longer. "Have you forgotten, in the years of conquest, that *our* people know Alyanya's blessing comes with the gift of blood, and that women in birthing face the same death that comes in battle? Do you not think it might be well for girls to learn discipline and courage, that our people never fall to ungenerous hearts again? You sound as if you thought it was a bad habit our women picked up from the magelords."

"But then they want to be yeoman-marshals, and the boys complain if the girls are better. They don't think it's fair." Sidis said this as if it answered all objections, then reddened as he realized, from the expressions around the table, that it didn't. Cob almost choked on a laugh. Some laughed aloud. Even Luap smiled. Sidis shifted in his chair, and finally shrugged. "All right. You're Gird's daughter, and no one can argue with you about what Gird said. I still think — but what does that matter?"

"It matters," Rahi said. "It always matters, because what you

174

really think will change the meaning of the words you say. If you think the girls are silly and glory-struck, while boys with the same visions in their heads are sensible and brave, every child in your grange will know it . . . and the sensible, brave girls will find a reason to stay home. And they will be as I was, good young wives to be trampled underfoot of the first tyrant who comes to the door." He started to speak, but she shook her head at him. "No, Marshal Sidis, you must think again. I do not want some child like me, some young girl whose mind is all on baking and weaving, as you would have it, left with no way to defend herself. Even my father, even the man who led the army to victory, could not defend me when an enemy came: *that* is the hard truth of it. There's nothing glorious about a soldier's death, but a victim's death is worse. My father saw it that way, finally: he had seen me near death, when I had no chance to fight, and if I had died on the battlefield, it could not have been worse."

Cob raised his hand, and Rahi sat down. "She's right, Sidis," he said. "It's the old way, after all. Some even believed that women taking up weapons caused less disruption than men, because Alyanya's Curse could not apply."

"I never heard that." It was not quite a snort, but close.

Rahi leaned forward. "You're not a woman. The Lady of Plenty, Alyanya of the Harvests, requires that blood be given for any use of iron or steel in planting or harvesting, isn't that so?"

"Yes, but — "

"And for a man, that means his own blood on the blade: shovel, spade, plow, sickle, scythe, pruning hook, even the knife used to cut grapes. Some folk said — in our village it was said, but I know in others it was different — that Alyanya required the same for using a blade on an animal. Others said that sacrifice was to the Windsteed, or even Guthlac. A man who withheld his blood would be cursed, in his loins and his fields. But for a woman, Sidis, the Lady had already had her sacrifice of blood; a girl cut her thumb once only, to promise the blood of childbearing later, and could use an edged tool with no more concern for Alyanya's Curse. Even in Torre's Song, it is the wicked king who is cursed for bringing steel to flesh, while Torre herself . . . "

"All right." Sidis turned up his hand. "I submit. We shall have granges full of girls, and lads who cannot keep their minds on the drill — "

175

"If you make clear to them that death follows stray thoughts as an owl hunts mice, Sidis, they should be able to follow the drill. If a girl can distract them, I would hate to have them in battle." Cob, again, with a look at Rahi. "For that matter, look at young Seri, in training here. If it weren't for her, I suspect Aris would wander from healing to healing, help Luap with scribes' work, and never take drill at all. That girl would make a yeoman worthy of any grange, and she's been nothing but good for a dreamy-minded mageborn lad with more talent than sense."

Rahi thought better of Aris than that, but she agreed about Seri. She knew that Seri had cheerfully dealt with a couple of lads who were at the age to see her as a girl, not a fellow-yeoman. Her Marshal had told the tale for a season afterwards. "She wasn't angry, and she didn't make any fuss," he'd said. "Just bashed them once each, told them not to be silly, and got on with it. Now they're her friends, and they've quit smirking at the other girls, as well. Do their courting at the dances, like they should."

Sidis still looked angry and stubborn; despite herself Rahi felt a twinge of pity for him. She hated being argued down, herself, and she knew he would have to come to this on his own before he would really believe it. She tried to think of some way to make it easier for him. Nothing came to her; she wished she had her father's power. Then she remembered how often he had stopped an argument with his fist, and a snort escaped her. Sidis glared.

"I'm sorry," Rahi said. "It's just — I remember Da — Gird — settling matters with his fist. I didn't like it, but here I am doing the same thing with words. I think you're wrong, Sidis, but you have a right to be wrong as long as it takes to change your mind. I don't want you agreeing with me just because I'm Gird's daughter, or Cob is one of the most senior Marshals. Gird himself thought we should talk things out, even if he stopped the talk sometimes; he was right in that."

"I don't understand you," Sidis said. "You change your mind —"

"No. I don't. But I won't try to change yours by force."

He still looked confused, but he nodded. When the time came to vote on the matter, he waited until he saw how the others voted. Then he shrugged. "It worked for Gird," he said. "So why not? We can always change it back if we're wrong."

And he tossed his billet on the pile for retaining women's rights in the grange organization.

After the meeting, Rahi was packing her things for the journey back to her grange when Sidis sought her out. "I wanted you to know it wasn't you I objected to, or any of the women who were actually veterans," he said. "But most women up where I'm from didn't fight — in fact, most of the men didn't fight. They see the grange drill as something imposed from outside; it's the women who've pestered me to send their daughters home."

"So they don't see the worth of it, eh?" Rahi sat down, and waved at him to do the same.

"Aye. It was on the edge of the magelords' holdings, and even I remember that things weren't too bad until after the war started. That's when our Duke — the Duke that was — raised the fieldfees and imposed stiffer fines. We had less bad to fight about, and more to lose, and there's feeling now that the grange system's as bad as the magelords' stewards ever were."

Rahi whistled. "Perhaps they don't think they need anyone at all, is that it?"

Sidis twisted a thong and untwisted it. "That's what it seems, most times. They're good folk, but they don't look ahead much, and they think they can deal with their own lives better than anyone else." He looked troubled, someone telling an unpleasant truth about people he cared for. "I've wondered myself, now the magelords are gone, what we need all this drill for. I come here, and you all seem to know things — it comes clearer, like. But how I'll explain it to them — "

"Maybe they should do without a grange for awhile." Rahi leaned back against the wall, watching his face. He didn't say anything at first. "If they don't want it, if they aren't supporting it — maybe they have to feel the need first. Da always said you can't convince an ox it will need water in the middle of the work when you show it a bucket at dawn. You could find another place . . . even here."

"But — " His hands worked the thong back and forth, back and forth. "It's losing, that is. Giving up. If there's a grange somewhere, it should stay — "

"Not if it's not wanted." Rahi felt her way into this argument, hoping she was right. "We're not here to make things worse, after all. The granges started because people wanted them. It's true there has to be some kind of law — if those folk come to market in a town with a grange, they'll have to abide by the Code. But if it sticks in their throats, why not let be?"

"The other Marshals," Sidis muttered. "They talk of their granges growing, of founding new bartons. They'll think I did something wrong."

Rahi opened her mouth to deny that, and then stopped. To be honest, *she* thought he'd done something wrong. He'd come into the war, and then his position as Marshal, without any real conviction. And if she thought so, others might as well. She could not reassure him with her dishonesty. "If you made a mistake," she said, picking her words as carefully as she would have picked through a bundle of mixed herbs, sorting them, " — if you did something wrong, it sounds to me that your folk have made mistakes as well. You couldn't have done all the wrong. Our whole system began with the people, the peasants. If they aren't with us, we have nothing. Pretending we do leads right back into what the mageborn did, all that pretense about the lords protecting the people, and the people serving the lords. If the folk in your grange don't want a grange, it won't be a real grange no matter what you do."

His brows had drawn together, but his hands were still. "Some do — at least — "

"If they want it, they will make it work. Think about it."

"What would you think, Raheli, Gird's daughter, if I let the grange go — closed it, or however it's done?"

Rahi looked past him, seeing against the far wall of the room a stream of images from the war, and the years after. What might it have been like, to live in a village with a better lord than Kelaive? Or with no lord at all? Could there be farmers, village folk, who did not understand in their bones what the grange was for, and how it worked? Apparently so. "I would think you had tried," she said. "I hear the truth in your voice. But it's not my decision." She could not tell what Sidis thought of what she said; he merely nodded and went away, leaving her to ride out of Fin Panir later that day still wondering.

She took that uncertainty with her back to her own grange, and looked more carefully at the people who did not choose to come. She had heard no grumbling for some time, but did that mean satisfaction? Or that people grumbled where she could not hear them? She was not surprised when a letter from Fin

Panir reported that Sidis's grange had dissolved, and he himself had given up his Marshalship. She hoped they would fare well, and hoped that her words had not formed his decision.

It was half a year before she came to Fin Panir again. Luap had finished his *Life of Gird*, and the Council wanted her approval. From the tone of the letter, she wondered what the other Marshals thought of it. They might have sent a copy, instead of a letter; surely it would have been easier to send the scrolls here, instead of dragging her to Fin Panir in the busiest time of the year.

A copy of the original awaited her in Fin Panir; the young yeoman who led her to a small room opening on an interior court pointed to it. "Luap said that was for you, as soon as you arrived."

Rahi stretched out on the room's narrow bed, and unwrapped the scroll. Luap's fine, graceful handwriting moved in even lines; she found it easier to read than her own crabbed script. "In the days of the magelords, in the holdings of one Count Kelaive, was born a child who would grow into Gird Strongarm, the savior of his people." Rahi wrinkled her nose at that. A bit flowery, not much like Gird himself.

She read on, her thumb moving down the scroll and holding it open. It couldn't be exactly like Gird, she reminded herself, because Luap hadn't known the young Gird. Even she had only village tales to rely on. But she felt uneasy, as if a hollow bubble were opening in her chest. She could not say, at first, just what it was, but something . . . something was definitely wrong. She put the scroll down and lay back, for a moment. Would anyone else notice it? Did it matter, when so far as she knew, no one else had survived from their village?

She picked up another scroll, and began reading. This was set during the war; Gird was enjoying a mug of ale in a tavern — she stopped again, trying to remember. Tavern? When had they been in a tavern? The drinking she remembered had been in various camps in the woods; by the time the army was taking towns, he had not been drinking that much. She looked at the scroll more closely. It was, she decided after a bit, intended to be funny: the great war-leader relaxing with ale, becoming excited, almost starting a fight. Her shoulders felt tight; she remembered how dangerous Gird could seem, in those rare drunken rages from her childhood. It had not been funny at all.

And worse than that . . . this was not real; she could think of no
time when it really happened. She scanned along the scroll,
looking for some reference, and found it. This was supposed to
have happened after the capture of Brightwater, and before
Shetley, but she remembered that time as clearly as the past half-
year . . . Gird had not been in any tavern; he had been off trying
to persuade brigands to join the army.

Luap had made it up. He had made up a good story, as men
often did, but then he had put it in this work, which was supposed to tell Gird's story for all time. Rahi felt cold, then hot.
How much had he made up? Was that what bothered her
about the first scroll? She snatched it up, and read it carefully,
with growing anger.

"You're not telling the truth!" Rahi's voice went up. Luap
managed not to wince visibly. He had been afraid she would
not appreciate what he had done, how he had turned the story
of an ordinary farmer-turned-soldier into the shape of legend.

"I am telling the truth — I'm telling what it meant. That's
what they need to know, not every little detail."

"It's a lie." She glared at him, Gird with brown hair and
breasts, the glare he remembered all too well. "You're making
it into a story . . . a song, like the harpers sing, that everyone
knows is just a tale."

"Raheli, listen! If the harpers change the kind of tree a
prince hid behind, because it rhymes — oak, say, instead of
cedar — that helps the listener remember. It doesn't change
anything important. The prince still hid behind a tree: that's
what matters. If they say half Gird's army wore blue, when it
was one person less than half, or almost two-thirds, why does
that matter? The point is that we won at Greenfields. That's all
I'm doing. I'm making sure people remember what it meant
— what his kind of life meant — and they won't make sense
out of the real details. You didn't yourself."

Would it work? For a moment he thought it had; her gaze
flickered, as she thought about her own reaction. But then the
angry glare came back.

"You're turning him into a lovable old gran'ther, using even
his lust for ale — "

Luap shrugged that off. "Most men like ale; it makes him
more human — "

"He *was* human! And his liking for ale cost us lives, you know it did."

"That's not the point—"

"It *is*, and it would have been *his* point. Was his point, at the last, remember? There's nothing good about it. . . . I remember after—" A long pause; he wondered which *after* she was seeing. "After my mother died, a bad stretch then; he came home drunk and sour with it, angry with everyone—"

"He had cause," Luap offered, sympathy he did not really feel.

"Everyone has cause," Rahi said. "But some do better. He did, later. And if you make it endearing, you diminish him— what it cost him to stop it, to change." In her eyes, *I never did that*, defiance but not quite pride. He knew she didn't, had sought, without admitting it, evidence that she was as fallible as Gird. As far as he could find out, she made none of Gird's mistakes; no drinking, no carousing, no wild flares of temper. Frustrating. He had never been able to maneuver Gird while Gird lived, and he could not maneuver Raheli, either.

He shrugged, as close to discourtesy as he allowed himself with her. "I'll change it back, then. You're his daughter; it has to please you—" He expected an explosion; instead he got a flat stare, and her nostrils widened as if she'd smelled something dead.

"I'm not . . . you're trying to make me feel bad about that, and I won't have it. He said you were slippery, and he was right about that." If nothing else. She didn't have to say that; it hung between them, something on which they agreed. She took a deep breath, and tried again. "I'm not asking you to improve the tale to please me; quite the contrary. I want you to tell the truth. Just the plain truth." If you can. He heard that, as if she'd shouted it.

"Even you don't believe the plain truth," he said, accenting "plain" just a little. "You weren't here; you're convinced it was something else than what we said."

She shook her head, the dark hair tossing back in a movement he remembered from his wife. His mouth dried. "*You* said things I found hard to believe—"

"Then ask the others! I know you did—"

She prowled his study, a thundercloud ready to burst. "What they said made even less sense."

His temper flared. "Then believe what you like! If I lie, and

181

the others talk nonsense, what will you have in the chronicles, eh? Shall we just forget him, and all he tried to do?"

"You know I don't mean that." Again that level gaze. "We can't just forget him. But — "

He would try sweet reason, though it had never yet swayed her. "You hate having to hear it from me. You don't trust me; you never have, not even as much as Gird himself did, and you wish you'd been here yourself. Well, so do I. Then you could tell me what to write, and — " He stopped himself from saying *and if you lie, it's your oath forsworn, not mine.*

"I would not have said to turn a dark cloud into a dark beast," she said firmly. "Even if I'd seen such a cloud."

"I'll change it," Luap said. He could always change it back. "I simply have no idea how to write of *that* cloud so anyone years hence will know what I mean."

"Do you know what you mean?" That with a shrewd sidelong look that took his breath away, the very look Gird had given him so often.

"I — no. No, I don't. It seemed — I told you — as if all the wicked thoughts and shameful fears in every heart had taken visible form, a black blight thicker than a dust storm. But *what* it was . . . I daresay only Gird himself knew. The words he spoke, that scoured it, lifted it, condensed it — those were no human words. I know that, and I've asked the elves — "

"And they said?"

"They found I could not recall the shape of the words, could not repeat them — and indeed, it was as if they slipped past my ears — and would say only that Adyan might be pleased with Gird."

"And then he died, while you stood there doing nothing." That was unfair; he seized that unfairness and cloaked himself in honest resentment.

"It was the gods' will; none of us could move. I cried — dammit, Rahi, I told you that, and others must have — "

"Yes." She had turned away. He waited. Finally she turned back; her eyes were dry. "You cried; I cannot cry yet. Tears are cheap."

He hated her. He felt he had always hated her; he willed himself to forget the times he had been sure he loved her, when (surely) he had only loved her father, and of her father only that part she herself could not share. "Your tears," he said formally, in as steady a voice as he could manage, "your tears you can name the worth of. It is your right. The tears of others you have no right to shame." He felt dark, dire, brooding as a storm-cloud low over the western hills. Great, and in some sense noble, to chide her about that, standing up for the tears (he could almost feel his gathering to fall) of plain, simple men who rarely cried, whose tears tore apart the rock walls of their souls, great floods that ripped mountains asunder. He looked up to find her watching him, that flat peasant stare (how had he ever thought it attractive?), that hard mouth with no sweetness, a dried haw withered on a dead stem.

"You're too poetic," she said. "You will make it all pretty, make all the patterns match at the edges, as they do in the rugs we took from the mageborn houses . . . better you should learn from village weavers, who leave one corner open for the pattern's power to stay free, and able to work."

"You don't understand." She didn't. She couldn't. She could but she wouldn't. He did not know which, but only that she did not understand.

"Nor you." Her back to him now, a back broader than a woman's ought to be, shoulders bulking more than his own. He had an excuse, a scholar's hours, but she had no excuse for looking (to his now critical eye) like a stubborn ox. "I'll see you in Council," she said, and left the room without looking back. Luap's mouth held a dry bitterness; he made himself sit back down at the desk, but could not find words to pen. Council meetings had been going so well, until now; Raheli would ruin all that, he was sure.

• Chapter Fourteen

And so she did. He did not know to whom she'd spoken when she left his office, or what she said, but from the way some Marshals looked at her she had spoken her mind. Whether about Gird or about him, Luap did not know. Others, who had heard she was in the city, but had not seen her yet, greeted her almost with reverence.

"Lady," said one, then actually blushed. "Rahi, I mean. Marshal. We're sorry we — "

"I know," she said, taking his hands in hers. It was, Luap thought, a very dramatic gesture. "Were you there yourself?"

"Not then, no — but I'd been out in the drillfields, and it didn't take long — "

"It's all right," she said. "I understand." Did she indeed, Luap wondered. Did she begin to understand what she was doing, with her fierce determination to leave Gird's life as blocky and unshaped as it had been in actuality? Why could she not realize that no story lived without shaping, without trimming here and filling out there? The point was to have Gird remembered.

Later that day, he hugged this certainty around him as he came into the Council meeting, expecting trouble from her, and those other Marshals who had not liked his *Life of Gird* as much as others. He had been able to hold them off by reminding them that Raheli, as Gird's daughter, must have some say. He had expected her to understand his purposes a little better than she had, to defend him to the others. Now — now it was going to be difficult.

Cob met him just outside the meeting room, and shook his head, though he smiled. "Luap, I could have told you not to try polishing clay. I know — you were trying to make the story fit the old songs, but you should have realized it would never pass Rahi."

Luap managed to smile back, shrugging. "I thought I'd

done a good job, until she raked me over about it. I really think that of Gird, you know. I think he's that special."

"Special, yes. But Gird's old gray horse — can you imagine it tricked out in flowers and braids and a golden bridle? It was a horse for such a man: strong and brave, not a fancy magelady's pony. So with Gird — he never wore a fine shirt to the end of his life, and knew better than to try it. You've put lace on a plough, Luap, and neither the lace nor the plough looks the better for it." Then Cob's arm came around his neck. "But I will say, Luap, that it's the most *gorgeous* story I ever read, even though not much like Gird. Life would've been easier with your Gird running things."

The others, once the Council convened, took the copies of the *Life* which Luap had made for them, and Cob suggested that Luap explain his work.

"You probably know already that Marshal Raheli, Gird's daughter, doesn't like what I've done." Better get that out of the way first; they would realize he was being honest. "What I thought — what I wanted to do, was write a *Life of Gird* that would live through the generations, and show why we reverence him. He did more than just raise the peasants in a revolt and win the war . . . we know that. He tried to make a way for mageborn and peasant to live in peace with one another. He tried to devise a fair law which all could use." He paused and drew a deep breath, looking beyond the table out the window into a darkening courtyard. "It seemed to me that Gird was too large to fit on my page; I could not find the right words for him as he really was. So I read in the archives, all the lives of the old kings and warriors, and what we know of the songs the elves make, and tried to shape what I wrote into something men and women could remember and chant by the fireside a hundred sons' sons' lives from now. Gird is a greater hero than any I found in the tales; it seemed to me I must show that in the way I wrote of him." He sat down, with a nod to Raheli, now calm and composed.

Marshal Sterin raised his hand, then stood. "I read Luap's *Life of Gird* two hands of days ago. It seemed to me very fitting for what Gird accomplished: perhaps more splendid than strictly necessary, but as Luap says, making clear to the future why Gird was great. It's true I found some of the phrases flowery, but if that is the mode in which men have always written of heroes, why not?" He sat down abruptly, as if he'd finished any argument. Raheli raised her hand, and at their nods stood in her place.

"He's a hero to you, to everyone: he *saved* everyone." She swallowed; her lips firmed. "He didn't save me." Before anyone could answer that, she went on. "Oh, I know, that isn't fair. He didn't want it to happen; he tried to fight and was outnumbered; he saved my life after. But the plain fact is that he did not save me, and what I remember includes that. My suffering was the price of his action; he waited until afterwards to start fighting."

Luap closed his eyes a moment. Against the inside of his lids, he saw his wife's face, the wife who had died — he had heard how terribly — in a village market square because he had not protected *her*. Gird had seen Raheli, but he had been able to heal her — or at least get her away — while his own wife . . . *You would not be* her *hero, if she had lived*, his conscience told him. I am no one's hero, he thought sourly, and opened his eyes again to find Rahi watching him with all Gird's intensity. Her face changed; he wondered what had come into his.

"I'm sorry," she said. "Your wife — "

"Never mind." He waved that away; he could not tell Rahi what he'd told Gird, that he had not really loved his wife until he saw her dragged away, weeping in fear and shame. He hoped Gird hadn't told anyone else, but he would not ask if she knew. "I can see what you're saying, Rahi, but do you think it is valid for everyone? He did not save you, as I did not save my daughter, but does that make what he did less important? Or less important that the future should know about him?"

Cob stood, and looked around the table. "Most of you know that I was with Gird from the first forest camp. Except for Raheli, there's none else can say that now. I was there the day he came, with his son Pidi and his nephew, a man near dead with grief but determined to make something come of it. And that's when Raheli still lay near death with woundfever and childfever, so though she is his daughter, I knew him longer as a leader in war." He grinned. "That's to stop anyone saying he knows what Gird would have wanted. I admit I don't. He was a plain man, and plainspoken, rough as the bark on an oak, but he knew as well as anyone the value of the old ways of saying things. And I've known our Luap from the day he first came, as well. To my mind, he's served Gird honestly all these years, and endured the taunts of them that didn't serve half as well. That's to stop anyone saying that what I say next comes from jealousy or dislike of Luap. It's not. I like him more now, and trust him more now, than I did that first year."

"Well then? What's your complaint?" asked Sterin, a bit flushed. Luap knew, as they all did, that Sterin had hardly met Gird before the war ended. He had organized and fought with a grange far from Gird's army; he had earned his Marshal's rank honestly, but resented the easy familiarity of those who had been Gird's friends.

"It's what I told Luap, before coming in here." Cob grinned at Luap, who could not help smiling back. Cob and Gird were wood from the same tree; whatever elevated Gird to greatness had been added to, not changed from, the essential peasant identity. "He's put lace on a plough; he's made Gird all smooth and easy, even his mistakes made decorative. Gird was a hero, right enough, but he was a plain man first: good bread and water — yes, and ale — not fine pastries and sweet wine. If the future knows him as a hero just like others, what good will it do them? He can help only those that remember him as he was."

"If he's remembered at all." Luap murmured that, not having permission to speak, but Cob turned to him sharply.

"Luap, he will be remembered. If not by your writing, then by fireside tales — and I grant — " He held up his hand. "I grant those tales and songs are likely to be even more astray. We've all heard some of them. But for this, for the story we most want told, I for one would like you to make it more like the man, plainer."

Luap nodded, expecting the vote that came. He would rewrite the *Life of Gird*, both now and again . . . and again, when some peoples' narrow ideas had died with them. He would not falsify — he *had* not falsified — what had happened, but he would choose his own way of saying it.

By the time they had settled other business, and finished the meeting, Rahi had cooled down. She came to him quietly, when the others had left.

"I know you don't agree," she said. "I know you thought you were doing the best for Gird's memory. You may think you'll outlive all of us, and maybe you will. But think about what Cob said, not my words alone. I am not that important; what happened to me happened to many, and I believe Gird would have come to his decision even without that. It might have made a neater pattern if Gird had been different. But he wasn't different; he was what he was, and it's that — the man he really was — that you must celebrate. The same man who did nothing all those years is the one who led us to victory, and at his death accomplished what his life could not. It makes no pretty pattern, but it's what really happened. He never asked anyone to believe something of him they had not seen; his *Life* must show what he really was, for that is what will help later."

Luap managed to smile. "I will do my best, Rahi." She asked no more, but went on out. He would do his best, his very best, to make Gird's life live in memory. She might not like it, but she might not be there to complain.

It occurred to him then that this might be another reason to move his people to the distant stronghold. There he could produce Gird's life as he knew was best, without interference. If — as seemed likely, given their age and health — he out-lived the older survivors of the war, he might find less resistance to his version of events.

The only problem was that he could not tell his people where he was leading them because he still had no idea where that land lay from Fin Panir. Arranha's curious method of determining sunwise distance had not been proven right in theory, let alone accurate. Besides, it would be not work for distance summerwards or winterwards. It would not help at all to start riding west in the hope of finding the place; as narrow as those clefts and valleys were, they could ride right past it and never find a thing. Perhaps he should ask one of the elves or dwarves who would be in Fin Panir for the spring Evener: surely they would know where it was.

A few days later, he found time to ask Arranha's advice. The priest's study, with its broad work table and two chairs, looked out on the little sunlit courtyard where he often sat. But the spring sun had not melted all the snow in the corners. The old man sat by the window, wrapped in a parti-colored knit shawl, in a chair softened with pillows, looking far more frail than Luap expected.

"Ask the Elder Races? Of course — that's what I said in the first place." Arranha did not look up from the scroll he was reading; Luap recognized his own handwriting. "This bit here, in your *Life of Gird* — are you sure this is how it happened?"

Luap felt himself reddening. "I'm changing some things," he said. "Surely you heard that the Council asked me to."

Arranha waved a dismissive hand. "That's to be expected. Nothing would please everyone the first time around. But I don't recall this conversation." He pointed, and Luap craned his neck to read the passage. He sighed.

"I was trying to make clear Gird's reasoning," he said. "At the time it seemed muddled, but later we could all see how it made sense."

Arranha looked up at him. "Luap, if you are telling the tale of people stumbling around on a dark night, you can't bring sunrise earlier so that you can see them stumble around. I remember this; Gird's reasoning *was* muddled, and it became clear later only because he himself straightened it out. If you make it too neat, it's not real."

Luap threw himself into the other chair in Arranha's study. "So I have been told," he said, trying not to let the resentment he felt color his tone. "Evidently I misunderstood the whole purpose of writing Gird's story. I thought the important thing was to have him remembered for what he did: freeing the peasants from oppression, establishing a new and fairer law, and his final sacrifice. I thought the details didn't matter, so long as people understood the structure of his life. That's why you can't write a life in progress: it has no shape yet. The shape you think you see cannot be the real shape."

"That's true enough, but — "

"But the Council — and now you — seem to think the details of the embroidery are as important as the design. I'm sorry. I thought making the whole design clear and easy to see was more important." He ran his hand up and down the chair's arm, enjoying even now the smooth curves and fine texture of the carving.

Arranha looked at him, that clear gaze which even Gird had found disconcerting. Luap remembered Gird telling the story of their first meeting, how the gaze of the old man's eyes unsettled him. "If you had been telling the story of a more conventional hero, I might agree: leave out the little inconsistencies. But Gird was in no way conventional, as we all know. He transcended all the easy definitions; he was a tangled mat of contradictions, heroic knotted firmly to unheroic. He fits no pattern, Luap, and it is that which you must make clear. Not trim and tuck and pad the old man to fit an existing model." He tilted his head slightly. "Why does this bother you? Why are you so determined to make Gird like any other hero of legend?"

Luap tried to subdue his anger, knowing that would move Arranha no more than it would have moved Gird himself, though for different reasons. His hands had clenched; he opened his fingers consciously, forcing himself to calmness. "Because I think that's what people remember. That's why the heroes of legend *are* alike, because that's what it takes for people to believe in them. If I told Gird's story exactly as it was, some would say he was no hero at all. They would disbelieve in his greatness precisely because it fit no pattern. Such a man, they would argue, could not have done those things; the gods would not work with someone who failed so often, and remained so muddled for so long. Even his death: think, Arranha — will any description in words of that cloud of malice and fear convince someone generations hence that Gird's death was more than a sick old man's vision? I can almost hear someone complaining that it was not enough, that he had done nothing to deserve the gods' favor, that cleansing all of us from all the dark desires of our hearts was less than killing a monster of flesh and blood."

"But it was, of course," said Arranha.

"Of course it was." Luap heard his voice go up, and took a deep breath. "It was far more than that; we all knew it who lived through it. But later — I think of those in the future, Arranha, who will not have even the shadow of a real memory handed down from grandparents. To say that Gird was, for most of his life, as confused, frightened, and ignorant as they° are will not make them believe in his greatness later. To say that he died uttering strange words, with no mark or wound upon him . . . well, so do many old people die, and if their families feel a sudden wave of relief and joy that the elder's struggle is over, that's no proof of the gods' intervention."

"So you do not trust Gird's own people to understand his real life?"

Luap shook his head. "No, I don't. I read all the old legends I could find, Arranha, and had the elders tell me the legends they recalled — of their own folk, not just mageborn tales. There's a difference, of course. The mageborn legends all name their heroes prince or king, princess or queen; the peasant legends are full of younger sons and daughters, talking animals, and the wise elder. But they still follow a pattern. The young hero looks like one — it's clear to friends and family that this is the hero. The hero never works with the evil he overcomes — he never submits to it. And he always knows what he's doing. I'll grant you, after knowing Gird I doubt this has always been true. But it's what people believed to be true, believed enough to remember. If I show Gird too different from that pattern, I don't think his legend will survive."

Arranha nodded. "Your reasoning is clear. But for that reason I suspect it's faulty in dealing with the life of someone who could no more reason than a cow can fly. Gird *felt* his way along, knowing the right as a tree knows good soil, by how it flourishes. In all my life, I never knew another like him, someone so infallible in his perception of good and evil, whose taproot sought good invisibly, in the dark. I learned from watching him that those with none of Esea's light — inspiration, intelligence, what you will — may have another way to seek and find goodness. Because Gird, as we know and can say with utmost respect, was not a man given to intelligent reasoning. Shrewd, yes, and practical as a hammer, but incapable of guile, which comes as naturally to intelligent men as frisking does to lambs." He laughed, shaking his head. "And I have only to think of Gird to find myself mired in agricultural images: listen to me! Cows that can't fly, tree roots feeling their way through the soil, frisking lambs — that's Gird talking through me, or my memory of him."

Luap could barely manage a smile in response to that. He felt colder than the raw early-spring day. He had not felt Gird's memory come alive while he was working on the *Life*; he had not felt Gird's presence at all, since the first days after his death. And if Arranha felt it, if others felt it, was that why they did not agree on his way of telling the story? Because they felt so close to Gird, they could not understand that distant ages would not have that feeling? He could not think what to say, how to ask the questions in his mind that troubled him without taking definite form. He waited a moment, one finger tracing the floral carving of the chair-arm, then reverted to his first topic.

"So you think I should ask the elves or dwarves where that pattern took us?"

Arranha's brows rose. "Yes, I said that. I admit I'm surprised you haven't already done so, though I suppose you've been too busy . . . "

"I felt — I wanted to finish Gird's *Life* first. But now — it will take me as long to rework it, and even then they may not like it. I just thought — "

Arranha's smile was sweet, understanding, without a hint of scorn; it pierced him just as painfully as Arranha's disapproval. "You just thought of your secret realm, a place of refuge. Quite natural. Yes, by all means ask them. But think of this, Luap: what will you do if they claim it as their own realm, in which we are not welcome?"

That had occurred to him before; he knew that was the root of his reluctance to ask. What is never asked cannot be refused: an old saying all agreed on. "The day I took Gird," he said, having thought long about it, "we saw at first only two arches, which I had seen before. But another appeared — "

"Gird saw this?"

"He saw three arches; I had seen but two, and saw two when we first arrived. You saw the third that is there now, with the High Lord's sigil upon it. When I told him there had been but two, he felt — I think he felt, for I admit he did not say it thus — that our presence, or at least his human presence, had been accepted." Luap had no idea himself what the appearance of that third arch meant, but trusted Gird's interpretation.

"I wonder if they'll see it that way. But better to find out now, before you take a troop out there and find you're intruding and not welcome. Will you ask the elven ambassador first, or the dwarves?"

"I had thought the elven. The legends say they're the Eldest of Elders."

"They will ask," Arranha said, "why you did not ask them before. Gird's will could not have withheld you past his death, not in their eyes."

Luap knew they would ask exactly that: another reason he had not asked.

The elven ambassador arrived a few days before the Evener. Luap had never been sure why the elves chose to recognize Gird or his successors; they had not, Lady Dorhaniya told him, ever come to the court in her lifetime. But from the first year of Gird's rule, an elf or two had come at

Midwinter, Midsummer, and the two Eveners, at first asking audience with Gird, and then with the Council of Marshals. Then the dwarves had begun to appear, on the same festivals, glaring across the Hall at the elves, who ignored them except to proffer an icily correct greeting. Some of Gird's followers preferred elves, and some preferred dwarves — the dwarves, Luap had heard, made good gambling and drinking companions. He himself found elven songs too beautiful to ignore.

This elf he recognized: Varhiel, he had said, was the closest human tongues could come to his real name. He stood taller than Luap, as most elves did, a being of indeterminate age whose silver-gray eyes showed no surprise at anything. He greeted Luap in his own tongue and Luap made shift to answer in the same. He had discovered a talent for languages, both human and other; he particularly enjoyed the graceful courtesies of the elves. When the preliminaries were over, Luap felt his heart begin to pound. He should ask now, before he changed his mind. . . .

"When Gird was alive," he said, "I found a place which might have been elven once."

Varhiel raised his brows. "Once? What made you think it is not still elven?"

"I found no elves there, or sign of recent habitation," Luap said. His palms felt sweaty. Why was this so hard?

Varhiel shrugged. "Perhaps it is a place we do not frequent; perhaps you came between habitations . . . but I doubt a place once ours would be abandoned." He picked a hazelnut from the bowl on Luap's desk and cracked it neatly between his fingers. "Where did you say this was?"

"I'm not entirely sure." Luap took a hazelnut himself, cracking it on his desk. He pushed across a basket for the shell fragments. "It's a long story . . ."

"Time has no end," the elf said. He leaned back in his seat with the patience of one who will live forever, barring accidents.

Luap wondered what it would be like to feel no hurry, no pressure from mortality. He pushed that thought aside, and began his tale. Necessarily, since the elf could not be expected to take an interest in minor human affairs, he left out much of it. He told of his first visit to the cave, of his discovery of his mage powers, and of the later discovery that the cave and those powers transported him somewhere.

"Say that again!" The elf's gray eyes shone. "You travelled — ?"

"Somewhere," Luap said, nodding. For a moment he felt he had been saying that word forever, telling one after another that he went *somewhere*, to meet the same incredulous response each time. "I don't know where. That's why I'm talking to you."

"Say on." The elf's wave of hand was anything but casual.

Luap tried to read the elf's expression as he described the great hall in which he had arrived, the arches out of it . . . and then Gird's journey.

"You took *another* there before asking our permission?" Luap had never seen an elf angry, but he had no trouble interpreting that.

"Gird was my . . . lord," he said. "He held my oath; all I learned went to him first." Then he realized that "there" had been said with complete certainty. "You know where it is?"

"Of course I know. And it is not a place for you latecoming mortals. You must not go again." The elf looked hard at him. "Or have you been more than those two times?"

"When Gird came," Luap said, side-stepping the question, "another arch appeared. One with the High Lord's sigil on it — "

"No!"

" — And thus Gird said our presence was accepted."

The elf stared at him. "Another arch . . . appeared?"

"Yes."

"When Gird came?" At Luap's nod, the elf sat back. "A mageborn human blunders into *that*, which we have kept inviolate for ages longer than your people, Selamis the luap, have existed . . . it is a clangorous thought."

"Gird walked through that arch," Luap said warily. He felt he must say it, but he did not know why he felt so. "He walked through, and then up the stair — "

"I hardly dared hope you had seen only the hall," Varhiel said. "And Gird would, yes — would have no doubt that he could walk through any arch he wished, or climb any stair, and I suppose he opened the entrance for you, did he? What was it like, your first view of that land?"

"It was blowing snow," Luap said. The memory could still make him shiver. Varhiel laughed.

"I'm glad. It is unseemly, but I take pleasure in the thought that at least one protection held against invasion. Now, I suppose, we must go to the trouble of destroying the patterns."

"No," said Luap. The elf's look reminded him he had no rights to argue. "Please," he said more softly. "Please listen — let me tell you the rest." As smoothly as he could, he told of his later visits, of the need for a place where the mageborn could train their powers to good, of Arranha's approval, and the Autumn Rose's. "They felt — we all felt — the holiness of that place, the great power of good that lies in it. This I'm sure would prevent any misuse of our powers, as our people learn to use them well."

"It is impossible," the elf said. "It is not your place; you did not make it; you do not understand those who did."

"But it is so beautiful," Luap said. He could feel tears gathering in his eyes, and blinked them back. Never to taste that pine-scented air, that cold sweet water? He could not bear that. Varhiel stared at him.

"You find that beautiful, all that bare rock?"

Luap nodded. "It eases something — I know not what — in my heart. And it's not barren — if you have not been there for years of human time, you may not know the trees that grace those narrow valleys."

"Canyons," Varhiel said. "That is what the Khartazh calls them, at least." He sighed. "If you find it beautiful, I am sorry to forbid it to you — but it is not yours. Even if I had the right to permit you, I would not, for I know why it was built, and under what enchantments it lies: it is not meant for mortals, and certainly not for humans. But I have not the right; you would have to have leave of the King — our king, of the Lordsforest, in the mountains far west and north of here — and I can tell you now you would not receive it."

"You could ask him," Luap said, in desperation.

"Ask him! You want me to ask the King to let a gaggle of latecomer humans inhabit a hall built by immortals for immortals? So you can practice your paltry powers in safety?"

Luap felt himself flushing. What he might have said he never knew, for the Autumn Rose came in at that moment. She had clearly overheard the last part of that.

"*I* will ask, of your courtesy, and as you are the ambassador, whose duty it is to carry requests from Fin Panir to your lord." Luap had not imagined that any human could approach elven arrogance, but the Autumn Rose angry came gloriously close. "Pray ask him, if you will, if he minds the corners of a deserted palace being home to those who have no other home, if they agree to be responsible for damages."

Varhiel stood. "Damages! Little you know, lady, what you say . . . little you know what damages such a place might sustain, or how to mitigate them. But as you command, and courtesy requires, I will take your message, and bring back his, which I am sure I could do without the effort moving from my seat. Yet you will have what you ask: the King's command, and speedily." He did not quite push past the Autumn Rose, yet she felt his movement, as a tree feels the gale that shreds its leaves.

She raised her brows to Luap. "If your meekness would not work, could it hurt to try my boldness? We shall see: I suspect Varhiel is not in his king's pocket any more than I am in yours, or the reverse. And you are a king's son; he owes you a king's answer."

"But if they're angry," Luap said. "If they never let us return — "

"Then we will find other mountains," she said. He wished he could believe her. He felt a cold wind sweeping through him; he could not bear to be barred from those red stone walls forever.

"Let's go there," he said suddenly. "Let's go now, before he returns."

She stared at him, eyes wide. "Luap — what is it? We can't go haring off to the cave now, and you can't get there by magery without those patterns . . . can you?"

"No. But — perhaps I could reproduce the patterns. It may not be the place, but the patterns laid there — " He wet his finger and began to trace a design on his desk. "See . . . like this, and this . . . "

She frowned. "Luap — I've seen that somewhere else."

"The design? You can't have."

"No, I have." She stood motionless a moment, brows furrowed. Then she looked at him. "Luap, come with me."

"Where?"

"Just come." She grasped his hand, and when he asked if she wanted to find Arranha first, shook her head. Down the stairs, outside, across the courtyard, and into the High Lord's Hall. He was halfway up the Hall toward the altar when he remembered what she was talking about. Incised in the floor

196

just behind the altar was a pattern he had never really noticed. "That's the same, isn't it?"

Luap bent over it. Here he dared not bring his own light, and the shallow grooves hardly showed in the dimness. "It . . . seems . . . the same," he said, tracing part of it with his finger. He dared not trace all of it, and vanish.

"In the old law," the Rosemage said, "*our* law, the man in a house has a better chance of keeping it. But you may be right that we need Arranha." Before he could say anything, she strode away, leaving him with his hand splayed out across the pattern as if to protect it.

Arranha, when he came, was inclined to shake his head. "It is not Luap's place, though he found it untenanted; we knew all along someone else had made it. If they forbid, we dare not object."

"But look at this!" The Rosemage pointed to the pattern. "It's *here*, in the most important place of worship our people had in the north. You told us this was the first of Esea's Halls over the mountains. If it is their pattern, then why is it here? If it is here with their consent, then Luap has an heir's right to it . . . to its use, at least."

"I don't know," Arranha said. "If it is the same pattern, then what it might mean is that they made some agreement with our ancestors. That doesn't explain why there were only two arches until Gird came, though."

"We could see if it works," she said.

"And if it didn't?" Arranha said. "I've never known you to be rash, lady, before this."

"*I'll* try it," Luap said suddenly. "If it doesn't work, then you will have the most excellent excuse to do nothing."

"You can't — " the Rosemage began. Arranha looked thoughtful.

"Perhaps you should. If it works . . . are you prepared to meet the elves in that place, by yourself? We could come along."

"No," Luap said. "If all three of us vanished, who would help the mageborn? We all know that I am one of the points of stress. Without me, some of our people would be quicker to forget their heritage and merge with the peasantry. If one of us must risk, I should be that one. You both have the respect of the Council of Marshals; you can do anything I could do for our people here."

"Well said." Arranha nodded. "Go, then, and Esea's light guide you." As he spoke, the pattern glowed in the shadowy hall, just bright enough for Luap to see that it was clearly the same. He stood on it, motioned them away, and thought of that distant hall.

And was there, on the dais.

But not alone. Under the arch crowned with harp and tree stood an elflord, crowned with silver and emeralds and sapphires: Luap could not doubt that this was the King, the Lord of that fabled Forest in the western mountains. Under the arch crowned with anvil and hammer stood a dwarf, his beard and hair braided with gold and silver. His crown was gold, studded with rubies. Luap could not doubt he was the king of some dwarf tribe, though he knew not which one. On one side of the hall stood a company of elves, facing a company of dwarves. All wore mail styled as their folk wore it, and carried weapons. In the center of the hall, a gnome in gray carried a great book bound in leather and slate. Varhiel faced the dais, only a few paces away.

"I told them you would come," he said. "Without invitation, without courtesy . . . see now, mortal, what you dare by intruding here. This is not your place: you did not make it, you do not understand it."

Luap surprised himself with his composure. "Is that your king's word, Varhiel?"

"You may ask him yourself," said Varhiel; his bow mocked Luap, but Luap did not respond. He looked down that long hall at the elvenking, inwardly rejoicing to see the hall filled and alive as he had always imagined it.

But before he could speak, the elvenking spoke; his voice held a richness of music Luap had never imagined. "Mortal, king's son you named yourself: what king claimed you?"

No human words could be courteous enough for speech with this king; Luap felt himself drowning in that power. His magery responded, seemingly of itself, and he did not suppress it, allowing his light to strengthen. "My lord, my father died while I was young; I have been told by those who knew both him and me that he was Garamis, the fourth before the last king."

"You claim the royal magery?"

Luap smiled before he could stop himself. "My lord, the

magery claimed *me*, when I had long thought I had none." He felt his mind as full of light as his body; he might have been burning in some magical flame. Was this Esea's light?

"Varhiel said you claimed that when you brought Gird here, a third arch appeared, and on that basis you claimed a right to use this place. Where is that third arch?"

Luap stared down the hall. Sure enough, he saw but the two arches he had seen when he first came. He felt the sweat start on his forehead. It had been there; it had appeared with Gird and had been there when he brought the Rosemage and Arranha. Now he could not see it. Surely it had to be there, between the others, where a blank red wall stood.

"Show us this arch," the dwarf said suddenly. "If you are not *nedross*." He did not know much of the dwarf speech, but no one could talk long with dwarves without learning something of *drossin* and *nedrossin*. He looked again, saw only the bare stone. But, his memory reminded him, the elves are illusionists. At once a rush of exultation flooded him. He walked forward, past the ranks of elves and dwarves, through the very current of their disapproval, their determination to exclude him. He walked past the gnome, who stepped aside without speaking. He thought of Gird, of how Gird had strolled down this hall as if he had the right to walk anywhere. Could he be that certain? Yes. For his people, he could.

He walked to the red stone as if he expected it to part like a curtain. Two paces away, one pace: he could see the fine streaks of paler and darker red, the glitter of polished grains. "Here," he said, laying his hands flat on the cold, smooth stone. "It bears the High Lord's sigil; in Gird's name — " His hands flailed in air; he nearly fell. On either side of him, the columns rose, incised with intricate patterns; over his head the arch curved serenely, with that perfect circle at its height.

He struggled to control his expression; blank astonishment filled him. He heard, inwardly, a rough chuckle that reminded him of Gird. *Did you think I'd let you make a fool of yourself?* Luap shivered; he knew that voice. He wanted to ask it questions, but it was gone, leaving his head empty and echoing. And no time. From their arches, the elvenking and dwarvenking had come to confront him.

"Mortal, I see the arch. I do not see why you should be allowed to use this hall." This near, the elvenking's beauty took his breath away; it was all he had ever imagined a royal visage to be.

"My lord, it was my thought — and Gird's, for that matter — that such a thing meant either the gods' direct command to come here, or their approval."

"For what purpose?" The arching eyebrows rose, expressing without words the conviction that no purpose would be justified.

"A haven for the mageborn —"

"You would use magery here?" That was the dwarf, a voice like stone splitting.

"This *is* magery," Luap said, with a wave that included the entire place. "How could one be here and not be using magery?" That came close to insolence; he felt his stomach clench, as if he'd leaned far out over a precipice.

The elvenking's eyes narrowed dangerously; Luap felt cold down his spine. "Mortal man, this is not human magery, but the work of the Elder Races, far beyond your magery —"

"Yet I came, and this arch appeared — I do not claim by my magery alone but with the gods' aid."

"And what gods do you serve?" Luap blinked; that was one question he had not anticipated. *The gods of my father, or of my mother? The gods of my childhood or my manhood?*

"I was reared both mageborn and peasant; I have prayed to both Esea and Alyanya . . ." he began. The elf interrupted.

"I did not ask from whom you sought favors, but whom you *served*."

How could any man say which god he served — truly served? He might think he had rendered service, but the god might have refused it, or not recognized it. Possibilities flitted through his mind, an airy spatter of butterflies. He could think of only one he had served, and that one not a god. "I served Gird, mostly," he said. The elf's brows rose as the dwarf's lowered; he had a moment to wonder if those were two ways of expressing the same reaction, or two different reactions to the same words.

"And it was Gird's visit that brought this arch," the elvenking said.

"Yes."

The elf looked at him so long in silence that Luap felt his knees would collapse. Finally he spoke. "You convince me that you are convinced of what you say. But you do not know what you ask. This stronghold was made for another, not you. It was built to ward against dangers you do not understand and could not face. If you live here, you may rouse ancient evils, and if you do, it would be better for you that you had not been born. Yet . . . if you ask me, knowing that you do not know, and knowing that I say your people would find better sanctuary elsewhere, I will grant you my permission. But whatever harms come of it will rest on your shoulders, Selamis-called-Luap, Garamis's son."

"What dangers?" Luap asked. "What evils? I saw a land of great beauty, breathed air that sang health along my bones—"

The king held up his hand, and Luap could not continue. "I tell you, mortal man, that you would be wise to choose some other boon from me. Yet wisdom comes late or never to mortals; I see in your eyes you will have your desire, despite anything I say. Be it so: but remember my warning."

"And you will not say what that danger is?"

"It is none of your concern." A look passed from the elven to the dwarven king, and returned, which Luap could not read but knew held significance. His anger stirred.

"And why is it not? If the gods led me to this place, as I believe they did; if Gird's coming hallowed it for mortal use, as I believe it did and this arch proves; if then you know of some danger which threatens, why should you not tell me, and let us meet it bravely?"

Another look passed between the kings; this time the dwarf spoke. "You believe the gods intended this: do you think the gods do not know of the danger? Are we to interfere with their plans? No: you have our permission; that is all you need from us, and all we give."

Luap realized suddenly that he was hearing the two kings each in his own language, and understanding perfectly, yet he knew he could not speak or understand more than a few courtesies of his own knowledge. Such power, he thought, longingly; his own magery was but the shadow of theirs. But pride stiffened him; he looked each in the eye, and bowed with courtesy but no shame. "Then I thank you, my lords, for your words. As the gods surpass even the Elder Races, I must obey their commands as I understand them."

The elf looked grim. "May they give you the wisdom to accompany your obedience," he said. Then he turned to the gnome. "Lawmaster, record all that you heard, and let it be as it is written." He strode up the hall, and when he reached the dais, the elves vanished. The dwarf king came nearer and looked up into Luap's face.

"You may be a king's son, mortal, but it will take more than that to rule in this citadel. You are not of the rockblood; you do not know how to smell the drossin and nedrossin stone. The sinyi care for growing things and pure water; we dasksinyi care for the virtues of stone; the isksinyi care for the structure of the law. Now ask yourself, mortal, what the iynisin care for, and what that corruption means. We will not forgive an injury to the daskgeft." He turned, and his dwarves cheered, then burst into a marching song. Luap could no longer understand their speech; he watched as they followed their king to the dais and vanished.

That left the gnome, a dour person who gave Luap a long humorless stare. "Gird should have had more sense," it said. "I am a Lawmaster: this is a book of law. Do you understand?"

"Yes, Lawmaster." Luap struggled with a desire to laugh or shiver. How had Gird endured an entire winter understone with such as this?

"In this book will be recorded the contract between you and the Elder Races. Do you understand that?"

He did not, but he hated to admit it. "If we wake this danger, whatever it is, they will take it ill."

"They will withdraw their permission," the gnome corrected. "You are, for the duration of your stay here, considered as guardian-guests, not as heirs. You have the duty to protect this as if it were your own, but it is not your own, nor may you exchange any part of it for any value whatsoever. Is that clear?"

"I — think so. Yes."

"You have the use-right of the land, the water, the air, the animals that live on the land and the birds that fly over it, but no claim upon dragons — "

"Dragons!" Luap could not suppress that exclamation.

"Dragons . . . yes. There may be dragons from time to time; you have no claim upon them. You are forbidden to interfere with them. You may not, through magery or other means, remove this citadel to another place — " Luap had not even thought of that possibility. " — And you must keep all in good

202

repair and decent cleanliness. You must not represent yourself as the builder or true owner, and you must avoid contamination of this hall with any evil. Now — if these are the terms you understand, and you accept them, you will say so now — "

"I do," said Luap.

"And then the sealing. You were Gird's scribe as well as luap; you know how to sign your name. As you have no royal seal, press your thumb in the wax." Luap signed, pressed, and the gnome laid over the blotch of wax a thin cloth. The gnome bowed, stiffly, and without another word walked to the dais, where he vanished.

Luap could not have told how long he stood bemused before he, too, went back to the dais, as much worried as triumphant. He arrived in darkness — not in the High Lord's Hall, as he'd expected, but in his cave . . . and realized he'd been thinking of it. Could he transfer directly? No. Back to the distant land, then to Fin Panir. The High Lord's Hall was empty; it was near dusk. Where had they gone, and why? Or had the elves wrapped him in such sorcery that years had passed, and they thought him lost forever?

"Almost," said the Rosemage when he found her in his office. "Four days is too long to stand waiting."

Quickly, Luap told her what he remembered of his meeting with elves and dwarves and the gnomish Lawmaster. He found it hard to believe it had been four days . . . but he could not remember everything. Something about danger, about *drossin* and *nedrossin*, about which of the Elders cared most about which aspect of creation . . . but none of that mattered, compared to the final agreement. The Rosemage grinned; she looked almost as excited as he felt.

"Well, then — and where is this fabulous place, now that we have permission to use it?"

At that moment, Luap realized he had not asked — that he had not been given a chance to ask. And he doubted very much that the Elders would answer any such question now.

Arranha was the least concerned about that; he was sure, he said, that he could figure it out by means of celestial markers. Luap, annoyed with himself for being so easily enchanted by the elves, grunted and left him to it.

● Chapter Fifteen

"What happened?" asked Aris, as Seri came out of the Council meeting room. She grinned, stuck up her thumb, and then put a finger before her mouth. They scurried down the stairs like two errant children, across a court, through another passage, and then found an empty stall in the stable.

"It went just as we hoped," Seri said, when she'd thrown herself down on the straw. "I'm glad you suggested starting with the history, though."

"Makes you seem older," Aris said. He sat curled, with his arms around his knees. It had been Seri's idea, all of it, but she had let him help her shape it.

"They had to agree with that, of course, since they knew it: that all the Marshals now were Marshals or yeoman-marshals under Gird himself, they'd all led soldiers in the war. And they had to agree that weaponsdrill in the barton, and marching in the grange drillfields, isn't much like battle. Even Gird had to get them out of the bartons and into mock battles before real ones. So they could see where I was going, and some of 'em — Cob, for instance — were already nodding when I said the granges needed something more. He started in to propose just what I'd planned, so I didn't have to bother."

Aris chuckled. "They'll like it better from Cob; he's one of them."

"And it doesn't matter to me," Seri said, with a wave of her hand, "as long as we have that kind of training. After all, he was *in* the war, not just scrubbing pots and carrying water like we were. He'll know better how to set it up, now he's thought of it."

"But about the other — " Aris prompted.

"You won't believe it." Her grin lit up the stall. "He had just gotten well started on laying out a training plan when the Rosemage raised her hand and said she thought perhaps I'd had more to say. Cob stopped short, shrugged, and asked if I did. So I told them about our plan — "

"Your plan," Aris said firmly. "I didn't think of that."

"My plan, then. I told them how future Marshals would need more training than just leading a gaggle of farmers around a hayfield, or even fighting in a mock battle once a year or so — that they needed to be real Marshals, well-tested before being given command of a grange — and Aris, they *listened* to me. I said it all, all we talked about: working up from yeoman-marshal, spending time in two different granges, and then talked about having a place for concentrated training." She paused so long that Aris had to speak.

"Well? What did they say?"

"Five or six of the older ones all started talking at once, about how they didn't have to worry as long as they had veterans, and how much it would cost, and that Gird never meant to have armies roaming around stealing from honest farmers — then Raheli stood up and they were all silent." Seri lay back in the straw and stared at the high roof far overhead. "You know, I never realized how much she's like him."

Aris sat up straight. "Like Gird?" He thought about it. They saw her only when she came to Fin Panir, and often enough only from a distance. They had heard stories, of course, but none of them made her seem much like her father.

"I know, it surprised me, too. All we'd seen, after all, was her from a distance, walking around. That great scar on her face, and her dark hair — she doesn't *look* anything like him. But when she looked at me, it gave me the same sort of feeling as the first time we met Gird. I don't know how to say it better than that she's an opposite of Luap."

"Warm, not cold," Aris mused, and looked up to see if Seri agreed. She was nodding vigorously.

"She has Gird's directness. I liked her at once, but if *she* was my Marshal I wouldn't dare try anything." She didn't have to elaborate on that; he knew about the tricks she'd played on her Marshal. It had been, she'd explained from time to time, the result of being separated from Aris. He had always kept her out of mischief. Not long after, they'd been reassigned to the same grange.

Now Aris came back to the main subject. "So Rahi stood up, and they were quiet, and then what?"

"She said it was a good plan. She said it should be in Fin

Panir, and each grange should have the right to nominate two candidates a year, but not all would become Marshals."

"But you thought three — "

"Two, three, it doesn't matter. The point is, she approved. And — what you won't believe — the Rosemage stood after her, and approved as well. *She* argued for including the study of law and the archives as well. Said that knowledge of war was only part of a Marshal's training; that Marshals had to be able to act as judicars and recognize all kinds of things going wrong. The two of them started in, then, and it was almost as if they'd pulled the details of the plan straight out of my head." She threw her arms out, raising a cloud of dust from the straw, and sneezed. "Of course, I know they didn't, but it means we were planning in the right way."

"Huh. If you said something that got the Rosemage and Gird's daughter working together, it was definitely right."

"They should be friends," said Seri soberly. "They would fit together."

"Luap doesn't think so."

Seri wrinkled her nose. "Luap couldn't do what he does if they did, is what he means. But it's what Gird would have wanted. Think of it — the Rosemage could lead her people — "

"Not while Luap is the king's son, and she's an outlander."

"He could *let* her; he could tell them to follow her, and not him. But he won't." Seri rolled over on her stomach and propped her chin on her fists, as if she were a child again. "He's ruining things."

"He's not!" Aris scrambled nearer and thumped her shoulder, then bent down to look her in the eye. "He's Gird's chosen luap, Seri: he is not ruining things."

She didn't budge. "You don't see everything; you're thick as bone some ways. I think the healing makes you see people differently. You don't see what they are; you see their needs." She rubbed the bridge of her nose for a moment before going on. "I don't think he knows it, I'll say that for him. I think he believes he's doing the right thing, what Gird would have wanted. But he got it into his head a long time ago that the Rosemage and Rahi were natural enemies, like a levet and a wren — "

Aris snorted. "And which of those two is a wren?" Seri smacked him.

"You know what I mean. He thinks that, and he can't see

that they're made to be allies. Not friends, maybe, but allies. And so he treats them as enemies, and they see each other through his vision, except sometimes like this."

"Mmm." It was something to think about. Did the healing magery give him such a different view of people? Or was it the magery itself? Could that be why Luap saw the Rosemage and Rahi as natural enemies? But he had no chance to discuss that with Seri, for someone was calling her. She rolled to her feet; he sighed and scrambled up after her. They had little time together these days, and he treasured the brief encounters.

"Seri!" Now the voice was closer: Rahi, Gird's daughter. Aris followed Seri out of the stall. The older woman laughed, the first relaxed laugh he had ever heard from her. "I might have known you'd be off somewhere with Aris."

"Yes, Marshal," said Seri. Her braid had come half undone again, and she had straw in her springy curls.

"Did you come up with all that by yourself, or did Aris help?" Now that she was close, Aris realized what Seri had meant about her being like Gird. A bluntness, but without any brutality, a sense of great strength in reserve, a warmth . . . he found himself grinning back at her, more at ease than he usually was with the older Marshals.

"He did —"

"No, Marshal, it was all hers — " Aris broke off as his voice clashed with Seri's and they laughed. "She will give me credit I don't deserve: we talked about it, but that's all."

"Gird said you two were great friends — but he sent you to separate granges for training, didn't he?"

"Yes, Marshal, but that doesn't matter." Seri might have said more, but another voice hailed them; the Rosemage moved across the stable yard, Aris thought, like one of the graceful horses.

"There you are, Rahi — and with the younglings. They're a pair, aren't they?" Aris felt like a colt up for sale at the market when the Rosemage shook her head at them. "Hard to believe the two of you could be our children, when you come to Council with solutions for problems the other Marshals haven't thought of yet."

Rahi had flushed, but now seemed relaxed and cheerful; Aris wondered what had upset her momentarily. He wanted to look at her scar; he wondered if he could heal it, but he dared not ask. "Fair enough," Rahi said slowly. "One for each of us, that way."

The Rosemage shook her head. "They come as a pair . . . we've learned that in Fin Panir, if nothing else. Gird himself separated them for a few years, in training, but even he admitted they were the closest he had seen outside a few twins."

Rahi grinned; Aris noticed how the scar pulled at her mouth, making the grin uneven. "They don't look much like twins," she said.

"We're not," Seri said boldly. "We're not alike, but we fit together. Father Gird said that was stronger than two alike."

The two older women looked at each other, a measuring look, brows raised. "That's true enough," murmured the Rosemage. "But again uncanny wisdom for one so young."

Seri shrugged, with a side glance at Aris. "It's not my wisdom, but Gird's."

"Well, yours or Gird's, it's true enough. Now I — we — need to talk to you." The Rosemage looked at Rahi. "Don't we? It's a nice afternoon for a walk in the meadow out near Gird's grave."

"And no one will overhear or interrupt," said Rahi, smiling. "Of course we need to talk to these two. I hardly know them except by what I hear from Luap."

With the older women flanking them, Aris and Seri walked out the west of the stable complex into the meadows beyond. Once well out of earshot of the stables, Rahi said, "You didn't say all you had planned, Seri; I could tell that. What else?"

"Cob said it well enough," Seri said. "The details don't matter — I mean, they do, but it doesn't matter who does it right, only that it's done. I know I'm too young to be telling Marshals anything, let alone the Council."

"But you were *right*," said the Rosemage. "That's what matters, not age."

"Well . . . it's like food. If I have it, I share it; if they eat it, it's nourishing. It doesn't matter who gave the bread and who gave the salt, so long as the bowl's full."

Rahi chuckled. "Peasant wisdom, lady."

The Rosemage pretended to stumble. "You're calling me lady?"

Rahi shrugged; Aris thought she was embarrassed. "I can't remember your real name."

"I quit using it; it meant something noble in our language I never lived up to." From the tone, she had never said *that* to anyone before. Rahi nodded slowly.

"And my name meant 'fruitful vine' — so I perhaps have no right to it."

"Rosemage," said Aris, trying to head off emotions he did not understand, "is a difficult sort of name to use — I mean in talking *to* you."

"You're right, it is. It's actually Luap's nickname for me, a nickname of a nickname." Aris noticed that the others looked as confused as he felt; she sighed and explained. "Your father knew this, Rahi, but I don't know if you did. The old king of Tsaia, the one I killed, had called me 'Autumn Rose' in a sort of jest. A bitter jest to me, for I loved him. When I killed him, I felt I had killed my old self, with its unsuitable name, as well, and I told Gird I would henceforth be the Autumn Rose in truth. Luap turned that to Rose Magelady, and then Rosemage. As you say, it's more a name of reference than one of address. Arranha told me I was being silly, and now I agree — but it's too late to change back."

"Never mind," said Rahi. "I can call you lady as the others do, without it hurting my mouth. I still have some questions for young Seri."

"Yes?" Seri, like Rahi herself, had seemed less interested in the Rosemage's explanation than Aris.

"You may be right to have the senior Marshals set out the plan themselves, but I'd like to know how you would have done it. Perhaps some of your details need to be included — and I'm a senior Marshal; I could see that they are."

"Oh." Seri paused a moment; Aris could almost see the thoughts in her head, busy and humming like a hive of bees at work. "Well, it seemed to me that we needed Marshals capable of leading out a grange against small problems, like wolfpacks or robbers. And then we needed Marshals, or perhaps High Marshals, who could lead groups of granges against invaders. I know it's peaceful now, but it was peaceful before the mageborn came — excuse me, lady — "

"No need," the Rosemage said.

" — And even though Gird won the war with ill-trained troops, and no cavalry," Seri went on, "it would be easier — it would cost less blood — to have better training and maybe some horse soldiers."

"Knights," said the Rosemage.

"Not too many," Seri said. "Mostly it should be yeomen, as it is now, but there should be a few whose parrion — guild? — it is to learn how to engage in wars, so that we have that knowledge when we need it."

"You would have the training place here, in Fin Panir?" Seri nodded. Rahi went on. "And you would have the Marshals — let's stay with that for now — learn what?"

Seri ticked the items off on her fingers. Aris was proud of her, the way she was staying calm when he knew she was bubbling inside. "First, the Marshals must be reliable, honest, hardworking: that's why I said they should have grown up in one grange, and then worked in another. They have to be old enough to become yeoman-marshals first, because you don't know if they're going to misuse power until they have some. Marshals shouldn't be bullies. Then they have to know the Code, and they need to know the Commentaries, too, because the Code's always changing and it probably always will. Marshals have to get along with everyone in the city — or town — all the merchants, crafters, and farmers. They may not be the strongest, but they have to be skilled in all the weapons our people might use, and they have to be good at teaching them. They have to know something about the mageborn, and about the horsefolk, and anyone else we find, because they have to judge whether there's been fair dealing."

When she paused for breath, Aris put in, "And she wouldn't mind if they were skilled in each craft, and born with every parrion in the world." Seri flushed red.

"It wouldn't hurt," she muttered.

The Rosemage chuckled; Aris thought she looked much younger than usual. "No, it wouldn't hurt, but how long do you think they could be in such training?"

"If they're made yeoman-marshal after their first year as senior yeoman," Seri said, "and then serve four years as yeoman-marshal, they'd be the same age as someone finishing journeyman training in most crafts. Surely a Marshal must have earned the same respect as a master in a craft, and most journeymen spend four to six years before they pass the guild. . . . "

"And in that four years they would have time for law and history and languages as well as military things," Aris said. "I think — we think — that Marshals should all have knowledge of healing crafts, as well. If they lead yeomen into battle, they should know how to treat wounds and camp sicknesses."

"So new Marshals would be over twenty-six," Rahi said. "Even thirty —"

"Weren't most of Gird's Marshals, appointed in the war, over thirty?"

"Yes, but that was a special case." Rahi looked thoughtful; Aris gave Seri a warning glance. Best let Rahi think it out for herself. "I wasn't close to thirty . . . but then . . . " Aris smiled to himself. He had expected her to see their logic. "You're saying that all Marshals should have that maturity, as Gird and his first recruits did?"

"Yes, because Marshals aren't just battle commanders; courage isn't all they need." Seri looked back and forth between the two older women. Aris watched them smile at each other, as if at the antics of favorite children.

"I think, Rahi, that these two have more maturity than some gran'thers I've seen." The Rosemage shook her head. "But don't you two get above yourselves, eh? I heard about the tricks you played when you first came, Seri."

"I wouldn't do that *now*," Seri said. Aris wondered. She hadn't meant any harm, and none had followed, but she could no more forswear mischief than he could healing. Tease, prick the pompous, and then hug the hurt away — that was Seri. "And besides, I don't know enough yet — I want to learn all the things I'm talking about — "

"And be the first truly educated Marshal?" The Rosemage whistled. Seri blushed, and Rahi reached over to tousle her already tousled hair.

"I keep telling myself it's a new world these younglings live in," she said. "It's not like where I grew up, nor you either. But sometimes it does startle me. I presume you know it's going to be hard, Seri?"

"Of course." Now she looked affronted. "It's supposed to be hard, or it's not any good. I'll be tired, and grumpy, and even scared — "

"And dirty and hungry and hurting, if we do it right," Rahi said, no humor at all in her voice now. "And you will be scared, I promise you that."

"And you, Aris — " The Rosemage broke that tense silence. "Do you, too, look toward being a Marshal?"

"I — I don't know. I want to learn all that Seri does, but — I'd like to spend more time healing, if I could. Teaching it, too."

"Mmm. It will be interesting. . . . " The Rosemage and Rahi shared a look Aris could not interpret, but turned the talk to other things until day's end.

Aris licked the grease from roast chicken off his fingers and reached for the bread. Seri pushed the loaf within his reach with her elbow; she was too busy eating her own chicken to free a hand. He tore off a hunk of bread, wiped his fingers, and ate that before saying anything. He had not been this hungry since coming to Fin Panir. Across the little fire, two of the yeomen with them grinned.

"I wonder what gave th' Marshal th' notion t'play this game," said one of them around a mouthful of bread.

"If I find out," said the other, "I'll knock his nob for 'im, that I will. My da told me it was more work than it sounded in songs, and he was right. We've climbed five hills a day, I'd wager, and haven't walked down but one."

"And that one muddy," said the first yeoman. "Wi' rocks at the bottom." He crunched the bone of his chicken leg and sucked the marrow noisily, then belched with satisfaction.

"Rocks!" said the second. "I'll tell you about rocks — " Then, as Aris raised an eyebrow, he fell silent. Their Marshal's blue cloak swirled past, then the yeoman resumed, in a lower voice. "Like to broke my legs, I did, and the old man says 'That's what eyes is for, lad, to look where you put your feet.'"

Aris gave Seri a long look; she blushed and wiped her mouth and fingers with bread. *He* knew where the Marshals had found that idea, and who to blame. He knew she would have confessed, challenging the man to thump her if he could, had the Marshals not told them to keep quiet about whose idea it was. Once they'd decided the idea had merit, it hadn't taken them long to put it into practice. Aris had been thinking of maneuvers in the spring, marching over soft green grass under warming skies. He had imagined himself setting up a clean tent to which the injured would come for treatment. Instead, the granges in Fin Panir, all four of them, were sent out in the cold after-harvest autumn storms, to practice moving engagements in the hills southwest of the city. Three days' march to the hills had taught them all how little they knew of supply and camp organization (the veterans enjoyed pointing it out) and the hand of days in the hills proper had been a revelation even to them.

Aris took another hunk of bread. So far he hadn't been scared, except of not keeping up, but he had been cold, wet, muddy, tired, stiff, and hungry. He hadn't been needed to heal anything worse than blisters and bruises, for which most of the yeomen had their own pet remedies. Instead of a healer's tent, he found himself carrying a staff just like everyone else, and doing the same camp chores he had done as a boy. Even though he and Seri had been with the peasant army, even though he had once lived a much harder life, the years he'd live in Fin Panir had taken the edge off. And tomorrow they faced the three days' march back, into the teeth of the winter wind. He wondered if they'd get to sleep tonight, or if the Marshals had some surprise planned for them, as they had on other nights. He hoped not. His eyes felt gluey.

Luap hardly believed what he saw, the Rosemage and Raheli eating elbow-to-elbow at the campfire, and both enjoying it. He was not sure what he felt. On the one hand, the two of them quarreling could knot his stomach. But on the other . . . he had always been able to move one by invoking the other's opinion. What if they really agreed? What if they became (he shuddered) *friends*? The Rosemage had always gotten along with Gird better than he did himself; if she made friends with Rahi, his whole rationale for withdrawing the mageborn could fall through.

Everyone knew how those two had loathed each other: if they could become friends, so could any other mageborn/peasant pair.

Beside them were Aris and Seri, a pair he already found inconvenient. He wanted Aris to come with him; he did not want Seri. But he knew Aris wouldn't leave her behind. He needed the Rosemage; he needed Aris's healing talents. He did not need Gird's troublesome daughter or that curly-headed young warleader who should have been born early enough to fight in the war.

He had come on this uncomfortable jaunt, he told himself, simply to chronicle the training exercise. Burdened with his sack of scrolls, his inksticks and pens, his folding table and a tent to keep them dry, he had not been tempted to take part in the training itself. Instead he instructed two of his more promising clerks in the art of field mapping, wrote up each days' notes as reported by the Marshals, and tried without success to devise a better way to render rough country visible on a flat surface. It had been tiring, difficult work, carried out under difficult conditions, but it had not been the same as clambering up hill and down to hold mock battles with another group of tired, rain-soaked yeomen. He knew that; he had been there in the real war. So he had stayed away from the evening fires, to avoid making his comfortable job any more insulting than it was already.

Tonight, though, the maneuvers were over — supposedly — and they would all march toward home in the morning. So he had brought out a jug of the peach brandy his favorite cook made, in hopes of sweetening the Autumn Rose's attitude. And there she sat, dirt and grease to the ears, joking with Raheli.

He walked toward them; young Aris saw him coming, and leaped up. "Sir — Luap —"

"Sit down, lad. You've worked a lot harder than I have." Other yeomen moved aside to give him room beside Aris.

"I wanted to ask you," Seri said, direct as always. "About those maps. Did you ever talk to the gnomes about mapping?"

How could the girl be that wide awake, that full of energy? Aris looked tired to the bone, but Seri — it must be the peasant endurance, Luap thought. He remembered Raheli brimming with energy when others had been too tired to move. And Gird, despite his age, had nearly always been the first up in the mornings. "Once, after the fall of Fin Panir," he answered. "They'd come to talk to Gird, and he showed them my copy of the map they gave him." He chuckled. "They weren't impressed. I told them I had had to do it without the original; it was lost in the flood outside Grahlin that time —"

"Was that when the well exploded?"

He looked past Aris into that bright, wide-awake face, and past it to the two older women. Was that tone just a bit put on? Did Seri have some purpose besides what he heard in the words? Rahi spoke up, as if he'd asked her to.

"Not exploded — but apparently the local magelord had magicked all the water in the river into it, underground, and sent it all out at once. It made an awful noise, and scared us silly."

"The water shot up in the air," Luap added. "Higher than any fountain, a column of water perhaps a man's height across. It was only a little mud-brick fort and when the water hit, it came apart around us. On top of us."

"And the next day we had a pitched battle we never should

214

have fought," Rahi went on. "Gird was too shaken by the flood, I think — he felt we had to hold the bridge. Cob's foot was hurt that night; he's limped ever since. And we lost others who'd been with us from the start — " She stared at the fire, her face grim. That fiasco and Gird's sullen, drunken response in the next hands of days had almost ended the rebellion. Seri looked from Rahi to Luap.

"What I meant, sir, was that I wondered if the gnomes had solved the problems you were having with the new maps. Do they have some way of showing the land, even when it's wrinkled up, so you can tell what part of a hill sticks out?"

"Not that I know of. By the time I had them to copy, of course, they'd been soaked and torn. We had to dig them out of the wet rubble, try to uncurl them without tearing them any worse, and then redraw them. Maybe there were marks that didn't show after that." Seri looked interested, alert, and — in another place and time — Luap would have been flattered by that alert interest. He had had few chances to teach her, but those few times he had enjoyed it. She came to everything with such enthusiasm, such eagerness to learn and do well, and those Marshals who had supervised her considered themselves lucky. But now he felt her intensity as a veiled threat — she and young Aris between them were up to something, and he could not decide what. Had they anything to do with the new friendship between Raheli and the Autumn Rose?

For those two were as amiable with each other as either with anyone else, now, and from the looks they cast at the youngsters, might have been their aunts if not their mothers.

"I brought something to warm cold hearts," Luap said, holding up his jug of peach brandy. "Who'd like a sip?" The Autumn Rose held out her hand, and he gave it to her.

After a sip, she handed it on to Seri. "Be careful, girl; it's stronger than it tastes. Did Meshi make that for you, Luap?"

"Yes; she spoils me." Safer to say it himself.

"True, she does," the Autumn Rose agreed. "Do you know I found her making spiced preserves one time, and she told me she didn't have enough for everyone — but when Luap came down the stair . . ." They all laughed; Luap managed a grin.

"It comes out even — the other cooks don't like me because she's so partial, and won't give them her secret recipe for the spiced preserves. I've thought of getting it from her, and telling them, just for peace in the kitchen, but — " He shrugged, and threw his hands out; everyone laughed, but with no sting in it.

"You know what would happen then," Rahi put in. "They wouldn't like you more, and Meshi would bang you on the fingers with a spoon every time you came in the kitchen. It is good; reminds me of my mother's preserves, but there's something else in it."

"Whatever it is costs enough to put cooks at each others' throats," Luap said. "I think one of the spices must come from over the mountains." He took a sip himself, that warmed him all the way down. Perhaps it wasn't a bad thing to have Rahi and the Autumn Rose friends. It seemed less threatening than it had, just as Seri's — or was it Rahi's? — ideas about the training of Marshals to replace those retiring seemed less threatening. He looked over at the girl — not really a girl, now. She would make a formidable Marshal in her day. He glanced at Aris. Would he take Marshals' training as well, or stick with his role as healer? He tried to imagine them both in middle age, and failed.

As sharply as a pinprick, his own vision of his stronghold intruded. He wanted to see Aris there, using his healing magery, teaching others how to heal. Seri did not fit. He had no use for a Girdish Marshal, a peasant with no more magical ability than any other peasant. What could she do? He wasn't going to raise and train an army; they would have no enemies to guard against, out there. Aris belonged, was one of his own people by birth and talent, and she did not belong. She would hold Aris back, prevent him from learning what other mage powers he had. If they did not marry — and he was sure they would not, though he could not have said why — it would be best for Aris to learn to get along without her, so that he could be with his own people. She would be happy enough in Fin Panir or elsewhere, busy with a grange.

How was he going to manage that? He watched Rahi and the Autumn Rose; clearly they, like Gird, thought the two belonged together. He would have to find some way of shifting them apart, bit by bit. He looked at Aris; the boy had deep circles under his eyes. This had taken more out of him than Seri; he was not, Luap told himself, as robust. He should be protected, his healing magery nurtured. That was too precious a talent to be squandered in mock warfare.

● Chapter Sixteen

"You're going," said Seri. Aris looked up from the scroll he'd been studying. Seri looked as she always did when she'd pulled off some mischief.

"And who's to be my guardian?"

"I am." She sounded as smug as she looked.

"You? But you're — "

She pointed to the badge on her tunic. "A Marshal-candidate in good standing, of known good character, approved by the Council. So we can leave whenever you like, and stay as long, and—"

To be free again — to ride out the gates, with Seri at his side, and no one to argue with him whether this one or that needed his healing more, no one to suggest he must conserve his power for greater needs — he felt a childish glee of his own, to match the sparkle in her eyes. "Tomorrow?" he asked, not really believing it.

"Good choice," said Seri. "I'll tell the cooks, and get our things ready. You finish that miserable compilation for Luap, and — I suppose you do have to tell him?"

"I should." Aris sighed. "But surely he knows — he was at the meeting, wasn't he?"

Seri rolled her eyes. "Meeting? What meeting? Can't a few Marshals get together and discuss minor matters without holding a formal meeting?"

"But then are you sure it's — "

"Raheli, the Autumn Rose, Cob, and Garig: is anyone going to argue them down? And they had discussed it with others — not *all* the others, admittedly, but enough to justify it. My directors agreed — in fact they had brought it up before I had. And Rahi did suggest we go on and leave now — quickly — before the decision caused comment."

Her look said even more: it usually did. "I could leave within a glass or so," he said softly. "I could leave Luap a note. We don't need that much — "

She clasped his shoulder, and leaned close. "Even better. We'll take an afternoon ride." She waved her hand, "I'll go get the horses ready."

Aris turned back to the scroll. He couldn't concentrate on it; he had read it before, and knew that nothing on it would help him. He rolled it carefully, slid it back into its case, and the case back into the rack. He rummaged on the desk until he found a scrap of old parchment, scraped many times and fraying, to write his note to Luap.

He felt slightly guilty for not taking the trouble to find Luap, rather than leaving the note in his office, but he did not want to discuss his plans with the Archivist. More and more, in the past year or two, he had felt uneasy around Luap, and he could not explain why. Seri, he knew, felt the same way. He put the note where Luap could not miss it, then went to see if Seri had left anything behind. His pack, rolled neatly, lay on his pallet, and his box held only what he himself would have left behind. When he ran his hand into the center of the pack-roll, he felt the hard edges of coins — so she had thought of that, too.

With his pack under one arm, he didn't look like someone out for an afternoon's ride — but then if anyone asked, he had permission to leave for longer than that. He remembered a Marshal saying once that an innocent heart was the best disguise, and on his way to the stables, no one seemed to look at him. Seri had both horses saddled, and her own pack strapped tight. Mischief lighted her eyes; her horse, catching the excitement, jigged sideways.

"I am hurrying," said Aris, to both horses as much as to Seri. His own snorted, as he snugged the pack straps, and mounted. He didn't have to ask which way — they would start as they often did, riding west and north into the meadowland beyond the city.

By sunset, they were out of sight of the city, beyond the range of their earlier rides in this direction. They had passed one village to the east, but now saw nothing, not even sheep, to indicate that another was near. Still, they felt safe; they could walk back to the city in one day if the horses pulled loose in the night. But the horses did not escape, and they rode off the next morning in high spirits. All that day they moved into country new to them, rolling land covered mostly in grass, with scattered groves in hollows and along streambanks. In the last span before sunset, they chose a grove near water to camp in.

"It's almost like being children again," said Seri. "When we used to go and make houses in the bushes, remember?"

"Yes, but now we know how to do it right." They had blown fluff from a seedhead for camp chores: tonight Seri had to dig the jacks, and Aris had to take care of the fire. Not that it mattered to either of them, Aris thought, but Gird's training held to the tally-group system, and it had come to feel natural. With the horses watered and fed, their own waterskins full, and their camp laid out properly, they settled in by the fire to talk.

"I wonder if we should take turns as guard," Seri said. "I know there's no war, and this is settled territory, but it's good practice —"

"Mmm." Aris leaned back. He had not ridden so many hours in a long time, and he knew he would wake stiff. "I don't sense any dangers."

"Nor I. But it's the right way to do things. I'll take first watch."

"All right." He looked at the fire for awhile, listening to Seri's footsteps on grass and stone. She went down to the spring, up the slope to the edge of the trees, and came back to the fire.

"Nothing now." He could feel her tension as if it was his own. In a way, it was his own tension, reflected like firelight. They both knew why they had needed to get out of Fin Panir, why they had needed to travel alone, but the years in the city made it hard to return to the easy communication of their childhood, when idea and response had flowed between them without barriers.

Seri sat back down with a sigh. In the flickering light, her face looked much older, and as heavily stubborn as Gird's had been. "Remember after Father Gird died?" she asked. Aris nodded. Because they were then training in separate granges, they had been able to talk for only a few minutes now and then — but they had had the same dream in the days after the funeral. "I always felt close to him," Seri went on. "From the first day we came. It was like having a grandfather of my own. Not that I didn't respect him, but —"

"It was much the same for me," Aris said. They had talked of this before; it was as good a way as any to ease into the real problem. "If I had been able to choose a father, I'd have chosen Gird."

"And then he died," Seri said. "Like any other father or grandfather, except it wasn't."

Aris looked at her. They had each tried to talk to the Marshals about it, and had had the blank looks given to those who have said something outrageous. They had learned not to talk about it, not to mention what was, to them, the most salient point of Gird's death. "I think," he said softly, "that they don't quite remember it. They know they felt better afterwards; they know they couldn't quite remember why they had been so angry — but I think they don't actually remember what happened."

"Luap does," said Seri. "Or he did, but that's not what he's put in his *Life of Gird*. He's made it a monster."

"How did you find out?" Aris had been wanting to see the *Life* for several years, but Luap gave him no chance.

"I heard from someone who heard Rahi complaining about it. She said he was trying to make it more like one of the old tales from the archives, one of the kings' lives tales."

Aris snorted. "That wouldn't fit Gird, no more than a crown would have."

"Rahi said he couldn't make clear what really happened, so he made up the monster so that people would understand. Only they won't, because that's not what it was."

"I wish he'd let me help," said Aris. "It could be written the right way, the way it happened. It wouldn't be easy, but that would be better than making up a false tale."

"Rahi said Luap can't see that — he thinks a false tale that makes sense is better than the true one no one will understand." Seri poked a stick at the fire, until sparks flew up. "Aris — do you ever feel Father Gird is still around?"

"Really? In person? Or just — feeling that he's there when he's not?"

"I'm not sure." She faced him directly. "Aris, those dreams we had after he died — those aren't the last ones I've had."

He wasn't surprised. Those hadn't been his last dreams of Gird, either. He nodded, and said, "Tell me about them."

"I can't, exactly. It's — it's as if he wanted me to do something, and I'm not sure what. If he *were* alive, he wouldn't be happy with Luap, that's certain . . . Luap's ruining it all."

That was the core of it, what they had needed to talk over far away from Fin Panir's many curious ears. Aris felt a cold chill down his back, as if someone had run a chunk of snow down it. "I know. And I don't think he knows what he's doing . . ."

"How can he not!" Seri had finally let go her anger, and now it blazed in his mind as brightly as the fire she poked into brilliance. "He's a scholar; he surely knows if he writes truth or falsehood. He was Gird's helper so long, he surely knows what Gird would have wanted. Gird wanted mageborn and peasant living in peace, one people. Luap swore *oaths* that he would obey Gird and follow Gird's will, yet he's doing everything he can to push mageborn and peasant apart."

"Not quite everything," Aris pointed out. "If he really knew he was doing it, he could do worse — "

"Not without the Council noticing. He's just being sneaky." She glared at him. "Or have you gone over to them as well?"

He stared at her, shocked and horrified. "Seri! I couldn't!" Tears filled his eyes; if Seri thought he would turn into another like Luap, he wasn't sure he could bear it.

"You spend so much time with them," she said, her voice hard. "You do what Luap tells you; you hardly have time for anyone else — "

"I'm here," he said. "I left Fin Panir in the turning of a glass, on your word — how can you think I *like* all that, you of all people!"

"Then don't defend him," said Seri, "when you don't believe what you say. D'you think I can't tell what you really think? But if you won't say it, even to me, even alone in the dark wild, how is that different from him?"

Aris struggled to control his voice. "I have tried to be fair," he said. "Tried not to . . . to make hasty judgments. I saw — I see — Luap and the other Marshals, all quick to say what someone meant, and sometimes I know that's not what the other meant. So I look for the chance that someone like Luap, doing something I would not do, has at least a good reason, in his own mind, for doing it." He swallowed the lump in his throat. "But — you're right — I don't like what he's doing, and I haven't liked it, and I haven't been able to do one thing about it. I'm too young, and I'm mageborn, as he is — "

"And half the distrust you meet is for him," Seri said, now less fiercely. "They're afraid you're another Luap. When you were younger, and you were out and around more . . . "

"Which is another thing," Aris said. "I want to do more healing myself; I want to go more places, and it's the Council — yes, and Luap — who insisted I stay close and try to train other mageborn to heal. It isn't working, and I don't think it will, but they won't listen to me."

"Why not?"

"Why won't it work? I'm not sure. The Autumn Rose says the healing magery was rare anyway; it failed first, when the mageborn were losing their powers. I've found only one who responded to the training —"

"Garin —"

"Yes. And he exhausts himself when he closes a cut; the one time he tried to heal a broken bone, he fainted partway through and slept for a week."

"You did that, when you were a child —"

"Yes, when I'd worked with all those sheep. But he's a man grown, older than I am. The Autumn Rose found a girl said to have healed her family members of headaches and the like, but what she was really doing was charming them — they didn't feel the pain as long as she was there. That's not a bad use of charming — I've taught her to use it on more serious things — but it's not healing. You remember that Gird wanted me to work with peasant healers to learn herblore, and with the granny-witches to learn hand-magicks. I've learned a lot more about herbs, and most of the women with a parrion of herblore say if I were a girl they'd trade my parrion, though they don't think much of a man learning it. The grannies have watched me heal, and I've watched them lay pains on a stone, and neither of us learned how the other did it. Whatever they do is not in their power to explain, or mine to learn — and the same for what I do. They don't sense the light of health and the dark of fever or injury the way I do, but they do feel the prickling in their hands."

"I suppose that's something," said Seri. She frowned. "So you don't think you'll be able to teach anyone?"

"I don't know. Some child, perhaps, will be born with the talent, and I can help train it. But it's not like reading or writing — it's not something everyone can learn more or less well — and since I didn't have someone to train me, I really don't know what the training should be like." Aris leaned away from the fire as a gust sent smoke into his eyes. "Nobody wants to hear that, though: Luap is still convinced I could teach other mageborn to heal, and the other Marshals still hope I can work with the granny-witches. They don't want me to be the only one — and I wish I weren't." He struggled with the sorrow that always came when he thought of that, of being the only one who knew what he knew. He could share his skills by using them, but he had no one who could understand what his life was like, what it felt like to hold that power in his hands and pour it out.

"We can't let him ruin it," Seri said. For a moment he didn't know what she meant. She nudged him with her elbow. "Luap, that is. We can't let him ruin what Gird wanted."

"How can we stop him, if the Council of Marshals can't? And it's not *all* his fault. Remember what Rahi and the Autumn Rose were like before you worked on them?"

Seri ducked her head. "They should be friends; they should have been friends all along. You know that."

"Yes, and I know they weren't. That started before we came, a long time back, from all the tales. What I meant is that it's not only Luap who has strayed from Gird's dream. It's a lot of them, even Rahi. They never saw it clearly, maybe." Aris wondered again why not, when it seemed so obvious to him. They were older; they had known Gird in the war. Why couldn't they all have seen that what he wanted was good? A swirl of night wind brought flames snapping higher from their fire, and a gout of sparks lifted into the dark. Aris tried to keep his mind from following them, from the trance of light, but remembered that only Seri was here. He need not worry. He lifted his hand, in one of their childhood signals, copied badly from the huntsman, and let himself go.

Sparks flying on a dark wind . . . he felt the glittering heat, the potential fire, in each spark, and its frightening vulnerability. So small against the cold, the dark, and yet so bright, so hot. Were there sparks of darkness as potent? Could darkness spread, as fire spread, from its sparks? He let that thought go, and rose instead with another gout of sparks, high above the starlit land. Most sparks lit no fires; most died to ash in the cold wind, and most that fell found no fuel.

He came back to himself slowly, slipping from trance to the ordinary musing of any mortals around a fire. The ideas that had seemed so definite against the dark slipped out of his mind. The fire crackled, hissed, murmured. Behind him, one of the horses stamped and blew. He felt his skin tighten all over, fitting itself to him again. Where had he been? Only a thin blue flame danced above the coals; he could not at first remember why he saw the fire from below, why he was curled on the ground instead of a bed. Then he felt Seri's hand on his shoulder, solid and warm, as if she were the hearth in which a great fire burned.

He took a long breath in, smelling the leather of her boots, the wool of his own shirt, the firesmoke, the horses nearby, even the wet herbs near the tiny creek. When he looked up, the stars seemed like a scattering of sparks . . . but sparks that would not die, that would never go out.

"And what did you bring back this time, Ari?" Seri's voice was almost wistful. He had never told her a story she liked better than one from his earliest childhood, and he had never been able to tell that story again. Like all the visions that came with light, it existed only in the moments of the trance itself, and his memory faded more quickly than a meadow flower.

"The sparks," he began, letting his tongue wander free. "If Gird's wisdom brought light, then the sparks flew out . . . but not all minds held the fuel to kindle them. Some would burn bright, but quickly die. Some would catch no spark at all. Many would come to the fire for warmth, but fear the sparks flying, lighting in themselves. . . ."

"But I feel it," Seri said. He turned over to look at her. He could see it in her, as he could feel it in her touch.

Aris pushed himself up. "You're right. You do."

"And so do you!" She sounded almost angry.

"I hope so. I used to think so, but — "

"But you've been listening to them. To *him*."

Aris shook his head. "No — it's not that. I think — I think Father Gird saw things from his own side — as a peasant — and so for peasant-born it's a little easier to catch his vision. It all fits. When I try to think like you, I see it clearly, but when I try to see it like Lady Dorhaniya, or Luap, I see other possibilities. Gird didn't have any reason to trust magery; even with me, he wished my healing would work some other way. He had no place for magery in his mind, no place it would serve the dream and not harm it. He agreed my healing was good, but he would not have agreed that being able to lift stones by magery was good. He would think how they could be used to hurt people. What I know is how much the magery hurts if you don't use it. Again, he understood that about my healing power, but I don't think he realized that it's true of *any* magery. It's like — suppose someone said to you, 'Don't lead. Don't learn. Don't question anything.'"

Seri had been scowling, but at the last her face changed expression. "No one could tell me that! I have to, it's the way the gods made me — "

"Yes, and the mageborn who have magery *are* that way, just as you are eager to learn, curious about everything, quick to lead. Remember our childhood? You got whacked with a spoon often enough for being — what did the old cook say? — nosy, bossy, always asking questions. You couldn't help it, but what do you think it would've felt like if you'd tried to change?"

"I suppose . . . I'd have felt trapped, like a wild animal tied in a barn. Ugh!" She shivered. "Why did you have to say that? I don't like to think about it."

"But when I tried not to heal, you said you understood. . . ."

"I knew you were unhappy, and I knew you would never do anything wicked, Aris, but I didn't imagine — gods forgive me, but I didn't really think what it might be like. I was thinking of the people who needed you, that you could heal." She leaned against him, as she had in childhood. "I'm sorry, Ari. It just never occurred to me."

"It's all right." He leaned back, comforted by her presence, by the familiar warmth and smell of her. "But can you try to understand, now, why it's so hard for the mageborn who have those talents to leave them unused?"

"I suppose." The doubt in her voice had no real solidity; he knew he had won his argument. He waited. In a few moments, she spoke again, slowly, thinking it out aloud. "And I suppose it's as bad — or worse — for Luap. Is that what you're saying? He's a king's son by birth, but he never got to *be* a king's son. They didn't know he had the magery; he never had training in its use. Yet he has it, and it's as restless in him as your healing is in you, or my curiosity is in me. I wonder if the royal magery would be stronger?"

"Arranha says it is, that when it comes it either comes in full or not at all — and that Luap has it. I don't think Gird ever knew how hard it was for Luap, or recognized how determined Luap was to be loyal to Gird." He felt Seri shift against his side, and then relax again.

"I suppose," she said again. "I would think that for Gird — but then, Gird never asked me to do anything but be what I am."

Aris snorted. "Except the time you were playing those tricks on your Marshal." He could feel her suppressed chuckle; it finally erupted into a gurgle of laughter.

"Yes . . . well . . . even then he didn't ask me to be different, just

225

reminded me that I was too young to know all the background, and too old to get away with it."

"I've always wondered — what *did* Father Gird do to you?"

Seri laughed again. "What do you think? Gave me a couple of smacks and told me to be glad he hadn't used his full strength. Told me to behave myself. If I wanted to be a leader, I'd have to set a better example to the junior yeomen — and that was true. It took me longer than I like to remember to straighten them out. They were a *lot* wilder than I was. 'Think you're clever now, lass,' he said to me, 'but what's to come of them if there's a real danger, and you're not there, and they won't trust the Marshal, eh?' Made me think, it did. He left me there another half-year, then put me in that grange down near yours."

"Good for both of us," Aris said.

"He thought so. You'd be a steadying influence on me, he said, and I'd be sure you didn't walk off a roof in a trance." Aris felt the twitch of her shoulder. "Come to think of it, he never did believe you could take care of yourself, any more than I do." As if on cue, Aris yawned, a great gaping yawn he could not smother before she turned and saw it. "And you can't," she said. "You were off there wherever you were, and you're half asleep now. Go on. I'll wake you to watch later."

Aris wrapped himself in his blanket, and slid into sleep as comforting as a hot bath, just wondering if Seri would wake him, or sit up all night thinking. The grip of her hand on his shoulder woke him to dark stillness; her other hand came across his mouth, warning. Before he moved, he felt some dire magery nearby. He slid a hand free of the blanket, and touched hers, tapping a message. Her hands left him, and he reached down and slid his own knife free. Where had he left the sword? Where was the danger? And from whom?

It felt like nothing he knew, no mageborn he had ever been near, not even his mother's last lover. Cold, ancient malice, a bitterness no love of life could touch . . . *iynisin*. Of the timbre of the elves who had so delighted him in Fin Panir, but of opposite flavor, this magery mocked all he had admired.

"Here's your sword . . . " Seri breathed, barely audible above the pounding of his heart. Aris flung the blanket aside and stood, staring into the darkness. He could just feel the warmth of the banked fire on one leg, but no gleam of coals lit the dark, and the stars' light seemed feebler than it had. The wind had died; he could hear nothing but felt one cheek colder than the other, proving the air moved. He felt Seri's movement at his back, a shifting from leg to leg more menacing than nervous. Then her quiet mutter of explanation: "I felt it first, then something dimmed the starlight. The horses aren't moving. Nothing is. I woke you —"

"I feel it," Aris said. "Iynisin." Saying the name aloud took great effort, but when it was out he felt less frozen. He bent and folded his blanket, felt around until he located the rest of his pack, and put it all well aside, in case they had to fight.

"The elves said that was a legend." Seri's voice wavered; he realized that she was really afraid. Seri? It was absurd; Seri had never been afraid.

"Doesn't mean it's not true." Aris moved to her voice, and leaned against her. His hands prickled; he laid one on her arm, and felt the demand of his healing lessen. She could not be sick — was he supposed to heal her *fear*? He let the power free, and felt it move from his palm to her arm, driving away whatever hindered her light.

Her *light*. Even as he withdrew his magery, knowing it had been enough, Seri burst into a glow as different from magelight as sun from starlight. Shadows fled away from them; Aris saw his own, black and dire, stretch to the edge of their hollow before he too caught light. His, though he had never seen it before, he knew to be magelight, the same as Arranha's. It had the quality of lamplight or firelight; he knew without trying that he could kindle wet wood with it at need. But Seri's . . . Seri's was light only, the essence of vision, of knowledge, of inward seeing and outward seeing. Aris pulled his mind back from its favorite pastime, and had a moment to think how they must look, two glowing figures on a dark wilderness.

Then he saw the iynisin. All around the hollow, everywhere he looked, the blackcloaks, the beautiful faces eroded by hatred to shapes of horror. He could not tell how many, but he felt the weight of their malice as if each glance were a stone piled on his flesh. As if they knew the very moment of being seen, they spoke — two of them, voices clashing slightly as if they read from a script.

"Foolish mortals . . . you have chosen an unlucky place and time to indulge your lust." Aris said nothing; Seri muttered, but

227

not aloud. The iynisin went on. "You stink of Girdish lands, mortals; you trespass on ours. As we cursed your dead leader, so we may curse you, if we do not kill you and feed on your flesh."

This time Seri answered them. "If you think you cursed Gird, you haters of trees, you erred; he died beloved of the gods."

"And his line died with him." One of the iynisin came closer; Aris could not see that the others moved. "Only sunlight spared him the full power of the curse, but that much held. And he ventured out only near dawn . . . it is long until dawn, mortals, and no sunlight will save you."

Aris felt a burst of gaity, unexpected and irrational. "Then we shall have to save ourselves," he said. "With the gods' help, if they find us worthy of aid."

"You cannot stand against *us*," the iynisin said. "See — " He pointed to the cluster of trees around the spring, where the horses were tied. Beyond, on the brow of the hollow, all the iynisin pointed downward. Aris stared: in the light he and Seri made, the trees shriveled, twisting in on themselves; their wood groaned and split. The new green leaves blackened, as if scorched. Under the trees, all the little green things that sheltered there shriveled as well. In the trees, one of the horses made a noise Aris had never heard. He felt Seri's back shiver against his; his sword felt loose in his grip as sweat ran cold down his sides.

"You call yourself a healer," another iynisin called. "Heal *that*, boy." They all laughed, a sound so close to beautiful that it hurt the ears worse than simple noise. Aris's hands itched, then burned; his healing magery demanded that he do something. But he could not go to the trees or the horses without leaving Seri, and he would not leave her. Could he do anything at a distance? He flung his power outward, toward the trees, but if it worked at all, it was the flurry of wind that whirled dead leaves from dead stems.

Not that way. The voice in his mind sounded impatient, like a master whose prentice had just done something wrong for the fifth time. I've never done this before, he thought back at it. *Think!* it bellowed. "Father Gird!" Aris said, almost squeaking in surprise.

"He can't help you," the iynisin said. The others laughed and sang, "He's dead . . . dead . . . dead . . . " And on that refrain they came forward, their black shadows streaming away behind them. Aris had just time to think what a ridiculous way this was to die, when he felt Seri lunge away from his back, and he nearly fell backwards into her. That stagger saved him; the blade aimed at his throat missed, and he had his own back up by then. He had not had as much training in weapon skills as Seri, but she had insisted that he go beyond the basics required of all yeomen.

His sword clashed on three; he was too busy to be scared, but a corner of his mind insisted he had no chance against so many. He had no time to remember exactly what he'd been taught. He had to thrust, swing, and thrust again; an iynisin blade slid past too fast for his response and he felt it burn along his side. He sagged to one knee; another blade caught his swordarm, slicing deep; his fingers opened, and the sword fell. He heard Seri gasp, and a dark form leaped above him. He grabbed a boot, and yanked; the iynisin fell, cursing, kicked back then scrambled out of reach. His hands itched, intolerably: he had no strength to withhold the healing magery. It leapt from hand to hand, almost brighter than his magelight, scalding first his wounded arm, then burning along his bones to reach his wounded side. With an intolerable wrench, his rib reknit itself, and the organs within returned to health. *So that's what Father Gird meant*, he thought, reaching for the sword.

Battle had now passed beyond him, for they had Seri backed to the rockface, her sword dancing in her own light, ringing a wild music off her attackers' blades. Her face had a withdrawn expression, showing neither fear nor anger. Aris ran forward, noticing how his light threw the iynisin shadows back into themselves, caught between the two lights. He thrust clumsily at the first black-cloaked back he saw, wasting no time in challenge. Seri had told him often enough he should spend more time in grange and barton: he would admit she was right, if they lived. This close he could see the blood on her clothes, sense the heaviness in her legs. He did not wait for Gird's admonition. To send his healing to Seri was the same as healing himself; he hardly slowed his attack on a second iynisin while closing her wounds.

They turned upon him again, but he fought through the ring to her side, taking another slashing blade across his shoulders. This, as he set his back to the rock, repaid his healing of it with a pain the double of its cause. One corner of his mind wanted to think about that: to wonder at the discovery that he could heal himself, to consider why it hurt, when none of those he healed had ever complained of pain. Between him and this curiosity stood the memory of Gird, who would not put up with nonsense in the middle of a fight. First things first, the old man would have said.

"I thought they'd killed you," Seri said. Then, before he could answer, she said, "Shift sides." She lunged forward, and he slithered sideways behind her. He had come up on her right, her strong side; she needed him at her left.

"I, too," Aris said, trying to look sideways and to the front at the same time. He wished he'd practiced whatever it was she'd just done to make an iynisin lose its blade. Something slashed the back of his hand, and he dropped the sword again. His tendons and bones screeched their fury at his clumsiness as the magery pulled them back into place and knit them into strength; in the meantime, the dagger in his left hand had shattered. He snatched frantically at the fallen sword, and got it up just in time to save Seri from a killing thrust to the side.

The analytical corner of his mind decided that the pain was healthy after all; it was the compaction of all the pain normally felt during normal healing. As healer, he had used his magery to lift such pain from those he healed; part of his exhaustion came from absorbing that pain. But he could not do this for himself. Better, the analytical function went on, like a prosy lecturer who does not realize that outside the classroom a riot has started, better to mend the real damage than soothe the pain, if that is the choice.

"ARIS!" Seri's shout brought him out of that, to see the black-cloaked iynisin fleeing through the twisted trees and over the rim of the hollow. From behind them, above the rock-face, a light stronger than their own held all starlight at its core. It was that, and not their fighting, that the iynisin had fled.

● Chapter Seventeen

Although Luap had been startled to find Aris's note, he realized that it might be wiser to bring up the idea of moving the mageborn when Seri and Aris were not in the city. They could only confuse the issue, and he had not yet formed a plan for convincing Aris to leave Seri behind. First convince the Council, and then talk to Aris. He rolled and unrolled a scroll as he thought about it. The details of the plan he had rehearsed so long flicked through his mind. How long, he wondered, would Aris be gone? Should he press for a meeting today? He thought not. Any appearance of hurry would plant some of those peasant hooves firmly in their muddled minds, ox-like. He remembered how it had been with his first version of Gird's Life.

He waited until the next regular meeting, two days later. The younglings, as he thought of them, had not returned. Some had noticed a column of smoke from far away, but that could have been anything. It was the season for storm-lighted grass fires, he reminded the worriers. And he had the feeling that they were unhurt, no matter what the smoke meant . . . they would reappear when they were ready, cheerful and sturdy as always. And inconvenient, no doubt.

The meeting began on a sour note, because a complaint of witchcraft had been referred from a grange-court. A group of sheepfarmers insisted that a mageborn boy had cursed their flock, causing all the lambs to be born dead. They had beaten the boy, who had responded with an obvious burst of magery, setting a hayrick afire. The local Marshal had saved the boy, but wasn't sure the first accusation was correct — and the boy, he said, would never completely recover from the beating. He had come, with the boy and two of the sheepfarmers, to Fin Panir to "settle this once and for all," as he put it. Luap winced; this would make the Marshals edgy about anything to do with mageborn.

231

He watched the sheepfarmers, tall husky men in patched tunics, sit on the edge of the bench in the meeting room, as far from the mageborn boy as they could. He didn't entirely blame them. It was hard to judge the boy's age — Luap guessed about twelve — because of his strangeness. He had mismatched eyes, one that slewed wide, and a constant tremor that erupted in a nervous jerk to his head at intervals. The eye that looked ahead had an expression Luap had never seen before, cool and calculating it seemed, though his mouth dripped spittle when his head jerked. The Marshal, balding and scrawny (had he really been the one who saved Gird from being trampled that time?), explained that the boy had had a bad name in their vill from the beginning. And it was his limp — not the slewed eye or the tremor — that resulted from the beating.

The farmers' testimony came in slow, difficult bursts of thick dialect; Luap knew they resented the questions he asked, but he had to know what they said to keep accurate notes. They knew their sheep, they kept repeating, and while it's true that sheep come into the world looking for a way back to the high pastures, they'd had a fair crop of lambs every year until this lad took a dislike to 'em, and for nothing worse than being told to keep away from Sim's daughter who was carrying her first and feared the evil eye. They knew he'd cursed the sheep because he said so — or at least he gabbled a string of nasty-sounding stuff that must have been a curse, and right then old Fersin's best ewe bloated up and died. Within a day, anyway, and it wasn't the season for death-lily, neither. Then the ewes started dropping lambs too soon, dead lambs, all of 'em, as if someone had fed them bad hay with birthbane in it, but no one had. Wasn't any birthbane nearer than a day's ride.

The Council looked at the Marshal — one of many named Seli, called for convenience Bald Seli — and he shrugged. "They called me in when the first ewe died, and accused this boy. I said don't be calling down evil you don't need — that ewe could've eaten something. None of 'em knew what the words meant, that he used. And they had no proof he was mageborn, only that he showed up years back with no family, and a scrap of good cloth for a cloak. Then the lambs started coming, all dead. They didn't call me; I heard from young — well — one of 'em's son, a junior yeoman. Thought I should know, he said. I went up there and found they'd pounded this boy so hard they'd broken bones, and then he'd set the hay on fire. The way I understand Gird's law is if the boy did magery first, he's wrong, but if he was hurt first, he could use magery to defend himself."

"Burning hay's not defense," muttered one of the farmers, as if he'd said it before.

"It made you let go of him," the Marshal said, as if he'd said that before, too.

"Is he truly mageborn?" asked Luap. The boy flicked him a malevolent glance that sent shivers down his back. Mageborn or not, the boy was wicked.

"I don't know," Bald Seli said. "He won't say. Isn't there some way to tell?"

Everyone looked at Luap. Would they realize that it was a use of magery to detect magery, and thus required a breaking of the law to detect a possible breaker of the law? No, irony was beyond them. He thought of sending for Arranha, but decided against it. He let a little of his power come forth, a mere trickle, and spread it as a net, imagining a silvery web before him. If the boy had mageborn blood, and such power, it should color that web. He leaned toward the boy.

"Are you mageborn?" he asked quietly. The boy stared past him, his skew eye to one side and his focussed gaze to the other. Luap turned to Bald Seli. "Can he answer questions? Has he ever talked with people in your vill?"

"Oh, aye," the Marshal said. "He never said much, but he made shift to ask for food, and answer yes or no. He didn't have our accent, but we could understand him."

"No, ye didn't!" The boy's voice was a peculiar skirl, rising and falling with no relation to the sense of the words. "Ye never understood me. Me. Never. Ye ask am I mageborn — I'm more'n mageborn. . . . " His words fell into a gabble Luap could not understand. The two farmers cringed against the wall.

"Careful, sir, he's doin' it again. He'll be cursin' the whole Fellowship next — "

To Luap it seemed that the boy's gabble was that of one who could not control his voice, like the very old who sometimes lost words and strength all at once. It did not sound as he had imagined cursing to sound, but the boy's cold gaze made him uneasy. He felt nothing in his net of magery to make him think the boy was mageborn — but he was not sure he wasn't, either. The babble died away; the boy licked the spittle off his lips with an eagerness that frightened Luap again. He wondered what Gird could have made of this; it was beyond him.

Cob came up with their solution. "Take him into the High Lord's Hall," he said. "And get Arranha. If it's a curse, that'll be the place to take it off. We'll know what we're dealing with."

Luap did not want to go, but he knew he must. He watched two Marshals carry the boy, whose tremors and twitches seemed less a struggle to escape than the way his body worked. Arranha met them at the Hall doors, and seemed no more upset by this than any of the problems people had brought him. He looked at Luap.

"He's mageborn, in part, but he was also born flawed. Both in his magery and in himself."

"Did he curse the sheep?" one of the farmers asked.

"I don't know," Arranha said. He asked the boy the same question, but got no reply. "Bring him up to the altar," he said then, "and we'll see if the god can shed light on our dilemma."

But as they approached the altar, the boy exploded in wild squeals and convulsive movements so strong the Marshals could hardly hold him. "He's frightened," one of them said. "Maybe he thinks we sacrifice people."

The farmers muttered, and Luap thought he heard one of them say "Only a mageborn would think of that."

"Put him down, then," Arranha said. They laid the boy down as gently as they could, for all his thrashing about, but he began beating his head on the stone floor. "We need Aris," Arranha said. He laid his hands to either side of the boy's head, but instead of quieting the boy screamed, a piercing noise that echoed in the high vaults of the Hall. Then he twisted around and caught Arranha's thumb in his teeth. Luap leapt forward, as did others, and somewhere in the struggle to unlock the boy's teeth from Arranha's thumb, the boy quit breathing. No one quite knew when, or why.

After that, and its daylong aftermath of confusion, grief, and anger, Luap expected nothing but trouble when he introduced his idea the next day. He led up to it as carefully as he could, explaining how a distant land could let his people learn to use their skills to benefit others, but he was sure their minds were full of the boy's malicious grin as he bit down on Arranha's thumb. When he paused, he heard exactly the disapproving murmur he had expected.

To his surprise, Raheli stood. The murmur stilled. Everyone peered to see Gird's daughter.

"I believe him," she said. Then she looked at Luap, eye to eye, gaze to gaze. "I believe him," she said more softly, and silence lay heavily on them. "My father — Gird —" As if they did not know, he thought. "Gird saw good in him; he was spared to serve Gird's Fellowship." In a long pause, no sound broke the stillness; he saw her take a long breath and wondered what would follow. "What is the reward of a faithful luap?" she asked. None answered. She looked around. "I will tell you, then," she said. "A faithful luap, one who serves without enjoying power, one who stands beside, in the place of, the inheritor, shall be recognized at last by the one he serves. He shall stand before him, and be given his reward, the respect of the people. This is Gird's luap: Gird will determine his reward."

Luap blinked; that could be taken two ways, and one of them he felt as a blade at his throat. "In the meantime," Raheli went on, "we can give our respect. I believe him, that he will take his folk to a far place and not breed up an army of invasion. You know I have not trusted him in the past. If his stronghold were nearer, I might be less willing to trust him now. But I believe he means what he says, and I believe the distance will enforce a truce between our peoples. My father wanted all to live in peace, but he himself could not find a way to let the mageborn learn to use their powers aright. That boy yesterday — if he had been brought up in a distant land, he would never have caused the trouble he did here. Arranha and Luap would have recognized something wrong in him. I believe Luap in this — that Gird agreed to let them go, and to this end." She sat down, and in a moment the murmur began again, this time in a wholly different mood.

For that, and for some other reason he did not fully understand, when the Marshal-General called on him again, he found himself speaking with less forethought and grace than usual.

"Marshal Raheli has said more than I would claim — that boy frightened me. It's true that I think our young people are best trained elsewhere — some place where we can be sure their power does no harm, that they have control of it, and know how to use it for good. But that boy — Marshals, I cannot claim to understand that."

"But if you had such a child, in your distant place, you would not let him come back here to cause trouble, would you?"

"No." He shuddered at the thought. "I don't know what we'd do — but we would not let him loose on the world."

"What about Arranha's thumb?" asked another Marshal. Many of them, Luap knew, liked the old man even though they would not follow his god. Luap shook his head.

"We don't know. If Aris were here, I'm sure he could heal it. But Garin is not as skilled, or as powerful. Arranha says if the Sunlord wants him healed, he will be healed, but he's feverish this morning."

Bald Seli had attended the Council, though his sheep-farmers had already headed home. Now he spoke up. "Maybe I should have let them kill him, 'stead of bringing such trouble on us."

Glances flicked at Luap, each a minute but definite blow. "Maybe — but I think you did right," Cob said. "You were trying to be fair; that's what mattered. And I'll agree with Raheli Gird's daughter, that if the mageborn had some safe place to teach their children, we might not have problems like this. At least not with the mageborn. It's not Luap's fault that the boy went wrong; for all we know he was cursed from birth."

To Luap's surprise, the other Marshals slowly came around to the same decision, and for much the same reasons. No one wanted to say good riddance to the mageborn — he was not even sure they thought that inwardly. Instead, the boy and his uncontrolled powers became the reason to agree that the mageborn needed a place to be trained properly. And they trusted Luap and Arranha to oversee that training and determine who might come back to the eastern lands.

"Will you take everyone? All the mageborn?" asked Bald Seli finally.

Luap shook his head. "I will take all who want to come, and try to persuade the younger ones that it's best. But some are too old, at least until we have established a settlement. Most of you know Lady Dorhaniya, for instance: she will certainly not come at first. Others are happy here, and get along well with those who are not mageborn — either they have no magery, or they are content not to use it. Unless you demand it, I expect they will choose to stay. Those who have little mageborn heritage, and whose families have no other mageborn blood, will almost certainly stay."

"I like that," Bald Seli said. "I remember old Gird saying we needed most to get along with each other; I'd hate to see that dream abandoned."

"So we'll give you all the troublemakers," Cob said to Luap with a grin, "and keep all the good ones — except you and Arranha, of course. And I suppose young Aris will come with you?"

Luap didn't want to start on that. "I thought to invite all mageborn who wanted to come —"

"But no others?" asked Raheli.

There was the crux of it. "I hardly thought any but mageborn would *want* to come," Luap said carefully. "Surely it would be as strange for them as a society wholly without magery is for the talented among us."

"But who'll do the work you mageborn don't know how to do?" asked Bald Seli. "Your folk don't know cooking and building and such, do they? They couldn't yoke a span of oxen and use a plough. . . ."

Luap nodded. "Some of those I think will want to leave are half-bloods, as I am . . . remember that I was fostered among farmers; I farmed, before the war." From the look on Bald Seli's face, he didn't quite believe it. Luap let a little humor seep into his voice, as he broadened his accent. "Aye, Var, coom up there; steady, Sor. . . ." His hands clutched imaginary plough handles, and his use of the traditional names for oxen brought smiles to more than one face. He grinned at Bald Seli. "My foster-father had me make my own yoke, same as anyone else. I've no doubt there are better farmers among you, but I made my crops and paid my field-fee and fed my family from my own work."

"I thought you'd been brought up in a big house." That was Kevis, who knew Dorhaniya.

"Only as a small boy. Then it was off to the farm, and no more big house for me until I came here." Luap glanced around the room. "I won't say all of us are farmers, or have such skills, but even for those who don't, it won't hurt them to learn." A shuffle of feet at that, agreement too strong for silent nodding. "We won't have to take the farmers and crafters you need here." Phrasing it that way, it could seem he was concerned for the welfare of those left behind. Which he was, in a way.

"But if someone wanted to come — I'm thinking, Luap, that if Aris goes with you, Seri will want to go too. You can hardly expect to separate those two."

"I wouldn't forbid it, certainly." Certainly not now, not when it could cause the failure of the whole plan. "But we don't want youngsters who wish they had magic powers wasting their time out there, when they could be learning good crafts here." Others nodded, seeing the point of that. "As well, since it is for our people to learn to use magery, it could be more dangerous for those without it. What I'm thinking of is more — more an outpost, say, where our people go for special training. When they have it, some of them — if you permit — will no doubt want to come back, and use their powers for good purposes." More dubious looks at that, eyes shifting back and forth under lowered brows. All the better: if they forbade mageborn to return, then it was not *his* fault that the peoples sundered.

"What about the archives?" asked another Marshal. "How can you keep the archives and lead your settlement?"

Luap relaxed. This was something he had planned carefully. "We have many good scribes now, those who can not only copy a text accurately, but understand how to organize the archives. I can't do both jobs — certainly not in the first few years out there — but I will always be available for questions. Frankly, I think my successors — those I will recommend — are as skilled as I am, if not more skilled. I will continue to write, of course, but I doubt you'll miss my contributions."

"But are these scribes Marshals?" asked the same man.

"No," Luap said. "Although there are at least three who have been yeoman-marshals and might qualify for the new training, if you felt it important. Certainly there are advantages in having an Archivist who is also a Marshal . . . even though I'm not."

"As good as," Raheli said. "We've granted you Marshal's blue, and the authority within the archives. I, for one, would prefer an Archivist to have Marshal's training."

The Marshals discussed that for a time, and Luap realized that they had made their decision, made it far more easily than he had ever expected. They would argue about when he should go, and who should be in charge of the archives after him, and how often he should report . . . but they were letting him go.

So he told Arranha that evening, trying to cheer him up. Arranha's thumb had swollen to twice its size, and a red streak ran up his arm. Suriya, the woman Aris had worked with in herblore, had come to poultice it, but so far without effect.

"She didn't have to tell me it was a bad bite," Arranha said. He sat with his eyes almost closed and the tense expression of real pain on his face. "I knew that, from the malice on his face, the way he ground his teeth on it, the way I felt."

"I wish Aris were here." Luap tried to sit still; he knew that Arranha needed quiet, restful companions.

"I, too. Young Garin has a lovely voice, but not a tithe of Aris's healing power. He eased the pain awhile . . . suggested I have Bithya in, that girl Aris worked with . . . but I'll wait. Perhaps I won't need her."

"Do you want us to send after Aris? Although I don't even know for certain which way he went."

"No . . . no, don't trouble the lad. He needs this chance to show what he can do somewhere else, and if the gods don't choose to send him back . . . " Arranha's voice faded. Luap felt a stab of worry. The old man could die of this, and then what? He needed him; they all needed him. Mageborn and peasant alike, they needed his wisdom, his determination to find the light in any tangled darkness.

"Rest now," he said to Arranha. "Is there anyone or anything . . . ?"

"No . . . don't bother."

Luap wondered if anyone else might help. Raheli, he remembered, had had a parrion of herblore. When he found her, she shook her head. "The woman Aris studied with knows more than I did, she and her daughter both. We talked about it."

"There's nothing more — ?"

"Not without taking his hand off, and that's chancy, as you know. Sometimes it saves lives, but some die anyway."

"I thought of sending for Aris, but we don't know where he went, and Arranha says not to."

"Arranha's getting feverish. But you're right, we don't know where Aris is, and we have no way to find him." Rahi sighed. "It seemed like such a good idea, giving Aris his chance to travel and test his healing — and he and Seri might make a good partnership, if they had time together — but now I wish we'd waited." She stalked restlessly about the room for a moment, then said, "Well — and when do you think you'll start resettling your people?"

"I don't know. I'd — you know Arranha and I had talked about it?" She nodded. "I depended on his advice, but now — "

"Now you may have to make all the decisions yourself. I hope not, for your sake as well. What will you do first?"

"Take others to see it. Start thinking how to make it workable — we should grow our own food, for one thing, and not have to transport it from here. There'll be plenty of work, hard work, to make it feasible."

She nodded. "There's something else: you need to think which mageborn to move first, and whether you want to gather them somewhere before you take them. Supplies for the first year or two, until your crops take hold. . . . "

"Supplies, yes." Luap grimaced. "Well — I did it for Gird; I ought to be able to do it now. But I don't even know how many mageborn there are, or how many will come."

But the familiar rhythm of planning comforted him in the days following, as Arranha grew sicker, the swelling worse. He began making lists: seed grain, vegetable seeds, tools for farming and tools for making tools. He knew of no mageborn smiths . . . could he hire a smith to set up there? And if he could, with what could he pay a smith's high fees? He found a master smith, and began asking the necessary questions; smiths were notoriously slow in giving answers. He went back to his lists. They would need a few looms — with skilled craftsmen and enough wood, they could easily copy the pattern looms. He paused, thinking. He had never worked wood himself . . . and that forest was very different . . . did that matter? Another question to ask a craftsmaster. He needed to know more about the skills of the people he would take — how many mageborn could weave, cook, plough, reap? So far as he knew, the work that needed doing — the work that would keep them alive — had never been done by magery.

Several times a day he checked on Arranha, who was unfailingly cheerful but visibly weaker each visit. To his surprise, others with no mageborn blood at all also visited. Rahi delayed her return to her grange and scoured the archives for anything on herbal treatments. Dorhaniya worked her way up the hill and arrived breathless and faint; Luap was afraid she would have a fatal attack as well. He insisted that she stay overnight in the palace; Elis agreed, and the next day Luap hired a cart to take her home. The men who had listened to Arranha's many lectures on light and wisdom came to stand by his door, peering in shyly but unwilling to intrude on a sick man.

Luap felt a deep guilt he could not explain. He knew it had not been his fault: the boy would have bitten anyone; he had been mindlost if not possessed by some evil. He knew it was not his fault Aris was gone — Rahi had confessed that she and the Rosemage and Arranha himself had connived at that. He knew it was not his fault that he lacked the healing magery. But he felt guilty nonetheless . . . somehow it *was* his fault — his fault that Gird's dream had not come true, and his fault that Arranha suffered for it. In reaction, he felt that his irritation was pardonable when one of the scribes made a mistake or spilled the ink. He got a morbid satisfaction out of scolding someone he would not ordinarily have scolded, and then lashing himself for being short-tempered.

He clung to his lists, and shared them with the Rosemage and Rahi. The Rosemage pointed out that he should require the mageborn to pay their own way, if they could: he was not a king, so he could not be expected to fund the expedition. Some of them were still wealthy; nearly all of them had something to contribute.

"They'd better," Rahi said lazily, leaning back on the cushions of a bench in the scribe's room. It was late night, and the scribes had long since ceased work. "If they don't have something to contribute, they'll starve."

"More than skills: money," the Rosemage said. "Clothes, tools, dishes, all that."

Luap had a sudden panic. "How are we going to transport all that? Either we have to take it to the cave, and try to stuff it in the chamber, or we have to take it into the High Lord's Hall — that doesn't seem right." He had a vision of the chamber choked with boxes, bags, sacks, bales of household gear . . . of the mess creeping across the floor of the great hall. Yet it had to be done: they couldn't make everything out there.

"It will work," the Rosemage said. "You don't have to do it all yourself."

"No, but — " But it had been his idea, his plan, and his place . . . his dream, in place of Gird's. If it came true, it would be his responsibility; he could not deny that. Gird had known; Gird had not started a war and then gone home to twiddle his thumbs and watch how it went.

"Scary, isn't it?" asked Rahi with surprising understanding.

241

He looked at her, and she smiled. "Back before you joined, that very first battle, Norwalk Sheepfolds . . . remember it from the archives?"

"Of course," Luap said. "Were you there? I thought — "

"No, I wasn't there. But it scared Gird — what he'd started. He wanted it; he thought it was the only way. But when it came, when he saw what it meant, that he could never go back and things would never be as they were, that scared him. And I thought that was what you were feeling."

"Yes," said Luap. "I suppose I am. I believe we have to do it, that it's the only way." The undefined warning the elves had given rose from his memory; should he tell them about it? No, for he could not tell them what he did not know himself. "If I'm wrong — if I forget something — "

"You can always come back for it. You will be coming back quarterly at first anyway, to report to the Council and check on the new Archivist."

"That reminds me." Luap rummaged among the scrolls on his desk, glad to be distracted with something more pleasant. "I think we should keep a copy of the records out there, as well, and a copy of my records there should be transferred to Fin Panir each year. You know we found that mice and damp had damaged many of the old scrolls. This way, we would have complete records in two different places."

Rahi snorted. "You would have all the world scribes, if you could. Think of the hours of work — "

"Yes, but good records are important. Without them, we wouldn't have been able to clear up the land disputes of the past few years, for instance. And if we had better records of the early mageborn invasion, we might know more about what happened to the magery, and why the transfer pattern is graved in the floor of the High Lord's hall."

"Very well, but you'd best take more farmers than scribes or you'll be hungry."

"What are you going to do about Aris?" asked Rahi suddenly.

"Do? We can't find him; we have no idea where he's gone. We can only hope he comes back before Arranha dies."

"I didn't mean that: I meant about taking the mageborn away. Do you think Aris will go with you?"

"Of course he will," Luap said. "He's mageborn — more mageborn than I am. He has the most useful of mageries."

"And Seri?" asked Rahi.

Luap shrugged. "She's welcome, of course; I said that before. I don't think it's the best place for her; I doubt any without magery will find it comfortable. But we all know how attached she is to Aris."

The Rosemage stretched and grinned at him. "Yes — though you did your best to separate them, didn't you?"

Luap felt his ears getting hot. "I thought it would be easier later, yes. Evidently you two don't agree, and I'm willing to admit I was wrong about them. So I suppose I'll have a peasant-born Marshal as well as a mageborn healer — "

" — And Marshal," Rahi said. "Aris will probably pass the Council when Seri does."

"Is he keeping up his drill that well? I wasn't aware. Two Marshals, then, one of each. That should convince the more stiff-necked on the Council that we're being well watched and not up to mischief."

The Rosemage scowled. "Nothing will convince some thick-heads. And they may not want to let Aris go; he's become very popular. If he does much healing on this journey, he will be under pressure to stay here. If Seri supports that — "

Luap shivered. "I hope not. Though to tell you the truth, if only he and Seri come back in time to save Arranha, I would trade that for having him in the new land."

● Chapter Eighteen

The light strengthened, spread around them. "Well met, kinsmen!" came a ringing cry, so like the iynisin that Aris flinched. Then he realized that this held the true music.

"Elves," whispered Seri. "But we aren't their kinsmen — "

"Those are," Aris said, fighting for breath. The aftereffects of healing clogged his mind; he wanted to fall in a heap and sleep. "The iynisin — " But the elves were dropping lightly down from above now, bringing their own light, in which their expressions showed clearly: astonishment and consternation.

"But you're not — " said the first, then his mouth shut in a straight line.

"Who are you?" asked the next, after a similar look and recoil. "How have you made that light? Is this some new human magery? Are you in league now with the dark cousins?"

Aris had not known he could make such light, and now he did not know why it vanished, with a sudden shifting of shadows. "I am mageborn," he said. "But— "

"I am not mageborn," Seri interrupted. "I am a Marshal-candidate, from Fin Panir, and I have no idea why the light came." She still burned with it, brighter than their elflight but as steady. "But we are not in league with those creatures; they attacked us as we camped."

"In truth . . . " What must be the leader of this group appeared now, striding down the slope and around to confront them. Elflight, Aris realized, cast none of the harsh shadows his magelight had thrown; its radiance softened the shadows of Seri's light, though it did not dim its brilliance. "You say you were attacked, by many?"

"Yes," Seri said. Aris glanced about but saw no bodies. He thought he had killed at least one of those he struck from behind . . . had they carried them away?

"If you were attacked," the elf leader said with such perfect clarity that it seemed an attack of language, "then why do we see blood only on your blades and clothes, while you stand unwounded? Or are you such mighty warriors that you can without danger engage a party of iynisin which might daunt even our band? For that matter, where learned you that name, which is not commonly used by mortal men?"

Around them now were the elves, all armed for battle as he had never seen elves: terrible and grim they looked, in the light of their magery. He saw some of them look at the trees the iynisin had cursed, and knew they would not forgive such an injury. He heard the cries of one who found their horses, and sang the news to the leader in that elvish tongue he had not learned. They will not believe us, he thought to himself. Here we are unhurt — they will believe we were with allies. His heart contracted. The elves had never loved or trusted the mageborn, and with good reason.

"Aris healed us," Seri said. She wiped her blade on a hanging shred of her tunic. "If you look, you will see he could not heal our clothes." Then she looked more closely at the smear on the cloth. "By — it has silver in it, this blood! Or is it your light?"

"Let me see," said the leader, stepping closer to her. He held out his hand for her sword; she handed it over as if to a Marshal, hilt first, across her fist. His brows rose, but he took it courteously, then looked closely, then sniffed it. "Well," he said. "It is indeed iynisin blood, lady, so whether it came from a quarrel among friends or a meeting of enemies, we give you thanks for it." He passed the sword to the others, each of whom examined it. The leader looked at Aris. "You *healed*, she said. You have the healing magery of your forefathers?"

"Yes, sir," Aris said. He held out his own blade. "And though I fought with less skill, I did spill some of their blood." His blade, too, the leader took and examined, then returned it, as another elf handed Seri back her blade. Aris wiped his own, and sheathed it, under those watchful eyes. When he looked up, the elf spoke.

"So you would say that you and this lady were beset by iynisin, and fought them off, and you with your power healed your wounds?"

"That is what happened, yes."

"A mageborn and a peasant together? A peasant with the power to call light? And it *happens* that iynisin come upon you in this place?"

Aris had no chance to answer; Seri broke in. "Yes, that is true. We came from Fin Panir, to — " She stopped, and

245

glanced at Aris. What they had been discussing was no business of elves. The elf waited, brows raised.

"Seri and I were friends before we came to Fin Panir," Aris said. "Before Gird died. I came to ask him to allow me to use my magery to heal, and he granted that, but put us both in training there. We have little time together — "

"So you rode a day's journey away to find privacy?" The elf's question implied only one use of such privacy.

"No, we're on a longer journey." Aris gestured to his pack, which one elf was examining with care. "I have been granted permission to travel, and test my healing in other places; Seri is my — well — supervisor. The Council wishes a peasant-born to make sure I don't misuse my powers."

"They let a friend have this right?"

"I'm a Marshal-candidate," Seri said. In her voice was the certainty that a Marshal-candidate would tolerate no misdoings from anyone, least of all a friend.

"And his lover."

"No." Seri shook her head. "We have never been lovers; we don't need to be lovers."

"Ah. Rare in humans, though I have heard of it. Well, then, young mortals who are not lovers, can you explain how you called upon yourselves the malice of iynisin, or why you called on us with your light? We thought it was elflight, and you beleaguered elves: we came to your aid. We had seen magelight before — " Here the elf looked at Aris. "We would not have come for that, but this light — " he gestured at Seri. " — is something we do not know and mixed with yours might be elflight." This time more gently, he asked her. "Are you sure you do not know how you called it?"

In that lessening of tension, with the elf's change of tone, Aris felt exhaustion sapping his strength again. Only immediate danger could keep him alert now, after such a day and night, after the healing power he had poured out. He heard Seri's explanation through a thick fog, and only realized he had fallen when someone caught him. Not Seri; he knew her hands. These were as alien as tree limbs: cold, strong, but not ungentle.

" — He's like this after healing sometimes," he heard her say. "Keep him warm — " He could not argue, but he could hear what they said, as they wrapped him in a blanket and laid him aside, while the leader still talked to Seri, and one of them stirred the fire and set the kettle back on it.

He listened to the voices, their sweet chiming voices and Seri's warm, practical peasant burr, comfortable as an animal's shaggy hide. She said nothing about Luap, but talked freely about her own training, Aris's training, the changes of policy that everyone discussed. Gird's legacy had been a government with few secrets, its issues argued openly in every market in Fintha. When the kettle boiled, he was able to drink a mug of the hot herbal brew, which opened his eyes and let him see that Seri's light had, at some point, gone out. Or back. She was telling the elf leader exactly what the iynisin had said, word for word as far as Aris could tell, and then describing the fight.

"I thought Ari had been killed; I'd been forced far enough away that I saw one sword go in — so I ran for the rockface. That way I had something at my back."

The elf leader nodded. "Wise — and this is your first real battle?"

"Yes . . . in the war, we were too young to do more than camp chores."

More raised brows. "You were too young to do camp chores, unless I read your age wrongly. But didn't you know your — Aris? — could heal his wounds?"

Seri shook her head. Her braid had come completely undone, and her hair looked like a wavering dark cloud. "No — he'd never healed himself before. We thought it worked only on others. When I saw him get up, I was as surprised as the iynisin. More, because they hadn't seen him; he came up behind them."

"I know why we didn't know I could," Aris said. His mind had caught hold of its familiar net of thought. They all turned to look at him. "It hurts — and the one time I tried it, that time I cut my hand on the sickle —"

"I remember," Seri said. "He was cutting wild grass for Gird's army," she said to the elves.

" — I thought to try it and it hurt a lot. So I quit."

"But it didn't hurt me," Seri said. "Or any of the others."

"No, and I think I understand that, too. You see —"

"Not now, Ari." Seri smiled to take the sting out of that. "You're not all the way awake yet." He was, but he wouldn't argue with her. If she wanted him to think it out somewhere else than with elves, he would. He sipped the bitter brew again, and wondered where her light had gone, and even more where it had come from. She shouldn't have been able to do that.

"What do you, young mortal, think of your friend's light?" That was the elf leader, pointing to him. Aris, in the midst of another sip, almost choked, and put the mug down.

"I don't know. I didn't know she could do it — I never heard of anyone coming alight but mageborn, and not all of them. And as you saw, her light was not the same color as mine."

"And you, she says, did not call light before: why this night, and not others? Did you never before need to see your way in the dark?" The sarcasm of the second question almost confused his answer to the first; perhaps Seri was right, and his wits lay more scattered than he thought. He hesitated, trying to gather them, before he answered, but the elves did not seem impatient. Only interested.

"We needed to see," he said finally. "Other times — it might have been useful, but I didn't really *need* it. Here — we felt the evil coming — "

"Did you call on the gods for aid?"

Had they? He could not quite remember. There had been a voice in his head — "Father Gird," he said. His voice chimed with Seri's, saying the same thing.

The elf leader frowned. "You're Gird's children? I thought only one of his children lived, a grown woman."

"Not really his children," Seri said, trying without success to smooth her hair. "But we called him Father Gird. Not to his face, it wouldn't have been respectful, but with each other."

"How old *were* you, when you left your homes?"

Aris tried to think. He wasn't entirely sure; the mageborn and the peasants reckoned age differently. "I had lost my front teeth," he said slowly. "I suppose we were — " He held up his hand. " — about this tall."

"Children!" the elf said. The elves spoke softly in their own language, a murmuring ripple, then the leader said, "So you called Gird your father?"

"Lots of people called him Father Gird," Seri said. "Or Gran'ther Gird."

"And you believe he spoke to you in your peril? How do you explain that?" Aris could not explain that, or the recurrent dreams he and Seri had had since Gird died. He shook his head. The elves spoke again to one another, and he tried to make sense of the beautiful sounds. He wished they would sing; he had heard elves sing at Gird's funeral.

248

He woke just at dawn, to find the elves standing in a circle around the two of them. Their elflight had drawn in around them, leaving Aris and Seri to the dawnlight. Seri looked as sleepy as he felt; in the cold predawn light, the dried blood on her clothes looked like smears of black mud. Aris scrambled up, uncertain of many things. The elven leader neither smiled nor frowned.

"We have no memory of any such as you," he said. "The blending of your lights last night . . . this is new. In all our memory, none of this lady's race has ever called such light, and we know no other living person with the healing magery among the mageborn." He looked at the cluster of trees, motionless now in their posture of anguish, blackened as if burnt, leafless, the ground beneath them ash-gray. "And there is the work of the iynisin, the un-singers, those who hate the living trees for the One Tree's choice. We found their blood on your blades . . . and I say we do not understand. We knew Gird, but we do not know you." The elves came together; their light brightened so that Aris could hardly see their faces. "We do not condemn you, for the iynisin blood you shed. But we do not commend you, for those trees which the iynisin blasted, and the creatures dead with them, and the spring now tainted. Heal that, if you can — if not, you have a long journey afoot, and the gods will deal with you."

The elves vanished, withdrawing their light with them; where they went, Aris could not see in the glare of the risen sun. He blinked; Seri came to him and put an arm around his shoulders. She was shivering; they both were. Around them, the new grass sprang, somewhat trampled but green and healthy; it stretched to the edge of the hollow. But the trees, and under the trees — all that was dead, not only dead but a death that held no promise of rebirth. Aris felt his mouth dry with fear as much as thirst. How could he heal that?

Gingerly, they moved into the twisted shadows of those twisted trees. The earth beneath felt dead, as if they walked on salt or iron filings. When they came to the horses — what had been the horses — Seri gave a choked cry and ran forward. Whatever magery the iynisin used had killed them as well, drawing them into strange unhorselike shapes as it worked, leaving the dead bodies hardly recognizable, the very hairs of mane and tail stiff as thorns. Aris moved past the horses to the spring, which the evening before they could have heard bubbling from here.

In its hollow, a plug of dirty wet earth like mucus, and a thin black stain along the line of the beck. It stank of death and decay, as disgusting a smell as the shambles in the lower market. Aris prodded the sodden earth with a stick that shattered in his hand. He was going to have to dig it out with his fingers. He shuddered; he did not want to touch the oozing slime. Behind him, he could hear Seri's boots scuffing the dead earth, the shriveled leaves. She was probably trying to do something about the horses, but he knew he had to clear the spring first. That was the earth's lifeblood.

He laid his hand just above the lowest part of the spring's hollow, trying not to smell it, and tried to feel his way into it. Nothing. Grimacing, Aris plunged his fingers into the cold, slimy mess and tugged. It felt worse than anything he'd ever touched. Gobs of cold stinking goo came off; he wiped the stuff from his hands on the ground beside the spring and reached in again. It's cursed, he thought to himself. There's nothing healthy in there at all; it's all gone wrong. Something warmer than the rest wriggled against his fingers and he almost cried out; when he yanked his hand free this time, he saw a dank tendril pull itself back into the muck.

Seri's hand on his shoulder felt as hot as a firebrand. "I hope Father Gird knows what he's doing," she said.

"He didn't do this," Aris said, wiping his hand on the dry earth again, and wishing he didn't have to put it back in there with whatever that was. "The iynisin did this." And us, he thought, because we came out here not knowing what we were doing.

"Can you heal it?" Seri asked, as calmly as if she were asking if someone could weave a fircone pattern.

"I'm trying," Aris said, putting his hand back on the damp hole. Was it any less slimy? Could he feel even a trickle of something that might be clean water?

"It doesn't look like it." Seri's face, when he glanced at her, gave no hint to any other meaning than the words themselves. "It looks as if you're digging muck out of a smelly hole — not healing a spring."

Aris felt a blinding rage, a white hot boiling fire that nearly escaped through his teeth. He clenched them, and looked at her through the flickering blaze. Her calm face . . . her eyes that were not looking at him, or the spring, or anything else. He saw the tears rise, glittering, in the early sun, and overflow; she did not even try to blink them away. His rage fled as suddenly as it had come. When he could get his breath back, he said "I can't reach my magery. You're right — I'm just digging and hoping."

"Aris!" She threw her arms around him so suddenly and so tightly that he lost his balance and they both nearly fell into the spring's hollow. "I'm *frightened*. I don't know what this means, what the iynisin were doing, what the elves meant — and the horses are dead and all the trees and there's no water and — "

She had never been frightened but once that he knew of; he had always relied on her. She had been awake last night when the iynisin came; she had fought with far more skill than he . . . and now she lay against him, shuddering all over like a frightened child. As they both were, he realized.

"I am too," he said. He could not even stroke her hair, not with his hands soiled by whatever curse the iynisin had laid on the spring. "I am, and I don't know what to do about it." For a long moment they huddled together. Oddly, saying aloud that he was frightened made the fright more manageable. It wasn't some nameless horror, some impossible alien presence: it was fright, the same ordinary fright that he had felt before in his life, worse perhaps because they were in real and not imagined danger.

As he thought this, warmth seemed to flow over him. He glanced up. The sun had risen well above the lip of the hollow by now, and its power seemed no less than it should be. He was frightened, hungry, tired . . . but alive, and warmer every moment. He shifted, and Seri too sat up.

"How silly," she said. "So that's what that kind of fright feels like. Ugh!" She shivered, but more as someone who steps unaware on spilled water than fear. "And it seemed to go on forever, but it couldn't have. . . . "

"No." Aris's hands had nearly dried. He looked at the moist hole, the gobs of wet muck he had torn out. "I wonder why I thought that would work. You were right; it needs real healing. And I can't."

"What if they come again?" Seri said. "It's daylight now; supposedly they can't come in daylight, but — "

Aris spread his dirty hands. "I don't know. We'll fight, I suppose, and if that's not enough, we'll die." Until he heard the words come out of his mouth, he did not know how serious he was. They might die; they might have died last night and if the iynisin came back they probably would. He didn't think the elves would come back to help them.

Suddenly it seemed ludicrous. Yesterday they had been

eager to leave Fin Panir, eager to ride out into the unknown and find adventure, and all in one night they'd had more adventure than he had ever imagined. And he was tired, hungry, filthy, and quite ready to spend the rest of his days playing scribe to Luap, if only he could get back there.

Or was he? He met Seri's eyes, to find the same speculative look coming back at him. She, too, had gotten more than she bargained for, but now she was coming to grips with it. He didn't want to go back and be Luap's scribe, the tame healer of the safe city, doling out dollops of power to close cuts and ease bruises and mend the odd broken bone. It wasn't contempt for those sick or hurt . . . it was simply that others could do that. Herblore and time would heal most of it, and the healers he'd been training could do the rest. No — he wanted to find out if there was something only he could do. He had wanted a challenge, and here it was, and he wanted to meet it. He felt a smile stretch his grimy face. Seri grinned back.

"We were idiots," she said. "We came out here expecting nothing worse than a stray thief, when we knew — we *should* have known — that these empty lands are empty for a reason. We were playing at being careful, and it nearly killed us. It's not maneuvers: it's real."

"Right." Aris stood up. The spring still stank; the trees still arched in anguish over them. "So how much water was left in the kettle when the elves left?" Very little, it turned out. Aris sloshed it thoughtfully back and forth, and did not pour it into the mug Seri held. "Wait," he said. "I'm thinking of something. Let's go up and see if there's dew on the grass."

Out of the hollow, the wide plain lay lush and green; the dew they could lick from the grass refreshed without satisfying. Aris looked back. In full daylight, the hollow looked even worse. They could not leave it like that, even though it meant spending another night far from any settlement. He hoped the dead trees would burn.

The column of smoke rose, oily and rank, from the dead horses and twisted trees. They had lighted it from their campfire, after carrying their remaining gear, including the kettle with its swallow or two of water, up out of the hollow. Seri, who had served with her grange's fire patrol, had told Aris which way it would burn, sunsetting, away from the city.

"And this season, with the new green, it should not go far, and be no worse than a storm-lighted fire."

It looked worse; the trees writhed in the fire as if they were still alive, popping and cracking and showering sparks. The smoke twisted, billowed, clear evidence to anyone as far as the horizon that something dire had happened. A back gust whirled it up Aris's nose; he coughed and shook his head. They waited; the fire burned away from them at last, the trees shattering into fallen coals. Without their shape, the hollow looked naked, vulnerable. Aris whispered an apology without realizing he'd done it until Seri looked at him.

"I was thinking of the Lady, of Alyanya," he said. "You remember what you told me, long ago — that the springs are sacred because that's where she gives her blood to the world?"

"Yes." Seri's ash-streaked face looked years older than the day before. He thought his probably did too. "And defiling a spring is like raping the earth itself. And all we can do is burn — " Her voice broke.

Aris looked away, blinking back his own tears. His gaze followed the smoke column into the sky; he grieved at its stain on what had been clean blue from one rim of the world to the other. It rose more gracefully now that it had consumed most of its tainted fuel, its black ugliness paling to gray as it burned slowly along the grass. "Come with me," he said finally, taking the kettle and starting back down the slope toward what had been trees.

"Wait, Ari — it's too hot." Seri caught at his arm. Then as if she had touched his mind instead, she moved with him. They said nothing more, even when the heat of fire beat on their faces, even when the coals they could not avoid scorched their boots. Aris found the spring's deep hollow surrounded by smouldering logs; he kicked one aside and knelt on the hot soil. The spring's outlet, first plugged by the iynisin's foulness, had burnt to a solid cake of muck in the fire. Aris tipped the kettle, as carefully as if pouring into a tiny cup. He knew no words to say, but he heard Seri chanting.

The first drop of water seemed to hang long in midair, sparkling in the light of the sun like a great jewel. Aris watched it hit the center of the original spring. It sat on the surface a moment, then made a tiny round spot of darkness. The next fell, and the next. Aris strained to hold the kettle steady, to have each drop fall exactly on the one before. He knew that was important, though not why. The sound of each drop falling echoed in his ears, as if they were hoofbeats, drumbeats, the tramp of armies . . . he had to keep the pattern, make the intervals regular. Drop by drop, he emptied the kettle and the dry, baked earth clogging the spring absorbed it.

When the last drop had fallen, and nothing happened, he started to shrug and stand. Then he felt his power return, as unaccountably as it had vanished. His hands itched and stung; he held them out over the single drop of moisture. Seri's hands gripped his shoulders; he felt her as a great reservoir of power, and drew upon it, trying to force a way past the obstruction. But it was like trying to heal a block of stone; he could tell he was doing something wrong. He sat back on his heels, enduring the torment of his unused power.

Then he realized . . . he had been trying *his* peoples' way, using force where violation had been the original wound. How could he use his power without repeating that violation? He tried to imagine it trickling out, as the water had, drop by drop, to be absorbed or not, as the spring — as the Lady chose. He cupped his hand gently over the damp spot, protecting it from the sun, the hot acrid air. A gust of cooler air brushed along his face. He looked up.

The smoke had shifted shape with the change in wind. Now it arched over him — over the spring — in almost the shape of a great gray horse. *Gird?* he thought. It could not be Gird's old horse . . . it was just smoke on the wind.

Thunder muttered; Seri's grip on his shoulders tightened. Another gust of cold wind made his skin roughen; he felt a sudden weakness as his power surged out of him as uncontrollably as a lightning bolt. He squeezed his eyes shut; when he opened them, rain stung his face. The sky had darkened; one of the spring storms, he thought, coming up unseen in the shadow of the smoke. Lightning flashed, so near that light and sound came together: he felt his teeth jar together. Rain fell harder, hissing on the hot coals that had been trees. Steam rose in swirls, blown by the wind. Perhaps the rain would waken the spring, when he had not. He huddled with Seri under the storm's lash, until it cleared as suddenly as it had begun. The last of the raindrops sank into that sterile soil; the surface seemed to dry almost instantly.

He felt a great tearing sadness. They had cleansed with fire, and the rain with water; he knew nothing else to do. He blinked the rain out of his lashes and looked up.

The horse standing across the hole that had once been a spring did not look like Gird's horse. It seemed made of air and cloud, storm and smoke, all the colors of the sky, and all the power of thunder. Its dark muzzle snuffed at the dry hole; its eyes accused. Aris found himself talking to it as if it were mortal.

"The iynisin cursed it; we tried to cleanse and heal . . . but I don't know how."

A sound between snort and grunt: a challenge. The delicate nostrils widened, sniffed at him, and over his shoulder to Seri. Then, with deliberation, one forefoot went into the hole. Aris could not see how deep; he could not look away from those eyes. He saw the quick withdrawal of the hoof, a flurry of mane and tail, then nothing as a final clap of thunder shook him to his face.

No rain followed; the sky arched unclouded overhead, with the sun halfway down the afternoon sky. In the arch of the hoofprint, as they watched, the damp earth darkened, sifted downward, and a line of silver appeared: the sky reflected in living water. Slowly, steadily, it widened to a circle, and the circle lifted to fill the hole. Aris felt something in himself that echoed that movement, something filling a hole he had not known was empty.

"Aris, look!" Seri tugged at his shoulder. He turned. Where there had been blasted, sterile soil, covered with ashes and the burnt remnants of trees, a few green leaves showed. It could not be; it was too soon. But there they were, looking exactly like young sprouts anywhere. Aris touched one lightly; he felt only the surging growth of a healthy young seedling just emerging from its sleep.

Seri reached back to touch the water in the spring; he wanted to stop her but was too late. She put her wet finger to her forehead, then the nearest seedling. "Alyanya's grace," she said. Aris echoed her. Whatever else had happened, Alyanya had chosen to restore her spring. The spring gurgled suddenly, almost a chuckle of amusement and content; its water overflowed the central hole and swept down the little channel, sweeping away ash and sticks. Aris wondered if they dared drink from it, or if that would be sacrilege; Seri had no such doubts, and with another brief prayer sank the kettle in the deepest part of the spring. "She doesn't want us dying of thirst and making another mess," Seri said. "Drink your fill."

The water tasted of water, clean and pure as any springwater.

255

Aris drank, and let it wash away the night's fear, the day's frustrations. When they had had enough, they went back to the gear they had left above the hollow. Not all had been destroyed in the fight, or in the fire; they had food enough for a day or so, and a change of clothes. Aris went to fetch another kettle of water, and found that the spring had swept the old channel clear as far as the deeper pool where they'd watered their horses the day before. He called Seri; they took turns bathing, with the other keeping watch above the hollow, and changed into clean clothes. Seri had washed her hair; it lay slicked to her head, braided tightly. Aris looked at the blood-stained rents in the clothes he'd been wearing. It was hard to believe that blood was his, that he had been wounded there, and there, and there, and yet was walking around in the sun with no wounds upon him.

"We should wash those before we mend them," Seri said, "but I don't know if it's right — "

"She's brought the water back, and it's — she might see it as another gift, our blood."

"It's smelly dirt, is what it is," Seri said. Aris looked at her, surprised. He had said something like that, long ago, when she'd tried to explain her peoples' rituals in building or reaping. Now she wrinkled her nose at him. "All right. I know better. But washing dirty clothes is not the same as ritually blooding a foundation."

"It might be, if we thought of it that way," Aris said.

"It's not the same. Else anyone could treat a spring as a common washpot, and claim to have a ritual in mind." She shook her head, and the first tendrils of her braid came loose. "But — we need to do it, and we'd best get on with it."

In the cold water of the larger pool, the dried blood melted into faint pink streaks and left rusty stains on the cloth. A smell of blood rose more strongly as the water soaked into the stains. Aris scrubbed at the gray shirt, the gray trousers, the blue tunic . . . he had bled more than he'd realized, and felt almost faint thinking of it. He did not look too closely at Seri's washing; he didn't want to know how much she had bled. Finally they had all the blood out that would come out, and wrung the clothes as dry as they could. Aris watched the clean springwater cut through the hazy pink, watched it clear gradually, in ripples and swirls, the last taint of blood from the pool. Alyanya must not be angry with them, if she kept the spring open.

They spread their clothes on the grass, up above the hollow, in the evening sunlight, and considered whether to start walking back to Fin Panir or spend the night near the spring. Aris yawned so, that Seri finally suggested napping awhile.

"You had no sleep last night," Aris said. "I had some — I'll watch first."

"You're half asleep already," Seri said. "You wouldn't be able to stay awake — " And in the end Aris curled up where he sat and fell asleep.

Sunlight woke them both. Aris stretched, blinked, and sat up. Why hadn't Seri wakened him? She was awake now, looking around with a puzzled expression. "I slept," she said. "I wasn't supposed to, but — "

"It's all right. We're here, we're alive." He felt completely rested, alert, better than he had felt in a long time, as if sleeping on the living earth had restored him. He stood, and looked down into the hollow. A thin haze of green covered the black scars of the fire; along the line of the brook, it thickened to a brilliant streak of emerald and jade. It had come back so quickly — how could that be? Was the damage done by the iynisin so superficial? He could not believe that; he had touched that earth, the agonized limbs of tortured trees — those had not been minor wounds. The elves had not thought them minor. So this recovery meant some power had intervened, restoring what it could not heal.

He felt an urge to go back to the spring one last time before they set out for Fin Panir. After they had eaten, he and Seri went down the slope, sniffing the fresh green smell of growing things that replaced the stench of death and burning from the day before. Even the horses' skeletons had crumbled, erasing the memory of their contorted, unnatural transformation and death. The spring rose, pulse after pulse of pure water trembling the surface, shaking the reflections of their faces as they leaned over it. Aris felt at one with it, with the power of Alyanya to bring life and growth, with the water and the growth of plants, with sunlight and the wind that blew through it, with Seri — as always with Seri.

When he looked up, two horses stood across from him, a bright and a dark bay.

● Chapter Nineteen

Two horses, where no horses had been. Aris shivered. Surely they should have heard horses walking up on them. One of the horses reached across the tiny trickle of water and nosed his hair. The other reached toward Seri. He and Seri looked at each other; he suspected her thoughts were the same as his. But neither spoke. As in a dream, he put out his hand, and the horse — his horse, the dark bay — nuzzled it. He turned away from the spring, and the horse followed. He put his saddle on it, as if he had the right, and the horse stood quietly, switching its long, untangled tail at flies. Seri, when he looked, was saddling the bright bay as if she'd done it for years. And the bridles — he had thought the bridles burned with the dead horses, but discovered the bridle — or *a* bridle — in his pack. It fit the dark bay as if made for it. Still without a word, he and Seri lashed their packs to the saddles, then mounted.

Aris turned the horse's head toward Fin Panir. It did not move. He thought about it. Was it a demon horse, sent by the iynisin? He could not believe that. But it had been sent by *someone*, he was sure. Perhaps he ought to be thinking what that someone wanted. He didn't really want to go back to Fin Panir now, he realized. He had something else to do, though he could not think what.

"I don't want to go back," Seri said. Her eyes sparkled; her cheeks had color again. "Let's go on, and see where these horses take us." She reined hers around, and it pricked its ears to the north, winterwards.

"Good idea." Aris rode up beside her. His horse strode off with a springy stride that made riding a pleasure. He knew he should be stiff and sore, but he wasn't. He felt he could ride forever. Seri's braid swayed to the movement of her horse. For a time they rode in silence. Aris puzzled over all the things that had happened, most of which made no sense to him, but he did not feel ready to talk about them out loud. He felt as if he'd

258

fallen into someone's story, as if powers he could not imagine were working on their own plans, using him as a stone on the playing board.

Seri spoke first. "If we were together like this all the time, it would help if you could fight better, and I could also heal."

Aris laughed. "It would be better if both of us could do everything anyone can do."

"I'm serious." Seri made a face at him. "If you were a better fighter, you wouldn't almost get killed right away — if you had, who'd have healed me? And if I could heal, then I could heal you — or someone else that needed it."

"I don't think good healers make good fighters," Aris said slowly. "I think it's — it's how, when I'm practicing, I can almost *see* the wound that I could cause. And I know what it costs me to heal it."

"Ah. Then that's why fighters — at least Marshals — should be healers as well. If we're to lead yeomen into battle, we should know what will follow. Not just what it looks like, but what it takes to heal it."

Aris shook his head. "But that makes it too easy, like the old stories of the Undoer's Curse: if you can make something right too easily, there's no reason to worry about doing wrong beforehand. Marshal Geddrin told me that, when I'd have healed every cut he got trying to shave himself: if I depend on you, he said, I'll never learn to keep a sharp edge and a steady hand."

Seri leaned forward and stroked her horse's mane where the wind had ruffled it. "But it's not easy for you; I've seen what it takes out of you. That's not the same as the Undoer's Curse. I still think there should be a balance. Those who must fight should also be healers, and those who heal should also be fighters. Otherwise I'm too proud of my fighting, and you're too proud of your healing. Or not you, maybe —"

"But the old healers are, some of the ones I worked with. You're right. Alyanya's the Lady of Peace, they say, and those who heal must never take service of iron . . . remember Gird, that time, when he told us about his boyhood? How his parents were angry that he wanted to be a soldier?"

"Yes, but it's Gird who healed the peoples at his death," Seri said, "and he couldn't have done that if he hadn't been a fighter first. Not because he wanted to kill people, but because

— " She looked far over the rolling grass, then shook her head. "I'm not sure how to say it. I just know it's true. He had to be a farmer *and* a fighter to do what he did."

"The service of blood," Aris said softly. "Both ways — I hadn't thought of it before, but they're related. To give blood to the fields, to bring the harvest — that's like giving blood to the people — "

"But it doesn't always work."

"Nor does farming. Things go wrong, in peace and in war both. But what Gird did, he showed that it's the giving that matters. You can't hold yourself back." Aris smacked his thigh with his fist as the thoughts boiling in his head finally came clear. "That's it, Seri! That's the link between healing and fighting: the good healer withholds nothing that could help. If I don't go because I'm tired or sick, or if I am unwilling to risk the loss to myself because I don't like the person who needs me, then I'm a bad healer. If the fighter tries to protect himself — herself — then that makes a bad fighter. Even the training, working on the skills — both are long-term crafts, practiced because they may be needed, not today, but someday."

"Yes," Seri said. "And the other link is that the fighter who heals will never forget the cost of it — and the healer who fights will never condemn others for fighting at need."

They looked at each other as if seeing anew. "I still don't know what this is all about," Aris said finally, "but somehow I don't think Arranha will be able to help us with it. It's too much of Gird for that."

They rode the rest of that day without meeting anyone. Aris had no idea, now, where they were in relation to Fin Panir, and he did not feel it mattered. He was going this way because he was supposed to go this way, and his horse agreed.

The next day, they saw sheep spread across a slope far ahead of them, and angled that way without talking about it. By afternoon, they were close enough to see the hollow below, with a tight cluster of stone buildings; they could hear dogs barking as the sheep moved down slowly toward the hollow.

"They must think we're brigands," Seri said, frowning. "They wouldn't be penning them that early, else."

"We'd better change their minds," Aris said, "or we'll be spending another night on the hard ground." He turned his horse downslope; Seri followed. From their height, they could see the scurrying figures, the dogs working the sheep far too fast . . . and one broke away at a gate, bounding up the hill toward the riders, followed by a dark streak of sheepdog. A shrill whistle from below brought the dog to a halt, growling, then it raced back down the hill. The sheep, moving with the single-minded intensity of the truly stupid, made for the gap between Aris's horse and Seri's. Seri flung herself off her horse and made a grab for it.

"Idiot!" Aris said. Grabbing a determined sheep is harder than it looks, and jumping on one from above is chancy at best. Seri had a double-handful of wool and a faceful of stony hillside as the sheep, bleating loudly, did its best to jerk free. Aris swung off his horse and grabbed for a hind leg, then the other. With the sheep in a wheelbarrow hold, Seri could get a foreleg and then they could flatten the sheep out and decide how to get her back down to the fold.

A bellow from below caught his attention — and there, making surprising speed up the steep slope, was a tall man and a boy, with two sheepdogs. "Let loose 'o my sheep!" the man yelled, when he saw Aris watching.

"She was gettin' away!" Seri yelled back. "We just caught 'er for you."

"An' sheep are born wi' golden fleece," the man yelled. "I know your kind. You catch sheep all right, and then ye make sure they don't escape — yer own stomachs." He waved the dogs on, and they came, bellies low, swinging in from either side. Aris started to rise, but then saw what the horses were doing. Each horse had put itself between a dog and the pair with the sheep — and the sheepdogs found themselves herded back as neatly as ever they'd worked a flock. The man and his boy stopped a short distance below. "That can't be," the man said, half in anger and half in wonder. "Horses don't do that."

"Ours do," said Seri, almost smugly. The sheep picked that moment to thrash again and kick her with the loose foreleg. "D'you want us to bring your sheep down, or will your dogs pen her for you?"

The boy came nearer, out of reach of his father's arm. "Aren't you robbers, then?"

"Not us," Seri said cheerfully. "Here — you take her." She beckoned, and the boy came up and got a foreleg hold on the sheep himself. At his soft voice, the sheep quit struggling; Seri stepped back and looked at the man. "I'm sorry we frightened

261

you," she said. "We're not robbers, even if Ari does have your sheep by the hind legs. We thought we'd help you."

"You could help me," the man said slowly, "by letting go of my sheep." Aris shrugged, let go, and stood. The sheep scrambled up awkwardly; the boy still had a grip on one foreleg. "Let'r go, Varya — let's see what these folk do." The boy let go, and the sheep stood, ears waggling. He said something to her, and she followed a few steps. Then the man whistled, and waved an arm, and the two dogs closed in on the sheep. She edged her way downhill.

"You don't act like robbers," the man said then. "But I never heard of honest travellers . . . where are you from?"

"Fin Panir," Aris said. His horse walked up and laid its head along his arm. He rubbed the base of its ear absently, and then the line between jowl and neck.

"Girdish folk? Is that why you're wearing blue?"

"Yes," said Seri. "We're in training to be Marshals."

"Whatever that is," the man said. He stood silent some moments, and Aris had almost decided to mount when he said, "You might as well come down wi' us for the night; I don't want your deaths on my conscience."

"Deaths?" Seri asked.

"Aye. There's things in the dark — surely you know that. We don't take chances any more, between human robbers and those other things, the blackrobes, and sometimes wolves and that, things running in packs. We'd have brought the sheep down early even without seeing you. Come on, now. No time to waste. There's chores."

The farmer showed no surprise when Aris and Seri both proved handy at the evening chores. Perhaps, Aris thought, he didn't know there were people in the world who couldn't milk, who couldn't tell hay from straw, for whom wheat and oats and barley were all just "grain." The farm buildings were larger than those Aris had seen before, well built and weathertight. They met the farmer's wife, his other children, all younger than the boy on the hill. And they ate with the family, sharing some berries they had gathered that day.

"So what brings you this way, Girdsmen?" the farmer asked. "Is it part of Marshals' training to wander around frightening honest farmers?"

"No . . . the wandering, perhaps, but not the rest." Seri

rested her chin on her fists. Aris watched the faces watching her, the children all intent and eager just because she was a stranger. The farmer's wife sat knitting busily, looking up only now and then as she counted stitches. "To tell you the truth, there's new ideas about how Marshals should be trained. Do you have a grange here?"

"Nay." The farmer sounded glad of it. "We had better things to do than get involved in your war and go around killing folk. We stayed here wi' our sheep, as farmers should. So all that about grange and barton and Marshals, all that means naught to us." He gave Seri a challenging glance, as much as to say *And take that as you please*.

Seri just grinned at him. "You were lucky, then. Aris and I had the war come upon us as children; we had to grow up hedgewise. Then Father Gird took us in — "

"Was that a real man, Gird, or just a name for whoever was leading?"

"A real man," Seri said. Aris could hardly believe that anyone doubted it; did these farmers never leave their little hollow? "He took us in, Ari and me, when we'd been living with farmers, because Ari has the healing magery."

"Mageborn!" The farmer glared at Aris; no one else in the room moved or spoke. "I let a mageborn in my house?"

Seri shrugged. "Father Gird let him in his house. And told everyone to let him use his magery. Healing's good, he said."

"Is it true, lad? You can heal?" The farmer's voice rumbled with suppressed anger.

"Yes," Aris said. "But not all things, though I'll try."

"Come on, then." The farmer heaved himself up from the bench, clearly expecting Aris to follow. He caught Seri's eye, and she rose as well. "What's that?" the farmer asked. "I thought you said *he* had the healing — why are you coming?"

"Gird said Aris must have someone to watch him," Seri said. "I travel with him for that reason."

"Huh. Don't trust him, eh?" By his tone, he approved: no one should trust mageborn.

"I do," Seri said, "and so do those who've worked with him before. But Gird set the rule, and the Council holds by it."

With a last grunt, the farmer led them upstairs. Aris had not seen stairs in a farmer's house before. He wondered if the farmer had taken over a small manor house. But he had no time to ask; the farmer flung wide a door on the left of the passage. There on a low bed lay a man near death from woundfever. "It's my brother," the farmer said. "He and his family lived here with us, and this is all that's left. They killed his wife and oldest child one night when we were out late, in lambing time. She'd gone out to bring us food. The younger children, two of them, died of a fever — they'd been grieving so, I think they had no strength. The others are with mine, of course. But a hand of days ago, maybe, he thought he heard voices outside, near the pens. He didn't wake me afore going out to see, and by the time I woke, and got outside, this is what I found. Heal him, if you can." His gaze challenged Aris.

"Do you know who did it?" Seri asked. The farmer nodded. "Aye. They blackcloaks, that the magelord used to keep away with his mageries. Cost us plenty in field-fee, it did, and we were glad to see him go, but we didn't know what our field-fee paid for until he was gone. It must have been his mageries that protected us, for now we see them, season after season, and if they keep coming, we'll soon be gone."

Aris knelt by the wounded man. He had been stabbed and slashed many times, but without a killing wound, almost as if the swordsman had wished him to live for awhile. The wounds drained a foul liquid that filled the room with its stench. "Did you try poultices?" he asked.

"Of course we did. D'you think we're all fools up here?" The farmer glowered. "M'wife's parrion is needlework, not herblore, but she knows a bit. She used allheal and feverbane, and you can see how well they worked. We took 'em off today, as it seemed to ease him. Please — " And now his voice was no longer angry. "Please, lad, try to heal him."

Aris was afraid it was too late, but his power burned in his hands. The women he had worked with had insisted on cleaning wounds first, before trying to heal them, but would he have time? He thought not: even as he watched, the man's flushed, dry skin turned pale and clammy, though he still breathed strongly. He looked at Seri, who stood poised as if for battle. "Seri — you wanted to know more of healing. Come here." Her eyes widened, but she came. "Think on this man as Gird would . . . a farmer, a father, beset by the evil that came upon us. Put your hands here — and I'll be here — and we'll see how your prayer works with my magery."

This time, the flow of power through his hands seemed like fire along a line of oil: both he and Seri came alight, as they had on the hillside when menaced by the iynisin. He heard the farmer stumble against the door and mutter, but he could not attend to it. Seri's hands glowed from within; he felt the flow of power from her, indescribably different from his — but he could direct both. He sent the power down the man's body, driving away the heavy darkness of the woundfever, then returning to mend the ripped flesh, the cracked bone, the torn skin. Seri's power, wherever it came from, seemed lighter somehow than his own, almost joyous. It seemed most apt against the sickness while his soothed the wounded tissues together. At last he could find nothing more to do, and leaned back, releasing his hands. Seri kept hers on the man's shoulders a moment longer, then lifted them. Instantly their lights failed, leaving the room in candlelight that now seemed darkness. But instead of the stench of rotting wounds, the room smelled of fragrant herbs and clean wind.

"What did you — " The farmer lurched forward, hand raised. Then the man on the bed drew a long breath, and opened his eyes. "Geris — " he said. "I — did I dream all that?"

"Dream what?" the farmer asked hoarsely.

"I thought — they came again. The blackcloaks. And you came, and I was hurt . . . I thought I was dying. . . . "

"You were," the farmer said. His voice was shaky; tears glistened on his cheeks.

"But I have no pain." The man looked down at himself. "I have no wound — and who are these people? Why have I no clothes?" He dragged the blanket across himself.

"Girdish travellers," the farmer said. "I — I'll get you clothes, Jeris." He turned and plunged from the room. The man they had healed struggled up, wrapping the blanket around him.

"You — will you tell me what happened?"

"Your brother asked us to heal you," Seri said. "We asked the gods, and it was granted us." Aris glanced at her. Was that what she'd done? He had done what he always did, using his own power. Like any talent, it came from the gods originally, but not specifically for each use.

"But — " The man shook his head. "Then it really happened, those blackcloaks? It seems now like a dream, an evil sending. They — they toyed with me; they would not quite kill me. And they laughed until I felt cold to my bones."

"Iynisin," Aris said. "That's the name we know for them. Evil indeed: we too have faced their blades — "

"And lived? But of course . . . you have healed me, so I, too, have lived despite the blackcloaks." The man still seemed a little dazed, which Aris could well understand. They heard the farmer stumbling back along the passage; he came in with shirt and trousers for his brother, and Aris and Seri edged past him out the door and went back downstairs. The woman and children all stared at them.

"He's alive," Aris said. "I've no doubt he'll be down soon." Two of the children burst into noisy tears and ran to hug the farmer's wife; the others looked scared. Then they all heard feet on the stairs, and the injured man came down first. His lean face still looked surprised, but he moved like a healthy man, without pain or weakness. Aris let out the breath he had not known he was holding. The farmer, heavier of build, stumped down the stairs after him.

"Thanks and praise to the Lady," the farmer said; his brother echoed him, then his wife and all the children. "Alyanya must have sent you," he said to Aris and Seri. "Did this Gird of yours follow Alyanya?"

"Alyanya and the High Lord," Seri said. Aris wondered at her certainty. He had always thought of Gird as following good itself, whatever god that might mean from day to day.

"And you are mageborn too, are you? I saw that light, which only the mageborn have. . . ."

"No," Seri said, shaking her head. "My parents were peasants, servants in a magelord's home. That light — I do not understand it myself, but it came upon me first when Aris and I were beset by those blackcloaks, as you call them."

"The gods' gift," the brother said. Aris wondered if he himself had looked like that when the elves came. "Are all Marshals, then, like you?" He looked at his brother. "Because if they are, Geris, perhaps we should turn Girdish; perhaps this is a sign."

"It may be a sign to us," Seri said, "or to you, but Marshals are not like us. They're older; nearly all are still Gird's veterans, those who led his troops in the war. I'm not yet a full Marshal; I'm in training. But Marshals are supposed to help and protect those in their granges; they study healing — at least the young ones do — but not all have more than herblore." *Yet*, Aris thought. Perhaps they would someday. Perhaps this has been a test given by the gods, instead of the Council of Marshals. He imagined future Marshals able to call light at need, able to heal. Perhaps the Marshals, and not the mageborn, would carry on his gift. It didn't matter, so long as someone did. He yawned, suddenly feeling the loss of strength that usually followed a healing. It had taken less from him this time. Because Seri helped? Because the gods were involved? He did not know, but he knew he would fall asleep here at the table in another breath or two.

Seri woke him at daybreak. He had been moved to a warm corner near the hearth, and covered with a blanket; he knew she must have told them to do that. Overhead, he heard muffled scrapes and thuds: the farmer moving around. Seri seemed indecently cheerful for such an hour. Aris scrubbed his itching eyes with cold hands.

"The horses are calling us," Seri said.

"They would be." Aris yawned again, and scrambled up, brushing at his clothes. They would be rumpled and smudged after a night on the floor. Seri opened a shutter, letting in the cold gray light of dawn. The farmer's boots thudded on the stairs. He paused when he saw them up, then shook his head.

"Now I can believe you're farmers' brats," he said. "Ready for chores, eh?"

Aris and Seri followed him outside. Heavy dew lay on the grass and bushes near the house, and furred the moss on the stone walls of the outbuildings. Seri drew buckets of water and Aris carried them to the different pens. When he came to the enclosure where their horses had sheltered, he stopped and stared. The horses snorted, nosing for the bucket. Aris poured it into a stone trough, still staring. The horses gleamed as if they had just been rubbed with oil. Of course he and Seri had rubbed them the previous day, but the girthmarks had showed slightly. Now nothing marred their glistening coats. Something tickled his mind, something he should understand, but it slipped away when he tried to follow it. A stronger flicker in his mind continued, strengthening, all through breakfast. Seri, he saw, felt it too.

"No," she said to the fourth or fifth invitation to stay. "No, we must go, today." And today meant as soon after breakfast as possible. Aris, moved by the same inexplicable urgency, took their gear out to the horses and found them already saddled. Seri, he thought, must really be in a hurry; he wondered when she had found time to slip out and saddle them.

They were well away before the sun entered the hollow, this time riding sunrising, into the light, as their need suggested. They followed a beaten track that ran along the high ground most of the time.

About halfway through the morning Aris said, "Do you think it's the gods, or Gird, or something else?"

Seri's frown meant concentration, not annoyance. "I've been trying to think. Up until the iynisin attacked us, everything seemed normal, didn't it?"

"I thought so. I was surprised that you'd gotten permission for us to leave, but nothing more."

"There was nothing strange about that; the Autumn Rose and Raheli and Cob all thought you should have the chance to travel and try your healing elsewhere, 'stead of becoming one of Luap's scribes. And they thought we'd do well together. Rahi said I'd been watching you heal even before Gird knew about it, so they might as well trust me."

"So it started with the iynisin attack," Aris said. "Or was it before?"

"Before?"

"When you were talking to me about Luap, about mageborn and peasant, and which I'd chosen."

"No." Seri shook her head. "It couldn't have been that."

"It didn't sound quite like you — the Seri I knew."

"How not?"

"Mmm. Angrier. And I couldn't believe you would stop trusting me, just because I tried to be fair about Luap."

"I'm sorry. I remember feeling suddenly furious, hot all over. You're right, that wasn't like me, most of the time." They rode in silence a few moments, then Seri turned to him with a strange expression. "You don't suppose . . . "

"What?"

"*Torre's Ride,*" she said softly. "It's a test, like *Torre's Ride* — could it be?"

Aris snorted. "That's ridiculous. It — " He grabbed wildly at

268

the saddle as his horse bolted, bucking and weaving. Seri's exploded too, pitching wildly and then bolting in a flat run to the north. Aris managed to stay on until his horse, too, gave up bucking to run after Seri's. His breath came short; he felt sore under the ribs, and the horse ran on and on. By the time it slowed, they were far from the track they had been following; a wind rose, whipping the grass flat in long waves, obliterating the pattern of trampled grass that might have led them back to it.

"And now we're lost," he said to Seri, who was hunched over, fighting for breath.

"I'm right," she said a moment later. "And don't argue again. It's a test."

"Fine." Aris waited until he could breathe more easily, and said, "And perhaps we should start figuring out what kind of test involves iynisin, elves, thunderstorms, and horses that come out of nowhere and run forever without sweating." For the two horses were not breathing hard, and no sweat marred their sleek hides.

"And a dying man who needs our healing." Seri straightened up and stretched her back. "And getting lost." Then she reached over and grabbed Aris's arm. "Look at them."

He looked. Their two horses had their muzzles together, and each had one eye rolled back to watch its rider. "*They* know," he said. "You mischief," he said to his horse. He felt its back hump under him, a clear warning. "No, I'm sorry. Don't do that again; I'll fall off. But you do know, don't you?"

"Gird's horse," Seri said. Her eyes danced. "These are the same kind." Her horse stamped, hard, and shook its head. "Or — similar?" Both horses put their ears forward and touched muzzles again, then blew long rolling snorts.

"Gods above," Aris said. "We are right in the middle of something — I wonder if Torre ever felt confused." He felt suddenly better, as if he'd solved the puzzle. But he knew he hadn't.

Seri grinned. "Remember when we were very young, and used to hide in the garden and tell stories?"

"Yes, and you always said you wished we could have a real adventure." Aris chuckled. "And I thought you'd grown out of that."

"Never," Seri said. "Nor have you; I remember who got

269

stuck up in the pear tree." Her face sobered. "Father Gird wants us to do something," she said. "And even if we hadn't stumbled into the iynisin; he'd have found some way to test us. He wasn't one to send untrained farmers into battle."

"We're supposed to be trained already," Aris said. "All those years in the granges, as yeoman-marshals, as Marshal-candidates — "

"So we've survived the tests. We've learned to share our talents. We're more ready now than we were." Seri looked cheerful; Aris hoped she was right.

"When we find out what it is he wants," Aris said. "If we've finished the tests." Seri grimaced and put out her tongue.

The two horses stiffened, then threw up their heads and neighed. Out of a fold of the ground rode a troop of nomads on shaggy ponies. All carried lances; the nomads called out in their high-pitched voices.

They came back to Fin Panir leaner, browner, and far more cautious than they'd left. The gate guards didn't recognize them or the horses, but when they gave their names said they were wanted at the palace. "Why?" asked Seri. Aris thought he knew; his hands prickled. He led the way, his bay picking his way neatly through the crowded lower market.

"Aris!" Luap, crossing from the palace to the Hall, stopped in midstride. "Is it really you? We need you."

"Who is it?" He was already off the horse; Seri slid off hers. A stableboy came running out; the horses let themselves be led away.

"Arranha. A few days after you left — " Luap told the story as he led them quickly into the palace. "We've tried everything — herblore, young Garin — and it's not enough. He hasn't died — I suspect that's Garin's doing — but his arm's swollen to the shoulder and he weakens daily."

Aris said nothing. He loved the old priest; he wondered why the gods had let him leave Fin Panir if Arranha was going to be in danger. When he came into Arranha's room, he stopped short, shocked. Arranha had always been "the old priest" to him; he had known Arranha was older than Gird. But he had been so vigorous an old man, so full of life . . . and now he lay spent and silent, his body fragile and his spirit nearly flown. Awe flooded him. Was this Arranha's time, and had the god he had served finally called him? He could not interfere with that.

He put his hands on Arranha's shoulders; at once the magery revealed the dangerous fever in the wounded arm. It had seeped even past his shoulder, into his heart. Aris let his power flow out. He felt the resistance of a deepseated sickness, and worse than that Arranha's lack of response. He had given up; although he breathed, he would not struggle against death any longer.

Seri put her hands on his; Aris looked up, surprised into losing his concentration. "We work together," she said. He nodded. He could feel her power pulsing through his hands and into Arranha. "Gird loved and trusted him," Seri went on. "Gird wants him to live; he must help Luap with the mageborn in the west." Slowly, Aris felt the sickness yielding, first from Arranha's heart, and then fingerwidth by finger-width down his arm. The swollen tissue shrank; the angry reds and purples faded. He could feel that Arranha breathed more easily; his pulse slowed and steadied. Finally, even the purple bite marks which had oozed a foul pus faded, and Arranha's hand lay cool and slender on the blanket once more.

Arranha opened his eyes. "You called me back. Why?" Then he seemed to see them clearly and his expression changed. "*Both* of you! Seri, when did you learn healing?"

She grinned at him. "It's not like Aris's; I have to ask Gird what he wants."

"Gird. But he's not —"

"He's not a god; I know that. But he lets us know what he wants done."

Arranha pushed himself up in the bed. "I might have known. He saved my life outside the walls of Grahlin, and now he's done it again; I wonder what he expects of me this time." His gaze fell on Luap. "Don't look at me like that, Selamis: I'm well now. I'll be with you in the west; isn't that what you wanted?"

Raheli watched the Council carefully the morning Aris and Seri were to come in to make their report. Already rumors had spread, as fast as light from a flame: Arranha healed, a mageborn and peasant working healing magery together. She and the Rosemage had already conferred; they sat on opposite

271

sides of the room where they could hear most of the murmuring and see each other. Luap sat in his usual seat, with fresh scrolls around him and his pen full of ink. The scribe he had nominated to take over his position sat behind him at a small desk; he would practice taking the notes.

But the Council concerned her most. In the years since Seri had maneuvered Cob into presenting her own plan for the training of new Marshals, the Council had changed character. Fewer of the rural Marshals bothered to come in to Fin Panir; some sent their concerns, and some ignored the Council until a crisis arose. Most of the Marshals who attended regularly had granges in Fin Panir or Grahlin, or vills within a day's ride of Fin Panir; they had plenty of yeoman-marshals to do their work while they attended Council. By the accidents of war, most of them had also been latecomers to Gird's army, gaining command because the earlier Marshals died in battle. Since they had not known Gird as well, they relied on the written Code, the growing volume of Commentaries, and Luap's version of Gird's life when considering some new policy. Raheli could still influence them, as Gird's daughter, as could a few others, but it grew harder every year. She had begun to regret her decision to refuse the Marshal-Generalship.

Aris and Seri appeared in the doorway. Both wore the gray shirts and pants of the training order, and the blue tunic of a Marshal-candidate. Raheli felt herself relaxing. No one could help liking those two; they had the cheerful steadiness that attracted goodwill. Aris looked tougher, his face tanned where it had been pale, his shoulders broader. Seri looked less concerned about him; she seemed full of confidence.

When they were called to account for their journey, they spoke in turns, but without formality: it did not seem rehearsed. Rahi had already heard part of the story the night before, but Aris's description of the iynisin curse on the grove and spring, and its healing the next day still awed her. When Seri told of the horses appearing, one of the older Marshals said, "Like Gird's old gray horse!" at once.

"We thought of that," Aris said. "But we are not Gird — we could never claim that importance."

"Nor did he," Luap said. Everyone stared; Luap rarely spoke in Council meetings, maintaining the distinction between the Marshals and himself.

"But go on," another Marshal said. "We can discuss this later. I want to know what happened next." So did they all, and questioned Aris and Seri about each least detail of their journey, including much that the two had not had time to tell Raheli. They had healed someone at a farm, they had found a tribe of horse nomads, and spent a few hands of days with them, learning their language and healing their sick. . . .

"Horse nomads? How could you learn so fast? And why heal them? We didn't train you and send you out to benefit them. Aris was supposed to heal yeomen who needed it."

Seri answered this time. "We cannot say how we learned so fast — it surprised us, and them, as much as it surprises you. But since the gods directed us there, they must have had some purpose. As for healing, that is the purpose of such power — to withhold its use is as evil as to misuse any magery."

"I don't like it," the Marshal-General said, scowling. "An honest peasant lass fiddling about with magery: that can't be right. I know you'll say Gird approved young Aris using his healing magery, under supervision. But that's not the same as Seri doing such things, calling light and all that."

Raheli spoke up. "Marshal-General, in the old days there are legends of our people having some great powers — consider the Stone Circles they raised. And Gird would have trusted peasants — especially someone like Seri who has served well in barton and grange — to use magery for the benefit of all."

"It's magicks, and magicks are evil," the Marshal-General said.

Raheli would have said more, but Seri leaned forward, smiling at the Marshal-General. "Sir, that magic by which Gird freed us all from fear and grief at his death: was that evil?"

"No, but — but that was not magicks; that came from the gods. Luap said so."

"And the gods granted this to me, sir — I did not ask for it; I didn't even imagine it was possible. It is not my talent. It is their gift. I would be ungracious to refuse it. Now if the Council requires that I not use it here, I will leave — but I will not renounce what the gods have given me."

That set off a stormy argument. Some said Seri was rebellious, haughty, ruined by spending too much time with a mageborn; others argued that she was right: if she had new powers, they must be the gods' gift, and she should use them.

Through this, Aris and Seri sat patient and quiet, though Rahi felt angry enough to bash some heads. She wished Cob had been there.

Finally, when the argument died of its own weight, the cheerful steadiness of the two young people had its effect, and the vote the Marshal-General demanded, to force Seri to give up healing, failed. In the days that followed, both returned to their former training duties so quietly that it seemed the storm had never occurred. Aris spent more time in the drillfields and barton, and Seri spent more time with him, learning herblore, but otherwise they seemed unchanged.

As the year rolled on, Luap and Arranha together planned for the great move. By word of mouth, the plans travelled the land, and mageborn survivors began to trickle into Fin Panir. The strong and young, those known to have magery, would go first and prepare the land for planting. One by one, Luap showed them what became known as the mageroad. He still worried that they did not know where in real space the stronghold lay, but he felt he could not wait.

● Chapter Twenty

Getting the first working groups funneled through the cave was almost as difficult as moving Gird's army, Luap thought. Aris had agreed to come to the stronghold with Seri "for awhile"; he would not say whether he would settle there permanently. In the wake of Seri's defiance of the Council, Luap chose not to press the issue. Surely they would find the new land fascinating enough once they had lived there for a time.

"*Here* we need not hide our abilities." The Rosemage eyed the canyon walls with a craftsman's look.

"The stronghold itself is large enough. . . ."

"For now. But it won't be. And we'll need tradeways: roads, passes, bridges. Look — " From her fixed stare, a line of light sprang to the nearest rockface a few spans away. A high screech ending in a *ping*, and burst of rockdust. A cylinder of stone wobbled, and fell out, leaving behind a clean, smooth, perfectly round hole. Luap stared at her, surprised once more. She reddened. "Of course, *you* could do more; I know that. And this tires me. But it will save our few numbers from spending all their time chipping stone."

It would that. Luap shivered, wondering if she were right in thinking he could do "more" when he had never imagined even so much. He shivered again, as the thought crossed his mind of what such use of power might say, to those with the ability to sense its use. As the smoke of a city could rise above it, reveal it, before its towers came in sight, could their magery make obvious their location?

"I wouldn't suggest it," the Rosemage went on, "if this were not empty land, unpeopled. The rockfolk never accepted human magic applied to stone; that was one of the quarrels the gnomes had with us." Luap had not known that; he wondered if she knew it as fact or legend. He wondered if the dwarven king he had seen would object; he wondered why he had been given no specific warning prohibition about that.

The Rosemage continued. "If the rockfolk lived in these mountains, we would have to have their permission."

"What about elves?"

The Rosemage shrugged. "They would not care; why should they? They work their magery with living things, not lifeless stone."

"Gird told me once of the blackcloaks, who seem elves but are not."

"Legends." The Rosemage stared not quite through him, and he shrugged.

"Some are true."

"Yes, and some horses fly. No one will argue that Torre's magic horse did not fly, or that the gods could not turn mountains on their heads if they wished, but we never *see* a mountain balanced on its peak. Elves are strange enough without making them into two kinds of folk —" She shook her head as he would have answered. "No — I have heard the tales, too. Bright elves that come by day, and dark elves that come by night; good elves living in trees and wicked ones living in holes of the ground and poisoning the roots of trees: children's tales. These people see duality everywhere, in everything, balancing a water hero against a sky hero, stone against tree, night and day, storm and calm. That alone shows it can't be true . . . it's too neat, a dance instead of war."

Luap drew a long breath, which tasted of nothing more dire than pine. The way Arranha had explained the original Aarean beliefs, the Rosemage's ancestors and his own had also believed in a duality, but one soon fragmented into a great arch of deities and powers, from the vicious to the benign. He had never really believed in any of them, until Gird. He was sure Gird had not lied about the dangerous being that had cursed him one dawn — Gird would not bother to make up something like that, assuming he had the imagination. But he had not seen it himself; Gird could have been mistaken. He had been, after all, only a peasant . . . he would not have known what it was, only what it told him. It might have lied, if it had been as evil as Gird thought. And he did not want the Rosemage's scorn.

"You have more knowledge, lady." Even as he said that, he wondered why his tongue chose *knowledge* over *wisdom*, which would have made the compliment stronger. He drew another long breath of air as clean and cold and empty of human scent as any he had ever taken. "An empty land . . . a fine refuge."

"Good morning!" That was Arranha, moving far more briskly than a man his age should, Luap always thought. Since Aris and Seri had healed him, Arranha might have been ten years younger. "A fine day. So, lady, you have the skill of stonework?"

The Rosemage smiled at him. "In a small way, Arranha." From her tone, she did not think it that small. He peered at the hole Luap pointed out.

"Ahh. Fine work, indeed; you have a straight eye. But you've done it the hard way; we don't need that precision in moving large blocks. We're going to need to move a lot of stone; best use the quicker ways."

"Quicker ways?" She was rarely flustered, but she looked flustered now. Luap took a guilty pleasure in that.

"With your permission." Not that anyone would refuse Arranha permission *here*, whatever Gird's folk might have said. Luap smiled and nodded; the Rosemage waved her hand. "There, then," said Arranha, pointing out the opposing rockface, a little distance down canyon. "Block the flow there, and we'll have a sizeable terrace to work with, once we have soil for it."

Arranha's mild expression did not change; the rock buzzed, then screamed like some dire creature mortally wounded. A dark line scored it, visibly darker and deeper with every heartbeat. Finally light flashed out from it, as if someone had poured boiling oil into its wound, and a chunk of red stone the size of a cottage leaned out from the cliff and fell gracelessly into the gorge. When it struck, Luap felt the shock in his boots and knees; a cloud of dust rose above the noise and every bird in the canyon took to the air. He had no time to watch that cloud vanish in the morning wind; the old priest had begun carving another chunk, and as it fell another. By the time Arranha quit, the low end of the gorge had a pile of broken rock chockablock in its neck, and the little stream had already backed up into a muddy pond. The Rosemage stood silent, arms folded, her brows drawn together.

"There now," Arranha said, a little breathlessly. "Yes, you can learn, lady. So can he." With his thumb he indicated Luap.

Not all could. Luap found it easy, and the Rosemage

difficult, but not more so than her finer carving. But some could not sense the stone's inner grain, and wore out their power on cuts that led nowhere, mere slits in the stone, while others could not score even a nail's path in the stone by magery. Aris, whose skill in healing no one matched, could do nothing with stone but carry the smaller chunks to be stacked somewhere.

Luap admitted to himself that he liked that. He, the king's bastard, had that power in full measure; he could carve his own castle, depending on his own abilities. Day after day he labored, never letting his growing excitement affect his concentration on the task. As Arranha had taught, he felt for the rock's own internal structure, the grain and interleaving of its substance, and concentrated his power so that it fell away as he wanted, and left sound walls behind. He learned to anticipate even the shattering that followed those falls, so that the very blocks fell readily to hand, for the builders to raise into terraces.

Others of his people had other magery; man-long blocks rose at their will, and eased into place. Sooner than he had expected, the framework in the small canyon had been done, and the lowest dam laid in the large one. The Rosemage had found a passable route to the lower lands southward, a matter of one low pass and a twisted canyon outlet where the little river ran knee-deep from wall to wall. Next year they would smooth that route for horse travel. No one knew what lay beyond, but the Rosemage and Arranha both insisted some humans lived there.

As nights chilled, and frost starred the pools of still water at dawn, Luap felt well content. He had made a good beginning; it was going to work. They could not plant the next spring, but the one after that he was sure they'd have enough level land for some grain. Gird's successor had promised food for four growing seasons; he should make it with one to spare. His careful planning seemed to lock into place like the blocks of stone forming the terraces; he took comfort in the evidence that his leadership was working.

Deep under stone the blackrobed exiles had long exhausted their own powers. Nothing they could do from within would free them, and through the ages the land around their prison lay vacant — a tangle of narrow canyons surrounded by deserts. Above, the battle scars of their defeat weathered away in winter snow and spring rain; grass and sedge, bush and tree, grew once more free of blight, until the few wanderers who came that way had no reason to suspect what lay imprisoned in one red mass of stone more than another.

Then into their prison of ancient magery the younger, less-skilled power came, fraying the barriers as if a caress from without were stronger than the many curses flung from within. Slowly at first, then more rapidly, the barriers withered. And silently, cloaked in that magery which even defeat could not wrest from them, the blackrobed spies went by night to search out their deliverers.

"Surely they have been warned," said their leader, when the first spy returned with his tale of mortal settlement. "Surely our noble cousins have told them — "

"No." The spy smiled, a smile that should have been beautiful on such a face, but was not. "For pride the sinyi will not speak our name; they have tried to erase all memory of us in the old lands. And they resented this one's ability to use the ancient patterns. He angered them."

"Blessings on him." The tone conveyed a curse instead. "And what did they say, those guardians of our . . . virtue?"

"Only that a great danger lay mured in this wilderness, which he would regret awakening."

The flash of bared teeth among them passed for humor; one of the others chuckled. "Oh, he will. He surely will."

"Not yet," said their leader. "Here we have leisure to purpose more than a hasty vengeance on our wardens. We can do much better, by Achrya's aid. Think on it . . . these mortals will settle and multiply, will they? Let them prosper. Let them plant their filthy trees, and reap many crops of fine grain, all the while fattening like oxen, like swine, for our feasting. Leave them without fear — for now. Let their prince, who is too wise to heed warnings he does not understand, take pride in his wisdom. May he rule long, I say, for his fall will be sweeter. We are free now; we can wait and watch this feast in preparation."

A murmur of delight, chilling in its intensity, followed his words.

"But there are hazards," the spy warned. "An old priest of Esea — of the Light, alas — has keen wits. And two of the younger mortals — one of them a true healer — have met our kind before. Or

279

suppose their prince dies before the feast is spread. They might all leave."

Their leader laughed aloud. *"You name hazards what I name treasures! The priest is old, you say: he will surely die before long. We are in no hurry. And they have a true healer, and a prince without the healing magery, a prince we would have live long in complacent prosperity . . . how fortunate for us. Here's a web to tangle those lightfoot cousins of ours, a jest to sour their hearts and silence even the forest-lord at the end. One shall snare the other, and never suspect it. Indeed the Tangler will be pleased."*

"But we cannot approach the Winterhall: that magery they did not touch, and it still holds strong against us."

Their leader smiled, then looked at each face in turn, the companions of his long exile. *"No matter. We have won, before ever battle be joined. Can you doubt that an unwary mortal, whatever human magery he may have, will fall to our enchantments? We need not enter the Winterhall, when we hold its prince's heart."*

Sunrise on Midwinter: Luap no longer shivered, having learned the bodily magery from Arranha. He stood, on the eastern end of the rock platform, looking southeast as rose light flushed the snow, as a high wing of cloud grew feathers of rose and gold, then bleached to whiteness as the sun flared, blinding. Behind him, the song rose up, the song he had vaguely remembered from earliest childhood, sung now by all his people. Not quite all, he corrected himself; all the ones *here*, the best of the workers of old magery. Deep voices, high voices, all in towering harmony that rang off the nearby cliffs, the echoes seeming answers from yet other choruses . . . his skin prickled. The words were nothing like the peasants' short rhymed Midwinter chants; he could feel the longer flowing lines twining around each other, statement and response, question and answer, full of power as the singers themselves. "Sunlord, earthlord, father of many harvests . . . " echoed back from the facing cliffs, and behind him the choir sang of "springing waters shining in the sun. . . . "

He alone did not sing; he had sung the invocation in the Hall below, at Arranha's direction, and now (also at Arranha's direction) he stood silent, looking at the land, listening to his people, being — according to Arranha — the tip of the spear the first light touched, the one through whom the Sunlord would enlighten his people.

"If you are clear," Arranha had also said, last night. "You must be clear, the crystal to gather the light and spread it abroad."

He would be that crystal, he thought, banishing from his mind the faint doubt he had heard in Arranha's voice. If Gird could become what he had become, if from peasant clay had come first that stone hammer to break the old lords' rule, and then that . . . whatever it was . . . that he had become at the end, surely he, Luap, could be that clear crystal point Arranha spoke of.

Light speared from the sun's rim, just clearing the distant mountain. He squinted only slightly. *Take it in*, Arranha had said. *Fear nothing light; the god cannot darken your sight; only you can darken the god's light.* Fine, but a lifetime's experience made squinting easy. Gird's voice, it seemed, came into his head with the thud of worn boots on hard-packed earth. *Easy? And who said leadership's easy, lad?*

He forced his eyes wide, and felt that his head filled with brilliant light, radiance, glory. Slowly, the sun crawled upward; he watched, not thinking now, returning only praise for glory. At last its lower edge flicked free of the world's grip. Behind him, the singers fell silent. He stood motionless another long moment, then remembered his next duty. Arms wide, welcoming, he let his gaze fall to the little altar before him. *Light to light, fire to fire, sight to sight . . .* the peasant chant intruded, and he had to strain to remember what now he should say. "Lightbringer, firebringer . . ." His own power's fire given to the eight carefully laid sticks, no conceit of actual help to the Sunlord, Arranha had said, but willingness shown. And he must make that fire the hardest of the several ways he knew. A flame burst from the sticks, unsustained by them, unconsuming: his own power given freely. They would be saved to kindle the first fires after Midwinter Feast.

He quenched the fire, and turned. Arranha nodded at him; the others smiled. Beyond them, their shadows stretched blue across the plateau almost to the cliff beyond. In his mind, their numbers matched those shadows; he could imagine the beauty of so many voices, singing the Sunlord's praises. This year they would fill the terraces they had built; this year they would plant for the first time, and then . . . then others could come. Others of his people, and in a few years children born here, would raise their voices in song to speed the turning year.

Back inside, he called the Rosemage and Arranha into his own room. "I will be going, in a few days. If it goes well — "

"It should," said Arranha. "They were friendly enough last fall."

"I hope it will." Luap paused to sip from the mug of sib the Rosemage had poured him. He had not expected her to become his servant, but she had been doing him such services since autumn. At first it had felt very strange, but now he enjoyed it. "But some may object even if we take the dirt from fallow lands."

"You can't take it from the cursed lands," the Rosemage said. "Remember — "

"I know." He waved at her. Most of the old lords who poisoned their lands had done so with temporary magicks, having hoped to restore themselves to power. But a few, in the final days of the war, had chosen to use long-lasting curses which even now could not be broken. Generations, Arranha had said, would pass before that soil bore healthy growth. Luap had seen the blighted fields, black as charred wood and far less fertile . . . luckily they were few. He would not bring that curse back here to work its evil. "It's still going to be difficult."

"I had a thought," said Arranha. Luap looked at him. From the tone it was one of those thoughts that caused them all to feel that their minds had been twisted into bread coils. He nodded, and Arranha, smiling as usual, went on. "At one time, our people had the power to make much of a small supply. As the Sunlord's light brings increase to the fields, or one seed makes many after the growth of a crop — "

"Argavel's Lore," said the Rosemage.

"Yes. And it came with the usual warning: the gods' gifts must not be used lightly. Some of our ancestors used this too greedily, and lost it. But I asked Gird one time — "

"You asked Gird?" Luap could not keep the surprise from his voice.

Arranha nodded. "Of course: he was a farmer, and a good one. The priesthood of Esea had preserved a verse at the end of Argavel's Lore which implied, I always thought, that the *elements* had been unaffected by the decree that mortals might not usurp the gods' power of increase."

"So?" For once, the Rosemage sounded abrupt with Arranha; Luap was glad his tediousness bothered someone else as well.

"So we could no longer make a pile of gold rings from the pattern of one, or a platter of bread from one slice . . . but we might, I thought, have the power to make two lumps of clay from one, or two gusts of wind from one . . . you see?"

"And what had Gird to do with that?" asked Luap.

"He let me try, with a lump of soil. And it worked." Arranha looked pleased with himself. Luap felt he was supposed to get something more from this than he had yet figured out.

"So you — took a lump of soil, and you got two lumps of soil?"

"Five, altogether. It's harder than it looks. One needs a matrix of some sort. I was using sawdust. Rockdust would be better." Arranha smiled again, and then shook his head. "Gird was not impressed. He said you could get good soil by putting sawdust and cow droppings together, every farmer knew that much."

At last it came together in Luap's mind. "But you're saying you could use some good dirt and the rockdust we have to make more? I would have to bring only one fifth what we need?"

"Better even than that. It didn't occur to me while talking to Gird, but I should be able to use whatever you bring doubled, and then redoubled, and so forth." Luap wondered if his face was as blank as the Rosemage's; Arranha sighed at them. "It's the same principle as my way of cutting stone." *How*, Luap wanted to ask, but Arranha anticipated this and went on. "Remember what I showed you about reflecting lines? Symmetry? This should work the same."

"How many of us can do it, do you think?"

Arranha shrugged. "As with the stone, we don't know. It may not be the same ones; young Aris may find multiplying earth more like healing than stonework, for instance. And it will not take many: doubling increases faster than you think."

Luap had chosen to return to Fin Panir after Midwinter Feast, and in the Lord's Hall before dawn. That should satisfy the new Marshal-General's finicky notions about magery, he thought. Everyone knew by now he traveled by magery; it was ridiculous to insist that he hide the fact. Particularly since he could time his arrival to alarm no one.

That had been his intent, at least, and he depended on his lookouts' report of the star positions to time his exit — but there was light enough in the Lord's Hall for a very frightened junior yeoman to see his arrival, and for Luap to see the youth's rapid flight, as well as hear it. Amused, Luap stepped from the incised platform below the altar and strode after him into the snow-streaked courtyard.

The yeomen on duty at the Council stairs were not amused. Roused from late-watch endurance by the boy's startled cry and plunge from the Lord's Hall door, they'd been prepared for something more dangerous than Luap: a demon, perhaps, or at least a ghost. Luap himself, familiar to them but not the boy, merely irritated them.

"You didn't have to scare the lad," said one, wiping his nose. "Comin' in th' dark like that — you could ha' been anyone."

Luap tried a smile, which made no difference in their expressions. "I'd thought coming before dawn would be the least trouble," he said. "I didn't expect anyone to be there — "

"It's after dawn," the guard pointed out.

"Here it is. Where I was, it will be dark another span. This is nearer the sun's rising, and I forgot how much." Actually he was not sure how much sooner dawn came to Fin Panir, but they need not know that.

"Huh. Don't think of everything, do you? Well, if it's the Marshals you want, they'll not all be up yet."

Luap thought of the years in which Gird was always up by dawn, at work by daylight. Some of the Marshals were like that still, but some, in Fin Panir, clearly relished the chance to lie abed warm on cold winter mornings. That had begun even while Gird lived, though the old man had not been above routing younger Marshals out himself.

"Something wrong, out there?" asked the other guard. He sounded hopeful. Luap laughed.

"No — all's going well, but I am supposed to report at intervals." The guards moved back into the windless angle of the building, and Luap moved through dim passages to the kitchen.

"You look fresh for someone who rode all night," said Marshal Sterin, hunched over a mug of sib. Another Marshal sat silent beside him. "Or did you come in late, and find a room?"

Luap chose a mug from the stack, and dipped himself a hot drink. "I came the mageroad," he said, not looking at them.

"But that still leaves you a long ride — unless you can come *here* — " By the change in tone, Sterin didn't like that possibility. His voice sharpened even more. "Or can you just flit from place to place at your will, regardless? I thought it was some special place you'd found, that made it possible."

"The Lord's Hall," said Luap, between sips. "The same pattern, or part of it, is incised in the floor near the altar. I thought you knew that." He could not remember which Marshals had been in Fin Panir the last time he'd come.

"Ah. So when you take the old lady, she won't have to ride a week to your hidden cave, eh?"

"No. That's why I came this way — " That was a reason they could accept, and even admire.

"How did you learn it worked here as well?"

Luap shrugged, and reached past them to a cold loaf; he could smell the morning's baking in the ovens. "Tried it once. I don't know what might have happened; my thought was that if it didn't work, I'd have come out in the cave anyway."

"Huh. Like jumping a horse over a fence in the dark," Sterin said, in a tone that suggested it took courage and stupidity in equal measure. Luap remembered now that he had been a stableboy before the war; he loved horses. "So — how do you like it out there? Is it good land?"

"It's rough," Luap said. "Mountains, narrow rocky valleys: it's going to be hard to farm, but it's ours."

"There's some won't mind thinking of the mageborn breaking their fingernails on hard work," said the other marshal in a carefully neutral voice.

"Work won't hurt us," said Luap. Let them think that, and gloat, while his people moved house-sized rocks with a finger's touch and magery.

Both men chuckled. "You learned something, your years wi' Gird," said the quieter one.

"And my years as a farmer," Luap pointed out. They looked as if they'd forgotten or never believed, but finally smiled at him. "When's the Marshal-General available?" he asked.

"Oh — time the sun hits the side court, he'll be done eating," said Sterin. "You don't want to bother him afore then

— but you'd remember." Luap nodded; anyone who'd tangled with Marshal-General Koris before he had two mugs of sib and hot breakfast inside him remembered it. That he'd been just as unpleasant to the magelords during the war, especially that morning at Greenfields, had won him a Marshal's shirt and later advancement. No one doubted his courage, or his willingness to work (once he was up and fed) but Gird himself had learned not to disturb Koris at dawn without urgent reason.

"You want *what*?" The Marshal-General stared as if his froggy eyes would burst. Luap still found it difficult to believe they had chosen Koris, even though he'd been at the election. If only Cob had not been so adamant about staying with his rural grange.

"Dirt," said Luap again, being patient. "Soil. You know: what you grow crops in."

"You're going to take *dirt* back to your mountain fortress by *magery*?"

Luap bit back a sarcastic remark about the practicality of taking it any other way, and nodded instead. Still, through the ensuing argument, he had a vivid mental image of a caravan loaded with dirt headed for an unknown destination. "With your permission," he said. The Marshal-General scowled at the courtesy, and Luap cursed himself. He had forgotten how rude — honest, they called it — the Girdsmen were, in their own land. Among his people, he found himself thinking, courtesy implied no weakness; he had acquired the habit of smooth speaking. Here it could only get him in trouble.

"Well . . . let me ask the others." The Marshal-General had run out of reasons, but he was not about to give in.

Luap bit his tongue to keep from explaining again that they would not take *much* dirt; it could inconvenience no one to take a little dirt from some disused farmstead. He could have simply taken it, without asking, except that he had promised Gird, a promise he had so far kept. But Gird would not have had to ask anyone; he would have given his answer at once, and that would have been the end of it. In his mind, Luap asked Gird, and Gird — his imagined Gird — growled assent, irritable at being disturbed for such a trivial matter. Luap felt better. Gird would have let him take the dirt, and this paltry successor to Gird's position would accomplish nothing with his indecision.

"You will excuse me," he said smoothly to the Marshal-General, not minding now that it ruffled the man so. "I have friends waiting, whom I have not seen in more than a season. When the Council has considered, perhaps you would let me know?"

Astonishment. Resentment. Envy. Anger. This was someone who would always end in anger, for whom anger served every need. "And where will you be," the Marshal-General asked querulously. "Here in Fin Panir, or off in that haunt of magery?"

Already such a reputation! Luap wondered what the man would have said if he'd seen them carving the very mountains to build their terraces, and smiled to himself. That smile came into his voice; he did not trouble himself to hide it. "I will be here, in Fin Panir, some length of days, Marshal-General. Working on the chronicles, and checking the copyists' work, as the Council requested. Should your decision take longer, I may be there awhile."

The Marshal-General sniffed. "We shall take what time we need, to consider carefully all that might result from such a choice."

Luap struggled not to think *It's only dirt* too loud. The man's eyes dropped again to his desk, then flicked up as if hoping to catch Luap by surprise. Luap met that glance with blandness. "I would not try to hurry you, Marshal-General."

Now the man flushed, and he rushed into explanation. "It's not just my decision, you know. I'm not like a king —"

"It's quite all right, Marshal-General," said Luap. They had no real hierarchy, having fought a revolution to end hierarchies, and had discovered the function behind tradition with dismay. Gird, taking a king's power, had never believed he held it, and in that belief had used it casually, as if born with the rod in hand. His successors, so far, had used it nervously, uncertain how much use was needful. Even Cob, who had seemed to understand the need for a single final leader, had not pursued his original plan. Luap smiled again at the Marshal-General, and left.

For all that he felt alienated from the peasants who crowded the streets, he enjoyed the city bustle. From the palace area, he

287

went down to the main market, noting how healthy, if rude, the population seemed these days. Red-cheeked men and women, bundled warmly against the cold, hurried to and fro, meantime trampling the snow to a dirty mess. When he came to the wider streets near the market, he found more signs of improved trade and order. An oxcart of sand almost blocked the street, and two men shoveled sand over a thick lens of ice. The inn where Gird had gotten so disasterously drunk looked busy enough; he heard singing from behind its windows. Loud voices in the streets, cheerful but coarse; half the words were those *his* people never used.

He had remembered where Dorhaniya's narrow house stood, past the market, and up one of the crooked streets on the lower hill. When he knocked, Eris answered the door, as stolid as ever, but she smiled briefly.

"She's doing better," she said. "I'll tell her."

"I didn't know she'd been sick," Luap said.

"Oh. I thought maybe that was why you came — "

"No, I've been out in the new place — surely she told you?"

Eris shrugged. "I don't pay that much mind, to be sure. She's getting on, you know. She did say something — about a new place, and we might go — but she'll never shift out of her own room, again, let alone move the household."

"But — " He said no more. He had counted on Dorhaniya, old as she was; something about her eased his mind in a way no one else did. To her, he was the prince, the legitimate heir to the throne, and while she agreed he must never take the throne, she still gave him the deference, the respect, she thought due his birth.

"I'll tell her," said Eris again. "Please — wait here — she'll want to see you, but she'll want to dress."

He waited in a stuffy little room hardly warmer than outside. Perched on a carved chair that seemed designed to poke him in the spine if he relaxed, he looked around at a room lit by sunlight reflected from a snowy back yard, perhaps a garden in summer. Gradually, he recognized the contents, the tools and supplies of a lifetime's occupation for a woman of Dorhaniya's class. Baskets of fine-spun yarn in neat balls, two standing tapestry frames, another hand-frame with a half-finished design placed neatly on a table under the window. He stood, after another vicious poke from the chair, and went to

288

the table. Outlined in a circle of blue, a white G and gold L intertwined, the stitches so tiny that, as with the altarcloth, he almost believed the design painted and not embroidered. He glanced at the frames. On one, another version of the G and L design, this one set in a blue rectangle bordered with red and white interlacing. To his eyes, it looked finished. The other, hardly begun, he could not interpret — something geometrical, he thought, in green and blue and red.

"She begs your pardon," said Eris, behind him; Luap turned quickly. "She wants to see you, but wishes to have me put up her hair. Would you like something to drink?" She had brought a tray with a tall, narrow silver pot; the scent of the vapor rising took him straight back to childhood. What had it been called? Something he'd never tasted, but served to the adults in the afternoon. "Selon, perhaps?" said Eris, touching the pot. Luap nodded, more curious than thirsty. It looked as he remembered, darker than sib, with a hint of red, but clear. Eris poured into a cup thin as an apple petal, and shaped almost flowerlike, of five lobes. He took it, inhaled, and smiled at her. The impulse came to confide.

"I haven't smelled this since I was a boy," he said. Her answering smile was clearly ironic.

"I don't doubt," she said, in a voice that halted any further confidence. "No more trade to Aarenis or Old Aare; my lady's had the sacks hidden in her grain-jars more than half her life. It was her husband's, the Duke's — part of the marriage settlement, it was, for my lady's father craved selon, especially in cold weather. Hasn't been any in the markets since I was a girl, not even for the richest mageborn. Yet my lady'd rather starve than sell it." From her tone and expression, it was clear that Eris had never tasted it, and that it would never occur to Dorhaniya to share, and that Eris would resent any questions far more than her lady's thoughtlessness.

Luap sipped. A strange flavor, that fit well with its aroma: rich, exciting, an edge of bitterness (though less bitter than sib, and needing no spoonful of honey to ease it down.) By the end of the cup, he felt rested, as if waking from a night's sleep. Eris had left the tray on the table; he considered pouring himself another cup, but resisted the temptation. Lady Dorhaniya might want to share one with him, and it would not look well if he had guzzled the whole pot. But the tray also held a small plate, of the same delicate ware, with tiny pastries; he tried one and found it delicious. He had not suspected Eris of being that good a cook. He ate another, then another.

"She's ready," said Eris from the doorway. She turned and led the way up a short flight of stairs, and showed Luap into a room in the front of the house, overlooking the street. He stopped just inside the door, appalled. It had not been that long — surely it had not been that long! Exquisitely clean and groomed as always, she lay against piled pillows, silver hair elaborately dressed — but no longer the spry elderly lady he had known. Only her eyes still looked alive, and even there, he thought, he could see the faint veils of approaching death wrapping her gently away from the world.

It could not be; he would not have it. He was making the safe place for her to live; she must live until he made it. He would heal her — he remembered then that Aris was in the new stronghold. Well, then, he would get Aris. He realized he was standing there, like any rude clod, saying nothing, and that she was smiling at him, the rueful smile of any grandparent observing a child in distress.

"You can't do it," she said, her voice as fragile as a frost-fern on the window. "It is not something you can cure."

"Aris — " he said.

She shook her head, once, very carefully, as if she feared it might come off. "No, my prince. Not even that sweet boy — man though he is — can defeat age. I'm glad you came back in time; I wanted to see you again."

He knelt by her bed, holding her hand in his and blinking back tears. It was hard to remember how he had resented her at first, when he felt she intruded on his childhood memories. Now it was as if he had always known her, as if she were part of his own family. "I wanted you to see it," he said softly. "I thought of you, as we carved the valley walls. . . ."

"I know," she said. "You told me. . . . I can almost see them in my mind, the way you said. A land made of castles, towers and walls, rose-red and pink and sunset-orange. I think of you standing there in the sun, atop a red stone wall, the wind blowing your cloak. Your place, your own land. Prince, if you never wear a crown, you will still have more than your father had, when you have your own land, at peace, with your own people around you."

In her soft old voice, the dream came alive; he forgot the surly guards, Sterin's doubts, the Marshal-General's obstructions. Already, the terraces lay green with springing grain, edged with vegetables, and fruit trees bore blossom and fruit on the same branch in a warm spring sun.

He blinked. Whoever did or did not have the power of charming men, Dorhaniya had it full measure, though he doubted she knew it. That vision had been hers, not his — for his included watchtowers on the height. "I came directly here," he said. "To the — to Esea's Hall; the same pattern is there, behind the altar. I could take you back, if only for —"

Her head turned slowly. "Prince, if you command, I will do even this — but I would not live to see it. Esea's light almost blinds me even now. Do not trouble yourself about me — think of the others you are working to save. Think of your friend Gird —"

"Gird?" The last person he wanted to think of right then, and the last he'd expected her to mention.

A sigh escaped her. "Prince, never forget him. He was — more than a man, I think. A great man, at the least. Peasant though he was, the gods gave him light to see beyond the rest of us. And he was your friend, though he and you might both deny it."

"I . . . would not deny it."

"Wise of you." She drew a breath, and let it out slowly. "If I cough, prince, do not fret. Just wait." He waited; she did not cough, but did not speak for some time. Then: "Gird loved you, but as a man loves a son he does not understand. And so his advice to you could not be precisely fitted — but it was not bad, for all that. You were his luap; I would not have you disloyal."

"Disloyal?" His heart sank. Could she possibly imagine all he had thought? Hoped? And would even she consider it disloyal?

"Downstairs," she said. "In the room where Eris left you. You saw the embroidery?"

"Yes, lady." Was her mind wandering?

"Prince, I charge you to take as your crest that symbol." It was as if a tiny child had spouted legal theory, or a wren had given voice to an eagle's scream. Luap felt his jaw drop, and hastened to shut it again. It was not a voice to bear argument. "Gird and Luap — your initials intertwined. I think of you as a prince, as indeed you are, but Esea's light shows me you will prosper as Gird's luap only. Stray from that at your peril."

"But, lady — why do you think — ?"

"Because — " Her old face crumpled, and her grip tightened on his hand. "Prince, I will not insult you — but remember an old lady's years. I had children; I had nieces and nephews enough, watched them grow through all the awkwardnesses of youth to adulthood, saw the same patterns in the adult as in the child, the same grain in the wood. It is not your fault; I could never blame you. But you know what I mean — don't make me say it!"

"I don't hate Gird," he said, almost whispering.

"That is not enough," she said. "You must love him. You must be his luap, truly his luap, before you can be the prince you are — or rather, the prince you were meant to be."

"To all but you, I have always been his luap."

"Then . . . to me also, be his luap."

"But, lady . . . you were the one who said I must be a prince; you encouraged me."

"Yes. I did." Her other hand plucked at the lace on the coverlet. "I did not always understand, until Gird died. I thought it was foolishness longer than I should have, all that about Gird's rule being one for both peoples. But it came to me when he died, that he was right: that was the only way. And if I encouraged you to think of your heritage, and that made you unwilling to enter into Gird's vision, then I was wrong and Esea may send me to the dark forever."

"You could not be so wrong," Luap said. He squeezed her hand. "You, who love the gods so much — how could they be angry with you?"

"Don't be silly!" Again that tone of authority that stung like a lash. "Selamis — no, *I* will call you Luap! If that will get through your thick head — how can you think of the gods as indulgent grandparents? If I cause great harm, then of course Esea will be angry with me. I only hope I have not, or that I can cure it."

"You have not caused any harm," said Luap firmly. If he could do nothing else, he would soothe the fears of this dying old woman. "You are quite right; I am Gird's luap. I loved Gird from the day I met him, served him as well as I could, and will continue to honor his memory to the day I die. Don't fear I could forget him."

She had fallen back against her pillows again. "You will use the crest I made?" she asked, her voice unsteady. "You will be loyal?"

He kissed her hand. "I will use it," he said. "I will carve it into the very rock, if that will please you. And I will serve Gird's memory as I served him in life." He meant that, and his voice carried all that conviction.

"Esea's light guide you," she said. She lay for awhile, eyes shut, breathing shallowly. Eris came in to sit beside Luap.

"It won't be long," she murmured. "Today, perhaps tomorrow."

Luap forgot time, and sat silently, holding that old hand with its soft loose skin, until the light failed outside. Eris went to fetch candles; when she came back, Dorhaniya's breathing had changed. She seemed to struggle, panting, then all at once lay motionless, each breath slower than the last. Luap waited long for the last, before he realized it had already come and gone. Beside him, Eris sobbed.

• Chapter Twenty-one

"You can take a wagonload of soil, but no more," said the Marshal-General when he summoned Luap. By his expression, he expected Luap to argue.

"Thank you, Marshal-General," said Luap, "for your generosity."

"And you can't take it from any working farm," the Marshal-General went on, "or from any grangeland. You must find unclaimed land, and take it there."

"Of course, Marshal-General."

"And take it out the *other* way — we don't want a wagonload of dirt in the Lord's Hall."

Luap started to say that a wagon wouldn't fit into the little cave chamber, and realized that was what the Marshal-General hoped he'd do. He bowed instead. "Of course, Marshal-General; that would not be fitting."

"*And,*" the Marshal-General went on, as if reaching for something at which Luap would balk, "and you will have a yeoman-marshal with you, to ensure that you take your soil as I said, from unclaimed land only."

Luap shrugged, as much in anger as resignation, but managed not to say what he was thinking. The Marshal-General stalked to his door, opened it, and beckoned to a short muscular woman wearing the blue shirt that most yeoman-marshals wore these days. Apparently he had already explained her task, for now he simply pointed to Luap and said, "Make sure, Binis, that he does what I said."

"Right, Marshal-General." She looked at Luap as if he were a thief on trial; he could feel his ears growing hot. He would, he decided, change her mind before he left, if he could not change the Marshal-General's. "When do we leave?" she asked Luap.

"After a friend's funeral," he said. "An old lady I've known a long time, a friend of Gird's — she died yesterday."

"Who?" asked the Marshal-General.

"Dorhaniya, who made the altar cloths for the Lord's Hall."

"A magelady," growled the Marshal-General.

"Gird thought of her as a pious old woman who cared more about the gods than any quarrel of men," said Luap, putting a bite in it. "He enjoyed talking to her—but you weren't in the city then, were you?" He regretted that even as it popped out, for it would do no good to remind the Marshal-General that he had never been close to Gird. The man scowled even more darkly.

"Even Gird made mistakes," he said.

"I must go," said Luap, "but we can leave at dawn, day after tomorrow. Meet you in the kitchen?" He looked only at Binis, who glanced uncertainly from him to the Marshal-General. The Marshal-General nodded, then she did.

"But don't try to sneak out without me," she said. "I'm a tracker; I would find you."

"That's as well," said Luap, "since we'll be traveling in the midst of winter storms. I will depend on your tracking ability when the snow flies."

The Marshal-General grinned at him. "That's right . . . how are you going to dig your soil while it's frozen? You can't use your magery here; it's against the Code and your own oath forbids you."

"I may find a place and come back after the thaw," Luap said. "I have no intention of breaking my oath." Before the Marshal-General could say more, he added, "And I will of course find yeoman-marshal Binis if that is necessary, so that she can supervise."

He turned with a conscious flourish and left the Marshal-General's office — Gird's office, as he himself still thought of it. He spent the rest of that day with Eris, and greeted those who came to speak of Dorhaniya as if he were a family member.

At dawn on the second day, he came into the kitchen with his gear packed and ready to go. Binis was gossiping with a cook kneading dough, an older woman who gave Luap an open grin.

"We miss you, Luap! Do you still like fried snow?" He saw Binis stare at the woman as if she'd turned into a lizard. So . . . not everyone remembered, or knew, that he had had his own friends here? That not all of them had left?

295

"Ah . . . Meshi, no one makes fried snow like yours. This Midwinter Feast I wanted to come back for it. I don't suppose you saved any?"

"Saved! Fried snow keeps about as well as real snow in high summer, as well you know. If you want my fried snow, Luap, you'll just have to come when it's ready." She flipped the mass of dough into a smooth ball and laid a cloth over it. "I suppose you want breakfast before you leave, eh?"

"Anything that's at hand." Anything at Meshi's hand would be delicious; she had a double parrion of cooking.

"First bread's out." In a moment, she had sliced a hot loaf and handed it to him with a bowl of butter and a squat stone jar. "Spiced peaches," she said. "From our tree."

"You shouldn't," he said, as he always had, and added, "but I'm glad you did. Spiced peaches again!" He let a lump of butter melt into the hot bread, then spooned the spiced peach preserves onto it. The aroma went straight to his head.

"You don't have spices in that godslost wilderness?" Meshi looked shocked.

"Not yet; I'll buy some in the market to take back." The first bite, he thought, was beyond price; his nose and his tongue contended over ecstasy. Then he noticed Binis standing stiffly to one side, and gestured. "Come, don't you like spiced peaches?"

"Never had any," she muttered, but sat across from him and took a slice of the hot bread. When she'd put a small spoonful on it, she tasted it; her face changed. "It's — I never had anything like that."

"Can't make much," Meshi said shortly, setting down two bowls of porridge with emphasis. "Takes time, makes only a little. Can't serve it all the time." *Or to everyone* came across clearly in the little silence that followed. Luap wanted to eat the whole jar of preserves, but took the hint and started on the porridge. Meshi's gift held even with that. She waited a moment longer, for courtesy, then took the stone jar back and capped it. "It dries out," she said. Then she turned to Binis. "He tried to talk me into going with them, you know. Flattered my cookery, said how they wouldn't have proper foods for the holidays —"

"We don't," said Luap.

" — And I almost went," Meshi said, as if she had not heard

the interruption. "But I had too many friends here who weren't going, and even for old Luap I wouldn't give them all up." Then she winked at Luap. "And, to tell the whole truth, I was scared of that magery — being taken by magic to some place I'd never seen gave me the shivers. So I couldn't. But I miss Luap, that I do, for he's one to notice who does the work, no matter what it is."

"He's mageborn," said Binis, around a mouthful of porridge.

"He's *half*," said Meshi firmly, giving Luap another wink. "Half mageborn, which he can't help any more than any of us can choose our fathers, and half peasant-born, which isn't to his credit any more than his father is to his blame. And I'll tell you this, Binis, to your face and in front of his, if you have the sense you should have, you'll forget whatever our Koris said about him, and look at the man himself. I was here when Gird was still alive, and Luap's worth a gaggle of your Marshal-Generals."

Binis looked at Luap, then at Meshi. "Was he your lover?"

Meshi glared. "He was not. Is that all you girls can think of, these days, but who crawls in whose bed?"

Binis shrugged. "You seem fond of him, is all I meant."

"I like him; I trust him; and it's not his fault he's in bad with the Marshal-General."

"Mmm." Binis was not convinced; Luap didn't know if Meshi's words had made things better or worse.

They left the kitchen, bellies full and foodsacks stuffed, and walked down to the lower city. Binis walked a step behind, Luap noticed, and would not come up beside him even though the streets were not yet crowded. He had not been surprised to find that the Marshal-General would not lend horses from the grange stables; he had arranged to hire mounts and a pack animal from a caravan supplier. He had no intention of walking those trails in winter if he could help it.

As much to annoy her as because he had planned to, he stopped to buy spices — perhaps someone out west would take the trouble to make spiced preserves — and tucked the expensive packets deep in his clothing. The horses he had arranged for were saddled when he arrived, two stocky beasts and a smaller pony. He lashed the foodsacks and their other gear to the packsaddle, and handed the caravaner the sack of coins. He mounted; Binis still stood, holding the rein of the other horse, with a dubious expression. Finally, flushing, she scrambled up so awkwardly he realizes she might not have ridden before.

"I'm sorry," he said. "Do you not like riding?" It was the most diplomatic way he could think to ask.

"Never did." She sat lumpishly, her stirrups far too long and her grip on the saddle too tight.

Luap caught the eye of the caravaner, who bit his lip and said, "Just wait, yeoman-marshal, and let me get at them stirrups. You looked longer-legged than that standing on the ground." The man adjusted the stirrups, then said, "Bein' as it's winter, you might want stirrup-covers, eh?" He ducked back into the stable entrance, and came out with fur-lined leather hoods that tied to the stirrups and protected their feet from the worst winds. They would also, Luap knew, keep Binis's feet from sliding too far into the stirrup.

By the end of the first day's riding, he wondered why he had ever thought midwinter a good time for this. They had had no more than ordinary winter weather, snow no deeper than usual, but they arrived at the village's small grange stiff and sore. Binis could hardly get off her horse, but flinched away when Luap tried to help her. Luap would have had more sympathy for her if she had not made it clear that she blamed him for her discomfort, as if he had chosen to travel horseback because she could not ride. The Marshal, new here since Luap had left, made it clear he thought they were both crazy to be riding around the countryside in the wintertime. He was inclined to blame it all on Luap's magery.

"You may be able to keep yerself warm wi' your magicks, but ye might have had some concern f'the yeoman-marshal here." The Marshal had wrapped a blanket around her; she gave Luap a venomous look out from under the Marshal's elbow. Luap wondered if it would help to tell them he had not kept himself warm — his feet felt frozen, despite the stirrup-covers. From the look on both their faces, they wouldn't believe him.

"I'll see to the horses," he said, and went out. He was tempted to spend the night in the grange's lean-to barn; the horses were friendlier than his companions. But they would probably think he was performing wicked magicks out here by himself; he had better not.

When he came back inside, he heard the murmur of voices; it ceased when they saw him. The Marshal's own yeoman-marshal had joined them. He looked at Luap with the same accusing gaze, and Luap knew they had been discussing the wicked mageborn while he was outside. He found it hard to swallow his supper of ill-cooked porridge and heavy bread amid barbed comments about the luxuries he must be used to. He bit back one retort after another; his jaw felt sore. He tried to remind himself that all peasants weren't like this — Dorhaniya's Eris, for instance, or Cob or Raheli. But these three, and the present Marshal-General, exemplified everything he disliked about his mother's people. By the time he rolled himself in a blanket on the floor (Binis, of course, had the spare pallet), he was thoroughly disgusted with them.

That day and night set the tone for the whole miserable journey. Binis felt the cold more than Luap, but remained convinced that he was using magery unfairly to keep himself comfortable. He had no way to prove he was not. As his anger grew, he would have used his magery that way if he had known how. He tried, surreptitiously, but succeeded only in giving himself a throbbing headache made worse by the glare off the snow. And he was just as cold as Binis, he told himself, but she wouldn't believe it. He remembered, with a burst of satisfaction that he knew was unwise, that the woman whose complaints had driven Gird to a fit of rage had also been named Binis. It wasn't the same Binis, of course, but this one might have been that one's daughter. He didn't ask. He preferred to imagine it, in the privacy of his own head.

They arrived, two days later than he had expected, in Cob's grange. Here, at least, the welcome was as warm for Luap as for Binis. Cob, always lamer in winter, stumped awkwardly into the snowy lane to greet them.

"Luap, you look like a frozen sausage. Get off that horse, and come in to the fire. Vre — " That was his yeoman-marshal, a brisk young man. "Take their horses around back. Bring the packs inside. Ah, Luap, I've missed you. That scribe you left in charge is slower than a pregnant ox at a gate. And who's this?" Luap explained that the new Marshal-General had insisted he have a yeoman-marshal escort. "You? What does he think he's about? No insult to you, Binis, but no one needs to watch Luap. Alyanya's grace, *Gird* trusted him. That ought to be enough for anyone,"

Luap took a step and staggered; he knew his feet were at the end of his legs, but he hadn't felt his toes since the village before. Binis, looking from him to Cob with a scowl, had made it to the grange door. Cob shook his head.

"You're going to look like me, if you keep that up. Need an arm?"

"No. I'm fine." He could walk, if he kept a surreptitious eye on his feet to be sure where they were. He made it to the door, across the grange, and into Cob's office. There a fire crackled busily on the hearth. Binis had already crouched beside it. Cob pulled a chair near, and waved Luap into it.

"Let him get his feet to the fire, yeoman-marshal — he's twice your age." Binis looked startled.

"But Marshal, he's a mageborn — he can use magicks to warm himself. . . . "

Cob snorted. "Does it look like it? Use your wits, Binis — he's famished with cold, as bad as you are." She looked at him, as if seeing him anew. Luap found it embarrassing.

"I'm warm enough," Luap said. Cob's welcome was as good as any fire, and his feet were already beginning to throb. Cob's yeoman-marshal, Vrelan, came in with the packs.

"Shall I fetch something to eat, Marshal?" Vrelan sounded eager to prove himself; Luap realized he was very young, probably born after the war. Cob sent him to the local inn — Luap had not realized there was an inn — and turned back to Luap.

"So how is the settlement coming? Will you get a crop in this next year?" With that opening, Luap could explain that he had come for fertile soil, and needed only a little. Cob grinned. "Take what you like — we've plenty in the grange fields."

"I can't do that. The Marshal-General specified I was not to take so much as a clod from farmland or grangelands, only from waste ground."

"Even if the Marshal offered?" Cob looked angry.

"That's right, Marshal," Binis said. Luap thought she would have been wise to hold her tongue. "That's what I'm to do, watch to be sure he doesn't take the wrong soil."

Cob looked at her; Luap recognized the look Gird had given that other Binis and held his breath. But Cob was not drunk, as Gird had been; he merely shook his head. "I didn't ask you," he said. "And I don't think that frog-eyed fool has the right to tell me what I can and can't do with a bit of earth from my own drillfields. He wasn't with Gird as long as I was." It was exactly what Luap had hoped he would say, all the long, cold, miserable trip from Fin Panir, but now he felt a hollow open inside him. Cob meant what he said, and he could take his soil and go home — but that would leave Cob in a mess.

"No," Luap said. "I didn't come here to start a quarrel between you and the Marshal-General."

"You didn't start it," Cob said, reddening. "That — " Luap was aware of Binis's interest, her ears almost flapping wide on either side of her head. And Cob had been Gird's friend, with Gird longer than almost anyone else still alive.

"No," he said again, and let a little of his power bleed into it. On Gird it had not worked; on Cob and Binis it worked well. Both sat quiet and stared at him. "I will not disobey the Marshal-General's orders on this, though I thank the friend who cared more to help me than advance himself." Neither of them said anything, and he was afraid he had put too much power on them . . . but then Cob shook himself, like a wet dog.

"All right," he said gruffly, not looking at Binis. "But I want you to know that I trust you. Now — where's that boy with the food?" He got up and left the office to Luap and Binis. Luap stretched luxuriously. The fire's warmth crept over him in exquisite waves; he could feel not only his throbbing feet, but a blanket-like warmth on his knees and thighs. He had not been this warm for days; the other Marshals had pushed Binis close to the fire. He glanced at her. One side of her face seemed flushed — from the fire or embarrassment, he could not guess.

"Are you warm enough?" he asked her.

"Did you really not have magicks for the cold?" she asked, without answering him.

"No," Luap said. He was not really surprised at her question; from the little they'd talked he had discovered her to have a literal mind and a tenacious grasp of the trivial. "I'm glad of a fire," he added, hoping this would divert her from the question he saw hovering on her lips. "If you are still cold, why not get a blanket?"

"I'm all right," she said. "Are you really twice my age?"

She was so predictable. She would ask next if Meshi were

301

really his friend, and if he had slept with her, and then why the mageborn had gone to his stronghold . . . and so on, no doubt for hours.

"I don't know how old you are," he said. She scowled at that, looking for trickery in it. "And I don't really know my own years." Which was not quite true, but saved discussing it. She scowled again, not because she detected a lie, but because she had not been answered.

"Is Meshi, that cook, really your friend?"

He uttered a silent prayer to any god who might be listening to bring Cob back into the room. She would go down the predictable list, and it would drive him to saying something he would regret. For the first time, he felt he really understood Gird's rage that night in the forest. He answered all in a rush. "Yes, she's my friend; we met during the war. And she's not my lover and never has been, just as she said when you asked her."

Binis looked shocked; Luap stared her down. Cob came in, followed by Vrelan with a kettle wrapped in cloths, which he unwrapped and put on the hearth. "Better stew than I make; the inn's cook has the true parrion. And new bread, and a pot of custard."

"Marshal-General says Marshals should make their own meals," Binis said primly. Luap closed his eyes a moment. Didn't she realize — ? Cob merely grunted, though his yeoman-marshal stared at Binis as if she'd sprouted green horns.

"I've cooked enough meals in Gird's army to last me, yeoman-marshal. When there's a good cook, who knows what she's doing, and needs the trade, I'm not going to eat lumpy porridge and soggy bread to please someone as won't get out of bed before midday. Gird could've milked a herd and ploughed two fields before Koris finishes breakfast." He dished out stew for everyone, breathing a little hard, and handed Binis her bowl with a stare. "And you go ahead and tell him, Binis, all I've said — he knows how I feel about him, and I know how he feels about me. But when all's said and done, he knows who fought beside Gird from the first day. I didn't *want* to be Gird's successor, but it was offered me. *He* had to argue his way into it."

Binis turned redder than the fire could explain, and ate her stew without looking up. Luap burned his mouth on the first bite, and slowed down. Cob was right — the cook had a parrion. Mutton stew could be almost as bad as lumpy porridge, but this had a savor he liked. Cob pushed over a half-loaf of bread and a dish of butter.

"You spoil me," Luap said, carefully not looking at Binis.

"No — we eat this well almost every day." Cob buttered a hunk of bread for himself and stuffed it in his mouth. Luap winced inwardly. He liked Cob, but the man had never acquired even as much polish as Gird. When he had refused the Marshal-General's position, he had apparently returned to his rural grange determined to be as much a peasant as possible.

Vrelan, meanwhile, sat in the corner opposite Binis, eating as rapidly as any hungry young man just past boyhood. He smiled shyly at Luap when their eyes met. *He will want tales*, Luap thought to himself. *He will want stories of Gird, and stories of my distant land — he's got those dreamer's eyes.*

Cob swallowed, then belched. "So — tell me, Luap, is that land what you hoped it would be?"

Luap nodded, and swallowed the stew in his mouth. "Yes — although it's even colder than this. I've never seen snow so deep. Luckily we need not travel in it, and the stronghold itself doesn't freeze. Though it's not really warm, either."

"Magic, is it?" This with a quick sidelong glance at Binis.

"No, the elves said it was the depth of stone. It stays about the same all year." Luap scooped up more stew before it cooled. His feet had quit throbbing and he felt almost sleepy. "We spent the time before snow building terraces," he went on. "Piled the rock up, had Arranha telling us how to level them."

"I thought you'd just level the valley floor," Cob said. "Isn't it a small valley?"

"Small and steep. Not just the sides, the floor as well. Level the whole thing and the new floor would be halfway up the mountains at the low end." Not quite, but it made a vivid image; Cob nodded, mouth pursed. "So we're doing smaller terraces, none more than three men high at the low end. Most less than that — it'd take too much soil to fill them otherwise."

"A lot of work," Cob said. "And so few of you — I suppose you found a way to use your magicks?"

Luap grinned at him. Cob would not demand, from a friend, but he was as curious as anyone else. "Yes, we did, though it still takes a lot of sweat and blisters. I must admit, it's good to see magery used the right way, for breaking stones and not people. And it keeps the few with magery too busy for mischief."

Cob shot another glance at Binis, who had finished her stew and was munching the end of a loaf of bread. "When you've finished, yeoman-marshal, you and Vrelan take back this pot and then check the horses. You can trust me not to let Luap out of my sight." His tone was pleasant but firm; she could neither resent that order, nor disobey it. Cob turned to Vrelan. "Since we have guests, get us a pot of their good ale, and see if they'll send a loaf of bread fresh from the morning baking." He gave the yeoman-marshal a few coins. Binis and Vrelan went out with the kettle, one cheerful and one scowling. When the outer door had shut behind them, Cob turned to Luap.

"There'll be things you don't want her repeating to the Marshal-General, I daresay, but you might share with an old friend. Tell me: did you find you had all the royal magery?"

For answer, Luap freed his light, and grinned at the expression on Cob's face. "I know — I shouldn't do that here, even though we are alone and you are a friend. You're a Marshal first, and I'm not supposed to use my magery. But I thought you'd like to see it."

"I'm glad for you, since you wanted it, but — glad to see it? — not really. Although it must be handy to have your own light, if you live underground. There are times I could use that. But — you built the terraces that way?"

Luap damped the light; the room seemed dark without it, despite the fire burning cheerily on the hearth. "We did," he said. "Some of us — it's strange, Cob, who has which magery. Our people have not tried to use it for work for a long time; I think that was a mistake. Some can move stones the size of this room —" Cob looked around, the whites of his eyes glinting in the firelight, as if worried that the room might take flight. " — And others can hardly shift a pebble. Most that have any magery at all can call some amount of light, enough to start a fire with. Aris, as you know, can heal. Were you in Council when he described his attempts to train others?"

"No. I missed that one." Cob prodded the fire and laid another split log on it.

"To make it short, he's found no one else who can do what he does. Some can heal lesser things, but at greater cost to themselves. He's hoping that some of the children will have that talent, that he can find it early and train it."

"I thought there was a girl — "

"Yes, so did the others — so did she, for that matter. It wasn't really healing; she could convince people they were not feeling pain, but what caused the pain got no better . . . unless it would have anyway. A useful skill, certainly, and a better use of it than charming someone into handing over their purse, but not true healing. Aris has worked with her, so she now recognizes when she needs to call him in and when it's safe to relieve the pain and wait for a natural healing." Luap sighed. "It's sad — the one magery we all wanted to have, that most people trusted, is the rarest. I had hoped to learn it; I can't. And Aris, so gifted, has little else but his light."

"I miss that lad," Cob said, shaking his head. "He loved Gird so, and Gird loved him like a grandson."

Luap felt a pang of envy and wrestled it down. Everyone liked Aris; he did himself. "We're lucky to have him," he said.

"And how's Seri doing, out there with all you mageborn?"

"Well enough. She has Aris, after all; they're still like two burs, though they don't seem likely to marry."

"Why not? Would you object?"

"Of course not," Luap said. "But since they came back from that long journey, back when she was still a Marshal-candidate, they've been different. I can't explain it, nor can the Rosemage, but we both recognized it."

"It's too bad," Cob said. "I was hoping their child might combine the two of them. Squeeze Aris and Seri into one person, and you'd have quite a Marshal-General." He stretched his legs to the fire. "You're looking better, now you've eaten — that sour-faced yeoman-marshal you're traveling with must have sucked the blood out of you."

Luap laughed. "It's not that. I didn't know she didn't ride, and she took it as an insult . . . and then she has trouble in the cold."

"She'd have died in the bad winter camps of the war," Cob said. "Or she'd have gotten over her foolishness. I hate to think of women like her becoming the next Marshals."

"How's Raheli?" That was the natural transition.

"Haven't seen her since the Council when she spoke for you. She'd mellowed a lot then, I thought. We talked a bit about Gird. I thought she should have been the next Marshal-General. She thought it shouldn't go from parent to child — but she has no children, so I didn't think that was a problem. She wouldn't do it, though."

"I thought the objection would come because — "

"Because she's a woman? So did I, though I don't agree. But she wouldn't take it. She nominated me, in fact, but — I don't know, maybe I should've done it. It just didn't seem right. I *knew* Gird; he threw me flat on my back the first day he came into our camp, and I'm no more fit to take his place than . . . than a cow is. Nobody is, when you come to it, but I couldn't."

The door opened, and the two yeoman-marshals came in, shivering. "A wind's got up," Vrelan said. "Old Dorthan says he reckons another storm's coming." Cob looked at Luap, his brows raised. Luap shrugged.

"I didn't like the look of the sky behind us today, but that's all I can say."

"You're welcome to stay all winter, if that's what it takes," Cob said. "But if a storm's coming, we've some work to do, with two extra beasts in the barn. No — " Luap had started to stand, but Cob waved him back down. "If this is a big storm, your help will be welcome come morning, but stay warm now."

"I'll bring more wood, at least," Luap said.

"If you're determined on it . . . there's a stack in the barton corner."

Outside, in the blowing dark, the cold wind took his breath away. Binis had gone with Cob and Vrelan; he found the woodstack on his own, and thought about moving some in by magery. But Binis might see, and that would do Cob no good. He lugged in several armloads before Cob returned. By then it had begun to snow, small dry flakes that stung his face.

Morning's light barely penetrated the blowing snow; Luap and Cob fought their way around the end of the grange and into the barn built against it, carrying buckets of hot water from the hearth. "We should have built peasant cottages, wi' inside ways to the cowbyres," Cob said, struggling to shut the door against the wind. The horses whickered, their breath pluming into the cold air. When they drank, their whiskers whitened almost at once. Cob nodded to the ladder. "If you can make the climb, it'll be easier for me." So Luap climbed into the narrow hayloft, and threw down enough for all the beasts at once, then climbed back down to help Cob feed them.

Later, the snowfall lessened, though the wind still scoured flurries off the drifts. All four of them went out to check on the poorer folk in the village. Luap had never had a clear idea of what a rural Marshal did when not holding court or drill. Cob apparently thought that a Marshal's job included everything no one else remembered to do . . . he was remarkably like Gird, Luap thought, in the way that he had made himself a caretaker for the whole village. He had Vrelan chop firewood for a family in which the man had a broken arm, and the mother was pregnant. He and Luap climbed up to mend a gap in the roof of one cottage, where slates had blown off overnight. Cob himself dragged one drunk out into the street and made him fetch clean water from the public well to clean up the mess he'd made on the floor, while the man's wife tried to make excuses for him. Binis, clearly astonished that Cob considered her available for such work, was kept as busy as the rest of them.

"It's like this," Cob explained after darkness had fallen and they were eating in the inn. "Some Marshals think we're just judges and drillmasters, but someone's got to do all the rest. Back afore the war, each village had its headman or headwoman, and in some places, even the magelords took care of their people. Everyone knew what needed doing and how to do it. They knew who really needed help, and who was a wastral. But the war changed that. People may not live in the village they were born in; we've got crafters and merchants and gods know what all, living all amongst each other. And whatever you say about one fair law for everyone, some things just plain aren't fair. You don't make it fair by treating everyone alike, either. That's all I do — what the village head would have done, or a good lord: either one. Know the people, know who needs help, and who needs a good knock on the head to straighten 'em up."

"But you can't do it all yourself." Binis looked tired, but less sulky than the days before. Perhaps work agreed with her; Gird had always said it was good for the sulks.

"No," Cob agreed, wiping his bowl with a slice of bread. "No, I can't do it all, not even with young Vre, here. But that's what I tell them on drill nights — just as in an army, we're all parts of each other. If you let your neighbor go hungry, he's not likely to help you when the robbers come.

307

Same way, if you're always asking for help, but don't give any, soon no one cares. I went after Hrelis today, you saw — the drunk. His wife's always coming for grange-gift, says he's sick. We know what kind of sick; Vre told me last night he was in here drinking and begging. So for him I have a bucket of cold water, but poor Jos, who got his arm broken helping someone reset a wheel, we'll do what we can for him. When his arm's mended, he'll be around here doing chores without anyone saying a word." He belched contentedly, and smiled at Binis. "But you're right — I don't do it alone. I don't have to check Morlan's widow any more, and I didn't have to find homes for the children whose parents were killed by lightning in the pasture last spring. This grange is beginning to function as a village should — with care and common sense."

"And that's the other reason you wouldn't be Marshal-General, isn't it?" Luap asked. "You had in mind what a grange should be, but you wanted to show it, not tell people."

Cob flushed and looked away. "I'm no more skilled with words than Gird was," he said. "It's what he did, after all. He showed us —"

"And yelled at us," Luap said, grinning. Cob's dream was not his dream, but he knew it came close to Gird's dream . . . and he could see it was a worthy dream. "But it's going to take unusual Marshals to do what you're doing."

Now Cob grinned back. "Oh — well, that young Seri, you know, she used to talk of things like this. Her and me and Raheli and some of the others: we were thinking what a grange is for, when there's no war. It can't be just to collect money to send to Fin Panir." Binis started to say something, then stopped. Luap wondered if Cob had convinced her; he doubted it. But Cob had convinced him.

That day and the next, with the drifts too high for travel, they stayed in Cob's grange and helped with his definition of grange work. Luap found himself able to admit he had picked a bad time to come looking for soil, but that he'd wanted something to work with for spring planting. "And I was with Dorhaniya when she died," he said. "I'm glad I was there, though I'd hoped she'd like the new place. . . ."

"Tell you what," Cob said. "Come thaw, I'll find you a place to take your soil — there's unclaimed land between me and the next grange south. If I understand it, we'll thaw here before you will, so you won't lose much time. How would that be?"

"I don't think the Marshal-General would approve," said Binis. Cob gave her a look Luap would not like to have turned on him.

"I didn't ask you, Binis, and I'm not asking the Marshal-General. If it's unclaimed land, he can't deny it: he's already given his approval. Whatever his quarrels with Luap, the law says he's made a contract, and he can't back out now."

"But we're not supposed to help —"

"We're not supposed to act like bratty children quarreling over sweets, either." Cob glared at her, red-faced. "D'you think this is what Gird wanted? We won the war; the mageborn aren't our lords any more. Now it's time for peace, and peace means helping each other. And you might remember that Luap here was Gird's closest assistant: he did more for Gird than any of the rest of us, including your precious Marshal-General."

Luap had not expected that strong a defense, even from Cob. It embarrassed him, shook his certainty in the peasants' opposition — a certainty that Binis increased whenever she opened her mouth. Now Cob turned to him.

"How about it — will you trust me to find you some good soil, within the Marshal-General's limitations?"

"Of course, I will," Luap said. "I will come back to Fin Panir in early spring — your early spring."

"Good. That's settled. It'll save Binis here from riding all over the countryside in winter — I don't suppose you can whisk her back to Fin Panir by magery, eh?"

"Alas, no. We'll have to go as we came."

It was as cold a trip as the one out, but Binis seemed slightly less hostile; at least she seemed convinced that Luap, too, suffered from the cold. Luap hoped that Cob would not get in too much trouble with the Marshal-General while he was gone . . . but when he considered the two men, he thought Cob would come off well in any contest between them. So he returned to the stronghold with the embroidery Dorhaniya had given him, determined to prove himself to Cob as well as his own people.

"Now we can begin to move," the black-cloaked leader said. "For mortals time runs swiftly; they become accustomed to safety, and cease to watch for danger. They hope all will be well, and hoping so, believe it to be. A year, two years, of peace, and they think peace eternal." He paused for the scornful laughter, like a rustle of dry leaves, before going on. "We must learn more about them," he said. "Especially the prince. We must know them better than they know themselves — not a difficult task. For each weakness, we will provide the appropriate temptation . . . and remember, if we can use what they call their virtues to entrap them, so much the better."

● Chapter Twenty-two

Luap returned to Fin Panir while the canyons of his own land were still choked with snow. This time, the guards at the High Lord's Hall merely shrugged when he appeared. The Marshal-General, he was told, was "in conference," too busy to see him; Luap found someone who claimed to know where Binis was. He went down to the lower city to visit Eris. Dorhaniya had left her enough to live on, she had said after the funeral, and her own skill at needlecraft would help.

"Sir," she said, when she answered his knock on the door. From her expression, she had not expected to see him again. Then she relaxed. "You've come for the banner?"

He had forgotten it, in the sorrow of Dorhaniya's death and the difficult trip with Binis. "No — or rather yes, I will be glad to have it, of course, but that's not why I came. How are you?"

"I miss her," Eris said. Then she stood aside and beckoned him in. "There's lots of them don't understand, you know. Why I ever stayed with her after the war, why I stay here now. She was just another rich mageborn, they say, just another foolish old rich woman." She led Luap back to the small sitting room he had seen before. "Of course that's true: she was old, and rich, and foolish, and mageborn, but that wasn't the half of it. You know: you met her."

"I know." Luap looked around. He had thought he could forget nothing he had seen, and yet he could not be sure nothing had changed. The embroidery frame was missing . . . but what else?

"I didn't stay just because she was rich, and I never wanted for anything while she was alive. It wasn't that."

"I know," Luap said again. He had never completely understood the bond between Eris and Dorhaniya, but it had nothing to do with gold or comfort: he knew that much.

"She was so — so dithery, sometimes. Her family — her own and her husband's — they both thought she was short of

311

wits. That's why her father sent me to her when I was just a child, and she had only married the year before. Keep her going, they said, as long as you can; she's got no sense of her own. But they were wrong." Eris sat down, and smoothed her skirt. Luap didn't know what to say. He felt that he should comfort her, but she needed nothing he could give. Except perhaps his listening ear, at the moment. "She knew people," Eris said. "She couldn't always say what she meant about them, but she knew what they were like inside. She knew her husband was a silly fool whose pride would get him in trouble with the king, but she never complained about it. She knew that sister of hers, the one who didn't marry Arranha, was mean to the bone, but she never complained about that, even when her sister cheated her out of her mother's jewels. I won't say she was never wrong, for she had a soft heart, but she wasn't wrong often."

Luap wanted to ask what Dorhaniya had thought of him, but he wasn't sure he wanted to know. She had seen through him several times that he knew of, commenting on fear or anger that no one else had ever seemed to see. She had scolded him, too; he would like to have known that he'd satisfied her afterwards.

Eris looked at him. "She liked you," she said. "She didn't think you were perfect, mind, but she liked you."

"I wish she'd lived to see our place in the mountains," Luap said. "I wish you would come." That popped out before he thought, and he wasn't at all sure he meant it. But Eris shook her head.

"I don't want to leave Fin Panir; I lived here in this house with her and it's got my memories. But I thank you for the offer; 'twas generous. She always said you were generous."

"Are you getting along all right?"

"Well enough. There's some as think I shouldn't be living in this house alone, that it's too much space for one person, but my lady left it to me, and the courts upheld that — " Luap had had to use all his influence there, for some considered mageborn wills to be invalid, and this was not an area Gird had thought much about. " — so I'll be all right. I may take lodgers, later, when I've decided what to do with the rest of her things."

She took him around the house, then, showing off the

treasures of a vanished aristocracy, things that had survived because Eris and Dorhaniya's other servants had defended the house and her. Much of it did not interest Luap at all: the cedarwood needleboxes carefully notched for knitting needles and embroidery needles of all sizes, the little bags of fine grit for cleaning and polishing the needles, the many boxes of colored yarn and thread, narrow bands of lace and embroidery for decorating garments, and small rooms full of Dorhaniya's best gowns.

"I could cut these up for the cloth," Eris said, rubbing the skirt of one blue and green brocade between her fingers, "but I can't bear the thought. No one wears such clothes now; they'd be used for patches, or rags, and it's a waste." They were beautiful; he remembered how Dorhaniya had looked, and how the mageladies of his childhood had looked . . . how their gowns had rustled, how he had reached out to finger the cloth, the lace, and been slapped away.

More interesting to Luap were the bowls and vases and trays, the sets of fine tableware, the silver spoons. "She had to sell some of it, the last few years," Eris said. "But most of it's here. You don't have to worry that I'd go hungry, sir, not with all this."

"I'm glad," Luap said. He would have felt obliged to help her some way, and yet he had no wealth to be generous with. He touched one of the bowls almost guiltily . . . as a child he had been delighted with the beautiful things he saw, fascinated by the fine detail of tiny carvings, the play of color and gleaming light in rich fabrics and embroidery. Other things were more important, of course, but he wished that Gird had not been so convinced that plainness was a sort of virtue in itself. The peasants had made beautiful things as well, as beautiful as they could within the limits of the materials they had. They had never had silver and gold enough to make it into spoons or dishes, but he had no doubt they would have . . . how could anyone not prefer the feel and glow of silver, which never changed the flavor of the food being eaten.

Eris watched him, musing. "She would have liked you to have some of her things," she said finally. "But she did not know what you would like; you never said much."

Luap shook his head. "How could I? As a child, I had one life, and in manhood another: there was no bridge between them until I met her. I found it hard to talk about, as you know."

"But your eyes speak, and your fingers when you touched that bowl. I have more than I need . . . would you take a few things, in her memory?"

"She made the banner," Luap said softly; tears stung his eyes. "I have no right to anything . . ."

"Nonsense." Eris brushed her hands down her apron. "You have not asked; I have offered. That makes the difference. And since you have no right, as you say, you have no right to choose: I will choose, and you will take what I give you." Luap wanted to laugh; she must have spoken in just that tone to Dorhaniya when that lady "dithered" as she put it. He could easily imagine her settling her lady's mind to a decision. If Dorhaniya had felt half the relief he did now, it was no wonder she had been as loyal to her servant as her servant was to her.

"Thank you," he said, feeling less guilt and more anticipation. "I do — I would be happy to accept whatever you choose."

"Very well," Eris said. "You'll take her needlework for you back this trip; I'll make my selections and have them ready for you next time. Not more than a quarter-year, either — is that clear?"

"Yes, ma'am," Luap said. She shook her head, smiling.

"And don't be saucy with me: you were her prince, but to me you're just another half-mage." The joy fell from him like a dropped cloak; she saw it in his face and came at once to put her hands to his cheeks. "No — I didn't mean it like that. I cannot feel for you what she did; I have no magery. But you are more than just another half-mage to me: you are a man she trusted and admired, a man who was kind to her beyond the requirements of his place. I would not give you anything of hers if I did not also respect and admire you, in my own way." She gave his head a little shake. "Though if you could laugh a bit at yourself, it would be better for you."

"I'm sorry," Luap said, tasting the bitter salt of unshed tears.

"No — don't waste your time being sorry. Go and do what you need not be sorry for." Gird's advice, from another peasant, but this one had given him respect and admiration; Luap lifted his head and smiled at her.

"I will," he said.

Binis in the spring was slightly less sour than Binis in deep

314

winter; she actually smiled at Luap briefly. He had debated walking the whole way to Cob's grange to accommodate her, but decided it would simply take too long. She had ridden it in bad weather; now she could ride in good. She did not argue or complain; perhaps she had anticipated this and practiced in the meantime. Despite the usual spring mud, they made good time, rising early to ride all day. They stayed in different granges than they had in winter, since they covered more ground each day, so Luap did not have to deal with the same Marshals. And this time, when they rode up to Cob's grange, Binis took both horses' reins without asking, and led them around back while Luap went in the open grange door. They had ridden late; Cob had started drill with three hands of yeomen who were bending and stretching together.

"Luap! I've been expecting you." He turned the group over to his yeoman-marshal, and came forward to clasp arms. "Where's your watchdog?"

"Putting the horses away," Luap said. Cob grinned at him.

"Getting her trained, eh? Using your charm on her?"

Luap winced and shrugged. "Don't say that; it sounds bad. And you know better. She rides better."

"She needed to." Cob looked him up and down. "And you could use some exercise, after days spent in the saddle, I daresay. Work out the stiffness, remind your legs what they're for?"

Luap groaned. "You — you're as bad as Gird himself. All right." He put off his cloak, loosened his belt, and joined the others. He had not really drilled in a long time; he had lost, he discovered, the suppleness he had had in youth and he could feel the tightness in his legs every time he leaned over.

But he recognized Cob's purposes. His yeomen might remember the man who had helped Cob in the blizzard . . . they would certainly remember the man who drilled with them, claiming no special place. He caught the sidelong looks; some of them knew his name. When Binis came in from putting up the horses, Cob asked her to lead the stick drill as if she were his own yeoman-marshal. Luap saw resignation and grudging respect on her face. She proved to be a reasonably good drill leader. Luap had not drilled with sticks in years; his palms soon felt hot. But he was determined not to quit, not with Binis leading. Cob limped around, giving advice to all, until he came to Luap.

"Take a breather; you're as old as I am, and this is young man's work."

Luap glared at him, half-amused and half-angry. "You got me into this."

"So I did, but I don't want you going back bloody-handed. I'd forgotten about the burn scars. You never did develop good calluses after that, did you?"

"Not on the one hand, no." Luap stopped, loosened his grip, and flexed his fingers. That would hurt in the morning; it hurt now. Cob took his hands and looked at them, lips pursed.

"Lucky we've a cold stream. Just wait for me." He stumped up to the front of the grange. "Binis, I want you and Vrelan to have them pair off for fighting drills. No broken bones, but a few raps in the ribs won't hurt my yeomen." Binis looked at Luap, and Cob turned to her. "You may not know it, yeoman-marshal, but in the war he had both hands burned. And you don't build callus on burn scars — I saw him try, in the war. Gird himself finally told him to drill only as much as his scars would bear. If you want to argue that — " He looked as dangerous as he ever had, Luap thought, a man sure of himself and his place in the world.

"No, Marshal," Binis said.

"Just keep in mind . . . Gird didn't say pain was good, only that getting good usually involved pain. Those aren't the same thing."

"Yes, Marshal." A dark flush mounted up her face; Cob put his hand on her shoulder.

"Sorry. We veterans can be rough-tongued; if I didn't think you knew what you were doing, I wouldn't let you supervise section drills." He gave her a little shake and came back to Luap. "Come on, now; we're getting those hands in cold water."

"You should have been a healer," Luap said. Cob had insisted that he keep his hands in cold springwater until his bones ached; then he'd put a salve on the worst places, and given Luap soft rags to wrap around his hands.

"I wish I were," Cob said. "You know, young Seri insisted that all Marshal-candidates learn something of herblore and healing. . . . I wish the gods would grant us just a bit of Aris's talent."

316

"I wish the gods would give everyone Aris's talent," Luap said. "He's always busy — too busy — and even working all day every day he can't possibly heal all he'd like."

"Is there no way to misuse it?" Cob asked. "Of course I don't accuse Aris — I know Aris — but if everyone had the power, could it be misused?"

Luap shook his head. "I don't see how. It can't be hoarded for self-healing; Aris can heal his own injuries, but it's painful, as is withholding healing from others. Aside from healing someone the gods want to call — Aris told me about a child kicked in the head, whom he healed but who never completely recovered — I don't see how anyone could misuse it. That doesn't happen often."

"Perhaps you're right. I know we need more healers, more who can do what Aris does. Herblore has its place, but it can't cure many things." Cob turned away a moment, rummaged in a basket, and came up with a lump of soil. "Here now — smell this, and see what you think."

Luap sniffed. It smelled earthy, alive, the way soil should smell. It was a dark, heavy clod, more clay than loam, but it would mix with the sand in the canyons, he was sure. "Good," he said. "In fact, better than good. Where's it from?"

"Southeast. Unclaimed land between granges, just as the Marshal-General required. I've found a cart and stout horse you can hire, although how you're going to get them into your cave . . ."

"I gave up on that," Luap said. "I'll take a sackful, or maybe two, on a pack animal. I can drag the sacks into position by myself." Or he could travel the mageroad alone, and bring back someone from the other end to help, but he did not tell Cob that. "We'll see what Arranha's *mathematics* does. According to him, we could start with this single clod."

"Good. We'll start in the morning, if that's all right with you." Cob leaned back in his chair. "Binis seems a bit less touchy this time."

Luap shrugged. "She's fine. The winter trip was my fault; it would have made anyone difficult."

"No — there you wrong yourself. You've never been one to complain about that kind of thing. But we'll see in the morning."

*   *   *

They arrived at Cob's chosen site, a meadow already greening, with new grass and pink flowers peeking through the dead grass of winter, by nightfall. Binis looked around. "Are you sure no one claims this, Marshal?"

"Very sure. I checked with the next Marshal over. There's a village blasted by magery between us, fields poisoned and dead, so there are fewer people than some years back, and neither of our granges spread this direction. This is just outside the dead zone, but you can see the land is well alive. Luap?"

Luap dismounted and dug his dagger into the turf, bringing up a small lump of thick dark soil. It smelled rich and fertile. "It's perfect," he said. He pulled out the two sacks he'd bought, and unlashed the shovels from the pack pony's saddle.

"You're not going to dig it *now*," Cob said.

"We're camping here, aren't we?" Luap asked. He grinned wickedly at Cob. "What was the first thing Gird taught all of us?"

"You give Vrelan that shovel and help me cook," Cob said. "I trust your cooking."

The next morning, Vrelan and Binis — she surprised Luap by offering — dug another narrow trench to fill the sacks with earth. "I know it's harder this way," Luap had said, "but a narrow trench will quickly heal; we don't want to leave the land open to harm." Soon they were done; Luap nicked his finger to produce a drop of blood which he squeezed into the trench. Binis stared at him, and he explained. "Alyanya's blessed me; when I was a farmer, I blooded my blade like everyone else."

They returned to Cob's grange that night, and the next day Luap and Binis set off for the cave, more than a hand of days away. He felt almost smug about surprising her with his willingness to drill, to dig a jacks trench, to offer his own blood in return for the earth. "I thought you would destroy all the old ways," she said as they rode. "*Our* old ways, I mean."

"Did you ever meet Arranha?" Luap countered. She looked blank. "The priest of Esea in the High Lord's Hall?"

"That old man in the white robe? No. They said he was a magelord who followed the Sunlord. That's what the war was against, magelords and bad gods."

Luap closed his eyes, fighting off a wave of anger. How could she be that ignorant, that stupid? "Arranha," he said between clenched teeth, "*helped* Gird fight that war. Arranha is the one who took Gird to the gnomes. You do know about that?"

Binis nodded. "They hated the magelords too, so they gave him pikes."

"No. They gave him training, and maps, and advice. Duke Marrakai of Tsaia gave him gold to buy pikes."

"*Duke* Marrakai? Gird took gold from a magelord? I don't believe it!"

"He did," Luap said. "And his son visited Gird after the war, in Fin Panir; Gird liked him." He glanced at Binis; her lower lip stuck out, and she looked like someone determined not to believe that night follows day. She was certainly not going to believe that Gird, hero of the peasants' war, considered a Tsaian magelord and his son friends. "But about Arranha: Gird rescued Arranha from the mageborn who hated him — the priests who really did follow bad gods, as you call them — and they became friends." He thought a long moment. "Binis — did you ever meet *Gird*?"

She reddened. "No, not to speak to. I saw him a few times, in the city, but he was . . . you know, he was the Marshal-General, and I was a child."

Hard to believe the years had gone that fast. Hard to believe that someone could be a yeoman-marshal, yet never have drilled with Gird, never have struck a blow in real battle. He'd known she was younger, much younger, but . . . *We're getting old*, he thought suddenly. *All of us who knew Gird; all of us who really know what that war was about, and who was on which side.*

"Were you in the city the day Gird died?" Luap asked. Binis nodded. "And did you feel it?"

"I felt . . . something," she said. "I remember how hot it had been, sticky. There'd been quarrels all day, up and down the street. My aunt got on me about something — I don't really remember — and I threw a pot at her. I knew it was wrong; I knew she'd tell my da, and my uncle, and the Marshal and they'd all be down on me again. I ran out the back way, up the alley toward the old palace, and I thought I'd run out in the meadows. They wouldn't know where to look. Everything was unfair; everybody was angry with me and it wasn't any of it my fault." Her voice had risen, remembering old grievances. Then her face smoothed out again, and her voice softened. "I remember . . . I'd run too fast, I couldn't seem to breathe, and I

319

felt squeezed somehow, like stones were on me. And then all at once it was over. Like a storm passing, but there wasn't any storm. Stillness, but not sticky, not so hot. Calm, I guess you'd say. I had stopped running, and now I thought I'd go back."

Luap was afraid to break her mood, so they rode in silence some distance until the pack pony stumbled, and he reined up and dismounted to check it. Binis stayed on her horse, and as he lifted each of the pony's hooves in turn, she went on.

"I didn't know what'd happened right then. Not till after I was back at our house. My aunt — she came to me as I came in, said she was sorry, and I was sorry too, for breaking a good pot. I felt — I don't know how I felt, except that nothing hurt inside, the way it had since my mother died. All the quarrels seemed silly, but not anything to grieve over. Just put them aside and go on. Later the Marshal said something about Gird having taken a kind of curse off us, but in your *Life of Gird* it's not a curse."

"No one really knows," Luap said. "If it was a curse, or an evil spirit, or just ourselves . . . but we know whom to thank for lifting it."

"Yes, but — but I still get angry. I still see things go wrong, things happen that aren't fair."

"Gird didn't heal us, the way Aris heals," Luap said, thinking it out as he spoke. He swung back up onto his horse and nudged it into motion. "Maybe he couldn't; maybe even the gods can't. But he gave us a respite, and a taste of what real healing is. I think we're supposed to do the rest."

"Hmph." Binis scowled again. "But we're not Gird."

"True enough. But Gird wasn't Gird all along." Which was, he realized, just the point Raheli had made about his *Life of Gird*. Could she be right about that? No. She had been right about many other things, but on that he would not change his mind. No amount of talking or writing would convince people who had not known him that Gird had begun as a perfectly ordinary man . . . they would simply decide that he had not been a hero. Just as Binis could not accept a Gird who befriended mageborn and Sunlord priests, later generations would deny either Gird's early life, or his later accomplishments. And he could not take the chance that they might deny what Gird had done. He must make sure that Gird lived through the ages as the hero he had really been, even though that meant shaping his early life. He wasn't pretending Gird had been perfect — he understood how people could love someone more for his faults — but Gird's life had been entirely too unformed to last as a story.

"Cob says the magelords mistreated you," Binis said. "So why didn't you turn against them?"

Luap turned in the saddle to see if she was serious. She was. "Binis — what else would you call joining Gird's army, than turning against them?" He had been so careful to keep himself out of the telling of Gird's life — he had been trying to make Gird the center, as he should be — but if people like Binis didn't even know what Gird's luap had done, perhaps he should make another revision. She looked unconvinced; Luap tried again. "Binis, Cob is my friend from those days — from Gird's army. We fought on the same side. The magelords killed my wife, my children—" As always, tears came when he thought of that; he blinked them away. Binis was the sort to think he had pretended grief. " — And I did turn against them, the ones who had done it. I have the scars to prove it."

"But then why did you take up with them again afterwards?" The depth of ignorance in that question took his breath away. How could he possibly explain? "I mean," she said, putting the final peg in her assembly of faulty logic, "everyone knows you're the mageking's son, and if you'd really turned against the magelords, you wouldn't have anything to do with them."

Among the rush of emotions came the cold thought that he'd never known one who needed Arranha's classes more: even he, not the brightest of Arranha's pupils, had learned not to use one word with two meanings in the same argument. Would she ever understand that the "them" he knew now were not the same "them" who had abandoned him in childhood and destroyed his family? Gird had known that. Raheli understood that; he realized how different she was from this sort of peasant, and how unfair he had been to blame her for the minds of those like Binis.

He even felt a trickle of pity for Binis herself, cramped into a narrow mind and unlikely to find a way out. In her, Gird's insistence that right was right and wrong was wrong, that compromises always cost more than could be easily reckoned, had turned to a rigid system unlike anything Gird himself would approve. What could he say to open a window in her head? Gird would have used his fist, likely enough, claiming that it took hard knocks to crack thick-shelled nuts . . . but that was not his way, nor would Binis learn that way from him.

"The people who hurt me, who killed my family," Luap said, "were killed in the war. I saw their bodies, many of them. The mageborn who survived were children and the very old, some women who had not even known me, let alone caused me harm. Should I hate them? Gird did not hate them."

"But they were the same sort. Magelords!" She made it a curseword. His magery growled within him, as if it could respond of itself to an insult. He fought it down, telling himself she was only saying what she had been taught.

"Are all peasants fair, kind people?" he asked instead. "Surely you've known some who cheated, who stole, who were unfair — ?"

"Ye-esss . . . " She dragged that out, as if it came unwillingly. "But they've been cheated by the mageborn; it's not their fault." She eyed him, looking for a reaction. "The Marshal-General says most real thieves and brigands are part-mageborn anyway; that's why they're too lazy to work and be honest." *That's why he doesn't trust you, half-mage*, was as clear in her gaze as if written on parchment.

"You insufferable fool!" Luap's anger roared past his knowledge that losing his temper would only cause trouble. This time it was not Gird; this time it was not someone he respected; this time — this one time, maybe — he was wholly justified, completely right, and he was not going to pretend a subservience and shame he did not feel. He would wipe that smugness off Binis's face, that sly satisfaction in catching him off guard, that intolerable superiority. "The Marshal-General himself has mageborn blood — is *that* why he can't get up until midmorning? Does that make him dishonest enough to steal from the grange-sets honest peasants have sent in to buy himself fancy foods rather than eat porridge and stew with the rest? Or didn't you know any of that?" By her expression she had not known, and didn't believe. "Look it up in the archives," he said bitterly. "*If* you can read. His grandmother was raped by a magelord, just as my mother was. It's in the records, the great accounting Gird held after the war. His own mother reported it."

"You made that up," Binis said. "It can't be true. Besides, the Marshal-General's special: he has a right to sleep later and eat better food."

"Really! Gird didn't . . . but then you didn't know Gird, more's the pity." That rush of anger over, Luap felt the first twinge of fear. Lazy, selfish, and misguided the present Marshal-General might be, but he still had to work with him. So far the Council had sided with Luap on the larger issues, but he must not strain their patience by angering the Marshal-General on minor matters. He looked at Binis with more loathing than she perhaps deserved. She was the Marshal-General's tool, less culpable because she was both younger and subordinate. He hated her. If not for his oath to Gird, he would use his magery now, and compel her to agree. He toyed with that idea for another furlong or so, imagining sending her back to the Marshal-General as a spy, as a mageborn tool. If she had said anything more, he might have, but she had the prudence of the naturally sly, and said nothing.

So the rest of the day passed, in uncomfortable silence. She asked once, in late afternoon, what grange they would stay at that night, and he replied that they would camp. He managed not to add, with the sarcasm he felt, that she should have realized that from the supplies he'd bought in Cob's village. He attacked the jacks trench as if it were a buried enemy, raising another blister on his hand, and she watched sullenly. They ate their supper in silence, and in silence passed the night and the morning's rising. Binis filled in the trench without commenting.

Luap rode in morose silence all that morning, inquiring of all the gods he could think of — and Gird — what else he could have done. The explanations and excuses looked shabby, spread out in his mind; he knew that Gird would have swept them away. Yes, the woman was stupid, smug, and difficult: that was *her* problem. He had not made things better with his flare of temper. He found himself arguing that Gird, too, had lost his temper with a difficult woman named Binis, but it would not work, and he knew it. All at once he was plunged into internal darkness, a wave of despair. How could he think of leading his people to any good purpose? Everything he'd ever done wrong came back to him in vivid pictures; he hunched over the horse's neck, wishing he could spew it all out and die, have it all over. The Rosemage would lead his people better. Or Aris and Seri, in partnership.

He had no thought of food, and Binis finally said, plaintively, "Aren't we going to stop and eat?" Another stab of guilt — had he compounded anger and rudeness with cruelty?

"I'm sorry," he said. "I — lost track of time." He reined in and looked around. At least he wasn't lost; he still recognized the shapes of hill and field. Beneath him, his horse sighed and tugged the reins, wanting to graze the fresh spring grass. "Yes. We can stop here, or go on a bit to that creek." He pointed.

"You look sick," Binis said with her usual tact.

Luap shrugged. "I'm sorry," he said again. He thought of apologizing for yesterday's anger, but Binis was not one to inspire selflessness; she absorbed it as her due. He dismounted, and let his horse graze. Binis found a convenient rock and settled to her food; he had no appetite for his, but realized he should eat anyway. He choked down some mouthfuls of bread and cheese. This would not do; they had several more days of travel together, and he had to find some way to get along with this woman.

He tried asking questions about life in Fin Panir; Binis gave short answers, and made it clear that he should know the answers already. He tried telling her about the war, how it had been to march these very hills and river valleys with Gird's army. She listened to that, but her questions revealed no grasp of tactics — he became very tired of her "Why didn't Gird just — ?" She seemed to think all battles were great set pieces, with armies lined up on either side; she was sure that any villagers who didn't support Gird's army must have been part mageborn.

"They were hungry and frightened," Luap tried to explain. "Someone had to stay and plant the fields, but if the magelords caught them sharing food with us, they'd be killed — worse than killed." He remembered the thin faces, the desperation, the bodies displayed on hillsides. "Look there," he said, pointing to an ox-team busy with spring ploughing. The farmer had made a grisly decoration of skulls turned up by the plough. Binis shuddered; Luap thought he might have pierced her determination to simplify the past. He hoped so.

By the time they reached the cave, in a misting rain, Luap felt her presence as a great weight on his neck. He made a last try. "We had several cohorts in here," he said. "Worse weather than this, but also early spring. Gird had a bad cold. Lots of us did."

"Which spring?" she asked. This time she took the shovel to dig the trench; he thought that was a good sign.

"The spring before Greenfields," he said. While she built a small fire in the familiar ring of stones, he dragged first one sack of soil, then another, back to the chamber. She did not offer to help. The feeling grew on him that this was the most significant of his visits to the cave: the season, the weather, and the sullen peasant were all the same. Binis could easily stand for some hundreds of her fellows.

He felt this even more when he discovered that she expected him to take the soil to his stronghold by the mageroad, then return and go back with her to Fin Panir to report to the Marshal-General. "That way I can be sure you don't return and steal more," she said. Luap wondered briefly if she had anything between her ears but malice and stubbornness.

"Binis, if I had wanted to disobey the Marshal-General and steal more earth, I could have come here in the first place and never travelled with you at all."

"You wouldn't have dared," she said. "You can't disobey the Marshal-General." She said it in the way she would have said that stones fall or water is wet, someone stating a natural law.

"*I* could," Luap said flippantly, and instantly wished he hadn't. He already knew Binis had no sense of humor. She was scowling now, as if he had insulted her. "Listen to me: I did what your Marshal-General asked because I swore an oath to Gird. Not an oath to obey his successor, an oath to support him, and do no harm with my magery to his people. I saw no reason to quarrel with the Marshal-General; I have fulfilled his requirements, and I am going back to my land." *To stay,* he almost said. But he would return, to continue his work with the archives, and he did not mean to cause more trouble than he had.

"I won't let you," Binis said. "You have to take the sacks there and return."

The sheer stupidity of it, her inability to see that she had no way to compel him, almost made him laugh. He thought of agreeing, and then not coming back, which might at least teach her something about the limits of her power, but in this place he could not lie to one of Gird's people, not even one he was sure Gird himself would have knocked in the head.

Gently, as if speaking to a dull child, he said "Binis, I am going and I am not coming back. You have food, two horses and a pony, and a clear trail. You're a yeoman-marshal and it's peacetime. You will be perfectly safe travelling alone, and there's a grange not a day's ride away. Now sit down and eat your supper."

"You're not going to do it," she said. She moved over to block his way to the chamber. Luap felt again the anger he had felt at Gird — and she was no Gird; he lifted his fist, and she blinked but stood her ground. He could not hit her. He had sworn not to use magery in this land . . . but it was gentler. His power flowed out and around her like honey around an ant; she struggled, but could not move.

"Farewell, Binis," he said, stepping past her. He moved quickly past her, into the chamber, and laid a hand on either sack as he called on his power.

● Chapter Twenty-three

"What does the prince fear?" the black-cloaked lord asked his spy. *"What does he love? These are the knots in which to bind him."* He had sent many spies, over the years, and learned many things he expected to use in the future. But he had not yet decided on the exact way to approach the prince and use him to destroy the others.

"He is a king's bastard — not ever acknowledged," the spy said. *"And like all such he doubts both his father's goodwill and the reality of his parentage. He fears ridicule — he fears disrespect — and he fears that he is not deserving of respect. He is beginning to fear age, as he sees those he respects dying or approaching death. He has a vision for his people, for this place, and he fears that as he ages he will lose control of them. That his vision will not survive."*

"And he loves?" The tone was contemptuous; they did not believe that *"love"* existed, but they knew others claimed to be moved so.

The spy shrugged. *"Insofar as he can, he thinks he loves his people. He believes they need his protection and wisdom; he takes pride in serving them. He is sure he knows best, and wants them to agree that he does. He loves his own will, but no more than many. He has a vision of himself as a great leader."*

"Anything else?"

The spy smiled; he had been saving the best for last. *"He was warned never to seek command, or take it; he was told he was unfit for it. Although he did not understand why he was considered unfit, he submitted to others. Now, having accepted the leadership here, he has broken an old oath. That is no consequence to us, but it bothers him: he will not let himself think of it, or admit that is what he has done."* Others laughed; such self-blindness offered easy access for their enchantments.

The leader's brows rose. *"Unfit for command? Not to our purpose. . . . I can scarcely imagine one I would rather see in his place. A bastard prince, a prince afraid of his own weakness, a prince afraid that age will erode his power, an oathbreaker . . . apt*

*for our purposes, indeed! He should welcome our aid as eagerly as
an overworked shepherd welcomes a well-trained sheepdog. So long
as he does not see the wolf beneath the dog's fur, we shall prosper as
he does. Let him think on his losses, and fear more: let him grasp —
and we shall have something for him to hold."*

Climbing up to the forested top of the mountain took
longer than Luap would have expected. He was winded and
sweaty when he finally made it over the rim and into the cool
shade of the trees. It had been too long, he told himself, since
he had climbed even as high as the terrace now below. The
Rosemage looked almost as tired, but Seri and Aris were bubbling with energy.

"It's easy walking from here," Seri said. "And we marked
our trail, the first time."

Luap nodded, still out of breath, and turned to look behind him, out over the rim. Now he could see much that
had been hidden from the level below, while whole clefts
and canyons had disappeared — they might have been
only surface cracks in the rock. Others showed more clearly; he thought he could see a narrow green valley up the
main canyon and then southward. Gird should have seen
this, he thought. Northward a great gray angular mountain loomed, very unlike the red rock around them.
Eastward, the higher mountains were white; he could not
tell if it was rock or snow.

"We haven't explored all of this yet," Aris said. "Only
toward the west, and only part of that. But we've found so
many things . . . trees like this in places, and in others low
round trees hardly larger than bushes. Grassy meadows, even
a little creek right up here on top of the mountain.

"And game," Seri said. "Tame enough to touch, some of
these animals."

"All right," he said, smiling at the Rosemage. "Let's see your
marvels."

The two led them along the southern edge of the trees,
where Luap could see between the trunks a plateau with
similar trees across the canyon. It was, as they'd promised,
much easier walking than the canyon itself; they reached
the low end before the sun had moved three handspans on
its way.

On this end of the mountain, no intermediate terrace broke its sheer cliffs. Luap crept cautiously to the dropoff and found himself staring down into a well of blue air, still shadowed by the cliff. Perhaps a bowshot away, a stone tower rose to a lesser height, partly eroded from the cliff behind. Below the steepest slopes, the hollow was filled with trees.

When he looked west, he saw across a lower cliff a vast low plain, with mountains rising from it in the distance. "Is that where you thought you saw a caravan?" he asked.

"Not from here," Aris said. "Come along this edge, now." He led the way around a cove or bay of stone, toward another outlying point; it occurred to Luap that this end of the mountain had a shape rather like an outflung hand, fingers of stone defining angled coves between them.

"That's what we thought." Aris pointed back to the tower. "We called that one the Thumb." The next prominence was farther away than it looked — everything in this country, Luap thought, was farther away than it looked — but from it he could look through a break in the western cliffs. "There's a stream in there," Aris said. "But it's not the same one that's in our canyon. It comes from the north, and cuts through to the west."

Through the break, he could see a pale line, like a scratch, in the even tan of the distant plain. "That could be a trail, I suppose," he said. "You saw something moving along it?"

"Yes. And if you look south — there — you can see what might be a town."

Luap could see nothing but a jumble of shadows that might come from a pile of rocks or low buildings the color of the plain. Certainly it looked like no town he had ever seen — but nothing out here looked like anything he'd ever seen.

"There's nothing green until the next mountains," the Rosemage said. "What could they live on? Is it just bare rock?"

"I don't know." Seri flung out her hands. "But I think we could find a way out of here . . . look." She leaned out and pointed. "If you come down the canyon to that lower fall, and then angle around the Thumb — that tower — and then up the slope that sticks out from this . . . then you're close to the stream that goes out through that cliff. It's rugged, but we could build a trail — "

"After we've made sure our cropland bears," Luap said firmly. "We aren't here to explore; we're here to settle."

Seri looked a little disgruntled; Aris spoke up. "But, sir — if we can get out, then others — those we saw — could get in. It's only good planning to know if there's a back door in your house, and how to secure it."

"Why would anyone come into such rugged country?" the Rosemage asked. "As level as that plain is — "

"What you said before: here it's green, and there's water. Or perhaps they hunt up here; surely we have more game than the plain."

"Hmm. Well, I don't see that we'll have people to spare for that this growing season. Perhaps next year. Although if trade is possible, there are many things we could use." Luap looked around. "Just as I see things up here that we can use. More timber, for one, and game."

"And we found pine-nuts very different from those on the taller pines," Seri said, her enthusiasm rekindled. "And other plants to eat."

Luap glanced at the sun, now well past midday. "Show us what you can on the way back; I don't want to be benighted up here." Seri nodded; she and Aris led away from the western cliffs back over the mountaintop. In some places, the ground was broken; scrubby bushes and small trees struggled among the tumbled stones. In others, the groves of tall pines rose straight from level rock; little undergrowth impeded movement or sight between them. They came upon small meadows in little hollows; in one of these a gray stag in velvet looked at them a long moment before stalking away. And by the time they had reached the eastern rim and the trail down, the mountain threw its shadow over all below, so that dusky rose rock melted into dusky blue shades, layer after layer. Far to the east the white cliffs of the higher mountains still caught the light.

The Rosemage climbed down the trail first, then Luap; he thought his legs would give out before he stood at last on the level stone of the terrace. And he still had to climb down the stairs to the main level of the stronghold. Behind him, he was aware of Seri and Aris, both still full of energy. He rarely felt his age — he had been younger than many of Gird's companions in the war — but now he felt the years that lay between him and the two younglings. Even between him and his own youth. That war, he reflected, had been years ago: they had been children, and he had had children. No wonder they were excited with each new hill and valley they found. He wished he had as many years left to enjoy this land.

He pushed that worry away. He was younger than Arranha, younger than the Rosemage. He would live to see his dream fulfilled. And these two would be part of it. In this mood, he was willing to grant Seri and Aris leave to explore farther, so long as they took their turn at the necessary fieldwork. Perhaps it would make them decide to stay; surely they would come to love this country as he did.

Arranha, at dinner that night, had his doubts about exploring the lands beyond the canyon. "Would it anger the elves or dwarves?" he asked. "Did they place any limits on your dealings with those folk?"

"They didn't mention them," Luap said. "They said I was not to claim ownership of this hall — or that I had built it. Of course I would do neither."

"That gray mountain we saw," the Rosemage said, changing the subject with less than her usual grace. "It looked to me as if it might have ores: did the dwarves say aught about that?"

"Not a word." Luap shook his head. "Why?"

"If there's silver, or gold," she said. "Even iron, for us to make our own tools and pots: you'll have no trouble getting a smith if we have metal. Or if we have gold to pay."

"That's much more sense than frolicking off to follow desert caravans around," said Arranha. "You brought the mageborn here to learn the use of magery in privacy, in safety. Involve us in someone else's business, and you're asking for trouble. But using the land's own wealth to trade back to Fin Panir, that's another matter."

"It's not far," the Rosemage said. "Even allowing for the way things seem close . . . I'm sure we could find a way to it.

Luap felt a vague discomfort; he had a vision of his folk flitting away in all directions like a flight of small birds when a cat pounces. "You're eager to leave, then?" he found himself saying.

"No — I don't think it's leaving," the Rosemage said, and gave him a steady look. "I think Arranha's right: our safety here depends in part on being unknown. We are few; surely whatever land lies there has more people in it. But if we can find materials we need, be they trees or metals, something to trade back to Fin Panir or hire artisans here, that makes more sense to me."

Luap raised his brows and looked at Aris and Seri, whose expressions wavered between wistfulness and chagrin. "And you two? You wanted to find out who lives out there, did you not?"

Seri gave the Rosemage a look. "It's — it's *practical*. In the military sense. Surely you see that we need to know who's at the back door, and how easily they could find us. Suppose someone's living in those western canyons — suppose they get a taste for the fish in our stream?"

"How far away do you think the gray mountain is?" Luap asked Aris. "Do you think it's as near as the western cliffs?"

"No — but I'm not sure how far." Aris looked worried, as he did sometimes when asked about things outside his competence.

"If it's just a matter of distance," the Rosemage said, "then the western cliffs — even that town Aris thinks he saw — are closer. I won't argue that. But there's nothing to the caravans and towns but danger — and the mountain might offer something better."

Seri looked stubborn. "It's dangerous not to find out what's out in the plain."

The Rosemage started to speak, then stopped, shook her head, and began again. "Seri — I know your Marshal's training covered defense; I know you are competent. But is this something you really think is important that way, or just an itch to explore?"

"We need to know," Seri said. She seemed to grow more compact, more peasantlike, even as they watched her. Aris leaned into the conversation.

"She's right — we do."

The Rosemage flushed; Luap felt a momentary tremor of excitement — was she going to lose her temper? She had not since they came, though he had seen her lips pinched more than once. Arranha spoke up.

"If the gods are telling you that, Seri, then there's no argument. You must find out, or someone must. We can look at the mountain later; it will still be there. Or one party could go each way."

"We can't have everyone going off at once," Luap reminded them. He felt again that vague disturbance inside, but had no time to attend to it. Later — later he would consider whether it had most to do with age or something else. Perhaps it was the thought of danger: danger either way, whether they left their neighbors unknown, or went to meet them. "Why not have Aris and Seri take a look at the western cliffs, see if there's any trail or road there? They need not explore so far as the town, not at first — not even leave the cliffs. That should take only a couple of days, I would think — ?" He looked at Seri, who nodded happily. "In the meantime, you — " He looked at the Rosemage. " — you could be planning your route to the gray mountain, perhaps from up on the high level. When they get back, you could leave, and not be too long delayed." He smiled at her. "Would that do?"

"Yes . . . of course. Arranha?"

"I don't even know how far my bones will take me," Arranha said, smiling. "Perhaps you should choose another, younger companion for the journey. Find me an easy trail, will you?"

"That I will. I have no more love than you for clambering over rough ground."

The mood around the table now seemed lighter, warmer. Luap basked in it; he had headed off a quarrel. "I'll check the schedules," he said. "Perhaps Aris and Seri could start tomorrow or the next day."

The lowest terrace in the main canyon had been placed just above a turn, where the canyon angled south away from a tributary stream. That far, the trail had been made smooth, and Aris and Seri had jogged down it easily. Now they turned north to follow the smaller stream around the Thumb. The tower looked taller from below. They came through the shade of the big trees that formed a grove where the streams met — not pines, this time, but broad-leaved trees whose deeply furrowed trunks and softly clattering foliage reminded them of riverside groves in Fintha. Small, bright-colored birds flitted through the leaves like butterflies; a bird they did not see gave a sweet rippling call. Up the smaller stream, the trees quickly disappeared and they walked among head-high bushes of juniper and thorn. Soon the stream disappeared, and though its steep bed rose steadily, it was incised even more deeply in the slope around it. They had started walking in the streambed when the water disappeared, because the thick growth close beside it made it impossible to walk on the bank. Seri, leading Aris up the narrowing bed, stopped suddenly with a little yelp.

"What?" asked Aris. He was not exactly grumpy, but the streambed seemed to hold every bit of the sun's heat, and he itched with sweat.

"That snake." Seri pointed; Aris looked past her. The snakes in Fintha were shy creatures, small brown or green serpents that looked like an old thong left on the ground until they moved. Here they had found similar snakes, though more brightly colored, curled on rock ledges. Aris had had to heal several snakebites. But they had not seen anything like the big yellow and brown patterned snake, longer than a man's leg and thicker than his arm, that moved with deliberation across the sand in front of them, worked its way up the bank, and vanished among the junipers.

"If that bit someone — " Aris said. He didn't know how to finish that. Was the snake venomous? In Fintha, snakebites were rare, and although some children suffered woundfever, no one died. Here they'd found that the bright-colored snakes could kill — the first person bitten had not bothered to have the wound treated, thinking it like the snakebites back home. But Aris could heal those bites, with no more drain on his power than a sprained wrist would cause.

"If they come that big, they might come bigger," Seri said. "I almost stepped on that one — for all its color, it looked remarkably like a stick until it moved."

The dry streambed led them back sunrising, into the sheltered cove between the Thumb and the next promontary. Sandy banks gave way to soil, then soil and rock. Seri climbed out, using the root of a pine to help.

"Plenty of trees here," Aris said. "Though it would be hard to get the wood back upstream." The search for timber had been one reason for this expedition.

"Until we build a road." Seri looked around. "Though it would really make more sense for someone to live here, at this end. I wonder how far back into the mountain the stronghold extends."

"Not this far." Aris looked across the slope to the mountain that blocked their view to the west. "If we could terrace this, it would give enough space for a pasture."

"Too far from the main settlement," Seri said. "Unless someone lives here to watch — they could be stolen by those folk below, or even escape." She drew a deep breath. "Well. We'd best go looking for that pass, if we're going to find it today."

That meant coming back out of the shady cove, into the glare of the sun, to scramble uphill between clumps of juniper. The ground here was shattered rock, obviously the outfall of the cliffs; in places it had worn to sand, but the nearer they came to the base of the cliffs, the steeper and more rugged their way. They seemed to struggle on forever, but the sun had not quite passed noon when Aris realized they were going the same direction without climbing. He was in the lead, then; he turned back to see Seri's head still below his, and a view that took his breath away. He stopped, panting, and waited for her to catch up.

"Look at that," he said, when she came up beside him. They were now, if he judged aright, at the level of the Thumb's base. Beyond it, he could see to the south, a better view of the canyon's new direction than he had had from the mountain-top. Looking north, the ends of the first two promontories showed clearly; he could not see the stream that had made its way among them to an outlet west, but he assumed that going downhill would lead him there.

They moved downslope and toward the next cove to find shade; both of them were unusually careful about the ground on which they sat. Aris thought that the people of the caravans might avoid these mountains simply because of the many things that stung and bit — that huge snake, the little crawlers with their poisoned tails. He said that to Seri, who shrugged it off. "Each land has its own hazards; I think it's the rough ter-rain. Horses would find it difficult unless someone built trails. And if they have no magery, building trails could take years."

Aris glanced back at the way they'd come. They could no longer see the Thumb, having come around the next outflung wall of rock — the pointing finger, he thought to himself. After a brief rest, they started off again, this time downslope and angling as much sunsetting as winterwards. They could see the notch in the western wall where the stream went through, but little of the land beyond.

"Should we head straight for it, or just go downhill to the stream?" he asked as they came out of the angle of the cove.

"It's easier walking up here," Seri said. "If we go to the stream, there'll be a lot of twisting about. And it looks as if deer use this — there's a trail here."

"Fine with me," Aris said. They worked their way down a rib of rocky soil that gradually narrowed on both sides, falling off more steeply to the north. Soon they were on exposed rock again, this time a ledge overlooking a sharp drop to another perhaps a man's height down on the north, though it sloped more gently to the south. "It didn't look like this from above," he said. Ahead, they'd almost reached the western wall, which came down in great steps to close off their ledge. "Maybe we should start heading for the stream."

Seri peered downward. The ledge below their ledge dropped to another, and then another. "If we get down, can we get back up? Remember that place up the main canyon . . . if someone came the other way, and dropped over, there'd be no way back."

"Not without wings," Aris said. "You're right; we'll go on to that wall. Maybe there's a way around." When they reached the wall, a narrow, well-scuffed trail seemed to lead along the very edge of the wall into the notch.

"My turn to lead," said Seri. Aris chuckled.

"You want to be the first to see out . . . go ahead then." Aris looked back at the rampart behind them, the steep rocky slopes changing abruptly to vertical walls . . . he could not guess how high. He glanced back once more as the angle of trail was about to cut off his view. Then he heard a confused noise in front of him, a muffled cry from Seri, and he ran forward.

The trail turned sharply back into a crevice of stone; Aris nearly went headlong over the edge. He dropped his stick and grabbed at the rockface. The rock he grabbed came loose in his hand but slowed him just enough that he could keep his footing. Then he could see them: Seri, struggling with two men, one of whom had a good grip on her braid, holding her head back while the other choked her. Aris charged, slamming the rock he still held against the first man's unprotected head with a satisfying thunk. The man dropped; Aris stepped on him with intent, and swung at the second, who had to let go of Seri's throat to block the swing. He didn't dare look at Seri; the man had a curved blade longer than a knife.

336

Aris shifted the rock to his left hand and drew his own dagger. The man grinned, and swung the curved blade in a complicated pattern. Aris ignored that, and threw the rock at the man's face, using magery to improve his left-handed aim. The man flinched aside, which gave Aris time to grab another rock. The man swung, not at him but at Seri. Aris lunged, trying to protect her, but he stumbled over the man he'd knocked out. Seri managed to jerk her legs aside; the blade rang on the stone but did not shatter. Aris pushed his stumble into a roll, hoping to get under the man's guard with his dagger. It might have worked, but the man stepped back too far and fell backwards off the trail with a yell. A series of thuds and clatters, and a very final-sounding shriek suggested that he would be awhile climbing back.

Seri was on her feet now, still gasping; Aris could see the purple bruises at her throat. She smiled at him, and waved him away. He wanted to heal her, but he understood — first make sure no more attackers appeared. He checked the man he had hit with the rock, who lay unmoving, but alive. Farther down the trail — Aris lunged and yanked Seri to the ground just as an arrow clattered against the wall where she'd been. Now that he was touching her, he could heal her; he struggled to keep the anger he felt from contaminating the healing magery.

"I'm fine," she said a moment later. "Stupid, careless, and clumsy, but alive and well." Another arrow rang on the rock just below them. "How many?"

"I don't know," Aris said. "I saw one with the bow, and another behind, but the trail twists. It's an awkward aim for the archer. Notice they aren't yelling at us."

"I did. No help to yell for, or other enemies?"

"I don't know that, either." He looked back up the trail. Had they really been so stupid, walking along an obvious trail without any precautions at all? Game trails, he reminded himself bitterly, go up and down to water, or connect food sources, not along ridges where people would prefer to walk. "But we can't get back up there without making a very good target, and even if we did there's that long open stretch of ledge." And all the way back to the stronghold, they would be leading trouble home. And hadn't both of them decided it was too hot to wear helmets, and that swords were awkward weapons not likely to be needed? Two sticks and Seri's dagger, he thought, might not be enough.

"So we have to settle it here," Seri said. In that tone of voice it almost sounded reasonable. Aris heard a faint noise and glanced up in time to see that the unknown archer knew about lofting his arrows into difficult places. No — *two* unknown archers: there were two arrows rapidly falling. Luckily, a wind-current near the cliff deflected them, and both fell harmlessly beyond the trail. Others, Aris knew, might not. He did not know if his slight magery would work on arrows shot by someone else. Seri touched his shoulder. "That man — the first one — had a bow over his shoulder."

Of course. Aris had not really looked at him, beyond making sure he stayed quiet. Together, they got hold of a foot and pulled the man closer to the cliff. An arrow struck the man only a handspan from Aris; the man did not stir. Seri reached for the arrow that had struck the cliff first. "Now we have two arrows," she said. "Unless he's got more." It was harder than Aris would have thought to wrestle the bow and string from the man's shoulder, and when he had it in his hands he wondered how a little twisted bit of a bow could be much use. But when he had it strung, he realized it was more powerful than most. He yanked the arrow free of the man's body, and set it to the string. It felt strange, but he hoped what he knew of the longer, straighter bows of Fintha would serve. He peeked around the rock and saw the other archer also leaning far out to look. Release . . . and a touch of magery as the archer, seeing the arrow on its way, tried to dodge. The man yelled then, in terror at seeing an arrow follow his movements. Aris saw two others get up and start running back down the trail; the man he had shot lay still.

"Odd sort of quiver," Seri said, behind him. He looked back; she had found six more arrows stored in a length of hollow bone.

"They ran," Aris said. "And wherever they're going, they'll report strangers up here. I think we should follow them." He was ready to say why they should do something so foolish, without proper weapons or anyone knowing, but as usual Seri understood.

Seri nodded. "Not good neighbors. And you're right; we don't have time to go back and get tangled in arguments. We need to know more before we tell the Rosemage anything about this." Aris was sure she felt the same pull he did, the same urgent call to follow the fleeing men.

Nonetheless, they would not be so incautious again. Aris retrieved his stick. They stripped the first man of his leather tunic, a small round shield, and a curved blade. He had dark hair and an unkempt dark beard; under the leather tunic he wore a long sand-colored tunic or shirt that left his muscular legs bare below the knees, and peculiar openwork shoes of leather thongs. Aris looked over the edge of the trail, and saw a crumpled figure far below; it didn't move. The dead archer, when they came to him, yielded another bow, another blade, and more arrows, as well as a helmet that didn't fit either of them until Seri tucked up her braid. She decided that the first man's tunic didn't offer enough protection for its weight and smell; they discarded it. The trail beyond that was both steep and exposed; Aris caught a glimpse of those they followed more than once. Now he thought he saw four of them. He thought about shooting across the angle of trail, but they were moving fast, and he was not sure how far this bow would send an arrow, even with magery behind it. He didn't trust his judgment of distance in the clear air.

● Chapter Twenty-four

The notch in the western wall had widened around them —
though Aris took only hurried glances at the land below
— when he heard horn signals echoing from the rocks around
them. He stopped, flattening himself against the wall. Here
the trail looped northward again, around the knees of the
mountain that formed the western wall; he could not see
directly west, but had a good view across the notch itself. He
saw nothing moving, though the horns seemed to come from
that direction. Sound could bounce off walls, he knew — could
it bounce around corners? He and Seri moved cautiously forward. He wondered if they could climb above the trail, where
the upper slope was now more broken rock than cliff.

"Yes," Seri said when he suggested it. "It's about time we
tried something sneaky." Aris tested the rocks; they seemed
firm enough. He pulled himself up into them, and worked his
way over the top of the knee, keeping low, until he looked
down on the next section of trail they had left.

He had been wrong about the number, or they had had a
trailing guard. Five husky, bearded men huddled on the trail,
speaking in a tongue Aris had never heard before. He didn't
have to understand the words to know they were worried and
afraid. The two with bows carried them strung, arrows in their
free hands; the other three had their blades out. From somewhere down the trail, Aris heard the noise of many men. He
flattened himself between the rocks, wishing that he'd found
gray rocks to match his clothes. He caught a glimpse of movement, sunlight glinting off metal. The general noise came
nearer, resolved into the scrape and tramp of boots on stone.
Below him, the huddle of five stirred. Their voices came up to
him, harsh and incomprehensible.

"Suppose they're rebels, like Gird," said Seri softly. She
looked almost as worried as the men on the trail. That had not
occurred to Aris.

"They attacked you," he pointed out. "Would Gird have tried to throttle you first, without asking questions?" Some of Gird's followers might, he thought. But if Gird had known, he would have clouted them; Aris felt no guilt at all about the man he'd bashed. Besides, the tension that had drawn him after these men had not been that of need, but of danger. He felt the danger now, far more from them than from whatever force was coming up the trail. "And you'd better take off that helmet — if I can see theirs — "

"You're right," said Seri. "Now — do we stay out of this, or assume the enemy of our enemy is a friend?" She had no time to say more. Around the corner of rock came a solid mass of men in rust-colored uniforms. As they caught sight of the five men on the trail, they let out a yell. One of the men below yelled back, the same word over and over. The men in uniform had bows, and drew them; the men below dropped theirs, and sank to their knees, arms wide.

"Fugitives giving themselves up," Aris murmured. That much he could understand, though not what kind of fugitives or why they had not left the trail to hide in the rocks, as he and Seri had done. More yells back and forth, all meaningless; two of the kneeling fugitives pointed back up the trail and said the same word repeatedly. He wondered what *biknini* meant.

"Telling about us," Seri said. "D'you suppose we were that frightening?"

"Perhaps — but I doubt we'd frighten that troop. They look well-trained." The bowmen were advancing in order, one step at a time, to someone's command. The fugitives knelt, their outstretched arms trembling. When the bowmen were perhaps twenty paces distant, and Aris had picked out the commander by his more elaborate uniform, they halted. The commander said something; the fugitives crept forward on their knees, arms still high, away from their weapons. One suddenly cried out, and tried to dash back up the trail. The two foremost archers loosed their arrows at once and the man staggered and fell, two black arrows in his back. The other fugitives stayed where they were.

Aris felt sick; watching someone else in danger was much harder than being in it himself. He watched the commander come forward, sunlight glittering on metal at his shoulder, on his ornate helmet, on the chain with a hanging pendant around his neck. Because the trail, even here, was scarcely wide enough for three men to walk abreast, he had to edge past his troop carefully. Unlike his soldiers, he had no beard, only long moustaches hanging below his chin. His heavy sword-belt of dark leather had a design worked into it in gold; from it hung a scabbarded curved blade on one side, and a short stick with a knobbed head on the other. He wore gloves and boots that matched his belt; the boots were knee-high, with tops turned down over them. Aris could see nothing of his face from above but the clean chin and drooping moustaches.

The captain and one of his soldiers walked nearer to the fugitives, and he gave an order, authority implicit in the tone. The fugitives shambled to their feet, one of them looking back to see their fallen comrade. The captain asked a question; the fugitives answered in ragged chorus, "Biknini!" Was that a plea for mercy, or a word for what they'd seen? Or something else entirely, an insult or curse? The captain gave another order, and the fugitives lowered their hands and put them at their backs; one turned, slowly, to face away from the soldiers. The captain yelled at them, and two more turned, grudgingly, partway. The fourth remaining stood as if frozen in place, trembling violently. The captain spoke to the soldier with him; the man pulled what looked like cord or thongs from his belt, and went forward to bind the captives' wrists.

He had just grabbed the wrists of the first man when Aris realized that the fourth was not paralyzed with terror but pretending it; he had drawn a long, narrow dagger from his sleeve. For the moment, the captain and the soldier with him were screening the fugitives from the archers; he no doubt thought the fugitives were far enough from their weapons, and sufficiently cowed, to make it safe.

That error nearly cost his life, as the first three fugitives whirled as one and grabbed the captain and his assistant; sheltered behind them, with knives laid against their throats, the fugitives began dragging them back up the trail toward their own weapons. The archers yelled, but wavered, clearly unwilling to shoot their own commander. Aris found himself standing before he knew it, and he and Seri yelled what later seemed silly, since the fugitives could not possibly understand, any more than they had understood the fugitives. "No, by Gird! Let them go!"

One of the archers let fly an arrow that wobbled up, then fell far behind them; it was clearly simple panic. The others, having glanced up once, kept their eyes and aim steady on the fugitives. The fugitives were not so steady. After one long terrified look, the one holding the captain let him fall and turned to run screeching back up the trail. Seri bounded up and across the hump, to cut him off on the far side. Two others cried out and fell to their knees, wrapping their arms around their head. But one paused to stab the soldier he was holding before he, too, fled up the trail. The archers got him before he made the turn, then ran forward to swarm over the kneeling fugitives and protect their captain. The captain scrambled up and looked up at Aris, calling out. Aris stood, expecting any moment to find himself full of arrows. Then his hands tingled; he felt the need of the wounded soldier. He met the captain's eyes and smiled. The man stared, spoke a word, and the archers lowered their bows. Aris pointed to the wounded man, then held out his hand, palm up. The soldiers muttered and drew back as much as the narrow trail allowed. The captain gestured: *Come down*, that had to mean. He held his hand up, palm toward his men, decisively. *No attack*. But did he mean it? Was he honest? Aris had to take that chance; he knew the soldier would die without his aid.

He came down the steep slope carefully, using his stick. The soldiers pulled back, leaving him room on the trail. They had bound the two fugitives tightly, with a loop from the wrists around the neck, and a guard stood over each one with naked blade. Aris went to the fallen soldier. He had been stabbed in the chest — Aris wondered why the enemy had not simply cut his throat — and he had already begun to turn blue; his breath gurgled. His eyes were open, but unfocussed as he fought for breath, but he saw Aris well enough to flinch.

"Don't be afraid," Aris said, hoping the tone would carry. "I will help you." He laid his hands on the man and felt the healing power flow out of him, a sensation that had become more powerful during his training. He could not explain it to others, but it could be as sharp a pleasure as withholding it was pain; although a difficult healing drained him, nothing else in his life gave him the same strong pleasure when it worked. He imagined the power surging along the man's torn blood-vessels, forcing out the blood choking his lungs and windpipe, mending every wounded tissue, restoring his strength . . . he noticed, in the vague way such things came to him, that the man also had a long-standing illness that recurred at intervals: this, too, the healing magery burned away. When he took his hands from the soldier's chest, the man blinked at him in astonishment: wide awake, obviously in no pain, and no sign of his injury but a short pink scar.

Aris looked around for the captain, and discovered that all the soldiers had also knelt, each with one hand on his head; the captain alone looked at him, astonishment clear on his sweaty face. Whatever he might have said was interrupted by Seri's shout from around the corner. "Ari! Come help me with this lout!"

"He will be fine," Aris said, to the captain, smiling. "I must go." He stepped over the soldier, who had not moved yet, and picked his way through the kneeling archers. Would they shoot him in the back? No. He made it to the corner and found Seri trying to drag the last fugitive by one foot.

"I whacked him in the head with my stick," she said, before he could ask. Together, they dragged the man back around the corner, where they found the soldiers just beginning to stand up; all promptly knelt again. "What is this?" asked Seri.

Aris explained. "And I suspect they think we're not human," he finished. "Perhaps they don't have magery." They dumped the fourth fugitive by the man the soldiers had shot, and Aris said, "I think we'd better make friends of these: it looks like they've been here awhile."

"Let's give them part of *Torre's Ride*," Seri said. "That's impressive."

They both held up their sticks, in the traditional gesture of minstrels who wanted everyone's attention, then began together the familiar old chant. "Hear now the tale of Torre, king's daughter, befriended of the gods, whose deeds divide the watches of the night. . . . " Together, they stopped and grounded their sticks. The captain stared, silent. Aris and Seri put out their right hands, palms up, and made a lifting gesture. The captain scrambled to his feet. Aris waved, indicating the other men, and made the lifting gesture again. The captain gave an order, and his men also stood, including the man who had been stabbed. The captain put his hand on that man's shoulder, then put his clenched fist on his chest, and extended his arm with hand open. That had to be thanks . . . heartfelt thanks? Aris thought so. He bowed, smiling at them, then turned to indicate the fallen fugitives: come get them. The captain smiled, and gave an order that sent two of his soldiers forward. Aris noticed that they left their bows behind; none now had arrows set to the string.

When the soldiers had dragged the fugitives back to the troop, the captain put out his hands, palm up. Then he pointed dramatically to himself, and said "Veksh." Aris wondered if this were his name, his title, or something else. The captain then pointed to one of his soldiers. "Veksh." So it could mean soldier, or man. Aris pointed to himself, and attempted the word with a questioning intonation.

"Veksh?"

The captain tossed his head, a gesture that could have meant anything to him but conveyed nothing to Aris. Then he pointed to one of the bound prisoners. "Veksh." So it probably meant man, not soldier . . . unless the fugitives were in a general class of warrior. And very likely the tossing head meant *no*. Aris pointed to himself again.

"Human. Mageborn."

Seri, following his lead, said "Human. Peasant." Aris hoped the strangers would not think that "mageborn" meant man, and "peasant" meant woman . . . he hadn't thought of that possibility until the words were out of his mouth.

The captain pointed back up the trail, then waved his arm . . . could he mean all that country? "Biknini." The fugitives had said that. The captain wasn't pointing at them, so it must not refer to individuals . . . a description of the land? Mountain, canyon, cliff? Aris decided that this was not going to work; he would try a more direct way. Moving slowly, he stepped nearer the captain, and with gestures indicated that he and Seri had been attacked by the fugitives and had killed three. Seri mimed her part well; the captain and his soldiers nodded as if they understood. He hoped that meant that a nod signified *yes*.

The captain pointed to Aris, then Seri — this time using a bent finger — and then made a circle with his arms, and threw the circle toward the distant canyons. Aris thought it was a very efficient way of asking if the two of them were all of their kind who lived over there. He shook his head, remembered that the captain had used a different gesture, and tried to copy the toss. Someone in the troop laughed; the captain turned on the unfortunate and said something scathing. Aris wished he knew what it meant.

Quickly, he used the same bent-finger point to indicate the captain, the man he had healed, and Seri and himself, then drew a circle with the same finger, and touched his chest. Slowly he made a fist of that hand, placed over his heart. He hoped they would understand that meant *friends*. Again the captain nodded, smiling, and repeated the gesture. He said something to the soldiers; one of them came forward with a bulging woven bag, and another with a leather bottle. Aris nodded to Seri; they pulled out the pouches they'd slung under their shirts. There on the trail, the captain offered a heavy loaf of dark bread, strips of dried meat, and water. Seri and Aris laid out salt, dried fruit, and their much lighter travel bread. The captain looked worried; Aris smiled at him.

"It is our custom to share," he said, as if the man could understand. "we will accept food from you, if you will accept food from us." He let his fingers rest on their food, and the others' food, then waved toward the captain. Again, the captain repeated his gesture, then very slowly reached toward the salt. Aris nodded, and himself touched the bread. The captain nodded. Seri reached forward and touched the water flask. The captain nodded again. Slowly, with great care, they exchanged bites of food. Seri almost choked on the water and told Aris, "It's not water; it's wine." The captain looked worried until Seri smiled at him. They each took a mouthful of each food: Seri, Aris, the captain, and the man who had been wounded. Behind the captain, his soldiers muttered softly.

And now what? Aris thought, as that ritual ended, and the four stood again. Do we just walk back up the trail and forget them? Or should we go with them and try to learn their language?

The captain clearly wanted them to come along. His gestures were unmistakable. Aris felt reluctance rise in him, a chill resistance. Seri shook her head decisively. "No; we are guardians, we must go back." Conveying that in gestures took longer, a pantomime that involved, in the end, the captain, his soldiers, and even the captives. Seri and Aris indicated that they, like the captain and his soldiers, were guardians who must not leave their post, who had pursued dangerous invaders, but must now return. Once the captain got the main idea, he nodded vigorously, then began a mime of his own. They would come back? They would meet with him? Such friends should stay friends. They could hunt danger together. He pointed to the sun, and held up one hand, fingers splayed: a hand of days, Aris thought. He wants to meet us here in five days. He offered gifts: a medallion from his boots, the flask of wine. Seri took off the little medallion she'd carved of cedarwood, with the interlocking G and L that Dorhaniya had devised. The captain accepted it with a deep bow, touched it to his forehead, and turned to his soldiers.

"We'd better hurry if we want to be back over the notch by nightfall," Aris said, with a look at the sun's position. Much of the upward trail would be shadowed already. Seri nodded, and they started back uphill, around the angle of rock that would hide them from the soldiers. It was cooler walking in the shade of the rock behind them; Aris noticed that even on the sunlit slope across from them, the trail they'd come down hardly showed. When they were well into the shade, he asked, "Do you trust them?"

Seri looked at him. "Trust them? Not like you, but I felt nothing evil, did you?"

"No, except from the ones who attacked you. Brigands, probably, who prey on those caravans." They both looked back, and Aris caught a glimpse of something moving in the broken rock below, toward the streambed. "Seri — what's that?" They crouched low, trying to see into the shadowed angles of the lower slopes. More movement, stealthy . . . someone darting from cover to cover, two hurrying a laden pack animal. . . .

Seri and Aris exchanged looks; the same thought joined them. "The *other* brigands."

"Those were decoys," Seri breathed. "They were supposed to draw off pursuit, while the main party went up the streambed."

"I suppose we're lucky," Aris said. "We could've run into that lot down there. There's probably more of them."

"We have to tell the captain," Seri said. Aris agreed, though he wished it had been earlier in the day. Now they could not possibly make it back to their own canyon by nightfall.

347

"If we can see them down there, they might see us," Aris pointed out. "And they'd expect their people to be a lot farther along."

"They might think we're soldiers, giving up the pursuit."

"We can hope." Together they marched in soldierly fashion to the now-familiar angle of rock, then back into the sunlight. Looking downward from here, they could see nothing below that looked suspicious; the stream's outlet, far to the west, looked like a dry, gravelly bed. And the soldiers were also out of sight already on the twisting trail. They hurried on, almost running, until they caught sight of the moving troop ahead and below. "Now do we call, or — "

"We call; I don't want to be shot by their very efficient archers." She grinned at him. "Let's give them *Torre's Ride* again; maybe they'll remember some of the words." They started in on that again, and at once two soldiers in the rear rank turned and gaped. They heard the captain's voice; the troop stopped. Aris waved, then pointed downward. The captain spread his hands and gave another order; his soldiers stood in their ranks as he toiled back up the trail. He looked disgruntled. Aris went to meet him, and tried to convey with gestures that they had seen many people, with pack animals, far below them as they climbed back. It took longer than it should have; the captain seemed determined to misunderstand. But finally it was clear he did understand. With his own gestures, he showed that it would take far too long to reach the foot of the mountain, find the trail, and follow that band of fugitives through the notch; he wanted Seri and Aris to lead him on the upper trail.

Seri and Aris exchanged glances. It would be dark before they got to the notch; on the far side that exposed ledge would be difficult to traverse without light, and the fugitives would see a light that high. Yet the captain's request made sense, from his point of view. And they were reluctant to have strangers moving into the canyons while they were here, giving no warning to their own people.

"Yes," Aris said, nodding. "Come now." He and Seri turned and again led the way upslope. Behind them, the captain and his troop seemed to make an incredible amount of noise. Not until they had marched some distance did it occur to Aris to wonder about the prisoners. He looked back but could not see them. They reached the place where he had seen the movement below, but deeper shadow now cloaked the lower slopes; he could see nothing. And in the time it had taken to find the captain and retrace their path, all the other party might well have passed. He pointed it out, nonetheless, and showed the captain with his hands how the fugitives moved.

From there to the notch was an uphill grind that tired even Aris and Seri. The soldiers had to stop repeatedly, and the sun had set well before they reached the place where Seri had been attacked, although enough skyglow remained to show the edge of the trail clearly. Scavengers had already found the bodies; Aris heard grunts and hisses as they neared it, and saw several dark blurry forms slither off the trail. He explained to the captain as if the man spoke their language; it was too dark to see most gestures or expressions.

The cold night wind had begun, and moaned softly through the notch, smelling of pine and wet rock. Aris and Seri led the way again, and in the last dayglow pointed out the ledge which they must follow to the base of the cliffs beyond. Aris moved out onto the ledge first. He could just see the ledges below in the starlight, one vague grayish slab after another, but he had to feel his way along. Seri, behind him, suddenly touched his back.

"What?"

"That glow." Aris turned, and saw the unmistakeable orange glitter of a fire in the distance, somewhere north and below.

"We still have to get off this ledge," he said. "Make sure the captain sees it, though." He made his way along gingerly, hoping that the large snake they had seen did not wander at night. The soldiers slipped, muttering what must be curses; their boots clattered on the rock until he was sure that they could be heard all the way back in the stronghold. Where the ledge slipped back under rocky soil, and scrubby trees began, he startled an owl. It flew away, hooting shrilly. "Now they must know," he said. Seri touched his shoulder again.

"It's farther than you think," she said. "Don't worry about it. Just let us get these men safely into some kind of camp."

Aris looked up at the looming cliffs ahead, their sheer flanks visible even in starlight. "The way we came," he said. "It'll be out of sight of that fire, and safe enough. One of us can go down the streambed to water." Soon the fire was hidden by a fold of ground, and then the massive projection of the cliff itself. The closer they got to the cliff, the colder seemed the air that poured off it, an invisible river. Aris led them to the edge of the forest; it was too dark to travel within it. There he waited for the captain; Seri put his hand over the captain's cold glove, and Aris pressed down: sit. The captain spoke softly to his men, and all sank to the ground. Aris felt legweary himself; he was glad to take out the food in his pack.

Somehow, even in the dark, they were able to share food among all of them. The captain assigned two men to guard, placing them where Aris suggested, upslope toward the north. Aris wondered whether to trust them, but he felt no warnings. He and Seri slept a little apart from the others, side by side, and woke stiff but rested in the first light of dawn. The cliffs across from them had begun to glow a dull orange, though the sun was not yet on them; behind, the taller cliffs of the main mountain were still deep rose, shadowed blue. In that dawn silence, he heard falling water, a merry irregular chiming like tiny bells. Following it, he found a spring dripping into a moss-cupped pool crowded with flowers, some the same as in the upper canyon, and one a curious lavendar bloom he had never seen before. He filled his flask, and showed Seri the spring.

The morning found the captain more suspicious and less amiable, if his expression meant anything. Aris had never before imagined how difficult it was to convey the simplest meanings with gesture alone. He knew the captain wanted to know if their people lived in the same direction as the fire of the night before. He wanted the captain to know that they did not. He wanted the captain to understand that either he or Seri should go and warn the stronghold, perhaps returning with help; he could see that the captain didn't want to let either of them out of his sight. Or perhaps he was not used to sleeping on the ground in his uniform. Aris knew that made some people grumpy.

He tried drawing a map on the ground with a stick: here we are, there they are, and over here are my people. The captain's expression did not change. Seri said, "Let's go with them now — they won't be worrying yet." She pointed north, where they had seen the fire the night before, and gave the captain a wide grin. His face relaxed; he shrugged, smiled, and gave an order to his soldiers. Soon they were on their way, around the first "finger" and into the next cove, angling toward low ground and the streambed.

By the time they found a reasonable slope down to it, the sun had cleared the cliffs to the east, and glinted off the stream itself. They saw no smoke; Aris thought that the brigands probably put their fires out in daylight, so that smoke could not betray them. Aris had spotted a trail that he thought the others used coming down from the high pass; he stayed upslope of it until they reached the stream, which here ran swift and clear, alternating rocky stretches, gravelled pools, and sandbars. Seri touched his shoulder, but he had already seen.

There on the damp sand were the hoofprints of several horses, headed upstream; the captain grinned and clapped Aris on the shoulder. "Kreksh," he said. The hoofprints went across the sandbar, and up into rocks on the far side. The captain walked his fingers along the near side of the stream; clearly he wanted to get behind the fugitives. Aris nodded; that made good sense. He still worried about sentries. He did not know this country, and the fugitives clearly did. They must have someone watching down their back trail. He tried to indicate this; the captain smiled, nodded, and mimed cautious sneaking through the bushes. Aris pointed to the cove that now opened behind them — why not go into the trees? The captain looked up at the cliffs, as if he expected trouble from them, and shook his head.

Soon enough, the streambed itself led them into the trees. Aris felt safer; someone perched overhead on a rock could not see through the canopy.

They heard the brigands, and smelled the smoke of their fire, before they saw them. Voices echoed off the cliffs; Aris was glad he had insisted that the captain speak to his men about moving more quietly. The captain could understand what they were saying; Aris could not, but he could tell that they were relaxed, not on their guard at all. Aromatic smoke and the delicious scent of cooking meat made him hungry; he tightened his belt and crept on, cautiously.

When he came to the edge of the clearing, it was obvious that these brigands had lived there a long time. Three log huts, low but sturdy, backed against the cliff, and a rail fence kept the animals from straying . . . a motley group of horses and mules. They had butchered a mule — its head was displayed on a stick; its hide had been stretched from a tree-limb, weighted with stones. Aris guessed that they stole the animals from the caravans, used them to transport their goods, then ate them.

The brigands themselves were swarming over the loot they had stolen, spreading it out in the sun to gloat over. Aris saw lengths of striped cloth, some in brilliant colors, rugs, copper pots, and small sacks that the robbers opened, sniffed, then tied shut again. He had trouble counting them, but thought the number must lie between fifteen and twenty. He thought all were men until a woman came out of one of the huts with a baby at her breast, and another woman followed her.

The captain grinned again, and sent his men around the clearing. He showed Aris, with gestures, what he planned: his men would attack from behind, forcing the brigands to withdraw the way they had come even if they escaped. His men would have the higher ground, and beyond the notch he would have reinforcements. Seri touched the captain's shoulder, and pointed to a trail that seemed to lead away from the clearing on the far side, then to herself, brows raised. The captain nodded, and Seri began to work herself into position. It might be only a trail to a jacks, Aris knew, or it might be an escape route.

The captain's signal to attack was that same horn call that Aris and Seri had heard the day before. It came from the cliff behind the clearing, magnified by the walls until it sounded like a fanfare. The brigands dropped their loot, looked around wildly, and bellowed. The hut doors opened; more women poured out, and a few men either sleepy or drunk by their staggering gait. Some of the men outside ran for the huts — to get their weapons, Aris guessed — but the soldiers cut them down with arrows, staying in cover themselves. Those not hit with the first flight threw themselves on the ground, behind any cover they could find, and tried to crawl to the huts. The soldiers ran out, yelling as if they had an army behind them. Some of the brigands broke and ran; two — who had swords in reach — tried to fight and were cut down. One of the fugitives charged straight at Aris and the captain, sword swinging. Aris leaped forward, evaded a swing, and thrust hard with his staff; the man fell, gasping, and dropped his sword. Aris kicked it away behind him, and looked for Seri.

Several brigands had tried to get past her; Aris saw only the final head-splitting blow which she dealt the last of them. Then the fight — it could hardly be called a battle — ended, with most of the brigands dead, a few bound hand and foot, and the women huddled together under the soldiers' guard. The captain strode up to them; the soldiers crowded around, laughing. One of the women screamed as a soldier grabbed her; Aris heard cloth ripping.

Seri and Aris pushed between them, and stood back to back on either side of the women; Seri said "No!" and Aris brought up his stick. The captain glared and said something, pointing to the women and then to himself. "No," Aris said. Behind him, the baby started crying, a thin pulsing wail; by the sound, at least two women were sobbing too. "No," Aris said again. "You can't hurt them; it's not right." He had no way to mime that; he hoped his tone would convey his determination. One of the soldiers muttered "Biknini daksht!" and grabbed at Aris's stick; Aris swung it out of his reach, and knocked him on the knee. The man fell back with a cry, and the others muttered louder, looking at their captain. He chewed his long moustaches, shrugged, threw his hands out and gave a command. The archers put arrows to their bows, and half-drew them. The captain pointed to Aris, then the women, then himself, and waved around at the archers.

One of the women said something more than a cry. The captain stiffened; his eyes opened wide, and he replied. The woman spoke again, in a low, hurried voice. Aris wished he had some idea what was being said. Whatever it was affected the captain; he bowed, stiffly, and gave an order that made his archers lower their bows. Then he bowed even lower and held out his hand. From behind Aris a woman stepped forth, wrapped in a blanket that now covered most of her head; her legs were bare and he thought she had on little under the blanket. She touched the captain's hand with the tips of her fingers and turned away. Aris saw wide-set amber eyes and a tangled mane of red hair. The captain shouted orders; his soldiers ran to the tumbled piles of loot and snatched up lengths of cloth. With great courtesy, the captain offered them; the woman took one and wrapped it around her, over the blanket, before walking into one of the huts.

"I think that's over," Aris said, lowering his stick. Seri moved around beside him; the women they had guarded eyed the cloth avidly, and when the captain nodded, snatched it up and ran for the same hut as the first woman.

"If only we knew what had happened," Seri said. She ran her hands along her stick, eyeing the soldiers. "Although I suppose we must now go with them, to make sure they don't mistreat these women on the way back — wherever that is. But if we're not back by tomorrow, our people will be worried."

Shortly the first woman reappeared, now without the blanket and wrapped in two layers of cloth that covered her to her ankles. She came first to Seri, knelt, and kissed her hand; then kissed Aris's. Aris was so astonished he could not react before she stood again and began talking to the captain.

He watched that interchange. Something in the captain's stance indicated that the woman was of equal or higher rank. A captive? He could not tell. The captain answered her, first briefly, then with a long spate of words that was, Aris finally figured out from the gestures, the full story of yesterday's chase and this morning's stalk.

Meanwhile the soldiers briskly packed up the rest of the loot, and searched the huts for more. The other women had straggled out with bundles and sacks; two more children appeared, both just able to walk. The soldiers loaded the loot on the pack animals, and looked from their captain to Aris and Seri. The captain looked at them, too, and spoke to the first woman. She pointed to the other women and nodded. The captain threw up his hands; the soldiers muttered, but unpacked one animal to saddle it for riding. The first woman and the two children rode; the other women walked, one carrying her baby.

Aris wondered what they would have done if he and Seri had not been there. He didn't like the thoughts that came to him. He had noticed that yesterday's prisoners had disappeared, and he was sure they were dead. He glanced at Seri, who grinned and nodded to the captain.

It was close to noon when the captain led them off toward the stream. They followed its windings deeper and deeper into the gorge that cut through the western cliffs. If he had had the leisure, Aris would have studied the odd colors and patterns of the rocky walls, but the captain, homeward bound, kept up a good pace. They stopped once to water the pack animals and eat the last of their food, but pressed on in the growing heat of afternoon.

354

The stream's narrow bed widened gradually; its water disappeared into a fan of gravel and sand. Aris looked back at the rampart of the cliffs far above; the mountains behind were invisible from here. They stood on a great hump of broken rock and gravel, the outwash of the stream, with a good view now of a cluster of buildings some distance away to the left. The captain looked back, and waved to them. Aris looked at the sun, about to dip behind distant mountains, and then at Seri. She still grinned, as usual, and it lifted his spirits. "Might as well," she said. "Maybe he'll feed us."

The captain had waved his shiny helmet, and blown his horn; soon Aris could see a mounted troop riding out to them. Well before dark, they were all mounted — on horses that seemed to Aris hardly larger than nomad ponies, though very differently shaped — and riding toward the town. The captain seemed unsurprised that Aris and Seri could ride; Aris thought perhaps he had worn out his surprise earlier.

The town, when they reached it, was a cluster of low, mud-brick and stone buildings crammed behind a stout wall perhaps two men high. Aris had not seen any green fields, though in the gathering dark he could not see clearly; perhaps its fields were on the other side. Its narrow gate had a tall, heavy wooden door. Men in the long, loose shirts like those the brigands had worn came out carrying torches to light their way. Inside the gate, the buildings jammed wall-to-wall. Women crowded the narrow streets, crying out when they saw the woman on horseback, and then shrieking even louder when they saw Aris and Seri.

355

● **Chapter Twenty-five**

Their first meal in the strangers' town combined new tastes with elaborate ritual. Aris could only hope that their hosts would not be offended by mistakes; he was soon completely confused about what was expected of them. They seemed to be part exhibition and part honored guest. He and Seri had been offered deep copper basins of warm water for bathing (the captain had mimed a bath for them); they had taken turns, glad to wash off the sweat and dirt of two days' journeying. Clothes, too, had been offered: long white robes with gray panels down the front — as close to the color they had been wearing, they thought, as the captain could find — went over wide-legged gray pants of the same smooth fabric. Aris found the robe deliciously smooth against his skin. He looked more closely at the gray panel, and realized it was brocade, glittering almost silver. Seri touched hers. "This is silk," she said. "Like the clothes Dorhaniya had, that Eris used to make those tunics for Luap." Their own clothes were taken away for washing — again, clearly mimed — but no one tried to touch their sticks or their daggers.

But the meal drove all concern for clothes out of mind. The captain had also bathed and changed; he appeared in a long robe similar to theirs, but in red and brown brocade. When he sat, on the pile of cushions placed for him on a colorful carpet, Aris noticed that he had dark silk pants under his robe. Aris and Seri sat on either side of him.

The room was lit by oil lamps and candles both, with polished metal reflectors used to make it brighter where the diners sat. On the other side of the room, a crowd of people stood, murmuring among themselves. Aris wondered who they were; the captain seemed to ignore them. Servants brought in low tables, then trays laden with food. The captain dipped into a mound of steamed grain and vegetables with a long handled utensil that had a flat, leaf-shaped blade, and offered Seri the resulting lump. She looked around for a plate or something resembling it; a servant held out a flat cake that looked like travel-bread. She took it, and scooped the food off the utensil; the captain repeated this ritual with Aris, who did the same. Then the captain ate a single mouthful, and waited until they had finished their serving. Every dish he offered first to one of them, alternating the honor.

Aris liked the steamed grain, but not the sour little leaf-wrapped rolls stuffed with meat and swimming in a sweet sauce, although he was hungry enough to eat it anyway. A bowl of crispy fries he realized with horror were fried insects; apparently the look on his face was enough, for the captain shrugged and turned away. When Seri also refused it, he shrugged again, dipped one in its accompanying sauce (red flecked with yellow and green) and crunched it, grinning. Another pile of steamed grain, this one colored a rich gold, and fragrant with even more spices. . . . Aris liked that, and the meat stew that came after it. Between each offering, servants handed him a cup of water and a cup of wine.

By the time Aris felt stuffed, after tasting several dozen different foods, all new to him, the table still held enough for a feast. The captain waved his hand, offering more of anything; Aris shook his head and patted his stomach, hoping the captain would understand. Apparently so; he clapped his hands and servants came to remove the tables. Other servants brought a small one, and on it put a loaf of bread, a bowl of water, a large book and a scroll. The captain smiled at Aris, then at Seri, and put his hand on the bread.

"Grish," the captain said. Aris blinked. He must be naming the bread, unless bread stood for something else.

"Grish," he repeated. Then he laid his own hand on the bread and said, "Bread." The captain repeated his word twice, and went through the whole thing again with Seri. Then he touched the water in the bowl.

"Sur."

Aris repeated that, and said, "Water." Again, the captain repeated the procedure with Seri. Then he pointed to the bread, and the water, and said "Bret. Waffer." Aris and Seri exchanged glances, pointed in their turn, and said "Grish. Sur." It was something, but didn't seem likely to lead very far.

Then the captain opened the book. Aris had heard of books:

357

Gird had reported that the gnomes used books, flat pages that could be turned. But he had seen only scrolls, although it was easy to see how one could cut a scroll into short lengths and bind them together. This book had not only writing — the script looked very strange, as if it were made of random brushstrokes, yet those vertical columns could be nothing else — but also pictures. Clearly drawn in black ink, brilliantly colored, they were both beautiful and informative. The captain stopped at a page depicting a group of riders on horseback prancing past a grove of pines. He pointed to one of the horses.

"Pirush." When Aris and Seri had both repeated it, he said, "Pirush. Nyai pirush." He held up one finger. "Nyai." Pointed again to the horse. "Nyai . . . pirush."

"One horse," said Aris. He held up his finger. "One — " and pointed to the tree, " — horse."

Two horses, it turned out, were "teg pirushyin." Two men on the horses were "teki vekshyin." One man on a horse was "nyaiyi veksh." One pine tree was "nya skur," and two were "tag skuryin."

With the aid of the pictures and a natural quickness, Aris and Seri made some progress even that first night. Their experience with the horse nomads helped, because although the languages seemed nothing alike, they had learned how differently thoughts could be put into words. The captain, also quick to learn, picked up their "please" although he offered no equivalent; perhaps he simply used it in situations where he'd observed them using it, without understanding. By the time the captain rose to escort them to their guestroom, they could understand his words, "Sleep — tomorrow more" as well as his gestures.

They slept well, wakening to find that someone had put their clothes — clean and dry — in a neat stack beside the door. No sooner had they begun to talk softly than servants appeared with more basins of warm water. Aris and Seri washed and changed into their own garments; Aris noticed a faint but pleasant smell of spice.

The next day, Aris felt that one of them must return and explain to Luap what had happened. His combination of words and gestures, with reference to the pictures in the book, seemed to convince the captain, who offered a mount and an escort. Seri spoke up suddenly.

"Aris — why not try duplicating the pattern — perhaps in the ground out there — and going the mageroad?"

"Because I thought you should go, and you can't use the mageroad alone."

"They won't know that; if they see you use it, they'll be convinced I have the same power."

"And we don't know if they'll consider it proof that we're the biknini." The biknini, in the book, were dangerous-looking monsters, capable of changing from a cloud to a collection of spikes, horns, and hooves, to apparent human form. "And we don't know if it would work."

"It's the quickest way," Seri said. "If it doesn't work, you can still ride the horse. As ceremonial as these folk are, they may take drawing it as a prayer of some kind."

"It will be," Aris said. It was too good an idea to waste, though. The captain led the way outside the walls. Aris looked around, noticing a green patch some distance away with trees around it. Grainfield? His newly acquired language deserted him; he had to point. The captain nodded, said something Aris thought he remembered meant "grain" and offered with gestures to lead him that way. Aris shook his head, and looked for a smooth, level space which he could use for the pattern. He found what seemed a good spot, and gestured with his stick: please get back from this. With captain and a crowd watching, he drew the design, and when Seri nodded, stepped onto it. Would it work? He thought of the stronghold's great hall, and with a familiar internal wrench found himself there. Luap, passing through on some errand, stumbled, then smiled.

"What — have you found another pattern somewhere? And where's Seri? I thought you two were off exploring together."

"We were," Aris said. "Where's Arranha? I need to talk to both of you — we've met the people out there to the west." He wished he had thought to ask Seri to protect the pattern — since it worked at all, it might work the other way too, and give him a quicker way to travel back and forth. Would she have thought of that? Probably. "Just a moment," he said. "I have to try something."

Luap stared at him in some confusion. "People? Where? And how did you get back here without Seri?"

"Please," Aris said. "Go find Arranha, and the Rosemage, and I'll be back shortly." *I hope.* He concentrated on the pattern he had drawn, on Seri's presence, and found himself back outside the town, where the crowd was arguing and waving their arms about, while Seri stood calmly by, arms folded. When he appeared, silence fell instantly; half the crowd threw themselves on the ground, another group turned and ran for the gate, and the captain blanched. "It works," Aris said to Seri. "I've asked Luap to find Arranha and the Rosemage. If you can protect this pattern, I can come and go using it. Is it safe for you to stay?"

Seri grinned. "Now it will be. I think the crowd was giving our captain trouble."

Aris didn't want to leave her there, in danger, but she insisted. He took the mageroad back to the stronghold and found Luap, Arranha, and the Rosemage all waiting for him. As quickly as he could, he told them what he and Seri had found, and done; despite his sense of urgency, it was a long tale to tell quickly.

"Luap, if you take my advice, we will let Seri and Aris learn the language before we take action, but in the meantime I will post guards at the western end of our canyon." The Rosemage had not bothered to repeat her earlier concern and point out that a possible enemy now knew exactly where they were. She turned to Aris. "Aris, can you describe the way to that upper trail well enough that someone can find it, or will you have to lead them?"

Aris shook his head. "I'd best lead them; it's easy country to get lost in."

"Then Arranha or I will use your pattern to visit that town, and bring Seri back. She should be able to explain that she will return later. What do you think?"

It felt right to him; he nodded. Not until later did it occur to him that Luap had said little, and made no decisions himself. Arranha, they decided, would be less threatening a visitor. He could bring Seri back, or stay a day or so: not more than two. The Rosemage went to gather the few trained fighters to follow Aris down-canyon, and Aris went off to fetch his own weapons from the armory, tell his prentices where he was going, and fill his pack. His mind buzzed with questions. How many people lived in the western plains, and where were those caravans travelling from and to? How long would it take to learn the language? Could they trade with that town? Were they peaceful folk?

He led the group down the canyon at a brisk pace. The Rosemage worried that the captain had already sent a troop of his own; Aris didn't think he would, but knew it was a possibility. He felt strange without Seri at his side, and wondered if Arranha were strong enough to protect her if things went badly in the town.

When they came to the notch, they had seen no sign of soldiers; Aris pointed out the route he and Seri had taken through the notch and then north toward the brigand encampment. The Rosemage, breathless, looked at him and shook her head. "You younglings! You covered all that ground and still had breath to fight and talk? At least I have some hard-won experience." She pointed out where she wanted the guardposts. "We need one of the stonecutters to come up here and carve them out; for now, we can build rock barriers of loose stone." She looked down toward the streambed. "You were right; we can't go straight down here without building another trail — but we'll put a lookout where he can see any approaches from the stream, as well."

By that night, Aris felt that no invasion could come from the town without being discovered. And the next day, Seri and Arranha returned; she slipped downcanyon to find him and tell him what had happened.

"Although the important thing is, the captain wants us to be allies against brigands. Makes sense to me; if brigands are living in that western end, they could be a threat as our people move down this way."

"What happened to the women we found?" Aris asked.

Seri made a face. "Hard to ask that; I don't have enough words yet. I tried, of course. If I understood what the captain said, one woman had been held captive, and her family is rich — they had a reward for her return. The others had been traveling with her, servants or friends or whatever. But I never saw them again, and the captain didn't seem to understand most of what I asked." She grinned. "Then again, I didn't understand most of what he asked, either. That book is impressive, but you can't draw pictures of the things we most wanted to say."

361

"What did they think when Arranha appeared?"

"They all threw themselves on the ground, even the captain. Perhaps they have more respect for old people, or perhaps they could sense he is a priest. Maybe it was his way of dressing, his long robes. But whatever it was, they treated him as if he were a direct messenger of the gods."

Aris punched her lightly. "In some ways, he is."

In the next day or so, after much discussion, Luap decided to let Aris and Seri contact the town as much as they wished, and encouraged them to learn the language. Since the strangers now knew about them, the original objections no longer mattered, and prudence alone suggested that they must learn more about these neighbors. He sent one of those skilled in cutting stone by magery down to carve guardposts where the Rosemage wanted them. Now that they had neighbors, he would need to think more like a ruler — a member of Council, he corrected himself — and less like the head of a family. His people's very existence would depend on decisions he made, how he managed relations with these strangers. Within a few hands of days, a trickle of information began to flow between the town and the stronghold, as Seri and Aris learned more of the language.

"They call themselves the Khartazh," Aris reported, the next time he came back. "They have large cities to the north, and a king rules in one of them. They trade with the Xhim, far to the south, and over still more mountains in the northwest to folk who live along a seacoast." He frowned, staring at the map of the stronghold which Luap had been working on. "It's hard to believe they mean north*west*; the great sea is in the east: we all know that. The Honnorgat flows into it, the Immerhoft Sea is part of it — "

"Perhaps it goes all the way around the land," Luap said. He did not really care where the great sea was; he had never seen one, except on a map. Aris, he thought, was like Arranha in one thing — his curiosity could take him away from the point at hand to investigate all sorts of unimportant trifles. If it weren't for his own ability to remember what really mattered, if it weren't for his prudent leadership, his people could find themselves hungry and naked because no one bothered with the boring necessities. He shook his head, banishing that thought: it was unfair. He had many able helpers, and Aris could be practical when necessary. Perhaps he had an illness coming on; he would ask Aris later. But Aris's next word drove that thought from his mind.

"The captain has reported to his king, of course," Aris said. "The king sent word that his ambassador will meet with you at your convenience." Another practical problem, Luap thought, yet to listen to Aris one would think he had produced a solution instead.

"How long will that take?" asked the Rosemage.

"The captain thought it would be sometime in autumn; he says the great lords move as slowly as mountains."

"Then we could still go to our mountain," the Rosemage said with a glance at Arranha. "The younglings have had their fun —"

Luap smiled at her. "I'm not sure it was fun — or was it?"

Aris shrugged, smiling. "Enough that I'll admit we've had our turn. At least it worked out well. But can you spare one of us to be in Dirgizh, learning the language, if the Rosemage and Arranha leave?"

They might as well get all their adventuring done at once, and have it over with before winter. Luap wondered that he had not noticed, back in Fin Panir, the erratic behavior of these four. Now that he thought of it, he had seen, without recognizing, an inability to stick to a task. Arranha had been a rebel among the priests — rightly so, considering that priesthood, but it proved he was undependable in some ways. The Rosemage, after all, had turned against her first lord; even Gird had found her hard to manage. And the young ones had followed no one's pattern; they were likeable, good-hearted, but of the same difficult, questioning temperament as Arranha. A shame, since they all had remarkable talents, but the gods made no one perfect. He would have to learn how best to use their talents without letting their limitations damage the whole settlement.

Gird, he thought, would have imposed his will with a hard fist, but he, Luap, preferred to use more humane methods. It was not for him to command as Gird had; he was not a king, though he was a king's son. He would not make the mistakes his father had made. He would temper firmness with gentleness, where it did no harm. Let them have a loose rein; let them discover for themselves that his reasoning made more sense than their wild intuitions.

So he was careful to keep an even tone as he answered Aris. "As long as they're back when the ambassador arrives. The fieldwork is well in hand; you'd be spending much of your time on other things anyway. Seri, I think you should go; Aris, as our only healer, needs to stay closer until his prentices have more skill. We had another snakebite while you were gone."

"But I can use the mageroad," Aris said. "I could go back and forth each day. Spend part of the day in Dirgizh, and part of it here —"

"I'm not sure that's wise," Arranha said, relieving Luap of the necessity. "What's often seen becomes common; the mageroad is presently a mystery to them, and should remain one."

"I wish we had a horse trail out," Seri said. "Then I'd have a reason to bring our horses from Fin Panir." She and Aris had left their horses behind at first, when the Marshal-General had baulked at letting so many animals into the High Lord's Hall to use the mageroad. Farm stock had been needed first, and after all they had little pasture and no place to ride but the main canyon. Luap had been surprised that they agreed without argument, but he knew they missed their horses. He, too, missed riding a good horse; the few plow ponies they had were rough-gaited and clumsy on trails. Still, bringing that up now was another proof that she could be as erratic, as faulty in judgment, as Aris or the Rosemage. What could *her* horse matter?

"The Marshal-General is not likely to let us bring more beasts through the High Lord's Hall," the Rosemage said. "Even those. And you know we've never fitted a horse into that inner chamber of Luap's cave."

"I know — but if we had them we could ride out there — and it would be quicker going back and forth —"

"Seri." Aris laid his hand on hers. "I know you don't want to be in Dirgizh alone — but is there more?"

"No — just a feeling. They keep talking about demons in here, demons haunting the canyons. What if something happens while I'm away? While the Rosemage is away?"

"I won't command you to go, if it so distresses you," said Luap; at his tone, Seri flushed.

"I'm a Marshal; I have nothing to fear." The look she gave

364

Luap had in it more challenge than respect. Then she grinned and relaxed. "In fact, it should be fun — they'll let me ride their horses, I can see how they drill their troops — "

"And you come back often and let me know," Aris said, almost fiercely.

"And Arranha and I will come back laden with gold and silver and jewels," the Rosemage said, laughing. "And we will all be rich, able to buy all those things in the market you've told us about. We won't have to dig the horse trail by magery; we can hire men to do it."

Luap thought they should have known better. If he had been asked, Arranha and the Rosemage would not have been his choice for the task of exploring the wilderness looking for gold. What did either of them know about it? Arranha, at his age, should spend his time in quiet study and prayer; the Rosemage, too, was no longer young, for all that she could wrap herself in magery so that none could see the silver threads in her dark hair, or the lines at her throat. But he could not argue with Arranha, who had been, in many ways, his mentor. He would never, he told himself proudly, use his power to overwhelm the old priest; if hints would not suffice, he would let Arranha do what he would.

The others talked on, their plans growing ever more grandiose and ridiculous. Luap listened, realizing his responsibility to protect them from themselves. They had talents he did not share, he thought with conscious generosity, but without guidance they would lead themselves — and everyone else — into a tangle of problems.

Aris busied himself, while Seri was in Dirgizh, by reorganizing his stores of herbs and bandages, teaching formal classes to his assistants and prentices, and exploring the main canyon for useful plants. When the Rosemage and Arranha came back from their mountain, when the ambassador had come and gone, and others could speak to the Khartazh as well as he and Seri, he hoped they could leave for awhile. The memory of the long rides with Seri, of the healings he had performed among the farmers, among the horsefolk, rose vividly in his mind. They could not stay forever in Luap's canyons; they had work to do in what he privately considered the "real" world. He missed Raheli and Cob; he even missed the Marshal-General.

Perhaps that explained why the Rosemage and Arranha wanted to explore the gray mountain — perhaps they, too, felt trapped in the canyon. He could not imagine Arranha lying about his motives, but — could anyone really take one look at a mountain and assume it contained gold or silver? The thought came into his mind that all four of them had been unusually distractible lately . . . he and Seri had felt a compulsion to explore the mountaintop, and then the western canyons, while the others took one look at that gray mountain and wanted to go there. None of them seemed to have time to talk things over, as they had when they first came, and when they did confer, their ideas went everywhere; they could come to few conclusions.

Had anyone else had similar desires? Aris intended to ask his assistants, but found himself instead confronted with an emergency that drove everything else out of his mind. Several children had eaten poisonous wild berries, and it took all Aris's skill and power to save them. By the time they were out of danger, he'd forgotten about his earlier concerns. He needed to find out which plants were poisonous, and make sure all the parents knew them; he needed to find remedies for snakebite and sting that could serve when he was not at hand. Luap was right, he thought: he had more than enough work to keep him busy right here.

● Chapter Twenty-six

Luap had no idea what to expect from the Khartazh ambassador. Seri and Aris had described the soldiers and their captain in terms of weapons and tactics. To his questions about what they wore, and what they looked like, they'd returned doubtful answers. "They're all sunburnt, of course," Seri had said. "Very brown."

"I think it's their natural skin," Aris had said. "Not just the sunburn. Perhaps a natural protection." Both had had much to say about the soldiers' gear, the use of headcloths to keep the sun from their helmets, the small, light horses they rode, the very different shape of their bows . . . but he had gained no insight at all into the men themselves. Nor had Seri been able to describe their language. She and Aris both were quick-tongued; they had learned the horse nomads' difficult speech with ease, and would no doubt learn this before anyone else, but she had spent the past hands of days in the west, with the Khartazh soldiers: she had not been back to teach him what she had learned. He would have to rely on her and on Aris for translation.

Although the captain Seri and Aris had met had told them it might be easily six hands of days before an ambassador would come ("at your convenience" Luap recognized as a term of courtesy, not a reality), in fact he had appeared in less than four. The earlier decision to allow Arranha and the Rosemage to go wandering off to explore the gray mountain now seemed less wise; Luap did not expect them back for days yet. In the meantime he was having to meet a royal ambassador alone, without their help, and it bothered him. He knew it had been his decision to let them go, but he had to fight off the temptation to blame them anyway.

He wished he knew more about protocol in royal courts. His was not, of course, a royal court, but the ambassador represented a king. He ought to show some magnificence, he thought. He had decided to offer the man a chance to rest and eat, if he wished, before their meeting; it was what he himself would want, after a journey up the canyon. He had a chamber prepared, with what luxuries they had brought, and hoped it would do. He had a sinking feeling that it would not.

Seri and Aris, in Marshals' blue, escorted the ambassador from the lower entrance to that chamber by a route that did not take him past the kitchens. One of Aris's prentices ran by the shorter way to let Luap know the man was inside.

"And he has moustaches down to *here*," the boy said, excitedly. "And four servants with boxes and bags and things, and — "

"Did you hear whether he would eat and rest, or whether he wished to meet at once?"

"He was glad of a chance to rest, I think. I can't understand his talk, but Seri and Aris seem to. Aris said he'd come talk to you in a little while."

Luap waited in his office, forcing himself to do necessary copywork to stay calm, until Aris appeared.

"Seri's staying beside the door," he said. "He's happy enough to rest first; he's used to riding wherever he goes, and that climb up into the mountains tired him. We should build a horse trail there, he said. I'd agree; if we ever want to trade, that would make it easier. He didn't think much of our horses when we got to them, but he rides well."

"What's he like?"

Aris shrugged. "It's hard to say. We barely understand each others' words; I think the captain we learned from has a different accent. He's very polite, but then that's what ambassadors are: it's his duty. He talked about some kind of demon that used to live in these mountains, but also about those who built the stronghold. They knew it was here, I think, but were afraid of something if they tried to come. Brigands, possibly; the captain said robbers had been in these mountains forever."

"I wish I could speak their language. It's awkward — "

"Perhaps not. He can't understand us, either. And misunderstandings can be laid on the language problems, not on any illwill."

"Do you have any idea what he wants? Why they sent an ambassador now, rather than letting that captain you met come talk to me?"

"If I understood them, they would consider that disrespectful. Once the captain had agreed that we weren't demons of some kind, he seemed to think we were something more than human. He would not dare, he said, to — I think the word means 'insult' — you by coming himself, when at the very least you should be welcomed by a royal ambassador, if not the king."

"What did you tell them about our settlement?"

"Not much — we're still learning the language. We tried to tell them that we had come from far away sunrising, and we had to travel by magery, not overland. That we lived in a great hall carved in the stone, and were friends of those who built it, not invaders." Aris looked doubtful. "I know that's not all the story, or exactly what you would have said, but it's the best we could do."

"That's fine — it may make us sound grander than we are, but that has its advantages. We don't want to be anyone's conquest."

"That's what Seri said, sir. Today, riding up the canyon, we could tell he was impressed, as much by the children playing in the stream and the fields as by the fields themselves. 'Is it safe?' he kept asking. 'You have not been attacked?' We said no, not by any worse than brigands, and his captain could tell him how we dealt with brigands."

"Good. We want peace with our neighbors, whoever they be. But trade could not hurt us, either." Luap stretched, easing tight shoulders. "Do you know anything of the way they spend the days? Would it be better to meet in the morning or evening?"

"I would think morning, not too early. Perhaps after an early breakfast?"

"Very well. I'd like you and Seri both to be there."

Luap chose to receive the ambassador in the great hall, where he had had two chairs and a table placed near the dais. The banner Dorhaniya had embroidered hung behind it. He awaited the ambassador in his Marshal's blue, which the Council had agreed he should wear even though his title was Archivist, not Marshal. He had shaved his face, since Seri reported that the captain had not had a beard, but the soldiers did.

Aris's messenger had brought word that the ambassador

was on his way, and had withdrawn hastily. Luap's heart pounded; he felt a great weight on his shoulders. If he failed, if this man became an enemy, all his people would suffer. He turned to the doorway, struggling to appear calm. A moment more . . . then Aris paused in the door, standing very straight. It had not occurred to Luap before just how impressive a man he had become.

"My lord . . . the Khartazh ambassador." Or how formal; in Aris's deep voice, that sounded as courtly as anything he'd ever heard, and his bow was as smooth as if he did it every day. He said something in a foreign tongue; Luap assumed he was repeating his announcement.

The ambassador came through the door, and seemed to freeze in place an instant, his eyes roving up and around. Then he bowed very low, spoke, and waited in that position for Aris's translation. "Great prince, it is an honor . . ."

"We, too, are honored," Luap said smoothly. "Will you come forward and take a seat?" Seri, not Aris, translated for him. He was surprised; had they worked this out between them? The ambassador looked paler than he had expected, and almost frightened. What had he thought he would see? He himself noticed the long moustaches, the face otherwise cleanshaven except for a tuft at the chin, the hair hidden in an embroidered cap. He was not quite Luap's height, and his build was impossible to determine, robed as he was in richness that reminded Luap of the wealthiest mageborn women. Layer upon layer of cloth, slashed and puffed, embroidered and decorated with chips of shell and polished wood . . . he rustled as he walked forward, then bowed again. But for all that, his eyes were shrewd, the eyes of a man used to judging others. They were a strange golden-brown Luap had not seen before.

Luap waited another moment for the man to seat himself, then realized why he would not: he, Luap, was assumed to have the higher rank here. Slowly, as if that were part of his own protocol, Luap stepped back and seated himself. Slowly, eyes watchful, the ambassador sat in the other chair. Aris moved to stand at the ambassador's right hand; Seri came to Luap's. In the doorway, the ambassador's servants knelt, laden with their boxes and bags. The ambassador spoke again, looking at Luap. Aris translated: "I have brought gifts from our king, not worthy for one of your rank, but we beg you will

370

accept them." The ambassador gestured, as if for permission, and Luap nodded. The servants came forward on their knees, and once in the hall began laying out an array of gifts.

A length of glowing scarlet cloth, edged in gold, tossed out to lie fanlike on the stone floor . . . a wide collar of black fur . . . a set of small pots of brasswork, with brilliantly enameled lids . . . a wide silver tray, on which a servant heaped mounds of preserved fruit, and smaller mounds of spices so pungent Luap could smell them from his seat. A belt of scarlet leather, stamped with gold sunbursts . . . matching scarlet gloves, deeply fringed with a gold sunburst on the back of each hand . . . and tall scarlet boots, stitched in sunburst patterns; the tops turned down to dangle tiny gold disks from them. Luap could not imagine how one could ride or work in such boots — they must be intended for ceremonial occasions. Finally, with a musical ringing, the eldest servant drew from its padded bag a necklace of many gold links and pendants, and laid it carefully on the black fur where it showed to best advantage. Luap tried not to stare like any farm child, but found it difficult. And what could he give in return? He had expected an exchange of gifts, but nothing like this. He had a few things from Dorhaniya's house that she had left him, but nothing so grand.

He nodded, smiled, and said "Our thanks for your graciousness; your people's workmanship is remarkable." That was too flat; he hoped Seri's command of their language was equal to improving it. He waited while she translated, then heard the ambassador answer, then finally heard Aris's translation of that.

"Prince, we are relieved to find you accepting these few gifts, all we had time to collect. It is the king's hope that you will grant us your blessing — " Aris looked uncertain; he turned and asked the ambassador something in his own language. Finally he resumed. " — the favor of those we think may be more than human, if not the gods themselves."

Luap had the uneasy feeling that he and Aris had both misunderstood something. But he went on as best he could. "We, too, would offer your king what trifles we have . . . nothing to equal this magnificence, but tokens of our friendship." The ambassador listened to Seri's translation of that with close attention; he seemed to relax a bit, and offered a tentative smile. Luap sat back in his chair, and sent Seri to fetch the gifts he'd made ready.

These she lay on the table between the two men. Luap himself unwrapped and displayed them — he hoped this would be taken for honor, not weakness. A sea-green bowl, in which Dorhaniya had once kept dried rose petals, filled now with the precious selon beans Eris had given him, a blackwood bow, and a richly decorated sword, part of the spoils of Fin Panir, which no Marshal would carry because of its origin and decoration. Luap had always enjoyed looking at it, but had to agree that it was better to look at than use.

The ambassador's eyes widened; he stared at the sword. "And the horse you rode yesterday," Luap added, "if it pleased you." Seri translated; the ambassador gave Luap a desperate look, then stood, his rich clothes rustling, and grasped the sword. Aris and Seri stared at him, both alert but unmoving. Luap wondered what he had said wrong. The ambassador said something that sounded formal, drew the sword quickly, and held it poised for an instant. Luap had that moment to think he was being attacked before the ambassador plunged the tip towards his own body.

"No!" Luap yelled, grabbing for the sword. Decorative it might have been, but it was sharp; it cut his hand to the bone. Aris and Seri tackled the ambassador and wrestled the sword away; Luap squeezed his wrist with his good hand and wondered what had gone wrong. Blood soaked his best gray trousers and splattered the floor; he could not wipe it up without letting go his wrist. He had bloodied the ambassador, too. . . .

"Sir!" The young men Seri had been training crowded the door. "What happened?"

"I don't know," Luap said through clenched teeth. His hand hurt more than he would have thought. "Help Aris with the ambassador — and don't hurt him. He wasn't after me; he was going to kill himself." In a few moments, two solemn young men were holding the ambassador, an easy task since he did not struggle. Seri had the sword; Aris came at once to Luap and took his hand.

"I can heal this," he said, with a sideways look at the ambassador. "Should we have him taken away?"

"No. Let him see." Whatever had gone wrong, Luap sensed, would not be made worse by a show of power. With Aris holding his arm, he dared to look at his hand. Two fingers dangled by a shred of skin; he saw bone and tendon laid bare.

"It's all right," Aris said. "Just relax." Easy for him to say, Luap thought — but he knew better. He leaned back in his chair, trying to relax, and let Aris work. The pain eased; he felt something tickle his hand, a feather-touch on the palm. When he looked again, his hand looked almost normal, if pale: the long gash was closing smoothly. It made him dizzy to watch; he looked past Aris to Seri.

"Do you know what happened?" She shook her head, and said something to the ambassador, whose reply was long and broken as she asked questions repeatedly. By the time she turned to him, Aris had released his hand; he felt no pain, and it looked normal except for the blood on his skin. The ambassador, he saw, was staring at it, wide-eyed; the man's servants had all put their foreheads on the floor.

"I think he thought you wanted him to kill himself," Seri said.

"What?"

"He keeps saying, 'He gave me the sword and told me to ride away.'"

"But that's not what we — what I — said."

"I know. But it's what it means to them. I think." Seri sighed, smoothing her tumbled hair. "He says if a king gives a servant such a sword — not a soldier's sword, but one with gold and jewels — it means the servant has displeased his lord and should kill himself. He was not sure that's what you meant, since you are not of his people, but the gift of the horse made it clear, because where could he ride that horse from here but to the afterworld? There is no trail back to his land."

"But I said the gifts pleased me," Luap said. "Isn't that what you told him?"

"I thought so." She asked the ambassador a question, and listened to his reply. "Yes, he heard that, but thought it was a joke — sarcasm. You liked the gifts so well you told him to die." Luap thought about that. What kind of people would think that way? Did he want to befriend people who thought that way?

"Tell him," he said carefully, "that among our people we do not make such jokes — we do not lie about things like that. The gifts pleased me. And among our people the gift of a sword is a gift of trust. Do you think he will understand that?"

"I hope so," Seri said. She talked, and the ambassador spoke to her, and she talked again. Luap watched the servants, who knelt motionless all this while. What kind of people had such servants? Abruptly, the ambassador yanked his arms free of the two young men, as if they had not been holding him at all, and threw himself at Luap's feet. All down his back, Luap saw, his outer robe buttoned with tiny black buttons . . . he realized the man could not reach those buttons himself; he could not get dressed without servants. Luap looked down; the ambassador had taken his boots in his hands and was kissing them. He felt sick.

"Tell him to rise, and sit in his chair," he said to Seri. He could feel the hot flush on his cheeks. "Does he still think I'm angry?"

"He thinks he's disgraced his king, and will bring war on his people," she said, before speaking again to the ambassador. This time he rose, shook himself to resettle his clothes, and sat once more in his chair, his hands linked in apparent composure. Those strange amber-yellow eyes stared at Luap as if trying to penetrate his mind.

"I'm sorry," he said, directly to the ambassador. "I am not angry with you. Please do not injure yourself. As you can see, I am not hurt." Bloody, yes, and confused, but not hurt. "Please ask your servants to rise; I will have someone show them where to take the gifts."

Seri translated that, and the ambassador spoke a few phrases to his servants. They set to work repacking the gifts, without looking up. The ambassador continued, speaking slowly, and waiting for Aris to translate each phrase. "It is my shame. It is my mistake. Do not be angry with my king. Great lord, let your vengeance fall on me, and not on my king. Great prince, your wisdom excels all; be merciful."

Luap put out his hand; the man flinched but did not pull away when Luap touched him. "Do not fear. I am not angry." He smiled, and thought of a joke of Gird's. "Don't worry: when I am angry, you will know it." Seri gave him a look, but translated that. The ambassador blinked, and stared, and then essayed a tentative smile. "That's right," Luap said, as he would have encouraged a frightened child crossing the rapids.

The ambassador spoke again, this time more fluently. "He asks about the healing," Seri said. "And perhaps I should have told you before, but Aris healed a soldier: the captain may have mentioned that."

374

"Tell him we have various powers, but this we consider the gods' gift," Luap said. The man listened to Seri, and made a curious but graceful movement with his hands as he spoke again.

"He says his king would be honored by our friendship," Aris said. "But, sir — there's a problem with that word. The captain told us there were different words for friends — if I understood him — according to rank and intention both. I'm not sure what this one really means."

Luap smiled at the ambassador again. "I'm not sure we need to know at the moment, and any kind of friendship is better than war. Tell him I wish to bathe and change, and have the blood cleaned up; perhaps he would like to rest, or walk outside, for awhile, and we can meet later." This suggestion, translated, seemed to calm the man more than anything else. He rose, bowed deeply again, and seemed rooted to his place. Luap finally realized he was waiting for the "great lord" to leave first. He was afraid to insist on anything else, for fear of causing another dangerous misunderstanding.

Even a bath and a change of clothes did not completely dispel his shakiness. Seri had evidently assigned her entire group of trainees to help him; one of them took his blood-stained clothes away to wash, and two more hovered outside his door, eager to help with anything he could imagine. He asked for something to eat, and got a tray of bread, sliced meat, and fruit. While he was eating, Aris came in.

"Seri or I will stay with the ambassador until we're sure he's not going to hurt himself," Aris said. "He seems better, but — "

"He scared me," Luap said. "I never saw anything like that."

"You saved his life," Aris said. "We were impressed."

Luap found himself smiling. "You never saw me in the war, did you? I spent most of it as Gird's scribe, but he trained me, and his training stays." He looked at his hand. "And I'm glad you were here, Aris; I'd have lost those fingers. I hope I'm doing the right thing."

"Saving him?"

"No. Talking to him at all. Making agreements, or thinking about it." Luap shook his head. "What kind of people can they be, to take a gift as a command to kill themselves?"

"It's the language problem," Aris said. "He seemed nice enough, on the way in. We just didn't understand him, and he didn't understand us. What did you think of his gifts?"

Luap looked at the bundles piled in the corner of his office. "Gorgeous, but the Marshals back home wouldn't approve. Those boots — !" He had a sudden urge to look at them again, and bent to unroll the bundles. "And this fabric — it must be the same stuff as Dorhaniya's dresses . . . silk, I think she said." He felt the scarlet material; it slithered through his fingertips like water, smooth and cool and slippery. "Look at it."

"Mmm." Aris touched it, then stroked it. "Lovely feel. They gave us clothes like this the first night we spent with them, only in gray and white. This would make a fine tunic for Midwinter Feast."

"Only with a fur undershirt." Luap found the boots, gloves, and belt curled together. He tried a glove, and found it short in the fingers, made for a stubbier hand than his. "Can you imagine what the Marshal-General would say if I wore these in Fin Panir?" The boots, he could see, were also too short. He shook them; the gold disks chimed softly together. But the belt almost fit; he could punch another hole in it. It looked garish with his gray and blue, he thought, but against the red silk it looked perfect. He laid the leather things aside, and found the little sacks of spices. "I'll have to take some of these to Meshi, the next time I go back to Fin Panir. I had no idea they had such spices out here."

"I wonder if that's where ours came from," Aris said, frowning. "The spice merchants rarely say."

"Still hoping for a land route? I suppose it's possible. But until we can talk to these people and be sure we understand what they say, we can't know." Luap sniffed the sacks, one after another. "I'm sure this is one of the spices she uses with peaches and pears both. I wonder if she'd come out here, even for a short while, and teach our cooks." He rummaged again, and came up with the little brass pots. Set in a row on his desk, they looked like a set intended for some purpose. Each had a slightly bulbous bottom, eight delicate ribs, and a flat lid. The brightly enamelled lids, in blue and white and red, fit snugly, but Luap pried them up. Inside, the pots had been enamelled in a dark but brilliant blue. The largest would hold perhaps two handfuls of grain; the smallest perhaps five pinches.

"They would store spices," Aris pointed out. "I've always seen spices stored in boxes, but boxes let in damp."

"I wonder if the designs on the lids mean anything." Those swirls might be letters or symbols, he thought, but in no script he knew. "I suppose we could ask the ambassador, first making sure he had no weapon at hand." Almost before he knew it, he had found the leather sacks of preserved fruits, and dipped into one. It almost melted on his tongue, a confection of honeyed fruit and spice. "Try this," he said to Aris, offering the sack. "Whatever it is, the merchants in Fin Panir would pay dearly for it."

Aris tasted the sticky brown lump and his face changed. "Anyone would. I can't imagine what it is." He began picking up the many little sacks and sniffing them. "Here's another — no — it's not the same. This is plums, I'm sure." Together they explored the contents of each sack with the slightly guilty pleasure of children rummaging in a pantry.

"I suppose these should go down to the kitchens," Luap said finally. He and Aris looked at each, then both burst into laughter.

"Not until Seri's had a taste," Aris said. "And then I think I might classify these fruits as medicinal. At least until we can figure out how to make them."

"You'd better go relieve Seri, then, before I lose all self-control and gobble the lot of them. What I should do is take a sample to Meshi — if anyone can figure out how to copy them, she can."

Aris left, grinning, and said he'd send Seri down; Luap decided he might as well unpack the rest of the presents and figure out where to put them. He had laid out the fur collar on the back of one scribe's chair, the silver tray on his desk, and had the gold necklace in his hands when Seri appeared in his doorway. He grinned at her.

"Did Aris tell you about the honeyed fruit?"

Seri gave him a look he could not quite interpret. "Yes . . . he said I should come taste it. That's — what are you going to do with that?" Luap looked down at the necklace.

"I don't know. I can't wear something like this. Perhaps the Rosemage can. Or perhaps we can use it for trade in your town."

"No, we can't do that. They'll be upset; it's the king's gift. Although you could sell it in Fin Panir." She looked thoughtful. "Although I don't think anyone in Fin Panir could afford it."

"Tsaia, then," Luap said. He let the necklace slide through his hands onto the silver tray, and picked up one of the sacks of fruit. "Here — smell this, then taste it." Seri sniffed, then poked in a cautious finger.

"It's sticky."

"Yes, and it's delicious." He watched as she tasted it, but to his surprise she didn't react as he and Aris had.

"It's too sweet; it'd be better spread on bread." She didn't taste the others, but did approve the spices, and looked at the set of pots with interest. "Those could be signs from their script," she said. "I haven't seen much but the captain's watch list and the book we mentioned, but the shapes are similar. Fat and thin squiggles, it looks like to me, but I daresay that's what our script would look like to them."

"While you're here," Luap said, "Can you start telling me about their language? Even a few words would help."

"We started on that back in the town," Seri said. She fished out a grimy scrap of parchment covered with tiny script. "Aris and I used this for notes — it's fairly hard to read, but I can copy it for you." Luap cleared the scribe's desk and chair for her, and decided to have the gifts carried up to his own quarters to get them out of the way. The youngsters were glad to do that, eager to handle things that had come from outsiders.

Luap made sure the ambassador was given the choice of eating in his guest chamber, or with the others; he chose to eat alone. Manners, thought Luap. We've already discovered that we don't have the same manners, and he doesn't want to offend. Luap himself took the notes Seri had made and started trying to learn a few words of the Khartazh tongue. He went out in the early afternoon, walking up and down the path reciting to himself. Words were easy; he'd always had a quick ear, so calling a horse a pirush didn't bother him. Seri had marked multiples: one pirush, two pirushyin. He practiced counting: not one or two pirushyin, but nyai pirush, teg pirushyin. The sounds felt strange in his mouth, as they had felt strange in his ears when the ambassador talked. But the structure of the language defeated him. He knew the language of the mageborn, which they thought of as Old Aarean, and the language of the peasants, which they called Speech. In between was the bastard tongue each race spoke to the other, now called Common. Each had its own ways of saying things, some easier than others. But this — this language seemed to make everything difficult. Seri had given him eight ways to say "Please come in" — not just a ranking from simple to ornate, but completely different words. Even the simplest greetings varied widely with the relative ranks of the speakers.

Thinking about the formality of the language, and what Arranha had told him about the Old Aareans, Luap decided that the Khartazh must be an old and very complex society. They would not be the same as the Old Aareans, but surely any old, complex civilization would have some attitudes in common. They were rank-conscious: that much was clear from Seri's first reports, and the language confirmed it. Wealth he could judge from the gifts he'd been sent, and attention to detail by the fine craftsmanship. They might or might not have magery — the ambassador's response to the morning's excitement could be taken either way — but they feared demons and had gods they respected. Arranha should have been here, he thought. Arranha would know how to interpret what they've already said and done.

He knew he could not wait for Arranha or the Rosemage. However the ambassador interpreted the morning's events, those amber eyes had been shrewd. The man would observe closely everything he saw, and report all of it. The longer he thought about the implications of that gold necklace, the silk, the heaps of spices, the set of pots, the more Luap worried that the Khartazh was more than it had seemed to Seri and Aris. What did they know of empires? He himself had read everything in the royal archives; he had listened to Arranha and Dorhaniya; he knew what Seri and Aris could not, how empires dealt with small princedoms on their flanks.

And it had been going so well. Why, he asked himself, couldn't the Khartazh have been some petty dukedom, no worse than a — a Marrakai? Why did it have to be what it so clearly was: a mighty and ancient empire, wealthy and sophisticated? And why did the ambassador have to come while the Rosemage and Arranha were off somewhere in the wilderness? He knew the why of that: he had agreed, in the certainty that nothing was going to happen until fall. So he would have to deal with this ambassador himself, and somehow convince the man that the mageborn were worth befriending and far too powerful to attack.

By late afternoon, he was ready to try again; he inquired and found that the ambassador had rested, eaten, and was willing to see him once more. His people had managed to get the bloodstains out of his good shirt and trousers, and get them dry again. His Marshal's blue tunic, so much thicker, had not dried; he put on one of the tunics Eris had made him. Remembering the ambassador's elaborate clothes, a length of brocade from Dorhaniya's dress could not be too formal. He wondered if he ought to wear the red leather belt, but decided against it; he had chosen his tunic for its color — the nearest to Girdish blue possible — and thought the belt looked garish with it.

This time, without the awkwardness of the gift exchange, things went better. The ambassador too had changed clothes; Luap realized that his blood must have splattered the ambassador's robe as well. Now he wore an over-robe of glistening black. Luap hoped it didn't portend anything dire. The ambassador bowed repeatedly on entering the room, but once he sat down seemed more relaxed. Luap knew he might be misreading the man's face, but hoped a smile meant the same thing for both of them.

To put his visitor at ease, Luap suggested, through the translators, that the ambassador might want to ask questions — some of which, he admitted, he might not be able to answer. The ambassador stroked his long moustaches and blinked. Then he said something which Aris translated as "Is this formal or informal?"

Luap thought about that. Either answer might be wrong, and give offense, but he had to answer. He turned to Seri. "Tell him it is informal, that I would not require formality from one to whom all our ways are strange."

The ambassador responded with a bow from his seat, and more apparent relaxation. "We are honored to be accepted without formality in your hall," was Aris's next translation of the ambassador's words. Before Luap could consider what that might mean in light of what he'd said, the ambassador went on, speaking in short phrases and waiting for Aris's translation. "It is clear that your people have many powers. Our king asks if you come in peace."

"Yes," Luap said, nodding. "We do not love war, though we are not without warriors." He hoped that would deter any aggressive tendencies; he watched the ambassador's face closely during the translation and his response to it.

"So our captain said." The ambassador let his eyes rest on Seri and Aris, one after the other, as Aris translated. "In our land, powerful lords rarely take the sword . . . it is common with you?"

Powerful lords — did that mean him, or Seri and Aris, or all the mageborn? "All our folk study weaponlore," he said, remembering Gird's sayings about peace and war; he paused there to allow Seri's translation to catch up. "We find it the best way to keep peace."

That earned a blink; the amber eyes narrowed, then relaxed. What he had said had gone home; he could only hope it was in the right target.

"Your folk did not build this hall?" was the next question.

"No," Luap said. "We are —" He had no word for it, really: they had not been given the hall, nor were they renting or borrowing it. "The builders," he said, "were our friends." That ought to make it clear: they had not built it, but they had permission to be there.

The ambassador sat straighter, if possible. After a long pause, during which Luap tried to think what he could have said wrong, the ambassador slid a thick gold ring off his finger and placed it on the table between them. Luap looked at the ring, and then at the ambassador. Was it a bribe? Another gift? A threat? A promise? The ambassador simply stared back at him. Finally Luap spoke.

"Your customs are different." He listened to Seri's words, which seemed a lot longer than that, and fretted at the need for translation. The ambassador looked anxious as he heard his version, then spoke again.

"He says that this ring is only a sign — a token — and that one more suitable will be brought later." A sign of *what*? Luap wanted to say. Aris went on. "He hopes you will permit the king to continue as your trusted steward. If you take the ring, he expects that you will not invade or use magic against them; if you refuse, he thinks you will conquer the Khartazh by force."

Astonishment swamped all other feelings, followed closely by triumphant glee. He had done it; he had bluffed an old, rich, empire into thinking itself menaced. But none of that must show; he felt the years of work with the scribes taking over. Blandly, almost casually, he said, "Tell the ambassador that I have no need for kingship of the Khartazh; his king may rule in peace. But I wear no man's ring — " Some memory of the horse nomad's ceremonial rings for Gird at his death came to him, and he held up his hands, thumbs upward. " — my thumbs are free."

Seri gave him a startled look before she began translating; the ambassador received those words with outward rigidity. Luap could tell he had made an effect. He felt another burst of satisfaction. Perhaps he was only a king's bastard, whose years in a palace had been far in the past — but it came back to those for whom it was natural. He was the prince, a true prince, with all the royal magery and the gift of command. He belonged here, dealing with a royal ambassador; he did not need the Rosemage or Arranha after all.

● Chapter Twenty-seven

After that, the real work began. The ambassador had maps, and could procure others. Luap tried not to show how fascinated he was by the maps, which used a marking system he had not seen before, dividing the land into squares. He saw at once how useful that could be, and noted the accuracy with which their mapmakers had drawn the cliffs he had seen, the delicate shading that made clear which slopes were steep and which gentle. Here was the technique he had needed so badly back in Fin Panir . . . the Council of Marshals would be glad to see this.

But the ambassador's use of the maps impressed him in other ways as well. The Khartazh traded overland to great distances; they had heard of lands far east, across a vast desert, but regular caravans had ceased some dozen years before. *The war,* Luap thought. Gird's war. They had been declining before that for several decades. *The Fall of Aare,* Luap thought, the hairs standing up on his arms. Could it be? The ambassador recognized the selon beans Luap had given him — yes, they had been part of that trade, and spice and amber had gone the other way. Now — the ambassador shrugged — now the caravans moved mostly north and south. The names he gave meant nothing to Luap — Xhim and Pitzhla and Teth — nor could Seri offer any hint of a translation. He asked again about the eastern trade: water was too scarce on the western end of the former route, the ambassador said, and profits too chancy. His shrewd amber eyes seemed to ask *What are you planning?*

In one moment of vision, Luap saw exactly what he would do. Here he had water, and safe shelter. That upper valley the Rosemage had thought of as horse pasture, with its opening to the high plateau above the plain: that would be the place for caravans to come. They would have to build a trail up from the desert below, and another into the western canyons and out to the town, but with magery they could do it easily in a few hands of days. Someone — Seri, he thought, or the Rosemage — would have to find a good trail from the base of their cliffs to the old caravan route south of them.

And then the caravans would come, bringing horses, cattle, craftsmen, harpers, goods to trade and a market for the Khartazh's spices and silks. Luap could imagine the whole stronghold full of busy, talented workers all enriched by the flow of commerce. He drew a long, happy breath. If only the Rosemage and Arranha would come back with good news of ores . . .

Instead, they returned too soon, for Arranha had collapsed on the journey, and the Rosemage had struggled to bring him to the stronghold alive.

"We had just reached the gray mountain's foot when he clutched his chest and fell," she said to Luap. Aris was busy with Arranha, whose shallow breaths hardly moved the covering upon him. "I knew the climb out of the canyon had been hard on him; he said he found it hard to breathe that night, and didn't sleep well. But I thought he was better, or I'd have turned back."

She seemed to want reassurance; Luap nodded. "Of course you would; you couldn't know."

"He's so old. I didn't realize; he's always been so active, so lively of mind. And now — "

And now he was dying. From Aris's expression, no healing would serve. Luap felt his own throat closing. "I should have let him go with you, and made Aris and Seri wait," he said; he knew that had had nothing to do with it, but it was all he could think of. Now the Rosemage put her arm around him.

"You know that made no difference. Neither of us . . . " She stopped, blew her nose and wiped her eyes, then went on. "Neither of us can stop age when it comes; not even royal magery is proof against time."

Luap felt something shift inside him — not quite protest, but uncertainty. Curiosity. Was that really true? Had anyone ever tried to hold back age with magery? With the *royal* magery? It might not work with the very old, like Arranha (though how had Arranha stayed so vigorous so long?) but perhaps it would work with someone much younger, still strong.

But the immediate problem swept that from his mind. The Rosemage needed care as well as Arranha; she had the hollow-eyed look he remembered seeing in survivors of daylong battles. Luap called for Garin, and someone to help the Rosemage to her chamber; when she protested, he overrode her. "We all love Arranha; Aris is with him, and I will be with him. But I don't want to lose both of you. Bathe, rest, eat — let Garin ease what he can. You'll be needed later."

"But — someone said the ambassador had come early, had been here — " She was trying to keep herself awake, upright, and focussed; she would not let herself escape duty for comfort, even now. Luap put his hand on her arm, and let a little of his power seep into it, and into his voice.

"It went well; everything's going to be fine. Go and rest. I will tell you all about it when you wake." In the influence of his power, she staggered a little, and Seri moved quickly to support her and lead her away. "Take care of her," Luap said to Seri: unnecessary, since Seri would never do less, but it let others know he considered Seri in charge.

Arranha sank quietly, without a word or change in his expression, all through that night. Before dawn, the Rosemage was back at his side; Luap was glad she had come while he was there. "What did Aris say?" she asked softly.

"That he was dying, that it was from old age, and that he could do nothing. I'm not sure that's true, because Arranha seems so calm — perhaps Aris eased him some way when you arrived. . . . "

"He had been calm since the first day. Then, he seemed anxious. He said things — but I wasn't sure he was aware of them."

"Said what?"

She shrugged, and hugged her robe around her more tightly. "I — I don't know if he meant it. Something about danger, about a darkness in the stone. But since he was dying, it could be that alone."

"Mmm." Luap thought about it. "When I climbed to the top of this mountain, I remember feeling that the light failed — but I thought it was being breathless from the climb."

"Yes, I thought of that. Especially coming back with him, places I had to carry him — my sight went dark more than once. That's why I didn't tell everyone at once and give warning. Even Arranha, who so served the light, might loose it at death for a time. Yet if it was a true warning, what was it about?"

"That mountain, perhaps? The gray one? Perhaps it has the gold you hoped for, but it's claimed by some rockfolk tribe; that would be danger, if we meddled with it."

"I suppose." She did not sound convinced, but neither was he. Most likely, Arranha's approaching death had shadowed his mind, and his words meant nothing to those who were not dying. She stirred beside him. "So — tell me about the ambassador."

He felt strange, sitting beside a dying man and talking of his own triumph — as he could not but see it — but it would pass the time. He kept his voice low, and began with the ambassador's arrival, putting in all the details he could think of. The Rosemage listened attentively, clearly glad to have something to fix her mind besides Arranha. When he described the ambassador's attempt to use the sword on himself, she gasped.

"And *you* caught the sword! What happened?"

Luap held out his hand. "I nearly lost fingers — you can't see a scar at all, for Aris healed it at once, but from here to here —" He pointed, then allowed himself a wry grin. "It hurt a lot more than I would have thought." Before she could ask more, he went on, explaining what the ambassador had thought, and what he himself had inferred from both the man's actions and his gifts. "A powerful ancient kingdom," he said. "More than a kingdom — more like the tales we had of Old Aare. They trade widely; I think they used to trade with Fintha in years past, perhaps before I was born. Powerful allies, if we are their friends, and dangerous enemies."

She looked worried. "I expect they will see us as easy prey."

"No." His power bled into that, and she looked at him with dawning respect. "They fear us now: they will do us no harm. Wait until his next visit; you will see."

She recovered her composure with an effort. "You are confident, suddenly." The warning not to be overconfident came across clearly.

He shook his head. "I saw the man; I dealt with him. Aris's healing power alone might have convinced them, or his use of the pattern to open the mageroad — surely you and Arranha realized that."

"I suppose . . . " Her voice weakened; Luap felt a rush of sympathy.

"You're still tired; let me fetch something to eat."

"No — I'm all right. I suppose — Arranha and I both felt they were hiding something — the ones we met in that town. Perhaps they were trying not to show their fear of the magery."

"That sounds reasonable. The ambassador seemed frightened even before we began, and if they have no magery of their own — if they cannot believe mortals have it — "

"You can't pretend we're elven!" She stared him in the face, shocked.

"Of course not!" Luap put a bite in his voice and she reddened. "We're mortals, not elves, and I could not pretend otherwise. What I was going to say — " He looked at her, and she looked away, still flushed. "Was that if they have no experience of mortals using magery, they may give us more respect for that reason. I went out of my way to say we were *not* those who had built the stronghold. Still, if they are in awe of magery, our few numbers will not be a temptation to them."

"Yes. I can see that." A long breath. "Now that they know we're here, whatever we can in honor do to convince them we're too strong to attack — "

"Exactly," said Luap. "If we must balance magery against numbers to avoid confrontation — "

"But we could not fight them," the Rosemage said.

"Of course not." Luap nodded. "The point is to avoid that — avoid it ever becoming an issue. They seem to think that because we are here, where their legends place demons or monsters, that we must have greater powers than we showed. Of course we must not masquerade as elves, or claim their allegiance. Not only would that be dishonest, it would place us at greater risk. But they found Aris's healing power, and the mageroad, impressive enough. If they think of us as a small but powerful folk, who want only peace and trade, they will have no reason to test our strength."

"I see," the Rosemage said. She looked again at Arranha. Luap thought his death very near; he remembered that slow cessation, breath by breath, from Dorhaniya. "Do you think we should call Aris?"

"Both of them," Luap said. "They will want to be here." He

rose and went to the door, where a boy dozed against the corridor wall, and sent the lad for Aris and Seri. Soon they came, sleepy-eyed and solemn. Aris nodded after he looked at Arranha.

"Yes — very soon. I could not heal him — " His shoulders sagged. Luap patted him as he would have a child.

"It's not your fault, Aris; no one heals age." The words felt familiar in his mouth, and he remembered that the Rosemage had said that first, many hours ago.

"I know, but we have no other priest. Who will perform the rites for him, and for the Sunlord?"

"I suppose I will," Luap said slowly. "What he taught me, at least; I am not trained as a priest of Esea."

"He was the last — " the Rosemage said, and then she was crying, her shoulders shaking. It echoed in Luap's mind: the last. The last priest of Esea, the last of his father's generation, the last link to the old world where his kind had ruled. With Arranha would die the knowledge that had comforted Dorhaniya — no one else was likely to know the rituals for making altar linens, or care. With Arranha would die memories of Gird shared by no one else — for neither Gird nor Arranha had told him all of the time they journeyed together to the gnomish lands. With Arranha would die quarrels among priests, theological disputes, conflicts of power, even such unimportant things as the questions he had asked Dorhaniya's sister, that drove her to anger. Arranha had connected him to his own past, had known the boy he had been, had known his father, had known men whose grandfathers came over the southern mountains from Aarenis, had been one of an unbroken priesthood stretching back to Old Aare.

Luap felt acutely aware of that loss. Gird's death had ended what he might learn from Gird, but there were still many peasants living in vills much like his, plowing fields, making tools, tending sheep and cattle. Arranha — what had been Arranha's vision, that died here with him? What had he thought, as a young man, would shape his life? What had really shaped it?

He stared at Arranha's quiet face, already as remote as a stone carving, and wished he could shake it to life and speech again. Now he knew the questions he should have asked — now, when it was too late. Now he knew what he did not know

— would never know. Elders died, he thought. Elders died, and with them their personal visions died. If Gird had died at Greenfields, as he had said he should have, Gird's vision would have died there too. It had lived on because Gird lived on, and when he died it began to fray. . . .

Luap shied away from that thought, forced his mind from the thought that different people — himself included — had striven to engrave their own visions on what was left of Gird's. Instead, he thought of himself as an old man for the first time. He would be old soon, the elder on whom the others depended, as he had depended on Arranha. Here, in this stronghold and the land around it, lay his vision. When he died, what would happen to the stronghold? To his people?

I did not seek command, he cried in his heart. *It is not my fault that it was thrust on me.* In that familiar echoing space, a comfortable warmth rose. He might have come to it by accident, against advice, but he had nonetheless done well. His people prospered, and praised him. Perhaps he had not been fit for command in Gird's day — he would admit that — but now? Who else could have done what he had done? He hugged that to him, comfort for his genuine grief, as they carried Arranha's slight body to its resting place on the mountaintop, where the first sun each day could find it.

He must not die until it was safe, he thought on the way back down. He must shape it now, while he could, with all his strength, and be sure he did not die too soon. He felt the weight of responsibility settle onto him . . . his people had no one else to depend on, now.

He spoke of this concern to no one. He might have discussed it with Arranha, in the old days, but Arranha was dead; in the days after the funeral rites, Luap found himself worrying the problem of his own mortality whenever the pace of work allowed. He was not afraid of death itself — he had proven that, he thought, in the old days, on the battlefields of Gird's war — but he wanted to accomplish something before he died. Gird would have approved, he thought. Gird, too, had dreamed of establishing a people in peace and prosperity — and that was all Luap wanted.

Always and ever, in the depths of his mind, the question tickled him: was it really not possible to hold back aging with magery? Could he not at least *try*? It couldn't hurt, surely . . .

not if he took care. Even the appearance of youth or ageless-ness might help impress the Khartazh, and the Rosemage had agreed that anything harmless which had that effect was good.

"And how is the prince, after the death of his priest?" the black-cloaked leader asked his spy.

"He has recently thought of trying his magery — his 'royal' magery, as he calls it — against aging," the spy said. "They have told him it will not work, but he is not convinced. And now, of course, he worries more than ever about the fate of his people if he should age too soon."

"I believe he will find his magery strong enough for that," the leader said. "He deserves a long and healthy life." The black-cloaked assembly laughed, their voices harsh as jangling iron.

A few days after Arranha's funeral, Luap called Seri and Aris into his office to look at the maps the ambassador had left him. Seri's eyes lit up.

"Imagine the effect of these in Marshals' training," Luap said.

"Do they have any of the old caravan route?" she asked.

"You remember I asked the ambassador that, and he said he would find out. But I have another idea. If we could find a practicable route from the upper valley down to the plain, it might be shorter and safer for caravans to come through there — and then through our canyon to Dirgizh. Then we would have someone to trade with, and a way for those who won't use the mageroad to visit."

Seri frowned. "Do we need that? It's a long way for anyone to come, and I doubt Girdsmen would . . . "

"I think they will," Luap said. "That trade used to prosper; as Fintha recovers from the war, Finthans will have more to trade. You know yourself the spice merchants do well. We could be trading now, if the Marshal-General weren't so op-posed to frequent use of the mageroad . . . imagine how easily we could sell the gifts the ambassador brought. An overland route should be acceptable to the Marshal-General."

"He's right, Seri," Aris said. "He's not opposed to trade; he's encouraged the trade south into Aarenis — " Luap had not known that; he wondered how Aris knew.

"And you want us to find a way through these canyons to the old eastern route?" Seri said.

"Yes . . . and I don't know whether you should begin by finding it from outside — from Dirgizh — or from the upper valley. But you're our most experienced explorers so far."

"We'll have to start now if we're to be done by winter," Aris pointed out.

"I hadn't thought you'd start this season," Luap said. "Until we have others who can speak the Khartazh language as well, I can't spare you more than a few days at a time."

"Then we'll start there," Seri said. "Aris can teach his prentices, and I'll teach the militia — "

"And me," Luap said, smiling. "I should learn Khartazh."

"And you," she said. "But you learn faster than most."

Even so, Aris and Seri managed a short trip into the upper valley. Deciding just where to start the climb out of the main canyon was hard enough. Two approaches ended in sheer cliffs they could not climb. Finally Seri climbed partway up one of the north-running canyons across from what they thought should be the best way.

"We didn't use our heads," she said when she came back down.

"Again?" Aris grinned at the expression on her face.

"It's not funny," she said. "We don't have much time and we've wasted too much. What we need to do is follow that game trail — " She pointed. "It disappears over that knob — "

"Which is too far to the right; the valley has to be right up over that fallen block."

"And we can't climb it. Think, Aris: the animals go everywhere. We follow the game trail and keep choosing the ones that go higher."

The game trail angled sharply up the steep slope; Aris found himself grabbing for rocks and bushes to help himself climb. By the time they were above the trees, he could see far down the canyon, and back up the one Seri had come out of. Above him, Seri's boots went steadily on, occasionally giving him a faceful of dirt.

"This is a lot worse than the trail to the mountain top," he said, gasping, when they stopped for a rest.

"We have more to climb." Seri tipped her head back to look. "Gird's toes: look at that. We should be goats to get up there — and how could anyone bring a caravan down?"

391

Aris looked down and wished he hadn't . . . the broken rock and loose soil below looked unclimbable. "We have to find another way out: I don't want to break both legs going down this!"

On the next stretch, they came out on rock that looked, Seri said, like cake batter or custard that had stiffened in pouring. It did not look like honest rock, Aris thought, and wondered what had formed those loops and layers. At least it didn't shift underfoot, and the angle of the corrugated surface made climbing easier. The slope eased; they could walk upright again, between odd little columns of the strange stone. Here Aris agreed — they looked exactly like the last bit of batter from a pan, dripping crookedly to one side or the other.

The game trails disappeared into a grassy meadow thick with late wildflowers — tall blue spikes and low red stars. Bees hummed past them busily. On their right, still higher cliffs rose; they seemed to be crossing a terrace that might, Seri thought, come out above the valley they sought. They could see a similar cliff face to their left; between, they assumed, lay the tumble of broken rock they'd been unable to climb.

From the meadow they passed into a pine-woods of trees smaller than those on the canyon floor, and came at last to a clear view of the upper valley. On either side, sheer cliffs rose from a level floor of green. A ribbon of silver wavered down the valley: a creek. They hurried down the slope before them, so much gentler than the one they'd climbed.

"It's odd that the rocks don't look the same on either side," Aris said. On the west, the same rose-red solid stone, streaked dark with ages weather, looked exactly like the stone found so far in the main canyon. But the eastern cliffs were subtly different — an oranger red, more mottled than streaked, conveying, he thought, some weakness in structure.

"I wouldn't make my home in that," Seri agreed, as usual, with the thought behind his words. "But that grass, and that stream — think of this for horses. It's perfect." She bounded down the last of the slope and ran out on the grass, only to fall on her face.

"Seri!" Aris ran after her, and tripped on the deep sand just as she had. She was up already, her expression rueful.

"Sand," she said. "It's not a terrace like ours at all." Aris, face down on the sand, eyed the patch of green before him.

"And that's not real grass, either. Sedge."

"Oh, well, it's got water." Seri strode off toward the creek, and he followed her. When he caught up, she was laughing. "Water, I said! Look at this — it's hardly a knuckle deep."

"Soaking the sand," Aris said. He looked all around, at the sheer walls, the almost-level floor of sand, the glisten of water that had looked like a real stream. "A very strange valley indeed."

It was, he thought later, as they examined it in more detail, like a flattened miniature of the main canyon. Its sand floor was not as level as it had looked from above; it had miniature grassy terraces, small dunes of open sand, little sedgy bogs near quicksand, even a small cluster of trees whose triangular leaves sounded like gentle rain in the breeze. They spent the afternoon working their way up the valley; the stream deepened upstream, against their experience, and acquired a gravelly bed. To the east, a tributary valley opened, but they could see it was blocked at the upper end by a sheer cliff. The way out to the south lay, if anywhere, up a ravine garish with orange stone and odd black boulders. They pushed themselves into that climb, unwilling to spend the night in the valley, though neither could say why.

They looked back once, from a terrace about halfway up the ravine, to see the valley looking once more like a level swathe of grass. Just above the ravine, they found a sloping pine wood . . . and more sand.

"It's softer than rocks to sleep on," Aris offered, when Seri's lip curled.

"And harder than rocks to walk on, and we do more walking that sleeping. It will take us longer to go where we need to go," she said. But they made a pleasant camp that night anyway, enjoying the knowledge that no one — no one at all — knew exactly where they were. Their small fire crackled and spat with the fat pine-cones and resinous boughs; the water they'd brought up from the valley tasted sweet with their supper of hard bread and cheese.

"Two of the most dangerous, alone, in our valley: we should take them."

"No. One is the healer. We need him, for the prince's downfall."

"Then the woman —"

"We cannot take one without the other, not without giving warning. Patience: trust the prince's weakness, and wait. Vengeance long-delayed is all the sweeter."

"The woman is dangerous, I tell you," the complainer said. "There's an uncanny stink about her, something like the old priest had. She doesn't like the valley; she senses something — and that against our strongest protections."

"Then we will have the prince distract her," the leader said. "She will do us no harm if she's busy somewhere else — or worried about something apart from our kind of danger. She is Girdish; such mortals concentrate their minds on practical matters, and dislike magery. If she senses something, let her think it is only that of other mortals, no more."

The next day Aris led the way out of the pine grove onto an open upland; to their left, a curious conical hill of rough black rock looked like nothing either of them had ever seen. Far to the west, they could see the mountains beyond Dirgizh. Ahead, they knew, was the drop from their block of mountains — but which was the best way?

Seri pointed to the black peak. "If we climbed that we could see more."

Aris shrugged. "It's higher ground that way. We might find rock instead of this sand." For the lower ground had small dunes of windblown sand, difficult to walk on.

They found the gentle slope toward the black hill much easier than the day before. Soon they were walking on rock again, rippled and curved like mudbanks in a stream. More and more of the land around them came into view. Looking back toward the upper valley and the main canyon, they could see only a jumble of red rock, cut with sharp blue shadows. The mountaintop above the stronghold stood out clearly, but not the canyons between. Southward, they began to see a lower plain beyond the mountains . . . and the high white cliffs of another mountain range to the east. Finally, as they walked among the jumbled black boulders of the black hill's base, they could see an edge.

Seri cocked her head at the black hill now close above them. It looked as if it were made of a pile of loose black rocks, some room-sized and most smaller. "Do you think we can climb that, or will it be like climbing gravel?"

Aris looked south, at a distant blue shadow he thought might be more mountains very far away. "Do we need to, now? I think we can find our way to the edge of this without it. I wonder how far that cloud or mountain is. . . ."

Seri looked. "More than a day's travel. In this air, more than two." She scrambled up the steepening slope of the black hill, dislodging a shower of rough black rocks, and slid down again. "Not worth it, you're right. I wonder what the dwarves would call this kind of rock." She picked one up, and hit another, experimentally. The one in her hand broke, and she yelped. "It makes sharp edges," she said, holding out her gashed hand.

"And you want me to heal it for you," Aris said, shaking his head. "Will you ever learn to wear gloves?" He laid his hand over the gash and let his power heal it.

"Peasants don't wear gloves," Seri said scowling, but her eyes twinkled. She shook her hand, looked at the rock, and shrugged. "Come on — we'd better get this done today. I've got to work on those junior yeomen — or whatever we decide to call them — when we get back."

They came to the edge before midday, an edge even more impressive than the drop from the mountaintop into the western canyons. Swallows rode the updraft, the wind whistling faintly in their wings, and veered away as the two came to the edge and looked out. Aris thought he had never seen anything so beautiful; a vast gulf opened before them, with nothing to bind the sight until the line where earth met sky. He knelt to peer over the edge, cautiously. A sheer drop he could not estimate, then spiked towers, then steep slopes and finally rubble flattening gradually to the glitter of a fast-moving river. He looked along the river's path, and saw that it disappeared into sand some distance downstream. Upstream — the breath caught in his throat. Upstream he could see what this cliff must look like — its match on the far side of the river rose from the sand, all shades of red, rose, and purple, and looking eastward he saw those walls converge. But above the red rock — where only blue sky arched in their canyons — were higher cliffs of gleaming white.

He looked at Seri, whose face he thought mirrored his own astonishment. "It's — beyond words," she said. "I can't imagine why the dwarves don't live here — why it's not full of the rockfolk."

He started to say perhaps they didn't know, then remembered the dwarven symbol in the stronghold's great hall. Of course they knew. And had they abandoned this — this vast beauty of stone so strong that it sang even to mortals? "Perhaps they loved it too well to tunnel into it," he said. "As the horsefolk leave some herds free-running."

"Perhaps." Seri stared awhile longer, then shook her head sharply. "Well. We're not going to build a trail straight down *this*. We'd better look for a place where we can. Maybe where the water comes down. . . . "

They worked their way east, staying close to the edge and looking over at intervals. This canyon narrowed rapidly at the bottom, while the upper levels were still far apart, and soon Aris spotted a sheer cliff with a waterfall. "That won't work," he said. "Even if it's passable from above, imagine that in a storm — it would wash out any trail we built."

They headed south and west again, crossing their own tracks, and found a place where a dry wash wrinkled the surface, deepening rapidly toward the edge. "It will be another cliff," Seri predicted. But when they looked, some flaw in the rock had formed a great fissure. Broken chunks the size of buildings stepped down toward the desert below. Aris looked at it doubtfully.

"I supposed we could try — go down as far as we could — "

Seri snorted. "We shouldn't be stupid twice in one year. We've already gotten into trouble — or what could have been trouble — when we used that robbers' trail without thinking about it. We're supposed to be Marshals — now think. If we go down, and can't get back up — "

"I could use the mageroad," Aris said, for the sake of argument. He enjoyed feeling more daring than Seri, rare as the chance was.

"If you slipped and cracked your head," she said, "I couldn't use it, and couldn't heal you. No — let's find some way to recognize this from below, and then figure out how to go around."

"From Dirgizh?"

"Right. From the old caravan route they spoke of. Now let's see. . . . " She lay flat, her head over the edge of the cliff, and looked toward the fissure, then the stream below. "It would be nice to have a grove of trees — "

"No trees," Aris said. He sat, his legs dangling over enough space to stack five cities cellar to tower, and looked over at the facing cliffs. Their fissure seemed to line up with a skinny spire of rock, much thinner than the Thumb, on that side. He pointed it out to Seri; her eyes narrowed.

"Yes . . . but from down there the line will be different. Let's see . . . we can see the stream, so if you stood on this side of it — "

"We should be mapping this," Aris said suddenly, wondering why they hadn't thought of that. Before she could remind him that they had brought nothing to map with, he said, "I know — we can't. But if we draw it on the stone several times, we should be able to remember it." He rolled back from the edge, and broke some brittle sticks from one of the stiff, spiny bushes that dotted the upper plateau. They drew what they saw, until both agreed on the proportions and shapes, and could reproduce it anew.

By then it was late afternoon; they would have trouble making it back to the pine wood by dark, let alone back to the stronghold.

"No one can see us use the mageroad here," Aris said. "Let's do it." Seri nodded, and he found a sand-covered stretch, back from the edge, and graved the pattern carefully with his stick. The late-afternoon wind howled up the cliff, blowing sand into the pattern even as he drew it; he had to rework the pattern with deeper grooves, and then decided to mark it out with pebbles instead. Seri wandered about at a little distance, looking alternately at the great space below and beyond, and at the curious black hill behind them.

Suddenly she stiffened, and said, "Aris!" He looked over, to see her staring back at the confusing jumble of rock near the upper end of the little valley.

"What?"

"Something moved." She backed toward him.

"Look out!" he said sharply; she had nearly stepped on the end of the pattern he had completed with pebbles. She looked down, moved aside.

"Sorry," she said. Her dagger was out, he noticed with some astonishment. "Aris, something's over there — "

"Too far to bother us, if you let me finish the pattern and get us on the mageroad."

"I don't like it," Seri said. Aris placed the last three pebbled, stood, and took her hand.

"Then we'll leave. Come on, Seri, it would be stupid to wait here for whatever it is; it's getting late, the sun will be in our eyes—"

"Oh, well." She relaxed suddenly, and stepped carefully where he pointed. "It's probably only one of those wildcats—"

And they were back in the great hall, where their arrival brought bustle and excitement, and a summons from Luap to tell him what they had found.

"So this is what we think, sir," Aris said, summarizing their long report. "We need to approach from the lower end, both to locate the old caravan route east, and to find out if that water we saw is good. Then we'll need to consult with the best stone-carvers — you know I can't do that — and it will take at least a season of work to cut a passable trail for pack animals, and make sure it doesn't fall. If we can go now to the Khartazh, and find out about the caravan, perhaps next summer — after the fieldwork's done — work could start on the trail down. And the trail from here to the upper valley, and the trail out to Dirgizh, which really should come first."

"But what about the distance overland to Fintha?" Luap asked. "Won't you need to go all the way to Fintha to be sure that's where it comes out?"

"We'll go to Fintha, surely," Aris said. "But we think the horse nomads will tell us about the eastern end of the trail — and the merchants in Dirgizh and the next town south may well know about this end. Convincing someone to try it may be difficult . . . but I've noticed the merchants show an interest in renewing that old trade."

"With your permission," Seri put in, "we'd like to start by going to Dirgizh, as soon as possible, and follow the old caravan route east — then turn north and see if we can find our notch."

"How long do you think that will take?" asked the Rosemage.

"Hands of days," Seri said. "We don't know until we've gone. But it must be done sometime—"

"And then we'd go to Fintha," Aris said. "Take our horses, and go visit the horse nomads . . . they liked us well enough before."

398

"What you're telling me," Luap said, "is that it will be more than a year before we have a way for a caravan to come here — let alone before one actually comes. Two years, more like, or even three. . . ."

The Rosemage shrugged. "When we started, remember, we didn't know if anyone would ever discover an overland route; I think even three years sounds remarkably quick."

"The question," Aris said, "is whether this is worth all the effort. People will have to work on the trails instead of other things — "

"It's worth it," Luap and the Rosemage said together. Then she fell silent and Luap went on. "No land survives long without trade," he said. "Especially one so limited in resources as this. If our people are to have a permanent place — for those who can't, or don't want to, return — then we must have trade."

"And overland trade," the Rosemage said, "will disturb the Finthans less than continued heavy use of the mageroad."

"I wonder if Raheli would come?" Seri said suddenly. "I would like to see her again." Aris noticed that Luap had stiffened, but before he could ask why, Luap relaxed.

"I doubt she'll leave her grange for us," he said. "But of course she would be welcome."

• Chapter Twenty-eight

Luap had made the decision to meet that first caravan at the upper end of the trail from the desert. All along the way, his people had planted bannerstaves; today the narrow pennants snapped loudly in a freshening wind. Blue and white, Gird's color and Esea's, alternated. He himself wore the long white gown they had found so practical in the dry heat of summer, and over it a tabard of Girdish blue. He had an uneasy feeling about that, but surely they need not ape the fashion of Girdish peasants, not out here. No one wore those clothes any more; he had put on that worn pair of gray homespun trousers and rediscovered how itchy his legs felt. So he had insisted on some garment of blue, for all of them, and most had chosen the simple tabard.

His scouts had reported the approaching caravan two days before. Last night's campfires had been at the base of the cliffs; soon they would be here. He was sweating, he realized, with more than heat. He wished he could see. Instead, he heard them first . . . the ring of shod hooves on stone, the echoing clamor of human voices, swearing at some unlucky mule. Then one of the youngsters waved to him, and he went to look over the edge. They were closer than he'd thought, toiling upward only a few switchbacks below, horses and men and mules all reduced to squirming odd shapes by the distance and brilliant sunlight.

One looked up at him, a face sunburnt to red leather, eyes squinted almost shut, unrecognizable. He had hoped for Cob, who had been, as much as any of them, a friend, but he had known how much Cob loved his own grange, how little he would look forward to a long journey into strangeness. The man's free arm waved, then he looked down again. Luap watched the slow advance. Seasons of waiting had passed faster than this; his throat felt dry, and he accepted the wineskin someone offered without really noticing it. The wine, cool and sweet, eased his throat, but the hot stone must, he thought, be crisping his toes. They would be even hotter, having climbed those sunbaked cliffs in the day's heat.

At last, the first of the caravan reached the top, two glasses or more after he'd expected them. Too late now to reach the stronghold by dark; they would camp in the pine-wood just below. Luap walked forward to meet the first rider, and proffered the wineskin. The man's horse stood head down, sides heaving. He was still convinced he had never seen the man before when Cob's voice came out of that swollen, sunburnt face.

"By the Lady, Luap, you've chosen one impossible lair . . . no wonder you travel by magery!"

"Cob! I'm glad to see you!" And he was, even now, even when he half-wished the caravan had not come, that he could sever the ties with Fin Panir. Of all Gird's quarrelsome and difficult lieutenants, Cob had been the first to shrug and accept him, and the only one whose loyalty to Gird's luap had never wavered except at Gird's command.

"And I, you: you could have come out to the grange, your last visit." That loyalty had not blunted Cob's tongue, reminiscent of Gird's own. Now he looked Luap up and down, as Gird might have done. "Gone back to magelords' dress, out here? That'll do you no good with the Marshal-General, Luap."

Luap felt himself flush, and hoped Cob would take it for the heat. "Try it yourself, out here — it's better in this heat."

"Not me. I'll sweat more happily in my own clothes." Cob took a long pull at the wineskin and grinned. "Ahhh. No need to ask how your vines are doing. That's good, sweet as I like it. How much farther do we go today?"

Again, like Gird, that ability to switch quickly back to the practical. "The Hall's a half day or more from here, for such a large group. I thought we'd camp partway; there's a good spring, and pine-woods. We brought food, in case you were running low. We can be there well before sundown."

"Good." Cob's gaze ran ahead. "Follow the banners?"

"Yes. Shall we wait to start until all are up?"

"No need. As long as someone's here to point the way and give encouragement."

Cob led his horse slowly over the rippled stone; Luap walked beside him. At first they did not talk; Cob seemed glad enough to look around. Then he began to ask questions. Luap explained, as best he could, the interlocked system of canyons.

"We don't go into this one much; the upper end, that we call Whiterock Gorge, has good hunting now that we've hunted out most of our own, but as you know all too well, climbing back up from the big one with game would be difficult."

"That makes sense. How deep is your canyon, then?"

"Not as deep as this, but steep enough going in. We'll go through a tributary first, a curious place. A rockfall let sand drift in behind it; we're hoping to improve the soil and use it for farming later. It would make good pasture: the walls go straight up from level sand, like a great wall. If we closed off the upper ends, our horses would be safe there."

"No wolves? No wildcats?"

"Oh, we have both, but our hunters have thinned them. The wildcat here reminds me of the old tales of snowcats in the southern mountains — remember them? These are gray; you'd think they'd show up against the red rock, but they don't." The bannerstaves here led off into deep sand; Luap paused. "I'm sorry, but we've a stretch of sand here; the rock takes you to a dropoff no horse can manage."

Cob sighed. "When I get back to Fin Panir, I will never complain about hard ground or cold again. We had three days of sand at a time on the way, and I learned about it."

"It's not long — just to that grove of pines." Best not tell him now that half the next day's journey would be on deep sand.

Behind them, the line of sweaty, tired men and animals stretched out; Luap could hear the creaking of saddle leather, the grunts and wheezes of tired animals; men complaining; the pennants snapping in the wind. It seemed to take twice as long to reach the grove as he'd expected, but they were all under its shelter by sunfall.

Those he had left to prepare a meal had created a haven in the wood: a central fire, cushions and carpets laid out for tired men to lounge on, stew, roast meats, and even fresh bread scenting the air. Picket lines for horses and mules stretched back into the trees. By full dark, everyone had gathered around the fire to eat and talk. Overhead, stars glittered brightly in the clear air; Luap almost decided to set no sentries, to emphasize the safety in which his people lived, but changed his mind. Gird's followers had learned prudence the hard way; it would do him no good with them to seem careless.

He woke in the turn of night, to find Cob beside him, holding his arm.

"Luap — are you *sure* there's no one out here but your folk?" Cob's voice was so low Luap could hardly hear it.

Luap pushed himself up, and yawned. "Not out this way. Why? Did the sentries call an alarm?"

Cob grunted. "Your sentries have become too used to safety: they're asleep. I woke up, went to the jacks, and went to speak to them — but found them curled up as comfortable as boys in a haymow. Then I felt something — nothing I could define, a cold menace — like the look a thief gives in a dark alley."

At that moment a cold current of air coiled around Luap's shoulders and down his neck. He shivered, then recovered. "Cob — you've not been in mountains before. The night air's colder than you think, and at the turn of night it feels colder than steel. More than once when we first came, one of us thought something dire had passed, but we came to realize it was only the cold. The night may be still when the sun falls, but later on, these movements of air come, as if they were alive. But nothing more."

"Huh." Cob's head, in the starlight, looked frosted; Luap could not see his expression. "Well. If you're sure. But you might have a word with your sentries, just in case."

Luap groaned inwardly. Get out of his warm blankets to rouse sentries to watch for nothing? But nothing less would satisfy Cob, and after all, the sentries were supposed to be awake. He nodded, pushed the blankets aside, shivering again at the cold. "I'll stir them up. If nothing else, all these horses might draw a wildcat." Cob rolled himself back in his blankets, and Luap headed for the sentry posts.

Cold, clear air chilled his face, his hands; when he breathed, his chest felt bathed in ice. Even under the pines, starlight trickled through; beyond the trees, he could see a silvery glow over the silent land. A horse stamped, in the picket lines, and another was grinding its teeth steadily. Luap heard nothing he should not hear, and nearly fell over one sleeping sentry in the speckled shade.

He shook the man awake. "Wha — what's wrong?" It was Jeris, one of the youngest he had brought with him.

"You're supposed to be standing guard," Luap said. "Marshal Cob got up to use the jacks and found you all asleep."

"I — I'm sorry." In the dark, he couldn't see Jeris's face, but the voice sounded worried and contrite enough. "There was nothing — and it was so quiet — and . . . and cold, and . . ."

"I understand, Jeris, but with all these horses we must worry about wildcats or wolves. We haven't cleared this plateau, you know."

"Yes, my lord." The words came smoothly; in the dark, off guard, Luap suddenly realized how that would sound to Cob and the others.

"Don't say that," he said sharply. "They don't use that anymore. Just call me Luap, or sir, if you must."

"But my — but, sir, it's not respectful —"

"Respect includes doing what I ask, doesn't it? Don't use 'my lord' while our guests are here. It will upset them." And would Jeris remember? And remembering, would he obey? Or would he, in the spirit of youthful investigation, ask Cob why it would upset them? Luap shook his head and moved to the next post. Sure enough, all the sentries were asleep, and as he went from post to post, Luap himself began to feel a vague unease. Wouldn't *one* have stayed awake? Wouldn't one of them have wakened at the turn of night to use the jacks, as Cob had? For that matter, why were all the travelers sleeping so soundly?

But he could not hold that anxiety when he got back to the clearing; he wrapped himself again in his blankets, finding to his dismay that none of his bodywarmth remained, and was asleep before he realized it. He woke at the sound of the cooks working about the fire; half the travelers were out of their blankets already. For a moment or two, he lay quietly, trying to remember what had bothered him in the night, but he couldn't. It was a morning as clear as the day before, too beautiful for dark thoughts.

They started early, before the sun could strike heat from the rock. Down from the pines, into a narrow rocky defile. When they came around a knob to see the little tributary canyon below them, Cob drew rein. "So that's your future pastureland. You're right: it's perfect. There's even water."

"And quicksand," Luap said. "But we'll work that out. Be sure you follow the stakes."

Down the length of that little valley, so oddly shaped with its nearly level floor and its vertical walls. Then up again, into the morning sun, to climb around the rockfall, back into the shadow of the main canyon.

Luap led the way down that steep slope, uneasily aware that the signs of magic in use were all about them, plain to be seen if any of the visitors wanted to notice. Would they? Would they know what those smoothly carven walls meant? Would they realize that the natural canyon had not been blocked by natural falls of stone, filled with natural fertile terraces ready for planting? Cob knew, of course; he had explained it all to Cob. And the Council of Marshals knew, in theory — he had come out here to train the mageborn in the right use of their powers. But he knew they had no idea what that really meant, and the common yeomen in this group would never have seen magery used in all their lives. How would they react? In his mind's eye lay the image of this land as he and Gird had first seen it . . . he could still hear Gird's dismissive "not farm land." Now each crop gave its own shade of green, its own texture, to the terraces: smooth green fans of grain, bordered by rougher, darker bushes yielding berries and nuts, a ruffle of greens and redroot vines. The fruit trees, just coming into bearing. . . .

"I thought Gird said this was no good for farming," said Cob, just behind him.

"We worked hard on it," said Luap.

"Mmm. You must have. You couldn't have taken this much soil, not through that little cave. Two sacks, is what I know you took."

"No, we didn't." He left that lying, and hoped Cob would do the same.

"Magery, I suppose," Cob said, and spat. "Well. It's what you came for, after all, isn't it? A place for the magefolk to do their magery without upsetting anyone?"

Even from Cob he had not expected that quick analysis and calm acceptance. Luap nodded. "Yes — although we had peace in mind more than magery to start with. And here it can't be used against anyone."

Cob peered up at the canyon walls. "No — unless enemies come upon you, which doesn't seem likely. The horsefolk don't come within hands of days of here, and who else could there be? Have you found any folk at all?"

"West of these mountains is flat land, with a caravan trail and a town — Dirgizh — that's a waystation for a folk called the Khartazh. They have a king somewhere north. They don't come into these mountains; they claim they're haunted by evil spirits."

Cob snorted. "Whatever you are, you're not evil spirits — unless they mean whoever was here before you and carved your original hall."

"I doubt it's either," Luap said. "Until we smoothed the trail, it was difficult for people, and impossible for horses. Robbers laired in the mountains just east of the trade trail and preyed on travellers; I think the king's men just didn't want to worry with 'em. It's easier to say mountains are haunted than to admit they're too rough for your taste."

"That's so. Like a junior yeoman I had in my grange back east, who was sure some mageborn had magicked his hauk. He could not believe he was really that clumsy and weak. It took me three years to convince him that he was his own curse. Speaking of that, how's young Aris?"

"Curse? Aris?"

"No, I'm sorry. He's his own blessing, I was thinking, unlike Tam back home. Are he and Seri still like vine and pole?"

Luap grinned. "Yes, but not married. You'd think they were still children."

"It may be best. Seri's not one to mother only her own children. What does she do?"

"She's our Marshal: insists on drill, cleaned those robbers out of the mountains between us and the trade route, set up guardposts —"

"Good for her." Cob's horse slid a little and he grunted. "You couldn't get out of here in a hurry, could you? Going up must be slower."

"That's one reason we'd like to keep some horses in that upper valley," Luap said. "Every time we take a party up and down this trail, we have to rebuild it. Foot traffic's not so hard on it; if we could climb up then ride out, that would help."

"The merchanters we travelled with kept going west and south; they say there's another trade route that way . . . and they've always wanted a shortcut. Do you think your — Khartazh, was it? — are on the other end of their road?"

"Oh yes. They talk about a time — probably before we were

born — when caravans went east to Fintha every year. As near as I can tell, that trade declined after the fall of Old Aare, and stopped almost completely after the war started. If that trade resumes — and I hope it will — I would like to see caravans here; it would be a shortcut for them, and good for us. That's why we built the trail you climbed up, from the lower plain; I hoped to bring in caravans. But the trails are so rugged, maintaining them would be difficult."

Now they were off the last switchback of the trail, into the pines. He watched as Cob drew a deep breath. "Ah — this is better. Some shade for my face, a cool breeze." Here, two horses could go abreast; Luap reined in to let Cob come up beside him. "This is the last time I make this trip, mind. You can travel the mageroad with no more trouble than walking out of a room; I'm not blistering my old skin again just to see you."

"I'll take you back the mageroad, if you wish," Luap said.

"We'll see," said Cob, eyeing the green terraces, the flowering bushes, the berries. "Maybe I'll just stay here and live off your mercy."

Luap pointed. "Up there — that's one of the lookout posts Seri had us build." Cob squinted upward, blinking against brilliant light.

"Good to see out of, but cold in winter, I'd think. And if a wind blows —"

"No one's fallen off yet." Luap enjoyed Cob's awestruck look. He liked knowing he'd surprised the man; he heard the murmurs from those behind with the same pleasure.

It was just on midday when Luap turned across the stream to the sunny side of the canyon; the walls seemed to shimmer in the light as if painted on silk. The little arched bridge, so delicate against the massive rock walls, rang to the horses' hooves. Cob stared at the narrow cleft of the side-canyon as if he could not believe it. "We're going in there?"

"Yes. It's not all a tumble of rocks; there's a trail." Again in single-file, they rode up, into the cleft with its hidden pockets of old trees. The lower entrance stood open, as always in good weather. One of Seri's junior yeomen stood guard beside it, proudly aware of his good fortune.

"Go in and tell them the caravan's come safely," Luap said. "We'll need help with the horses."

"Yes, Luap," said the boy; Luap was glad for once that Seri's young trainees tended to scamp the courtesies. He slid off his horse, and took Cob's reins.

"Here — go on in and let Aris put a salve on your face if he can't heal it. I'll water your beast."

"I'm all right, here in the shade." Cob leaned against the rock, watching the others come up, and Luap handed the reins of both horses to one of his people who had come running out. That one did murmur "my lord" as he took the horses away; Luap hoped Cob hadn't heard it. Another appeared with a tray and tall cups of water slightly flavored with an aromatic fruit from Khartazh. Luap handed one to Cob, who was looking up at the great pines, around at the rock walls. "I wouldn't have believed it without seeing it, that's certain. And how you've managed to raise food in it — that's another wonder. Gird would have been proud of you, Luap." He sipped the drink, then smiled and emptied the cup. The servant took it and refilled it.

"I'm glad you think so." He wondered if Cob would still think that way when he'd seen how comfortable a life he and his people had achieved in so few years.

"Luap . . . I'm not here to check up on you." Cob's shrewd glance widened to a grin as Luap felt his face burning. "There — you see? You *did* think I would act as the Marshal-General's spy."

"Sorry," Luap muttered. So he had heard the servant's words.

"You should be! When have I ever agreed with him? No, if you and your folk are happy out here, and living comfortably and at peace, this is what I hoped to see. And if you transgress some one of the Marshal-General's many little rules, he won't find out from my report — not that he could do anything if he did. You're growing your own food; you're not taking anything from the granges any more."

"I see him when I report," Luap said. "I suppose I've come to think of you — of the others — as mostly like him."

"We're not. At least, not all of us. So settle down, will you, and quit looking so nervous. If you're playing prince out here, and all your people kiss your feet, it's your business. I won't, but if they want to, they can."

Luap forced a chuckle. If only he could believe that — but Cob, he knew, would not lie. Perhaps he did have a friend in this sunburnt old peasant. "I confess, then, to allowing more deference than I would have in Fin Panir."

"Deference! Is that what you call it?"

Luap shrugged. "If you mean showing respect —"

"For rank and not for deeds. Yes. Although I suppose you have shown them deeds enough, out here, even if those deeds were magery." Cob nodded to the growing cluster of Girdish riders now dismounting and milling about the stronghold entrance. "We're making a tangle here — where would you have us go?"

"Which is greater, fatigue or curiosity?" Luap countered. "We have guest chambers, of course, and bathing chambers to wash off the trail grime. Or you can begin with food. Or you can let us drag you all over, showing off."

"I must admit food sounds good," Cob said. "I want to see that grand hall you told us about, but then food . . . and that lot had better start with something to eat." He beckoned to a younger man. "You may remember Vrelan, my yeoman-marshal."

"I do indeed," Luap said, smiling. Vrelan looked old for a yeoman-marshal now, and he wore the blue tunic of a Marshal.

Cob nodded. "Yes, he's Marshal Vrelan — just finished his training this last winter. We're finally training Marshals faster than establishing new granges, so we old ones can have replacements and the younger ones can get experience before taking on a whole grange. Considering my age and failing health —" by the tone of his voice, he was quoting someone he did not like, " — the Council decided that a younger Marshal should come along to report on your settlement. The Marshal-General would have sent Binis —"

Luap almost choked. Cob was grinning broadly.

"I thought that would get your attention. But I insisted on Vrelan, for his expertise in horsemanship and wilderness travel; Binis still rides like a sack of redroots." He cleared his throat and spat.

"Marshal Cob!" That was the Rosemage; Luap was surprised that it had taken her this long to appear. He had half expected her to meet them in the upper valley. She hugged Cob, then turned to Luap. "Seri says there's another gang of robbers holed up in those canyons somewhere; the Khartazh had a caravan attacked north of Dirgizh. We got the message yesterday. She's taken half the regular guards the long way around, and I'm about to leave to take the high trail and try to spot them from above. She wanted me to wait until you were back in the stronghold with your guards."

"Is Aris with her?"

"Yes, but Garin's here if anyone in Cob's group needs help."

"Then I suppose we'd better set the usual doubled guard, and let you go. Who's your second this time?"

"Liun, and he's up on top checking all the guardposts. He'll be down to report to you."

"Well, then." Luap shrugged at Cob. "I'd better get to work; come along if you like, and we'll get something to eat as we go past the kitchens." He felt almost pleased by the otherwise bad news. Cob would see how well Seri and the Rosemage had organized the militia; he would see busy, hardworking people, not idlers. The Rosemage turned away and strode rapidly up the passage. "Just let me tell Jens — " Quickly he gave his orders to one of the boys to provide food and a guide for Vrelan and the others. Then he headed for his own office, with Cob trailing.

It had become so natural to him that he hardly remembered his first feelings of awe and nervousness at being underground. Cob's wide eyes and quick breathing reminded him. "It doesn't bother you at all?" Cob asked, when Luap looked back, having just remembered Cob's lameness. He slowed, waiting for Cob to catch up, then forced himself to stroll as if he were not in a hurry.

"Not any more. It did at first, but we've been here now for several years and the walls don't cave in and the light never fails." He pointed out store-rooms, kitchens, the great water reservoir, as they passed them, and explained where the cross-corridors went. They came at last to the corridor behind the great hall, and the chamber where Luap had chosen to do his work. His scribe had heard him coming, and was looking out the door.

"Ah, Luap: did the Rosemage find you?"

"Yes — she's on her way. Where's the Khartazhi message?"

"Here, my lord." He handed over the woven pouch, like a miniature rug, in which such messages were carried. Luap opened it, and looked it over. The king begged his assistance in the capture or destruction of lawless robbers who had attacked two caravans in the past *thirg* — a thirg, Luap knew, was about six hands of days. The king's captain thought the robbers might number fifty — an unusually large band. The message finished with the flowery compliments he had come to expect in any communication from the Khartazh. "We could not send a formal answer, my lord, until your return . . . the messenger is waiting."

But Seri had already gone, as if she had the right to anticipate his commands. Luap wondered why some were born with the will to act, and others always awaited permission. "Then I'll dictate it now," he said. "Or — better — write it in my own hand. This is Marshal Cob, by the way, an old friend from Fintha. Why don't you fetch Garin, while I'm writing, and see if he has some salve for sunburn?"

"I can go," Cob said. "No need to bring anyone to me." Luap saw his gaze flick around the room, noticing the thick patterned carpets, the wall hangings, the stone ink-dishes, the racks of scrolls. He smiled at Luap. "I'm glad Vrelan will see this." Just enough emphasis on Vrelan to make his meaning clear to Luap . . . a visit from Binis would have been a disaster.

"I won't be long," Luap said. He pulled a clean scroll from the rack kept ready for him, and stirred the ink his scribe had been using. Cob nodded and withdrew; Luap hoped Garin could ease that sunburn—it almost made his own face hurt to look at it.

By the time Cob came back, he had finished that message to the king's captain, and seen his messenger on his way. He had also approved the revised watch-lists Liun submitted, and suggested to his personal staff that they minimize the formal courtesy for the duration of Cob's visit. The scribes flowed in and out of his office with reports, messages, requests; he dealt with them easily, as always, sensing around him the whole settlement in busy, organized activity. When Cob came in, Luap smiled at him and said "Now — you must come see what I found when I first came by the mageroad."

Cob's reaction to the great hall was as strong as Luap could have wished. He looked up and around. "This is . . . this is . . . it's all magery?"

"No — not now; it's real enough. It was done by magery, though, and not by ours. The Elder Races built it; they have never told us why, or why they abandoned it." No sense in repeating the vague warnings he had been given; if he didn't understand them, Cob certainly wouldn't.

"And those are the arches." Cob walked toward them, as Gird had, with perfect assurance that he could do so. Of course, he had not come by accidental magic. Cob looked up. "Harp, tree, anvil, hammer . . . and the High Lord's circle. This is the one that appeared when Gird came?" Luap nodded. "I'd have been scared," Cob said.

"I was," Luap said. "Do you want to go up and see it from above?" He nodded at the spiral stair.

Cob shook his head. "Not today; my foot's climbed as far as it wants. Let's go find one of those kitchens full of food, eh?"

Luap smiled, and led him slowly back the way they had come. Cob seemed to notice everything. "Big as this place is, I'm surprised your people are moving out into the canyons: why do the work to dig out a separate dwelling?"

"Convenience, mostly. It may not look it, but the lower terraces are a half-day's walk down the canyon: it's easier to live beside the fields. And it's like the old palace at Fin Panir . . . living in a small house is easier. To have privacy here, you have to spread out into all the levels, but when you've done that, you're a long way from the kitchens or the bathing rooms, or even a way out. Some things we have to do here, but families, in particular, seem to want their own dwellings."

"Ah. And do they make these dwellings the old way, or by magery?"

"By magery, for the most part. Most are small, one room deep and several wide, just in from the rockface. You saw the way this stone breaks, leaving wide arches? They build within that, using magery to help shape the broken stone into blocks and then lift them to form walls." He grinned at Cob. "They're very odd-looking houses, by eastern standards, but they're comfortable. Tomorrow or the next day I'll take you visiting."

By the next morning, all the travellers had rested and were eager to satisfy their curiosity. Some went out to the terraces in the main canyon to see how the mageborn farmed; some explored the passages of the stronghold itself, getting lost repeatedly. All climbed the spiral stairs at least once, to look out over the tangle of canyons and have the locals point out where they had been riding the day before.

"When will Seri and Aris be back?" Cob asked Luap at the midday meal. Luap shrugged.

"I don't know. It depends on which canyon the robbers are in.

Look — " He put his hand down on the table. "This — my hand — is the mountain we're in — as if we were in the wrist. On the west end, six fingers stick out, with canyons between them — they could be in any one of those. That's why the Rosemage went up here — " He pointed to his knuckles, " — to see if she could spot them from above and let Seri know."

"Why not have a permanent settlement there, and then you'd know?"

"It's the size: you don't realize how far away that is. And those canyons face west, picking up all the summer winds, very hot and dry: you can't farm in them." Luap reached for another slice of bread. "We're very few, you know, in a very large land."

"So you do this king's work for him, catching his robbers . . . ?"

"They'd prey on us if they could; some tried." Luap remembered those early encounters with an echo of the same fear he'd felt then: his people were so few, so vulnerable. "Once the Khartazh realized we were settlers, not brigands, it made sense for us to help keep those canyons clean of trouble."

"Ummm." Cob blew on his stew, as if it were still hot. "And what do you get from this agreement?"

That was, of course, the problem. "Not a great deal yet," Luap admitted. "But we can grow more food here than they can in the desert below the mountains. We take in fresh food to Dirgizh — the nearest town — for trade; they have superb weavers and smiths."

"Do they know you're mageborn?"

Luap pursed his lips. "They know we do some magery; I'm not at all sure they understand what 'mageborn' means to you and me. The king's ambassador, when he first came, saw Aris healing. They have legends, they say, of the builders of this stronghold, and at first thought we might be those beings, or their descendants. We haven't tried to conceal our powers, but neither have we tried to exaggerate them." Much. He thought Cob would probably not approve his strategy of subtly encouraging the Khartazh to think the powers they saw were the least of those actually held.

"They're a very formal society," he went on. "A very ancient, complex empire by their own account, and their craftsmanship and language support that. In our encounters with them,

413

we have had to adopt a more formal, ornate style than is common in Fin Panir." He let himself chuckle. "I confess I rather like it — it's like a dance, making intricate patterns."

Cob looked at him. "I can see you would like that, but do the patterns mean anything?"

"All patterns hold power," Luap said. Cob's eyes widened; he realized he'd quoted a proverb learned from the king's ambassador. "The elves say that," he said, which was also true. "That's what they said when I asked how the mageroad works, why the magery alone wouldn't do, or why those without magery could not use the patterns. Patterns hold power, and those with power can both find, and use, the power in patterns."

"The patterns of language and manners as well?" Cob asked. "Are you saying that those with the most elaborate manners have the most power?"

"I — never quite thought of that," Luap said. He liked the idea; certainly it had been true in Fintha before the war. Would the peasants, who now had the power, develop more elaborate manners because they had it? Or did it work only the other direction? "I did think that the patterns show where the power is, in a way. The Khartazh, for instance: they have different ways to say something depending on the ranks of the people involved. That reveals the way their society is organized; if you know there are eight ways to say something, you know there are at least eight different ranks."

"Or eight different crafts," Cob said. "Each has its own special terms."

Luap wondered if he were missing the point on purpose, and decided not to pursue it. He wanted Cob to see how much they had accomplished, how well they were doing, not quibble over the interpretation of Khartazh social structure and language. "Would you like to see the farm terraces this afternoon, or would you rather visit one of the outlying homesteads?" Either one of those should provide plenty of innocuous conversation, he thought.

Cob frowned thoughtfully. "I'd like to see the farmland, I suppose. See what you've made of those two sacks of earth. But — is it all in the sun?"

"Not all of it. We'll take care of your sunburn." Luap asked the cooks for a loaf to take along, and led Cob down the side-canyon, back across the bridge, and into the shade of the pines.

"We can stay in the shade, here, while I explain what we did. In another glass, the sun will be off this terrace, and you can dig in it if you wish." He leaned against a tree-trunk and Cob leaned beside him. "Gird was right, in what he said: there was not a flat bit of earth in this canyon larger than my hand. But there was water — the stream — and Arranha knew how terraces worked. Now the little terraces you know — the ditches and dykes every farmer uses to keep wet fields drained and slow runoff on slopes — are the same idea, but we had to build bigger ones. The rocks came from the walls, by magery as I told you before. Then we had to shape and place them, some by magery and most by hand. That left us with a series of rock walls across the canyon — and notice all the terraces are fan-shaped, with curving walls."

"Because straight ends wouldn't stand flood?"

"Right. The canyon widens downstream — it doesn't look much like it, but it does — so the terraces reflect that shape. But what we had when I came to you for soil was a lot of broken rock heaped into the walls that now form the lower edge of each terrace. Look upstream there — " Luap pointed; Cob leaned out to see a curving, breast-high wall. "Downstream, the terraces are lower; the stream falls less rapidly. That wall is thicker than it looks — Arranha told us how far back to slope it so that it would hold. But that left us with spoon-shaped hollows to fill with soil. We had broken rock for the base, and plenty of sand — good drainage — but nothing with which to make good soil for grain and vegetables."

"So you brought two sacks of earth, about enough for two healthy redroot plants. . . . "

"And doubled it by magery. And doubled that. And doubled that. I know — " Luap held up his hands at the look on Cob's face. "I know, it seems impossible. It did to me. The only reason I rode off with two sacks was that Binis was with me, and I wanted to be free of her more than I distrusted Arranha's numbers. The short of it is that the mageborn used to have the power of doubling many things, but lost it — for misuse, of course. Some fool couldn't resist doubling gold and jewels, and another tried to increase crops. But earth was not

415

under the ban: we could double a clod of dirt to two clods, and that two to four clods, and so on. Arranha said it would be enough, so we tried it. And it worked."

"But doesn't it take — I mean, I thought the larger the magery, the more power it took — the more it cost you."

"That's true. Supposedly the doubling should have been the same no matter what amount we doubled. But we couldn't think of it like that, so as the amounts grew larger, it was harder. What we had to do was double small amounts many times." Luap grinned as he remembered just how difficult and time-consuming that had been. He explained to Cob, who after awhile began to see the humor in magicians having to haul one sack of soil a few feet, double it, and haul it another few feet and do it again. "And when I think that I almost dumped it out loose — that would have been a real mess. If we'd had to move it shovelful by shovelful from one terrace to another —"

"How long did it take?"

"Longer than I planned for. We didn't make a full crop that year." He pointed. "We didn't finish upstream from that one, or go farther downstream than — the third, there, with the tall tree beside it."

"What about wood? I notice you haven't cut this area recently."

"We get most of our wood up on top — the very top of the mountain is heavily forested. Down here, we use the trees for shade — as you see — and as shelter for the herbs we need. Aris has found that some of the natives are also medicinal, but we have gardens of the same ones you'd find in Fintha."

"But as your population grows, will you have enough cropland?"

Luap shrugged. "If not we'll spread into neighboring canyons, as I said. This year we should have a good surplus. In another few years, the fruit trees should be bearing, too."

Cob nodded; if he was the friendliest of the Marshals, he was also the one Luap respected most, and most wished to have respect him. The rest of that visit went as Luap had hoped, although he and Cob were both disappointed that the Rosemage, Aris, and Seri did not return until the last day before the caravan must return.

"It was all very complicated," the Rosemage said. "They

416

asked if we could give testimony at the trial, and then there was a message from the caravaners, sent north from Vikh, the next town south. Had you arrived safely, they wanted to know. The captain had to hear all about Cob and the new trail — he thought we would fly them in by magery, I think. Anyway, it all took much longer than we expected, or we'd have come back by the mageroad, if only for a day. We have messages from their king, by the way."

"And I have a letter for you, from Raheli," Cob said. He handed it to the Rosemage, who opened it and began reading.

"I wish I'd known," she said ruefully. "This needs an answer — I wish I could take time off and visit her —"

Luap, who had opened the king's message pouch, shook his head. "Not now, I'm afraid — he wants to send his heir to visit. We'll have a lot of work to do beforehand."

"One thing after another," the Rosemage said, shrugging. "Tell her I will come as soon as I can, Cob — and I *wish* we'd had more time."

But if they would return safely by the overland route, they must leave now. Cob would not take the mageroad and leave others to travel the hard way, and they all knew how the Marshal-General would react to the sudden eruption of horses, mules, and people into the High Lord's Hall. The Rosemage went with them to the edge of the mountains, and watched until they were safely down into the desert below.

"We'll be back," Cob bellowed cheerfully from halfway down. "Or someone will."

"They grow rich and fat," one of the blackcloaks grumbled. "Year after year, and for how long? Their horses foul our valley; their caravans clatter and gabble, loud as a village fair. Let us have a good feast now, and forget the rest."

"Are you truly one of us, or a half-mortal fool?" hissed the blackcloaked leader. "We have no reason to hurry: the fatter they grow, the greater the feast to come. The more folk who come, the more kingdoms or empires involved, the more chaos will follow their downfall. We shall topple not one princeling in a canyon, but all with whom he trades, if we bide our time and prepare. Will the eastern lands blame Khartazh? Will Khartazh believe it a plot of Xhim? Some mortals, at least, will think it a plot of the sinyi. Dasksinyi may turn against irsinyi . . . all is possible. In the

417

meantime, we observe. We listen. We gather from their idle talk much we can pass to others."

"As long as the sinyi don't find us first," the grumbler said, undaunted. All hissed, a long malicious sibilance as chilling as wind over frozen grass.

"If the sinyi do find us," the leader said, "if the dasksinyi or irsinyi find us, it will be because some one of you was clumsy . . . some one of you was hasty . . . some one of you could not obey my commands and thought to outwit me. Then it would be better for that one to be brought before the forest lord, than before me." Silence followed; after a time he said, "Is that understood?"

"Yes, lord," came the response.

418

by the time he could make peace, no one would listen, but he had valued any help he ever got. The wisdom of Gird, all of the learning of the best, spread counsel by copying books in the land. Never long happening, somehow the lopsided form made sense neither as well as inequality? He lived on and on, and he was not the way the laws were changed in that important, known—only thing, but around in Oral side.

● Chapter Twenty-nine

Years passed, peacefully enough. Each summer a caravan came, bringing news from the eastern lands that seemed increasingly irrelevant. Late each summer they left, taking with them the copies of the Code, of commentary and history, and taking also the memory of a high red land peopled with grave, courteous folk. As time went on, a few stayed, some of mageborn parentage and some not, but all intrigued by a way of life so different from their own. Craftsmen, finding a market for superlative skill; scholars; judicars intent on pursuing fine points of law; even a few Marshals, unhappy with changes in the Fellowship.

Some disliked the stronghold and its inhabitants intensely. They claimed to sense evil; they blamed the mageborn for using their powers. Their companions laughed — in the face of that peace, that prosperity, that hive of diligent workers who quarrelled so seldom and shared so readily, such suspicions reflected on those who voiced them. Perhaps the old magelords had been evil, but not that child charming a bird to sing on his finger. Not that woman whose magery lifted the bundles from the pack animals and set them gently in a row. The suspicious never returned — and some did not survive the trip home, having angered their companions with too many arguments.

For the first ten years or so, Aris and Seri travelled often, sometimes to Fin Panir, where their adventures furnished the substance of many a fireside tale and song. Their other adventures, in distant Xhim, on the vast steppes, no one knew but themselves and the gods. Luap worried, every time, that they might not return. Later, they spent most of their time — in the end all of it — in the stronghold, for despite Seri's warnings, the mageborn did not maintain active watchposts or keep up militia training unless she was there. They depended on the Khartazh to guard them on the west, and on the desert and mountains to protect them on the other sides.

By the time Cob died, Luap's position as a distant, powerful, but valued ally had become secure. His version of Gird's life, of the history of the war, spread copyist by copyist throughout the land. Power kept him young, something he concealed from each year's visitors as well as his own folk. He lived on, and the other witnesses to Gird's *Life* died, one by one, until he was the last who had fought in that army, who had known anything but the end of Gird's life.

The Council of Marshals even invited him back to be Marshal; his refusal won him support as a moderate, modest man, although the more violent said it proved his weakness. He noticed, in reports of the gossips, that Raheli's influence lasted beyond her own death. She was blamed for a militant and violent strain of Girdish rule that Luap was sure Gird would not have approved. He ignored the counter-arguments that she had compromised with Koris and his successor only to ensure that women retained their rights in the grange organization, that she herself, and her followers, had been moderate. Rahi's death left him free to write Gird's *Life* as it should have been — he would prove he was right, and she had been wrong. Aris and Seri still held Gird's original dream, and something in Aris's clear gaze kept Luap from openly admitting that he had no intention of reuniting the two peoples, not now or in the future. The others were content to leave the eastern lands to their own affairs.

Luap's calendars of the western lands, meticulously kept though they were, interested Aris little. . . .

Aris climbed the last few steps to the eastern watchtower, aware that he no longer wanted to run up them. He didn't feel older, but he was, when he thought of it, acting older. He put down the sack of food and the waterskin without speaking to Seri; she was watching something in the eastern sky, and she would speak when she knew what it was.

In the changeable light of blowing clouds, the stone walls and towers seemed alive, shifting shape like demons of a dream. Clefts and hollows in the rocks gave them faces that leered and mocked the watchers, faces that smoothed into bland obscurity when the light steadied. Far below, he could hear the moaning of the great pines; up here, the wind whistled through the watchtower openings.

He felt on edge, his teeth ready to grip something and shake it, his hands curling into fists whenever he wasn't thinking about them. It was ridiculous. He was a grown man, the senior healer with students (none too promising) under him, too old for such feelings. He glanced at Seri, then stared. He rarely looked at her; he felt her presence always, so familiar that he did not need to see her. But now: when had gray touched that wild hair, and when had those lines appeared beside her eyes, her mouth? From vague unease, he fell into panic. Seri *aging*? Getting old?

As always, she reacted to his change of mood before he could move or speak. "Aris. What's wrong?" Her eyes were still the clear, mischievous eyes he had always known; her expression held the same affection. He shook his head.

"I — don't know. Something just — "

"I'm on edge too, and I don't think just from you." She turned to look out again, the same direction. "Maybe it's this weather; it's hard to see, hard to judge distance, even for landmarks I know. I keep thinking I see shadowy things flying in the upper canyons, something moving along the walls — but of course those are the cloudshadows, blowing all over." She sighed, rubbed her eyes, and sat down abruptly. "Whatever it is, if it's not nonsense, can't get here before we eat our dinner."

Aris unwrapped the kettle. "Kesil and Barha brought back a wildcat and two stags; we have plenty of meat in this stew. And the bread is today's baking; Zil wanted you to have this fresh. He tried something new, he said. I'm to slice it from this end." Seri spooned out two bowlfuls of stew, while Aris sliced the narrow loaf. "Ah . . . I see . . . he filled it with jam."

"Before baking? Let me try." Seri took a slice and bit into it. "Good — better than spreading it on after. And perfect with this stew."

Aris leaned back against the stone wall, noticing how its chill came through his shirt. Soon time to change to winter garb, he thought. He munched thoughtfully, carefully not thinking about how Seri looked, which was harder than it should have been. He found he was thinking of how everyone looked: how old or young everyone looked. Babies born the first few years had grown to adulthood . . . men and women who had been much older now looked it, white haired and wrinkled. Men and women his own age — he did not pay that much attention to, outside of sickness, and they were rarely sick. He frowned, trying to count the years and *see* the progress of time on some familiar face. Luap? But Luap had not aged at all. Had he?

Seri's warm shoulder butted against his. "You're worrying again. Tell me."

He put down his bowl of stew, still nearly full, and saw that Seri had finished hers. Her hands, wiping the bowl with a crust of bread, were brown, weathered, the skin on the backs of them rougher than he remembered. When he looked at her face, the threads of gray in her hair were still there, *really* there. "You're older," he blurted. Seri grinned, the same old mocking grin.

"Older? Of course I am, and so are you. Did you think this magical place would hold us young forever?"

"But you — you never had children!" He had not thought of it before, but now it seemed so obvious, with all the others having children, with all the children growing up around them.

"Did you want children?" Seri asked, eyes wide.

"I never thought about it," Aris admitted. "Not until now. I just wanted to heal people. . . ."

"That's what I thought," said Seri. She nudged him again. "You had other things to do, and so did I."

"But — " He could not say more. He knew what "other things" she had had to do; she had had him to look after, to care for when he pushed his healing trance too far. And she had shared in the same tasks as all the adults not busy with children: planting, harvesting, taking her turn at guard duty, drilling the younglings, working on whatever needed doing. She had many skills; she used all of them.

"Aris." Her strong hands took his face and turned it toward hers. "Aris, you are not like other men, and I am not like other women. We were never meant to be lovers and have a family like everyone else. We are *partners*; we are working on the same thing, and it's not a family."

"I suppose." A cold sorrow pierced him, from whence he could not say. Was he an adult? Could an adult have gone on heedless of time, year after year, pursuing his own interests and ignoring the changes around him? Was that not a child's way?

422

"Think of Arranha," Seri went on. "He gave his life to his service of Esea. He could never have been a father. Think of the Marshal-General." He knew she meant Gird by that. "Did he marry and have another family? No. Or his daughter Raheli?"

Aris stirred uneasily. He had always wished Rahi would let him try to heal her, and had always been afraid to ask. Now it was too late; she had died without children, and he knew she had wanted them.

"Besides," Seri said, chuckling. "If everyone had children, as many as they could, with your healing powers, the world would be overrun with people. Would the elves like that, or the dwarves? And where would the horsefolk wander, if farmers moved out onto the grasslands? No, Ari: it's better as it is. You didn't think of fatherhood; I didn't care that much. If it makes you feel better, think that I took you as my child."

Aris felt his ears go hot; it did not make him feel better. He cleared his throat and said the first thing that came into his head. "But Luap hasn't aged."

The quality of Seri's silence made him look at her again. Eyes slitted almost shut, mouth tight, she stared past him into the wall. Then her eyes opened wide. "You're right. I hadn't thought. He's older than we are; we thought he looked old when we first saw him. And he *hasn't* changed. The Rosemage — "

"Some, not much." A few strands of white in her hair, a few more lines on her face . . . but that wasn't something he looked at, or thought about, much of the time.

"*He's* using magery." Seri's tone left no doubt which "he" she meant, or that she disapproved. "I didn't know he could do that. Will he be immortal, like the elves?"

"I . . . don't know." Aris had never considered that use of magery; he could not imagine its limitations or methods. "He must get the power somewhere — for something like that — "

"But you know I'm right," Seri said, her eyes snapping. "You know he's doing it — it's the only explanation."

"I suppose." Other possibilities flickered through his mind, to vanish as he realized they could not be true. Long lives bred long lives, yes: but not this long with no trace of aging. The royal magery itself? No, for the tales told of kings aging normally, concerned that their heirs were too young as they grew

423

feeble. Could he be doing it without realizing it? Hardly. Ari
knew Luap to be sensitive to subtleties in those around him
he must have noticed the changes, the graying hair and wrin
kling skin, and known his own did not change. "I must talk t
him," he said. "He must tell me what he's doing, and why."

"The *why* is clear enough," Seri said. "He doesn't want t
die, that's all."

"I don't think so. I think it's more than that. You know h
always has two plans nested in a third; for something like thi
he must have more than one reason."

"He won't thank you for noticing," Seri said, taking the las
bite of her bread. "Not now."

Aris knew she was right, but felt less awe of Luap than h
had for some years, now that he knew whence that unchang
ing calm had come. "I'll be back," he said, "to tell you what hi
reasons are."

"If he'll give them." She handed him the empty pot and cloth
Aris took them and fought the wind back to the entrance shaft.

Usually he met Luap several times in an afternoon, withou
looking for him, as they both moved about their tasks. Now h
could not find him. Aris looked in his office — empty — and i
the archives — also empty. He carried the pot back to th
kitchen, where Luap sometimes stopped to chat with th
cooks. They took the pot without interest; Luap was not there
They didn't know where he was . . . and why should they? they
said, busily scraping redroots to boil. Aris looked in his ow
domain, where he found the others busily labelling pots of th
salve they'd made that morning: the task he had given them
No Luap, and he had not stopped by while Aris was gone
Back down to the lower level, where the doorward at the lowe
entrance said yes, Luap had gone out some time before. He
often took short, casual walks; he would be back soon, the
doorward was sure.

Aris took the downward slope toward the main canyor
without really thinking about it. Luap might have gone acros
to visit any of those who had hollowed out private homes ir
the fin of rock across from the entrance. He might have gone
for a dip in the stream, though it was a cool day for that. But he
walked most often out to the main canyon and across the
arched bridge, so Aris took that route.

The main canyon, under the blowing clouds, looked as strange as it had from above. Aris paused on the arch of the bridge, and looked upstream and down. The wheat and oats had been harvested; the stubble in some terraces had already been dug under, while others looked like carding combs, all the teeth upright. Around the edges of the terraces, the redroots and onions made a green fringe against the yellow stubble. Down the canyon, he could see the tops of the cottonwoods turning yellow. Upcanyon, a few of the berry-bushes had turned dull crimson. For a moment he thought he saw a wolf slinking among them, but it was only a cloudshadow, that slid on up the canyon wall like a vast hand.

But no Luap. Aris walked on to the pine grove on the south side of the canyon, and found a child bringing goats back . . . the child had not seen Luap. He came back across the bridge, telling himself that he was being silly, that not seeing Luap for a few hours meant nothing. But his heart hammered; he could hear his own pulse in his ears.

"Aris — you're needed!" Garin waved at him as he went past the storeroom where the herbal remedies were kept.

"What?" His voice sounded cross to him; he saw by Garin's surprise that it sounded cross to others. "I'm sorry," he said. "What is it?"

"A child of Porchai's has fallen down the rocks — you know they've made that new place, the next canyon over — "

"I know it." And he'd told them to be careful, with three young children, all active climbers.

"A badly broken leg, the word is. The runner came in just after you were here before."

"I'll go," he said. "No, you stay — I'll take one of the prentices." He chose the one who had the sense to have a bag packed ready — Kevye, that was — and strode out. He would certainly find Luap when he got back.

The shortest route to the Porchai place lay through a tunnel cut through the fin that separated the two narrow canyons. Aris disliked the tunnel; he had argued against making it, despite the distance it saved those who lived on the far side. But convenience and speed mattered more to most people than his concerns about safety. The tunnel was cleared and lighted by magery; most of those who had need to go from one side-canyon to another used it. Aris rarely did, but could not justify leaving a patient in danger just to satisfy himself. He strode through quickly, hardly noticing the stripes of red and orange in the rocks on either side.

Irieste Porchai met him as he came out, crying so he could hardly understand her. "You said be careful of the dropoff and we were, I swear it. He was climbing up from the creek and slipped — turned to look at something, I think."

"It's all right. He's awake? He can see?" But he could hear the child now, fretful whimpers interrupted with scream when anyone came near or tried to move him. He moved quickly to the sound, and found a small child lying twisted on the ground, the bones of his legs sticking out through bloody wounds. He knelt beside the boy, and put his hands on the dark hair. First he must be sure nothing worse had happened.

"Lie *still*," Iri Porchai said to the child. "It's the healer, Lord Aris." Even at the moment, he wished she had not used that title; he'd never liked it. But he'd never convinced the mageborn not to use it.

The child's head rested on his palms now . . . he let his fingers feel about through sweat-matted hair. A lump there and a wince: a small bruise. He felt nothing worse, and his hands already burned with the power he would spend. He let the child's head down on a folded cloth someone had brought and ran his hands lightly over the small body. The child looked pale, and was breathing rapidly: pain and fright, Aris thought. All the ribs intact, and no damage to the belly or flank. He looked more closely at the legs. Both were broken, and both breaks split the skin; on the left, one bone stuck out a thumbwidth; on the right, the child's flailing had drawn the bone ends back inside. With all that dirt on them, Aris thought. This would not be easy, even for magery. Aligning such badly broken bones, healing the ragged tissues . . . he would be here until after sunfall. He looked up at his prentice. "Kev — you'll have to steady his legs for me; we must be sure the bones are straight."

"Don't hurt me!" cried the boy, trying to thrash again.

"It won't hurt," Aris said, "if we get them straight in the first place." He wished he had Gurith's power of charming the pain away; this would hurt until the healing was well begun. "Come now — we'll be quick." He nodded to Kevre and to the adults who would help hold the boy still.

426

As Kevre moved the boy's legs to a more normal position, the broken ends of bone disappeared back into the wounds; he yelped but quieted quickly as slight tension kept the ends from wiggling. Aris laid his hands on the boy's thighs, and let the power take over.

His years of training and experience melded with that power so that now he knew what he had not known in his boyhood: he knew how the broken bones lay, how the thin strands of tendon and ligament had twisted, which of the little blood vessels had torn. He could direct his power more precisely, even into both legs at the same time, working down from the knee-joints, first aligning all the damaged bits of tissue, then forcing them to grow together, to heal as if they had not been broken. The bones were the easiest; they were easy to visualize, and being rigid were more easily controlled. Harder were the blood vessels and tendons, the torn muscles and ripped skin. Hardest of all were the innumerable bits of dirt, any speck of which could cause wound-fever. Slowly, methodically, Aris directed the flow of power, concentrating on each minute adjustment. He knew by the boy's relaxation when the healing had progressed enough to ease the pain, but he was far from finished.

When the power left him, the child lay silent, watching him with bright brown eyes. Dark had come; magelight glowed around him from a dozen watching adults. Aris drew a long breath. He had not quite completed the healing before his power ran out; the bones and other tissues were aligned and firmly knit together, but he had not been able to replace all the lost blood. "Wiggle your toes," he said to the boy. A frightened look, that said *will it hurt?* as clearly as words, then both feet moved, and all ten toes wiggled. He looked at Irieste. "He'll need a lot of your good soup," he said. "As much liquid as he'll drink, and good meat to help replace his blood. I'm sorry: my power ended before I could replace that." He felt dizzy and sick, as usual, but he knew he would be all right. Kev helped him stand; his knees felt as if someone had hammered on them.

"Lord Aris, you need to eat something. . . ."

I need to sleep, he thought. But he could not fall asleep here; he must not worry the family. "We'll go back, Kevre." He leaned on Kev's arm more than he liked, and yet he could walk . . . how was it that he had used all his power, but had not fainted from it? His mind worried at the question, as if it had importance just out of reach. The family followed him into the tunnel, which he suddenly saw as an orifice in the body of some vast animal. Like walking into a blood vessel, or a heart . . . the prick of fear woke him enough to make walking easier. In that light, the red rock streaked with darker red and orange looked entirely too much like something's insides. He staggered, climbing down to the creek, and Kevre steadied him. In the stronghold, he wanted only a bed. Seri appeared and started to ask a question, but her face changed.

"Ari! What happened?"

Kevre answered for him. "A healing, Marshal Seri; two broken legs. He's just tired. . . . "

"He's more than tired." Seri's arm around him renewed his strength; he could lift his head, now, and focus on the faces around him. She helped him to his own room, and pushed him onto his bed.

"I'm better," he said, smiling at her. She did not smile back; she was chewing her lip.

"You look half-dead," she said. "Kev says your power ran out before you finished the healing?"

Shame washed over him. "Yes. The boy will be all right; I finished the main part of it, but I couldn't do it all . . . it was just gone." Exhaustion clouded his vision; now that he was down he could not imagine how he had stood and walked so far. "Sorry . . . " he murmured, and let himself slide into blackness.

When he woke, Seri sat curled in the corner of his room, wrapped in blankets. He tried to throw back his own covers, and she woke up and blinked at him. "So — you're alive after all."

"Of course I'm alive. You know I sleep after a difficult healing."

"I know that ten years ago you would not have called a child's broken legs a difficult healing."

Aris frowned, trying to remember. "I suppose . . . it's part of getting older. I don't have the strength I had."

Seri unwrapped herself and stood up. "I think it's something more. Remember what we were talking about yesterday?" He didn't; he felt that his head was full of wet cloth, heavy and impenetrable. "Luap," she said, leaning close to him. "Luap staying the same as the rest of us aged."

The conversation came back to him dimly, like something

428

heard years before. "That can't be right," he said. He wanted to yawn; he wanted to go back to sleep.

"It is," she said. "Come on — get up and eat." She pulled the blanket off him, and yanked on his arm. Aris stood, stiff and sore, and let himself be prodded down the passage, in and out of a bath, and into the kitchen.

"Breakfast's long past," said the cook on duty. "Where've you been?"

"He was healing last night," Seri said firmly. "He exhausted himself, and we let him sleep it out."

"Oh. Sorry." She spoke to Seri and not to Aris. "What does he need? Something hearty, or something bland?"

"He's hungry, not sick. Meat, if you have it."

"I've the backstrap off that stag; I was saving it for the prince." The cook looked at Seri again, and said, "But Lord Aris can have it; it'll give him strength." She pulled a slice from the deep bowl where it had been soaking in wine and spices. "There's soup, as well, in that kettle there — " She nodded at it. Seri filled two bowls, and brought them back to the table as the cook worked on the venison steak. She grabbed a half-loaf of bread from the stack on another table and tore it in two pieces.

"Here, Ari — get this into you." Aris sipped the hot soup, and felt its warmth begin to restore him. The fog before his eyes thinned; by the time the cook laid a sizzling steak in front of him, he was alert and hungry. He began to feel connected again. Seri said nothing, just watched him eat, and when he had finished the steak she handed him another hunk of bread. "Come on, now, we're going out."

"Out?"

"Yes." With a cheery thank-you to the cook, she led Aris out into the passage that led to the lower entrance.

"I should tell Garin where I am," Aris said. He had no idea how late it was, or if Seri had told his assistants and prentices where he would be.

"Not now," Seri said. Her grip on his arm might have been steel. He strode along beside her, more confused than worried. She slowed a little as they neared the entrance, and nodded casually to the guard she had insisted on posting there. She led Aris downstream toward the main canyon, but turned off the trail to a hollow between two trees. They had often sat there to talk in privacy; the stream's noisy burling in the rocks just below ensured that. Aris curled up in his usual place, with the tree-trunk behind him and a twisted root as an armrest; Seri stretched out, her head near his knees, her booted feet on a rock. "You went looking for Luap after we talked," she said. "Did you find him?"

"Not before they called me for the healing," he said. Suddenly tears filled his eyes. "I failed, Seri: I didn't have enough power. And who will follow when my power fails completely?"

"You did not fail," she said. "Something stole your power."

"What?"

"Listen. Yesterday, I felt something dire, remember? I've felt it before; I've never found anything I could point to. But when I started thinking about it, I realized that you've been having more trouble with your healings in the past few years — since we quit travelling, in fact. I looked up your records last night. Garin helped."

"You?" Seri's dislike of poring over archives had long been a joke between them.

"Yes. And since you insisted that I keep accurate notes of guard reports, I could put those together. I hadn't really noticed, but my comments about feeling an evil influence have been more and more frequent — and correlate with your most difficult healings. No — " She held up her hand as he opened his mouth to speak. "Wait and hear the rest. Think about it. Why haven't we noticed that Luap was not growing older? And how can he do that? You told me once that for the body, aging meant injuries unrepaired, illnesses not completely healed. You said that of course healing couldn't keep someone young — but what if it *could*? Suppose Luap gets his power from you — and that's why he's not aging, and you cannot heal as you did five years ago?"

"It can't be," breathed Aris. He closed his eyes; he felt as if he'd been kicked; his breath came short. It could not be; it was impossible. But inwardly he was not sure . . . or rather, he was sure that in some way Seri was right. "Not on purpose," he murmured. "He couldn't — he wouldn't — "

"Aris, you cannot stay young forever without knowing it. He must know what he's doing. I'll grant this might not be the only way. It could be his own magery, or something the elves granted him. Something else could be sapping your strength. But taking the these things together . . . why couldn't you find him yesterday, and why did someone need your healing just then?"

Aris stared at her, even more shocked. "You don't think he made that child fall!"

Seri reddened. "No — I suppose I don't, really. But it happened just when you were about to confront him, and I have not seen you so drained since you were a child. And I must tell you, I have had a prickling all along my bones since yesterday. There's danger coming."

Aris stirred restlessly. He knew something was wrong; when he thought about it he had to admit he had been losing strength for several years. He had thought of that as age, when he thought of it at all. He had shrugged it off; his powers mattered only as they served the community, not in themselves. But he could not imagine Luap deliberately risking him — the most powerful healer — the way Seri suggested. Luap might be willful, even devious, but he had never been stupid.

"How could it be?" he asked. "I don't think it's true, but if it were true, how would it work?"

"I don't know. If we knew when it started —"

"We do." Aris realized that he had known that without knowing what the sign meant. "Remember the first time the king's ambassador came?" Seri nodded. "He commented then on how young Luap looked for his age; he said something about those who do not grow older being the wisest. I thought he meant the elves."

"I think he did. He meant the ones who built the stronghold."

"Well, I heard Luap talking to the Rosemage after Arranha died, and saying how lucky he was to look younger than he was — that it gave him an advantage in dealing with the Khartazh. He asked what I thought, and I said that age seemed to be loss of resilience — the skin stretches out, the joints stiffen. It might, I said, be like a failure to heal. We know that those badly wounded often seem older, even if they live. If it were possible to heal all injuries, even those so small we don't notice them, wouldn't that hold off age?"

"I doubt it," Seri said, scuffing the pineduff with her boot. "If it worked that way, everyone you healed would get younger."

"And you're right; they don't. I said so then, and the Rosemage said the gods meant time to flow one way, not slosh back and forth like water in a pan. But it might have given Luap an idea. If you're right about him, I think that's where it started."

Seri frowned. "But he doesn't have the healing magery. At least, you never thought so."

"No. The royal magery, yes: you saw him carve the canyon with it, and he can do many other things. But I've never seen him heal."

"Because healing is giving," Seri said, as if she'd just thought of it. "You pour out your own strength; Gird recognized that. Luap doesn't. He conserves; he withholds. He tries to do right; we've both seen him do the right thing where someone else might not. But it's calculation — he must figure out the right thing and then try to do it — he can't just feel it and do it, as Gird did."

"He's not selfish," Aris said quickly. Then, as Seri watched him without saying anything, he said, "Not in the usual ways, I mean. In times of shortage, he takes no more than his share. He lives simply, compared to any of the Khartazh officers."

"Would you give a wolf credit that he eats less grass than a sheep?" Seri asked. "And I am convinced he took your power, made you less able than you were, risked not only you but all who depend on you for healing. For that matter — " She rolled over and stabbed at the soft duff with a twig. "For that matter, how do we know that no children have the healing magery? Suppose he's stealing it from *them*? Before you could detect it, perhaps without knowing it — "

Aris shivered. He had a sudden vision of a hole in the bottom of the great water chamber . . . all the water swirling out that hole, eventually, if it were not refilled by rain. Had that happened to his power? Had Luap known, had he thought he was taking only a little, the overflow, and unwittingly taken from the very source? Or had he known — no. He could not believe that. He studied his hands, aware now of the signs of middle-age as clear in him as in Seri. "I think," he said slowly, "that something never existed in Luap that Gird had . . . as if a young tree grew with a hollow core, as those giant canes do, but then thickened around it. No one could see, from outside, but if that inside were what Gird gave *from*, then Luap might have nothing to give. He might try — as he has — but no one can bring water from a dry well."

"Whatever the cause, it was wrong," Seri said. Then she sighed, and scraped her hair back, looking at him with worry in her eyes. "And there's you. What are we going to do to restore your power? And the others: how are we going to find out how much else is wrong?"

Aris squirmed against the tree's bark. It felt comforting, that great vegetable existence at his back. "*If* you're right, the first thing to try would be the freeing of my own power. You say you noticed a change after we quit travelling?"

"Yes — within a year or so, at least."

"Then we should travel."

"But we can't — we can't leave the stronghold now!" He had never seen her so anxious. "I told you, I sense some evil. We can't leave them here, without help — "

Aris tried to feel around inside himself, the self he had thought so familiar, and find the hole out of which his power fled. He could not; he felt opaque to himself, and wondered how long that had been going on. Years? He could not tell. "I don't think I can free it here, so near him — and I don't know how far we'd have to go." When had they last been as far as the western canyons, the town beyond? He could not remember. Seri reached out and took his hand.

"You will do it, Aris. Look — let's try the mountaintop."

Exhaustion washed over him. "Today? Now?"

"Yes." She held both his hands; he felt as if warmth and strength poured out of her and into him. Very strange; he was used to that process going the other way. "Now," she said, pulling him up.

They reached the foot of the stairs without anyone commenting. Aris looked up the spiral. "All those steps," he said. Then he grinned at Seri. "I know. Gird wouldn't put up with whiners. If you're beside me, and old Father Gird will help — " He felt better, ready to face the long climb to the first plateau.

They came out into the midday light, another day of blowing cloud. Aris felt the wind pushing him sideways, but fought with it until he reached the trail to the high forest. He looked up, wondering if the rocks meant to look unclimbable, or if it was his fault. He made it up, grunting and puffing. The backs of his legs ached. Seri came up as lightly as a deer, he thought. She spent more time out of doors than he did . . . and why? he wondered. When had that started? It wasn't as if the mageborn were sickly, always needing him. But the accidents seemed to come just as Seri was starting somewhere, or when they'd planned a day away.

He headed off into the trees, taking the short way to the western watchpost. Seri caught up with him. "Let's go north, to Arranha's cairn."

"It's a long way," Aris said; he didn't feel like walking that far. Hard to remember that at first they'd come up every Evener to lay a stone on the pile.

"So? We're trying to find out if either of us can come out of the fog up here."

They had walked some distance when Aris realized he was moving more easily. He had warmed up, he thought . . . but it was more than that. He was breathing deeper, without strain; his head felt clearer. The racing patterns of light and cloud no longer seemed ominous, but playful. He noticed flowers in bloom up here that had gone to seed in the canyon below; he remembered years when they had always climbed the mountain to see the last wildflowers bloom.

Seri swung her arms and did a skip-step. "It may have nothing to do with Luap, but I still feel happier up here."

"And I." With renewed strength, he probed at himself, feeling again for anything wrong with his power. Vaguely, fuzzily, he sensed something wrong *there*. He prodded it as he would have a sore spot: how deep, how big, how inflamed? The familiar sense of something resisting the flow of healing magery . . . but this time resisting the flow *in* . . . he wondered if patients felt this.

He did not realize he had stopped, until Seri took his hand to tug him on. "Don't stop — it's getting better."

"Yes, but I — "

"A little farther. I'm feeling it too." She went on, and he followed, until his head cleared with an almost audible *snap*. He blinked; everything seemed brighter, the colors of leaf and bark and stone more sharply defined. Seri slowed. They had been walking in mature pine forest, the trees spaced well apart, with the sun slanting in between them. When they stopped, Aris could hear nothing but the wind in the pine boughs overhead. There before them was the pile of stones; some had fallen in the years when no one came. Aris stooped to replace them.

Seri rubbed her head hard with both fists. "It feels *strange*, but good. And you?" She picked up another stone and placed it.

"The same. Rather like a long fever breaking." Aris stretched out between two trees; he felt both exhausted and full of life. He wanted to eat a huge dinner, sleep, and get up well again. "And you were right," he said to Seri. "I won't accuse Luap, not yet, but *something* was interfering with my magery. It must have happened gradually — "

"And now," Seri said, sticking to the practical, "what are we going to do about it? About him?"

"Do? I — don't know. Did you find out what had been done to you?"

"Oh, yes." Her expression was grim. "Good, loyal Marshal Seri had to be kept from taking Aris out on misguided quests: she had to be convinced we were needed here, even though I should have seen that everything I tried to do, Luap managed to undo."

Aris thought about that. "I still don't think it can be Luap by himself. Something else must be involved."

Seri nodded. "And I think I may know what. Remember how the Khartazh worried at first that we might be demons in human form? All their legends said these mountains were full of demons. What if they were right?"

Certainty pierced Aris like a spear of ice. "And Luap didn't know — "

"No — although I do remember Arranha saying once that the elves had given him some kind of warning no one could understand."

"So your feeling of evil somewhere . . . could be that. It could have been spying on us all these years, making some plan — "

"And perhaps invading Luap's mind, making him prey on your power — " Seri shivered, and shook her head. "Which still leaves us with the practical problem of what do we do? They won't listen to us; we can't get them away, even if that is the right answer. I can try to cajole Luap into letting me double the guardposts, make some patrols, but it won't be enough if what I suspect is coming."

Aris looked at her. "We can either leave now — as soon as we can — and hope to strengthen ourselves enough at a distance to come back in force — or we can stay, and try to resist the influence here. It depends on how long we think we have; I suspect we have very little time."

"Yes." Seri gnawed on the side of her thumb like the child she had been, raked at her unruly hair, and sighed. "I should have realized earlier — "

"No." Aris was as surprised as Seri when his light came and

flooded the space between the trees. "We don't have time for that; we must put aside regrets and guilt and do what we can now."

For the first time in many years, her light matched his; he watched the old confidence and courage flow back into her, the old enthusiasm kindle.

"They know," the black-cloaked spy said. "That Girdish woman Marshal —"

"I told you we should have killed her before now —" hissed one of the watchers.

"And I forbade. She kept the healer happy, unaware. What does she know?"

"That their prince has not aged, and that the power for that came from the healer, and not from the prince. That some magery prevented anyone noticing."

"And the healer?"

A soft unpleasant chuckle. "The prince had a sudden urge to go here, and then there — where the healer and woman did not think to seek. And we arranged a diversion —"

"Without asking me?" the edged voice of their leader brought absolute silence to the chamber.

"Lord, we had to do something. . . ."

"So. And you did what?"

"Loosened a stone beneath a child's foot; he fell, and required the healer. Such things are easy now, the way the mortals have burrowed into the stone. They have prepared their own doom, even as you, lord, said they would. We sapped more energy from the healer as he worked, and no one knew. He will sleep long, and waken tired and confused. It will give us a day, perhaps two."

"So . . . now, now at last we may act. True, the game has lasted just over a score of years — but for some of them it has been a lifetime."

A shiver of delight, hardly audible, disturbed the silence with the faint rustle of black robes. Eyes and teeth gleamed. They knew already which would go where, and do what. Immortal hatred burned in their eyes, immortal pride. Vengeance at last on the proud sinyi who had imprisoned them; vengeance at last on the mortals who had dared to meddle in immortal quarrels; vengeance on the foolish prince, and his more foolish followers. Through the stone itself, rotted from their malice, they moved in darkness and silence.

● Chapter Thirty

The guard on the eastern post saw the smoke dark against the first glow of dawn, and sent for Seri, who sent for the Rosemage. By then the light had strengthed; they had to squint against the glow of the rising sun. The Rosemage eyed the smoke columns and said nothing. Seri said, "That's all the way to the head of the canyon, lady. Duriya and Forli are up that far. . . ."

"And the others?"

"The caravan route, the upper valley. Probably the other part of it, where we've been pasturing the horse herd."

"And your assessment?"

Seri scowled. "If we had enemies, if someone wanted to cut us off from the east, that would do it."

"And if they wanted to move on us, they'd be coming down, from higher ground. Like a spring flood."

"But we don't know yet it *is* an enemy. Or who."

"You smell trouble as clearly as I do, Seri." The Rosemage, in morning sunlight, looked like an image made of silver and ivory, her hair concealed in a shining helm. "And I, since our lord Luap is not qualified in this, at least, will take a troop up the canyon to see what it is."

"Not alone," Seri said.

"No — but if it is magery of some sort, I will know it. I will send word."

"If you can," Seri muttered. "*They* haven't, unless that smoke is their warning." She meant those who had chosen to live at the head of the canyon, carving their home where the seasonal waterfall could make a glittering curtain for its porch. And those who lived in that first valley along the caravan way.

"Perhaps that danger surprised them," the Rosemage said. "It won't surprise me." She strode away, to the entrance of the stair down to the great hall. Aris, ignored in this exchange, sucked his cheeks.

437

"She *is* a warrior," he said to Seri. It was half-plea, half excuse.

"She is," Seri said, "but she's a long stretch of her life from a war. As are we all."

"She's the best we have," Aris said. Then, with a look at the expression on her face, he added, "Barring you, of course."

Seri turned on him. "Me! Don't be ridiculous. Aside from grange maneuvers, I have never been in battle, or commanded; I have the training, yes, but that's all. What I know — what I feel — " She stopped, brooding away eastward toward the distant columns of smoke. "I could have, Ari — and I can't tell you how I know, but I'm right in this. It was my parrion, but no one wanted it, and I had to find my own way to it . . . and now, when I'm older than Gird was when he commanded, now our lives may depend on it. Because you're right, even though it is ridiculous: I am the best we have. Better than the Rosemage, because like Gird I know what I don't know."

Aris touched her arm. "Seri — it's all right. It will be all right. It could be a fire, some child careless in learning magery — "

"No. Three fires, the same day, almost the same time? Have you forgotten our talk yesterday? No, it's an attack, from whom or what we can't know. But we had best find out."

Far below, the clatter of horses' hooves echoed off rock walls, coming to them as a confused stutter. A thin shout and the sweet resonance of a horn call reached them: the Rosemage must have flown through the halls, he thought, and put a flame on someone, to be out and moving so quickly.

"Find me a replacement," Seri said. "She's our commander, but if she doesn't come back — " Aris made a warding sign without thinking; she scowled at him. "This is not a child's game, Aris. Hurry."

Whatever the Rosemage had said, as she passed through, had affected the mageborn as a stick would an anthill. Aris heard the noise before he was well down the stairs, and met half a dozen on the way up. One only had the armband of a trained lookout; that one he grabbed and held until the boy actually met his eyes. "Go up, and do whatever Seri tells you," he said. "You're on duty now." Then he himself went on down. He knew what she would want; he could start seeing to it. And he could prepare himself for the healing that would be necessary.

In the great hall, no one ran: it never occurred to anyone that running was possible. But Aris hurried, stretching his long legs, and then jogged steadily along the corridors, dodging those who tried to grab his sleeve and ask questions. He caught a glimpse of Luap, who was surrounded by a sea of bobbing heads and waving arms. He saw a sturdy yeoman, half-mage, whom Seri respected, and waved him over. "Seri'll be coming down," he said. "She'll explain; wait for her, but tell anyone she would want."

In the kitchens, the cooks were heading toward the lower entrance; Aris called them back. "We're going to need food," he said firmly. "We'll have people coming in; we'll have marching rations to prepare — "

"The Rosemage took all we had — " grumbled one.

"Then start making more. In case of wounded, I'll want broth and soup, and I'll need space at one hearth for a row of small kettles of herbs."

"Stinking stuff," said another cook. "We won't have that in here — "

"You will," said Aris firmly. "I can't heal everyone; we'll need poultices and draughts. I'll send in one of my prentices with the kettles." He smiled at them until they withdrew, grumbling, to their hearths and ovens. A moment later, a messenger bearing Luap's armband came in with the same orders, but found the cooks at work. "C-commendations, then," he said, looking around with obvious surprise. "The prince thought you might have been upset."

The head cook glanced at Aris and away. "What, then — does he think we've no common sense, to know what's needed?"

Aris walked swiftly to his own quarters. Jirith, his steadier apprentice, was laying out an assortment of healing herbs. "Good lass," Aris said. "I might have known you'd be at work."

"I wasn't sure where to do the steeping," she said. He could tell by the tension in her jaw that she was alarmed, but her voice stayed steady. "The lower kitchen is closer to the main entrance, but the upper one to the infirmary."

"The lower," Aris said. "We'll clear a store-room for use down there, if we have many wounded. Gods grant we don't." His mind tossed up the things he remembered from Gird's war, when he had not yet known he could heal. As if it were yesterday, he saw those wounds, heard the groans and screams, smelled the rotting bodies before they could be decently buried. This time, he thought, I know what to do. This time it won't be the same.

The Rosemage swung into the saddle of her gray horse, hardly aware of the turmoil her passage through the stronghold had generated. She felt at once vindicated and elated; she had *warned* Luap that all was not well; she had felt something, and he had insisted it meant nothing, and now — now she would prove she was right. Behind her, other hooves clattered on the stone, other riders mounted . . . she did not look back; she gave them the trust that they would be ready when she gave the command.

Outside, sunlight had just reached the bottom of the cleft into which the lower entrance opened. She could smell the resinous pines, the damp earth, the living air that always seemed fresher than the air inside. She sniffed, but caught no hint of any smoke but that of the lower kitchen ovens, fragrant with baking bread.

Two hands of men . . . that was all she had. It would have taken much longer to muster a larger number, so had the settlement spread from its early years. Had they counted on that, whoever they were? Were the smoke columns warnings, lit by their own people, or triumphal, defiant acts of a victorious enemy? Two hands of men — enough for casual brigands, but — she nudged her horse, and rode forward, out into the sunlight — not for anything serious. And her instincts told her this was very serious indeed.

Outside, turning downstream to the main canyon, she did glance back. Two hands, mostly full mageborn, with the lances they used against mountain cats and brigands, with swords and bows as well. She unhooked her signal horn from her saddle, and put it to her lips. The sound rang off the stone, echoed crazily from the main canyon wall across from the mouth of their smaller one.

She wondered if that had been wise, though they had used horn signals for years. Whoever caused the smoke would know someone had noticed, that someone was coming. But they might have known anyway — it might hearten defenders, help drive off attackers. She didn't believe that, but she hoped it.

At the main canyon, she held up her hand and the others gathered around her. "We cannot surprise them," she said. "Speed is our chance to do some good. But if things go badly, someone must get back to warn the others." She looked around, gauging their reactions. None of these were old enough to have fought in Gird's war. Some had helped drive the brigands out of their holes above the Khartazh caravan route; others had traveled with the caravan east, and fought horse nomads. She hoped that would be enough. She settled on the youngest. "You, Tamin: you stay well behind, and if I fall, ride back as fast as you can to the stronghold."

His young face looked even younger with the effort to be solemn, to live up to this. The others too looked serious enough.

"We will ride first to the head of the canyon; that's the shorter way, but we'll leave Tamin at the caravan trailhead. That way he can't be cut off. We have no idea who this might be, or what, so stay alert." They nodded; she turned her horse, crossed the stream on the terrace dam, and made her way up the shadowed south side of the canyon. Coming down they might have to trample crops; going up she was careful to use the trailway.

If it had not been for the smoke columns — the one at the canyon head visible even from here — she would have enjoyed that ride. The trail, two horses wide and well-packed after years of use, required no great skill; her big gray muscled its way up the steeper sections with ease. A light wind sang in the pines, and swayed the grain as they rode past it. They passed the narrow openings of the other two side canyons running north, all three separated by ribs or fins of rock that seemed slender in comparison with the great block which lay over the stronghold. Yet each was broader than the length of Esea's Hall in Fin Panir. She peered up at the canyon entrances, a little higher than the trail in the main canyon. All looked normal there. Should she stop to look? No, they must find out what the smoke meant, first.

The trail lifted over a hump of rock, and the caravan trail snaked back, up the first switchback. Ahead, the trail to the head of the canyon wound around house-sized blocks of stone at the outfall of the upper valley before angling left to clear the base of the mountain that formed the valley's eastern wall. She could not see from here what caused the smoke; it had changed color as they rode, and now the thick column thinned to a faint stream of ash-gray. And from here, close under the steep slope, she could not see the smoke that must have come from the upper valley itself.

"Tam, you'll stay here. No — wait — go across the stream, where you can see anyone coming down the caravan trail. Give us a warning, if you do, then go back to the stronghold and warn the others."

He nodded, and reined his horse away from the others. The Rosemage watched as the horse picked its way carefully across the stream, here fast-running over a rocky bed. She remembered when all the canyon had been that way, only small deep pools interrupting the stream's noisy rush. Tam turned, on the other side, turned, looked far above them, where she could not see, and waved. She was proud of him; he remembered to make that wave a signal, to indicate that he'd looked and found nothing amiss. She waved back, and legged her horse on.

She felt the skin of her back prickle; more than sunlight made her neck itch, her skin feel tight all over. When she had first come into this empty land, so vast and strange, she had felt this way often. They were so few; the land could swallow them and not even notice. But years had dulled that feeling; she had become used to the solitude, the wide sky, the great canyons empty of everyone but themselves. Now she felt again as she had that first year, when every rock seemed to shelter an unknown menace.

As they moved from the shadow of the cliffs to the broken rock beyond, sweat began to trickle down her sides, under the mail. She could never see very far ahead, and worried more and more that they might be ambushed. But nothing stirred, and no strange sounds alarmed her. The trail was narrower; although it had been built wide enough for two horses abreast, it had not been maintained as well. The horses plodded on, steadily and quietly.

Beyond the broken rock, the foot of the valley wall narrowed the canyon again. The stream here gurgled pleasantly, narrow enough to step across in most places, edged with mint and a plant with starry golden flowers. The trail wound back and forth across the stream, hardly more than a footpath. The Rosemage stopped and turned in the saddle.

"We must leave the horses," she said. "We can't fight horse-back up this way, and we dare not be trapped where we can't even turn — "

"They cleared a forecourt, like, below the fall," one of her troop said. "There's room to turn there."

"Yes, but not in between." She didn't like this, any of it. Leave the horses and they might be stolen, or spooked. Take them, and they could be attacked easily from above, with bows or even rolled stones. And why hadn't she thought to leave the horses with Tamin, back at the trail division? Now she would either have to leave someone else to guard them, which meant having only eight with her, or tie them and hope nothing happened. She had lost her wits, she thought angrily. It was hard to think, hard to make any decisions; she half wanted to turn around and ride back to the stronghold. She dismounted, ending both the internal and external discussion, and the others dismounted as well. "We'll tie the horses," she said. If something spooked them, sent them back down the canyon, it would at least warn Tamin.

Despite everything, that walk up the steep trail to the clearing below the falls reminded her again why she loved this country. All along the creek, more of the starry yellow flowers, more tiny ferns, more beds of fragrant mint. Tiny golden frogs splashed into the water, arrowing across pools not much larger than a kettle to flip themselves onto a sunny stone. The canyon walls closed around them, making each stretch of trail a private room, almost a secret.

She could well understand why someone might want to live here, even though in flood or in winter snow it would be impossible to get out, to join the others in the stronghold. If she had had no responsibilities, she might have wanted to live here herself.

They came around a last twist to the clearing, a grassy circle edged along one rock wall by the merest trickle of water. The Rosemage stared. The last time she had seen it, fruit trees and vines had been trained all around the margin in rock-walled terraces above the seasonal floods. Those trees had been hacked to the ground; their green wood, slow-burning, had fueled the smoke that rose as if in a chimney, straight up the cliffs past the dwelling. They had not smelled it before, but now acrid smoke stung her nostrils. Behind her, a mutter rose; a wave of her hand silenced it. She let her eyes rove up the cliff, ledge by ledge, looking for any movement, ignoring for the time a trickle of darker smoke from the dwelling entrance. Nothing . . . no movement, no sound, until her gaze flowed into the sky and found dark wings already circling.

She moved cautiously around the clearing, keeping close to the wall. The trees had been cut with axes, the marks clear on their short stumps. A few branches had escaped the fire, their blossoms and tender leaves already wilted from the day's heat. Some of the carefully laid terraces had been broken apart, the stones flung several arm's-lengths. It could not have been done by stealth; it would have made considerable racket, to echo off the cliffs on every hand. The mageborn must have heard it — why had they done nothing? Because they had been killed first? She did not look forward to what they might find in the dwelling itself.

The lower, obvious entrance led to a small stable, carved of the rock. Here the families had kept goats and a couple of sturdy ponies to pack their fruit down-canyon and other supplies back up. Normally it was closed by a heavy door of thick planks; these were shattered almost to splinters. The Rosemage knew before she entered that the animals were dead; she did not expect the savagry with which they'd been flayed and butchered. Most of the meat had been taken, and the innards strewn to smear every bit of wall and floor with stinking slime. Here, for the first time, she found a footprint in the bloody mess: it could have been human, by its size and shape, a foot cased in soft leather, not boots with heels.

From the stable, an inner stair led up into blackness. The Rosemage considered, decided to use the outside approach to the family's own chambers. This, outside, meant climbing a series of ledges, zig-zagging up the curving cliff. When she had visited before, a notched log had served to cross one gap which now required a careful leap.

The main entrance had served as a front porch, a low stone wall protecting small children from the drop to the clearing below. No water trickled past it now, but she remembered how beautiful it had been when the falls ran. She glanced out, down-canyon, surprised as always at the way the land hid its real shape. From here, the side-canyons were invisible; she could not tell where the stronghold lay.

But she could not stand gazing at lost safety, not now. She waited until half her band had made it that far, then called her light. It flickered for a moment as shock blurred her mind. There they were, the two families, the bones unmistakable through charred flesh, square in the entrance to the rest of the dwelling. A few ends of wood indicated that the household furniture had fed that fire. Stinking smoke trailed along the cave floor and made her cough. She moved forward.

"We have to know," she said. "Maybe someone escaped, maybe a child found a hiding place — " In her light, she could see walls smeared with blood and filth and smoke. As she edged past the smoldering pyre, she realized that the passage had been systematically dirtied with the corpses before they were burned — she hoped they had been corpses then, not still living. Nausea cramped her belly, her throat, and she fought it down. She had to remember how the cave dwelling had been laid out. She heard someone retching behind her, but the stench of death and burning was so bad nothing could make it worse.

Two families, both fairly young; they had shared this passage, a dining hall, a large kitchen with two hearths, and the wide space behind the waterfall. On either side of the passage had been each family's sleeping rooms and private space. She could not remember all of it; she wasn't sure she'd been shown all of it. She went into the first opening she found, on the left, and found the remains of a loom, smashed, and the cloth ripped away, hacked and smeared with blood. In the next, only the splinters of whatever furniture had been there, probably to fuel the fire. Someone had walked through the pool of blood on the floor before it dried, leaving footprints like those in the stable. Chamber after chamber, on one side the central passage or another, had only destruction, blood, the smell of horror.

Her mind could not take in the whole thing. It seemed to fragment, to split into five or six minds, each attending to only one part of what she saw and heard and felt. Had they been surprised? Had anyone fought? Where had the attackers come from, and who were they? Could she find more clues?

In the kitchen with its double hearth, its concession to the kitchen rights of two women of equal rank, she found the first sign of resistance. A pothook, marked as if by a sword-slash. A

broken knife, stained with blood. The Rosemage sniffed it
trying out what her magery might tell her. A strange odor
seared her nose, woke terrible fears. Not human, not this
blood. But what? She called the most experienced of the
huntsmen, who sniffed and then shook his head.

"Nasty, lady, you're right about that. But it's nothing I've
smelled before, not here or anywhere. It has a . . . a tingle in it,
a ringing, almost a sound."

"It's wicked," the Rosemage said. She felt something in the
atmosphere as a smothering wave of evil. "And it knows we're
here."

But nothing more happened, as they searched each chamber carefully. They found no survivors, only the bloodstains
where each had been killed and gutted. They found no clues
but the odd-smelling blood on that one blade, and the
evidence of the pothook that the attackers had used swords.
And the sense that some great evil, some cold and incalculable
menace, lurked about them.

The Rosemage was almost surprised to find that it was still
daylight outside when she came back to the ledge behind the
dry waterfall. Her head ached; her mouth tasted of smoke and
death. The others were all white-faced and grim.

"We must find out if those in the narrow canyons are safe,
and warn everyone," she said. "Belthis, you go — tell Tam
what we've found, and rouse the stronghold. Then check the
first of the side canyons. Those two oldest lads of Seriath's
were planning to live there this summer; they'd started a rock
shelter last year. Get them out of there, if they're alive, then
make sure the next side-canyon's safe."

"Should those people leave?" asked Belthis.

"No. Remember — the west wall of that's the east wall of the
canyon outside the stronghold, and there's the tunnel." The
next side-canyon east had seemed a good place to expand the
settlement's living quarters, but it had proven inconvenient to
have to go around the spine of rock between them. The
Rosemage wondered just how far along that tunnel had
come . . . she had not kept up with such things lately. But if
they lost the upper canyon, if an enemy attacked, that tunnel
could be dangerous.

They must not lose the upper canyon — they could not, if
they only knew what they faced. And she must find that out,

before worse came upon them. "Go on," she said to Belthis. "Have Tam talk to Seri, as well as Luap, about defenses. Messengers must go today to the lower canyon, to the western valleys."

He gulped. "And what shall I say about you, lady?"

"That I am trying to find out what manner of enemy we face." She followed him out from under the ledge, into the cleaner air that still smelled of smoke, and wished she need not stay.

Aris had chosen his room, and had his healers at work making it orderly and handy, when Seri came to find him. She was wearing the mail she had ordered from the Khartazh, and it jingled slightly as she moved. The expression on her face combined decent concern with pure glee.

"I had the word out before *he* said anything." Her eyes sparkled; though she was trying to stay solemn, she looked very much the mischievous child she had been.

"How many?"

"Not as many as I'd like." She scowled a moment, thinking, then went on. "We've lots more who could fight — who may have to fight — but of the ones trained solidly, either Girdish or magery, we've fewer than twenty hands — a bare cohort." She didn't say why; she didn't have to. Luap had decided, when the Khartazh proved true to its treaties, that they did not need a large armed force. Training took time from more important things. "Of course I don't suppose there's ever been a commander who didn't want more soldiers," she added. Then, looking at him closely, "And how are you?"

Aris shrugged. What bothered him most was Seri going out to fight; they both knew that, and there wasn't any use saying it. "I'm following our plan." The one he and Seri had worked out together, in case Luap's assumptions about the safety of the region were wrong. The Rosemage might be Luap's ranking military commander, on the strength of her background, but Seri had trained the young men and women, mapped each canyon, and planned the details of defense. She had also, in the early years, led more than one expedition against the brigands.

"Good. If nothing interferes with her, she should have a messenger back here by midafternoon, at least. Then we'll know something — " She paced the small room, her hair springing free with every stride. "I've got the old guardposts all manned, messengers on the way west — "

"To the Khartazh?" Aris asked. That had been a decision point in their plan, one they had argued over, taking opposite sides in alternation. Seri shook her head.

"Not just yet. I want to hear the Rosemage's report." Then she flushed, aware what that sounded like. "I mean — "

"I know what you meant." Aris grinned. "You *are*, you know. You might as well admit it."

"Luap hasn't said anything," she muttered, still red.

He could think of several reasons for that, none of them good. He felt once more the emptiness, the coldness, he had felt when he realized that Luap was using magery to extend his own life. Images raced through his mind, all ugly: an empty skull, rolled along the stone by a high wind; a headless man staggering, falling, dying. If Luap had lost — whatever made him a leader, whatever made him care — then they were all lost. And what kind of leader would choose to live long, and watch his people age and die?

Not Seri. He had another clear vision of her, from one of the early raids against brigands, leading the way up a narrow ledge. She might have stayed back, knowing her value to them as a trainer, or even commander, but she always led — she never pushed. She would have been, he knew, a better leader than Luap; in her own land, in distant Fintha, she would have made a good Marshal, and probably come close to Marshal-General, for everyone liked and trusted her. But here, Luap's refusals constrained her, like a plant grown in too small a pot.

Luap, when he came down, looked both calm and elegant. "The Rosemage can easily handle any little raiding party of brigands," he said. Aris looked at him, thinking what one of the cooks said aloud.

"And if it's not just a little raiding party?"

Luap smiled, "Then we can gather everyone in here, and defend it; once those doors are closed, no brigands can open them."

"But the crops — " someone said.

"We can replant; we can trade to Khartazh if we need to. We have reserves of both food and money. And if it's some invading force, horse nomads gone crazy or something, we can call on the Khartazh for aid." That smile again, confident and calm. "As you know, we have close trading ties there; the king has promised to be our brother."

Seri poked Aris in the back. When he didn't move, she poked him harder, then hissed in his ear. "Ask him to — " But Luap was already talking again.

"I know there are some of you who would like to see me call out our guard. Seri, I know you've been training them for years — " Aris dropped his hand and grabbed Seri's wrist even before she moved. He knew how that tone would affect her. " — But we don't yet know what we face," Luap said, reasonably. "Better to give an early warning and let families pack up their goods on the chance they might have to come here."

As if a heavy iron trapdoor fell on stone with a great clang, Aris felt something *shift* in his head: something final. From the expression on Luap's face, he had felt something too, and all the mageborn crowding around had the same startled, wide-eyed look.

"What was that — ?" began someone. Aris felt an icy certainty, and again saw it mirrored in the other faces. He knew what it was; he knew . . . and by the time they had reached the great hall, others knew it too.

There, each beneath the appropriate arch, stood two figures that Aris knew at once were rulers of their folk. More than their rich clothing, or their crowns, their bearing proclaimed their sovereignty. The elven king carried a naked sword in his hands; the blade glowed blue as flame. The dwarf king bore an axe with the same light. Both looked grim and angry. Between them, but not *in* Gird's arch, stood a gnome all in gray, holding what seemed to be a book bound in slate and leather.

Luap went forward to meet them, as an aisle opened through his own people. Aris followed close behind him.

"Selamis Garamis's son, you have broken your word with us; you have loosed that which we bound long ago, in spite of our warnings."

449

● Chapter Thirty-one

Aris felt a cold wave wash him from head to foot. He had not known Luap had made a contract with elves and dwarves — what contract? The elven king continued.

"We revoke our permission; we lay a ban upon you. The patterns of power you enjoyed will not longer suffer your use. You must scour the evil from this land, or be forever mured in this hall."

"But what *is* it?" Luap asked, all in a rush. Then he took a long breath and said, more slowly, "My lords, I do not know what you mean. We do not yet know what the smoke portends; my people have gone to find out. We have waked no evil that I know of — "

"Then you are blind and deaf, mortal, and your pretensions of power all are lies! You were warned; you were told to beware your neighbors, to walk softly and keep watch: you have not. The very air stinks of evil; the rock tastes of it; the water; the trees wither in its blast — and you claim you do not see?"

"But then — if you revoke your permission — you want us to *leave?*"

The dwarf spoke. "Mortal, we could wish you had never been, save that that would be to walk with cursed Girtres Undoer. What you have done cannot be undone; it must be mended, if that be possible, by the one who broke the covenant. Thus we command, who have that right."

"But — how? What do you mean?" Aris could hear the tremor in Luap's voice, and smell the sweat that sudden fear brought out on him. He himself stood watchful, wondering.

The elf spoke again. "You are barred from the use of the patterns to make your way elsewhere, lest the evil you waked travel with you, and bring dishonor on the patterners. You are forbidden permission to live here, where you have polluted a holy place with evil; the living water and all green things will no longer do your bidding. You must fight free on the land's skin, cleansing it from the evil you waked, or die here — your deaths payment for what evil you have done."

Aris could not see Luap's face. His voice, when he spoke, was low and halting. "You — cannot condemn all these for my failure, if indeed I failed. Not all are guilty; we have children, young people. . . . Let them escape by the mageroad; I will stay and fight. . . . "

"A people abide the judgment of their prince," the gnome said in a colorless voice. "If the prince errs, the people suffer: that is justice."

"But it's not *fair*!" Luap cried. "You have never told me the nature of this evil — I don't even know what I did, or did not do, or what it is you speak of!"

In the silence that followed that outburst, Aris heard running footsteps coming toward the hall. One of the youngest of the militia ran in, gasping, bearing a broken knife in his hand. Without ceremony, he said, "This is it! This is what the Rosemage found!" Luap turned his back on the kings, and reached out a hand.

"Let me see that." The young man held it out; Aris intercepted it as a strange, almost-forgotten smell tickled his nose. Luap scowled, but Aris brought the broken blade to his nose and sniffed.

"Iynisin," he said. Luap recoiled, snatching back his hand. Aris turned to the kings. "This is iynisin blood — is that the evil you meant? Are iynisin the evil, or the servants of it?

The elvenking spoke. "You are right, mortal, in your surmise: that is iynisin blood, and they are now awake and powerful in this place, where once they had been banished and trapped in stone. Your prince paid no heed to our warnings; one by one he broke the terms of that agreement by which we gave permission, and used his magery in ways no mortal should. Now the evil has come upon you; now the pattern comes to its necessary end." For a moment, compassion moved across his face like a gleam of light between clouds. "We take no joy in the suffering of those innocents among you, but we cannot risk evil escaping from hence to ravage wide lands. Escape may be possible for some of you — but not by magery. Those roads are closed until another of your people comes by land."

"We have caravans every year," someone said.

The elf smiled without mirth. "They could not come up the trail from the great canyon against iynisin arrows; you have lost the upper valley. It will be long, even in our perception, before a Finthan walks into this hall."

The gnome spoke again. "I, the Lawmaster, witnessed this contract the day it began; I witness now that it was broken by Selamis Garamis-son, and that the lords of elves and dwarves declare it void and state the penalities openly. So it is, and so it shall be recorded." He took from among the pages an irregular cake of wax. "This was your seal, Selamis: it, like your word, is broken." He dropped it, stepped upon it, and ground it with his heel. Aris noticed that Luap had turned white as milk.

And with no more words, they vanished. Luap stared around him; his eyes seemed sunken in his head. Those who had rushed to the great hall stared back, but no one dared speak. Aris moved forward. "Let the prince have his peace," he said. "Go to your homes and prepare for whatever comes; gather what food you have, what you can carry — "

Murmuring more and more loudly, casting looks back, they went, at first slowly and then all in a rush. Luap stood alone in the midst of the great hall, silent and motionless. Aris looked at him, then shook himself. They didn't have time now — he had to find Seri and await the Rosemage's return.

"What will it take to recapture the upper valley?" asked Luap. It was after the turn of the night; the air tasted bitter and stale. Aris wasn't sure if that was the lurking evil, or simple exhaustion. They had been in conference for a long time, Luap and all the older inhabitants, with explanations and non-explanations flying back and forth.

"Were you listening?" the Rosemage said, her voice edged like steel. "We cannot take the upper valley with the forces we have, not if we bring everyone in from the western valleys, not if we ask aid from the Khartazh. Which, by the way, I would never recommend."

"Why not?" Luap had laid his hands palm to palm, a gesture that meant he was withholding blame for the moment only.

"Luap, the king could not hold these canyons before we came; he could not do it now. We are his friends so long as we are useful, and we have been useful because we drove out the brigands that preyed on the caravans. Even if he would help, and could help, his price would be more than I want to pay."

"We have gold," Luap said.

"It is not gold he will want, but lives. Which of our people will you send into slavery?"

"Nonsense." Luap slapped the table. "We have gold; we have other wealth. We are not poor wanderers —"

"Strength is your heritage," Seri said suddenly. All heads turned toward her; Aris stared. "Arranha told Father Gird that, remember? Your people believe that the strong take, and prove their strength by taking. If you lack the strength to protect your own, what does that make you?"

The mageborn went white to the lips; silence held the room. Seri looked around, meeting each gaze with her own challenge.

"What the lady has said, and what the Khartazh king will see, is that you — we — are no longer a strong ally, to be respected. If we cannot hold these canyons, we come out of them suppliants, beggars, no matter what wealth we bring with us. Can we stand against the Khartazh on open ground? No: and so that wealth can be taken as easily as you once took the land from the people of Fintha and Tsaia. The Autumn Rose does not trust the king of the Khartazh, nor do I."

"But some are already living there; some have married into families —"

Seri shrugged. "It may be they will fare no worse than other foreigners who settle in his realm — but they will no longer be favored foreigners, when this citadel falls. We must hope for mercy; we cannot demand justice."

"Then what do you suggest?"

"We must try to send word to Fin Panir and stop the caravans: perhaps one can get through, by following the main stream out its gorge. That route is passable, though difficult. We must use what magery we have to seal off the upper valley — and the upper end of the main canyon — and hope that gives us time for the children and those who cannot fight to make their way elsewhere."

"But where? If we cannot go back to Fintha — and you will not seek aid of the Khartazh — where else can they go?"

"They cannot go back to Fintha by the mageroad, but some,

453

if we are careful, might make it overland with a returning caravan. Some might go to Xhim."

A growing murmur of dismay. The older mageborn knew they would not be welcome in Fintha, not as long as the present Marshal-General ruled. None of them wanted to face the long journey to strange and unknown lands.

"There must be another way!" Instantly several other voices echoed the first man. "Have you even *tried* the mageroad?" asked another. "Why should we believe elves?"

"It won't," Aris said. "Can't you feel the difference?"

"I'm going to try," said the man. Luap started to stand, but said nothing as the man walked quickly to the dais, stepped onto it, and closed his eyes. Then the man fell, as if someone had hit him hard; he made no sound but lay crumpled on the dais. Aris went to him quickly, felt for his pulse, and looked back at the others.

"He's dead." Someone screamed.

"*Silence!*" Luap rarely raised his voice; now it rose above the scream and commanded them all. Aris wondered how much of his royal magery went into it; he felt his own throat close, refusing speech. "I will confer with the Rosemage, with Aris and with Seri," Luap said. "You will await my decision. Go now."

Luap dressed for the conference with care. If he looked slovenly, they might panic; his people — any people, he reminded himself — relied more on appearances than they might think. White and silver gray, to remind them of his power, touches of rich blue to comfort any who still worried about Gird's view of things. He combed his dark hair — still unfrosted — and congratulated himself on his decision to preserve his youthful vigor. They would need a strong man, not an aged one, to bring them safely through this crisis. Most of them seemed not to notice, but if anyone did — if anyone, in a panic, mentioned it, he could point out that it was proof of his great power. It could not be as hopeless as the elves had said; nothing was hopeless. He had survived too many things in his life to believe that, and his experience mocked the despair he had felt earlier. What a fool he had been, to let those things upset him.

It bothered him that he could not quite think what to do

what solution might come, but he was sure he would in time. He might even find a solution the elves had not thought of. They so hated their once-relatives that they had refused to admit the problem . . . if they had only *told* him, from the beginning, like any honest person would, all this could have been avoided.

He found the beginning of the meeting tedious. The Rosemage gave her report not once but a dozen times, answering the same questions over and over. Each head of a family had to express shock, dismay, worry. Somehow they managed to entangle old grievances in the present emergency, dragging in all sorts of irrelevancies. Why could they not see that there was no time for this? He quit listening, and began trying to plan some effective action. The next caravan would arrive in the spring; they must get control of the upper valley by the time it was due. They could not fight successfully in winter . . . his eyes narrowed, as he tried to think where in the upper valley a small force could shelter for the winter, to be sure the iynisin stayed away once evicted.

"What will it take to recapture the upper valley?" he asked in the next pause. He hoped that would get their attention and force them to think about the real problem, not who made what minor decision a decade before.

Everyone stared; the Rosemage looked as angry as he'd seen her in years.

"Were you listening?" she asked. He let his brows rise; he stifled the urge to say no one had said anything worth listening to, and let her rattle on. They were too unsettled yet, he decided, as the Rosemage and Seri refused to consider going to the Khartazh; they were still full of complaint, unreasonable, unready to think their way through to answers. When Keris Porchai insisted on testing the mageroad himself (Porchai, who had been slower to learn its use in the first place than most of the mageborn) Luap let him go; when he died, that was the perfect excuse to end the meeting. He would take his few chosen assistants and see if he could knock sense into them in privacy. He would need all of them, and they must quit acting as if he were a half-wit.

He used his power on them, as he rarely did, for the sheer pleasure of seeing it work: one word, and he could silence them all, even Aris. They obeyed, as they had to, leaving in a rush. He wondered if they knew how lucky they were, to have had a gentle, unambitious prince. Until now. Now only his ambition could save them; he would have no more time to be gentle. He led those he had named to his office, and turned with what he intended as a calming smile.

Instead, he faced rebellion. Hardly had he begun to explain what he thought of doing, when the Rosemage flashed out at him.

"You have not aged: surely you know this."

"Of course," he said smoothly. "It served its purpose. . . . "

"You used the royal magery for yourself!" The Rosemage glowed, as full of light as a fire, as the sun. "What might have held that evil away from the entire settlement, you used to spare your own years —"

"I held the evil I knew or suspected away from here *by* using it so, by seeming ageless: have you forgotten how that convinced the king's ambassador? You are the one who reminded everyone how dangerous the Khartazh empire is. *This* evil knew nothing about."

"And you stole that power from Aris —"

"No." Luap shook his head. "My own magery served well enough. I would not have taken aught from him."

"But you did," Seri said. "Did you not realize that he has less healing power now than a hand of years ago?" Her voice conveyed utter certainty.

"It cannot be." Luap's face sagged; he felt as if all his years had come upon him at once. "I would not have done such a thing. It's impossible."

Seri shook her head. "It is not impossible, and it is the only explanation we have. Aris's power has waned, year by year, and you did not age. Let the Rosemage test your power, and she will find the flavor of his. Perhaps you did not know. . . . "

"You had no healing magery of your own," the Rosemage reminded him. "How, then, have you remained hale and strong so long? You must realize that the healing magery and control of age are closely allied." Her voice shook; she was, Luap realized, very near tears. "It may be too late, but you must release your magery to its proper purpose."

"It is too late," Luap said, looking at his fingers. "The elves say that, and I believe them: they make unsteady allies, but they do not lie, and they know more than we of the iynisin." He attempted a smile. "I have not even seen one."

"I have," Seri said. He had not known that. Her blunt face, weathered from years in the brilliant sun and dry wind, had lost the bright promise of its youth, but nothing could dim her eyes. Now, as she looked past him into the memory where that iynisin had been, he felt a pang that was almost guilt. She should have stayed in Fintha with Raheli; he should even have allowed Aris to stay, if necessary. She was Gird's child as much as any of his blood; she belonged there, and she might die here, because of his selfishness. If, indeed, he had been drawing on Aris's power. He still could not believe that.

"Let me see," the Rosemage pled, her long hands reaching for his. He seemed to see her doubled, the beautiful woman she had been when he first met her, overlaid by the woman she had become. When had her hair gone silver? When had those lines marred the clarity of her cheek and jaw? An insidious hum along his bones urged him to ignore all that: what did it matter, after all, if one woman aged? He could lay an illusion over anything unpleasant. The important thing, surely, was his reign, his kingdom, his power.

Then her hands grasped his with a touch like fire. He could feel her power in his wrists, her magery only just weaker than his, her skill in using it as great or greater, for she had had the early training. Swift as light moving across the face of a cliff, picking out each hollow and ledge, her magery swept along his nerves, into the chambers of his mind. He could not sense what she found, but she recoiled in horror, eyes wide.

"You — you do not even know, do you?" Her voice was a whisper hardly loud enough to hear. Seri, after a quick glance at the Rosemage, stood alert, as if ready for battle.

"What is it?" Seri asked, not looking away from him.

"He . . . was invaded." The Rosemage scrubbed her hands on her robe, as if to remove the touch of his skin. "I cannot tell when — or I might, but it would take longer. You were right; he has been drawing on Aris's power, though I do not think he knew it. I am not sure how much Luap is left, to be honest."

Luap felt something stirring uneasily deep in his mind, like a hibernating animal prodded in its den. What was it? He tried to explore, to do for himself what the Rosemage had done, and met a vague reluctance — no opposition to meet head on, but the sensation that things would go better if he didn't bother. "I don't know what you mean," he said to the

Rosemage, in a voice he hoped was reasonable. "I am the same Luap as always."

"No," she said, with a decisive shake of her head. "That you are not, whatever you are."

He wanted to scream at her, insist on it, but Seri stood there poised for anything he might do. She looked less angry than he would have expected to find that he had been stealing power from her beloved Aris, but he knew she was dangerous. He tried to gather his magery around him, the comfortable cloak he had had all these years, and the Rosemage stirred.

"No," she said, as if she knew what he was thinking. "No, you cannot do that, not again. I won't let you."

The sleeping monster stirred again, then arose, flooding his mind with its anger. "You!" he said, not knowing or caring if he spoke his own thoughts or those of the thing within him. "*You* not let me? You old woman, I mastered your magery years ago, when first we met: you should remember that. And I can master it now." It was in his hand, as reins in the hand of a master teamster; he could feel the power straining to be free to strike. His light filled the chamber; his will —

And Seri came alight. He nearly gaped in astonishment. *A peasant*? Had she been mageborn all along? But her light met his and did not mingle; his eyes burned. Where had he seen such light before? He squinted against it, his eyes streaming tears.

"You will not harm her," Seri said. "The gods will not permit it."

"It is too late," the Rosemage said. Luap looked at her; she struggled against tears. "I served one bad king: I killed *him*. Now I have served a bad prince through another exile. I will not kill you, Selamis, but I will serve you no longer. I will serve what remains of our people, and kill only those creatures of the dark. Fare well, Seri and Aris: if you ever come again to Fintha, I hope you bring peace between our peoples. As for you, Selamis, I can neither curse nor praise you; I pray instead that Esea's light will show you what you have become, and the High Lord will judge fairly how far you consented." She pushed past Aris, out into the corridor. Luap could not doubt it was for the last time, that she meant what she said. She had never said anything she did not mean. He wanted to scream after her, beg her to stay, but the shadowy presence inside him forbade it.

"What did I do?" he asked himself as much as those around him. "What went wrong?"

Seri, still alight, came near on one hand, and Aris on the other. "Perhaps," Seri said, "it is what you did not do. Give me your hand." He would have refused, but she had it already; Aris took his other hand, and they joined theirs. In that instant, he saw the thing within him, which like a soft maggot had found his hollow core, soothing and comforting him as it nestled there, growing to fill what emptiness it enlarged. Now a mailed and glittering malice, the self's armour against self-knowledge, raised its claws in mock salute and leered. He knew it chuckled in delight, its long purpose fulfilled.

"*NO!*" Not so much scream as moan, with all the intensity of the feelings he had not felt for years. He squeezed his eyes against the sight, but for the eyes of the mind there are no lids. Shame scalded him. Seri's light, and Aris's, flooded his mind, left no shadowy corners, revealed everything Gird had revealed those long years before, but worse. Tears ran down his face; he remembered all too clearly trying to tell Gird he would have been a better king. Better? The presence in his mind mocked him: Could any have been worse? Had any kin of his, any of those royalties whose prerogatives he envied, ever been as feckless, as vicious, as to let such an enemy into such a sanctum? "I'm sorry," he said; the echo of the many times he had said that reverberated through his mind.

He would have been glad to die, but death was not offered. "Is this what you wanted?" asked Seri. He shook his head; that was not enough. He had to answer aloud.

"No," he said hoarsely. "It is not."

"Did you know what you were doing?"

"No." He remembered all the warnings, and how sure he had been that he knew better, that he had outgrown those warnings.

"Then throw that filth out," she said. Luap stared at her, surprised he could see her through his tears. Throw it out? How could he? "You must," she said, more gently, as if she could see every thought in his mind. "You must; no one else can."

He had no more strength; he felt it running out of him like blood from a mortal wound. "I can't," he whispered.

"You were Gird's friend," Aris said, unexpectedly. "You can."

All those times he and the others had faltered to a halt in

459

mud or hot sun, certain they could not march another step
and Gird had bellowed at them, rain or sweat running down
his weathered face . . . and they had taken the next step, and
the next. If Gird were here, would he dare say "I can't"? No.
He could almost hear the old man's gruff voice, feel that hard
fist once more. He had to try again. "Get out," he whispered to
the presence within him. "Get *out*!"

You'll die came the response. Its sweet poison soothed; he felt
himself responding as he had, unwittingly, all these years. *You
have no chance but me*. Disgust at himself, and the memory of
Gird, gave him strength to resist.

"Get OUT!" He felt Aris and Seri joining their power to his,
yielding this one last time to his command as his magery
proved too weak . . . and then the presence, whatever it was,
fled away down the wind of his anger.

And left him once more empty, hollow, guilty, hardly able to
stand. Seri and Aris supported him; as his strength returned
he could see them more clearly. No longer "the younglings"
he had both admired and envied, but weathered and graying,
well into middle age.

"I can't — I don't know what to do." His voice came out
rasping and feeble as an old man's.

"You've made the right start," Seri said. "Now you might try
asking the gods."

Luap winced. He had not, he realized, really asked the gods
anything for a long time. He had never really wanted to know
what the gods wanted of him. He had spent those times in the
yearly festivals when prayers were normally offered giving
complacent reports on his own genius, looking for praise in
return. Now he had no choice; unpracticed as he was, he must
ask. He let them lead him back to the great hall, and tried to
fix his mind on the gods he hardly knew.

● Chapter Thirty-two

He knew at once it was no dream, not as he had dreamed before, and his first thought was that Gird had not warned him what meeting a god was like. Where had the space come from, he wondered, in which he hung suspended, like a thought in some vast intelligence? At once his mind clung to that notion, and began elaborating it, an activity he recognized even as it continued: protective flight into logic, the mage's trance.

A face appeared before him, a man's face of near his own age, he thought. Unlike dreams, it carried no emotion with it — a stranger's face, weathered by life into interesting lines. It stared aside, not directly at him, and he watched with his usual attention, looking for clues to character and motivation. A face used to command, to the obedience of others, to hard decisions . . . it was turning now, toward him. Eyes a clear cool gray met his, *caught* his, across whatever gulf of time and space lay between them. Commanded him, as they had (he could tell) commanded so many others. Now he could see the head above the face, bearing a crown — a *crown*?

A king. A king's face, and not the one he had seen last, dead, on the trampled earth of Greenfields. And not Tsaia's king, past or present, nor the black-bearded king of the Khartazh: those faces too he knew, and this was something else. A god? He thought not, though awe choked his breath. He tried to look aside, and could not. Slowly, inexorably, the rest of the man's figure became visible. A king in green and gold, the gold crown in his hair shaped of leaves and vines. Something about the clothes seemed foreign, strange: he could not say what. Slowly, as the drifting of morning fog, he began to see the room around the man . . . its panelled walls, its broad table littered with scrolls and books, its carpet like a garden of flowers, manycolored. Someone else . . . across the room, a woman whose weathered face wore a curious ornament on the

461

brow, a silver circle . . . but in a trick of light she seemed to fade and he could not see her. The king said nothing . . . did he see Luap as well as Luap saw him?

Then, "You." The king's voice, deep, resonant, carrying power as a river carries a straw. "You are part of it; you will help."

He did not want to answer a wraith, a dream, whatever this was, but from his mouth came the honest bleat of fear he felt. "I can't." Even if he'd wanted to, he had no more help to give, not even to his own people. Could he explain *that* to a wraith, a messenger, whoever this was? The iynisin could not get in, through no power of his but the original power of those who had sculpted the fortress . . . but he and his could not get out.

"You will wake them?" That voice came from the glare he could not see, where the woman had seemed to stand. The king's face turned aside, and Luap almost sagged in relief. It was like facing Gird again, on his worst days — and worse, that he had now failed at what he'd promised.

"I must," the king was saying. "They close the pattern. I cannot explain — "

"No matter." For an instant, Luap could see her again, this time as if through a white flickering of flame. She had a smile that rang aloud, louder than laughter would have been; when she chuckled, softly, he realized again that his senses were rapt in some strange magic. "I think you've missed your mark, sir king. What you seek to wake has not slept."

"What?" The king looked again, deep into Luap's eyes, a look he felt as a sword probing his vitals. "How can that be? I sought along your memories, to find the place — "

"While thinking of the reason you sought them, a reason many lives old, did you not?" The king's eyes never wavered from Luap's, but he nodded. The woman went on. "You found what you sought, then, but — Gird's teeth, my lord, I can't understand how you will get them out, and still leave what we found."

"Nor I." The king took a breath, and let it out slowly, now watching Luap with obvious wariness. "You — " and there was no doubt which of them he addressed. "You are of Gird's time, are you not? And someone who knew him?"

Luap was not aware of speaking, but he knew he spoke in some manner the king understood. "I am Luap."

"Yes." One word, in that tone, and Luap wondered what the king saw in his face. What Gird had seen? He hoped not, but the king's next words were not reassuring. "You are not . . . what legends made you."

No time to ask that, not of such a king. "I was Gird's friend, until his death; his chronicler, after."

"You have Aarean blood."

He could not help it; his chin lifted. "I am a king's son." He did not trouble to explain which king.

"And your mother — ?"

Damn the man. Luap struggled once more with the envy that never died, and said, "A peasant woman. I never knew her, past infancy."

To his surprise, that stern face softened a little. "I am sorry. My mother, too, died when I was young, and I had a . . . difficult time."

Difficult, Luap thought bitterly, could not have included being tossed out to fend for himself in a peasant village. "I have the royal magery," he said, uncertain why he said it.

"I suspected you might. Some of you, at least." The king turned away again, and spoke to the woman. Luap wondered again why she was so hard to see, for a white fog lay across her image. "If you're right, and we have opened a gap between times as well as places, how should I proceed?"

"I have no idea." The fog intensified, then she appeared, much nearer, peering past the king's shoulder. "You truly are Luap?"

He found it hard to answer, even in this nebulous state. "Yes. . . ."

Her eyes widened; humor quirked her mouth. He was reminded, for no reason he could imagine, of Raheli in one of her rare good moods. "Gird — understood you, did he?"

Tears flooded his eyes and ran down his cheeks before he could blink them away. What he might have said vanished in the storm. Her brow puckered; the ornament centered it, serene and unchanging.

"It's all right," she said. "Don't worry . . . he understands."

"Who?" asked the king.

"Gird. He shelters you as well, Luap." He had thought the king's voice commanding; he had never imagined a woman with such power. Light and tears blurred his vision to a white glow. "It will be well," she said; her voice came to him as a warm arm around his shoulders. "King's son, listen to the king." Then he could see again, the king's face expressing rue and tenderness. For her, he was sure.

"Lady — dammit, Paks, you will unnerve me, as well as him."

"Sorry, my lord." She had moved from his sight, though he knew, as if he could see, that she had stretched out in a chair at one end of the table.

"You aren't really sorry." It sounded like an old quarrel between them, worn comfortable with time.

"No — but he needs your help, as you need his. Tell him, sir king." She did not need to say "then listen" aloud; it was implicit in her tone.

The king raised his brows; Luap's knees would have shaken if he had been aware of them. Not a man to anger, he thought wildly. As bad as Gird. As good? Not another one, he thought; gods save me from heroes! As if she had heard his thought, the woman chuckled again, out of sight, but with no scorn in it.

"I am Falkieri, Lyonya's king," the king began. "You won't know of me — and was Lyonya even a kingdom in your day?"

"Ah — I had heard tales — " Such tales as no one believed, he'd always thought, but so had the iynisin been, until they attacked. And what did the man mean, "in your day — "? Was this foreseeing, this trance? He had thought that gift lost utterly; even the Rosemage, even Arranha, never suggested he might have that power.

"Good. I am half-elven, and if the old tales be true, and your father was a king, then you are half-Aarean. Is that so?"

Half-elven. He had never heard of mortals and elves together; his skin shivered at the thought of the iynisin who waited outside the hall's protection. "My father was a magelord, sir king — " Odd way of speaking, that seemed, after the Rosemage's description of court life, after the florid formality of the Khartazh. Plain, even. "They came from Aare, but old Aare is no more. So they say, who have traveled the south; I have not."

"Magelord . . . and that means?"

"Some of the mageborn retain the powers all once had. I myself have some — but much diminished, if the tales be true, from those with which the magelords came."

The king sighed. "As I suspect it was my magic that called

464

ou, it is but courteous that I explain why. Your ancestors, ing's son, had long abused the powers they held before they ame to this land. No blame to you, but when the pot's broken, t matters not who spilled it — all must clean. Long and bitter vars have followed every trail your ancestors took; the Seafolk hey raided and scourged from the eastern coasts fled seaward, ind found this land, only to find your people moving into it rom the mountains. Generations of war — which I, as a young man, helped to fight. Injustice on injustice, which I now eel called to redress."

"You?" That got out; Luap clamped his lips on the "alone?" hat would have followed.

"I have an heir. Several, in fact. I have a trustworthy Regent — " The king's glance went aside, to where the woman sat out of Luap's gaze.

"And Council," she put in. "You know my limitations."

"If Gird sends you elsewhere on quest now — " the king began.

Another warm chuckle. "I'm not *that* old; you were still commanding the Company — "

"But — "

"And I'll make no promises I can't keep." Luap flinched, and hoped the king didn't see. From something in her voice, he knew it as truth: she had never made promises she couldn't keep, and had kept promises he didn't want to contemplate.

"I know. And you know my meaning. King's son, I am going back to a place where I made grave errors; I will try to put them right. I need your help, and that of your people — Gird's people — to bring justice to Aarenis and even to Old Aare. Now — "

As if that pause released his voice, Luap heard himself asking "Who is she?"

"A paladin of Gird," she said, a bright shape once more wavering at the king's shoulder. "Does that grieve you?"

She had chosen the very word. Whatever she was, he could not be. "Paladin?" he asked, clinging to the unfamiliar word.

"Gird's warrior," the king said. "Sworn to his service, under his command."

Awe choked him again. "You've —*seen* — him?" Faster than speech could be, the hope ran through his mind that Gird had not mentioned him; shame made his ears burn.

"In my heart," she said, bringing a fist to her chest. Now h
could see clearly; a big fist, scarred with work or war, and a fac
that had seen a life's trouble without hardening to bitternes.
A yellow braid hung over one shoulder. "Don't worry," sh
said again. "Gird will help you."

Even the Sunlord wouldn't help him, he thought miserabl
If this was foresight, no wonder the gift disappeared; it woul
drive him mad, one more instant of it. He squeezed, trying t
close his eyes, but could not. "Not me," he said, with difficulty
"I — erred. Stupidly. Again. He warned me, but I thought —
could read, you see. I was smarter."

"Smart enough to cut yourself with your own sword?" aske
the king. His smile was rueful again. "I did that, too." He flick
ed a glance at the woman. "We kings' sons have much to learn
from peasants, Luap."

The rush of laughter came as suddenly as the tears, a
despair; he gulped it down. "So . . . so Gird said. And Rahi." A
the king's look of incomprehension, he added "Gird'
daughter."

"I never knew he had a daughter," said the woman; Luap
winced, suddenly quite aware of the reason. He had left Rahi
out of the chronicles where he could, helped by her own belie
that being Gird's daughter meant nothing special. If these folk
were indeed from far in the future, when some at least of the
records must have been lost, Rahi's part might have vanished.

He could think of nothing to say about Rahi. He could
think of nothing but his guilt, and the iynisin outside, waiting.

"You're afraid," the woman said. "What is it?"

Her voice soothed, warmed. "Iynisin," he said. Best get the
tale over with quickly; this vision had lasted a long time
already. Without sparing himself, he told of the decision to
move all the mageborn to the canyons, and how he and the
others had used their powers to smooth the way, to make the
canyons liveable. Then of his dealing with the Khartazh, and
his decision to use his power — he thought only his — to keep
him young. And then the iynisin, whose influence at first
escaped notice, until that morning's attack, and then of the
judgment of elves and dwarves that sealed the mageroads
against them.

They stared at him, the two faces unlike but the same
expression.

466

"We will die," he said, facing it for the first time. "All of us. If we can't go out to plant and harvest, or trade . . . we will starve."

"What would you?"

"Escape, of course. Can you — "

"No." The king's face was grim. "I have no magicks to bring so many so far, from such a length of years. What I had thought to do was wake those found sleeping in your Hall — " Luap opened his mouth, and the king raised a hand to silence him. "Paks saw that, years ago. I presume that was you and your remaining warriors. She traveled by the pattern — the mageroad, you call it? — back to Fin Panir, where the Girdsmen rule; I had thought to ask you to go that way, or to another end — for some went elsewhere, the time Paks used it. But you are not now sleeping in that hall — at least, the man I talk to is not — "

"Sir king." The woman's voice carried power again; again she reminded him of Raheli. If Gird's daughter had been fair instead of dark . . . he shivered, suspecting that she was Gird's daughter in a way he had never been his father's son. "If he is not sleeping, yet we found him sleeping — if peril threatens which he cannot escape, and fighting will not serve any good — Gird knows I understand the iynisin — " She turned to Luap. "They captured me, for a time." Luap shuddered; her eyes were steady below the circle on her brow. "Perhaps you can suggest a way for him to save his people in that enchantment."

The king's eyes came alight. "And then — "

"And then perhaps a call to wake will actually awaken them."

"But — " Luap cut that off. To sleep but awaken only to another danger, to whatever distant war the king had in mind, to waken only to more guilt, more peril . . . what purpose was that? Even if it could be done, why not simply die, and be done with life? Despair seized him again, and all he could remember were the numberless lies, the many times he had dodged trouble, to let it fall elsewhere. The face of his dead wife before him, for the first time in years; he heard his daughter's pitiful cries as they dragged her away. He could hear his own voice, the perpetual whine that Gird had accused but he had never heard. And he had robbed even Gird's daughter of her due, in shaping the chronicles as he had. He would be better dead; he would only ruin another man's dream.

"All the others with you?" asked the woman. She had read his thought again, or it showed on his face for all to see. Now she shook her head slowly. "No — they can have a better death than that, to fall once more because you fell. And for you, too, death is not the answer."

"How?" All his rage, all his sorrow, all his weakness; they knew everything now, or should have. "I was their king; I failed them!" He squeezed his eyes shut, trying to hold back the tears, then stared at her through that wavering pattern. "How many? Tell me — how many were left?"

"I . . . don't remember. Fifty, perhaps. A few more or less. I was not counting them, and the High Marshals left them in peace."

"We have more than that — some hundreds — " He could not reckon them up; their faces flickered through his mind too fast to count. Somewhere they had records, he was sure of that. "Children, parents, old people . . . not just warriors. . . . " He shook his head. "Few warriors; we were a peaceful people." That too was his fault; guilt squeezed him harder.

"Yet there are warriors with you," the woman said. "Two of them: who are they?"

He had forgotten: the dream or vision had taken him so far away that he had lost any memory of Seri and Aris standing near, holding him. He tried to see, tried to remember, but the woman went on as if he had spoken, her voice suddenly lighter. She spoke to them, not to him, some greeting that they answered, though he could not really hear it.

"I should never have been a prince," he said, not knowing to whom he said it. Perhaps to himself, perhaps to Gird's memory.

The woman spoke to him again. "What do you mean?"

"Do you know what my name means?" he asked. Irony flavored the thought, even now.

"Luap? It's your name: that's all I know."

Luap looked for mockery on her face, and found only compassion and mild interest. "It means 'one who holds no command,' " he said. "Or 'one who does not inherit.' Some called bastards that, when they meant to be kind. I was Gird's luap — his scribe, his helper, his friend — but he forbade me command, and in the end I took the name of my position. Then he died."

"Killing the evil monster," the woman said, nodding.

"No. That's what I wrote, thinking it more understandable than what he did do . . . and what that was I cannot say: you would have to have been there and experienced it. But he died, and released me from my oath — or so I thought. As you see I sought command. And this is what came of it."

"You — oathbreaker?" That was the king, for whom command had no doubt come early and with no qualifications. "You seized your command against your oath to Gird?" No doubt, from the tone, what the king thought of that.

"At Gird's death, he said he was wrong — about our peoples." There was too much to explain, no way to make it clear. Luap found he could say nothing more, though his memories clamored for expression. "I thought," he said finally, "that he meant I was free to bring my people here, and take command here — only here — if they agreed. And they did." A long silence; he saw both faces clearly. "I was wrong," he said then. "I thought I would be better than my ancestors; I was worse. And I don't know what to do. Aris and Seri — " He could only hope that the woman now knew who Aris and Seri were. " — told me to pray, and when I prayed, I saw you."

The king grimaced; the woman laughed — not cruelly, but in genuine amusement. "I doubt it will be so easy, Luap, but are you willing to try?"

"Try *what*?"

"If you got into this by taking command you should not have had, relinquish it."

"How?" How could anything lift that weight from his shoulders? Who would take it? Yet he longed to hand it over, all his pride with it — anything, if only the wrongs he had done could be undone.

She grinned at him, and he could not help but feel better. "*There is* a king," she said. A real king, she did not say, but meant. "Would you follow such a king?"

That was the king he would like to have been; a last stab of envy took his breath, a last certainty that *that* king had had an easier life, and then he felt the tears running down his face. "I would," he said.

"Then be the luap you were: give Falkieri, Lyonya's king, command, and obey him."

Could he trust this stranger seen in a dream? Luap shrugged; he could not trust *himself* — this man, he was sure, could be no worse, not if he had a — what had she said, "paladin of Gird"? — to help him. "I will," he said, and looked the king in the eyes. The king looked back; Luap would have flinched if he could, but then the king's eyes warmed.

"Tell me about your people," he said. "Tell me about your land, and what you know that might help us save them."

"This is what you must do," the king said finally. Luap nodded. He felt eased, though it was not over. "Your people must go — now — tonight — with your paladins to guard them."

"My paladins?" He had no paladins he knew of, nothing like that woman with her strange ornament and her laughing eyes.

"Paks says your Marshals are paladins: Seri and Aris, is it? Yes. They must go with them, or your people have no chance at all. Then you will need some for a rear guard, who cannot expect to escape."

"The militia, I suppose," said Luap. His lips felt stiff. Seri's militia, he might as well have said, for he had had nothing to do with it for years.

"You will stand guard," the woman said. "Where we found you, on the stone arch there above the entrance of your Hall."

"There isn't an arch," he said. "The mountain falls sheer. The arches are in other canyons."

She shrugged. "By the time we come, it will be there; I saw you as a vast guardian shape, protecting that approach and the upper entrance from all harm, in Gird's name."

Luap would have protested: he wanted death, not an eternity of waiting, of the memory of all his errors. He wanted to ask how long he would stand there, how many hands of years. But he had given his oath; this last short time he could be true to it. As if she understood, the woman smiled at him.

"You loved this land," she said. "You will be able to see its beauty all those years." She did not say how many; perhaps she did not know. Despite himself, through all his guilt, that brought him joy. It was a mercy too great, and bought at too dear a price; tears scalded his face again.

"And I will need the use of your royal magery," the king said, as if asking for the use of a spoon or knife. "I must command your people, through you, and this is the only way."

"I — very well," Luap said, hardly able to speak. "Go ahead." He was aware of his voice, speaking the king's words, but it seemed to come from some distance, as if he hung suspended between the vision and the place his body stood. He heard himself explaining, asking for volunteers for the rear guard, directing everyone to go now, to snatch up only what they could carry. Aris and Seri looked stubborn, and would not have gone with the others if something — he could not know what — had not intervened; he saw their faces change. Sorrow fought with hope, reluctance with eagerness. Seri embraced each of her militia in turn, then turned to Aris; hand in hand they led the others out of the great hall.

Then the king's magery and his own twined in the last acts of power, preparing the enchantments that would let his survivors rest, that would place him once more where he had first seen his kingdom and imagined himself a king.

He stood poised on a great stone arch on the eastern end of the mountain; he could feel neither heat nor cold, neither wind nor rain nor snow, neither hunger nor thirst. Above him, above the clouds that blew past in the seasons, the stars wheeled in their steady patterns; he knew them all. Beneath him, in the hollow heart of stone, his warriors rested at peace, until they should be called to rise again.

Beyond his mortal vision, but within his dream, on the dark night his watch began, he had seen the fragile human chain make its way down the canyon. He had seen the glowing figures of those he had not recognized as more than Marshals; he had heard the cries of those who fell; he had known that some lived, that some survived to reach far Xhim and the sea beyond, and a few — a very few — returned to the eastern lands to tell of a disasterous end to his adventure. But they had all been children when the stronghold fell, and their tales, though he could not know it, were dismissed as children's make-believe and soon forgotten.

He knew when the Khartazh soldiers came to visit, and found demons abroad once more, and saw the western canyons fill up once more with brigands who preyed on the caravans of the west. He knew what they said, how they mocked the folk who had once lived there, who had disappeared so suddenly.

He stood guard on the stone, year after year and age after

age, bound to that place by his own magery and the magery of those who built it. In time the iynisin retreated to their lairs of stone; in time the trees grew again, in time the snows and floods of years tore down the terraces and left the canyon once more "no good for farming," as Gird had said, with all the soil so carefully placed scoured from the canyons to dry and bleach on the desert far below. In time the stone beneath him crumbled, leaving him suspended on a vast arch of stone. He could not tire, but he could hope for an ending, a completion of the pattern once begun, a better completion than he had himself designed.

He knew it would come, because he had begun it. The paladin would come, and restore the mageroads; the king would wake his warriors. Then his long watch would be over; he would be freed to go before the gods. He knew that would come, because the king had promised, and the paladin had given her word, and they were not liars: he could trust their oaths. It did not depend on his.

It is said in Fin Panir that the first paladins came out of the west, in a storm of light, riding horses so beautiful they hurt the eyes to see. A man and a woman, it is said, but no one remembers their names.

The End

Paksenarrion, a simple sheepfarmer's daughter, yearns for a life of adventure and glory, such as the heroes in songs and story. At age seventeen she runs away from home to join a mercenary company, and begins her epic life . . .

ELIZABETH MOON

THE DEED OF PAKSENARRION

"This is the first work of high heroic fantasy I've seen, that has taken the work of Tolkien, assimilated it totally and deeply and absolutely, and produced something altogether new and yet incontestably based on the master. . . . This is the real thing. Worldbuilding in the grand tradition, background thought out to the last detail, by someone who knows absolutely whereof she speaks. . . . Her military knowledge is impressive, her picture of life in a mercenary company most convincing."**—Judith Tarr**

About the author: Elizabeth Moon joined the U.S. Marine Corps in 1968 and completed both Officers Candidate School and Basic School, reaching the rank of 1st Lieutenant during active duty. Her background in military training and discipline imbue The Deed of Paksenarrion *with a gritty realism that is all too rare in most current fantasy.*

"I thoroughly enjoyed *Deed of Paksenarrion*. A most engrossing highly readable work."

—**Anne McCaffrey**

"For once the promises are borne out. *Sheepfarmer's Daughter* is an advance in realism. . . . I can only say that I eagerly await whatever Elizabeth Moon chooses to write next."

—Taras Wolansky, *Lan's Lantern*

* * * * *

Volume One: Sheepfarmer's Daughter—Paks is trained as a mercenary, blooded, and introduced to the life of a soldier . . . and to the followers of Gird, the soldier's god.

Volume Two: Divided Allegiance—Paks leaves the Duke's company to follow the path of Gird alone—and on her lonely quests encounters the other sentient races of her world.

Volume Three: Oath of Gold—Paks the warrior must learn to live with Paks the human. She undertakes a holy quest for a lost elven prince that brings the gods' wrath down on her and tests her very limits.

* * * * *

These books are available at your local bookstore, or you can fill out the coupon and return it to Baen Books, at the address below.

SHEEPFARMER'S DAUGHTER • 65416-0 • 506 pp • $3.95 ____

DIVIDED ALLEGIANCE • 69786-2 • 528 pp • $3.95 ____

OATH OF GOLD • 69798-6 • 528 pp • $3.95 ____

or get all three volumes in one special trade paperback edition,

THE DEED OF PAKSENARRION•72104-6•1,040 pp•$15.00 ____

Please send the cover price to: Baen Books, Dept. BA, P.O. Box 1403, Riverdale, NY 10471.

Name_____

Address_____

City_____ State_____ Zip_____

Anne McCaffrey
vs.
The Planet Pirates

SASSINAK: Sassinak was twelve when the raiders came. That made her just the right age: old enough to be used, young enough to be broken. But Sassinak turned out to be a little different from your typical slave girl. And finally, she escaped. But that was only the beginning for Sassinak. Now she's a fleet captain with a pirate-chasing ship of her own, and only one regret in life: not enough pirates.
BY ANNE MCCAFFREY AND ELIZABETH MOON
69863 * $5.99 _____

THE DEATH OF SLEEP: Lunzie Mespil was a Healer. All she wanted in life was a chance to make things better for others. But she was getting the feeling she was particularly marked by fate: every ship she served on ran into trouble— and every time she went out, she ended up in coldsleep. When she went to the Dinosaur Planet she thought the curse was lifted—but her adventures were only beginning. . . .
BY ANNE MCCAFFREY AND JODY LYNN NYE
69884-2 * $5.99 _____

GENERATION WARRIORS: Sassinak and Lunzie combine forces to beat the planet pirates once and for all. With Lunzie's contacts, Sassinak's crew, and Sassinak herself, it would take a galaxy-wide conspiracy to foil them. Unfortunately, that's just what the planet pirates are. . . .
BY ANNE MCCAFFREY AND ELIZABETH MOON
72041-4 * $4.95 _____

Available at your local bookstore. Or you can order any or all of these books with this order form. Just mark your choices above and send the combined cover price/s to: Baen Books, Dept. BA, P.O. Box 1403, Riverdale, NY 10471.